PARKE GODWIN

"A SUPERB STORYTELLER."
Sacramento Bee

LORD OF SUNSET

"GODWIN HAS CREATED A STORY THAT IS
BOTH VIRILE AND TENDER and in which
his love and reverence for the myth of England
plays an active part . . . *Lord of Sunset* is a
symphony of eleventh-century voices,
realized with Godwin's dramatic skill."
Susan Shwartz, author of *Shards of Empire*

"ENTHRALLING . . .
Godwin brings Harold and Edith powerfully to
life as lovers fated to be swept up
in the turmoil of a changing England."
Booklist

"FASCINATING . . .
Godwin is a genius at his craft . . . He bewitches
his readers and holds them spellbound."
Rendezvous

"*LORD OF SUNSET* IS A BOOK I KNOW
I SHALL READ AGAIN."
Morgan Llywelyn, suthor of *Lion of Ireland*

Other Avon Books by
Parke Godwin

BELOVED EXILE
FIRELORD
THE LAST RAINBOW
ROBIN AND THE KING
SHERWOOD
THE TOWER OF BEOWULF

LORD OF SUNSET

PARKE GODWIN

AVON BOOKS ◆ NEW YORK

AVON BOOKS, INC.
1350 Avenue of the Americas
New York, New York 10019

Copyright © 1998 by Parke Godwin
Cover art by Jeff Barson
Library of Congress Catalog Card Number: 97-50346
ISBN: 0-380-81064-6
www.avonbooks.com

First Avon Books Mass Market Printing: August 1999
First Avon Books Trade Printing: July 1998

AVON TRADEMARK REG. U.S. PAT. OFF. AND IN OTHER COUNTRIES, MARCA REGISTRADA, HECHO EN U.S.A.

Printed in the U.S.A.

WCD 10 9 8 7 6 5 4 3 2 1

Acknowledgments

My deepest thanks to generous individuals for their personal help:

Phoenix McFarland for the videotape of a modern handfasting ceremony.

Frank Barlow, Emeritus Professor of History, Exeter University, for permission to quote from his translation of *The Life of King Edward* on page 88 of this book.

As always, to Persia Woolley for critiquing these pages and keeping me simple when I wanted to explain too much.

SOURCES: The Anglo-Saxon Chronicle.

Barlow, Frank. *Edward the Confessor*. Oxford: Clarendon Press, 1970.

Barlow, Frank, translator (anonymous). *The Life of King Edward*. Oxford: Clarendon Press, 1992.

Buckland, Raymond. *The Tree: The Complete Book of Saxon Witchcraft*. York Beach, Maine: Samuel Weiser, 1974.

Davies, John. *A History of Wales*. New York: Penguin Books, 1995.

Howarth, David. *1066: The Year of the Conquest*. New York: Penguin Books, 1981.

Stenton, Frank. *Anglo-Saxon England*. New York: Oxford University Press, 1971.

Persons of the Story

Edith of Shaftesbury, called "Swan's Neck," Harold's handfast wife

Edward, King of the English

House of Wessex (at Bosham):

  Godwine, earl of Wessex

  Gytha, his countess, kin to the royal house of Denmark

  Eadgytha, * their eldest child, queen to Edward

  Swegn, their firstborn son, heir to Godwine, made earl in the west, 1045

  Harold, second son, made earl of East Anglia, later of Wessex, crowned King Harold II, 1066

  Tostig, third son, made earl of Northumbria, 1055

  Gyrth, Leofwine, and Wulfnoth, the younger sons

House of Mercia:

  Leofric, earl of Mercia

  Aelfgar, his son, later earl of East Anglia, later of Mercia

  Aldyth, daughter to Aelfgar, married Prince Gruffydd ap Llywelyn, later queen to King Harold

  Edwin, son to Aelfgar, later earl of Mercia

  Morcar, Aelfgar's youngest son, later earl of Northumbria

Aelard of Denby, thane in Sherwood Forest

---

* Harold's wife and his sister were both named Edith in history, but to avoid confusion in narrative, I've used the archaic form of the name for Queen Eadgytha

Glossary

Some contemporary terms in this work might benefit from definition.

hide: a unit of land, varying in different parts of England but generally between 100 and 120 acres.

thane: a title of rank, hereditary after three generations, for a landowner of at least five hides or the equivalent in other wealth. Most thanes owed fealty to their earl, while Crown thanes like Aelred were sworn to the king.

staller: a lesser court functionary.

vavasor: a mounted knight, though "knight" was not used in Normandy at the time.

Foreword: The Setting

After years of Danish rule, Edward's coronation in 1043 restored to the English their ancient West Saxon line of kings. In his late thirties, his native tongue almost forgotten, Edward was half Norman in blood and all in character. He inherited a realm whose people high and low wanted their own nation and laws again. While Edward never grasped the uniquely independent nature of his folk, Earl Godwine of Wessex never forgot it. The anointed king and the master statesman must inevitably collide.

Harold was Godwine's second son, by contemporary accounts a fine soldier and administrator, an outgoing and affectionate man. Of all Godwine's sons, Harold was most like him, but never dreamed he would inherit his father's earldom, let alone Edward's crown, or the price destiny would exact from him.

Historians may argue his motives and actions against those of Duke William of Normandy, but one clear and touching truth about Harold has survived to become legend. Though forbidden by Church law to marry her, he loved only one woman all his life. Her name was Edith. She lived twenty years with him, bore his children, and she, not his queen, was at Hastings on that last day.

BOOK I

Edith

1 • Edith

Fourteenth October, 1066

All day, from midmorning and the first quarrel of war horns to the ragged, thinning cries as night came down, the sound of the battle came to me from half a mile away. I didn't want to look, though from Caldbec hill above the wood where I waited, I could have seen my husband's place by his standards, the Lions of Wessex and the Fighting Man.

The two monks of Waltham Church who attended me left the trees often, climbed the hill, then hurried back to report. Our army held, the Norman infantry was hurled back again and again, nor could William's mounted knights break our shield wall—hour after hour while the sun rose higher, hovered, then sank. As the October day went to its grave and England with it.

I didn't need to see. The battle was there, stark and clear behind my eyes: Harold rallying his housecarls and the men of Kent and Sussex. His stocky brother Gyrth everywhere at once, the great ax on his shoulder, crying for William of Normandy to come against him. Leofwine shouting encouragement to his men, Harold's nephew Hakon racing a lathered horse, carrying messages between Harold and his brothers. They'd never fought men on horses before and didn't know how, only how to stand and die. Toward evening I built a small fire against the autumn chill. The monks came and went, no longer eager when they returned.

"It is hard to see now, lady. Some of our men were

3

lured out and cut off. We could not see the king's standards. The battle is in doubt.''

They said nothing more nor needed to. Darkness hovered over the field and my heart like an ax already falling.
When the wind brought the smell of blood from the field,
I went with the monks to the top of the hill. We could
see nothing but the small horn lamps weaving like timid
fireflies about the ridge where the last of the battle had
been—and three Norman horsemen approaching us. They
had no trouble seeing us silhouetted against the last line
of scarlet sunset thinning under night.

I recognized Hugh Malet when he halted by us, one of
William's most trusted knights and lifelong friend of Harold. The other two men might have been squires. Hugh's
long oval shield was badly battered, his mail coat torn at
the hip. Hugh hooked a thumb under the nosepiece of his
helmet and bared his head. ''Lady Edith. I thought you
would be—''

''The queen? No, Aldyth is not here.'' We stared at
each other through dusk, neither of us young anymore.

''We heard his wife had come.''

''So I have, Hugh. Did you think I would not? Is it
over?''

''There is fighting north of the field, but yes.'' I heard
the exhaustion in his voice and the halting reluctance.
''The duke's tent is pitched on the ridge. *C'est fini.*''

I remember that moment: the chill October air, the
horses snorting, unsettled by the smell of blood, the scrape
of Hugh's mail as he dismounted. Streaking down out of
the blue wall of night, a single burning star died in red
sunset. The wind had shifted, and somewhere to the north
a shouting of men and the high scream of horses faint and
far, as if they were already ghosts. ''And Harold? What
of my husband?''

Hugh's hesitation answered me before the words; not
yet the sharp pain of loss through me, only the closing of
a last, leaden door. To whatever end, Harold saw this day
coming years ago, clear as the comet that burned over
England in Easter week.

''Edith, *je regrette.*''

"Gyrth and Leofwine, what of them?"

The knight looked down at his boots. "Gyrth, Leofwine, Hakon . . . all, Edith."

I couldn't trust myself to speak just then. *All? How will Gytha bear it? I have lost one husband while she now sees five sons go into the ground before her, four of them within the month. How does a woman bear that and still hold with a merciful God?*

"Duke William sent for the queen. He needed to . . ."

"To what, Hugh?"

Half English on his mother's side, Malet was one of the few Normans of whom Harold spoke well. A measure of the man's humanity that he could fight a long day against us and still send his heart out to my loss. "To look and tell him if it is Harold."

Can't Bastard see for himself? "I see. In the queen's absence, the king's first wife must serve. Help me to horse."

One of the squires held the horse while Hugh legged me up. I walked my mare after him away from the wood and down one gentle slope to climb another. As we neared the long ridge where Harold's army had made its stand, the sounds of women rose on the night air. Across the marshy valley on the opposite ridge, the fires of William's main force were building up for the night. Below us the distant lanterns bobbed back and froth, the wives and daughters of Kentishmen. Like me, they had huddled on the fringes of battle and now searched for their own among the bodies. So many of them, the lanterns wandering, pausing to illumine a woman's face as she knelt and peered then rose and moved wearily on, or hovered and found. There were only the slow-moving lights and voices blurring together in one long keening of grief and names.

We came to the large tent. Hugh Malet helped me down. As he guided me toward the entrance, a servant scuttled in before us, bearing chunks of freshly broiled meat on long spits.

We left the monks outside and entered. Among the nobles around him, some sitting to table, others eating on their feet, William would have been recognizable from his singular height, tall as Harold and of his age, but broader and heavier. He had about him an air of absolute command that pervaded his most casual movement or utterance, controlled but never completely relaxed. He and Harold had admired each other, vastly different though they were. Where Harold used power as a tool to be picked up and then laid aside, William *was* power; that and his life were stamped on him, the look of a hunted wolf, defiant but wary.

A much harder man than my Harold, this bastard duke who in a few weeks would be crowned our king. Now he was just a foreigner who had ripped away the greater part of my life, a massive soldier in torn and mud-spattered mail, finishing the last of a hasty meal. Seeing me enter, he wiped his hands on a rag and came to greet me, inclining his head in courtesy. "Queen Aldyth. I am sorry to meet you in such circumstance."

"So am I." I didn't try to hide the edge in my voice. "But I am not Aldyth. I am Edith of Nazeing. Harold's *first* wife."

His reaction, and that of the other Normans, was obvious in their physical relaxation from courtesy. They discarded it like a stone. Among them were names soon to be too familiar to Saxons: Odo of Bayeux, Fitz-Osbern, Guy de Ponthieu, who once imprisoned Harold and would have held him for ransom had not William sent rescue. Ponthieu snickered openly at me. William showed less surprise than impatience. "Malet, you said the queen had come."

"So I thought, sire, but Lady Edith—"

"Never mind." William brushed the matter aside along with any need for consideration toward me. He sat down without offering me a chair. He had ridden and fought a long day. The effort to conceal his fatigue was not entirely successful. "His leman will do."

"I am his *wife*." I did not lower my gaze from his face. "The Church would not marry us. You and your duchess were long denied marriage for the same reason. We were within their forbidden degrees of kinship. We have more humane laws. Written laws," I stung him. "You would not understand."

"Nor would Rome," William grunted contemptuously. "Yes, Harold spoke of you once or twice." His eyes flicked over me with no more regard than if I were Harold's concubine, but Malet came to my defense.

"His honorable wife, my lord. They were married in the handfast tradition. By their law it put no bar to Aldyth as his queen."

William growled, "It matters little for what I need." He beckoned for wine without offering any to me. He spoke the execrable Norman dialect of French. Now and then I caught the telltale effort at self-correction illiterate men will make when speaking to someone whose grammar is reproachfully correct to their ear. "Your French is very good for a Saxon. You were educated at Bec, no? Paris?"

"Wilton Abbey."

William gulped down the wine, tossed the cup in the general direction of a servant, and rose. Beyond the tent walls the night wind dirged with the voices of the searching women. Sisters to me in grief, I envied them. They at least could hurl at the air and God what I could not voice before these cold-eyed foreigners.

"Woman, we have Harold's body."

No, don't let him see my pain. The ground gave way and I fell and fell and yet stood upright before these thieves. I would not allow them to see me die.

"You will attest it is he," William said.

My mouth opened but no sound emerged until I forced the effort. "You would know him."

"Of course. That is not my reason." William nodded at Hugh Malet. "Tell her in English. Be sure she understands."

"Lady, already our prisoners are talking," Malet explained. "They are sure Harold escaped with the men who withdrew to the north. Others will carry the same tale. They cannot believe he is dead."

"Come," William beckoned to his lords. "Fetch lanterns."

They fired horn lamps from the candles on the table. I

felt near to fainting and silently blessed Hugh Malet for his offered arm. "I wrapped him in my own cloak," he murmured to me as William led us out of the tent. "It was the least I could do for a king who called me friend."

Dreading every step, I was led around to a lightless area to the rear of the pavilion where the dim outline of a single soldier leaned on his pike. As light flooded over him I saw what lay at his feet. "Hold the light closer for her," William ordered.

The scarlet cloak was voluminous and yet seemed to cover the body too completely, the figure queerly misshapen—

I'd girded myself but could not stifle the cry when the soldier turned back the covering. They had not left my husband in one piece. The great wound had obliterated the features of the severed head.

My countrymen still say Harold never died, that he will return like Arthur. Each time, down the long years when the faded flag of that hope has fluttered by, my heart has run out-of-doors to troop foolishly after. "Have you heard? The king lives! He is in Denmark . . . in Chester. He goes as a blind man, hiding his face, but 'tis he. Many have seen . . ."

No, hush the tale and furl the tattered flag. I had loved and lain by this body for twenty years, borne his welcome weight and the sons he gave me, knew it in every dear part and line. I saw the mole below the navel, or where the navel had been. Torn away with one of the long legs and that between in which I'd gloried with my own flesh. Sickness rose in me but passed as something colder took its place. I felt Malet's hand gentle on my shoulder but shook it off, glaring up at William. "Yes, it is Harold. Did you fear his very manhood so much? Even that had to be yours?"

Something flickered in William's eyes and in his reply a kind of appeal. "Some of my men . . . it was impossible to hold them back when so many of their own had died. But the man who did that has been turned out of my service in shame. He will never know favor again. Harold . . . I never knew a better man. I was his friend,

I thought him mine. Woman, he *swore* to me. On the holiest relics he swore to be my man in England, my voice for the succession. Today, before the battle, when I searched for a way around this—all this death, Harold said he had no choice.''

His emotion splintered on the insanity of it. ''In the face of my clear right and God's will, no *choice?*''

I knew what he meant, William, but you never will. Even now in my age with my husband dead and my boys gone, I can find in words no more than Harold could. Why do we anoint our kings with chrism, call them sacred, and then hedge them round with thickets of law? Why are our riddles and peasant songs gay and bawdy while somber, muffled drums beat through our poetry? I only know, as he did, deep in the blood, that we won this isle five hundred years past and live in the iron belief that it is ours.

I rose with an effort from my husband's body, feeling a hundred years old. ''Ask of God when you stand before him. May I take Harold home?''

William said adamantly, ''No.''

''Has he not been desecrated enough?''

''It is not that. I will not make a martyr of him.''

Harold was that when he fell. ''Duke William, I beg this of you. His body and those of his brothers.''

''For the others I care not. Take them where you will, but not Harold. God's face, woman, it is not vengeance. This is where Harold betrayed me, betrayed God by usurping my crown. I will not deny him Christian burial.'' William looked pointedly at Malet. ''But there will be no stone over him, nothing for men to remember.''

So said the man who was to rule us for twenty-one years. He did what was necessary, but as he hovered there over the remains of the enemy he most admired as a man, he must have known England was yet far from won, whatever his claim. Every mile he advanced would be fraught with uncertainty, and years before our country lay bleeding at his feet. But I tried once more.

''William, let a balance be brought. Whatever weight his body, I and his mother will match it in gold if you let me take him home.''

William bent and slipped the cloak over the body. "He was dangerous alive. He will be dangerous for some time dead. I dare not allow it. You have my reasons. Go home, woman. Malet, help her find the brothers. See she is provided for her journey."

He broke off suddenly, twisting about, glaring into the dark. "Those damned women out there! Will they never be still? Ponthieu, go shut them up."

"No, my lord. By your leave," Hugh Malet said. "Let us suffer them as we can. You have won the crown with honor. That honor will not deny their grief."

"Yes, yes—but if they would just be *silent*."

Never again silent nor still, I thought over Harold's body. *You'll hear them until you die, and your children after you.*

I drew my mantle closer about me as the night grew colder. *Win our crown, William? Not yet. That bitter round is not easily won nor worn. I hated it young and hate it still, for it's killed my love, sucked him down, and drowned him even as it raised him up. But write his name with Arthur's and as large. By every law and hope of our people he was the one chosen, fated to draw our Excalibur from the unforgiving stone. Betrayed you? How could he not without betraying that far beyond you and far greater? Foolish Willy Bastard: In a moment when the hawk stood hooded and jessed on your arm, you made it swear never to fly.*

Oh, enough. There would be weeping later, years of it, but to break so before men like these would be another defeat. I heard a clatter of horse and men's urgent voices from beyond the tent. In a moment a thick-set, middle-aged soldier limped into the ring of light, the mail covering his right thigh torn and seeping blood. This Norman every Saxon knew: Eustace, Count of Boulogne, whose arrogance and brutality at Dover fired the ready tinder of rebellion and drove Harold into exile with all his family. Eustace was typical of his breed, not tall but bull-broad, built more for the brief, violent exertion than the long pull. From his words with the duke, he had led the squadron of horse that pursued the remnant of our army north.

"Where are the rest of your men?" William demanded.

Eustace leaned on Ponthieu's shoulder. "Coming in, what's left of them. They tricked us."

"Tricked how? Where?"

"Too dark. We couldn't see. They lured us toward the wood with their torches. Some of us had the sense to be cautious, but most never saw that evil ditch before they went over into it. Just—fell, men and horses, piles of them. The English had longbows. They couldn't miss."

Eustace saw one man shouting orders to the archers as they sent flight after murderous flight into the helpless mass of men and horses at the bottom of the ditch. The count and his remaining knights spurred around the ravine to flank them. Eustace felt gingerly at his damaged leg. "I took an arrow graze. Not deep, but nasty. I need a surgeon."

"Not yet." Only when William was done with him; until then Eustace could damned well bleed, but first he'd finish his report to the duke's satisfaction. "What man led them, could you see? Harold's brothers are dead."

Eustace saw the leader's shield but didn't recognize it. "No one of note, just one of those—what do they call them?"

"Thanes," I said.

"Yes, one of those," Eustace confirmed. "A bossed wooden shield devised with an oak tree."

William snapped at me: "You know it?"

"No. There are many thanes."

A blithe, glorious lie! I knew the device on that shield, and my heart rose up on the dark like Phoenix, sorrowed but singing. Aelred of Denby, that knotty, shire-drawling man out of Sherwood Forest. Yes, it would be men like him, and this William, crowned or not, would face their like again and again when he ventured north of London. There would be submission here, resistance there, treacheries back and forth, but the Aelreds would draw their line and die behind it for five years before William could wear his crown in peace, if he ever did.

Aelred. He was my small victory as Hugh Malet escorted me and the monks to horse for searching out dear remains among the other grieving women, and the long journey home. The first time I set eyes on Aelred Brihtnothsson I met Harold as well, in Winchester in the winter of 'forty-five. A peal of bells from the Minster church for the marriage of Harold's sister Eadgytha to King Edward—

2 • Edith

And my first breathless, gay-giddy presentation to the high folk as a young lady, Thane Teinfrith's daughter from Shaftesbury. I drank good wine at dinner in the women's gallery overlooking the palace hall, but who needed drink when I was already tipsy on the stir and color, the music, the clamor of the hall, and the once-only wine of being sixteen?

Heaven smiled on England in that provident year. From Land's End to the Scots border, there was a new spirit alight in England, our own bright banner unfurled again. Out Danes, in Saxons! Edward, a true son of our own royal house, sat on our throne, and devil the Dane or any other who tried to wrest it from us again. A king must have sons to carry on his line, and to that purpose no prospect brighter than Earl Godwine's daughter Eadgytha.

She was (I would tiresomely declare at any mention of her name) a distant cousin on my father's side, educated at Wilton Abbey not far from Shaftesbury. I was fortunate to be among those daughters afforded an education and luckier still to go to Wilton, considered best for studies. My parents' motives were not scholastic. Long peace gave us leisure to cultivate ourselves, and since the new generation of highborn sons was taking to literacy, they saw it as a long step toward a better marriage for me.

From the day I arrived at the abbey, a child of ten shy-stammering in a Dorset accent, Eadgytha was my big sister, and disapproving of the meat pies I smuggled into the dormitory on fast days.

"You're a walking stomach, Edith. How you last between one meal and the next without fainting is a mystery."

Precise about table manners: "A woman of gentle birth should always show immaculate deportment at table, if only as good example to the men about her. Clean your fingers in the ewer."

"But I just washed them."

"No matter. Let those about you see that your hands are freshly cleansed. They will have less reservation about sharing the common dishes. And *never* scratch your head or any other part with the hand you eat with."

She was stern about missed prayers, the pet frog in the chemise case meant to carry my psalter, unforgiving about my language when an ill-cut quill blotted my French or Latin. "Devil and damn!"

"Girl, I'll be at that tongue of yours with strong soap. You'll need more than God's grace to enter heaven. You'll need a good lawyer."

Next to "Eada" I was a weed by a willow and in absolute awe of her. She had that West Saxon blond, sapphire-eyed beauty foreigners think typical of us, where I was short and dark, plump and plain. When the question of a consort for Edward was raised, the greater families turned out their daughters like goods at a market fair. Earl Siward of Northumbria had no daughters, while Earl Aelfgar's Aldyth was still a child. *Sweet Aldyth. Sin or not, I have pondered much on heavenly oversight wherein death takes so many infants at birth and yet missed her.*

Eadgytha stood first on the list. Her father, Godwine, was the most powerful man in the Witan, Eada a ripe twenty-four with a queenly demeanor long before the crown settled on her brow. She was given a royal escort of thanes and housecarls from Wilton to Winchester. I rode in the rear with her women of honor and nuns from Wilton through a bone-chilling day and a half. Eadgytha was escorted to chambers in the palace to await her wedding the next day.

I stood with my parents far back in the crowded Minster church as old Eadsige of Canterbury invoked the traditional blessing on the royal breasts and womb of our new queen. I cheered with the lustiest—*Vivat! Vivat Regina in aeternum!*—and dropped a curtsey as Eada passed on Edward's arm to banquet separately in the Minster refectory with the archbishop and other prelates. My mother, Hildre, accompanied the queen as part of the escort, but I begged by virtue of my (very) grown-up sixteen years to join the other girls of my age in the palace hall gallery.

What a day for a convent girl who rarely saw any men but priests, let alone dazzling young bucks, and so many of them. As far as Rome it's said our youths are the most beautiful in the world, and surely they were that evening in Winchester. Too excited to taste what I ate or drank, I goggled down from the women's gallery at the feast of male splendor lounging at the long trestle tables. There were so many men of rank that monks, priests, and minor court stallers had to eat anywhere they could jostle and wedge their way in. Below me, in sheer magnificence, the coming generation of England's lords caroused riotously or yawned in elegant boredom. Here and there their ranks were punctuated by Norman knights. We girls giggled at the ridiculous way they cut their hair, close-cropped at back and crown, letting only the bangs grow over their forehead, where our men wore it to luxurious shoulder length. The foreigners reminded me of half-plucked chickens.

At the high table King Edward sat flanked by his three greatest earls, Siward, Leofric, and Godwine of Wessex. They were virtual kings in their own lands "and no love lost betwixt any of them," Teinfrith said. Edward's three great hounds ready to strain at his untested leash and, by common gossip, Godwine least loved or trusted by Edward. I'd glimpsed Godwine only once in Shaftesbury, and of his sons knew only Swegn by sight. However distant our blood tie, the king's disfavor seemed flat unjust to me. I was a Wessex girl, by God!

My companions were hotly debating who was the prize male morsel in the eye-feast below. One or two held for Swegn Godwinesson, who had recently been made an earl in the west. Looking up indolently, he answered one girl's bold smile with a brief but open invitation. Swegn didn't attract me, but the stunning youth next to him—

"That's Tostig, Edith. Swegn's younger brother."

"Don't point at him, ninny. He might see you."

"But isn't he gorgeous?"

"I suppose," I condescended casually, having never laid eyes on the boy until that moment. "Cousin of mine, didn't you know?"

Pure hypocrisy, for devastating Tostig was. I went weak at the sight of him: just my age, his long raven hair meticulously curled about an alabaster forehead, more beautiful than any boy had a Christian right to be, as if heaven had conceived no feature without symmetry, any flaw unthinkable. For the first time in my life, my heart actually fluttered. That evening a lifetime ago, Tostig was Adonis, but at sixteen, adoration is a spring shower, drenched at noon, dry by one. I was in love with him for almost an hour.

Eadgytha's father rose in his place at the high table beside Edward, raising his cup in a toast to his king. A portly man of about fifty, the whitening hair sparse about his pate, Godwine wore a habitually benign expression. Later and closer, I recognized the watchfulness of the statesman. He moved heavily with the girth of well-fed years, but his mind and spirit were yet nimble dancers.

The earl drank his toast, which Edward barely acknowledged, and sat down, saying something to the young man on his right. This must be Harold, the other son I'd heard of, for the resemblance was strong. Harold's fingers drummed distractedly on the board. In listening to his father he wore that air of forced attentiveness people assume when they would rather be elsewhere.

"Oh, Edith. Pity."

The girls near me clucked over my accident. Absorbed

in the scene below, I'd reached into the dish of poached eel and trailed sauce over the lap of my kirtle.

"No, let be." I waved them away as they tried to dab at the stains. I'd attend to it myself in the lavatory set aside for women. Hurrying down the gallery stairs, I collided with a gangling, sandy-haired boy just reentering the hall. He lurched unsteadily and reeked of ale, a country lad come to town in his old-fashioned long gown over baggy trousers of homespun.

"Eh-h," he drawled. "You're the lass coom from Wilton with the queen. Saw you in church." He gestured expansively at the festive hall. "Flamin' woonder this. Never been south of Nottingham before."

That I could well believe. "Edith Teinfrithsdohtor. My father is Thane of Shaftesbury."

"Aelred Brihtnothsson," he gargled at me. "*My* da's Thane of Denby." Which, as Aelred flourished the title, clearly denoted the vast gulf between his eminence and my abyss.

"Ah. Earl Beorn's man?"

Aelred seemed put out at the assumption. "Brihtnoth's a Crown thane, girl. Given his coronet by old Canute, mind. We take no orders from any earl. Your lord would be Godwine?"

"We are proud to say so and to be his kin."

Aelred's gentle, sleepy blue eyes flicked up the hall to the high table. "You mind that old fox. Meet him with thruppence, you'll part with two, he's that crafty. Give y'good e'en."

That was Aelred who became thane in northern Sherwood Forest on his father's death. He commanded the last resistance at Hastings and died fighting against William in the last English stand at York. Loyal to Edward but a sometime thorn in the royal rump, Aelred was mild beside his son, whom the Normans later called a devil and we a hero. You must have heard the songs about Robin of Sherwood.

I cleaned my kirtle in the lavatory, closed my mantle with its brooches, and started back through the cold dark toward the hall. As I passed across the barely lit vestibule two young men strolled out of the banquet hall, likely for a stretch and a breath of air before having at the feast again. Swegn and Tostig. I caught my breath and, girl-foolish, froze timidly behind a thick post, hating myself for the awkwardness, but what if Tostig saw me gawking at him?

"Well," said Swegn, "our big sister is married to Edward. *Laudamus,* glory to God. We are now in bed with England."

Tostig snickered. "You would put it that way. Could she hope for a better match? From a practical viewpoint, could we?"

"Oh, Edward will do. Hunts well enough," Swegn allowed. "Awfully pious for my taste."

"You and taste were ever strangers," his brother retorted with tart humor. "As for piety, I could have grown a full beard since you last heard mass."

"Ah, priests rub me the wrong way. Exhorting us to chastity while they're plowing girls themselves. Or each other, which is worse. Hypocrites. Never mind my soul, little brother. You want to concern yourself, worry over Harold."

"Why? He's been uncommonly sedate and unusually sober all week."

"That's it."

"You've lost me. That's what?"

"Sober and miserable when he arrived, miserable and sober since. I'm worried. He's barely said a word to anyone."

"Then for once we won't have to carry him to bed," Tostig yawned. "Great sack of rocks when he's that far gone. He's an earl now, and right under Edward's nose there in Anglia. He ought to take that seriously."

"That's my point," Swegn pressed with audible concern. "More than serious, he's gone dead melancholy. You know Harold. When was there a time when he couldn't find a joke in everything? The state of the world, even seagulls over Hastings beach. 'Listen,' he says to me. 'They're laughing.' All I could hear was the din of them. What's a stupid gull got to laugh at? 'Maybe us,' he said."

Swegn paused to emit a sonorous beer belch. "I'm bound something's happened to him, something he's taken hard."

"For a change." Tostig started back toward the hall doors. "Come on, I'm parched. I need another draft."

They shouldered through the doors and disappeared. I waited a discreet time and then climbed the stairs, strolling along the gallery until I looked directly down on Godwine and the brother who must be the object of Swegn's concern.

Eada always spoke of her brothers with that privileged judgment the firstborn use toward younger siblings. She doted on Tostig, who could do no wrong. Swegn was the arrogant one—in Eada's case the pot blackening the kettle—and Harold the idler too fond of his ease, too quick to charm, too slow to act toward anything worthwhile.

How did he seem to me that evening long ago? I saw a well-made young man, stylish in the short blue tunic then fashionable, elegantly draped in a mantle of scarlet. Not a male beauty like Tostig or as sharp of feature as Swegn. An open, friendly face, I thought, or it would be in lighter moments. A generous mouth made for the laughter Swegn said he found in everything, though now the whole cast was heavy with sadness and . . . hurt? Harold looked as if someone had struck him hard across the face, wounding and dazing him.

A serving woman placed a dish before him. He flashed her a smile of thanks absently as he might pat a favorite hound, but when he did, something warm and genuine shone through. The woman departed, and the warmth died like a hearth doused with water.

Suddenly Harold lunged out of his chair and, with a curt nod to Godwine and the king, strode down the hall and out the doors.

3 • Harold

It's over and done, boy. You did what you did. The girl, well, that's sad, but there it is and a good lesson to you. From now on be more careful where you wet your wick. You've a future and far more important matter to concern you."

More important? I could only stare at Godwine before rising abruptly. "By your leave, sir." I bowed shortly to King Edward and left the high table. For the only time in my life, I had to get away from my father. Of course he was right in the long view, but how could I utter then what I suffered when I barely understood any of it myself beyond the clammy guilt that clung to me like wet wool? I stumbled out of the hall, away from light into kinder shadow.

Eirianell. Her voice witched me before the rest of her. When she stood before me and throatily murmured that name, I heard four distinct musical notes.

"Eirianell, my lord. From the countess's manor in Devon."

A Welsh slave sent with a complement of servants when I assumed lordship of East Anglia. My mother had inspected my new manor at Nazeing and found the hall drearily in need of brightening. Spare tapestries were dispatched from other holdings, along with skilled weavers and dyed wool for more hangings. Eirianell, perhaps a year or two younger than myself, was among the loom workers.

I won't deaden guilt by exalting her memory, although I did at first. I'll see her clearly, her skin olive but seeming fair against the blue-black curls that tumbled wild down when freed from pins and veil. Sweet midnight about her face and shoulders, a sweeter, wilder forest between her thighs. A poet might say she rode Cupid's arrow to my heart—might, but we're dealing in truth. In the May flush of my eighteen years, Eirianell struck me much farther south. I fell feverishly in lust, reached for her like wine because she was there, willing and intoxicating, after the example of Swegn who had already fathered several accidents, and no great matter to Godwine beyond urging a certain economy. Such slave girls and their get were sold off or tucked out of sight on this or that manor at the far end of Wessex, families compensated, warned to silence, and there an end.

Eirianell was the first and last of that for me. I already had some repute for offhand charm and an easy nature. Very little mattered to me then, court jester to life itself, a boy earl vastly impressed with himself, idle and uncaring, a new-molded bell not struck until Eirianell came. If I'd thought for one moment beyond myself . . .

God amercy, Swegn and I rarely thought then. We were the sons of Godwine and Gytha, and to us so much came early and easily. Gytha was the kinswoman of King Canute, joining us by blood to the royal house of Denmark. On Godwine's side distinction was less clear. My grandfather Wulfnoth may have been a Sussex thane, likely of no great account. On him and more remote ancestors, Godwine was silent. The omission is eloquent if you know our national character. Given the reach, all men seek power, and England allows men of ability to advance. More than ability, Godwine had political genius, working with shrewd diligence to become first voice in the Witan under three Danish kings and then Edward, to have his older sons ennobled and his daughter crowned queen, guiding us toward power through the shoals of rival houses and shifts of royal mood. Through Godwine's influence, Swegn and I were created earls by Edward two years after his coronation. Swegn was twenty-one, I eighteen, Tostig next in line and already chafing for what he lordly and loudly considered his due, and three more cubs at home, Gyrth, Leofwine, and baby Wulfnoth waiting their turn.

Self-made and a hard game played for every gain, God-wine lavished on his children all the advantages wealth and long peace could offer: Wilton for Eada; tutors in French, Danish, history, and religion for his sons. The province of the clergy, education in England had become the fashion of the rich, but Godwine had sober purpose in endowing us. We must learn to think, not merely react. From the age of twelve or so we older sons spent several months at court each year. Godwine placed us near the font of power and provided the resources to deal with it. When I knelt and pressed my forehead to Edward's knee in fealty, I knew at least what an earl should be.

Eighteen then, the new toy lord of an apprentice earldom, without Swegn's wildness or Tostig's self-righteousness. As a boy I followed Swegn everywhere, and although he was older Swegn always came to me, confiding, cursing, and melancholy when the slow-grinding world couldn't keep pace with his mercurial moods: now arrogant and invincible, now despairing or miserably repentant. In any victory he blazed with high spirits that could vanish quickly as sunlight behind April cloud. If deep love shone from his eyes for those he held dear, a devil glared forth as well. I saw both in one day while visiting him in his new hall at Gloucester, shortly after his elevation to the rank of earl.

Older huntsmen present that day still speak reverently of Swegn and his feat in the Forest of Dean. With huntsmen, kennelmen, beaters, and hounds, we had trailed a boar toward a densely thicketed part of the wood. He was easy to follow: big, the cloven hoofprints deep in soft earth and loam. By the spattering of dried blood, he'd been scored earlier in the day by another animal. Any boar might take a dog or man down with him, but wounded you could count on it. Swegn's master huntsman advised us to break off and try for other game.

In fine fettle and full of ale, Swegn and I scorned the advice and pressed on, hounds baying and near mad with the freshening scent of their quarry. When the kennelmen finally let them slip, they bounded forward in a straight run, we crying after, bending low under tree branches, in and out of copses, until we caught sight of them circling and snarling about a dense hazel thicket. When we reined in, by chance I was between Swegn and my man Botulf, who carried our heavy boar spears.

"Gone to ground he has," Swegn exulted, reaching toward me. "Quick, Harold. Spear."

I leaned far out to take it from Botulf, misjudging the distance, and carelessly slipped my right stirrup. In that deadly space of a breath the boar broke cover. My horse reared at the sight and smell of him, and I barely had time to clear the other stirrup before I hit the ground hard. The men shouted warnings as the beast, with a piercing squeal of rage, slashed a razor tusk along one hound's hide and then charged straight at me.

Never have I sobered more quickly. A boar's tusk can slash a thigh to the bone or rip a man's body from groin to breastbone in one maddened pass. In an eye-blink I would be dead, the last sound in my expiring ear the screaming murder about to sweep me from the world. Then the scream blended with a deeper roar as Swegn, mad as the beast, launched himself out of the saddle and dropped squarely onto the animal's broad, heaving back, clawing for a hold about its thick neck, the other hand snaking the knife from his belt.

The boar staggered as my brother's weight struck him but recovered and began to charge at anything that moved, racing in circles with two hounds hanging from his ears and Swegn stabbing again and again at the tough hide of its throat. Botulf pulled me safely back while the spearmen hovered helplessly, unable to use their lances without endangering Swegn. We gaped, unbelieving: one screaming animal clinging to another in a mad, twisting dance. Then Swegn's knife must have dug an opening. No longer stabbing, he pushed the knife deeper and deeper until finally the boar, with a wet, gurgling sound, collapsed, its blood steaming in the dry bracken.

I bellowed at the spearmen: "In! Save him!"

They bounded in, kicking aside the dogs that tore at the dying boar's wounds, thrust their spears in behind the shoulder. When the boar lay still, they pulled Swegn out from where the carcass trapped his legs. Knife and hands red, my brother wove on his feet like a man only half awake, then stumbled toward me, reaching to clasp me to him. "It's all right, b-brother," he stammered fiercely. "All right. I've killed it."

"Christ, you could've been—"

Swegn only crushed me to him, trembling violently. "Tried to hurt you . . ."

As we rode home to his hall with the trussed carcass needing six bearers, my man Botulf ranged beside me and pointed with his chin to Swegn riding ahead, his horse difficult to manage with the blood smell on his rider. "Never saw the like, sir, nor any t'others. No man could do it, not and live."

But Swegn had feared for me alone and held me hard enough to hurt.

That evening, with no ladies present to mind our mouths or manners for, Swegn's hall was a pandemonium of raucous young spirits. Called to give the cheer, Swegn bounded onto a table, flagon in hand, anointing all within range with its contents. "May it well become you!"

Charged with more than human energy, my brother gained the dais in a running bound, vaulted over the high table to fling himself down beside me. "Wonderful day, a *capital* day. You there, fill my cup. Drink, Harold. Let's get weepy, maudlin drunk."

What else after such a day, such a rescue. Hours later when we'd all stuffed and drunk deep, we listened to Swegn's Welsh harper. A master of his art and instrument, the man had a genuine tear in his voice, for on this night, his cheer fading with each draft of ale, Swegn would hear only songs of the sad heart. The tables fell silent, listening, Swegn very drunk now and mourning for his Agatha. Swilling my Welsh whiskey, I was as far gone but unmoved by sentiment. I'd not yet felt any sadness I couldn't walk whistling away from, and how does one describe color to the blind-born, music to the deaf?

As the harper played and sang, Swegn's melancholy deepened and darkened, leaving him desolate as he was jubilant before. When such humors took him, my brother was the very pall on the funeral bier of fortune. Try as I might to change the subject, he doggedly returned to Agatha, battened on her as he had the boar. Pale, pallid to say Swegn agonized. Swegn Gethseman-ized. The humors never balanced in him. Any or all could riot across his heart in a breath. Swegn loved or hated without measure. As a brother I'd always known his love, near fatally proven that day, but there was that sometimes in his mien and eye that prudent men feared, none more than Swegn himself. A unique form of hell to see your own fault clearly, yet helpless as it consumes you.

He mumbled over his ale, "Agatha wouldn't see me."

I suppressed a yawn. "No hope then?"

"Gives me hope one day, takes it back the next."

Since their first meeting I'd heard more of Agatha than I needed to know. A few years older than Swegn, she was abbess of Leominster Abbey. Her religious house lay within his earldom. To Swegn the fact that Agatha was a bride of Christ was no more insurmountable than a hand-fast marriage.

"Nothing left for me without her," he declared hollowly. "I'll give up my holdings and leave England."

"Ah, you're dumb as bread."

"I'll go to Denmark or Norway," he gloomed. "Or even through the mists to Russia or Constantinople to throw my useless life against the infidel Turks."

"Bit much, all that." I hiccuped. "Sailing off devil knows where just because a woman you fancy belongs to a nunnery."

"Just because, my little brother says." Swegn wagged a prophetic finger at me. "Just wait. Your turn will come."

"No, but just hear yourself: 'Oh, my heart is riven, so fair and yet so far is she.' "

"You bastard, what do you know?"

"Brother mine, I owe you my life today, but how many buckets have you wept on my sodden shoulder in praise, poetry, and pain over Agatha? I concede she's a paragon, on earth a sacred icon, in heaven counsel to angels. Where Agatha walks, when her delicate foot deigns to touch mere soil, no weed but only blossoms spring."

Swegn turned to me, more dangerous than I had the

sense or sobriety to realize. "That's enough. You're very entertaining sometimes, but not tonight. Let up."

"Lord love me, can't you laugh at yourself just once? Where's the hindrance? Take the woman if you must, top her, tup her, and be done."

All I heard then was a short, vicious growl, then I was jerked out of my chair and slammed on my back across the table amid a scatter of jugs and bowls, Swegn's dagger stinging the skin of my throat as it had the boar's. The crash alarmed the others. Botulf sprang up and hurried toward the high table. "My lords, hold. Hold!"

"I said *not funny*," Swegn hissed closed to my face. "What say you now?"

Nothing came to mind. His eyes were terrible. In them I saw no question or hesitation, blank of all but murder, sure as he'd done the boar. My courage declared immediate holiday. Everything deserted me but my wits. "I say it's very difficult to drink in this position. May I get up?"

My remark drew nervous laughter from the men, dissolving some of the tension. The blade lifted from my throat, but its edge was still in Swegn's eyes. "I'll forgive you because you're drunk."

"Not at all." I wilted back into my chair and the remnants of dignity. "I can still see only one of you." I draped an arm beerily over his shoulders. "Look, you know I love you. It's always been you and me against them all, but your suit is hopeless. You haven't a prayer with Agatha."

"She loves me."

"Aye, let her love till the sun burns blue, she's still a religious."

"I know, I know." Swegn's narrow face contorted with real pain. "Why am I so cursed?"

I pulled him to me. "My dear brother."

"*My* brother. But to have all and have nothing at all."

"Pray it won't earn me another blade at my throat, but your heart has no middle ground. Everything's either brilliant or dark. Nothing at all? You'll be Wessex one day."

My brother sat back, staring into distance to a place beyond sadness. "How if that should change?"

"You're the first son."

"What if Wessex lights on you?"

"Me?" The notion was laughable. "Tostig harks to astrologers, not me. Do I look like destiny's child? Shag off."

Swegn only stared into his drink. "I love you, but you're blind. And you've no feeling for another's pain."

At eighteen none at all, the world my unending revel. I loved to laugh and too often at the expense of others, careless of my target or the wound. So I rode to Nazeing in East Anglia and a new earldom not earned but bestowed as a gift or privilege, closely followed by letters of advice from Godwine. My father had grave reservations toward some of our new king's policies, particularly Edward's predilection for lavishing English lands on his Norman friends. Nonetheless, Godwine charged me to cooperate fully with the royal sheriffs in East Anglia. Difficult not to. Edward held more estates there than I did, and his officers teemed like fresh game. There was more law than crime and little for me to do but let the stewards collect my rents, approve matters already seen to, or dispense justice in the hundred moots. In the first week, my cardinal show of authority was sentencing a "piecemeal" baker in a village near Waltham.

"Piecemealing" is a grimy practice but as common among bakers as selling short-weight bread. Housewives would bring their kneaded dough to be baked in the shop, but while the baker diverted their attention, his apprentice would pinch off and hoard as much dough as wouldn't be missed. I gave the baker and his "pinch" the prescribed sentence. They were bound on a wooden hurdle and drawn by slow oxen through the village with the offending evidence tied about their necks, to be pelted with dung or mud by their outraged customers. Not lethal but highly unpleasant and precisely just. Property and possession are the cornerstones of our law. Theft is not winked at. The baker suffered minor punishment; most thieves lose their right hand. Godwine wrote approvingly:

Edward says you show good judgment. I wish Swegn could boast as much or at least control his temper. He quarrels with Edward's Norman friends and those of Earl Ralf at every turn.

Judgment? By the time Father's compliment reached me, I was further sunk in folly than Swegn at his worst, and the folly's name was Eirianell. She did little tapestry work for me. Those were the first heady days of power and wealth in my own right, intoxicated with my own image and then, from the night Eirianell's touch first burned me, with hers.

If I'd had then the knowledge of women God gave an observant clam, I might have noticed how often the girl was about. I encountered her in the corridors, on the stairs, in the hall, somehow just passing the mews when I brought a new hawk out to the weathering block. Always at such times she would modestly drop her eyes, but not all at once before she passed by with my permission. I'd noticed her as a man will, the sensuous movement of her body under the kirtle, the full mouth and deep-set black eyes too knowing for one so young—and her invitation finally became clear.

And why not? I thought. Eirianell was beautiful, clearly available, and I would at last have something to boast of to Swegn.

One late evening in deep, green summer twilight when I went down from my chamber to the hall for a last draft of mead to help me sleep, I sat alone with a single candle at a lower table, when Eirianell was suddenly there before me. Why she was up so late or there in the hall never occurred to me, only that she came out of the shadows beyond the candle glow, her unbound hair like part of the darkness framing her face, a little half smile on her lips, the black brows questioning curves in charcoal.

I answered her smile without a word, yet in that glance between us there were recognition and acceptance. Eirianell came to cross behind me. Her fingertips, trailing across my shoulders, tingled through the thin linen of my shirt. I rose and turned to her, and as if it were the most natural answer in life, Eirianell flowed into my arms.

Lost from the start. Every part of Eirianell, every element that made up the woman of her witched me, made me drunk. The hot pressure of her inner thighs, the fire between them, the husky music of her voice at my ear, the whimpering sounds as she neared her climax, forgetting English and then her own tongue as her nails raked down my back. The rage between us in our hunger, and the sweet, brief languor before we took fire again, falling asleep only as day lightened. That night, the next, and most following.

My body needed hers. Those few nights when she was gone from my bed, the pillows and linen smelled of her and made me ache and yearn, wishing before day was born for it to die and bring her to me again. She never questioned, just came. We spoke little, for little was needed except the contract of flesh and flesh. Doubtless Godwine knew from the servants he'd sent. The matter of Eirianell was an open secret in my hall, though my father declined to mention it when he wrote:

Though the wedding is to take place Wednesday, twenty-first January, Edward's dream of a new abbey at Thorney occupies him more than any thought of Eadgytha. He agreed to the marriage without comment, yea or nay. On other matters he gives in here, stands stubborn there, but it is still impossible to take any close measure of the man. Toward me his courtesy is rimed with frost, no doubt the old business about his brother. We must show our loyalty while nature takes its course with Eadgytha to provide an heir. Edward's nature is not a trusting one. Because Canute created me and married me to Gytha, I am suspected of being Denmark's snake in England's bosom. Arrant rot, of course. All foreign claims to our throne must be ruled out by a son of Edward and Eadgytha.

The youngest and least significant of Edward's earls, I was neither summoned nor missed at Christmas court, but Swegn was needed that year by the Witan and king regarding recent trouble in Wales. My brother's measure of Edward was clear and direct, buoyant with the healthy cheer of his better moods.

"Edward? A damned invisible wall around him. No one gets really close, nothing excites him except hunting and mass, never looks you in the eye with a simple answer to anything. Has to be reminded by his chamberlain how to dress, and as for women? I think Eadgytha will have far more solitude than any woman wants.''

In January we had cold, clear weather for Plough Monday, the holiday when local boys black their faces and haul an old ploughshare through the lanes, collecting gifts of meat, cakes, and ale to eat in the local tavern, or to gouge a mark before the portals of the ungenerous. Lords never intruded on this custom, wisely honoring the sentiment that they as well as commons should know and keep their place.

So I rode that day for sheer good spirits, hawk on my wrist, Eirianell wrapped in furs on a fine mare beside me. I cried halloo! to the sooty-faced scamps of Plough Monday, tossed them a few pence, and wished them a good feast. We rode long that day, perhaps too long, for Eirianell appeared unusually spent when we returned to the hall. That she might be indisposed never occurred to me. *I* felt wonderful, therefore the world surely must.

With Eirianell sharing my bedchamber, it had become our custom to take supper there when there were not guests in the hall. Only after ordering the meal did I notice that she was more silent than usual. Eirianell drifted about the chamber, absently touching this or that object, not looking at me. When supper was laid I waved her to the table, but she came and curled up in my lap instead, face pressed into my chest.

"Now what's this? Not hungry?"

"No," she whispered. "Talk to me."

"Of what?" I stroked her back casually as I would one of my hounds, already picking at the food before me. "Want to romp first?"

Her dark head moved slightly against my chest: no.

"Why not?"

Eirianell only nestled closer, urgent. "Be with me."

"Come on, I'm hungry."

"That can wait."

"Well then, what's got into you?"

"You have." Eirianell sat up and looked directly at me. "My courses have stopped, and I have been ill these three mornings. There is no doubt. There is a child."

Quite honestly I was less surprised than annoyed at the

news. I shifted her off my lap and into her own chair, pouring wine for us both. "Well."

Not much of an answer and Eirianell knew it. She sat looking down at her hands. "No more than that?"

I couldn't think of anything more at the time and convinced myself I needn't. "Of all the times for this."

In three days I must meet my parents at Silchester and travel on to the royal wedding. Eirianell's condition hardly meant disgrace, but I simply had no time or inclination this month to spare her any more thought than a kennel bitch about to litter.

"Harold, I—it is not that I ask anything for myself."

"I never expected this."

"But it has come."

That silent, searching look again. What in hell did she want of me? I retreated from her, rising with my goblet of wine from the table. "You know how these things stand. No promises. I owe you none. Your child—"

"Our child."

"If acknowledged," I reminded her sharply. "And that's not likely. It can have no place in my house."

"That is not what I ask."

No tears, only that grave probing, perhaps for some quality she hoped to find in me now. "My folk were slaves to the countess, your mother. They were never mistreated, nor was I. God and Saint David have been merciful. I have never known want, only kindness. Here I have known . . . it is that I am asking the same for our child. Not your name, only your kindness."

"Eirianell, listen to me—"

"No, Harold. Hear me." She rose slowly and came to me, placing her hands on my shoulders, still searching my face. "Do you think I was drawn to you, came to you so readily that first time because I saw beauty alone? Many things I saw but gentleness surer than all the rest. Need I saw and some of that arrogance your kind always harbors, ill-fitting because it is not truly your nature. But the gentleness and the need were true and fitted into mine."

I found myself wanting to back away from her. "Eirianell, we've given each other much comfort and pleasure, but don't make it more.''

''But it is more,'' she said. ''Men have taken me before, but with you I gave.''

I had to turn away from her. Kindness and regard? That was fair and little enough. ''I'll see you have your freedom, a house and a woman to look after you when the time comes, and a wet nurse if you need one. Later you can return to Devon or perhaps take service with my brother Swegn. He'd be glad to have you.''

Eirianell didn't speak at first. When she did, her voice was quietly anguished. ''Away from—?''

''I think it best.''

''You would send me away?''

''Aren't you listening, damn it?'' I was handling the matter badly, not taking command, where Swegn would have her out the door and be damned to her. The girl would not see facts. ''After this week I shan't be here that much. I'm a Crown servant, girl. When the king whistles, I come. When my father beckons, I run. I *must*. I won't have time for you or any child. If it is mine.''

I might have struck her. How easily the young kill one another with a word, a look, a fear. *If it is mine*. How could it not be when Eirianell had scarce spent a night apart from me since the beginning?

Her silence grew to another presence in the room. I turned to see her unmoving in the candlelight, a sad judgment in her eyes. ''At least you're not dissolved in tears, there's a mercy.''

Still, still as death standing there. Only the candle flames moved and our shadows shuddering on the wall. Eirianell spoke so softly I barely heard her. ''I do weep, my lord.''

She turned and left my chamber.

The end is purgatory to remember, worse to tell. Quickest said is best. That night in the dark, empty hall below, Eirianell hanged herself. Of how they came to tell me in the morning, hushed and reluctant to touch the body, how I myself cut her down, I will not speak. In three days I had to meet my family. I went through the preparations numb, not daring to feel or knowing what emotions would savage me given the chance. Yes, pack that tunic. Yes, those horses will do. I stoppered the good wine, opened the whiskey, and deadened my heart while the women laid out Eirianell, washed and dressed her, and the regretful priest came, shaking his head for what he could not give her.

"We are sorry, my lord. She was so very young. But Canon law is clear."

"What are you saying?" I stared into the fire, drunk since lifting her body down. *"What?"*

"The manner of her death. She cannot be buried in consecrated ground."

"Cannot . . . ?" With all the rest, I hadn't recked that consequence, that horror. I couldn't speak, only waited for the nervous priest to go on.

"My lord, we will render what we can, but . . ."

But precious little allowed by God's precept. I glared at the little cleric with his plump belly and comfortable living, and thought: *you sanctimonious bastard,* and opened my mouth to spit it at him, but the judgment wouldn't fly, just rooted firmly in myself where it belonged. "Do it then, whatever you can. Get out."

Liquor could no longer keep out the winter chill of remorse. That Eirianell took her own life damned her eternally, doubly for the child murdered in her womb, and I would join her there.

I saw gentleness more than all. Over and over her voice and my last sight of her before she slipped out of the chamber and the world. No man alive has not turned craven before a truth he couldn't face. Riding to Winchester at my father's knee, I was coward enough, vile enough to reason away the guilt. After all, I did no more than any other man would with a willing girl, and hadn't I treated her well? Didn't I offer to care for her and the child where dozens like me would spit on her?

Eased by this I defiled myself further. From the first her spell was on me, her body a love philter coursing through mine so that I could hardly call my will my own. How could I know this was not deliberate? The Welsh kept many of the dark old ways. Could Eirianell not have been a witch?

To my meager credit, I ground the thought into the dust, remembering the truth. Not that I refused to acknowledge the child, but that I would send her away. The truth was plain in that moment before she left me and went to die, and I was blind.

Eirianell loved me.

No, I—

Loved me. Enough to choose that noose of twisted linen and waiting hell rather than live with loss. Later and older, Eirianell might have dealt with it. That night when it mattered, neither of us could.

Can you remember one moment, one heartbeat when, as a helmsman turns the steerboard hard, your life heels over from one course onto another? One truth like a wedge between what you are but can no longer be? I felt part of my soul tear away and fly guilt-shriveled home to pierce the earth over Eirianell and settle forever by her where she lay. There must be confession and chantry prayers for her deliverance, but whatever penance, *I* took responsibility for her death and, in that moment if yet far short of a man, I was no longer a selfish boy. Human folly must be God's schoolroom. Anyone who's not been a fool for something, some love or dream, has led no more than a shadow of life.

So I hunched there in the gloom of the gallery stairs, letting flow the tears that would not come before, already translating Eirianell's name to lament, stabbed with a hundred proofs of my guilt. I buried my face in both hands and sobbed—

"Harold? Cousin?"

The high, sweet young voice startled me. I wiped at my eyes and looked up to see the round, serious face of the girl bent close over me.

"I'm Edith Teinfrithsdohtor. Are you ill?"

From that dismal point in time nothing would ever be right again. With one deep, shuddering cry, I buried my face in Edith's breast like a balm and a prayer to God.

4 • Harolo

Edith cheered me through that dreadful wedding week until her warmth and eagerness began to thaw the winter in me. We could talk easily, but whenever I tried to tell her of Eirianell, the words stifled in my throat. I could only be grateful for the mercy of her presence.

At sixteen she was no beauty, a spring flower only half opened to morning, wistfully envious of Eadgytha's womanly poise. We didn't fall in love but rose to it, the difference between a quick, hot blaze and the steady glow of coals.

She remained at Winchester until Easter court as one of my sister's maids-in-waiting, writing to me often. The pain of Eirianell faded slowly, but Edith made it bearable. I make no comparison between them. At seventeen, Eirianell had been a woman. She was moonlight and deep shadow, Edith the morning sun rising and ready for life, chafing at the need to return to school, wide-eyed at the new world of royal court life. Her letters, written on whatever scrap parchment she could beg from the queen's scriptorium, were forwarded with Eadgytha's. Their styles were as different as the two themselves, my sister's cadence and composed:

Our Edith sends her missive with mine. I believe she is becoming restless at court. Tostig has been much help to me in my duties. For yourself, I urge you emulate him and discharge your offices so as to make the king and our father proud of you.

Edith's letters surged with the energy of her, much underscored for emphasis, blotted here and there in the wake of her speeding quill. I thought to ask her to Nazeing, but she might enjoy Bosham more. Teinfrith often traveled there to render Godwin's Shaftesbury revenues, so I urged Edith to come with him if at all possible.

Oh, I would be thrilled to come, I *will* come, and many thanks. Court was exciting at first, but now, to be frank, I am bored, and only extravagant shopping relieves the tedium. Papa sent me a purse and Eada another, so I had a *fortune,* almost four shillings. I bought a new pair of shoes and was going to buy a crucifix in Gold Street, but there was the most beautiful brooch I've ever laid eye to, and I was lost. Pray you don't account me a vain goose, but it is a burden to be decorous *all* the time and to hear so many masses in a day as we must do at court. At Eada's suggestion (ergo royal command), I've gone to confession so often that my conscience is scrubbed, rinsed, wrung, and hung out like the wash. Eada is so busy, at times it seems she wakes the kingdom and puts it to bed at night, just as she managed us girls at Wilton. Audiences in the morning, sitting on the canon councils, seeing that the king is properly dressed. Oh, yes, I have been formally presented to His Majesty. He is *very* dignified. I look forward to seeing you, dear Harold, wishing only I *didn't* have to go back to Wilton first. I feel I am growing *old* here.

In private Edith's impression of Edward was more precise. "He's—well, he's *dim.* Pale skin, pale eyes, moves about the palace like a sad ghost and looks quite through you as if you weren't there."

Before midsummer I rode with Botulf and a small escort of carls to my parents' manor at Bosham, where Edith would be coming with her father.

Bosham, where I was born and raised, stands on a finger of green land jutting out into Chichester Harbor. The sleepy village with its teeming marshes fringes the tidal inlet where boats rise at high water and heel over in the mud at low, like contented sows in a wallow. Less than a hundred yards from the shore at full tide is our church,

Holy Trinity, already ancient when great Alfred was crowned.

Home to me was always sound and smell as well as sight: the derisive squawk of ducks on the water adding their discord to the constant chick-chick of magpies, and geese waddling and honking through Bosham village, and ever the salt smell of the marsh and sea. As boys Swegn and I sailed with the Bosham fishermen, lofted our first hawks over the marsh, learned sword and shield in the nearby meadows.

Some thought it strange for Godwine, always at the center of English affairs, to choose such a backwater for his home, but Bosham's location is deceptively strategic. London, Winchester, and Gloucester are accessible by land or sea. One or more of Godwine's keels always lay at anchor, ready on an hour's notice to carry him wherever needed. From the shore the worn path leads up past the church and the village of fishermen, weavers, armorers, blacksmiths, and all the craft folk who served the manor. A short half mile beyond the village are the low walls and gates of home itself. There are stables and mews, storage houses, a barracks for housecarls, guest bowers, and two kitchens, one to serve the main hall, though Godwine and Gytha preferred the smaller when no large company was present. In the summer all the casement covers were propped open. The fresh tang of sea air flowed through the little hall, rippling my mother's prized tapestries and over the comfortably cushioned chairs and benches.

Gytha had a rare feeling for homes and saw them as objects of love to be nurtured carefully as children. When she first came a bride to Bosham, both halls were deplorably run-down, thatch-roofed, leaky when it rained and frequently smoldering from firepit sparks. Gytha had the thatching stripped away and replaced with solid tiles. Declaring the halls themselves dark and stodgy, she broke out one wall in each, replacing the small, cramping doorways with generous round arches. She sent to her native Denmark for wood-carvers and presented Bosham church with an exquisitely carved altar, embroidering the cloth herself. She insisted on fresh flowers every several days in spring and summer. Cottagers delivered new rushes regularly, and servant women were kept busy cutting sweet herbs to crush and sprinkle among them and to scent our bath soap.

By that year Godwine and Gytha had been through much together, with harder trials and deeper sorrows to come. Many nobles looked askance at both: Gytha as kin to the Danish power that still coveted England. Godwine came to power through the Danes, and many suspected his motives and leanings. Wherever his loyalties, his love went to Gytha and us, his children. Family came first with my parents. Edith felt it straightaway, the aura about Godwine and Gytha. They relished each other's spirits and company, and one sparked the other. They'd weathered royal climates both fair and foul. If Godwine was first in the south, he was not loved by Edward or the north. This added a bite to my parents' wit, and if they seemed ever to share some edged joke between them, the jest was brittle as glass, treacherous as court politics.

"There they are!"

As the long keel hove in sight at the mouth of the inlet, Botulf and I cantered our horses out onto the low tide mud. Just forward of the mast, the small figure waved frantically to me. We waded the horses farther out into the shallows as the keel glided close.

Teinfrith might have been shocked at his daughter's eagerness. I'd intended to lift her over the beam onto my horse, but Edith hopped nimbly over the sidewale, devil take new shoes or kirtle hem, and splashed toward me to spin merrily about in my arms before I legged her up into the saddle.

"Dear Edith, most welcome."

As I led her by the bridle she twisted about to see this, wonder at that, call gaily to her father. With so much life in her, Edith could not keep still for long. She held up her wrist as in hawking, inviting a low-flying gull to perch—"Come, bird!"—and cried after as it ignored her: "Your loss, then."

Like one long in pain who is grateful and surprised

when it ceases, I knew how much of a pall had lain over me since Eirianell's death and how quickly this vibrant girl could sweep it away.

Edith

Much of my gaiety that first day was sham. I was terribly nervous about meeting Harold's parents, especially his mother. I needn't have been. When he presented me to Countess Gytha, she tilted back my chin and traced the line of my throat with one finger.

"*Svanneshals*," she murmured. "You have the graceful neck of a swan, Edith. The earl will be up presently, but now come and meet my savages. Boys, come in!"

There was kindness. Gytha ravished me from the start, where she might have crushed me with one arch frown, false smile, or the slightest nuance of disapproval. She allowed me not one moment's discomfort. To me Gytha was always more queenly than Eada, with a strength so assured it never needed display.

Easy to see that Harold and his brothers took their height from both sides of the family. I had to look up at Gytha. She must have been a great beauty in her youth, for she was still striking. Vitality sparkled in her light-blue eyes, and there were far fewer lines in her fair complexion than time might have etched. In faith I think more noble English harridans envied her looks than questioned her loyalties. Her light-red hair still showed no grey, though Gytha admitted to me much later that she assisted the illusion with judicious touches now and again. I've done the same since. We need a few vanities to keep us human. As Gytha presented her younger sons to me that day, I had the impression of a great, tawny mother cat proud of her kits and contented with her life.

So I met Gyrth, Leofwine, and Wulfnoth, thirteen, ten, and nine years of age. Teinfrith politely asked if the earl intended Gyrth for the Church. Gyrth quashed that decisively.

"Oh, no, Thane," he piped. "Father's going to make me an earl."

Not the king, mind you, but his father. These cubs already took power and place for granted. Teinfrith reminded Gyrth that Edward might have some voice in the matter.

"Well, I suppose," Gyrth conceded grandly as his true king appeared at the top of the stairs. "But it's Father who says about everything."

Gytha stretched a hand to her husband. "Come greet our guests."

Godwine came first to Harold and embraced him. "Well met, son. How goes Anglia?"

"Oh, royal and dull."

This was my first close sight of Harold's father: far too heavy, but carrying his bulk with a massive grace. He had the largest head I've ever seen on a man. With a full growth of hair the effect would have been leonine, but that pate bore only a meager whitening fringe about the back and ears. Godwine said that for all his good fortune in life, heaven stinted the hair to keep him humble. If so, heaven failed. Humility was no part of Godwine's nature, but in its place caution and farsightedness had given to this great, benign bear of a man a watchful benevolence. Godwine played at the high table of English politics and won more often than he lost because he knew the weaknesses of his opponents.

He greeted Teinfrith warmly. "So glad you've come. Give me all the news from the west."

"My lord, this is my daughter Edith."

Gytha herself took my arm and presented me to Godwine. "Edith, whom I have named Swan's Neck on the instant, lovely as she is."

And eternally in her debt for the grace.

Gyrth and Leofwine wanted to dine with the family but were banished to the large hall to eat with the housecarls. "They badly want manners still," Gytha apologized, leading me downstairs from the solar to the light, airy chamber made ready for me. "My barbarians still regard food as missiles against each other, and Wulfnoth finds soup best eaten with his fingers."

The countess sent a servant woman scurrying to ready a bath for me and personally shepherded me on a sunlit walk to the bathhouse. Gytha towered over me, but as we strolled I noticed she shortened her stride, consciously lessening the difference in our heights. I was glad to be alone with her, needing to ask a question in confidence.

"Lady, I thought to make something for Harold's birthday, but I don't know the day. In April, isn't it?"

"So it is," Gytha smiled. For a moment I had the impression she would have said something more. "April twenty-fifth. I'd hardly forget the day or hour. Harold and Tostig were both born on that day, three years apart. Lady Day it was, the sexton ringing terce with far too much vigor. The bell bothered me terribly. Harold was enough of a task to bear, and I was *not* feeling charitable. Tostig came in the evening toward vespers."

Gytha paused to pluck a yellow cowslip from beside the walk and set it into my hair. "There. The color becomes you."

I asked her what might be a suitable gift for a young earl who apparently lacked nothing.

"There are wants and wants," Gytha considered. "Not another hawk, he's a mews full of them. Nor drink, for he's far too much of that as is, and I lay that vice to Swegn. They were inseparable as boys. In truth, little *Svanneshals,* if you have enough maturity and sense of responsibility to spare some, that would be most helpful to my son."

Gytha halted outside the bathhouse. She seemed to read me through and through and perhaps approve of what she found. "So we've come so far, have we? Personal gifts, no less. You won't have an easy time, my dear. Perhaps you know that already?"

"I think I know Harold."

"Do you? I think he has the depth Swegn lacks, but of course, Harold will do anything to hide it. Most like his father in that."

"That is a blessing, lady."

"Blessing perhaps, but rarely a joy. Come, your bath will be ready and you may take as long as you like."

So I did, indulging in the bath, soaking the fragrance of the scented water into me after the long journey. Just before supper was laid, Harold called for me, bathed and changed, his hair freshly oiled and curled about his face, eager for me to approve of everything at Bosham. "How do you like my family?"

"Family" seemed inadequate for such people; say rather a pantheon. "They are wonderful."

When he moved closer, smiling, I thought he would kiss me. I'd often imagined that, how it would happen the first time—but then, as so often at Winchester, that curious shadow fell over Harold's face, and he hesitated. Quick as it came, it lifted. He took my arm. "Mother's laid on music with supper: fiddle, pipe, harp, Irish drum, the lot. Must warn you though. Father will talk court matters and Mother will try to see he doesn't eat too fast or too much. Always does when he's worried. He had to oppose the king again and—oh, devil that now. I *am* glad you're here."

To my delight there was nothing formal about supper in the smaller hall, only four long tables, the first for family and guests, the others for servants. The hall buzzed with contented conversations underscored by the musicians. Godwine did indeed eat too much, but with an air of preoccupation, and I asked Harold what had passed with the king to bother him.

"Robert Champart."

As if that rendered all transparent. "Champart? Sounds Norman."

"Frightfully."

His arch inflection made me giggle. Harold had the trick

of accenting the serious with the frivolous. Prominent in the center of the table was a block of polished fruitwood a foot long and perhaps half as wide, the sides showing the three Norns in relief. On it rested a delicately carved and gilded stem that curved gracefully up into the petals of a rose. Teinfrith had taken the trouble to advise me before landing. When the rose was displayed at table, anything said there was not to be repeated beyond it. I felt honored and very grown-up to be trusted in the matter under discussion between Godwine and Teinfrith. Gruffydd ap Llywelyn, Prince of Gwynedd, was a neighboring power to Swegn and had sounded the young earl on an expedition next year against a rival prince in the south.

"I've advised Swegn to go," Godwine said. "Not that he required any prodding. Half of Wales on Edward's side and in his debt is better than all of it against him."

My father was less at ease with the strategy. "For now, perhaps, but you can't trust the Welsh. They'll turn on anyone, even their own."

"I daresay no more than we," Gytha ventured. "Just more emotional about it."

"That's the living truth." Godwine drained his third cup too fast and held it over his shoulder to be refilled by a hovering servant. He rolled the red wine around his tongue critically, then with obvious pleasure. "We should compliment Manni on this vintage. From Normandy?"

"From Acquitania," the countess said. "An excellent year."

"Touching Normandy," Harold wondered, "whatever's become of that poor little duke of theirs? Has he managed to stay alive?"

Godwine set down his cup. "Young William? Still breathing, God knows how. Every one of his vassals is out to grab the duchy."

In the west we'd scarce heard mention of the fugitive duke. To include me, Harold quickly glossed the situation. Duke Robert had died when his heir was only seven, an illegitimate boy whom none of the great Norman lords wanted to recognize and whom any and all would gleefully dispatch when they found him. No more than eighteen, with few loyal men, William was seen by most English wagers as dead before the end of the year.

"Got four shillings on that myself," Harold said. "Though Bishop Stigand is always lured by long odds. He thinks the boy has a chance."

Only one, as Godwine saw it. "If he can cross Epte into the Vexin, it's in King Henry's interest to support him."

Gytha brought the issue closer to home. "Will Edward support him, do you think?"

"Not if I can prevent him." Godwine canted his large head in concentration. "Listen: that figure in the harp. Lovely."

The plucked, limpid notes drifted over us. The earl rubbed two fingers over his broad forehead. "Edward is inclined to help, but he's not yet that secure at home, and for once Northumbria and Mercia side with me. While the Normans fight each other, they can't make trouble for us."

That wisdom passed with no comment. We are not sentimental where our security hangs in the balance. We'd rid ourselves of Danish kings and influence and were not about to allow any foreigners such foothold again. This was the deep feeling of most English, from the earls and thanes down through the commons, and all looked askance at Edward's Norman sentiments and friends.

Countess Gytha laid down her knife and cleaned her fingers daintily in a ewer. "The duke's cousin to Edward, isn't he?"

"Yes," Godwine frowned. "Through Edward's mother."

"Poor Emma. She's seen enough ill luck."

"And caused enough, my dear."

Gytha smiled down the table at me where I sat close to Harold, our fingers twined beneath the board. "Never be a queen, Edith. The game is not worth its candle."

The elderly steward Manni approached the earl with word from the gate porter. There was come a mounted party of five, four English monks and a Norman knight. "On royal business, they said, but from the bishop of London."

"Let them in." Godwine sighed in resignation. "I expected this, Gytha. You wonder why I can't digest properly? Edward has appointed Champart to the bishopric in the face of the Witan. We all opposed, we argued ourselves blue, but . . . damn him, he did it.''

"So like our royal lord," Harold muttered over the common dish we shared. "He wants Godwine to know he's beaten by rubbing his nose in—Malet!"

Harold sprang up from the table as the visitors entered the hall, four mud-spattered monks and a vital, broadshouldered young Norman of about Harold's age. Harold rushed to greet him heartily, silencing the musicians with a gesture. "Malet, most welcome. We met at my sister's wedding, remember?"

"I do, my lord."

Harold presented the knight to his parents with a flourish of admiration. "Father, Mum, this is Hugh Malet, the finest horseman in Europe, possibly in the world."

Malet actually blushed, protesting modestly. He spoke far better English than most Normans, and less accented. "I think the earl has yet to see our finest riders."

"Nonsense, you're wizard. I saw you in the tiltyard below the palace. Father, Teinfrith, you should have seen him. Mounted in full mail without a hand on the pommel, and then, sword in one hand, shield in the other, jumped this great, fat horse over a wall. No hand on the bridle—how in the world did you *do* that?"

"All done with the knees. Pardon, Harold." Malet inclined his head in respect to Godwine and proffered a cylindrical leather case. "From the king, Your Grace."

His duty discharged and the four bedraggled monks hovering at some distance, Malet was presented to Teinfrith and to me. "This is Teinfrith's daughter, Edith, whom I—to whom I am cousin."

I caught the quick change of direction in midthought, hoping Harold had meant to blurt *whom I will marry.* The sort of thing a woman would catch and cling to. Or worry at. Wasn't he sure? Were there second thoughts about us? Doubts?

But then Godwine handed the parchment to Gytha with a snort of disgust. "Damn."

"The bishopric?"

"Yes. Edward is kind to inform me so speedily."

Gytha rose and offered her hand to Malet. "Please refresh yourself and be our guests tonight."

"*Merci, Comtesse.* The monks are fatigued."

Harold had praised Malet more than once, not only as a splendid rider but for having truly that sense of honor all Normans boasted but seldom demonstrated, save in matters of their own rights—proving, as Harold complacently asserted, the dominant English in his friend's blood. Certainly Malet had maturity, good manners, and ability. Though of no great family, in later years he became Duke William's liaison at Edward's court. At the moment his reluctance was evident as he beckoned one of the monks before Godwine. "From Bishop Robert, Your Grace."

The monks, not recently tonsured or shaven, were as uneasy in their charge and under Godwine's dubious gaze. One of them opened a leather pouch and set a parchment on the table before the earl. "Regarding certain episcopal lands at Merton, my lord."

"Indeed? Already episcopal?"

"And other holdings at Wimbledon. Bishop Robert claims that the livings noted are part of his see and asks that you return them at once."

Godwine scanned the minute chancery script. "Asks? From his tone, the good bishop demands. These lands have been mine since Canute invested me. What in hell is he thinking of?"

Obviously embarrassed, the monk hastily sought refuge in authority. "As Your Grace can see, the king endorses the de—the request."

Godwine rose heavily and returned the schedule to the bearer. "The Witan will rule on this. By law, little monk. Until then, Champart does not demand of Wessex." Godwine's manner lightened quickly as it had clouded. He grinned cordially at the pained monk. "Not your sort of errand, I'd think."

"No, sir, it is not."

"You are all welcome. Take some supper. Manni, see to their needs and quarters."

Harold stayed at table to entertain Hugh Malet, leaving me alone until nearly time to retire, but I felt far too stimulated to sleep. I walked out by myself to watch the guards' lanterns bobbing to and fro in the last of summer dusk, bathing my face in the cool wind wafting up from the harbor.

I'd wandered almost to the gate, savoring the soft quality of Sussex summer, feeling at once very grown-up and still terribly unsure. I loved Harold, and how would that change me? Would he marry me after all? Did I know all of him? Did I know myself that well, or much of anything beyond home or Wilton?

"Edith?"

Harold came down the path to wrap one arm around me. "I thought you'd gone to bed."

"No, it is too lovely and peaceful here. Thank you for letting me come. But why was your father so upset about the Norman bishop? A little land, a few livings?"

"Not the land but the precedent and the scheme behind it. Edward's intent is clear as it's dangerous. He fills as many offices as he can with Normans. They're flooding into England, and Godwine is the bulwark of the dam."

Then more lightly: "See what you're kin to, love?"

"At least I shan't be bored."

"I'd say not, but peaceful? Look there, Edith." Harold pointed back toward the hall. "See that light on the ground floor? That's my father's scriptorium, his sanctum. He'll be awake long after the last servants are snoring. Trying to stay one move ahead of Edward and men like Champart."

"As I live, I've caught him out. At last Harold sounds serious about something."

"It is serious. It's war. Always subtle, so far bloodless, but very deadly war by the king against Godwine."

"But why? Your father's first in Edward's council."

"In a word?" Harold turned me, guiding me back toward the hall. "Edward thinks his power derives from blood-right and God alone. For most men, that's an impressive pedigree. Not having heard himself from the Almighty, my father tends to disagree. Oh, it's been coming, Edith. Now it begins."

5 • Edith

Cupid may be blind, women are not. If time proves
we shot at poor game, never think we didn't choose
our mark. There were contradictions in Harold and
in me as I learned living with him, and no anger like that
sprung from love. We gave and took high happiness and
deep hurt, as in any real marriage.

But that was later. Think now how happy we were that
lovely summer at Bosham. Harold then was a man to share
his happiness, though not yet any sorrow, and that became
for me a door still closed. As summer wore on I learned
to mark those brief, dark parentheses in his good humor.
Our days at Bosham were gay-ribboned with blue skies
and golden sun. The choice minds of England such as
droll, dry Stigand shimmered at the table, wit bounded
like a ball between Godwine and Gytha. Harold and I rode
every day, he ever with a favorite hawk on his wrist
whether he lofted her or not. As we drew closer together,
the hawk remained hooded and idle more and more.

Before Saint Michael's Day in September my father had
to return to Shaftesbury, and I went reluctantly back to
Wilton for the last of my schooling. With nothing in my
mind but Harold, I did poorly in French, worse in Latin,
a disaster in Scripture, where the winter severities of Paul
melted in my heart's June. Mother Werburgha wrote to
Eadgytha that I no longer applied myself. I lived for Harold's letters, and when I daydreamed of him, two pictures
always came: one day at Bosham when he paused to taste
the flower-sweet air for its own sake, then turned with a
wordless smile to share the moment with me; the other,

earlier, hunched on the gallery stairs in Winchester Palace, weeping and clutching himself to me.

But from what wound he couldn't share?

"Whatever troubles you," I urged, "there's no thought you need fear to tell me, nothing so terrible I would turn away from you."

Forward of me, almost a declaration. Harold said only, "Heaven itself will turn from me, Edith."

How curiously age works on memory, steals from now and pays back from the past with interest. I lay down my needle or shears for a moment and lose them for a half a day, yet a memory thirty years lost will return vividly, all its significance clear, though obscured at the time. It was the day after Hugh Malet came from Bishop Champart. The three of us were taking the sun, lazing in a meadow beyond the manor, Harold's man Botulf grazing the horses by the yonder rill. Malet wondered how on earth our soldiers could fight astride horses so small. Lying in my lap, Harold just laughed.

"Where have you been? Have you ever seen us fight from the saddle?"

"I do not see how you could," Hugh judged, giving Harold's horses dubious inspection. "They are not horses, more like large dogs. Your feet almost drag the ground."

Harold closed his eyes while I wove bits of clover into the dusky gold of his hair. "Never gave it much thought, but it's just not done."

"Common soldiers go afoot, but not lords and vavasors."

"It doesn't sort well with the spirit of the sword."

Hugh had never heard the phrase. A Norman vavasor would die of shame to be set on foot beside lowly kerns.

"Nonsense. Spirit of the sword." Harold bounded up and hauled Malet to his feet. "The will to close with your enemy eye to eye, foot to foot."

Hugh scoffed. "Outmoded and inefficient."

"Oh?" Harold wandered a few steps away then called to Botulf down at the rill. "Eh, lad! Fetch Sire Hugh's shield and one for me. And two practice swords from the armory."

What followed then was a triumph to Botulf and I dare-say a revelation to Sire Hugh Malet. From the moment they set to, his long oval shield, designed to protect the off leg while mounted, was awkward on foot, where Harold's round shield was everywhere at once, unpredictable as the flight of a butterfly. Laughing, adding friendly jibe to injury, he stepped back from the panting Norman and tossed his sword aside. "Come, attack. I'll use shield alone."

Irritated now, Hugh rained blows like hail, but wherever they fell, the round shield was there, Harold's feet dancing precisely, always balanced. Then Hugh's sword spun, a blur in his hand—

"La!"

—but never landed. Harold hurled the shield into its path and himself at Hugh's middle. Caught unaware, Hugh found himself off his feet and on his back, blinking up at his friend.

"Ta ta *ra!*" Botulf crowed. "Victory to England!"

Some of the wind knocked out of him, Hugh sat up, gruffly trying to salvage some dignity. "Well played, well played, but were we mounted, I would have destroyed you."

So you did at Hastings, you and your kind. They were outmoded, they were yesterday against your tomorrow, and welcome to it.

I must not think of that but find those silly shears. . . .

Oh, beyond wonderful! Harold sent an invitation to visit him at Nazeing early next summer, properly companioned by my mother. We could spend the latter part of the season at Bosham if I wished. If I wished? I dashed home to Shaftesbury at Christmas, besieging Hildre with the news before the wet cloak was off my back.

"You must come, Mama. Absolutely must."

I urged my suit again after supper in the hall while the servants cleared away scraps and the bread trenchers. "Say I may, Papa, and Mama can come with me?"

Hildre glanced at the servants and lowered her voice. Servants loved to gossip, nor were some above selling information when there was a market. "There's been trouble."

"What, what?" I'd heard nothing at secluded Wilton. My heart plummeted. If no summer with Harold, then no life. "Father?"

Teinfrith kept his voice low. "That business of Champart. Godwine's carls routed the bishop's men from Wimbledon. No one badly hurt, but the Witan backed Godwine. The king isn't pleased, and as for Champart, he came close to seizure."

Teinfrith reckoned the matter wouldn't boil over, but you never could tell about Normans. "Arrogant donkeys would rather fight than eat. Downright boring if they weren't so dangerous."

Hildre must have cast her vote for my cause. We had my father's leave to go if Earl Harold would provide an escort of his housecarls.

When I left Wilton that spring Teinfrith was gone from Shaftesbury. Earl Swegn had marched with Prince Gruffydd against the southern Welsh prince, and my father was occupied with establishing a new system of post riders between Bosham and the west. One fine day toward the end of May, Botulf pranced through our gates at the head of ten mounted carls to escort Hildre and me to Southampton. From there we would travel by calm summer voyage up the Narrow Sea to Thames and River Lea to Nazeing.

Botulf alighted and stripped off his baldric, indicating that he and the men expected to sit at table. All his life Botulf's gait was somewhere between a lurch and a swagger, as if his long bones were too loosely connected. He was a *geneat,* the highest peasant rank below that of thane, Harold's standard bearer with the occasional duty of escorting the earl's guests. Tow-haired Botulf farmed a few acres of yardland at Holyfield near Nazeing, mostly leaving the labor to his own bordars and cottagers, preferring to ride with Harold. This furnished frequent escape from his stolid wife who, from the age of fourteen, had regularly presented him with children who regularly died at birth. She had broken his nose with an iron pot on his twentieth birthday. They were colorfully mismatched.

Scarce older than Harold, Botulf was always more impressed with his station than ever his lord was. Nothing unusual; there's no commoner in the world more snobbish than an English peasant, none more conscious of place and propriety. In those early days I'm sure Botulf felt Harold's light approach to a serious world reflected on himself. If Harold carelessly mislaid his dignity, Botulf was always there to snatch it up, brush it off, and drape it properly again.

"I'm sure Botulf wishes for a straighter nose," Harold confided to me once. "He'd love to look down it at me."

Botulf bowed to Hildre and me, so correctly he must have practiced, then ruined the effect by wiping his mouth on the back of a brown hand. He flourished at the ornate wagon sent for us, painted in scarlet and gold, the Wessex colors. "You'll have a lovely ride to the port, but it's been a thirsty one for us."

"I thought as much," my mother invited. "All of you come into the hall."

A rough lot for manners, but on their best behavior while we were in their charge. Botulf allowed no straggling or slacking between Shaftesbury and Southampton Harbor, where the manned and provisioned keel waited. He would sail with us. The rest of the escort would change horses at Bosham before returning to East Anglia.

"My lord hopes he hasn't neglected anything for your ease," Botulf said as he helped us into the boat where the tough, sun-browned young lithsmen waited to cast off. Indeed, Harold had thought of everything. I was gratified by his thoughtfulness and delicacy. A small tent had been rigged in the stern for our privacy and stocked with choice wine, fresh bread and butter, cheese, and even grapes from Brittany.

Botulf turned expectantly. "Ladies, if you're quite ready."

In bubbling spirits, I rattled his composure with an impulsive kiss on his astonished cheek. "Sir, tell them to *move* this vessel."

Oh, he was beautiful waiting on Lea bank, fists planted on his hips. I was so eager to close that final distance that

I would have gladly seized an oar and outpulled the liths-men. But there'd been choppy water in the Narrow Sea and Hildre had been faintly green until we turned into Thames. I let my heart race ahead, pointing Harold out to her.

"There he is!"

"I know, child. I saw him at Winchester."

Saw and approved, I prayed. Earl or not, I so wanted her to like him for himself as he stood there in a brilliant short yellow tunic, bare legs, hair bound back with a strip of gold cloth. He waved as the keel glided in toward him.

"Hal-*lo,* Cousin. Well done, Botulf, all of you." As the rowers shipped oars, Harold sprang onto the foredeck and strode aft to us, bending to kiss my mother's fingertips. "Lady Hildre, most welcome."

My qualms about Hildre's first impression vanished on the instant. When Harold smiled at her, the genuine plea-sure glowing in his eyes would have devastated a stone saint.

"And my learned Edith"—with a more than cousinly embrace for me. "My sister hears you neglected your stud-ies this year, but I won't believe a word. Come. I've a poor place but brighter while you're here."

The manor at Nazeing was a mile or so north of Wal-tham Church, where we halted to give thanks for a safe voyage, then rode on. So I came to his home, the place he held for Edward on the edge of Epping Forest. Not nearly so inviting as Bosham, the manor had a temporary aspect, no more personal than a porch crossed toward a chamber beyond. It had been held by too many young novice earls looking to better elsewhere and scarcely inter-ested in improvement or even maintenance. By Hildre's lights, nothing was done right or smartly. Some of the servants had been sent from family estates in Wessex, some were local folk, but all so idly overseen that my mother turned her eyes to forgiving heaven in the first few days. Laundresses got nothing really clean because no one corrected them. Chamberwomen forgot to set new candles much of the time, and we had to do with ends until I spoke to Harold about the matter.

"He's a lovely man," Hildre sighed. "No more house-broken than a horse."

So are most men until they marry. His cooks were excellent, there was a blessing, but service haphazard. Visitors were few. Now and then priests came from Waltham but rarely thanes or reeves from the neighboring royal manors.

"They don't deem it wise to know me," Harold shrugged. "Edward's liege men know what he thinks of my family and any who befriend us."

Like Botulf, I felt this reflected on myself and resented it. "King or no, who is this half-foreigner to disapprove of us? I say devil take him *and* his Norman favorites."

"Excellent sentiment," Harold agreed. "Let's conspire in that much treason."

He escorted Hildre and me through ancient Waltham Church, built on the foundations of an earlier one and with its own miraculous history. In Canute's time his officer Tovi was granted the local manor and hides, and brought from his estate in Somerset a great black stone cross that shed the blood of martyrs when scratched or punctured. The church's endowment of relics was small but powerful to the devout: several bones from the body of Saint Dunstan and a fragment of cloth from his garment.

Moving from place to place through the cool, pillared nave, Harold's enthusiasm sculpted his vision with widespread arms. "We'll build a transept with an apse for the dean. It will be a collegiate Church, no cloistered living for the priests but out among the folk so they'll always know their needs. We'll do away with the side vaults and crypts." He loped across the chancel and spun around to me. "And here, the altar."

And just there they did put your altar, my love. When that unforgiving William allowed your poor bones to be brought home, I laid you to rest where you shone in my eyes on that morning so long ago.

He was so eager to please me and my mother, I was sure an offer of marriage would shortly follow. Hildre saw what was shaping, a clear-headed west-country mother who knew the true moon from its shimmer in the pool of a daughter's fancy, and finally said so as we sat up in the big bed by candlelight, carefully arranging her hair under the nightcap. Hair was a bother here in Anglia which was far more humid than the hills of home.

"Clearly he favors you. On the face of the matter, it is ideal. Your father is close in Godwine's trust, and Harold is the highest-placed second son in England. But," she sighed, "some say the least competent."

"Not so," said I, loyal to the heart.

Hildre sniffed, tucking the last limp strand beneath her nightcap. "The least ambitious anyway. They all grew up spoiled if you ask me. Hardly knows how to manage Nazeing let alone an earldom."

"Oh . . . pooh."

"Common knowledge, child. He's well liked but lightly regarded even by his sister. An untried horse."

That about the estate was true enough. Harold's casual neglect of the hall outraged my domestic instincts. "Don't you like him?"

"Did I say as much? There, put out the candle, no sense wasting. Yes, I like him," Hildre allowed out of her tidy soul. "But I couldn't live in such dither, and as I brought you up properly, you can't either."

I snuggled down close to the safe warmth of her. "I could do far worse for a husband, but how better?"

"Come so far, have you? Lambkin, listen to your mother." Her arms went round me as they always had and held me close. "Your father and I are not against the match. We'd not hoped so high for you, but what kind of match? The Church will never marry you."

"They will."

"You're blood through Teinfrith. Consanguine."

I squirmed free to bounce up on one elbow. "Stuff. There's a horde of cousin degrees 'twixt us. Any road, that's got round all the time. Earl Godwine will see to it."

Sure as the Second Coming, and there an end. Satisfied, I lay back peering up into darkness bright with my future. All would be well, would be capital. Facts were far from me and Harold that summer. Tomorrow we would ride again. . . .

On an evening in July I grew up all too suddenly. The cloudy day had been cool for summer, with a storm from the northern sea passing close by to the east. Mother and I came down for the evening meal, waiting at the high table for Harold to appear. The hall filled with his servants and stallers, musicians tuned their instruments, the fiddler plucked a few trembling notes to find his mode. The overcast day so darkened the hall that candles were lit, fluttering in the draft from the open windows. Beyond the timber walls, the wind cried eerily under the plaintive sound of the fiddler's strings.

By custom Harold must give the cheer, and to begin without him would be an inexcusable breach of manners by a guest. We waited but he did not appear, nor had his steward any idea where the earl might be. We cleaned our fingers in the ewer for the third time as the lower tables, packed with travelers, itinerant monks, and mendicants, grew restive, furtively pinching off bits of bread and cheese from the platters before them.

"He's been detained, Mum. Most like in his chamber. I'll fetch him."

The upper story was dark but dim light spilled from the partly open door to Harold's closet. I rapped lightly. "Harold? Are you there?"

No answer. I pushed in the door. Several candles burned on a table and the door to the outer stairs stood wide, wind bending the candle flames flat in its draft. Harold had been here and would presently return. Or, if he was detained longer, perhaps he would not mind after all if Hildre gave the cheer this once to his hungry household.

I turned to go—then stopped still, arrested by an instinct strong as a hand on my shoulder. Harold's bedchamber was indifferently tidied as all the other rooms, but a woman had put her mark on this place. A woman lived here, or had, and this room was her center.

Does he have a mistress who comes at night? Poisonous thought, but it wouldn't leave me. Harold's female servants were all older and reassuringly plain, nor had I any hint of anything like that since coming to his hall, even when growing physical awareness of him compelled me to wonder. But this room screamed the presence of *her*, whoever she was. If you say I should have left the room then and there, you may be a mannerly man but certainly no woman.

She was easily found. On the prayer stand there was a jewel case carved from ivory, containing a silver penannular such as Welsh women use to fasten their cloaks, rings of gold and silver made for fingers far smaller and more delicate than Harold's. In an open clothes press, beyond shame now, I found an embroidered work basket with thread and expensive needles. There was a sachet of lavender still fragrant, and a shriveled Spanish orange studded with cloves that still perfumed the carefully folded garment beneath. A woman's nightdress of finest linen, piped at the throat and narrow cuffs with samite embroidery masterfully worked into conceits of bluebells and rosebay. Under the smell of clove, the gown still retained the fainter musk of its owner.

"She made it herself."

My heart skipped a beat as I whirled about.

Harold stood in the open outer doorway.

6 • Edith

My neck and ears burned hot with shame. Caught like the pilfering thief I was, pawing through his life. Harold stood very still in the doorway, the silver goblet in his hand. Behind him, in the unnatural darkness of the storm passing over, the wind muttered like a troubled ghost.

I longed for him to say something. Below in the hall,

tabor and bone flute struck up a lively measure. I stammered lamely, "They've begun supper then."

"Yes. I sent word." Harold moved into the chamber. He took the nightdress from me, laid it back in the press, and closed the lid. As he passed I smelled the whiskey on him.

"I'm so sorry. You were so late to table, I came to fetch you."

Harold sat down heavily on the bed, hunched over his knees. He'd dressed for supper in a short yellow tunic, but his knees were smudged as if he'd been kneeling in damp earth. Silent still, not accusing or apparently angry at my intrusion, not even in the same room with me. In a year I'd come to love the open, gentle nature of this man, but now he was a blank wall. I writhed, desperate for him to say something, to look at me at least.

"I know I shouldn't have. There's no excuse for this."

Nothing from him, not a word.

"Harold, please speak to me."

"She's dead."

"Who?"

"Her name was Eirianell."

She's not dead, Harold. She's everywhere. This room cries out of her. What a roil of feelings! When my shame ebbed, I felt foolish and angry and somehow betrayed, as if I'd caught him in adultery. He just sat there with no sign that he knew or cared I was with him.

"My regrets about supper. I was elsewhere." He drained the cup. "Such times go better with a drink."

"Teinfrith says only Welsh and devils can drink whiskey, but you seem to hold it well."

"Patient practice. Sometimes I have to . . . go away. The dress, these other things, I don't know why I've not got rid of them."

Rest her soul, I was glad that much of her was gone. It is a shock at seventeen to grow up so much in a moment, but that evening I had little choice. In the midst of dream-fashioning a life, the reality was here before me. Very unsure of myself, I sat next to Harold, not wifely close or yet too far, so that he could touch me if he chose.

"Only natural if you loved her." Oh, there was hollow generosity. Her name sounded Welsh: servant or slave, which said much in itself. These things happened between young lords and such girls, but she must have been much more to him, and I was jealous of that, dead as she was.

"Loved her? Bless you, Edith. You're fine and good." Harold saw the goblet was empty and simply tossed it away. "If I'm for hell, it won't be for hypocrisy. I didn't love her. I didn't care a damn about her."

"I think I understand." Asinine: I understood none of it.

"It was some time ago."

Some time—oh, God, was that—? "Was she why you wept that night in Winchester? Tell me what happened."

His smile was no more than a mirthless parting of his lips. "Catalogue my sins once more? I've prayed so much, lived with it so long, were it not a double sin, I could honestly confess being bored with guilt itself. Let it rest."

"No." That much a woman I was already. "If I do, this will always be between us."

"You have the stomach to hear it out?"

By God, did I not! "If you have to tell."

He spoke hesitantly at first, as if wary of the sharp edges of each memory he touched. Then faster, running the gauntlet of his purgatory to be the sooner done. So I learned the pathetic truth of Eirianell and her unborn child, the need for Harold she could never put in words until too late, his rejection, and the death she chose. I thought: Jesus and Mary pity her and him now in his misery.

"I never loved her," he summed in a flat voice, "but there was a moment when I could have been kind. I could have been a man."

All the woman in me went out to him then. *Don't*, I yearned, *don't suffer*. I'd stored up such proper, soothing things to say, but all that emerged now was a fluttering gasp of nervous laughter. "All . . . all the things I wanted to ask, as what are your intentions toward me? I suppose I should wonder, but all I can think of now is, for all we're close, I can't even touch you, and—"

His arm went round me and Harold pushed me gently

down onto my back, his face very close to mine. "This is my intention. I want to marry you."

He gave me a moment to stare up at him in joy and astonishment before his mouth pressed down softly, beautifully on mine, starting a wave of warmth that coursed all through my body. What can I or anyone say about that first sharing between two people meant for each other? Minstrels try but ever muck it up with words. All I remember is that something in both of us relaxed with that kiss, opened, and we lay close together on the bed, truly able to touch now. I felt far better and much relieved. Call it feminine practicality. Whatever was past, Harold was here with me now, and in our law possession carries the court.

"Well, finally."

"What's this 'finally'? Surely you knew."

"How could I? You never *said.* Even Hildre was beginning to wonder."

"Well, I assumed—"

"Pox on your *assume!*" I smoothed a finger over his mustaches, darker than his hair. "Sometimes you're dumb as bread."

"I have so much reason to love you, Edith."

"Pretty words. Give me a reason."

"With you it's so easy just to be me. I can laugh with you or not be ashamed to cry."

"Can you?" My hands crept down his side. "Can you truly?"

I chucked him in the ribs. Harold convulsed as if arrow-shot. "Don't!"

"Don't what?"

"I'm ticklish—no, no, Edith, now stop."

"I thought so." And I assaulted him vigorously. "Ticklish, is it? There!"

"Stop, *stop.*"

"Nay, I'll have you beg."

"I'll beg, I'll beg," he gasped, helpless and writhing.

"Beg by all the saints!"

"By all the saints and the ven—now stop—venerable and the blessed, *stop.*"

I relented and Harold collapsed against me, gasping.

"Well, now I know how to hold rein on *you*."

"My lady countess," he laughed, his breath warm against my throat. "Achilles had his heel; with me, it's tickling. I cry you mercy."

I traced my finger again over his lips and down his throat. "Buy that mercy with another, for it would be a mercy to me if you cleaned your chamber of old oranges and cloves and rings and—"

"I promise." Then again, meaning it: "I promise."

"Then I'll tell Mother—" Oh bless! *Mother!* I'd forgotten her and everything else. She'd be asking questions about my long absence. At least now I had an answer. "We should go down to supper."

The piercing blast of a horn at the gates made me jump. Harold grumbled, "Now what in hell is that?" He slipped through the outer door and returned immediately, kicking the portal shut. "Five riders just coming in."

"Who?"

He didn't know. Not Godwine's men but apparently not strangers, being readily admitted by the porter. In a moment an imperious male voice rose above the dull noise of the hall below. *Where is the earl? Quickly, I say!*

Booted feet pounded up the stairs two at a time. One vigorous rap swung the unlatched door in, and there loomed Tostig like the storm he'd ridden through, blue cloak mud-splashed, the long raven hair below his Phrygian cap plastered about his neck. He barely glanced at me before going to Harold. "I've come from London. Swegn's had complete victory in Wales."

"That's very good. Fine. You know our cousin Edith?"

Tostig tore the sodden cap from his head, nodding to me. "Lady."

From his manner, Swegn's victory was the smallest part of Tostig's agitation. "Harold, we must speak privately."

Clearly Tostig considered me an outsider and beneath confidence, but Harold gently corrected him. "Edith is our kinswoman. You might as well be first to know she's to be my wife. Now what's wrong?"

Our betrothal bounced off Tostig like a pebble off a wall. I couldn't tell whether he was angry, frightened, or both. "Well. You know how Edward reveres the Church?"

Harold sighed. "How could a body forget?"

"And the sanctity of her daughters?"

Harold's expression went tight. "Oh, Jesus. Agatha?"

"The nun, yes, if that's her name." Tostig shook out his wet hair like an irritable hound. "I don't know, it's all a filthy muddle. Swegn came home through Leominster—drunk, I suppose—and took the woman from the abbey by force."

My mouth dropped open at the sacrilege, but Harold only stared at his brother. "And?"

"And what? That's it and bad enough. For all of us. The king's already screaming for trial and conviction. Rape, Harold."

"No."

"You know what they can do to him?"

"I said no." Harold paced back and forth with the vigor of his denial. "I don't—I'll never believe that. I know him better than you do."

Tostig almost screeched at him. "Tell Edward that! Swegn took a nun from her consecrated house, carried her off, and bloody *raped* her."

When Harold looked at me, I must have been easily read, horrified and fascinated all at once. "Right now Swegn needs our coolest heads and our loyalty. Who've you talked to about this? None but Eada, I hope."

"And there enough. She's sick with it."

"Where's Swegn holding Agatha?"

"God alone knows." Tostig undid his cloak and just dropped it, sagging down into a chair. "'He's fled home to Bosham, but she's not with him."

"Are those Edward's men who came with you?"

"No," Tostig growled wearily. "Sister's. I think they can be trusted, but I'm not sure. Bosham's the only safe place for Swegn now short of a pitched fight with Edward's men. Perhaps if Father can reason with that fool something can be saved from this. You and I'd better ride early tomorrow. Father will want us."

"Surely. Swegn needs all of us now."

"*He* needs?" Tostig burst out. "What about the rest of us? What about me? Sister has her place, you have yours, and what will I get now? It's not right."

His indignation was shot through with selfish fear. I stared at the beautiful, spoiled boy whom I could have adored only a year before. He seemed so much less beside Harold.

"You may know Swegn," he said with raw conviction, "I know our pious king. Swegn may have done for us all."

Harold

The only calm about next morning was the tranquil sunlight mocking our urgency. In the way of these things, the news of Swegn was all over the hall amid a deal of smothered whispering, Botulf tight-lipped and livid. For myself, a turmoil of emotions, fear for Swegn and what this could do to all of us, but gladness for myself. At last Edith knew what I'd carried so long on my soul and would marry me notwithstanding.

We breakfasted early before departure. I couldn't apologize enough to Edith or her mother for the sorry matter that called me away, but promised a visit to Shaftesbury the moment I could to speak to Teinfrith. Then we had time only for hasty chapel and to provide a boat for their return to Southampton, servants scurrying like a line of worker ants to pack and stow my guests aboard while Tostig chafed at the delay. I rode with Edith and her mother to the boat waiting by Lea bank, Botulf trailing behind and muttering beneath his mustaches.

Before they boarded, I took Hildre's hand. "Lady, once again my deepest regrets."

"Oh, hardly your fault. Just an unhappy confusion. Do come to us soon." Then she added with a twinkle of meaning, "Teinfrith will welcome you on merrier business."

I looked at Edith, who glowed with the happiness I felt. "And I."

Hildre said seriously, "You know it won't be easy for either of you."

"God give you fair passage."

Edith's mother curtseyed to me and went off to leave us to our farewells. I hugged Edith close in a rush of tenderness. "I'm glad you want me."

"And did you doubt for one breath? I thought you'd never get round to the asking."

"Having you here has been—"

"Wonderful," she finished firmly, putting a forefinger to my lips. "Wonderful, but no more old ghosts?"

"None, Edith."

She gave me a canny smile. "*None,* says he, and I'm thankful your 'none' is none too lush, else I might have doubts. Listen: Of Swegn, then—is it as bad as Tostig said?"

"I'll wait to hear that from Swegn."

"Surely Eada can help soften the king's anger in this."

"Perhaps. I'm sorry," I apologized for the hundredth time. "I'd meant to say more and happier before you left."

"And you did." She raised on tiptoe to kiss me. "Just be about cleaning out that chamber of yours. Including the dust."

"Done."

Edith seemed pleased. "Then we shall be married and have ten children and nary halt or fool among them."

"And ride the downs in the sun, grow old, and die of pure peace, God willing. Oh, love, there'll be time, so much time for us, I promise—ach, your mum's calling."

"Come soon, Harold."

"I will." We started away from each other. I took two

strides up the bank before realizing I'd not said when I could come. As I spun about, so did Edith, both of us with the same thought—

"When?"

"When?"

—and caught ourselves, merry at our own open excitement. "Aren't we a pair?" Edith trilled.

"You'll have a long letter by post rider this week."

"And by swifter back," she sang out as one of the lithsmen handed her into the boat.

Riding back to Nazeing, Botulf asked out of his worry, "Will the king war on your father?"

"If it were that simple." If any of it ever was.

To balance the queen's men, I took Botulf and two other carls to ride with me and Tostig. We could leave my sister's men in London. I didn't trust them. Once in the city they might detain me for Edward on some pretext or other. We skirted east of Bishopsgate, sweating with the heat from the marshes, and through East Cheap to London Bridge by the least-traveled streets late that night.

I breathed easier when we crossed to Southwark. Though we and the horses were nigh spent, we pushed on to Southwark manor where we were safe on Godwine's lands and within his walls. Tostig and I shared a small room. By the single candle, as I watched him say his careful prayers before sleep, I wondered how far I or the family could trust him. Rape, he said, as if he already sat on the court judging Swegn.

"I've always known the truth of him," Tostig pronounced the morning we left Nazeing.

Indeed, brother? There's rare knowledge. It's hard enough to see both sides of a truth and that neither can prevent cause from falling toward effect like a hanged man from the gallows tree. Though you would have eagerly volunteered judgment on all of us, had Christ delegated the office, you were never the man to measure Swegn. You didn't know his loving, savage heart, didn't watch that many nights through with him while he bled over the woman. Before Eirianell I jested myself at the intensity of his passion, suggesting a leech to bleed him of such thick humors. After passing through the fever myself, I knew that siren-sickness and how the drunkard will reach for the killing draft while fearing of its ravage.

But for Tostig, whatever vices he had were yet so virginal that condemnation came easily.

Where was the original flaw in Tostig? Name any virtue men admire, any charm to make women grow breathless, draw them together in one form, it was Tostig's. The comeliest son, most devout, a faithful husband, able soldier, and yet he might have been more human if once someone could have made Tostig laugh at himself. All his life he saw himself as the hero denied his stage. He lived in the pregnant light of expectation, his fond sister's paragon, his future trumpeting where mine merely nudged and beckoned. Like Gruffydd ap Llywelyn, now king of Wales through Swegn's strength and soldiering, Tostig never had the smallest doubt of greatness due or that it would come. When that destiny mocked and fled him, I think he went a little mad.

I was fearful for Swegn, but concerning Agatha I could remain a little more detached, hardly knowing her then. She was the daughter of a Leominster sokeman with no dowry to spare for a younger daughter. Agatha was packed off to the near abbey for a nun. Swegn met her in 'forty-three when he took possession of his new earldom. She was a year or two older than him, but Swegn was smitten. Why and how? I can't say. No one outside a marriage or a love match can gauge what happens within. Swegn declared her beauty and her soul beyond any compare or words to express, which I thought excessive. Agatha was comely, though nothing I'd walk a mile to view twice, with a generous, well-shaped mouth made more for kissing than prayer. Whatever her spiritual objections, they must have fled west howling when she met Swegn. Perhaps it was an aura of danger about him, the hint of violence to erupt in the best breath. Whatever, he woke something in her unstirred by Jesus, and Swegn was never one to leave bad enough alone.

But he did *not* rape her. I didn't believe it then or now,

not after listening for hours to his agonized tales of their meetings, tense with self-denial, his pleas, her resistance and final yielding in a moment of forbidden sweetness only to tear away from him in a hell of repentance that forswore itself at his next touch. So he told me, and there was Agatha's account later. It was mad, it was pitiable. And it was the truth of them. So Agatha waited in hiding and Swegn at Bosham, choosing Godwine's wrath over that of Edward and the Church, which would fall on him and all of us soon enough.

At noon of the third day, favoring tired horses, we came to the gates of Bosham manor. One of the carls sounded the greeting horn and, presently, out from the stables, Father's grooms hurried to meet us.

Tostig pointed. "Look, Mother's coming, too."

Gytha appeared in the entrance to the smaller hall, our brothers Gyrth and Leofwine coming to either side of her like small fish bobbing to the surface of a pond. A son on each side, Gytha hurried down the walk toward us, followed by a waiting woman. Gytha threw some remark over her shoulder and the servant turned back to the hall. She and Godwine were not by nature secretive, but serious family troubles were kept from the household at large insofar as possible.

I hailed Gyrth, who was fourteen now, just at that age between boy and youth when he moved with the grace of a three-legged horse, while Leofwine, still a child, skipped at Gytha's side, waving and calling to us. He broke away and churned down the walk to collide joyously with us. Tostig caught him up roughly and mussed his hair.

"Mother." I gathered her close in my arms. Glad as she was that we'd come, I could read the strain in her face and by the simple twist of her hair done up with combs rather than the usual meticulous plaiting.

Gyrth greeted me with the portentous air of someone who knows things are bad in the family and liable to get worse, aware he was part of it and being very mature.

"Where's Father?" I asked him.

Gytha answered with flat meaning: "Planning a way out of this."

"If there is one," Tostig said.

"And Swegn? I'd hoped he'd come to greet us."

"Your brother is in his old bower," Gytha told me. "Godwine wouldn't see him until you arrived."

"Yes, that's wise," Tostig reflected. "Eada worries for you all. She's sent a letter with me."

Presented with the message, Gytha did not break the seal, but looked to me. "Swegn wants to see you immediately you've come."

"Good," Tostig said firmly. "I've a word or two for him."

"I daresay, Son, but he asked for Harold alone. Come talk with me, for I see so little of you these days."

Gytha and Tostig moved on to the hall, Leofwine hugging his big brother possessively about the waist while Gyrth hung back with me as I made arrangements to quarter Botulf and the carls.

"You're getting on for a man," I admired. "They'll be cutting new clothes for you soon."

"Ah, they've done that for a half-year gone. Nothing fits for long. Is it that bad with Swegn? They haven't told me much."

I looked down into my brother's solemn face and could have said no, Father will take care of this as he does everything, but I could see the first easily read lines of the uncomplicated man Gyrth was becoming: provincial but unshakeably loyal, blessed in a lack of complexity. I could not dissemble with him. "It's bad, Gyrth. But we'll win through."

"He looks dreadful, I know that much. What did he do? Didn't he beat the Welsh for the king? Tell you flat," he confided in a voice that squeaked with the last of boyhood. "The king's in it deep. Sent a messenger two days ago, a Crown thane demanding Father deliver Swegn."

"Oh, it will all sort out." I put more confidence into the words than I felt.

"Tell Swegn I'll take it ill if he's not to supper. He's kept to his bower since he got here."

"You mean you're civil enough to be risked at table now?"

Gyrth stuck out his tongue at me and blew out his cheeks in a farting jeer. "So I by God am!"

I walked on alone toward Swegn's bower beyond the larger hall. Deliver him by royal command. That meant his appearance before a daunting consistory of churchmen, probably dominated by Champart flanked by other Norman priests. Eada could have done much for our brother, but Tostig said she was speechless at Swegn's desecration— oh, rare day when Eada fell mute—and no merciful word when she found her tongue again.

Dear sister, you are one of those women the world will always revere as Good, though by the proper sentiments and ever the right thing done, you speed tragedy on its course.

The bower door was barred. "Swegn, it's me. Harold."

I heard him move within. The bolt shot back. Stepping from bright noon to the shuttered twilight within needed a moment to adjust sight. The room smelled stale. Swegn slumped in a chair in the darkest corner, hands clenched before his mouth. His cheeks and chin had not been touched with a razor for days, and the peasant clothes, shapeless dun tunic, and loose trousers were far from clean.

"You look like someone's stable boy."

Only his eyes moved. "Being careful. Dear Edward's men are searching for me in case I'm not here. I rode alone and light."

The foul air stifled me. I moved to prop open the shutters.

"Don't."

"Stinks in here."

A listless gesture of assent. "As you will."

In the light, the haggard sight of Swegn shocked me, eyes too bright and wild where all else sagged, as a man might slump in exhaustion from prolonged rage or passion. Perhaps in my brother's case, all that and more. As he hunched there shaking a little, I thought that if anyone appeared the victim of rape, it was my unmanageable Swegn.

His voice was a horse whisper. "Are you my true brother?"

"You ask that?"

"I know what you'll think."

"You don't."

"What they'll say at court anyway. What they'll do. Don't believe them."

"This is me, Swegn." I dragged a stool from the table and sat close before him, capturing his hands in mine. They were cold. "I'll believe you before any others."

"I love Agatha, and she loves me—must love me. But it was not rape."

A nice distinction in the case of a bride of Christ, but that wouldn't help Swegn. His fingers tightened about mine. "It was always the two of us against the world. You and me, remember?"

"Always, the way we used to play in the old villa. You were England's golden king and I your good, loyal carl. But this time it's not just another wench to be put away."

"Think I don't know that? I've got to give her up and I can't. She must go back, and now she can't."

"Heed me, damn it. The sooner you return her—"

He said it with a tender concern I'd never heard in him for anyone but me. "Agatha is ill."

"You have physicians."

"She's pregnant."

I could only drop my tired, ill-slept head in my hands. "Oh."

"The child makes her ill. I won't move her now. And to what if I did? A penitent's cell to pray on a stone floor and be lectured with holy fustian by dried-up old men? Help me, Harold."

"How?"

"I don't know, just . . . be there for me tonight. I don't know what I'm going to say before Godwine. Be near me."

God, yes, for the good it might do. I needed sleep myself, but still the unpleasant thought intruded: Swegn had not uttered one word of concern about the family's feelings or the vulnerable position he'd forced our father into.

Perhaps he couldn't think clearly at all now, hunted by the king's dogs and gone to ground.

"Pregnant. That knits her up properly, doesn't it? Only you would aspire to make a cuckold of Christ."

"Will you *listen*?" Swegn burst out. "Will you for once think before you make a joke of life? Life hurts, boy. You'll learn that someday."

I already had, but in his blundering way Swegn was facing his problem more honorably than ever I did, who now owed God for more deaths than my own. "Forgive me."

"Harold, I—" His voice smothered behind clasped hands. "I hurt."

"I'm here." I put my arms around him, holding my brother close to protect him. "And Agatha? Where is she?"

"Never mind. Safe."

So even I was not to know that much. "You know Father must give you to Edward."

Swegn lunged out of the chair to the open window, letting the sun pour over his face as a man parched might gulp cool water. He'd lost so much weight in a short time, the drab peasant clothes hung loose on him. "Our noble king. I distinguished myself in the fighting, did they tell you? Honored and respected by Gruffydd ap Llywelyn. All Wales bows to him now, while I have put him neatly in Edward's pocket. And that psalm-singing son of Ethelrede can see nothing but mortal insult to his precious Church."

"If Edward forgets your worth, trust me to remind him."

Swegn stared out the window. "It's tonight after supper. Stand by me, Harold?"

"Need you ask?"

"And don't judge."

My shoulders ached with fatigue. I needed a bath and sleep before then. "Is there some wine?"

He filled and offered me a cup of summer wine mixed with fruit juice. "Don't judge me. There's more than any of them will know. Listen and help me to understand."

7 • Swegn

I love two people in this world. Only Agatha answers
my need, only Harold knows my heart. I'm a ship
foundering in a storm, can't think but only rage, *rage*,
but I must stand before Godwine tonight with some semblance of reason. A small, sane part of me knows what
I've done and its price. I've thrown my family into the
hazard against Edward's own dice. Mind says I must care
about that, but Heart can only cry out for what it needs.

Why must I answer to Edward and the dry-dust Church?
You greedy God, Agatha never wished to be a nun. Yet,
chained by vows, no touch or glance passed between us,
no joy not stained with your filthy, cursed guilt. Was joy
ever such agony? We clung and parted, repented, resolved
to end it, then rushed together in rapture and pain. Now
there's our child to come. So be it and damn all else.

Brave words. So be what? What are you, Swegn?

I don't know; I've never known, only felt. Godwine,
my so-called father, you should have seen me against the
Welsh. Gruffydd said I led and fought like a king. My
own men hailed me as first man in the west, clashing
spears against their shields. Man? If they knew how much
of woman's warring in me, teetering back and forth with
the man, neither strong enough to conquer for good and
all.

I was born too late. The blood of Canute boils in me,
rage that must spend itself, hunger that must feed *now*
until I am sated. That done, the melancholy woman droops
in submission, crying to be loved. I wonder is it so with
the hardest of men, this need for a softness somewhere?

71

They've done with supper. Godwine will summon me soon. I must put my mind to that. . . .

But my heart goes back to a room and a time when Agatha first gave herself to me, pure woman casting off nun's purity, and then turned to me in the dim light, and I worshiped with more heart in that moment than in a month of masses. A time when I lay with her, delighting in her hands slow-smoothing along the length of my body. A time to ask nothing but pleasure in the curving line of her shoulder, thighs, and limbs tapering, dim, and dimmer in the fading light, darkening the delicate tint of her nipples swelling to my kiss against the whiteness of her skin. Her face pales to shadowed ivory close to mine. We lie silent as the distant bells ring vespers, letting God and guilt intrude only to be routed again by our fierce hunger, and then guilt itself is honey to our joy.

Harold has loaned me his best long gown, scarlet piped with gold, the Wessex colors. The garment is loose on me. I've wasted while he's put on muscle. I couldn't wrestle you down easily now, brother, but I could finish you if need be. As often as I've searched your eyes, I never saw the wolf there, only love of life and blessings you've always taken for granted, while I must somehow turn and tear at what I love. God help me, gentle me, give me rest. If I am damned, I am still lost in her.

Dear, lighthearted, innocent Harold. What a gift to be so simple, what a mercy not to burn too hot with life. Thank you for your trust and love. I must stand straight before the man you call father, but without Agatha I am only half a soul.

The summons comes. Dutifully we assemble before Godwine in his sanctum—Gytha, Harold and I, Tostig and young Gyrth, who is now old enough to share in family concerns, if only to learn. Don't reckon me too shameful, little brother; not until you've been there yourself. Tostig is immaculate as usual, his hair and first aspiring mustaches carefully oiled and curled. Whatever his virtues, as boasted by Eadgytha, they have never precluded vanity.

Beyond the open windows the summer twilight pales slowly. Only two candles are needed, playing shadows over dusty corners. This chamber has never been tidy within my memory. Only a few servants beside the steward are allowed in, and those not often. It is the heart and brain of Wessex, lined with shelves of rolled parchments, here and there an expensive bound volume.

Tostig draws Gyrth to the old refectory table, dark with generations of monks' meals served or spilled on it. There's the scribe's desk where Manni does the estate accounts, and the one decorous piece of furniture, an intricately carven chair "acquired" from Queen Emma when Edward dispossessed his meddlesome mother after being crowned. Godwine leads Gytha to the chair, then stands before the large calfskin map that dominates the room. England and Wales, the current earldoms outlined in iron gall ink, fine quill work detailing roads, towns, and distances in hours by horse or boat from Bosham. A clear picture of where, what, how many, and how far. This rotund, amiable bear of a man has a mind to outspeed Mercury, yet I chafe under him. He wants me to sit over the board morning to night, absorbed in the game of power and kings, planning so many moves ahead. Godwine used his power to make me earl but will not trust my competence when it shouts in his ear. Where is your heart, Godwine? Did you once burn for my mother as I burn now?

Loyal Harold stands beside me by a window. God, I'm tired, burned hollow. I think of Agatha with weary pride and pray she is well. When a man is born within an iron destiny, he cherishes anything won by the naked lump of himself alone.

Mother is speaking. I try to listen while Agatha's voice caresses my mind. *Come home soon. I am so afraid without you. No fear when you hold me, but then when you go . . .*

Gytha looks tense and strained. My heart would go out to her were it not tethered elsewhere. Beautiful Gytha, get on with it.

"Your father and I have only so much to say. You will do what is required without argument, do you hear? First remember what you are and who set you so high. If your father is the ablest man in England, he is also the most maligned. The envious slight his gifts and magnify his sins.''

As if his sins needed enlargement. *Your father,* she says without so much as a blush. Mother, were I that true a Christian, I would deem you as damned as myself. You are handsome still and must have been ravishing younger. The tale whispers the name of my real father.

"See clearly the damage you've done," Gytha urges. "It is Godwine the king strikes at here."

Godwine waves that aside. "We expected as much. Our king is as free with condemnation as he is with alms."

"And alleged miracles," Tostig comments tartly.

"Look at the map, Swegn. See the field and the game."

I know the field, old man, and I can see through the game to how skillfully you've danced through twenty years of intrigue under four kings to keep your balding head on your shoulders and power intact. You didn't emerge clean, but I admire the footwork.

"The position of your earldom was not idly chosen."

Anything but. Together with Harold, we hold the richest third of England. With Wessex as base, Harold in the east, and me in the west, our holdings sweep north like the curving horns of a bull. I border on Leofric's Mercia, the holdings of Beorn Estrithsson, Ralf of Mantes, and Wales. I can counter any of them swiftly across any border in the event of aggression. Through fast post riders or keels I can send news to Bosham or receive it in two days. In no more than that I stabbed deep into southern Wales with Prince Gruffydd. By comparison the northern earldoms are isolated, Harold's Anglia a tranquil backwater.

But now the bull stands to lose one of his horns, and I see beyond thoughts of Agatha to the cold consequences of my act and still cannot renounce her or say the thing was ill done. Never.

"You did well in Wales. That may weigh in your favor," Godwine says. "But you have a perverse genius for turning triumph into disaster."

"Not half," Tostig puts in. "Edward has maps, too, and Bishop Robert."

"Tostig, be so good as to allow me." Godwine

squelches him. "I've been at this for some years now. You, Gyrth! Are you paying attention?"

Laboring manfully to comprehend all this, Gyrth sits up straight. "Aye, sir."

"Not nodding off after all that supper?"

"No, Father."

"A good deal of which missed your mouth by the look of your tunic," Gytha clucks. "Lord, the wash with that boy."

Godwine's eyes are not stern as he plies the boy. "What do you see in the situation, Son?"

"Don't know, but . . . we're in trouble?"

"We are that, nor can we win just now. Nothing for it but to lose as little as possible. Swegn, mark me."

Without rising, Godwine's voice carries unquestioned command. "You will do whatever the king demands: donatives, public penance, found a charity, build a church at Gloucester, whatever. When we meet Edward, I want you so humbly contrite as to make Christ look like a lecher. Clear?"

"Sir, I wish to speak."

Harold cautions me softly, "Not now."

"You will use few words before the king and all of them penitent. He'll demand you send the woman back to her abbey, but I want that afoot by tomorrow morning and done when we meet him. That may go some way toward patching up this mess. Where is she?"

I hesitate while Gytha presses me. "You know she must be restored."

I look at Harold and see in his open face more sympathy than I would have hoped even from him. "I can't put her away."

Then that deceptive, dry calm that has frozen so many of Godwine's peers in the Witan. "Aren't you hearing well today?"

The lion could gut me were his claws extended; instead I am merely held down like an unruly cub, but his eyes are cold winter beyond a fire. "Well?"

"I love her."

Winter turns to exasperation over an obstinate child.

"What in hell does *that* matter? You were always in love with one or the other."

"She bears my child."

Silence. Gytha shades her eyes with one hand. "Wonderful. Perfect. We can't buy off the problem this time. Send her back."

Tostig's brows lift in arch amusement. Gyrth is doubly fascinated, learning much of the world tonight. Somehow I want even your young mercy, brother. Don't condemn me until you've burned in the same fire.

My head weighs a stone on my shoulders and takes effort to raise. "*My* child, Godwine. When did you or Edward command and I not obey? May I never have anything of my own?"

"When have you not? How many of your undying loves have I not paid for and tucked away? Don't give us self-pity, there's no time. Where's the woman?"

"I can't."

"You mean you won't."

"As you will."

Tostig leaps up, slamming a fist on the table. "For God's sake, Swegn!"

I barely glance at him. "Our embassy from court."

"And not the most comfortable place to be, thanks to you. The woman is nothing. Her family is nothing. What can she bring you but shame and her miserable get?"

"Tostig, shut up!" Harold orders.

He won't, not him. "Think like the lord Father's made you. Like a man!"

"A man?" I have to smile at the little courtier who's never put blade to anything but his dinner. "*You* would school me to manhood? Your tongue's your undoing, Tostig. Someday someone will have it out."

"Not you, Swegn." His hand drops to rest on his dagger hilt. Yes, this one does have the wolf in his eyes. Not yet grown into his killing teeth, but the instinct is there.

"Must I suffer correction from this puppy? One more word and I'll give him a benefice of knuckles."

Harold moves between us, warning. "Steady on, now. Tostig, if you can't help, don't hinder."

"Tostig will have his part in this," Godwine says. "I believe he's to hunt with Edward at Dean, true?"

"Yes," Tostig says with no enthusiasm. "I'll be taking more lectures than game."

"That's your function this month," Godwine instructs as if the matter were self-evident. "You'll suffer his sanctimonious tirades and let him see you are stunned and shamed at your brother's crime. You will assure him of our eagerness to make this good. To that end"—the earl's eye skewers me like a target—"you will restore Agatha."

"My son, enough," Gytha prompts me. "Harold had the same problem and dealt with it as he should."

I can only blink at my brother in surprise. "What?"

"Tell him, Harold."

Not Harold, not common sense incarnate, that laughing heart. "Tell me."

Yes, it's there in his eyes, a shadow I've never seen before. "What happened?"

Every word is a pain to him. "She was with child. I put her away. The slave girl Eirianell."

"Oh, a slave. That's different."

But he blazes at me: "You goddamned stupid ox! She hanged herself, that's the difference."

Stupid indeed, cruel in ignorance. "I deserved that. Forgive me."

"If I could be so easily forgiven. How much of my soul is owed to hell for her, I can't say. Father needed me in Winchester. She was . . . inconvenient."

"Harold, I never—"

"Never mind. You're needed now just as I was."

"Why didn't you tell me?"

"Why?" He turns away from me. "Do you think I'm proud of it?"

"Nary a whisper we heard at court," Tostig purrs. "My, my."

Gytha crosses herself. "Mercy on her soul."

"And on mine." Harold means it. I can only hold him close and tight in my arms as he hovers there miserable with self-loathing. It's not the end, I want to say, only that you've soiled your hands on the dirty world at last.

"Hours today you listened to my troubles and never a word of this."

"Swegn, please. This is not the time."

"Why didn't you let me help you?"

Harold pulls away from me savagely. "Christ, can we leave weeping? You know what you must do."

I lean close to him, our foreheads touching, close as we always were. "*You* tell me I must?"

"I do. God help me, I wish I could say else, that I could say to hell with all but Agatha, go to her, love her, rejoice in every moment with her and your child, but I can't. You can't. We're earls, royal officers. There's too much at stake. Agatha at least has life. Let her live it. Go on your face before Edward, but get it *done*."

Yes, let's end it. So tired of fighting, drained. What else can I do? "She's at Gloucester."

"I'll send a boat in the morning." At last Godwine permits himself to sit, settling his heavy bulk on a stool by round-eyed young Gyrth, who is certainly learning the ways of the world this day. Godwine ruffles the lad's hair. "Tired, son? We all are. Let's go to bed."

But before sleep comes, staring up into the dark, I know I've put my word to a promise I can never keep if honor itself drove all else out of me with whips. I cannot give her up—no, nor go prostrate for pardon to Edward or his suet-faced bishops.

Forgive me, Harold, and understand. If I'm forsworn, it's the most honest thing I've ever done and only a little more shame.

8 • Harold

When I went to fetch him early next morning, Swegn was gone, promises forgotten, his word worthless, and only a pitiful brief note on a scrap of vellum left for me in his bower:

H/ I know I am wrong but can't help myself. Curse me if you must, let Godwine forgive if he can, but never say you didn't know my heart in this. Honor is easier to leave. I must be with her. S/

No time for confusion or dismay. Godwine sent Teinfrith to Gloucester in haste. Edith's father returned the news that Swegn had sailed for Bruges with Agatha and a company of his carls, leaving us to clean up the mess he fled and pay its price. Oh, sweet Edward must have rejoiced. He could now attack his old enemy from the unassailable fortress of outraged Christian morality. From Eada only silence, while Tostig asserted bluntly what he dared not say at court.

"Swegn is unfit for his rank, but who's to have it in his place, Harold? You . . . or perhaps me?"

On that day of disgrace, he was right. He spoke of a stain on our family while I only felt something die in me. Swegn could never be trusted again.

We'd had nine days to deliver Swegn. On the last day, as Godwine, Tostig, and I rode north with a small escort of carls, I felt for my father as never before. He faced Edward now with no defense against the charges. I imagined too clearly how our king relished the prospect as he waited us on the downs near Dorking on the Chichester road.

Two riders appeared on the hilltop just beyond us. I cantered ahead of our party toward them. One of the horsemen waved to me and started down the hillside at an easy lope, followed by his squire. I spurred forward gladly, recognizing the hammer device on Hugh Malet's shield hooked to the squire's saddle. This would be a bad day for my house, so thank God for a friendly face.

"Harold!"

Knee to knee, we clasped hands. "Hugh, I'm glad to greet you. Where's the king?"

"In the valley just beyond that rise."

I waved our company to come on. "Who's with him?"

Beside his usual court train, Edward's party was distinguished and indicative of his intent toward us. Three earls: Leofric of Mercia, my cousin Earl Beorn, brother to King Svein of Denmark, Ralf of Mantes, and (we should have known) Bishop Robert Champart. No private rebuke, Godwine was to be pilloried before his peers. As Malet and I rode down the hill, I wondered which of them would profit most from Swegn's dishonor.

A narrow spur of oaks jutted out onto the downs, and in the shade of its verge, our two parties drew up facing each other, we bareheaded in respect, Edward gaunt, stern, and erect in the saddle, wearing the lightest of his crowns, a simple gold circlet.

To encounter our king for the first time, you saw a man of goodly height with a somber, ascetic bearing that made him appear older than his forty years, though this was deceptive. Edward was an excellent horseman and his passion for the chase almost equaled his zeal for the Church. Never trained for kingship, he had nevertheless shown royal ability in his first three years. Perhaps the profound disparity between his continental mind and that of his English earls confounded them. Godwine read him best.

"As in swordplay, Edward waits for you to launch a blow, then fades aside and thrusts where you're not."

Some men called Edward blessed. Certainly he yearned toward holiness as a beggar toward a good meal, and yet there was something in the man, beyond the echo of cloister and sanctuary, that could not resist revenge, a brittleness of nature that nursed grudges and too often sank to spite. He lacked the leavening of common clay, and so most men, being more of sod than sanctity, found him maddening.

The horses nickered and shuffled about, dropping their heads to graze. A large insect buzzed by the ear of Edward's fat priest-scribe who batted at it with a rolled parchment, and I wondered what doom waited us within its sealed loops.

Godwine bowed his head. "Hail to our king."

Edward stared stonily. "Wessex. Anglia," he acknowledged in his thin, high-pitched voice. "You were charged to render Swegn today. I do not see him."

"Sire—"

"Is the woman returned to God's house?"

"My lord." Father's posture was straight in the saddle, though I knew the effort that cost a heavy man long more used to the council chamber than riding. "They have left England. They are in Bruges."

Edward leaned forward, gloved hands resting on the saddle crupper. "My command was not clear?"

"Sire, the woman is with child."

The king absorbed this with a glance at Robert Champart. "Sin upon sin. You disappoint me greatly, Godwine. What security in all Wessex if its lord cannot manage one unruly son? I have too often been turned aside by your arguments, which were ever smoother than honest."

Smooth enough yourself and indirect as usual. Both Edward and Champart looked like cats contemplating a cornered mouse.

"What will great Wessex say to me or Holy Church?" Edward goaded. "What defense, what mitigation for your unspeakable son? So the proverb holds after all: The fruit falls not far from the tree. I have ignored or passed over, for the sake of the queen his sister, the nature of her ungoverned brother. I now declare him outlaw, his title stripped, and his lands to be settled on more deserving lords."

Godwine walked his horse out to halt between our two parties. "I expect no more in justice. I ordered him to return the woman. We had his promise. I make no excuse.''

"He *defies* me!" Edward's voice rose to a querulous screech. "He defies Holy Church!"

"I ask no clemency," Godwine said. "Let his lands be given where my lord pleases, but in stewardship—"

"No, Godwine."

"—against his return and restitution. Swegn has had no trial by any court."

Champart laughed aloud at the notion. "We have never been friends, Godwine," he declared in heavily accented English. "But one must admit you have a certain . . . gall? If that is the word. Restitution? Archbishop Eadsige would have him labor barefoot to Jerusalem and back."

Edward said, "Godwine, do you think us feeble-witted or uninformed? I knew last night from my people in Bruges that Swegn was there." He paused to include Leofric, Champart, and Ralf in his glance. The anger washed out of his countenance, and his tone became reflective. "And that he intends to sail for Denmark when his unholy get is born. Why Denmark, Godwine? What might he intend in Svein Estrithsson's court?"

Earl Beorn reined his horse forward and wheeled about to protest to Edward. Implication hung heavy as lead seals from the king's question. Swegn never trusted our cousin, though I'd formed no opinion. Young as myself, Beorn seemed a fair and competent lord who gave Edward no cause to question his loyalty.

"No, sire," he denied vigorously. "I take oath that my brother has no ambitions in England. If he shelters Swegn, it's no more than I would do for Harold or Tostig in kinship."

"That's as will appear," Edward muttered dubiously. "And a weighty oath from a foreign house so lately on our throne. Resume your place, Beorn. Godwine, your son has finished himself. Scribe, read our proclamation."

Across that hostile intervene, my father stoic before me, I studied the faces of his rival earls—gristly, taciturn Leofric, Ralf closed and unreadable, Beorn shaded with resignation, divided in his own way as myself, and Edward's unmistakable triumph. A butterfly danced impudent and carefree before me, and I thought fleetingly of Edith. As the clerk began to read, the enormity of our loss crushed in on me.

"Edward, by the grace of God King of the English to his earls."

His intent was indeed clear, his solution shrewd. If he deprived Swegn, he would shower no other lord with too much largesse. Some of Swegn's estates went to Leofric, some to me, one to Tostig in deference to the queen, a portion to Beorn, but none could concentrate trouble to the Crown anywhere in the rubble of Swegn's ruin.

"With our advice that you think on the proper object of loyalty," Edward admonished us. "Read on."

Now the adder's sting. Not only did a large piece of the confiscation go to Church revenue as fine, but Edward's dear nephew Ralf would hold a long swath through the heart of Swegn's land clear to the Welsh marches, a Norman wedge between Godwine, Leofric, and Beorn. My brother's folly had broken us in the west.

"My lord, I thank you." Beorn sounded as grateful as a man discovering the marks of leprosy on his skin. Leofric said nothing, obviously regarding the added estates as his due in the checking of a rival power. Only young Ralf was genuinely pleased.

"Merci, mon roi."

No, it was unjust. If Edward didn't see the weakness in this dispensation, surely I could. Godwine was constrained to silence, Beorn in a delicate position, but insignificant Anglia could bark a little at someone's heels.

"Sire, please hear me." I put spurs to the horse's flanks and walked it forward to Godwine's side. My father's glance said it was unwise to speak at all, but on this day I started learning to be a statesman of his mold, declaring confidence where I had none, clothing a half truth in the trappings of a greater good.

"No detraction from Earl Ralf, but in this distribution, my lord makes him a marcher lord. Earl Ralf does not speak Gruffydd's language or know his customs, where Swegn has personally bound the Welsh prince to our king.

Whatever Swegn's weakness, who can deny his strengths? Ask Gruffydd himself, who swears there is no better soldier in the west. Now Gruffydd will see a trusted, proven ally replaced by a total stranger."

Gratifying to see Tostig move up to my off side, raising his voice with my own. "Lord king, Harold speaks for me."

Ralf edged his horse out toward me. Men on both sides grew suddenly quiet. "Does Anglia question my competence?"

"Not at all," I said. "I question the policy."

"You whelp!" Edward exclaimed. "You'd snap at me? Godwine, is this how you manage your sons?"

Godwine tried to silence us with a stern look and a word. "Peace, both of you."

Ralf snickered, but his amusement glinted with a challenge bent on me. "Perhaps Anglia wishes to try my worth."

I was ready for him. "I'll try a question, my lord earl. Say for sake of argument you commanded the late expedition in aid of Gruffydd. Say as well that you are an equal prince. You meet, as he and Swegn did, across a river. Who crosses the water to honor whom?"

To Ralf the matter was obvious. "He is the client. He must come to me. To England."

"Right, sir—and wrong. My brother knows Gruffydd well. He is a force to be reckoned with and the set of his life and mind are as far from yours as the other side of the moon. Because he is a Briton, because he has many chieftains before whom he cannot lose face in the smallest things, because he wants his harpers to have honor to sing of, because he is painfully aware of a thousand years of warrior ancestors, because he considers *all* of us foreign invaders and hates our guts on principle and doubly because he needs you now—you obligingly cross the river and pay him honor."

Tostig allowed out of the side of his mouth, "Impressive. Keep it up."

So I would. "That is how my outlawed brother won Gruffydd ap Llywelyn's gratitude for our king. Believe

me, Ralf, Gruffydd wouldn't give a damn for your competence if he felt one instant's disrespect. The revered Au-
gustine lost the British bishops for nigh seventy years
simply because he would not rise when they approached
him. Whatever Swegn's failings, he took such pains, he
served our king well and got it *done*."

"So if I condemn a murderer," Edward countered, "I
must be lenient for that he had good manners? You heard
our will. We have done—though you speak to the point
about failings, Harold. The queen has told me of you and
your cousin in Shaftesbury. We do not deem a marriage
suitable. By God's Lamb, none of you seem to know properly where to bed."

Edward wheeled his horse about and threw his last commands over his shoulder. "Tostig, the queen desires you
return to London with us. Godwine, tonight I will rest at
your own estate in Merton. We hope your steward is
prepared."

With that he simply rode away with the earls and the
rest of his party. Godwine sagged in the saddle and my
heart went out to him in a rush. "How is it, Father?"

"Sometimes you must take a blow and swallow it. We
will speak later."

He rode away. Tostig offered me his hand. "You
spoke well."

"And you timely. I was surprised."

His too-delicate mouth twisted in a sly grin. "Did you
believe all you said?"

"Mostly. You?"

He shrugged casually. "Oh, I knew there wasn't a
prayer for Swegn, but we needed a show of unity. Edward
will be more impressed by that than condemning our own
blood, deserved or not."

I'll say this for Tostig: Yet little more than a boy, he
was nothing if not self-possessed. "Well, you're richer for
it anyway."

"My new 'estate'? You've seen that misbegotten cab-
bage patch. No one will get rich from that, Harold."

"You can hold it for Swegn. I'm going to steward what
the king gave me and send him the revenues."

"To hell with that! It's not much but it's mine now." What Tostig said then I think he could not keep back. "Always you and Swegn. Why? Why were you always against me?"

The strain of the last few days took its toll. I sagged like Godwine with our defeat. What my brother asked I couldn't have answered then had my soul stood in the hazard. "If I gilded Swegn just now, it's what I had to do. For what it's worth, I wish you'd been born first. Swegn might say the same now. Give my love to Eada. Fare you well."

"*Well* indeed," Tostig grumbled, gathering his reins. "You'll be heir now while I go back to kissing the royal arse."

"What do you think Godwine just had to do?"

And didn't Edward savor the moment. We heard later from the steward at Merton, lamenting the carnage. The royal party had battened several days on the small estate, eating and hunting the place clean as maggots on a mortified wound. Hayfields were trampled and villages ungently handled. Now Edward turned his chill, calculating disapproval on Edith and me: not suitable.

One way or another our king evened all scores.

9 • Edith

The times and all else weighed against Harold and me. Swegn gone in disgrace, Harold's position still unclear, our happiness could no longer be the sole consideration. On Godwine's map, there was no forgotten corner of the land where we could walk together and let the world pass by. Swegn's heedless flight was only the beginning.

"Oh, Edith, Edith," Harold's letter cried out to me. "My poor brother is plaiting the rope to hang himself. There is a great empty hole in me where he deserted us."

Poor Swegn indeed! Though I wouldn't meet Agatha for some years yet, what heart I could spare from our own dilemma sped to her. She had courage and a strong constitution, no more of a nun at heart than I would have been. Any Christian could pity: doubly damned both here and hereafter, living in that knowledge day by day, ill with the pregnancy, frightened, swept up by passion with only Swegn's love to sustain her in lands not always friendly to her kind. They had limited funds, were surely charged too much everywhere, and their presence in Count Baldwin's court was politically delicate to say the least. Agatha endured a difficult confinement, bore her son in the cold, wet spring of Bruges, then swaddled little Hakon and followed Swegn on as his star fell and fell.

So long as there was a hope of holy marriage for Harold and me—and far beyond that hope in truth—Teinfrith and Hildre gave us their full support. Harold appealed to Bishop Stigand while I fretted away fruitless hours with our priest in Shaftesbury, but we were lost from the start. Eadsige of Canterbury had already excommunicated Swegn and Agatha, and brushed aside Harold's suit for papal dispensation. The canon law has stood for five hundred years since Justinian declared any union incestuous between kin closer than the seventh degree.

"Got round all the time," I'd said and so blithely believed. Not without time and influence, my girl. Duke William and Matilda of Flanders were yet blocked by the Church for the same reasons. Petition after petition Harold dispatched to one pope or another—they came and went so rapidly in those days—all to no avail.

"I doubt the letters ever got to Rome," he concluded gloomily. We planned and hoped so desperately, and what we did while hoping became our life.

In the autumn after Swegn bolted from England, Harold and I met at Winchester. Edward was off hunting, leaving

Eadgytha alone with her servants as he did most of her life. We intended a plain appeal to her aid. In those early days we really believed we could prevail. Eada was a strong (and strident) voice in Edward's council; surely she would see our need and take it up.

I'd seen her only once since leaving court after her wedding. Eada came with her train to render a donative for the student girls at Wilton Abbey. Married a year then, she spoke of her royal husband with proper affection, but some things women cannot hide from each other, though then I couldn't have put a precise name to it. A woman who feels loved has a glow about her, so that merely fair or even plain becomes its own beauty lit from within. It seems to me now that Eada labored to paint that image for the world. Her conventional sentiments rang hollow, lacking the warmth to give them proof. I was still a girl, but to the maturing woman in me, aching to be with my chosen husband, Eada painted with a broad brush over drab sorrow.

But Edward must have been nagged to distraction by Godwine's strong-willed daughter. Of commanding height and presence, in public she pictured the submissive and obedient wife so lauded by the Church and so praised by Edward's monk-biographer:

Although by custom and law a royal throne was always prepared for her at the king's side, she preferred . . . to sit at his feet, unless perchance he should reach out his hand to her, or with a gesture of the hand invite or command her to sit next to him.

Written when she was nigh forty-five years of age and, I suppose, more resigned than anything else. Actually the throne was always hard on her hips and back. At Edward's foot, Eadgytha combined dutiful devotion and relief. The king saw much more in private, as I did that day in Winchester when the drooping flower showed her thorns. For God and Eada were always right. God might have second thoughts in an eternity or two, but Eada never. If Swegn was the untrainable hawk from Godwine's mews, Eada was a true peregrine.

Winchester is larger than Shaftesbury but arrayed much

the same, sloping eastward from the top of a hill down to little River Itchen. In those peaceful days, the timbered royal residence nestled companionably among ordinary streets of shops hard by the river. I remember that morning well: sailors singing bawdy songs as they unloaded fish along Itchen's banks, Harold and I gobbling pork pies at a stall, giggling as we dripped some and had to dab our clothes clean from a bucket of water, and then the time came for us to meet with Eadgytha.

Many of the court were away with Edward. The palace was quiet, dark, and chill as we climbed the stairs toward the queen's privy chambers, passed on by a series of terribly self-important stallers and butlers, to wait finally on a hard bench for far too long. One of the queen's Norman waiting women appeared in the entrance to Eadgytha's audience chamber: Clothilde, the daughter of some petty baron with ancestry and arrogance that went back almost as far as her family's unpaid debts. She inspected us with fastidious disapproval, from Harold's mud-splashed shoes and cloak to the dubious cut of my veil, then disappeared again. From within we heard a brief exchange in Frankish: Has Gervin come? Oh? Yes, you may admit them.

"The Lady of England will see you now." Clothilde ushered us in and retired.

Eadgytha's audience chamber was more austere than inviting, the far wall dominated by Christ in majesty, right hand upraised in the sign of the Trinity over a prie-dieu on which an ornate psalter lay open. To one side her audience chair, and in the center of the room a heavy table on which various parchments and correspondence were arranged in two stacks.

Eada stood by a tall clothes tree draped with the most sumptuous garment I'd seen since the pageantry of her wedding, an amice fit for a pope done in fine linen and trimmed with gold set about with precious stones. If Christ consorted with beggars, whoever wore this wrought fortune would not. My old mentor was gowned in pale blue with a white veil. The Virgin is often painted so. By happy chance, blue was also blond Eada's most flattering shade, and well she knew it.

She gave the amice a last tug and opened her arms to Harold. "Dear Brother, welcome. You're looking fit."

"Your Highness." Harold bowed. "Good morning, Sister."

"And Edith. How you've grown."

I hoped my curtsey was graceful enough. "Thank you, Lady."

"Come, let me kiss you. I'm in good spirits today. Abbot Gervin is come from Saint Riquier." Eada spun away in a swirl of weighted hem to run the rich material of the amice through her fingers. "He's been such a good friend to Edward and myself, I've had this made for him. Isn't it perfect? The jewels are from my privy purse."

"Very grand," I ventured.

"Did you receive my letter?" Harold plied. "We wouldn't intrude on you, but—"

"Yes, yes." The queen searched quickly through the smaller pile of correspondence and found one near the top, scanning it quickly. "You say you have Stigand's support."

Not a strong point, as we knew. Stigand had been openly critical of Edward and the Norman faction around him. With the letter in her hand, Eada settled herself in the audience chair, yet even seated she gave the impression of standing taller than anyone present, an illusion bred into her long before she wore a crown. I edged closer to Harold for moral support.

"I have spoken with the king and again, as you asked, with Eadsige of Canterbury." Eada lowered the letter into her lap like a defeated flag. "Neither will hear of any dispensation."

"But did you add your voice to ours?" Harold pressed. "Did you argue for us?"

"I thought it best not to, Harold. They would say I was influenced by love over law and policy, and true enough. My dear, rash brother and my old friend from school. My heart goes out to you both, but . . ." Her hands fluttered more with the indication of helplessness than its fact. Eada never fluttered, she swooped. "Edith, my dear, I can only counsel you to patience and propriety. If I can't aid in this, I can surely find you a worthy husband."

What did she say? No, *no,* this was too important for courtesy now. "I don't want another husband, Eada. This is my husband. If he were only a poor thane with a leaky roof to his hall, I'd go to him."

Harold's arm firmly circled my waist. "Or if Edith came to me with no dowry or shoes on her feet."

"Oh, Harold. You have no more sense of responsibility than Swegn. You always lacked ambition; now I see you lack clear mind. And you, Edith. To be the wife of an earl requires as much sacrifice as to be a queen. Always duty before your happiness, and those duties may very soon change."

"You mean supplant Swegn?" Harold translated. "When the sun sets in the east. He's still heir."

"Don't be light, Harold. You're always verbal and clever at the wrong time. Edward loves the Church. Swegn could not have profaned her more by spitting on the True Cross. He is an animal."

"No more than I, just unthinking."

"Unthinking," Eada echoed. "I daresay you'd call Noah's flood a heavy spring rain." She launched out of the chair to her prie-dieu to gaze up at the figure of Christ, her voice no longer cool but unsteady with strain she could not conceal. "I must bear much. Edward heaps this on me, did you know that? He never hesitates there, as if I were part of the injury. Listen to me, both of you. You've felt little of the heat from this matter, yet you ask further help and indulgence. To Edward, not Swegn alone but all our house has done this thing. We're Godwine's children, that is enough for him. Does my charming brother realize that if he is needed in Wessex, his marriage will become an important choice of state policy? Brother—have a care where you place your loyalty and love. Swegn has written his own doom."

"I know," Harold conceded bitterly. "I was there. Edward made our father crawl for it."

A soft tap at the door, then Clothilde opened it a few

tentative inches, reminding the queen in a tiptoe voice, "*Ma reine?* The abbot of Saint Riquier."

"*Merci, ma petite.* Give me a moment and then send him in. Harold, I have audiences."

"Of course." Harold stepped back and bowed as I curt-seyed, both of us deeply disappointed. Nothing had changed, nothing went forward for us. "We thank the queen for her grace and counsel. Come, Edith."

But Eada stayed us. "Wait and see this. Gervin is a dear friend. The king may soon have to take sides against Normandy, but I can at least keep their clergy close in love. Such is *my* duty. You will see how profitable state-craft can be when things are properly done. Ah, *mon cher* Gervin, come in."

In view of the grotesque incident that followed, our acquaintance with Abbot Gervin was brief, not even af-fording us the chance to be presented. I remember a short, tonsured cleric with a pinched and prim set of features. Eada swept down on him before he could speak and wrapped him in a warm embrace, cheek to cheek as she had done with us, but with far different reaction. Appar-ently the abbot's vows regarding women extended far be-yond mere celibacy. The little Norman blanched at the physical contact and recoiled so hastily he seemed to have torn himself from the queen in revulsion.

Harold and I were speechless at the *faux-pas,* but then the silly fool made it worse. "Lady," he flustered, compo-sure fled to the winds, "if—if you please, it is unseemly. I may not . . ."

Gervin faltered into silence. Eada was confused only a moment, then something darkened her blue eyes like a thunderhead on a fair horizon. "May not what, pray?"

Gervin stammered some more, totally off balance while Harold and I kept tactful silence, trying to be invisible. The gist of his apology seemed the unsuitability of such an embrace with any woman, let alone the Lady of En-gland. He should have shut up. The thunderhead became Eada's whole sky, something I'd never seen in her before.

"Unseemly?" She pronounced the word like damnation, looming over the hapless man in the terrible weight of majesty. "Un*seemly*? How dare you throw my friendly greeting back in my face! It is you who forget your place. Nothing—" The knuckles of her long fingers were white as her fists balled—"*nothing* a queen does but it is correct, little man. You may go."

Poor Gervin writhed in embarrassment, paying the price of his principles. From pure sympathy Harold tried to rescue him. "Lady, I am sure the good abbot—"

"Sure?" The rampant lioness now suffused the gracious queen, and I saw the fierce arrogance that proved her less Godwine's daughter than the sister of Swegn. "You come for gifts at my hand, then rebuke me before my own family? Then see here, monk."

Eada lunged at the clothes tree and tore the amice from its arms. "This was to be your gift, but if you are so loath to touch a woman, even a queen, then God my witness I'll find someone to wear it who's a man as well." She flung the rich garment into a corner. "Leave us!"

The anguished Gervin opened his mouth to speak, but the queen's hand came up, cutting him off like the sweep of an executioner's ax. "Leave—us."

Nothing for it. Gervin had the wit to bow and retire without a further word. I could only stare at Eada as she threw herself into the audience chair, one hand covering her mouth as if to dam what must break forth. The anger passed. She looked up at us with a rueful smile of appeal. "Doing things properly, I said. I made a proper muck of that, didn't I? Edward will insist I apologize."

"You did lay on a bit." Harold grinned at his sister. "He looked like he'd been kicked by a mule."

"Yes, yes, I'll have to give him the amice anyway. But if you only knew."

Harold went to soothe her, and in a moment of openness, Eada pressed her face into his hand and clung so while her eyes implored us both. "I am smothering. Dying, fading out. Sometimes I could just scream at all of them."

10 · Edith

No and no and *no*, such was the color of that autumn for Harold and me. When we saw that nothing would avail, our choice became clear and hard. We must marry, if at all, without the blessing of sacrament. Hildre was quick to point out the vast difference between Harold's countess and his mere wife in civil law. These lectures were conducted behind closed doors, not stern, but closely concerned for my future. Swegn's banishment and the dismembering of his earldom were defeat for all loyal to Godwine, nor could we ignore Harold's altered position.

"He could put you and your children away at any time," Hildre warned.

Teinfrith took a longer view. "He may have to, child. Look at facts. Swegn's ruined. The entire Witan's against him."

I prayed Swegn would come home, somehow compose with the king and be restored. From a girl who simply fell in love with a man, I had become that year a woman living in the direct path of a country's fate and hating every moment of it.

"What will your marriage value be if Harold must leave you?" Hildre argued.

"Facts are facts," Teinfrith hammered doggedly.

"She *knows* that, Husband."

"Does she? If Harold succeeds Godwine—and better him than Swegn, I say—his marriage choice will be important to the country. A tie with Mercia or Northumbria, even some foreign court."

Impatient of theory, my mother brought it back to my reality. "Then love you or no, Edith, you'll be quickly divorced or no more than his concubine."

I wish I could say that I stood like a heroine, ready to give all for love and not count the cost, but I knew Agatha's forlorn plight and wondered would it someday be mine. To find love in marriage was an ideal beloved of poets, but to people of Harold's station, the ideal was more good luck than expectation. Frightened and unsure of all but my feelings for him, too young for guile, I wrote to him of my fears:

—**that you would marry me as a kind of penance toward the girl who died, show kindness to me only because you denied her, as if to redeem yourself with God. If this is so, tell me *now*, for we've troubles enough, were we the truest loves in all the world. Love truly or truly not in your deepest conscience, my dearest. You will say I fear for nothing, and I will believe you because—oh, I so much want to, but I have my pride and price which will not be paid in cruel kindness or a husband's guilt. Write to me soon, for Christmas will be dark without you, and the Yule block will give neither warmth nor cheer.**

Harold

Edith's letter fetched me up short like a catchpole about my neck. Why did she have to say this when it was shamefully true in part? So many confessions and donatives I'd made that Stigand's poor thrived on my guilt. There would be a chantry in my new church at

Waltham where prayers for Eirianell would be said daily. As for that overgrown grave where my beech woods met the near meadow—when I read Edith's honest fears, I knew the time had come to lay the last flower, beg the last forgiveness, and walk away, plucking the lesson of mercy that grew from Eirianell's dust. To turn a corner, make an end to guilt and love Edith for herself as she deserved.

Dear Edith, how young we were, remember? If God had made us wise then as well, surely some frugal steward angel would have reproved the extravagance and sent to have it back. What happened had to happen.

I rode to Bosham in December, needing Godwine's counsel and Gytha's wisdom amid problems that smothered me up like fog on Thames. Any consideration of Edith and me always came back to Swegn. Cut off from his income, always spendthrift, with a family and following to support, he must be desperate. The third-quarter cash rents from his estates forfeited to me I had sent to Bruges with as much extra as I could spare. As his fortunes, so ours. Godwine advised patience and caution. Yes, I might handfast Edith, since that in itself would be no bar to a later marriage—

"If you take my place."

"Always that," I fretted. "Both of you talk as if Swegn were already disinherited or dead."

Godwine returned, "Is that so unlikely?"

"Edward is changeable, Father."

"Not in this," Gytha denied flatly.

"Swegn writes repeatedly to the king. He promises anything if he may be restored."

"As he has so often promised reform to us." My mother moved to take Godwine's arm. The windows of the study were open, washing pale winter sunlight over the map of England that dominated the chamber. "It is fine of you to send him aid, but you won't be able to afford that if you handfast Edith."

"No canon law can annul us."

"But Edward and the Church can fine you to the bone."

I recalled Edward's barbed comment to me at our summer meeting. Edith and I might indeed be poor for some time. Easily thought but needing some time and effort to comprehend. There had always been enough money, enough everything. The child part of me still refused to believe Edith and I would be blocked forever or that Swegn could not come home, that all things could not be again as before. That day in my father's study, I learned that nothing resolves itself and nothing is free.

"Is there no help for Swegn then?"

"Son, listen," Gytha urged gently. "Remember the apple tree you loved to climb, that always smelled faintly sour with the fallen fruit going to rot on the ground? We could never take many healthy apples from that tree, though we tried for years. The blight was in the roots. So with your brother. Soldiers under his command, Bishop Ealdred, all have sworn there were times when Swegn seemed possessed."

"The blight's in that thought, Mother."

"No." Godwine led his wife to a chair and stood behind her, one hand on her shoulder. "Tell him what Ealdred said."

Gytha twisted the kerchief in her lap. "Really, it hardly—"

"Tell him, Gytha. Tell Harold how much his brother loves us. How loyal he is."

Gytha hesitated. Clearly she didn't want to speak any of this. "Bishop Ealdred wrote to us in shame what Swegn confided to him over too much wine, I suppose. That he was not Godwine's son but out of me by King Canute."

Oh, Jesus. I had to sit down. The lie was dangerous as it was despicable, branding Gytha an adulteress and Canute guilty of incest with his own niece. Small wonder then that so many English ladies gave bare minimal courtesy to the highest woman in the realm, save for her daughter. Swegn would do this to her?

"Since Ealdred of Worcester loves gossip far more than he does our house," Godwine suggested, "surely Edward and others have heard. This is what he fears if Swegn goes to Denmark, that he'll use this to gain their support."

"But how, Father? The damned lie insults their whole royal family. It's blind mad."

"So is he." Godwine moved heavily to the firepit at the far end of the chamber, spreading his hands to the warmth. "Oh, yes, he was sorry and all but groveled before your mother. Swegn will always be sorry."

"And we always believed him," Gytha sighed. "Now it's too expensive."

"I knew as much this summer when I could say nothing before Edward and the earls. He's lost, Harold. He'll fail in Denmark, fail if he returns. As usual, he takes everyone down with him." Godwine turned his gaze on the large map with the new red swath of Earl Ralf thrust through Swegn's lands like a dagger sunk clear to the Welsh border. The sound of his thought was distaste and resignation. "Marry your Edith, but remember what it will cost you."

"And her," my mother added. "Edith is a fine girl. There's good stuff in her."

With all I'd heard, I could barely think clearly. "Then you'll disown Swegn?"

My father looked older then than I'd ever seen him. "I can never do that. We swallow the disgrace and get on, but he's passed over. You are my heir."

We were silent a moment. There was only the crackling of the fire. *There it is, Edith.* I felt a surge of ambition like bread rising in an oven, before seeing the price of the prize. The entire south of England mine, the richest lands, an army of thanes and their followers, myself no longer a second son but a power to challenge anything Edward might field against me—and with these, all Godwine's enemies, including our pious liege himself. Edward always blamed Godwine for the death of his brother Alfred. Many accepted this tale and made sure it was published abroad. Godwine never spoke of it, nor had I ever dared to ask, but the contention remained a deep, bleeding rift between my father and the king.

"Whatever you tell me, sir, you always have my loyalty and love. If I'm to be Wessex after you, there's that I must know."

Godwine put his hands behind him. "We've had much unpleasant truth today. Why stop now?"

"Alfred."

A look passed between my parents. Godwine's smile was slight and sad. "Poor, unhappy Alfred. For a dead man he has a long shadow."

Unaccountably I was calm and composed of a sudden, almost as if some mind beyond my own were thinking for me. "I said you have my love. If I have yours, give me truth now. Mother, you need not stay."

"Listen to him: already standing under the Lions. My son, you do not dismiss me. I've heard it all before. Once more will not wrench my heart."

Godwine asked her, "Harold was how old then?"

"Barely ten."

"And a subject of Canute's Danish empire."

Common knowledge. Canute took England from feeble Ethelrede, married his queen, Emma, and set about absorbing our divided people into Denmark's future. He had Harthacanute by Emma and Harold Harefoot by a second wife, a mere concubine, some said. Meanwhile Emma already had young Edward and Alfred growing up in Normandy.

"Dynasties are a mess," Godwine opined bluntly. "The trouble with royal blood is that it has rights with or without royal ability. The problem of our people is that we've always resented foreigners, especially on our throne."

"And yet you supported Canute," I reminded him. "He created you."

"My rank and fortune, yes—and a wife worthy of a king, but beyond that he could unite England. No other man could touch him for ability then, nor, unfortunately could either of his sons. Harefoot was a galloping disaster, so was Harthacanute after him. Rulers are *made,* not born, and the best of them have known that since before Caesar. Young Alfred did not. God alone knew what he hoped to accomplish, but he landed on my coast, ostensibly to visit his mother at Winchester. Harefoot set me to arrest him and . . . do what was necessary."

"Necessary? Including execution?"

"I excuse myself nothing. The country was on the brink of civil war, torn between Harefoot and Harthacanute, confused enough without another prince to further muddy the waters. I was the king's earl. I did what was needed."

Then at Guildford, Harefoot's own men relieved Godwine of Alfred's custody and took the prince to Ely, where he was blinded and died shortly after.

"Then you were not present, sir?"

"No, thankfully."

"But, did you know what would happen to Alfred if you turned him over?"

Godwine's eyes had long since faded from clear blue to a kind of clouded grey, perhaps from too much gazing on a brutal world, but now they evaded nothing. "You have a gift for the heart of things."

We stared at each other, not father and son now but equals between whom there could be no pretense, not even of kindness. "Did you?"

"Yes, I knew it would happen. Harefoot was a butcher, I his servant, a sword in his hand. If I'd delivered Alfred myself, he was still doomed. He came at the wrong time. Notions of justice, guilt, or right were luxuries then. I did what I had to."

What men must do. What a cruel time and a brutal king commanded, and so never directly guilty but never truly innocent. In the same vein, I must deny Swegn and take his place for reasons beyond either of us.

Never say I envied you, Brother. Never say I wanted this, but damn you to hell, what devil turned you so false and weak that you dragged our mother through so much dirt?

But for the stubborn love that wouldn't let go, he had to be torn out of my heart. Like foolish Alfred, what could he bring home but more confusion and harm? I must deny Swegn for my parents' reasons. He cost too much.

I walked alone the rest of that day, through the village, around the marshes that bordered the inlet while the wind blew and the tides came and went. I prayed on the cold flagstones of Trinity Church—tried to pray, but the heart of prayer, like stones, flew at Swegn.

Damn you, I wanted so little and knew so little. I prated at you righteously that duty was our life, when mine was not yet in the balance, never counting how little of a little we may keep ourselves. Now I could envy the freedom of a gull and know why their cries sound so much like laughter. Nigh comic to think I am advanced because, in the matter of one woman, you couldn't keep your trousers up. You made the bed but Edith and I must lie in it.

Never come back, Swegn. As you once brooded, sail beyond the mists and disappear like the ghost ship you are.

Then if I must be a power instead of a nobody with a loving wife, so be it. If I must be a miser in my time with Edith, so little to her, so much in dealing with Edward, dark in his crypt of a soul as ever you were mad, so be that. I take your birthright, Brother, because you've broken mine forever. As Edith, I have my price. If my life must be thrall to destiny, Edith will be part of it come what may, but damn you thrice again, Swegn. Damn you and Edward, damn his bloody crown and all it devours for so little in return.

From that day nothing would ever be the same. A few days later I rode for Shaftesbury to claim Edith for my wife.

11 • Edith

Wherever the Welsh girl lay buried in Harold's heart, I knew he loved me when he rode through three days of winter rain to ask my hand. Sing heigh ho the holly for the twelve days of Christmas and to hell with King Edward and his bishops. Ten days before Christmas when the rain turned to stinging sleet whips to lash at our walls, Harold stumbled into our hall in the midst of supper, Botulf at his side and both of them chilled through, to stand before Teinfrith, water from their sodden cloaks puddling about their boots. Harold looked haggard but happy, knowing his mind. There before my parents and the delighted servants, my love stripped off cloak and baldric and spoke his mind.

"Thane Teinfrith, I'd have Edith to wife. We won't have the Church with us, but there's the law."

My heart leaped up and I would have followed it winging like a lark to him, but Hildre restrained me with a firm hand under the board.

"But I want to, Mama."

"Of course, but with dignity, Edith. The bargaining is first, and that's your father's place."

Shivering wet, Botulf was miserable as a chilblained hound, beseeching, "Thane Teinfrith, may I have a warm cup and a place by your fire?"

Invited to sit, Botulf lurched away on frozen feet to find blessed comfort. Harold plowed the wet-straggling hair back from his forehead and asked me directly, "Will you have me then? Been a long cruel ride and not to hear you say no."

"As if I would."

Oh, I remember every moment of that evening, every hour to the time we departed after Plough Monday. Cheers broke out from the servants' tables, fresh casks of ale were broached, wassails raised to Harold and me, raucous predictions of a Christmas such as Shaftesbury had never seen. Harold joined me at the high table and we pledged one another from the same cup.

Teinfrith leaned between us over the backs of our chairs, speaking for our ears alone. "We can't help hearing rumors. Are you to be Wessex, my lord?"

Harold put his hand over mine; what he said carried no pride or pleasure. "I'm afraid so."

"What then of my daughter?"

"Teinfrith, I've lamed my horse and nigh done for myself and Botulf getting here." Harold slumped in his chair, utterly spent from the journey. "Edith will always be my wife and provided for. Shall we draw the contract tomorrow?''

"Agreed. Then I must find the right parties to perform the handfast ceremony. There'll be some charge involved and''—my father added significantly—''a great need for discretion.''

There would that. As daughter to Shaftesbury's thane, my marriage would be no less noticeable than a forest fire. Neither our bishop nor the mother superior of the convent could be invited, nor any of my dear teachers or friends at Wilton.

"Darling Edith," Harold said, "we'll be expensive.''

"We're worth it.'' But then and later I wondered bitterly: Why could our joining not have been as simple as the love that inspired it?

The storm blew itself out before morning, the sun only a half-opened eye in the east when I fetched a cup of hot cider to Harold's bower. He was already yawning and grumbling.

"Damned Botulf kept me awake all night with his snoring.''

On a pallet in one corner, Botulf lay like the dead, mouth wide open, still thundering prodigiously. Poor man, he'd drunk so many healths to us last night, he needed assistance to bed.

"Here's to warm you.'' I put the cider by and hugged myself to Harold in the bed. "And myself to help. It snowed last night and the whole world is white. The men are dragging in the Yule block.''

The last snow was feathering down from a windless sky, and Harold must share it with me. "Come! Up and dress, you lout.''

"Such a hurry?'' Harold drank some cider, smiled sleepily, and wrapped me in his arms as I buried my face in the warm man-smell of his neck.

"Papa will have breakfast before the bargaining. What's my bride price, pray?''

"What indeed? What will I give for my pearl of great price?''

"And the right to love me solely and selflessly all your life, mind."

"I'll give . . . a broken pot ill-mended."

"Beast."

"Used trenchers. Bread sops from last week's hunt."

"Miser."

"Shaved pennies from a false moneyer."

"Oh, it's a true lover, I can see that."

"And in the contract, that you can never be beaten on holy days or through Lent."

Botulf snorted, reared up and over on his belly heavy as a fallen tree. I dealt Harold a good one on his lean rump. "Up!"

When he joined me outside, we stood for a moment in the magical dawn light that poured gold over the new snow, watching four of my father's foresters coming through the stockade gate, straining at the chains that towed the great Yule block, a whole section of oak trunk cut months ago by a sokeman clearing new land, the wood marked for our hall. The block would burn through the Christmas season, servants and cottagers would beg the embers as protection against thunder and lightning, and even the cold charcoal would be mixed with water as a cure for consumption.

In the faerie hush of that morning we were children again, scampering out to greet the men, hauling with them to drag the log to the hall, all of us lustily singing *heigh ho!* and *"Call Home the Sun"* as we and Welsh alike have done since before history was written. And when we fetched up by the doors, panting and cheering, I'm bound there were never two happier young people in all England.

"Good plighting, lord!" the men roared as Hildre came out from the hall with cider for them in a clay jug. "Good bridal, lady!"

"Your father must speak to Earl Harold after breakfast," Hildre informed me meaningfully. "You'll count linens with me."

"No, please." Harold wiped the chain rust from his hands and drew me close to him. "It's not the custom, but I wish Edith to be present. We know what we do and its cost. From the first, there've been few secrets between us. From today there'll be none."

"I want to be there, Mama. I know the law as well as Papa."

"It seems very forward. Sometimes I think we spoiled you. But as the earl pleases."

I gave her a grateful peck on the cheek and skipped after Harold.

After breakfast Harold and I were again summoned to the hall by Teinfrith, together with Anfrith, the plump little reeve of Shaftesbury, who would record and witness the marriage contract. With some sense of the formality of the occasion, my father wore his best long black robe with the small gilt ax of his rank thrust through the belt. He opened the proceeding with a loud *harrumph!* that startled the hound drowsing by the firepit. It was clear Teinfrith intended to protect his rights as well as my own.

"Daughter, you know you may not be forced to marry where you mislike any part of the agreement?"

Sitting to one side, hands demurely laced in my lap, I attested I misliked not a jot. Anfrith duly recorded the match as of my choosing.

"My daughter has perpetual right to her morning gift. Agreed, your grace?"

The gold ring? Of course he agreed. Pick, pick, pick. Let me get *married*.

And so through the early morning as the winter sun grew brighter outside. My right to second marriage if widowed, my share of all household goods or the forfeit thereof if I married within a year of my husband's death. Oh, no fear at all. I never married again, nor will I.

"Now." Teinfrith sat back and folded his hands over the ax at his belt. "Let it be written that Edith keeps all items of bedchamber she brings with her."

Standing before the table, the tedious legality was beginning to amuse Harold. He winked at me. "Agreed. I'll not go to law over a featherbed."

"Good, good. Now we come—umph—to the bride price. Edith is my only child and precious to me. How dear is she to you, then?"

"More than I can say, sir."

My father nodded approvingly. "But for the sake of the law, please try."

"Shall I bandy superlatives, Teinfrith?"

Father was not to be put off. "My lord earl—how much?"

"The cash rents from two villages," Harold proposed. "For two years."

Teinfrith frowned and seemed offended. "Did you not say Edith was dear to you?"

Papa the old fox. *Dear* in this sense we take from the Danish *dyrt,* meaning expensive.

Harold spread his hands. "Edith is worth a city's price and more, but I have a household and soldiers to support."

"Three villages for three years," Teinfrith posed.

Harold's show of hesitation was admirable. "Anglia is not rich, Thane."

"Your grace will not wring my heart out of a fair bargain. Three."

"Oh . . . done."

"And," Teinfrith raised a litigious finger, "the equivalent in Wessex should you succeed to Wessex within that time."

"Villages of my choosing," Harold parried.

"So I lose no value thereby."

"Done."

"Anfrith, record it."

I couldn't help giggling. "Better than a broken pot, love."

Teinfrith looked around at my intrusion. "Eh?"

"Nothing, Papa. I spoke idly."

"And now for Edith's personal maintenance from the date of the marriage. You have thought on that?"

Harold had. I was to have the rents free and clear from specific hides tilled by the villages of Nazeing and Eppingham, rendered quarterly by Harold's stewards.

Teinfrith thought that fair but not to the point of forgetting eventualities. "And the equivalent in Wessex later?"

"Larger and even more suitable."

"Reeve, put that down. More when his grace becomes

Wessex. Generous, my lord. Very generous, but how much more?''

"Half again that in Anglia.''

I stared at my love and swallowed hard. The rents from two prosperous Anglian hamlets would not make a woman rich but certainly more than comfortable in her own right. Not at all shabby for a convent girl with four gowns to her name and two of those just everyday. I remember it for the secret laughter between Harold and myself while Papa was being so cautious of my welfare. I was only a thane's child; trust me, had I been more exalted the bargaining could have gone on for months.

"This, ah, steward who will render her accounts.'' Teinfrith steepled his fingers. "He is honest?''

The mischief flickered in Harold's eyes. He leaned over the table, sober-serious as my father. "As yourself, Teinfrith.''

"To the half-penny?''

"To the farthing.''

"No sticky fingers? You must have a care to that.''

Now it was Harold's turn to feign injury. Did Teinfrith think that the earl of East Anglia, young though he was, had no grasp on his own lands? "You wound me, Thane. I'm the law in Anglia next to the king. Sticky fingers are detached from greedy hands and that quickly.''

Teinfrith approved. He sat back, fingers drumming on the gilt ax head. "So. Now, what will you ask from me?''

What indeed? Our wealth was loyalty to Earl Godwine, not much in cash or kind. Then Harold did something I'll always love him the more for. He grinned at Teinfrith and completely changed mood and direction. "Tell you flat, sir. I don't much care.''

That took the wind out of Papa's sail, though he recovered with admirable speed. "Oh. Well. It should be in some proportion, so you realize I am not rich and this has been a thin year. Two years, actually.''

"Do you now wring *my* heart, sir?''

"Nay, I speak truly.''

"And I would not incur the sin of greed.''

"Therefore?''

"Oh, make me an offer."

"Well . . ."

"Have you a penny about you, Teinfrith?"

My father spluttered behind his drooping mustaches. "Sir? I've heard you have a certain lightness of wit, but we're doing business here. A penny? You think I offer my only daughter without the legal gift?"

Harold dismissed it with a slighting gesture. "Ah, well. You spoke of thin years. Make it sixpence."

"By God! You'll not find me niggard. You shall have the marriage gift our ancestors passed from wife to warrior lord, not a jot less. A new sword, a baldric *and* coat of new mail."

"Let it fall below the knee."

"Until you flamin' well trip over it, if y'want."

"Done."

"Reeve, write. Edith, come."

I was there beside them as Teinfrith poured two cups of mead. He and Harold signed the marriage contract and the reeve witnessed.

"Pour the wax, set the seal. I think I drove a keen bargain," Teinfrith congratulated himself. He and Harold linked arms and drank as new-bonded father and son.

"You did indeed, Thane Teinfrith."

"Ah, but you're not a horse trader. You should have held out. I would've settled for two villages."

"Come to that, you could've had me for the penny, for I love Edith that much." Harold offered me his cup to plight our troth, and I drank happily from where his lips had touched the rim.

"My love," I whispered, "you're flat outrageous."

"So I am."

So he was. He often gulled greater men than Teinfrith with the same careless charm and the careful mind behind it.

12 • Edith

"Look, they're coming."

Harold pointed to the sharp bend in steep Gold Hill that bordered the convent wall. Three men and a woman were descending to meet us through the last light of winter afternoon. The cold wind stirred the hood of my cloak, and my mare snorted as she scented unaccustomed smells from the town.

Teinfrith had arranged the meeting in very little time, considering the delicacy of the matter. No, Botulf might *not* attend Harold this day and took it ill his lord would not confide in him. None were told more of this than necessary.

I had never knowingly met Wicce folk before nor were they ever discussed in our hall. That morning Hildre took me aside for what, by her secretive manner, I thought was to be the usual instruction toward my wedding night, which I'd rather omit for both our sakes. To be maiden is not to be naive. A number of the nuns at Wilton had been married before taking the veil. Sister Martha Veronica answered our fascinated questions with bored authority. After twenty years with her husband, marriage to Christ was a rest. She needn't abide his snoring at night nor scrub his endless wash.

But that was not my mother's drift. "They'll meet you before vespers. If you recognize them, don't call them by name. There will be four of them. Each will have a part in your handfasting."

A day of learning all round. Teinfrith and Hildre had

apparently known the Wicce folk for years, their existence an unspoken fact.

"They are your father's best ear to the minds and needs of the country folk. So they do no harm, Teinfrith protects them as any other lawful householders."

As they neared us I did indeed know them. One man and the woman I recognized as a silversmith and his wife, plainly but well dressed in muted earth colors. The other two men were familiar to sight, local merchants seen often in our hall.

We dismounted as they approached, and Harold held our horses. The four arranged themselves before us, the priest and priestess, as I supposed them, directly before us, flanked by the other two.

The priest was a man of middle years and a quiet dignity, his manner not cold but reserved. From his wife I had the impression of intelligence and considerable strength.

"Your Grace and lady," the priest greeted us. "There seems some service we can do you."

"We would be handfasted," Harold said.

"So we were given to understand." The priestess's voice was low and melodious. "But we must be cautious. How stand you on our Craft?"

"As Teinfrith. As Godwine who is your earl."

The barest smile from the priest-silversmith. "Your Grace says much in few words. For one whose name means 'friend of God,' your father has a formidable number of holy enemies."

"So does the pope," Harold returned, delighted with the man's keenness. "When bishops say mass, my father is tolerant. When they try to steal his lands, he's downright narrow-minded."

The woman's lips parted in silent, appreciative laughter. "My young lord is already a realist."

"Lady, I am learning."

"Then you see our position. We have performed handfast often in circumstance like yours, and Thane Teinfrith has been our protector as citizens. We must ask that consideration of you." The woman looked closely at Harold. "You understand, my lord?"

"Teinfrith has always shielded us with silence and discretion," the silversmith declared. "Now we hear you are to be Wessex after your father."

Ah, now they were, just as Harold and my father, not warlock and cowan, but merely two Saxons talking bargain and price while my feet got cold.

"First your silence before all."

"Of course."

"No names on the marriage register but yours, the bride's, and the reeve."

"Agreed. And?"

"When you succeed as Wessex—as on occasion orthodoxy takes the Church like fever—your promise to protect any householder in Shaftesbury who may need it from such an ague."

With my toes growing progressively more frozen, I didn't realize the import then, but have often since. *Seax-Wicce,* our old religion, was still too widespread among country people for the Church to threaten seriously, though they made trouble now and then. Like the Jews of London and York, this silversmith and his followers must be thrice honorable and visibly more law-abiding than their Christian neighbors. Now he asked a promise that might cost Harold dear later. All his life men said my love was too free with promises. He broke none to me and only one that mattered to England, and that because he cared more for all of us than his honor or, possibly, his own soul.

"Done," he said.

"In writing, Your Grace." The small man beside the priestess spoke for the first time. "One copy only, over your signature and seal, to be kept by us."

Harold grinned at him. "Signed in blood?"

"If my lord inclines to the exotic; otherwise ink will do nicely."

"So be it," Harold pledged. "So you keep my peace and work no harm. There's a fee?"

"None to you," said the silversmith. "Thane Teinfrith was generous as always. Unless you've a penny about you."

I saw Harold's surprise, then his bark of laughter rang

out on the cold air. Father must have told them of the bargaining. Harold and the priest shook hands warmly. "Until the bridal, my lord and lady."

My toes were painful cold now despite the thick wool stockings. I longed to stretch them close to a warm fire. "Please? When can it be?"

The priestess lifted her gaze to the moon already bright in the late afternoon sky and waxing toward full. "Within these four days, no later. Until then, merry part."

She stepped close and kissed me on the brow. "Be happy."

We were married three nights later, though we would have wed in the dark of the moon on the most ill-starred night of the year. Our hall was ready, the first preparations for the wedding feast set out by midafternoon. The priest assured us there would be no impediment so long as an ample space in the center of the hall was left clear. Their full circle would be present, plus Anfrith the reeve, Harold and I, and my parents. For the circle's security, not ours. Our servants and cottagers were plaintive with disappointment, especially since so much extra work was asked of them in preparing the feast, and yet they understood when given the nature of the wedding. I gathered these rites were more familiar to our tenants and servants than Holy Church would care to imagine.

Botulf was apprehensive when he learned in full. "Oh, ho, when the wrong people get wind of *this.*"

An enormous number of tallow and beeswax candles were dipped and rolled; the parish church went begging that week. If excluded from the wedding, all would be welcome at the feast to follow, not only servants and tenants high and low but extra tables would be set out for as many as could be crammed into the hall, while those who lacked a place would find more than the usual broken meats and loaves freely dispensed at the kitchen door. Mother was everywhere, badgering the cooks, fretting over supplies promised but not arrived, upstairs and down betwixt hall and bridal bower, counting linens twice over, seeing to the hanging of holly ropes in the hall—

"Don't put it there. It goes *there*. And use smaller nails. It's holly you're putting up, not a gallows."

—and finding time that afternoon before the wedding to bathe and dress me herself. Normally I used our bathhouse, but today the great staved tub was carried up to my own closet and filled before Hildre barred the door. She would let no one else prepare her child for wedding. She lit three candles, for it was already darkening outside, and laid my new white wool gown and undershift on the bed. Beside them she set the new mantle of light blue, the shade I loved so when Eada wore it, wondering if it would complement someone plain as myself. Mother would not let me lift a finger—

"Let me, child."

—moving from clothes press to bed with a silent, tender preoccupation. Her hands, as they set out the new stockings and shoes, had an eloquent reverence that sent a surge of love through my heart.

By the gown, Hildre set out the chemise case and belt which would carry my psalter. I wore it for many years, so well and cunningly was it made of pigskin with eyeholes and loops for household keys, shears, awls, and the small case of precious needles handed down since my grandmother's time. It was a gift I'd not expected. Chemise cases were bought ready-made but Hildre had made the extra loops and eyes.

"So beautiful, Mama."

When my mother turned to me, something I'd rarely seen before brightened her eyes in the candlelight. "Right, my girl. In you go."

Briskly said but nothing hurried about her hands as she undressed me and helped me into the tub. When I reached for the soap, she had it first and gently worked it over my back and shoulders. The hot, herb-scented water made my skin feel wonderfully sensuous as always. I can't reckon how many fancies my absolute but yearning virginity had indulged in such baths. I stood up and let Hildre wash me all over, feeling at once like a woman grown and a little girl come all too soon to what I'd thought I was ready for.

"Mama? Am I fair?"

"Fair what?"

"You know."

Her smile was softer than usual. "Oh, two legs, two arms, two breasts, one head. You won't cause the hens to stop laying or a husband to leave home."

"Oh, *Ma*ma."

"There now." She kissed me as I sank back into the water like a doomed ship. Undoing my hair, she said quietly, "Were I a man, I'd be wedding you myself. You really love Harold so much, then?"

"He's the other half of me."

"Oh, there's deep." Hildre worked the comb through my hair. "No questions?"

I flinched inwardly. We're not to have *that* lecture, are we? "Sister Martha Veronica was married once. She used to tell us things."

"Oh? You know what to expect?"

"Aye, Mum."

"Purely from listening, that is?"

"Hardly else."

"Hardly. And not nervous?"

"Not about that," I lied shamelessly.

"Well, there's a wonder. I was." Hildre brought the wide towel cloth to wrap about me. "Your father was so anxious he couldn't do much, and I was a bit distracted myself. A little wine helps."

I remembered Harold's chamber at Nazeing, how it cried out that other woman's presence. That gave me a chill moment. What if his love for me were not that sure after all? What if he measured me against the Welsh girl and found me pitifully wanting? Or if he mourned her yet despite all? Damn her, what spell did she work on him?

"You don't think Harold's changed his mind, Mama?"

"Not a bit of it. They all have their doubts on this day. Harold is a good man, Edith. We are truly happy for you."

"You thought he lacked ambition."

"Before you father became thane, no one thought he'd make a decent hedge warden. Wait, I think they've come."

Cart wheels creaking in the courtyard and the sound of voices raised in greeting and welcome. The thing was begun. Am I fair? Will he find me so? Find or not, we're for it, girl, and no mistake.

I looked down at my body, hoping by some miracle to see all those endowments men called beauty and found not much beyond a sturdy young body, good skin, straight legs, and over it all the health of an ox, but for pleasing a husband? Confidence quailed and fled.

"Raise your arms, girl."

Hildre slipped the undershift over my head and then the white wool gown.

So many years ago. So much less to fear from love than kings.

13 • Edith

I'm *not* nervous."

My voice squeaked as I pulled away from Hildre in the readied hall. The dozen folk of the coven waited as their circle was prepared, our servants whispered just beyond the closed doors like mice behind a tapestry, and the thing was here to be done. Not nervous? I was a storm of feelings: happy, excited, quietly hysterical, icy-handed, and numb. Standing with my father, Harold looked much the same.

I know little of the old religion or those called witches who attended our handfasting, except they appeared no different from those I saw at mass of a Sunday, and some of them I had seen there quite often. Their dress was peculiar to this ceremony: earth colors, green, yellow, or brown except for the priest and priestess, who wore white tabards over their regular clothes. All carried traditional seax knives.

The circle "thane," one of the men we'd met with the priest, set the book on their round altar with the salt, water, candle, and sword. He unwound the long knotted cord that belted his green tabard, and measured nine feet from the center to each of the four points of the circle. When the ring was cast, an opening was left, candles were set about the circumference, and we were called into the center to stand before the altar.

In truth I remember more of it now than I did in the giddy, dazed hour that bound my life to Harold's. Hildre and Teinfrith standing to one side with Anfrith the reeve, the circle thane announcing our intent, their scribe stating our names in a clear voice. "Harold Godwinesson is the man and Edith Teinfrithsdohtor is the woman."

Facing Harold, the priestess asked his name again and his desire. He sounded a mite stiff but managed not to stumble over the ritual words. "To be made one with Edith in the eyes of Woden and Freya, and of God the Father, Christ the son, and the Holy Ghost."

These folks do not swear by Christian deity but were not surprised when we asked to include our own. Apparently this happened often when they handfasted those of our faith.

Now the priestess took the sword from the altar, setting the point to Harold's breast. I heard his oath through a haze.

—in love, honor, and sincerity . . . may the seax pierce my heart should I not be honest in all I declare.

The sword was passed to the priest, who touched the point to my own breast as I repeated the oath. Then the priestess sprinkled the two silver rings with salt-purified water and handed them to us. After so many years I don't recall the words of advice they gave us, except that they were simple, wise reflections on the natural differences in men and women, the storms that would surely come and as quickly pass; of giving and receiving, of expected weakness and true strength, each in its season.

"Make love often and with joy and know truly that you are one in the eyes of the gods and of Seax-Wicce. For love is the law and love the bond."

From all the circle: "So mote it be!"

We turned to each other, awkward and dazed. Harold dropped the ring before fumbling it onto my finger. Somehow I managed to get mine onto his, then we just stared at each other, unable for the life of us to remember what came next.

The priest coughed discreetly. "Kiss her, my lord. It's done and we must clear the temple."

We kissed numbly as we looked. The priestess raised the great sword, the coven folk their seax knives. The gods were thanked for attending. "The temple is cleared."

In a trice the circle was dispelled, altar and candles taken up, tabards removed, and all became simply guests looking to a happy feast. Hand in hand with Harold I received the embraces of my parents and the good wishes of all while the first joy poured like sunlight through fog into me. *I'm his wife. I am really his wife. Jesus and Mary, forgive us. We would have gone to church if we could.*

Then Hildre was everywhere with peremptory orders for the feast to be brought in *now* and look sharp! The hall was suddenly full of people, a roaring tide of voice, and pounding at the outer doors.

"It's the guests from Shaftesbury," Teinfrith called. "Porter, let them in."

But I ran ahead of the slow porter and threw open the great doors myself as the musicians struck up lively in their first tune.

"Come in!" I sang to the eager faces there. "Happy Christmas and merry Yule. Come in all!"

No, I couldn't stand still; the inviting sweep of my arm carried me about in a thrill of music and happiness until I was facing Harold. "Oh, come and welcome, my good lord."

We ate little at the feast, Harold and I, but danced ourselves foot-weary into the small hours. Some were carried away from the merry battle of that board, others staggered away leaving the ruins of roast boar, honey-basted chicken, spitted doves, ale barrels drained of their last drop. Many were still gorging when Harold quietly left the high table. Shortly after, Hildre and her women led me out amid cheers and good wishes and dressed me in new night clothes for the bridal bower, a large chamber over the hall usually kept for important guests.

At the door I kissed my mother good night and hugged her close. "It has been so beautiful, Mama."

"And more to come. Good bridal, daughter. Your husband is waiting."

I pushed the door in and closed it behind me. Four candles burned, two on either side of the bed. Harold sat at the foot in his nightshirt, warming his feet by a peat brazier. I will always be grateful that he wasn't solemn at all now, smiling at me like the friend he ever was. He rubbed at his toes. "Well, hasn't this been a day?"

"Feels like three."

"Sorry I dropped the ring. My hands wouldn't seem to work right. Well?"

I didn't move. "Well what, then?"

"Going to sleep there by the door? Much warmer over here."

I came slowly to sit by Harold, stretching my feet out to the peat warmth. Somehow I couldn't look at him straight on just then, couldn't tell him what I feared all of a sudden. "How is it with you, Harold?"

He took my hand while considering the question. "Like I've gone charging at a boar without a spear. How with you?"

"The candles are terribly bright, aren't they?"

Harold rose and blew one of them out. "Better?"

Not really. "What I wanted to say . . . this is a path you've been down but I've not. I mean, after all of them, after—"

"Edith." There was the old lightness in his voice. "You're not an enemy castle to be stormed."

"Oh, I—" Then everything came out in a rush. "Just I've never grown tall and comely like Eada, and I don't sway like she does when she walks. Even at Wilton she looked like a queen, and you're used to beautiful women and—"

"Stop now. You'll have me asking the bride price back."

"And I'm not that slender," I agonized.

"Nor high as Caeser's Tower nor wide as Thames mouth. For God's sake, be still before you disappear altogether. Wait now." He got up and blew out another candle. The room softened toward friendly darkness as he came to kneel by me again, taking off my shoes and massaging my stockinged feet before the brazier. I began to feel welcome warmth flood through me.

"I was flat scared all day before the wedding," he said, not looking at me. "Men nattering at me with musty bridegroom jokes, Teinfrith too hearty, telling me not to be nervous and making me more so. Then when the pipe struck up that first dance measure and I caught your eye and led you out before the folk—ach, Edith, we've been drowning in people all week when it's really just us. You and me as it's always been." Harold lifted my chin to make me look at him straight. "And always will be. All this foolishness about Eada and other . . . I could give you morning gift now, I'm that pleased."

I so wanted to believe that. "Are you? Are you really?"

"Never lied to you and don't intend to start now. We'll be poor the while; dear Edward will see to that. There'll be much work for both of us, but as much love to see us through. I promise that."

He made me bold enough to ask. "Are you scared now too?"

"Right enough," he snickered nervously. "I may have been down a path or two, but not this one, and it's fair awesome."

Once more he rose and snuffed the last candles, leaving only the soft glow from the brazier, and I realized I'd stopped trembling. Harold lifted me to my feet, kissed me lingeringly, and then began to unlace the throat of my nightdress. "I love all of you, Edith. Now will you please leave fretting and let me be a husband? Not like I've done this every day."

I slipped the gown over my head and let it drop with one last prayer. His eyes traveled over me, and I was so intent on finding not judgment but joy in his eyes that I misread altogether the gleam there.

"I have a great desire . . ."

I swallowed. "Yes?"

"To see if you're as helpless ticklish as I am."

Then I knew what I'd seen in his eyes: warm laughter that beckoned me to share with him. Nothing he could have said or done, were it ever so tender, could have quicker made me his just then. And so it was with us, despite so many years and forced partings, frustrations, pain, and anger as the wise priestess foretold, through all our lives.

I stretched out on the bed. "Come find out," I dared him.

Our fire burned long into the night and so did we.

We lingered blissfully at Father's hall through Epiphany and Plough Monday week, busy with plans and packing and discovering each other. On a sparkling January day when sunlight found jewels in the new snow, we ran like children about the courtyard, pelting each other and Botulf with snowballs. The snow was too dry for balling tight and all we managed were great flurries of loose snow scooped at each other.

A horn sounded at the gates and Gyrth Godwinesson rode in with several of his father's carls and a wagon bearing gifts from Godwine and Gytha. Under the six lions, the scarlet-and-gold banner of Wessex, in a new blue cloak wide as an ocean and grand for swirling, a fine new dagger gleaming in his belt, Gyrth was his parents' loving embassy, verging on fifteen, grave and grown-up with me and very impressed with his first charge. I bounced up onto the wagon, round-eyed at the treasures from the earl and countess. There were casks of their best wine, a present of money for Harold, bolts of fine linen and woven wool for me.

"Look what they've sent!"

Harold didn't care at the moment, busy wrestling his little brother with fierce affection while the carls crowded into the hall with Botulf to tell him the news from the east.

Grunting and growling, Harold and Gyrth slammed up against the wagon and left off only at my beseeching. If there was never any brood or blood so cursed with division, they loved as deeply. The brothers stood there by the wagon, bareheaded with the wind whipping their long hair about, and Gyrth gave us the news from Bosham. The king already knew of our marriage.

No surprise to me. "And took it how?"

"Badly," Gyrth said.

"And Eadgytha?"

"Well, as we heard, she wouldn't say a word against you." Then in a rush of hurt and confusion: "And not a bleedin' word *for* you either. Pardon my language, Edith, but it's true."

"Well, the king warned me last summer. Let's go in." Harold lifted me down from the wagon as Gyrth brandished his new dagger. "Got a wizard balance. I can sink it home at six paces every time. Oh, yes," he broke off with a secondary item almost forgotten in the excitement of greetings. "News from Normandy. Didn't you wager with Stigand on the barons 'gainst their duke . . . what's his name?"

"William. So I did." Harold drew both of us close under each arm as we trudged through the snow toward the hall. "Well?"

"Well, you lost. Father says William won."

"Ach, you're joking. He hadn't a prayer."

"No, but he had the French king on his side. A grand pitched battle they say. I forget where, but he bashed them *good*. They know who's duke in Normandy now, I'm bound."

Harold shrugged. "So I'm out four shillings. Wouldn't have thought it, but I'm glad the fellow's got on. Gyrth, tell one of the carls to byre the oxen. Don't leave them out in the cold."

"And you must be by me at dinner, Gyrth," I commanded. "I'm your sister now."

Four shillings; that's all the loss you were to us then, William. You rode victorious from Val-es-Dunes, and if you were at last duke in fact as well as name, what was that to me? I was Harold's wife, I possessed his heart and body, and who needed a countess's coronet? Who needed the empty name?

BOOK II

To Wake
the Lion

14 • Harold

Heigh-ho for the lye and ashes! From Edith's arrival at Nazeing, my dreary hall took on new life and cleanliness. For the first week the servants were scrubbing high and low. I could be grateful my bride was a country girl who'd learned good housekeeping from Hildre. She brought in younger servants from local villages, kindly pensioning off the eldest dodderers to neighboring steadings as cottagers with few duties. Perhaps it was the memory of Eirianell that put her small foot down in the matter of slaves, especially the Welsh women. I had a few left and had become fond of them.

"But Edith, they're like family."

"No."

"One?" I wheedled. "For your chamberwoman?"

Edith's soft chin went very firm. "Particularly not in my chamber. Send them off."

"You'll get nowhere with demanding."

The chin softened again as she came close to me. "If I asked, then? If I entreated?"

Like the cobwebs from the rafters and dirty rushes from the hall floor, the Welsh disappeared from Nazeing, banished by my wife whose own Dorset speech now and then lilted with their music. I'd rid my chamber of any lingering hint of Eirianell. Where I over-looked one small silver penannular, Edith did not. She gave it to one of the departing slave women. A clear statement: If no countess, she was sole wife.

I ate better for a start. Under Edith's close managing of

the kitchens, I put on half a stone of weight from relaxation and simple happiness with this girl of whom Eada once despaired regarding decorum; who secreted meat pies on Wilton fast days and boarded an ailing frog in her chemise case only to bury it later with reverent prayers. I found that tale more amusing than the live frog she put into our bed one night.

"Gah!" Out of the bed in one convulsed leap. "What in hell is *that?"*

Sweet as she was, and bare as Eve in the peat fire's glow, I swear I could have kicked her. Edith just rolled about the featherbed, helpless with laughter, offering up the bewildered reptile to me.

"Give it a kiss. Might turn into a princess."

Then I was laughing and tussling with her because she was outrageous and we were young. The frog was duly dismissed and we turned to each other in the firelight. Happiness? The day, the night, the very air I breathed was music. I felt I had never lived before this. When we rode to church at Waltham or through the villages where folk were preparing for the spring's stirring of the earth, they hailed Edith as *hlaefdige*, though none knew we'd not been priest-wed.

Happy but poor. This was brought home to us when Bishop Stigand, one of my few real friends in Anglia, relayed Edward's message by one of his priests a week or so before Lady Day, the end of the year's first quarter. The command was both royal and ecclesiastical. Stigand's personal note conveyed his distaste for the errand:

—that you set aside as payable to our king and the archbishop those fines in cash here set down.

The young priest handed me the schedule with a reluctance equal to Stigand's. "My lord, the bishop says that any small assistance he can render in this . . ."

"Thank him for me, but we shall cope. Please take some supper."

I went to bed that night with a knot of worry in my stomach. Between them, Edward and Archbishop Eadsige would have half of everything due in cash and kind for the first two quarters of the year. The first of these was due, and Edward's message left no leeway:

We advise you to be as prompt in payment as you were lax in the sacraments.

Edith sat up in bed by candlelight, combing out her hair, her movements languorous and her eyes far away. "What has the king left us?"

I showed her the schedule of payments demanded.

"We're expensive." She said no more than that. Her comb resumed its crackling passage through the dark brown hair. "We'll just have to manage."

I hadn't the smallest notion how. Certainly, we would not burden Stigand, out of Edward's favor himself. I lay down beside Edith and put my hand over her warm stomach under the covers.

"Edward," Edith pronounced with solemn conviction, "is a pious shit."

The way she said it shattered my gloom. I had to laugh while her eyes remained fixed on some thought far beyond the annoyance of our king. I hugged her to me, not caring just then how thin most of this year would be. Payments owed to Teinfrith in the marriage agreement would have to be smaller over a longer time.

"We can use the rents from my own hides to help," Edith reasoned, still in that distant tone. "Papa needn't know."

"Where are you tonight?" I asked, up on one elbow. "You seem miles away."

"Not so far, love," Edith breathed dreamily. She put her comb aside and snuggled down beside me. Her eyes were huge and dark so close to mine. "Just very happy."

"Share with me? After the royal love note, I could use some."

"We'll have a child in October."

I rolled over to gaze down at the radiance in her face. "You're sure? So soon, then?"

Edith kissed my nose. "You wonder, the way we've worked at it?"

A child out of us. No, I can't say how I felt just then.

The joy was too great; such happiness must grow over weeks and months.

"Blow out the candles," Edith whispered.

In soft darkness we lay together, watching the red shadows from the peat brazier dance along the rafters.

Edith murmured: "Lady Day soon."

"And Edward will be sending to collect."

"No, that's not what I was thinking. Ever since I was sure of the child, it's been in my mind how simple truth shows in all things, in the old religion as well as the Church, if you think on it."

"Oh, heretic."

"Not a whit. On Lady Day, the angel told Mary she had conceived God's son. On this same day the old Welsh folk say the goddess returns, and our folk used to celebrate the quickening of the earth by Freya. So then is it mere chance they all come at this time?"

Who could answer that? Edith spoke of things beyond my ken. After a time, she said, "And now I quicken, too. I think they're all one in the end."

Deliciously drowsy with my face buried in the sweet nest of her hair: "I'll put it to Stigand."

"No need, love. I know."

We fell asleep so very close together, the three of us, Edith and I and our gathering child.

Edward was not trained toward kingship but learned quickly with his canny instinct for survival. He had spent twenty-five years in one continental court or another and knew their ways to check an unruly vassal: in the purse. His reeve came to Nazeing to collect, then the delegation from Canterbury. I flinched and paid, but Edward was far from done with me.

Easter that year came only a week after Lady Day. Our spring was warm. Hen blackbirds pecked the earth for worms, and April trailed a brush of color over the meadows. I was seeing to my hawks with the mewskeeper when the first "incidental" visitors announced themselves at the gates. Thirty priests, reeves, and others from several of Edward's estates on their way to Canterbury. They battened on us for two days in a flurry of chicken plucking, egg gathering, stable fodder and fresh meats exhausted. Our whole home estate was nigh eaten clean as Edward had done to Godwine's at Merton.

Scarce a week later a party of Edward's men descended on us with the news that the king himself would be passing through Nazeing soon on a progress of his Anglian holdings.

"Our house will be honored." About as honored as a sentenced convict. "May I know when?"

The monk messenger could not say exactly. His Majesty went where and as he must—which meant dear Edward wanted me to wonder and weary in anticipation. We did. Hall servants scurried over the Nazeing estate, my carls rode to my other holdings for whatever they could spare. Muttering sentiments close to treason, Botulf took two keels to Godwine's closest Kentish estates for whatever they could part with in stores and provender.

"What is he *doing* to us?" Edith agonized as four servant girls hurried past with fresh rushes for the hall. She plucked up one long stem and slashed at the wall in frustration. "We'll survive, but it's oatcakes and barley soup after he goes."

We did our best not to lay more of this burden than necessary on my thanes and peasants, but some was unavoidable. Their May festival was soon, and I'd received concerned advice from the college of priests at Waltham about heathen practices. I replied with gracious thanks and little heed. The folk had already touched our hearts with their generosity, volunteering early payments of rent in kind not due until later in the year. They needed something in reserve until the first vegetables came in, and a little besides for the Maying.

As for heathen practices—if a pagan May tree went up in a village here or there or a tipsy Jack in the Green cavorted in the ploughed fields on May night—well, I couldn't be everywhere at once, could I? The growing firmness of Edith's lower belly reminded me of what she'd guessed about gods: *They're all one in the end.* If that's heresy, I've answered to worse.

On Saint Mark's Eve when the sky chattered with birds returning north and the cuckoo, no more responsible than Swegn, left her eggs in borrowed nests, Edith and I went to vespers mass at Waltham. We had much to pray for, chiefly that we survive the king's visit.

"I've baked a divining cake," she told me. Edith grew up closer than I to country folk and their customs. If she only half believed, that half weighed more than her disbelief, and the superstitions were affectionate keepsakes in her heart.

Late that night we were alone in the deep-shadowed hall with only one short candle end for light, hoarding our good ones toward the coming royal siege. Edith set the cake between us on one of the lower tables. As the small light washed shadows over her high, healthy coloring, I couldn't help but remember another night and a different face come out of the dark—less vividly now and with only a phantom pain. Edith put three glass beakers before us, a wedding gift from Gytha.

"Best glasses?" I appreciated as she poured the wine. "Why three?"

The edges of her mouth curled in tender mischief. "Oh, for him who will come."

"And who's that?"

"The old folk say." Edith vanished down the hall into darkness. I heard bolts drawn and the outer hall door creak open, bending the candle flame in the draft. When Edith returned she cut the small cake and we each took a bite. The wheat and barley meal had been liberally salted.

"Part of the magic, love. Dorset girls bake these today and leave the door open. The man who comes in to share it with her will be her future husband."

"What if he doesn't?"

"Then she'll see him in a dream."

"Tell him I saw you first."

"No. I saw you first." Edith's fingers closed over mine like a protection. "So if I dream tonight, perhaps I'll know if there's to be boy or girl in October. What would you wish?"

"Now? No more than what fills my eye in the candle's light. Come to bed."

A lovely moment, my need and her eagerness to fill it—then voices and footsteps without, and the porter's nasal voice from the darkness. "Earl Harold? Messenger from the king."

I gaped at the cake. "It works!"

Edith winked. "Infallible."

"Well, we know he's not here for your hand. Fetch another candle."

The young man strode into the light, scabbard rattling against his thigh. "Sir."

"From the king then?"

He was barely Tostig's age, tall and lank, the new sword and baldric a contrast to his worn yellow tunic. "From him, sir. Aelred of Denby."

"Sit, Aelred. When will our lord be here?"

"Should have been now." Aelred dropped gratefully onto the bench beside me, reeking of his horse's sweat and his own. "Lord love me, I'm that tired."

I poured the third beaker full of wine. He drank it off in one noisy draught. "We left Bishopsgate early this morning, but the king tarried in East Ham, then his horse threw a shoe some miles down Lea, so he's put up with Thane Sigward there."

Mind, that was Aelred's drift. The northern brogue takes time to sort out in a southern ear. Aelred was a thane's son from Sherwood, I learned. He looked it, one of those forest lads who live in the open most of their lives. But for the good-humored blue eyes of the midland Saxons, his fair hair and long body betrayed a deal of Dane blood. Youngest and lowest-ranking in the king's train, Aelred drew the duty to ride ahead, saddle-sore or not. Sigward was doubtless as glad to see the king as I would be tomorrow.

Aelred stood up as Edith returned with the candle end, lighting it from the first.

"Give you good even—oh!" she brightened. "I know you. We've met but I can't think where."

"Winchester, lady." Aelred bowed stiffly. "The king's wedding."

"Of course. Welcome."

Over wine, Aelred allowed he was glad for our marriage, volunteering that he too was new-plighted. "Maud her name is. A carl's daughter from Mercia."

Lovely, but I had more present worries. "How many with the king?"

"Three score or so." He didn't notice my wince, wiping his mouth on a road-grimy sleeve, innocently unaware of Edith's aversion to that particular lapse of delicacy. "Be here well before noon, I'd guess. That Norman bishop's come, too."

"Champart."

"And the king's to hold a council here, my da says."

"Then my father's with him?"

Aelred dropped his eyes. "No, sir."

Nor Siward nor Leofric. Godwine had been present at a London council, but Aelred could tell us no more. Perhaps the wine and fatigue of a long day in the saddle relaxed him toward confidence, or the flinty northern style of it which could chill hot soup.

"My da don't hold with yours on most matters. Or the king always. Sherwood's our land. We mind out for our own folk, but with all these foreigners comin' in—well, Brihtnoth's heard things these last days."

Edith plied him. "If there's that we should know, please tell us."

"Only what my father told me to say to the earl." Aelred looked me squarely in the eye. The northern men are disconcertingly direct sometimes, a manner that can be mistaken for insolence by those not used to their ways. "Brihtnoth's no quarrel with you, he says."

"I am glad. We've never met. Trouble?"

"Walk soft about Edward, he says. And that Norman bishop."

The mewskeeper jessed the goshawk to my gauntlet. She was a young one, just off the weathering block and near ready to hunt. Time for her to become accustomed to riding my wrist.

Servants hurried between kitchen house, stable, and hall in frantic final preparation for the royal visit: the last plucked chickens, extra fodder for the stables, freshly rolled beeswax candles for the hall.

I twisted about in the saddle, calling, "Botulf, Aelred! We must be going."

They were to ride with me down to Lea landing to meet Edward's party coming from Sigward's steading. But Aelred, a willing but infrequent horseman, simply could not hurry, and Botulf's contrary mare did not want to bear a saddle this morning and had to be convinced.

While I waited, Edith came out from the hall bearing a stirrup cup for me. She moved slowly, not wasting her strength. This day would be an ordeal through which the king's earl and his harried lady must turn grimaces to smiles.

Edith handed me up the cup, watered German wine and juice pressed from the last of our good apples. "Waltham bell rang terce a good hour past. It's well gone nine. They'll be at the landing soon. But no fear, love." Her smile flashed more bravely than Edith must have felt this day. "Nazeing will come through splendidly. I pray. What doves we had in the kitchen cote are on the fire. I don't *think* I've neglected anything."

I drained the cup and gave it back, catching Edith's hand a moment in mine. "Kings come and go, but when I look at you I can never doubt God. How does the babe?"

"Better than I. I didn't sleep that well."

"Did you dream a boy or girl?"

"Neither." Her smile clouded as she bent her head over the cup in her hands. "A strange dream."

Just then Botulf and Aelred walked their horses out of the stable. Time to go. "How strange?"

Edith's brows knitted as she tried to recall what was nearly faded away as dreams do at morning. "The king. It seemed he . . . he cursed you. Yes, that much is clear."

"Been doing that all year, girl."

"But even as he did, Edward clutched at you like a

drowning man. What do you make of that for a Saint Mark's vision?''

She was genuinely troubled by the vision, a west-country girl to the heart. "Edith, were there more salt in that cake, you'd have dreamed dragons.''

"Oh, get along.'' Edith slapped the gelding on the rump and I moved off after Botulf and Aelred.

15 • Edward, Rex Anglorum

His mistress is young and fresh. I cannot even in charity call her his wife, but the girl keeps a good hall. Nazeing never looked so well turned out. Bishop Robert and I have stayed long enough to exhaust their resources. This will teach the pup, bring him to heel, and let him know whom he flouts. First his unspeakable brother, and now him. It's the Godwine in them, surely, or perhaps the wild Dane. Yet . . . this Harold, I must study him more.

It is a burden to be the chosen of God as I am, a king pacted with heaven at my coronation, yet I had no thought to that at first, nor did I choose sorrow to walk with me all my days.

My mother, Emma, has always been a domineering shrew with a penchant for marrying kings. When Ethelrede sired me on her, he swore he would prefer me to his other sons for the crown, and all his earls took oath to accept me as king. When she married Canute, Emma demanded the same security of him, that no son of any other wife would come before me.

I was the anointed, but God would test me beforehand as He did Job. That same year I was sent into exile with my brother Alfred. There I was marooned, of an age between child and boy, wondering why, if chosen, I should be so homeless, so alone and unloved. I came to see how Emma used me, used all her children to keep power herself. You think I didn't enjoy leaving the bitch without stick or stone to her name? Godwine said I was too harsh. The serpent chides a king for cold blood? Oh, I restored her somewhat afterward, but now Emma knows who wears the crown. Be good, Mother. Sit up and beg. I'll throw you a scrap from my table. I learned early there is no love in this world a man can trust save God's, and no hurt or hate like that where love should have been but wants. Such men as I can return over and over to the places of childhood, but never feel we have come home, only that something, if ever there at all, was lost and gone forever. We fumble and sift through memories like an old trunk, sure that *something* was there once, perhaps at the bottom. But it isn't.

How did I grow? See a boy kneeling alone in the shadows of a Norman church, stone floor cold on his skinny knees and an ache of loneliness in his heart. A wanderer prince, anointed but abandoned, promised by God but not a sign from Him for all my prayers.

And then poor Alfred murdered. I loved my brother, Godwine. You will answer for him in heaven. See two little boys alone in a strange place, needing to learn the tongue of indifferent strangers. Disinherited, purse-poor children with barely the value of pawns, then isolated youths with none but each other for solace. Such brothers turn inward to each other. They create their own tongue and meanings wherein one glance or single word, the other can read volumes.

When I left England, I was a boy and you, Godwine, were Canute's dependable lackey. When I returned, you were power itself, but I will bring you down. Your star wanes, you grow old. You make mistakes. You will stumble and fall. That animal Swegn was a boon of sorts, but cunning and caution be my watchwords, as I doubt not they have ever been yours.

So Harold is now to be your heir. *Bien,* he impressed me last summer, but I am in no haste to take his full measure. Time and fortune are on my side. You want to reestablish the Danes here, I know you do. Why not? They created you, raised you up from common beginnings. Up Denmark, down Edward! One is not surprised. A number of crowns fancy they stand to inherit mine. I am like the rich widow wooed for her lands. I flirt and flatter, lean to one and now the other, let each think himself favored while I commit to none. An old game but ever an effective one. Baldwin of Flanders is too powerful, a threat by sea. For the time enemy Danes become allies, Norman friends foes at the stroke of a pen.

And what do they watch anxiously here and abroad as a sailor peers through fog for a guiding star? My wife's belly. If Eadgytha bears a son, they must all go claimless, but I know what they are saying high and low. Why does not the queen conceive? Is she barren? Is the fault in the king's loins? Is he unnatural?

Hardly. I have ridden and hunted all my life, hale as any man. There were women along the way despite exaggerated clerical repute of my chastity which they hung on me like luggage on a mule. There is some truth in this though not all from virtue. Years now since I had any keen appetite for women. Where the young heart yearns, the older may come to yawn. I am forty-two but more than that in sorrow since a painful time in a desolate year when I knew my own mother could make me a pawn in her own game.

Think on that if you would know me. In a month, a day, a moment, a boy sees what his natural love would deny as unthinkable, that a mother could so distance herself from her own flesh and use him. From that hour, Emma, how could I trust you ever again or anyone so closely? Cruel woman, you'll go to God soon enough, before Whom your sins may smack of murder, for you killed love in me.

But the Witan nagged at me. A king must marry. Still, it is to laugh when one sees how absurdly I am painted. On the one hand the celibate king reputed by some clerics to be unknown to women, on the other expected to stand diligently at stud to produce an heir. And poor Edward in the middle, neither wholly one nor the other. I sat in those early councils listening to Godwine and the others with difficulty, no longer fluent in English. To speak truth, I marked none of the gilded daughters they put forth for consort. This one danced well and graced a table, that one had a talent for singing and embroidery, another was said never to be so joyous as when at prayer, still another had ancient blood and manors in her own right. When the choice lighted on Godwine's daughter (and what did that cost the old Satan of Sussex in promises and silver?) I was not sufficiently interested to object.

Eadgytha's accomplishments were vaunted to me: a prize of learning, wizardry with a needle, the darling of our clergy. Duly she was brought to court for approval. I was impressed by her poise and learning, less by other traits. She speaks a purer French than mine and ever lets me know it, corrects me continuously in front of others. Her mind is swift and of steel like her cursed father's. She reveres the Church but deals with some of its servants like the arrogant chatelaine she is. That grotesque affair of Abbot Gervin required delicate handling, not to mention expense in gifts.

Life with Eadgytha is not always difficult. The woman has fine qualities. She is a devoted wife and able consort, but one senses in her restless energies a soul aspiring far beyond a woman's natural station. She has far too much to say in council and more in private—

"Where *did* you get that disreputable old robe? I ought to give it away for alms. And if you must wear those old shoes, let me have them cleaned. You never scrape off the mud when you come back from Thorney. They're filthy; sit down, I'll have them off. Now, as I was saying, my plans for Wilton. I'll bear the expense from my own purse and jewels and—Edward? See? These shoes have walked their last mile. The soles are near to coming loose. Don't you ever notice what you put on?"

Like a child in leading strings, I drown in solicitude morning and night. You wonder that I leave so often to hunt or just to breathe for one unmanaged moment?

But the Crown must have an heir. I have addressed the duty less frequently of late. Not that Eadgytha repels me, nor that she is unwilling. It is a distressment I can confide to no one, least of all herself. For all her beauty, she looks so much like that old adder who begot her, it's as if I embrace the father himself. She *unmans* me. Feature for feature, she is Godwine: the cut of chin, the quick, infectious smile below cool eyes that instantly detect and impale your every weakness. To think a son of mine might in the smallest part mirror that hated face.

Oh, but Godwine would love to have a royal grandson. For Eadgytha, she has his ambition but not quite his patience or wile. I do not hate the woman, but so much of the time I simply cannot bear the sight of her. Those arms entwining my neck remind me of a noose.

And you, Harold, who are to be Wessex when Papa Snake dies, heaven haste the day, what are you? Where once I saw an indolent wastrel idling toward shiftless manhood, now I see a man extravagantly in love with a woman who can never be your countess and whom God bars as wife. I remember her at Winchester: a shy, plump child awkward in curtsey. Now there's a sureness to her, a radiance I've never seen in Eadgytha nor my own reflection. The notion is fugitive, but were I born else, I might change places with you, Harold. Yes, take your warmed life for the chill of mine and see what shape cold duty and colder destiny made of you.

But today in your hall I saw something Eadgytha may never have glimpsed or guessed in you. You are an idealist. Admirable, but you are also secular like your father. More than disquieting, that is dangerous.

I called the council in Harold's hall after the servants had cleared the midday meal, taking my place on the dais. My chancellor Regenbald rapped three times with his staff.

"My lords, draw near. Pray silence for His Majesty."

The crowd of them separated into two distinct groups. To one side stood Champart and my steward Esgar, my crown thanes and their chief carls, and the priests like fat black crows. To the other, Harold and that knobby-nosed fellow who bears his standard, his Anglian thanes, and . . . oh, yes, Bishop Stigand, who has been very critical of me. Loyal to Godwine, they say. We must watch him.

"My lords, you well know my mind and I yours in purposing to suspend the burdensome tax we have for years paid to Denmark. It is the last shame borne from the days of Danish kings on our throne. Last week in the Witan, all confirmed this resolve, save one. All opposed the fifty ships Denmark asks against Magnus of Norway, save Godwine, who surprises no one in this. Earl Harold?''

He stepped forward from the ranks of his men. "Sire?''

"You were the only earl not present at that council, though we well understand how a new dalliance may keep a young man at home.''

Eddies of rough laughter from my thanes, dutiful snickers from the priests. Harold's retort bore a subtle challenge.

"Do you speak of my wife, my lord?''

"Wife indeed,'' Robert Champart broke in. "From disobedience, the earl passes to insolence.''

"Insolence? Bishop Robert, I can barely afford ink to write the word. The Church has well seen to that.''

That was a cask I needn't broach at the moment. "But we would know where you stand on the Danish issue.''

"I say end the Danegeld. No to the tax and no to the ships.''

That caused some murmurs in the hall. I put it to him: "You gainsay your own father?''

"We've thrashed out the matter. Godwine has his reasons. I have my own.''

"Sans doute,'' Champart conceded with a tinge of disdain. "One longs to hear them.''

Harold's eyes barely flicked over the man before he addressed me. "You are sworn to England. I took oath to you because you are England.''

For some reason he winked at the rough cub from Sherwood and grinned at his standard bearer. "Godwine considered the suspension of the tax hasty. The Danes need our help now and he thinks we can profit from that need. Cautious perhaps, but I say no. Never. I stand for England now, not thirty years past. Devil take foreign claims or threats. Our king will give us an heir to succeed. Until then, let Danes and any others know we've taken back our house and keep it well.''

"Damned right," someone muttered. I couldn't tell who but the sentiment found favor with more than one present on either side, while Champart looked vexed.

"Behold," he goaded. "Our host reveals himself a—what is the word?"

"There are several, but *patriot* will do." I leaned forward to Harold, making my point clear. "One can always brandish a cause where personal fealty runs thin."

"A country lover?" Champart trumpeted. "Then I would know one thing, Earl Harold."

"Just one?" Harold's expression altered subtly. He bent on Bishop Robert that damned English look of amused superiority that infuriates even me at times. "Were there time and inclination, you might have more. But what?"

"We know the sentiments of Wessex, who has never endowed so much as his own parish—"

"Nor sent any of that parish hungry from his door."

"—and you yourself have conjoined outside canon law."

"From which your clergy have reaped a profit while shaking a moral finger at me," Harold shot back. "What's the question?"

Champart was surprised, I think, to meet such razored resistance, but they're all a sharp-tongued lot out of Bosham.

"Tell us plainly, my lord earl. Do you honor Mother Church?"

"I am rebuilding ours at Waltham."

"You equivocate!"

"As Your Grace does, choosing 'conjoined' over 'married.' "

"More sinful men build chapels than pray in them," Champart countered. "Do you love the Church?"

Their exchange had turned by degrees more heated until Champart's last question was like a sword striking on iron. Harold did not even blink. He'd learned his father's trick in debate of the effective pause and the voice suddenly lowered but clearly heard.

"When she *is* our Church, Your Grace. And when she loves England in return."

My God, they cheered him then, his own men and many of my own English. Well, all Europe knows I inherited a land of indifferent Christians, but patriots are unreliable servants for a king, a blade that may turn in the hand and wound the user. I daresay Judas could have argued his reasons just so. You do not serve a cause or an idea, Harold, but myself.

I say no. Never. I stand for England now.

Not his king but the dim thing beyond me he loves. Speak of unnatural. There is only one kingdom, Harold, and that is God's. Below that, loyalty must be to your sworn lord, else the house has no mortar to hold one stone to the next. When you put the state before God, you place Man before morality, his fleeting earthly life before his redemption. Madness.

Yet, how he glowed saying it. One expects such light in saints, not secular fireflies. Did I ever love anything in this world so much? If so, I've forgotten. There is God's will and mine. By the tools he gave me, patience and wile, I will prevail.

As for loving? I am not cut from such cloth.

16 • Harold

Edward's message was clear. For the rest of that year, I was paupered and lay low as a fox gone to ground. If I hawked in the meadows along Lea, my heart was not in the cast, nor could I look forward to autumn hunting with much pleasure. Edith worried me. Although she and the physicians assured me again and again of her sturdy health, I became fiercely protective, forbidding her to climb stairs unnecessarily or any physical exertion months before she grew heavy with the child.

"For heaven's sake, go ride," she implored at last in exasperation. "One would think *you* were carrying the babe."

Sometimes I felt so, even to occasional stomach pains. There were other concerns I wouldn't burden Edith with now. Godwine's fortunes sank while Edward's rose on a tide of luck and grasped opportunities. Edward saw only the straight path that was *his* way. He would have done well to learn from the Romans. Caesar might conceive a road built arrow-straight from city to city but had the good sense to leave the laying down to engineers.

In the middle of October, Gytha came to be with Edith. Actually, she was more help to me. The child was late. Edith had predicted the fourteenth of the month, but day followed day with false twinges which she took for labor before they faded. She was far stronger than I that hellish week. My hunters idled in their stalls, hawks went unflown, while their owner chewed a thumbnail down to the bleeding quick in his hall.

At midmorning of the twentieth, Edith's labor began in earnest. After three hours and no news, I was a miserable wreck.

"Does it always take so long?"

"And longer," Gytha assured me, calm over blackberryleaf tea.

"I ought to do something. I can't just sit here and wait. And you should go back to her."

"I've been with her all morning," Gytha protested. "And the midwife has not left her side. Do let me finish my tea; my feet are tired."

I rode to Waltham Church to pray fervently for Edith—and for Eirianell in the bargain. Like Edith, she would have endured all this, the heaviness and discomfort, the ordeal of labor and the hazards of birth itself—all for me? Too much for any man to say *for me.* When the very bones of the earth rend and grind against each other in earthquake, can such agony be to narrow human purpose?

Life and God have larger motives. In Edith as in Eirianell, this was for something far greater than me, than we two.

After making extravagant promises to God that no man could keep short of sainthood, I rode home to Gytha. No news yet. Nothing. I wanted to scream.

"There are no problems, Harold," Gytha warranted. "Honestly, the girl will have to nurse you and the child together, the way you're working yourself into a state."

But I was sure she was keeping some imminent disaster from me. "We're quite ready, you know," I said for the tenth time, striving to bolster the pitiful remnant of my confidence. "Everything's been foreseen, even a wet nurse if she needs one, a priest from Waltham is coming—and where in hell *is* he? He should be here now."

At such times fearful men can be absurd. "You must be with her when the child comes. Botulf will be without the door that no one puts a changeling in her arms."

"Oh, really!" Gytha set aside her tea and rose with patient resignation. "That sort of thing passed with the Elven folk. You are foolish."

"Please."

"Your father wasn't half this trouble."

"Then why do you look so worried?"

"I am not worried."

"You are, I can see it."

"Not for Edith."

"What then?" I fairly screeched at her. *"What?"*

"I was thinking of Swegn."

With Botulf vigilant by the door, the small, crumpled face next to Edith's on the pillow was no one's son but mine. Ours.

"How is it, Edith?"

"Not so bad," Edith breathed like a weary child on the point of sleep. "But isn't he beautiful?"

I inspected my son through a mist of welling tears. No unnatural mark or flaw of any kind I could see, but a child just born looks so *unfinished*. Nevertheless, Godwine Haroldsson surpassed angels in my sight.

I left Edith and went to find a place where I could let

the tears fall until I was wept dry with gratitude to God and so much else.

My fines were rendered in full, the wrath of Edward and the Church assuaged for the time. Early in May when the hawthorn bloomed in my meadows and cows gave rich milk, Mercia was torn by earthquake and laid waste by plague among men and cattle. Ranting priests declared this God's unrelenting anger at the spiritual sloth of England at large and "certain high-raised lords" in particular.

"Meaning me," Godwine interpreted. "If I'm the mark, God took very careless aim. I must send condolences to Leofric."

Botulf took the charge more personally. "Tell you flat, I'm tired of being thrashed for what I ent sure I've even done, for a start. That Norman bishop at London, he's behind it."

Somewhere between Godwine's skepticism and Botulf's resentment, you had the English attitude at large. Calling such catastrophes just offended our commoners' sense of fairness. Enough was enough, damn it! Didn't they keep the laws, pay their rents promptly, and refrain from (excessive) poaching? Such grim judgment might have held in the bad times thirty years gone, but England was at peace in her heart and a right paradise compared to Normandy. What earl today would think to rise against his lawful king? What thane or carl would fight against other Englishmen? Disgraceful. Unthinkable.

"No," they concluded, shrewd finger aside their red noses. "That's Norman ways. Didn't they try for years to kill their own duke, and him just a boy? Just luck and God's mercy they couldn't. Mark me, there's too damned many Normans in England already and no good will come of it."

Meanwhile Godwine made a concession toward peace with Edward. At the queen's request, he allowed my youngest brother, Wulfnoth, to join her household. Eadgytha's letter of summons was condescending as ever:

It is our wish that Wulfnoth be educated with us for

**the Church and to those refinements of court which he
can only lack at Bosham.**

"By God, but she's too much," I fumed to Edith as
we rode Lea bank through a June afternoon. " 'Only lack,'
she says. That infuriating, self-satisfied—"

Laughing, Edith rescued me. "Oh, say it before you
burst."

"Bitch!" My horse shied at the force of it, but I felt
better. "Eada insults our parents, as if they're provincial
clods and brought us up as such."

"Easy on," Edith soothed. "Perhaps it's a good thing
for the boy. How old is he now?"

"Twelve almost. That's not the point. Most annoying
woman I ever knew."

"But never a happy one, Harold."

That was stone truth. Eadgytha was hardly blessed with
the happiness we had. Edith glowed with contentment. For
some time after Godwine's birth, she fretted over the extra
weight of her pregnancy not melted away fast enough, and
I loved even that small vanity in her. Lying beside her after
the baby had fed at her breast and dozed between us, no
human joy could come close to mine, let alone the barren
portion given Eadgytha so far. She *was* the mirror of womanly virtues as the Church preached them, *was* devout and
devoted to Edward, her accomplishments lauded. The opulent
robe of state she fashioned for him in gold, rubies, and pearls
dazzled court and visitors alike. They twittered over her skill
with a needle but never the energetic mind that wrote excellent prose and passable verse. Born a man she would have
been a natural and dominant leader, the vessel of her life
navigating a different destiny.

"Quite right." I leaned toward Edith and grasped her
hand. "You're very wise."

Edith pointed downriver. "Look there. Just rounding
the bend."

A courier craft, fourteen rowers and a canopied seat aft
bearing a corpulent staller, his thick legs splayed wide,
gown turned back to cool his fleshy thighs. He wiped the
sweat from his fatty cheeks and batted irritably at the
marauding insects that teemed along Lea banks.

I stood high in the stirrups, waving. *"Hoch,* staller. Here!"

The bank was thick lined with reeds in both directions; no place for the staller to land without sopping himself.

"Afraid you'll have to," I advised with cheerful malice.

He slung the leather pouch about his neck and went over the side. The water was deeper than he thought. He floundered considerably before hitting firm ground.

"Poor fellow," Edith giggled.

"Edward's inconvenienced me enough. His turn."

Up the bank he puffed, clearly put out. I let the little tub stand there sweating and soggy, regarding him like something escaped from a midden heap. Ruefully, he inspected his linen gown, soaked nigh to the waist over ruined shoes.

"The earl *could* have put me in on better ground."

"Sorry. Didn't think it was so deep just there. What have you for me?"

He opened the pouch and handed me a folded dispatch bearing the chancery seal.

"You will all refresh yourselves at Nazeing," Edith invited the lithsmen and their disgruntled passenger. "Harold, what is it?"

I passed her the message. "Norse raiders in the Narrow Sea. The king's joined the fleet at Sandwich. I'm to raise my fyrds and ride tomorrow."

17 • Harold

Edith led that evening's supper while I sent riders to Sigward and my other thanes, munching a quickly roasted dove as I hurried between armory and stables. In the midst of this, another messenger pounded in with sightings relayed from our coast. Norwegians, no mistake. Twenty-five fully manned longships. They'd put in at Keswick for water, taken a few hapless folk for slaves, then made south again, lured by the richer ports of Kent. My good luck there, but those they took were *my* folk.

An undercurrent of nervous excitement ran through my younger carls. Their first war adventure! The novelty was dimmed for me by the fact that I must command in battle for the first time. Men would judge my conduct keenly and talk of it long afterward for good or ill. I longed to have Swegn riding with me now. Whatever he lacked, my brother could fight.

The raiders' banners were known. Their chiefs were Lothen and Yrling, no doubt lustily sung as heroes in their home fjords, though we had other names for them. They'd already got rich taking slaves and plunder from our shores, but this time fortune deserted them. Edward's fleet at Sandwich deflected them from the Kentish coast. The swift raiders made southwest for Pevensey. No luck there either. They'd barely taken on fresh water when Godwine's local thanes came down on them like angry bees from a threatened hive and sent them scrambling back to their ships.

None would mourn the fate of such arrant thieves, but their predicament can be reconstructed. They were rowing without much rest. What fresh meat they carried must have quickly gone high in the sun, while supplies they'd counted on, the fat sheep of the Sussex downs, were all safe in cotes for the June shearing. The raiders were now sweating at their oars on no more sustenance than oats, dry bread, and beer. Their raid was becoming a matter of pride for Yrling and Lothen, who then made the disastrous error of pulling west for the Isle of Wight, no more than eleven or twelve miles from Bosham.

What they didn't reckon was the speed of couriers between London and Bosham, post riders pounding down old Stane Street through Chichester to alert every thane in Sussex. The raiders saw a ready host everywhere along the shore, including Wight. They lay off Chichester Harbor overnight, then at first light tried a quick stab into its marshy mazes. By now their water and food were running out. In the narrow channel between Chidham and Bosham they could hear the clangorous alarm of church bells and see the swelling ranks drawn up against them on either shore. Fighting men in mail flanked by the peasant levies and, over them all, the Wessex standard furling in the breeze like the twitching tail of a furious cat.

The finest keels in the world, drawing no more than three feet of water, they must have had barely a foot to spare when they withdrew toward Selsey Bill. Another long day waiting for dark to slip through the fleet from Sandwich, then pulling for home. Not only a failure but a message to Norway's King Magnus, who might be tempted by our throne: England's shore is beautiful, but so is the poisonous foxglove.

But these are Norse. Valor in battle is more important than slaves or booty. How it must have stung them later to hear of Godwine's laconic dispatch to Edward: *The Wessex lions have scattered the Norse lambs. The southern coast is clear.*

This is how and why the Norse came to Slaughden, a last foray to take home something beside defeat. All we knew in East Anglia at the time was that they were returning north. From Godwine's example I'd had coastal and interior maps of Anglia prepared, including roads and main towns. In the hours before we rode, I pored over these, trying to predict where they might beach. Harwich or Felixstowe? Too heavily defended. Aldeburgh? Perhaps, or even farther north at Southwold? These last were most likely.

All Nazeing was awake and astir before daybreak, the kitchen fires stoked, a priest come sleepily from Waltham to say a hasty mass, horses saddled, armorers ready. Thane Sigward rattled in with his small detachment of mounted carls. Edith could not join us in the hall. She was weaning the baby, and he was cranky. Edith relinquished him to a serving woman and hugged herself to my chest in farewell.

"Dearest, you're not worried, are you?" She searched my face. "I don't want you to worry about us."

"No time for that," I said truthfully. "That's the blessing of haste. I'll be home before you've time to miss me."

"Never that soon."

I went off a martial virgin to war, Botulf carrying my standard, thanes and carls following. We made east toward Witham to gain the Roman road that ran all the way to Colchester.

Roll a ball of wet snow down a steep bank, see it grow with each turn. So we gathered, thanes joining us as we passed through their holdings. Because speed was essential, we would not call the fyrds in great numbers, only those local troops along our route and the coast as we came to them.

Speed and logic, yes. How efficiently the Roman legate with a network of roads and disciplined legions could plan so many miles a day toward his objective and actually achieve it. Our Saxon fault is that thanes will come at their own speed, gathering reluctant carls and farmer-soldiers from the sheepcotes and fields. We planned a general muster at Wherestead, one of my estates southeast of Ipswich. Before that, in my novice impatience, I'd drawn up a schedule of our passage, so many hours to each point, so much time for rest. Good luck, Harold. Things never work out so well. This horse is improperly shod and costs you time, that one goes lame and more time is lost finding a remount. Carls straggle off during rest, looking for beer and women. Thanes must search and curse and kick them out of taverns back into the saddle. The older ones would rather be home, not impressed by young boasting or an untried earl. We arrive in Colchester, horses and men spent. More time bedding the lot down wherever we can. One thane is very late in joining; another doesn't appear at all. Where is he? So it went. By the time our column turned off the road toward Wherestead, the Ipswich bells were ringing vespers.

"Should have been here by noon," I fumed to Botulf. "Someday there'll be real trouble and England will lose because it's too damned early to get out of bed."

"We'll never raise the coast in time," Botulf despaired.

Or know for sure where the bastards would land. I joked

with the men to hide black doubts as we strained the resources of little Wherestead to feed us.

In the end, they went neither for Aldeburgh nor Southwold but a huddle of thatched huts on a narrow spit of sand. If we had any victory that sad day it was owed to a fisherman who slept off his beer in Aldeburgh, and a dutiful *geneat* on a spavined mare, both nameless to me and history.

At midsummer the sky barely darkens before lightening again. We were on the move before that, planning to raise Witham by the hour of prime. There we would be with the levies under the Crown thane Wulfwig.

The air was heavy and flower-sweet as we rode, the warm beginning to a hot day. Botulf twisted about in his saddle. "They're straggling again. The last of them must be more than a mile back."

No surprise. Even with sleep and rest, English carls are not used to much sustained riding, and I was pushing them. Botulf sent a rider dashing back to prod them on. When we heard church bells from Wickham and Rendlesham, I felt a little better. We hadn't lost *too* much time, but should rest the horses in Wickham. No. No time. Rest them later. So much to remember and anticipate. Would I ever carry command naturally as Father or Swegn?

As we passed west of a small wood, we heard the sour blast of a hunting horn. Two riders emerged from the trees, hurrying toward us. Just behind me Sigward shaded his eyes to make them out. "That's old Wulfwig."

I saw a swaybacked mare laboring in a kind of frenzied waddle under a shire-wide barrel of a man. Wulfwig and his *geneat* toiled up to us. The thane was far past prime with yellow, food-stained mustaches and untrimmed hair shooting out from beneath a dented conical helmet. His mail looked to be as old as the owner, but freshly scoured of rust. Both he and his middle-aged *geneat* carried old swords in battered scabbards, throwing axes tucked into broad belts straining over well-fed bellies.

Wulfwig wasted no time on greeting or prologue. "Forget Wickham, my lord. The Norse are down Slaughden. You must turn east.''

Without further parley we urged our horses to a brisk trot to join with Wulfwig's waiting men. He told me the story as we rode, a man who obviously liked the gravelly sound of his own voice. At the point where I would have begged brevity, I reflected that Wulfwig carried a thane's ax before I was born, and so kept silent. It seemed there was this unlucky fisherman from Slaughden . . .

''No luck at all this week, as if the fish saw him coming, but no mystery there. The fool's only sober of a Sunday.''

Out of dire necessity—not a man to be moved by less— he fished longer and later, taking his boat up to Aldeburgh where he put in to rest, and one drink led to another.

When you go to bed drunk you sleep deeply but not long, so there's the fisherman pushing his boat out for home around matins bell with morning already eating away at night in the southeast. He's sweating over the oars when he sees the morning smoke from Slaughden fires and as well the long, lean keels lying off his village. Aching head forgot, he pulls for shore, beaches, and from the fresh high watermarks along the sand, he knows the tide's about to ebb. He runs to the village elder, one of Wulfwig's *geneats,* gives him the news, and off goes the messenger to raise alarm with his thane—

''And here we are,'' Wulfwig concluded as our weary horses began to break gait. ''I've only three carls, the rest fyrd, but they'll be waiting the other side of Tunstall Forest. Two score, maybe half a hundred.''

No matter. The raiders wouldn't all land. At worst we would outnumber them. I could feel my stomach tighten with fear and excitement both, but as we cleared Tunstall and saw the milling knot of fyrd men on the meadow beyond, my mind cleared suddenly, a dead calm within battle nerves as they ran toward us. Not regular soldiers but farmers in soiled, torn linen and Phrygian caps and ragged wrappings about sturdy brown legs. They were armed with no more than staves and spears or old scrama-sax swords. Here and there among them, a hacked wooden shield most like passed down from a grandfather. They waved and shouted as they came, flailing an urgent message to us: "There. Northeast. There!" They panted up to us and gasped out the news. The Norse were after water, right enough, but two keels had rowed up Alde estuary for whatever else they could snatch quickly. Slaves, I thought. Not much else worth the taking.

"Up Alde then?" Old Wulfwig squinted at the still-low sun and turned to me with a yellow-toothed grin. "Then we may have them good."

"How? What, man?"

"The tide," he cackled. "The tide. It comes fast and goes faster. We don't go for Slaughden but there!"—his arm shot out. "Straight to the estuary. Two miles, no more."

God smiled on me that day, giving me a clear head to see the thing plain. Where they were, how far, and what to be done. "Botulf!"

"Sir!"

"I want all our horses in line, three ranks deep. Bring them up. I don't care if they're tired or dying from the heat. Bring 'em up."

As he galloped off, I demanded of Wulfwig, "What ground between us and the estuary?"

"Flat as a bride's first bread."

"And the estuary bed? Sand or mud?"

"Some mud, mostly sand."

Then if their keels had been caught, if they were grounded, we could maneuver to cut them off. Wulfwig sent his fyrd men running back toward Slaughden village while I guided our massed horses at best speed northeast. Tide comes and goes fast, Wulfwig said. I'd seen it all my life. Our whole coast along the Narrow Sea is a huge tidal area where river mouths and broad estuaries sink to shallow pools with mere rivulets meandering to the sea.

We saw them well before reaching Alde side: the two grounded keels heeled over in no more than a foot of water. As Wulfwig shrewdly guessed, they'd miscalculated time and tide in their greed. Forty or fifty men plodded along the sand with casks and skins of water. Others herded tethered men and women to be sold as slaves. More of them disappeared to the east toward Slaughden.

"Not today," I ground out. "Not today, you bastards."

"They almost made it," Botulf purred pleasurably. "God rot them all."

The raiders had seen us and were running now, leaving the slaves and water, clawing swords from scabbards. I wheeled my sword forward, riding for a point to cut off as many as we could. We pounded down the bank, my men roaring challenges at the pirates. Half our force under Sigward blocked those to our west while the rest of us dashed after those scurrying out toward the village and their own boats.

We lost more men than we should have, not skilled in fighting from the saddle. Some men toppled and fell in swinging at the fleeing Norse. I cut my way through anything in my path, bent low over the horse's mane, Botulf and Wulfwig scything and screaming close behind.

In the end we cut off perhaps a score, breaking out onto the beach at Slaughden. I saw the raider keels lying half a mile and more out at low tide, a few lucky Norse wading out to board.

For those twenty or so, they stopped running, knowing they had no hope. Sigward's men were already closing in behind them and we blocked their way forward. As we dismounted—a strange silence. All my senses went sharp as a new-honed knife. The knot of pirates, swords drawn and shields up, gathering together, waiting for us and death. The smell of brackish water and dead fish. Blood on my sword.

One of them actually grinned at me and swung his arm in invitation. "Come!"

We closed with them. The man who chose me was not tall but a rock, but already spent from running. I stepped back as he came at me, but his foot turned in a treacherous patch of mud. In catching his balance, his round shield swerved just far enough aside for my blow. Even as he went down, cursing me, his blade slashed out, slicing across my lower leg.

For the rest it was over quickly. We were a wild-looking

lot, the older men silent, the young ones like Botulf fever-lit with a fire half fear, half rage. Botulf pointed at my leg with a hand that shook violently. "You're bleeding."

I looked down at the wound from a great distance. The damned thing might have been in another shire; I felt nothing. From the village huts, frightened folk peered out at us. West to the estuary the sand was littered with bodies but not enough for old Wulfwig. He lurched forward across the sand, cursing the boats in a voice that went tremulous with the burden of tears. In the nearest keels, some slaves had already been dragged aboard. Wulfwig's folk, already lost to us. I stumbled heavily toward him, wanting to lie down there in the sand and sleep.

"Too late," he choked.

"No, man. We've saved most of them."

He was weeping, the awkward tears of an old man whose best, by his own heartbroken measure, had not been near enough. "Those were my folk, Harold."

And we would see none of them ever again. To know that, to stand there helpless while they stared forlornly back from the already moving boats.

Wulfwig fell on his knees sobbing. "Christ . . . Christ."

All I could do was hold him as the insolent keels backed water and turned north. The wound in my leg began to burn.

Sigward rode up and slipped wearily off the horse, stepping among the dead Norse on the sand. "We've got some of them wounded but still alive back there." When he turned to me, his eyes held a clear question and already a judgment.

"They shouldn't be," I said. "Kill them."

18 • Harold

Another June come, another year gone, and my Edith pregnant again. Little Godwine was toddling now, unsteady in his nurse's leading strings as he wobbled about the stockade yard. If he was dear and comical, so was Edith. To birth in August, her natural brisk gait gave gradual way to a waddling progress that reminded me of Wulfwig's old horse. I had her favorite chairs specially cushioned, for sitting down had become for Edith a process difficult as rising.

This time I resolved not to drive everyone into a frenzy with worry. We were young and Edith healthy. Those June days at Nazeing, cushions were brought from the hall and we would laze the morning out, listening to my vociferous son trying to talk. It's flat amazing, that time just before a child can form words. Godwine was *stuffed* with them, running wild through a growing mind, but the messengers between thought and mouth were yet so new, we'd need angels to interpret.

"Edith, listen. He said *milk*."

"He said *mull*."

"*Milk!*"

My heir resolved the argument. "*Muk*."

No matter. Each outburst would be answered solemnly by us, and when we had to burst with laughter and the child's efforts, we always tickled Godwine to include him, squealing, in the mirth.

By the good Lord we were happy. Not even Edward could lower my spirits when once again his couriers rowed up Lea with the summons to council at Winchester.

* * *

The royal residence at Winchester is ancient, mostly of timber, drafty and not at all grand. The "great" hall is more designation than description. All of Edward's earls had been summoned, so that we and our followers filled the chamber.

The hall was already crowded and noisy when I, Sigward, and Botulf elbowed our way in. Edward had not yet appeared; he knew the value of making men wait. I inclined my head to Ralf of Mantes and received the same in cool response. Lean, grey Leofric chopped his head up and down to me, and grizzled old Siward of Northumbria drew me aside for a word. Surprising: A word was about all I'd ever had from him when he spoke to me at all. He drummed his fingers on the heavy gold chain about his sloping shoulders and breast. "Have you seen your father this morning?"

"No. I just arrived."

"I saw him at Eastgate. Look to him, Harold."

Odd sentiment from Northumbria. They had never been friends. But the old earl's frown was one of concern.

"What's amiss with him?" I asked.

"He looks ill. Give you good day." Not a man to waste two words on one meaning, Siward turned away to his own men. I shrugged off the notion. Godwine never was, never would be less than vital. A morning's indisposition, no more. Possibly too much wine. But then Botulf touched my elbow.

"Wessex is coming."

Just then entering the hall with Teinfrith and several other thanes. I'd barely taken a step toward him when Edward's bustling steward Esgar climbed onto the dais and placed an embroidered cushion on the chair of state. I shouldered through the press to take both my father's hands. His look and their touch shocked me. They felt like cold clay. Godwine's ruddy cheeks bore the pallor of grey mud, his eyes dull and unfocused. "Father, what?—"

He cut me off curtly. "Nothing. The king's coming."

He moved heavily away as Regenbald the chancellor

rapped for silence with his staff. "Give ear! His Majesty Edward, by the grace of God, King of the English."

As the Red Sea for Moses, the company of us parted down the middle for our liege lord. I whispered to Teinfrith, "What is it? Father looks like death itself."

"He shouldn't be here," my father-in-law frowned. "He almost fell down in Eastgate."

When Edward passed, my father bowed. Even that habitual movement was effort for him now. He straightened slowly, ashen, and faced the dais erect as he had for three previous kings.

The council opened with minor matters quickly disposed. Edward spoke more confidently than in his first years, in a thin but clear voice. One had the impression, more and more over the years, that he spoke like God in a monk's dream, from a great distance. Certain men previously banished and now suspected of trafficking with Flanders were reconfirmed in outlawry until time should clear them. And Edward would strike a new penny next year.

"Stamped with the cross of Him for Whom I hold this charge."

Pious as always, but get on with it. My father shouldn't be on his feet at all.

"Now to our chief business."

Which was England's present duty in the sea blockade. The so-called Lotharingian League was for England a conflict in name only. We were aligned with Henry of Germany, Svein of Denmark, and Pope Leo against Flanders, Normandy, and France. The causes were remote from us. Baldwin had besieged the emperor's castle at Gelderland, flaring a few skirmishes along their borders. Most English felt our involvement a waste of time and money but for two elements wherein, for once, I agreed with Edward. One, the Vatican sided with Henry—not surprising since the German imperium elected our popes, an avuncular arm about His Holiness' shoulder and ever a hand at his throat. Two, and crucial to our sea trade, Norse pirates were using Baldwin's Flemish ports as forward bases for raiding. Edward's policy was cautious and shrewd. To wound a Fleming mortally, a lethal thrust through his purse. We would strangle Baldwin's own sea trade until he found the Norse presence too costly.

Siward of Northumbria would patrol the northern coasts, Earl Leofric to support him with men and money already pledged. The Danish squadrons would form the second line of blockade out from Caister.

"For the third line, the earls Harold and Beorn will join our own squadrons at Sandwich and be at sea in five days."

Five days. In ten, June would be nearly spent. The child would come soon after Lammas. I prayed Edith need not bear it alone while I mucked about at sea, but all in God's hands. We earls were the Crown's tools, the price of the gold chain on my breast.

"And Wessex will be our postern gate, deploying between Wight and Pevensey."

Good. Father could direct the ships from home while resting in the care of Gytha and his physicians.

Peter the royal chaplain gave a brief benediction to our enterprise and the council closed. Once more we parted for the king to pass. As Edward came to us, he paused. Father's condition was apparently obvious to him as to me.

"We hope our lord of Wessex is not indisposed."

Godwine straightened at a cost I could reckon with my own eyes. "I am fit, sire."

"We are happy to hear it." Edward's solicitude was chilly. "Your son Wulfnoth applies himself well to study. He is a joy in the queen's household."

The king passed on. Godwine tottered and might have fallen had I not steadied him. He protested with strengthless hands. "Get away, boy."

"No. You should not have come."

"Just light in the head for a moment, no more."

There was more indeed. I'd never seen him look so *old.* "Please sit, sir."

"I said get away. It's nothing. Comes and goes." His fingertips fumbled at both temples. "Sometimes there is pressure here. Help me to bed."

Walking unsteadily between Teinfrith and me, Godwine

murmured, "Did you mark that mention of Wulfnoth? With his usual finesse, Edward is showing his power and that we will bend to it at his pleasure."

No time to say good-bye to Edith. I sent a messenger and rode straight for Sandwich. For the first time, I seriously wondered how long my father had to live. He had lighted the sun and turned the world each day since my birth. The Wessex sky shrank over me, the green downs went drab. Life was leaving Edith and me less and less room to live.

19 • Harold

C an't hear it now."
Cloak-wrapped against damp fog, Beorn, Botulf, and I stood forward at the prow of our keel, trying to hear the strange ship's horn again. In a line out from Sandwich Bay, our ships blew their horns regularly, keeping position by sound, but the three-note blast we listened for now was not one of ours.

Long auburn hair hanging about his cheeks in wet strings, Beorn was concentration itself. Botulf looked like a hound with strong scent in his nose but no sight of quarry. Aft of us, only the first rows of lithsmen were visible at the oars.

The strange horn sounded again.

"There." Botulf's arm shot out at a point off our steerboard bow. "Closer."

"Moving dead slow." Beorn slipped back to my side. "Botulf, pass the word to stand ready."

My man moved away, blurred, and then swallowed by the mist. On the benches the rowers looped baldrics over their shoulders, and unhooked shields from the side wales. The sea had been calm all day, our keel barely rising and falling on gentle swell. Now we heard the muffled wash of oars. Flemings wouldn't have signaled. In the monotonous weeks of patrol, not one had been sighted. As Edward's observer with the Danish squadrons, Tostig said their crews were fishing and gambling to relieve boredom.

Once more the invisible stranger signaled, very close now. They could easily hear my hail. "Hallo! What ship is?"

The prows came out of fog like two blades through white wool. "Sheer off! Back your oars, *back!*"

Ghost oars dipped and backed, then rose high as the rowers shipped them. The first keel bumped along our side as the second eased along the other. By their lines they were Danes for sure, but with the dragon prows unstepped.

Someone hailed in a singsong English: "Who is there?"

"Wessex," I shouted back. "On our king's service. "Who are you?"

"Godwinesson's service."

I grinned at Beorn, relaxing. "Tostig. Hallo the boat there! Tell him to come aboard."

Beorn pointed forward at five more dim craft now visible ahead. "Why would Tostig pull seven craft out of the line?"

Then the lean figure cleared our sidewale in one agile bound. The man who strode forward to clasp me to him was not Tostig.

"Swegn. What—?"

He only gripped me tighter while I searched over his shoulder for answers in Beorn, who was baffled as myself.

"Brother." Swegn devoured the sight of me with fever-bright eyes. "And Beorn. So long since I've seen a friendly face."

Beorn swung him around in a rough embrace. "You madman! How did you get by the Danes?"

"I didn't. They asked a deal of questions but finally let us through."

"Where bound?" I asked.

"Bosham."

"Father's ships are out between Pevensey and Wight. He's been ill, Swegn." And whether the sight of my prodigal brother would be physic or more sickness, I couldn't tell.

"Come aboard," Swegn urged, pulling at me. "Agatha's with me." His heartiness seemed hollow and forced. Swegn was thin, just gristle and bone in my arms. He bounded onto his own deck. "Harold, come see my son!"

Beorn muttered, "What in hell is he doing here?"

"I don't know. Send all's well to the other ships. They'll be wondering."

"You know he can't land."

"No, but I want to know why he's come back."

Futile by any road. I should turn him back. Swegn was forbidden England on pain of death or prison. Dishonored, desperate, but still my brother; that shouldn't weigh now but it did. I jumped onto the other keel and walked along the deck among the rowers. They were nondescripts, Danes, Norse, and Swedes beyond their prime. Too old to be royal lithsmen but well-enough armed for a quick raid, if that were Swegn's intent. Mercenaries, the sort scooped up from every northern port between Roskilde, Oslo, and Jadar.

By a small leather tent rigged in the stern, Swegn waited beside a cloaked woman who held a child wrapped in a blanket. "Lord Harold," she said in a strong west-country accent. "May God be with you. It is good to see you again."

"And you, lady."

Her face within the cloak hood was young yet, stronger than comely, as I'd always thought, but etched with the hardship of recent years. "May God be with you as well, Agatha."

"My son." Proudly Swegn took the boy from his mother. "Hakon, this is your uncle Harold."

About three now, Hakon stared at me a moment before losing interest. I drew Swegn aside. What showed in Agatha's face was writ large over all of my brother. His clothes were very worn and mended more than once, his hair overgrown. More unsettling than any of this, there was in his intense stare the off-putting glare of the fanatic.

"What will you seek at Bosham? Be straight, we've not much time."

"I must see Godwine."

"You broke your word to him."

"Harold—"

"And he had to answer for you. All of us, we paid for you."

"That's all past. He'll speak for me."

"Speak what, fool? Your outlawry is pronounced by the king. You finished yourself. Turn your ships about. Go back to Denmark."

"No."

"I can't let you through, useless if I did. Godwine's disinherited you. Goddamn you, why do you wrack us like this? Go back where you came from."

"Disinherited?" Swegn only blinked. The notion might once have ignited him to violence. Now it seemed to make no impression at all. "He's lectured me before. He'll see me restored."

Is there a word for frustration so commingled with outrage and plain disgust? Swegn heard nothing, understood less. "Wessex goes to me."

Swegn's mouth twisted in a smirk. "You?"

"Me. I didn't want it, but there it is."

"You could bear the Lions better than I?"

"Could I dishonor them more deeply than you have? For God's sake, you've left nothing unbroken behind you. Nothing."

My brother and I faced each other in a dense fog on a slate-colored sea in the middle of nowhere, all of it unreal as his hopes of restoration. My boats called back and forth, the horns a lonely sound. Then another long prow slid alongside and grappled to us.

"Lord Swegn, are you there? The boatmaster must speak with you."

Swegn swore softly. "What's wrong now?"

"Do we sail south or what?"

"Coming." With an impatient shrug, Swegn moved off. "Mercenaries. Not a damned one you can trust."

When I returned to Agatha she was just emerging from the tent shelter to sit on the edge of the half deck. "Hakon is ill, and no wonder. All this traveling, so much of it in foul night air. We are fortunate to find you, Harold."

"Agatha, I have to turn him back. For all the world, as I love him and care for you, I can't let him through."

The woman did not show any disappointment, only accepted with stoic matter-of-factness. Agatha was a farmer's child. She had the broad feet of one who'd walked and worked fields through early life. She had been a capable abbess, anchored in all things to the real and practical. There was strength in the rather heavy line of her jaw. Once in her life she slipped that anchor and reached for the impossible. She might have reached anywhere better than for Swegn, but there she'd grasped and held.

"Then I don't know where we can turn. Godwine is his last hope. And you. You were kind to send the money."

"Go back to Svein's court," I urged, grasping at straw hopes myself now. "It's better luck than you think. Beorn is here; he can send a messenger with you to his brother. Yes, that's what we'll do."

Through all this Agatha only shook her head in bleak denial. "He can't go back."

"With Beorn's safe conduct—"

"He cannot. Svein sent him from court with a price on his head if he returns."

That should have surprised me, but didn't. "What happened?"

"You know my husband. There are no reasons but his own. He sued to Svein for a fleet to argue by force, if necessary, for his place in England again."

Sweet Jesus, he was deranged. Did he think Godwine would defend him against Edward in arms? I pressed Agatha to me, feeling miserable. "Tell me all."

"King Svein welcomed us to court as guests and kin, no more. But well enough is never enough for Swegn."

"Aye, he's a genius there."

Little by little, as Swegn felt more secure, he made

much of his blood tie to Svein. Men began to wonder at his reasons and his claims. Then the Danes allied with Edward against Flanders. When Swegn asked for ships, Agatha herself called it sheer folly. The alliance was fragile enough, Svein's own crown barely recovered from Norwegian incursions. Edward's suspension of the Danegeld was clear sign of England's mood. Svein would be a fool to grant the ships. His council laughed Swegn out of the king's presence, but not before he cursed them all and swore he would come again and in such state as to make the old gods quake in Valhalla.

"Mad," Agatha concluded "They could have killed him there before my eyes, but they just laughed the more. Svein gave him ten days to sail from Roskilde. We used the last of our money for these few ships and such men as you see."

She stood up, wrapping the shabby cloak closer about her thin body. "God alone knows where we can go if not to his father." She looked off into the fog. "It's as if we are not part of any real world anymore. Swegn is the first person I ever truly loved and needed in this world, but even that sometimes . . . I have felt dead for so long."

Pity Agatha. If virtue can't grow from sin, certainly wisdom can. Had she a little more experience in loving men before she met him, Swegn might have been far less of a temptation, sent on his headlong way with a kindly word. But the thing was done. She needed him.

And myself? Call me coward. For her sake and the child's, I wavered and changed my mind. Someone else could pronounce Swegn's final doom. When he returned to us, grumbling about men hired rather than honestly sworn, I gave him the chance he begged.

"Hear me well, brother. Edward's ships are in a line out from Dover. Don't try to engage them."

"With men like these? Thank you, Harold."

"Never mind thanks; just listen. Turn east by south, give it two hours steady rowing, then south and west again. If the fog holds, the Dover squadrons may not sight you."

I saw what passed for a remnant of hope in his face. "For my family I must thank you."

"Go on." I clasped to me what was left of him in my heart. "Get out of here. Good luck."

Back on my own ship I found Beorn, and together we watched the long dim shapes of Swegn's forlorn fleet back, turn, and disappear into fog. Leaning over the side, I tried to sort out my feelings, whether I'd done right. Mostly I felt miserable. "Beorn, did you know your brother had banished him?"

"Only that he'd sailed for Oslo. Just hearsay."

The sound of oars grew faint and was gone, washing Swegn out of our lives. Strange to feel old at twenty-three, staring at a white wall of mist I hoped would hide Swegn long enough for him to reach Godwine's ships.

My cousin spoke after a long silence. "A man can't forget his kin. Blood is much. Nevertheless, if Godwine urges that man's restoration, I'll speak against him. How will you?"

I only stared down at dark water the color of regrets, sick at heart.

20 • Harold

We lay at Sandwich far into July. Our thanes grew anxious to be gone home, worried at each splatter of rain, praying for dry weather inland during hay harvest.

Edward's base on the grassy cliffs above the beach was a sprawl of tents and mud now, gone filthy with horse droppings and the unwashed lot of us. Below, relief boat crews tossed pebbles at gliding gulls, fought among themselves, and fermented in boredom as we did. Royal estates and Godwine's holdings alike for miles around were strained to provide food and forage, and rations grew worse every day.

Botulf and I sat outside our tent in salt-stiff linen shirts and baggy trousers, grumbling at duty as soldiers have done since pharoah's infantry. I'd heated water for shaving over a small fire. Botulf poked irritably with an iron awl at the wet rust on his mail.

"There's more men down from the bad food and water," he said. "Small wonder. My wife's fed dogs better than we've had this week."

"Can't last forever," I hoped. "Have you seen the king today?"

"No," Botulf grunted. "That young snot steward, Esgar? He said the king's beset with a cold."

Which meant no audiences today, not if a man wanted pleasant answers. Nevertheless, the earls ought to ask in a body how long we must stay here. Neither Flemings nor Norse had been on the Narrow Sea in all our watchful weeks. At home Edith was within days of birthing if she hadn't brought the child already. I should be with her.

The sound of a horn pulled our attention to the two sentries at the cliff's edge. They'd been yards apart, strolling back and forth, bored as ourselves. Now one trotted toward the other who pointed out to sea with his spear and blew another blast on the horn.

I dried my face on the tail of my shirt. "Botulf, go see what it is."

He loped away to the sentries as Beorn and Tostig rounded a tent to join me. Beorn was disheveled as myself. Even Tostig, who will outdress God at Judgment, was seedy and unkempt.

"What is it?" Beorn plied. "Danes, I heard someone say."

Botulf returned, rubbing at his crooked nose. "Eight keels."

Some premonition urged the question in me. "Swegn had seven. Is it he, you think?"

"Dane ships by their lines." Botulf was certain. "Seven of them anyway."

"Just the duty ships coming in," Tostig guessed. "Tired of this as I am and wanting to go home."

Botulf looked from me to my brother, shaking his head. "The leading ship flies the Lions. Your father's aboard."

Men already hurried toward Edward's pavilion. The whole camp stirred like a sleeper rudely awakened. Tostig and I ran to the cliff edge. Yet far from shore, the eight keels advanced, one slightly forward of the others and flying the scarlet and gold of Wessex.

Tostig rubbed at his stubbled chin. The line of his mouth tightened. He knew Swegn had slipped through our patrol but tactfully had not told Edward. "Well, at least we won't be bored *this* morning."

From the first horn summoning us to the king's presence, the camp mood convulsed from lethargy to apprehension. No one knew what would ensue. Edward's household carls surrounded his tent in arms. The lot of us groomed ourselves hastily. Some, like Ralf of Mantes, buckled on mail, but there I balked.

"I'll not arm against my own father."

Arms were not needed. Most of Godwine's men remained on his ship. Those few who trudged up the cliff path with him and Swegn wore no weapons beyond daggers. We were a bedraggled lot, waiting for them before the king's tent. Esgar had set the chair of state outside and Edward took his place without ceremony, red-eyed and snuffling into a cloth. He'd thrown an opulent robe over his dun tunic and donned a simple gold circlet for crown; no other state would he afford my father.

At the head of his dozen, Swegn at his side, Godwine marched through our assembled company and halted. My brother strode on to throw himself, face to the ground, at Edward's foot.

"I hail my liege lord and ask his mercy."

Edward wiped at his red nose. No one spoke. I caught Godwine's eye; he looked better than at Winchester but still far from well. *Why are you here? Whatever you're doing, it's dangerous. He's not worth it.*

"Godwine," Edward wheezed, "will you ever grow infirm enough not to amaze us with your presumption?"

Swegn rose and stepped back. "Lord, I asked him to bring me in peace."

"To what purpose? You know your condition."

"To make amends to the Church and my royal lord. To render whatever the abbey of Leominster demands and what penance I must, so that your clemency might restore my lands."

Already a lost cause, I knew. I shot a glance at Earl Ralf. He'd have a bone or two to pick on that score.

"And the woman?" A small rent in Edward's dignity as he sneezed wetly. "Not that Christ would want her now. You have been judged. Godwine, take him out of my sight."

My father stepped forward. "Edward, my lord, and you earls of the realm. My son's had no hearing. Even a murderer may be heard before sentence."

Lacking much of its old strength, Godwine's voice that ever played on words like a dulcet flute still riveted attention. "Were he to stand trial and were the Church not involved, his offense would mean no more than civil fine. Men have appetite and women are willing; is not this common among men of the world? For Agatha, she's hardly the first to leave a religious life more blithely than she went to it from choosing other than her own. For Swegn, what man here has not faltered over a fetching eye or loved with his whole heart where whole reason would snatch him away? Agatha is in my countess's care at Bosham to go where and when she will; if back to her vows, none will stop her."

"And her bastard?" Edward queried.

"Sire, my father speaks for me," Swegn spoke. "I love Agatha but cannot command her soul in this. I sue only for pardon, penance, and my return to your service."

"He is contrite," Godwine warranted. "I well know some of you here have no love for me and mine. But own in conscience, lord king, that my house has bent as dutifully to your correction as it has ever answered your call to service. Recall what Sussex cost the Norse last year and how Harold taxed them at Slaughden.''

And at what cost, I added silently as the image came unbidden: old Wulfwig sobbing on the beach for the few he couldn't save.

''Never did thieves limp so beaten home. Recall that Swegn—appallingly stupid at times, I grant—is still the only Saxon warlord the Welsh respect and fear.''

He might well have slapped Ralf across the face. The earl spat out his denial. ''No so, old man!''

''But it is,'' Beorn contradicted. ''Harold said as much two years ago.''

Ralf wheeled on my cousin, bristling. ''Your meaning?''

''You're a foreigner, Ralf.''

''Said the Dane.''

''You've never troubled to learn Saxon ways in the west,'' Beorn said. ''If the Welsh raid again, what English could you levy who've not been insulted already by your arrogance and that of your Norman and Boulognese knights?''

Ralf would have answered hotly but Edward checked him. ''I will have silence! Earl Beorn, do you argue for Swegn's return?''

''No, sire. Only for his honest worth which once was much.''

''I ask that restoration,'' Godwine declared. ''Whatever restitution, it shall be rendered. Swegn is needed in the west.''

I couldn't believe what I heard. Penance, yes. Pardon, perhaps. Let Swegn build a mile of churches—but restored to power? *You were the teacher, Godwine. You don't make such mistakes.*

Edward took his time in reply. ''If I were so foolish as to restore him—and I'd be safer falling on my sword— what of you, Earl Godwine?'' Edward toyed with the linen cloth while Ralf lowered like an imminent storm. ''You disinherited him by writ sealed in our chancellery. Would you put aside Harold and reclaim Swegn once again?''

I saw it all in that charged moment: Beorn and Tostig confounded as myself, Ralf of Mantes one breath away from attacking Swegn. And my father in his own terrible agony.

"Father," Swegn beseeched. "Speak for me. Harold—"

"Uncle, no!" Ralf thrust forward to confront Edward. "I will not give up one hide to him."

But for Godwine and myself, everyone began to shout at once in squabbling babble through which Regenbald pounded futilely for order, but I saw my question clearly answered in Godwine's eyes. What man has not faltered, he asked. That included himself now, as warped by stubborn love as ever Swegn would be. Godwine loved him as I did, though he'd be our ruin as he was his own. Some part of me that dealt not at all with love noted the watchful Danish jarls. Svein Estrithsson would hear of this and no doubt rejoice. An England troubled in her own house was one less worry in Sjaelland.

"I said *peace!*"

On his feet now, Edward thrust out a royal arm to command our silence. His warning finger swept back and forth over all of us. "Giving? Not giving up? Who will and who won't, say you?" His reddened eyes glared balefully. "What is to be given *I* will give. What is denied *I* will deny."

We fell silent. I'd heard Edward's temper could be towering. Good or ill, it was the anger of a king. He sat down again.

"Reserving that place—" as his mood shifted mercurially from wrath to something I read like calculation—"we will put the issue to our earls present."

Swegn made another appeal. "If begging will serve me best, then let me beg of you—"

"Leave off," Edward snapped peevishly. "You make a poor embassy."

Swegn nodded humbly. "Poor in everything, my king. But Wessex left a sick bed to bring me here. I can thank him for that much. I've no practice in humility, so it comes hard for me. All I can do is entreat your trust in my restoration." My brother hung his head. "Failing that, I ask only land to live on. A thane's value, no more."

Edward studied him behind hands folded over his lips. "Quite right: Humility does not suit you. Lords, we would hear your minds in this. A trial is asked. Shall he have it?"

Ralf's vote was predictable. "No. Outlawed he is and must remain."

"Earl Beorn?"

"I also say no. With regret."

"To all, Cousin?" Swegn challenged him, humility gone up in smoke. "Pretty words, Beorn. Sue for my worth but profit from my loss. Aye, as *you* have, Harold."

Beorn strode out to confront Swegn, not angry but sick with it as I was. "Then with the king's leave, take them back. Live on them for all I care, but be no earl in England."

"Be damned then." Swegn turned to me. "Harold, I always had your trust. Will you speak for me?"

Hard truth made me craven just then. I couldn't meet his eye. "No, Swegn."

"What?" Swegn came close to me; for him then, Edward and all others about us had ceased to exist. He couldn't believe such betrayal. *"You* deny me?"

"I have to. You think it's easy?"

"Not one word?" So Jesus must have reproved a kissing Judas at Gethsemane. "Not one breath for me?"

Christ, can't you see? "Not this time, Brother."

Our voices were low, private now. Swegn whispered, "Before God, there was never a day I wouldn't lay down my life for you."

"Save one." I kept my own reasons buried and my voice even, but truth still came out harshly. "One day at Bosham when you promised Father, promised me. When you broke your word and dishonored all of us."

"You know why. Not even a pinch of trust left?"

"In what? From what store? Agatha told me how penitent you are, how humbly you'd have come if Svein had given you the ships. No, Swegn." I had to turn away from him, and that felt like dying. "There's nothing left."

"From your own brother." Edward shrugged with a

there-it-is gesture of conclusion. "Swegn Godwinesson, you have had the hearing you craved. Being a merciful rule, we will raise no hand against the former abbess of Leominster or her child. For yourself, we allow you four days to quit our realm, never to return on certain pain of death. So say the earls, so says England."

Regenbald's staff came down like nails driven into a coffin.

Edward Rex

Now have I seen all the world's wonders. They are divided, and Godwine declines. The old lion's wit's as worn as his teeth, and where once he reasoned, now he dotes. The sun shines on poor Edward, for which I thank Providence.

Who would have thought the old man would overrule his own best interests for love? Or guessed so much hard resolve in Harold? The pupil bests the master, though I saw what it cost him. Well, for the time his purposes and mine walk hand in hand. But is Harold truly for a whole England, or merely the whole of England to be Harold's?

Excellent question.

The last of Swegn. Oh, I pray it's no fault in heaven to relish Godwine's loss. Your move, Fortune. Play what piece you will, the game's already mine. Give us pipe and tabor! Despite this wretched cold, the king's in a mood to dance a little.

21 • Harold

Before retiring to his couch, our saintly Majesty, rubbing salt in the wound, laid a task on Beorn and me. "Being of his blood, my lords will escort Swegn directly to his ship. Four days, Godwinesson."

My father looked shrunken as he bid Swegn farewell, like a once-healthy fruit squeezed dry of its juice. "I did try, Son."

He might have said more but his infirmity overcame him. I helped Godwine to my tent and let him rest on my cot, dragging a stool near. Only a moment before I must go, but my father needed every bit of comfort and heart I could give him then. "Sir, I wanted to say—"

"No need. You were the wiser statesman today."

"Hang that. I wanted to say that I love you very much. And for what I had to do, I'm sorry." So miserably sorry that I wanted to hide under a rock.

Lying with his eyes closed, Godwine smiled feebly. "Thank you. I put love before reason. Inexcusable."

"Don't." I wanted to hold him, weep for him. "Don't blame yourself. If he was worth it once, he's not now."

Some of the old amusement curled in my father's wan smile. "Rather a shock to find myself awash in paternal feeling. But his mother wished it."

I might have seen that. Despite all, blindly, stubbornly, they would have him back. "Rest here before you go. Botulf will tend you."

"Just for a little." Godwine pressed at his temples, wincing. "What tedium life can be. My physicians say

I must give up meat and wine and be bled to cleanse my humors.''

"Perhaps you should."

"I will. When there is time."

I pressed his hand and rose. "Beorn's waiting."

"Harold, he . . . it tore your mother's heart out to see him."

And she knowing what contempt for her lay behind Swegn's false kiss and ingratiating smirk. But he was flesh and blood out of her own. Honor can die quickly, but love is hard to kill. I glared at Swegn where he waited by Beorn, and felt the anger build in me. *You hurt them. You hurt her.* "Time to go, Swegn."

Silent, the three of us, going single file down the cliff path, then our shoes crunching over the loose beach pebbles. We passed Godwine's ship. In the prow Teinfrith raised one hand to me, or perhaps a last salute to Swegn, to what he had once been.

The mercenary keels were beached south of the king's squadrons. Some of Swegn's crews cooked their midday meal amidships, others simply idled and waited, leaning over the side. The tide was coming in, already lapping close about the grounded prows. Swegn's boatmaster hailed him from his own ship, a one-eyed man with a deep scar trenched across the empty socket. "Lord Swegn, we sail now?"

Swegn swept an arm out at the crewmen on the beach. "Get them aboard."

"That man with the scar." Beorn was certain. "I've seen him in Roskilde. My brother put a price on him."

"A price or a rope for all of them," Swegn said. "I didn't have time or money for better. Harold—why?"

"Don't waste time. Get aboard. God go with you."

"And may He go from you." Swegn damned me more bitterly with his eyes than the words. "My loyal little brother. Godwine spoke for me. Why couldn't you?"

"Swegn, it's done. Go."

"Why couldn't you? You might have swayed the others."

"Where Father could not?"

"You have your own reasons," Swegn insinuated.

"There are things I would not say now."

"No doubt. You covet my place. Don't pretend you regret this."

"More than you know." That much was honesty. All I could see was Gytha, how she must have suffered when he came and more when he went. "Take my hand and say farewell."

Swegn only stepped back from me, smiling coldly. "Look to your own shores, Anglia. I may put in for water."

"Don't threaten me. You'll fare no better than the Norse."

"Cousin, you must sail." Beorn put a hand on Swegn's arm only to have it struck viciously away.

"Don't touch me!"

All this in plain sight of the grinning boatmen. Some things should not be aired before strangers. "For God's sake, go with some dignity."

"To hell with dignity," Swegn seethed. "To hell with all of you."

I should have recognized that blank-eyed demon bent over me long ago when Swegn laid a knife to my throat, but my own anger was heating beyond caution. "You want reasons, you want why? First you dishonored and humiliated our father."

"*Your* father."

"Stay, I'll come to that. Agatha told me what happened with King Svein. You're a bloody wonder for brains, you are."

I felt control slipping away with every dangerous word. Beorn tried to prevent further conflict. "Stop this, both of you."

But I shoved him away this time. "No, he wants reasons. I'll not let him go ignorant. Break a hundred vows, bed a hundred nuns, I'd have loved you still. But what you did to Gytha, that filthy lie you put out about her and Canute, that will take seven years scrubbing and still leave a stain."

"How do you know it's a lie?"

The taste of sick revulsion rose in my mouth, a breath away from murder, seeing my brother and a madman who must believe his own poisoned lie. He actually smiled at me with the challenge.

"How do you *know*, little brother?"

My fists balled at my sides. "Don't say any more."

"Beware of you? When I wiped your runny nose for years? Your father was only the king's creature. Mine was the king himself."

I don't remember willing the blow. My fist just went back and out with my shoulder behind it, smashing into Swegn's face. He went down on his back. The boatmen roared with laughter, glad for any diversion. Swegn sprang up, drawing his dagger and lunging at me in one flowing motion. I stepped back instinctively at guard, but the loose pebbles slid underfoot.

"No!"

In the instant I needed to recover, Beorn was between us, still unable to believe Swegn would use the blade. The needle point caught at the join of neck and shoulder and drove in deep.

Before heaven, I don't believe Swegn knew clearly what he did, only that something prevented him from reaching me. He struck again and again as Beorn sank to his knees and collapsed.

Swegn stared down at him. I've seen men woken from nightmare, not yet in the real world until the undertow of red dream ebbs from their mind. So my brother woke slowly to where he was, to me and the men watching and the mocking screech of gulls overhead.

And Beorn at his feet. The dagger fell from his hand. He backed away. "Harold, I . . ."

I stumbled the few steps to kneel beside my cousin. Beorn's eyes were open but saw nothing. I scooped up the dagger and flung it at Swegn's feet, past fear, past all now. "Use it. *Use* it, then. Me you wanted, right? Go on. Finish it."

Swegn only covered his face, his right hand flecked with Beorn's blood. "God forgive me."

"He may but I won't. You'd have killed me easily as you broke your worthless word."

"Brother . . ."

"You're no one's brother." I covered Beorn's face and shoulders with my cloak. "No one's son."

Leaning over the ship's side, the one-eyed boatmaster commented, "Oh, don't they smell of the real world now? Where do we sail, Lord Swegn?"

"Sail?" He lurched away toward the boat like a man turning from life to cross Styx, and I cared not whither. He was carrion to be washed from my heart. As the oarsmen backed water, I heard footsteps running toward me, then Botulf loomed over me where I crouched with Beorn's body in my arms.

"Love of mercy, what . . . ?"

The horror in his face mirrored mine. All I could think was that I must be the one cursed to tell Father.

Edith

He came home that August in a strange kind of exhaustion, different and older than the husband who'd left me to serve his king.

I took to bed in those last days before Magnus was born, less concerned then for the child than the too-silent man who sat by me through the tedious hours. Before the pains began, Harold lay with his face against the high mound of my belly, one hand pressed to the flesh wall between himself and the coming child.

"It will be well, dearest," I promised him over and over. "The first is always hardest. You'll see."

"I want to feel it move," he whispered, fingers spread and tracing the life to come.

Only when he could tell me about Swegn did I understand his fierce need for this life in me to make up the death in himself.

22 • Tostig

May I put in a word? That is, if you can tolerate the intrusion of an obscure third son. Why do men speak of my brothers but never of me? If Edward was chosen of God, the very stars conjoined in my destined birth. Never say I am not loyal to family, meager though the rewards have been. Swegn had a certain brute valor but no mind, and Harold is noble . . . I suppose. Swegn was an earl at my age, Harold belted at barely nineteen. When is *my* turn? Is my portion ever to be less? Neither of them has been at best more than provincial lord and heroic only by happenstance. I who am at the fountainhead of events, who see most clearly how all things come together and with what meaning, must live under Edward's frowning scrutiny, beguile the time with Eadgytha, listen to little Wulfnoth garble his Latin, and feed my starveling ambition what scraps are flung to me.

I am twenty-two. When is my life going to *happen?*

"Keep your eyes and ears open," Godwine counsels. "Heaven may be fixed and unchanging. We have no reports from that realm, but here the game shifts constantly."

Shifts daily. Two years since our blockade of the Narrow Sea and Swegn's murder of Beorn. Godwine perseveres in the Witan, Edward plays his own crafty game.

Nothing and everything has changed. William of Normandy now rules so firmly in his suzerain that his blood claim to our throne through Edward's mother, Emma, must be taken seriously. Those perfumed courtiers who flit between Baldwin and Edward report William suing to the count for the hand of his daughter Matilda. Jeweled hands aflutter, they gossip that she'll have none of him. Cooler heads say she will when Baldwin's price is met.

That peerless servant of God, Robert Champart, is now archbishop of Canterbury, virtually equal in power to Edward, and Godwine's bitter enemy. Even less chance now for Harold to marry his Edith properly. Well, he knew what he did. He chose the woman out of love; there's indulgence. He should have put her aside like his Welsh whore. Fornicators are not to be admired, but in the matter of Edith, a little sin would have been a large saving. I have never known that hunger when it could not be sated in an hour, confessed in another, and on my shriven way.

The center of power has shifted from eclipsed Denmark to Flanders and Normandy. With Champart at his ear, Edward sways toward the latter and the ties of his youth. Godwine urges a treaty with Flanders. Then, he reasons, whatever William's claim to England, his potential father-in-law is not an ally but one more treaty-bound obstacle.

Shrewd, even brilliant, had it come to pass. Wonderful were we a nation with every nose sifting the air for danger. But we are an island. Within our shores are myriad islets of earls and thanes indifferent to all that does not directly concern them. In Mercia, Earl Leofric ponders mainly what title he can manage for his son Aelfgar. *Fool* would be my modest nomination. In wild Northumbria, Siward is an aging watchdog whose traditional enemy is the marauding Scot, not some fledgling Norman duke. For the commons and lesser thanes in their remote steadings, London and Winchester are a world away, Normandy and Flanders beyond the sun. Importance to them is good weather for planting and harvesting. Disaster is a cold, wet summer. Wonder is the acquisition by their church of a saint's knucklebone, higher thought the question of whether or not Edward's bath water really cured a woman of wens, and could they possibly acquire some.

Godwine is not heeded in council. They think his day is past, yet he broods over the game. Ambitious as an oyster, Harold rusticates at Nazeing with a son hanging from either hand, while I see daily the changing game, the subtle or bold moves of the pieces. I see tomorrow happening around me.

In Maying time when Winchester grew pleasant, Eadgytha summoned me to her chambers. *Vitement*, Clothilde added; there was news of great import.

My sister sat with three of her women at embroidery. A fourth pressed limpid chords from a small harp.

I bowed. "Lady, you sent?"

"Tostig! Yes." Eadgytha sprang up with more happiness than I'd seen in her for many months. Her marriage was the one subject she would not discuss with me, as if words were needed. A court can keep no secrets. The royal union was not happy, not sad, but for the most part simply not.

Today she evinced her old energy as she dismissed her women with little sweeping gestures, then, when we were alone, kissed me with urgent tenderness. "I've a surprise for you. Come look."

She led me to a table cluttered as usual with correspondence and the court business of the mints, which she personally supervised for Edward. "It was not mere fondness that gave you my love from the first. You have a destiny, Tostig. You glow with it, lit from within. See."

Eadgytha spread the broad new parchment before me, covered with celestial diagrams and the minute script of Roland of Rouen, her astrologer. "I always knew such fortune would unfold for you. Great trials, but greater rewards to come, and soon. Read."

By what I read, the portents were not only incredible but imminent. Roland foresaw my betrothal to a woman of the highest place, preceding higher rule. Very soon my stars would pluck me from obscurity into prominence, though elevation would have its price. There would be great troubles later, mostly through the misunderstanding of my virtues and motives by lesser men.

I looked up from the glittering future to the present pride in my sister's eyes. "Is he sure? I mean . . . 'high rule'?"

"Roland is never wrong."

But he could be maddeningly ambiguous. "Harold was born on the same day."

"Three years earlier and at a different hour."

I scanned the forecast once more, trying to comprehend and believe. For what Roland saw, I'd always had the ambition and the strength of mind. I am the most competent among Godwine's children, yet now I felt a sudden timidity. "He could be wrong."

"Roland? Never."

"Never? Who foresaw that Harold would replace Swegn? What else could 'high rule' mean?"

"Tostig, don't be dense." Eadgytha dropped into her audience chair, laughing with tender exasperation. "We love our brother, of *course,* but he's a fool. What high marriage or high rule for him? His qualities are sterling but plain. He's a loyal, loving man. He adores Edith, which is sweet but inconvenient, since he can never marry her. He is serviceable in Anglia and will doubtless be so when Father dies, but as to destiny? A cipher."

He had been no cipher at Sandwich. Who would have credited the stern will in him who had loved Swegn before all others?

Eadgytha beckoned me to her. "There will be other earldoms. When fate takes your hand, don't drag your feet."

I sat at the foot of her chair as I had for years as a child.

"Will you trust your sister?"

"You know I do."

"Keep secret about this for the nonce. Mark Roland's word. Smaller men will always misunderstand and fear your excellence."

No worry there. I'd always been a miser in what I divulged to anyone. The more they knew, the more to use against you with ill intent. I would keep the future and my motives close. This was the first earnest toward believing the forecast. Who could ever misunderstand Harold, whose nature was open for all men to see?

On the other hand, I had seen flashes of something in him more complex than Eadgytha would guess. Depth? Secret purpose? He might be one of those master deceivers so open they're closed, hiding all in apparently hiding nothing.

I wrapped my arms around my beloved sister's knees. "I'll speak no word."

"And we will build on this," she promised.

As foretold events fell one by one into place, I doubted less the more I wished to believe. By one of his most trusted thanes, Godwine sent letters delivered into my hand. Gytha's note invited me home to Bosham. Godwine's was to be destroyed after reading.

Edward has spies in Bruges, but they are mostly Normans and may tell him no more than William wishes him to hear. Not entirely trusting Edward's judgment, the Witan needs one of our own to observe Baldwin's court and what William does there. You served well in your first charge at Sandwich and may again now.

The mission required someone of name but not so prominent as to raise any suspicion. A younger son of Baldwin's old friend, traveling for pleasure and broadening. Edward's leave would be easily obtained. I was only added expense in the queen's household; he'd likely hand me out the door himself, Godspeed. Godwine would furnish ample funds, his only stricture secrecy. Neither Harold nor even Eadgytha were to know my real purpose. I loved my sister but more than all I wanted Father's respect and trust. To show my motives the more innocent, Godwine suggested I might court Baldwin's younger half-sister, Judith.

—somewhat older than you but one of the highest-placed eligible ladies west of Rhine, an excellent connection and step to your own advancement. Come to Bosham first, as your mother wishes. We will speak in detail before you embark.

Could I doubt further? Proofs are not always writ bold

but in subtleties as well. Roland told true. At last *I* came forward. *I* was at the center. Father needed me then, perhaps even more than he did Harold.

To Flanders, led by a brightening star.

23 • Tostig

I am to observe in Bruges, and that I do. The Flemish build more in stone than we; even in summer, Baldwin's palace is cool and damp. His court is more sumptuous and sophisticated than Edward's, and Baldwin himself approaches middle years with an ease of power so natural, the iron fist rarely shows beneath the glove of charm. He speaks English, Danish, German, and Frankish fluently, one of those men who give the impression of an intimate equal on first meeting. He has seduced the world in this way, a listener who learns more than he divulges while the guest, gulled with courtesy, lets slip far more than intended. I am entertained as the beloved son of his friend Godwine. The soul of tact, Baldwin referred only once to Edward's blockade as "our late difficulties."

Lady Matilda has a mind of her own but none of her father's diplomacy. She is the smallest woman I've ever seen and the most willful and imperious. She leads William a merry dance in his despairing courtship. On Monday she'll have none of him, Tuesday she might. She chides his rude Norman accent and manners in the morning, invites him to ride with her in the afternoon, to attend her without fail at dinner . . . then sends that she is indisposed. "Come closer a little farther away," is her maddening message to his suit. "Quit me a little nearer." Her wit could shave a tough beard close or draw blood. To see her with William, fierce little terrier bullying a boar hound, one concludes the obvious. If Matilda weds him, Normandy will have ten times a duchess and Willy Bastard a handful.

William himself is not so easily read. At first glance a physically massive young man, deliberate, no lightness or poise about him. His wooing of Matilda is dogged, if frustrated. I could not draw him out. With my pleasing manner and looks, he thought me at first a rival for Matilda's hand, and indeed the little vixen flirted openly with me sometimes to further the impression.

Lumbering, illiterate William seems insecure among older and more powerful men, but I sense in him an elemental strength surely forged in the constant peril of his early years. He is the very opposite of Harold: distrustful by nature, nothing of jest or lightness about him. He labors at social grace like a woodcutter with a blunt ax. Where Harold will wrap a serious thought in a joke, William's attempts at wit plummet like stone and lie expiring while he explains the point and why it's funny. One might dismiss him as a boor but instinct says look closer. There is something about William more than merely tedious. *Relentless* is closer to the mark, his will already formidable. He has forbidden private war among his unruly vassals and is strong enough to enforce that edict.

Most disquieting of all, there's that about William that is not young, nor ever was, one feels. So I smile and play the shallow English fop to his man of destiny. But he's made a careless slip: Sometime in the near future he will make a visit to Edward in the courtesy of kinship.

"We are cousins, as you know."

"Indeed? Hadn't heard." When all England had heard for years, but let him think me a vacant dolt. Edward is childless and his sister's husband, Eustace of Boulogne, is already in England sniffing out his own piece of our throne. What vanity prompts you foreign lot to think England yours for the taking? Ambition knows its like, William, and I have your measure now. You'd have the bloody lot if the world let you. Better my crown than yours.

But I smile at the duke, lift the perfumed orange to my nose delicately, bow, and excuse myself. *"Adieu,* your grace. The count's sister expects me for a game of *lourche."*

Which I lose gracefully, commending the lady's skill. Judith pleases me sufficiently in that nothing about her displeases me. By liking and calculation—in a profitable match the latter must never be neglected—she is perfect for me, if a few years older. Judith is tall with a high complexion and reddish-blond hair and thin brows which I am sure she plucks to arch high, giving her a perpetually quizzical expression. Matilda the glaring exception, Fleming women are like Fleming horses, large and built for breeding. Judith has an agreeable disposition, made all the more so by her value as the sister of Europe's most powerful magnate.

While I am not her only suitor, Baldwin inclines to me. I suspect he considers the match a convenient paternal hand in England. If Matilda marries William, Baldwin's other hand will be in Normandy. A shrewd politician; small wonder he and Godwine have vast respect for each other. By rank and nature Judith will complement my destiny as a precious relic sets off the pommel of a fine sword. *Tant mieux,* if Baldwin gains a stake in England, our children will be like grappling hooks over Flanders' beam. Yes, Godwine will be pleased.

My stars held true. Baldwin's consent only sealed in wax Judith's open eagerness. Our betrothal was announced, emissaries dispatched to haggle the contract, and I would sail for Bosham in the last week of August. Other suitors were disgruntled, William openly surprised, muttering something contemptuous about English foppery in Judith's hearing. "Where are their vavasors, their warriors? With their finery and long hair, they are more like pretty girls."

"It must be so in England," Judith concluded warmly. "You are the handsomest man in my memory."

"William should beware of such 'girls,' " I laughed.

"It would cost him dear to dally with us. Until our wedding, lady."

So home with my "pretty" head full of intelligence for Godwine. Baldwin's intentions toward England: watchful but benevolent. William's? Ambitious, perhaps dangerously so. William's strengths: formidable. His weakness: lack of political experience and guile, unable yet to mask his intent behind diplomacy. As with Harold and Edith, the Church bars his marriage to Matilda because of consanguinity, but the sure word is that Baldwin will prevail, Rome will have its price and Flanders will pay it.

A superior report. I'd missed nothing. Be pleased, Father. Be proud of your son who served you and England well. Listen to me, then. Lord a-mercy, do I become what Edward so scathingly called Harold? A patriot? Pleasing thought for a passing moment, but . . . hardly. Like everyone else in this very hard world, I want what's mine.

Godwine had given me two of his best ships, fifty-five footers, one of them fitted to carry the horses and luggage of my train, manned by his most experienced lithsmen. We stood out from Bruges with the morning tide and a fair wind for the Kentish coast. Edric, my boatmaster, estimated we would raise Sandwich in a few hours if wind and weather held.

When we passed below the cliffs at Sandwich, the wind still held out of the northeast. Edric took full advantage of the stiffening breeze but worried at the clouds building south of us, reading them from long experience.

"Spoiling for a squall. We'd best put in at Dover and wait her out."

Only common sense. In a storm men can rule themselves by discipline, but horses are difficult to transport even in calm sea. The seven or eight tethered in our second boat could break loose with hell, broken bones, or drowning to pay.

Only twelve or so sea miles to Dover, but by the time we rounded the shallow headland, there was a high sea running. Worse, the wind shifted without warning and blew out of the southwest. Edric ordered sail reefed and

oars broken out. By now the tide was turning. Our lithsmen rowed against the wind, the current no longer with
us. When we raised the beacon smoke from Dover light-
house, we were already drenched in the leading edge of
the squall. Beside me at the starboard beam, Edric pointed
at the smoke over Dover valley.

"That's not any beacon fire."

Not that dirty pall darkening the already turbulent sky.
"There's fire in the town. Have the men arm, Edric. The
tide'll let us beach close. When we do, we move fast,
clear? Pass the word."

Some of the off relief were already buckling on mail
and slinging baldrics. "They're from Dover," Edric said
with a tinge of my own apprehension. "This is their home.
You think it's a raid?"

"We'll find out." Almost surely a raid; the smoke was
more than accidental fire. Too much of it. Partly in royal
jurisdiction by law, but in loyalty Dover looked to Godwine for justice. Whatever happened in the town, Father
must know swiftly.

When the keel scraped bottom, I leaped over the side
and splashed through the shallows to shore, followed by
Edric and more than a score of his youngest and best.
Whatever help we would have been was too late. The
houses still burned. A few people carried buckets, no
longer in frantic haste but exhausted despair. Dover
sprawled in shock, able only to lick numbly at its wounds.
Whoever had done this was gone.

One by one my men collected about me. Some of them
from Dover ran to houses, calling for family or wives. Or
found them lying in the streets.

"God's mercy," Edric choked. "Even children."

Trampled in the mud beyond us were the bodies of as
many women as men and several children, one no more
than a swaddled babe. The nauseating smell of wet charred
wood was acrid in my nose. I wanted to be sick but these
people would expect more of Godwine's son. Today *I* was
Wessex to them. Not Godwine or Harold but me.

*Find the facts if anyone can tell you straight. Think fast,
then act. They are all watching you.*

The Dover men who'd fought and survived sat or knelt in the mud by fallen friends. One stood apart, a thick-set older man with an ax in one hand, a longsword in the other. It was a Norman blade, far too expensive for any Saxon householder.

"You there! Fellow!"

He looked back at me, through me, dull-eyed. Edric and I went to him. The rain was falling harder now, fires hissing in the wet. Somewhere a woman wailed. We stood there, the three of us, and I saw just beyond the grim sentinel, the row of dead Normans and Boulognese laid out in a line.

The man said in a lifeless voice, "I know you. Godwinesson. Should've come sooner."

"Just luck and weather we put in at all."

"Tell the earl . . ."

"I will. Speak, man. What happened?"

He told us in fragments of sentences begun and trailed off, still drained by the fray, which must have been brief but savage. Bad as I thought and much worse. These were Count Eustace's men. They'd come to the town from Canterbury not two hours past, just rode in and demanded lodging. Foreigners who didn't know or care about the rights of householders.

"There was my friend, a mercer. Known him all my life, best wares, best house in town. Look, there it is . . . was. They rode in and some foreign scut just walks in like't were his own, says he's staying the night, if you please. My friend went to throw him out and the bastard wounds him with a dagger. In his own house, mind, and wait till Godwine hears of that. Well, he showed that dirt how a blade is used proper, stuck'm in the ribs for good."

Eustace and the rest found themselves surrounded by a roused town with blood in its eyes, and rode out. Dover thought that the end of it, but they came back in arms, riding through the streets, killing and trampling everyone in their path. They broke into the mercer's house and killed him.

"On his own hearth they murdered him. We closed ranks against them. Did what we could." He pointed at the line of corpses. "Nineteen of them, more of us. Christ, even children."

Eustace and his men finally retreated the way they came, toward Canterbury. The townsman prodded the body at his feet. "This one lived long enough to curse us."

Edward would punish Dover for this outrage to his brother-in-law. So he would, I knew. The grey knot in my stomach expanded. I saw the whole thing with cruel clarity. The matter would spread like the fires these folk fought now without someone to speak in their defense.

I voiced the next thought without meaning to. "Well, it's been coming. Best bury these carrion. Your midden ditch will do and no need to be nice about prayers."

"Prayers?" The Dover man spat on the body at his feet. "If they're gone to the king, that's a long ride. The king's at Gloucester."

Yes, Eadgytha wrote me he'd gone with most of the court to hunt in Dean Forest. Eustace would have to cross the width of England from the Narrow Sea to the Welsh marches, and that with some of his men wounded.

Godwine must be prepared. I must give him the time.

"Edric, we can't do much now. Rest here tonight, sail with first light, but I want everyone aboard well before that."

"Hard pull getting here." Edric turned a doubtful eye toward the choppy sea. "The wind will still be against us."

"To hell with that. We'll row all the way if we have to, you hear me? Every damned one of us, all day and all night."

A hard pull indeed to Bosham with the wind against us. We'd do well to raise Chichester Harbor by evening of the second day. "We'll row shorter turns, all of us. For now, help put out the fires. Quarter us where you can. And pay for all we use."

I'd done what I could for the time; some pride in that as I contemplated the face of the dead vavasor. *You're a rare fool and Eustace another. Not that you'd care alive or dead, but you may have begun a goddamned civil war.*

All plans, all policies, all intents narrowed and converged on little Dover now.

24 • Harold

God bless Tostig for once. He stumbled ashore at Bosham, hands cracked and bleeding from the oar he worked hard as any lithsman to reach Godwine with time to spare. When the king's rage broke over Wessex, the south was ready. From Edward came the furious command: Godwine must answer for this insult to royal kin and punish Dover severely. Back to the king from Godwine: He would answer with all Wessex at his back to thrash the matter out, but would *not* punish the town.

The alarm went out. Beacon fires blazed from hilltops and church bells alarumed from Somerset to Kent. Men left fields and threshing floors to assemble under their thanes. The whole south rippled like sinew beneath the skin of England. I would sail Thames west to meet Father in the Cotswolds, where the wind blew cold over the heights and colder with what I knew was coming. No issue had ever been so clearly drawn, a test of the law of England against the power of nobles over defenseless commoners. An insult to royal favorites versus an outraged people's sense of right. No middle way this time. The handwriting was clear on the wall and our backs to it.

Every keel under my command lay in a line along Lea bank, loading men, horses, and stores. Priests from Waltham went up and down the embarking lines, offering benediction prayers for us and England. Botulf loped back and forth like a harried sheepdog on the flank of a contrary flock—

"Move, you people, *move!*"

—while Edith left our boys in the covered cart and came to say good-bye, something we'd said far too often since our marriage. No need to tell her how bad things were. My wife had a mind and eye to see, but I put the best face on it.

"It's only a show of strength, Edith. Once Godwine has a chance to reason with the king—well, no fear. Sigward will mind Nazeing. He's ample men."

She was not so easily cozened. "Don't."

"What?"

"I don't need false cheer. Godwine won't give in this time, will he?"

"He can't. Not on this."

"Then it's war?"

"Not yet. Edward heard only the foreigners' side of it. All Father wants is a fair hearing."

"Fair!" Edith stamped her foot, blazing at me. "You reck he'll get fair? I am so tired of seeing you go and go and go, so sick of you gone from us. The boys are so little, each time you come home they must learn to know you all over again. And I hate sleeping without you. God a-mercy, sometimes I wish it were only that Welsh girl you were off to. I'd only have to worry about pox and lice."

"Edith, it's more than family this time."

"It's always more, isn't it? I wish you were a farmer. A peddler, anything. We'd be happier."

So did I more than once. All I could do was hold her as Botulf called out, "My lord, all boats ready."

"Aye, coming. Kiss me, love. I'll be home before to-day's milk is ripe for cheese."

I helped Edith up into the wagon and hugged my boys with a pang. Little Magnus could only gurgle at me, but Godwine gave me a hearty, wet kiss and a laugh.

"You mind your mum and nurse now. I want to hear only good of you when I'm home."

I touched Edith's cheek once more. "It will be well."

Both of us knew I lied. The outcome of this would be victory or ruin.

*   *   *

Between Tetbury and Beverstone the hills rise high, cut through with valleys thick with beech woods, their leaves turning in the first autumn chill. In the valleys, more than a thousand of our men were deployed in a semicircle on the high ground where the commanders' tents were pitched. Distantly to the north on other hilltops, we could see the fires from Edward's camp. Not so many as ours. For the moment we had the advantage of numbers, but still ordered more fires lit to add illusion to our strength.

Evening, 7 September, 1051. In Godwine's spacious tent we were a weary lot over supper, Father and I, Tostig, Teinfrith, and Botulf. Ridden or sailed, most of us had sped the broad width of southern England to be here. None of us could say what would befall when we confronted the king, but all knew what couldn't be allowed. Such knowledge silences men, makes them eat with more thought to the morrow than the wine gone tasteless in their mouths.

The braziers warmed us, but outside the night wind mourned like a new widow where sentries shivered at their posts. We heard a distant horn, sounded again minutes later and closer. Godwine turned the wooden cup in his fingers.

"From the king, I presume."

Tostig nodded. "Come to tell us what we already know."

Such envoys were common practice. Edward would send requesting parley while his messengers estimated our numbers and disposition where they could, anything they could ferret out. Beyond the tent we heard voices in challenge and response. I stepped outside the tent. Farther down the slope our men had stopped a mounted party of six, five of them carrying torches. In the wavering light I recognized the massive figure of their leader, and ducked back into the tent.

"It's Earl Siward."

Even in the dark one could identify Siward's heavy stride set off by the chink-chink of his old-fashioned scale armor. Then he filled the tent entrance, throwing back the hood of his long, black cloak. He chopped his white head up and down to Godwine. "My lord."

"My lord." Godwine indicated the table. "We're just at supper. Will you take something?"

"Thank you, I will not."

Godwine eased back into his chair. "Pardon me if I sit. A strenuous day."

"You're yet ill," Siward observed bluntly.

"Well enough. Please sit."

"No. Thank you."

"Will the king parley?"

"Tomorrow as he says. On the Bristol road. But he demands hostages."

Godwine might not have heard. "Botulf, pour me some more wine."

Botulf stepped nimbly behind my father to fill the cup lifted over the earl's shoulder. "No, Siward," Godwine said at length. "No hostages. Edward already has my son Wulfnoth. A 'guest' of the queen but forbidden to leave court."

"Godwine," Siward said heavily, "you realize what is at stake?"

"Clearly. Do you and Leofric?"

Siward hesitated, then shrugged. "This is a southern issue. It's between you and Edward."

"You know what happened. You know it's more than that."

"You have always been a man of reason." Siward's response betrayed ambivalence, reluctance. Northumbria and Mercia were here by royal command alone, hardly inclination.

Godwine drained his cup and set it by. When he looked up at Siward, I saw the steel usually sheathed in mellow tact. "Not this time. Well you know, well you've seen how I've backed up, backed off, backed down for years in the name of reason and peace. How all of us have bitten back frustration before that man and his foreign favorites. But not this time, not possible."

"I will sit, thank you." Siward dropped heavily into the chair Botulf drew up for him. "In the matter of Dover, all Edward's heard is Eustace and his yapping followers. They say you ordered the town to resist.''

The denial burst from Tostig like a whip crack. "That's a lie. I was there. I saw what happened.''

Siward stilled my brother with a glance. "You speak for your father, boy?''

Tostig stiffened. "I am no boy, sir.''

"Certainly not,'' Godwine interceded smoothly. "If you wonder how we mobilized so swiftly, it's because Tostig moved even faster. Well done.''

My brother straightened with pride. Until that moment, I never realized how much he might have thirsted for Godwine's smallest approval, like parched soil yearning for rain.

"Leofric and I have been ordered to send for reinforcements,'' Siward said. "It's that serious with Edward. Eustace and his rutting knights are with him.''

"And what others?'' I asked.

"Earl Ralf with as many as he could levy, mostly Norman cavalry. And Champart.''

Godwine chuckled sourly. "Our tireless prelate of Canterbury. Wouldn't seem like Edward without that thieving son of a seamstress at his ear. Have some wine, Siward.''

"You're a keen one for making light of what's dark.'' Siward took the offered cup and gulped at it. "There's worse. Champart's noised about that you plot against Edward's life as you did Prince Alfred's.''

I might have ignited at that myself, and I think Siward was for once aware of having been too frank in the wrong company. He dropped his eyes. "His words, not mine.''

Godwine smiled at me. "We really must do something about that saintly man.''

"Canonize him,'' Tostig suggested. "At the neck.''

Godwine rose with an air of conclusion. "This is not a hostage situation. The king will require none, nor will I. What hour tomorrow?''

Siward lifted his bulk out of the chair, fastening the cloak with its heavy gold brooch. "At noon.''

He took Godwine's hand, not warmly but in courtesy to a respected equal. "If this goes to arms, are you prepared for outright war? Eustace wants it. All the outlanders do.''

"Readier than Edward, but no one wants that. Not you or Leofric, not one thane or fyrd man. Reason, Siward? If we give way on Dover, it's not my house burning alone but all of us. Men like Eustace—yes, and busy young William surely as I breathe—will see an open door into England.''

"Don't I know that?'' Siward snorted. "I could have told Edward as much, but what use? He's half Norman in blood and all at heart.''

Skilled at reaching for truth behind men's words, my father asked, "Did you try?''

"As if he'd listen. He's never trusted you.''

"And you, my lord? Do you distrust my motives in this?''

Siward lifted the tent flap, then let it fall. Telling hesitation in such a blunt, determinate man. "I could, Godwine. You're too clever by half—but wrong in this? No, I can't say that. Scots I'll fight any day, but you and I are too old to start killing our own over foreigners. Give y'good night.''

After Siward departed, Godwine called for his cloak and summoned me and Tostig to walk with him. Out in the wind scouring the hilltop, we faced toward the far pinpoints of light from the king's fires.

"At noon,'' Godwine mused. "Very late.''

"Our king is a man of fixed habits,'' Tostig offered. "He rises at prime and hears mass before breakfast every day, sick or well. A long one,'' my brother amended from experience. "Then he bathes and dresses, and only then will he see any but those of his chamber or his chaplain.''

Godwine nodded as if confirming his own thoughts. "So nothing moves until midmorning.''

"What *I* think,'' Tostig asserted, "he's giving himself time to deploy his men. We don't know how many.''

"We know enough.'' Siward's words flashed bright in my memory. "Remember? Siward said he and Leofric had been ordered to send for reinforcements. They couldn't possibly be here yet.''

I estimated we faced Ralf's men, the king's household-ers, Eustace's party, and whatever numbers the northern earls brought with them on such brief notice.

Tostig grinned with cold satisfaction. "Then we have him."

"Having him is not the matter," Godwine advised. "Of course, it helps. Harold, pass the word. I want every man mounted by sunrise and all infantry formed and ready to march."

By the time Edward heard mass and emerged from the royal bath, he would already be outmaneuvered and out-manned. We went to bed far more confident than we should have.

25 • Harold

Just before noon our scouts sighted Edward's force moving southeast in a long column toward the Bristol road. By that time our men were in place on the hill-tops commanding the road or in the wooded valleys hard by. Godwine had first planned a show of numbers but changed his mind in view of the ground. The thick-wooded valleys were ideal for ambush if one were needed. Most of our force was hidden with perhaps only two hundred horse, foot, and archers arrayed on the upper slopes. Our bowmen were the south's finest, men from the forests of Ytena and Andredsweald. If ordered, they could volley a lethal hailstorm into Edward's ranks.

God forbid that. We wished only for the king to hear us out in honest reason where until now he'd heard only our enemies. Edward was devious, but far from mad. If he saw himself mated in one move, his own choice would be caution. From our hilltop, Godwine, Tostig, and I made out Edward in the lead as he reached the road and turned west. At Father's word I signaled them with the horn slung from my belt. The Wessex standard-bearer and three accompanying carls trotted their horses down the slope toward the road.

Godwine leaned from the saddle to clap Tostig on the thigh. "Let's to it, son Tostig. Stand with your brother and me."

Clearly meant as warm confidence, but Tostig bridled. "You thought I would not? Did I not stand *for* you at Dover?"

He touched spurs to the bay's flanks and cantered away toward the colors. We could only stare after him. Like violence in Swegn, you never knew when Tostig might turn hostile.

"I'm bound," Godwine vouched. "He'd take umbrage if someone offered him the crown in the wrong tone of voice."

My brother did acquit himself splendidly at Dover and received Father's thanks—though perhaps in Tostig's particular need, not near enough. He was clearly impressed with himself; the world might be more so were he less.

Where the road cut through a shallow notch between two hilltops, our parties met. Edward paced his horse to within a few yards of us, flanked by Earl Ralf, Eustace, Leofric, Siward, the chancellor Regenbald, and the archbishop, Robert Champart. Behind them the Boulognese and Norman knights fanned out to either side, fully armed, their helmets with the iron noseguards masking all humanity in their faces. Toward the rear, the column began to expand, men and horses trickling out on either side of the road, but in no good order. We retained the tactical advantage. We bared our head to Edward but remained mounted. The king surveyed our few visible men on the slopes before speaking.

"Godwine, as always you age us before our time. In this business of Dover, I have few words. You will harry the town one end to the other for their insult to Count Eustace."

"For what you instigated!" Champart fairly yelped. "Can you deny you instructed Dover to resist the count's men?"

Godwine answered evenly. "Of course I deny it."

"Encouraged then."

"Nor that, but knowing the truth of the matter from my son who was there, I commend them."

I tried to gauge their mood. The Boulognese and Normans looked eager to fight, Ralf of Mantes less so. He was Eustace's stepson but Edward's nephew and, more, an earl who dealt mainly with other English nobles. Siward and Leofric were silent and clearly uncomfortable, distancing themselves as far as possible from the dispute.

Edward said, "Earl Godwine, I have given you a command."

"I cannot punish my folk for defending their homes and rights. Over thirty of them were killed."

"And nineteen good men of mine," Eustace reminded him. "I did no more than teach the pigs a lesson they deserved."

"And with exemplary courage," Tostig remarked with honeyed acid. "Dover's women and children are known for their ferocity. *Mes compliments."*

A few guffaws from the English on both sides. Earl Leofric started to laugh, then masked it lamely as a cough. Eustace swore under his breath and spurred at my brother. Tostig drew as well, bringing up his shield. Swiftly as they moved, Leofric was quicker, seizing Eustace's bridle. I nudged my horse forward to block my brother. "Tostig, no. Peace."

Order restored, but hardly peace. The brief outburst charged all of us, drew us tight as a bowstring, within a breath of violence. I touched the horn dangling at my side, hoping my mouth wouldn't be too dry when needed.

"Rein your son," Edward advised Godwine. "My patience is at an end."

"Then let this—kin of yours rein his temper. He's not in Boulogne now."

"Your whelp called me coward," Eustace frothed. "If it's battle he wants—"

"What we came for is justice," I barked for all to hear. "For Dover more than ourselves."

"Harken to our patriot," Edward smirked. "Our national conscience. Anglia, you are hardly in a position to dictate."

"To negotiate, my lord." Godwine nodded to me. "Now."

I lifted the horn and blew. Before the last note died away in echo from the hills, a roar grew under it, a roar and rush as hundreds of men erupted from the woods, galloping or running up the slopes in ordered detachments behind their thanes to take up precise positions above us. Mailed and mounted carls, the archers calmly jabbing arrows into the ground before them, fyrd men hurrying to form ranks behind the horse.

At the same time our remaining horses snaked out in a long line on Edward's left flank. Eustace's men and the Normans reined their heavy mounts to stillness. I couldn't resist something of a smirk myself, having placed the hidden elements so efficiently that even the bellicose Normans, those lords who make knighthood into a martial religion, knew they were boxed and helpless. We were ready, they weren't.

Edward acknowledged, "Our turn to compliment you, Godwine."

"To Harold, sire. He placed the men."

"Ah, yes. Anglia: a bottomless trove of unguessed abilities. This alters nothing. You will discipline Dover or see more justice than ever you desired."

My father made to answer, but it was as if God put a finger to his lips. I saw him blink, then that telltale fumbling at his temples. He made no sound but went white with the effort against obvious pain. *Please,* I prayed. *Not now, not here. We need him.*

When he spoke his voice was clear but drained of strength. "No, sire. I cannot."

"You hear!" Edward stood up in the stirrups for all to see. "Wessex refuses his sovereign lord!"

"So they do," Godwine said in a tone barely above a whisper. "Edward, we're not going to be foolish about this because we can't afford to. Count Eustace is ignorant of common rights in our country. Even I would not force myself on a private house. Had he asked hospitality and, speak of miracles, offered to pay for it like any experienced visitor, he could have avoided this. You earls, you thanes and householders, tomorrow will judge us for what we do today. Let it not be in shame or folly. Dover can be a small fire smothered here by our common sense, or a conflagration to burn more than one little town, believe me. I must help Dover rebuild; for that, I could ask damages and wergild of Eustace. I will not. In return, do not ask me to do something so unjust. So vile.''

"Vile?'' Eustace, count of all Boulogne, could not believe his omnipotent ears. "Brother-in-law, will you suffer such mutiny? If such a thing happened in my lands, that miserable town would cease to exist.''

"No doubt,'' Godwine answered levelly, "and the ground sown with salt for good measure. Edward, have you thought to the consequence of this? If I punish a town still bleeding, I won't have a loyal man left in Wessex. Nor will you, sire.''

Leofric spoke up then and bless him for it. "That is true.''

"You say that, Mercia?'' The rising spleen was audible in Edward's challenge. "You who sacked Worcester for Harthacanute when two of his carls were killed there? You think this unnatural?''

Godwine answered in Leofric's stead. "*I* remember Worcester and can imagine how Leofric must have felt, duty or not. Royal discipline done on a Saxon town for Saxon crimes. Believe me, I take my oath now: Had Dover been attacked by any folk within Wessex, the malefactors would be swinging in the wind long before this.''

"I am your king!'' Edward shouted, voice rising still higher. "Eustace is my kin by marriage.''

"And a blight on the land.''

I thought Godwine had lost his temper, too, but though the words cut like a razor, they were level with cold conviction. "A blight, Edward. You have brought them like a Trojan horse into England and made them lords over your own folk. You have let them build castles while spitting on our laws. One foot in the stirrup and the other on English necks. You have—"

"Enough!" Edward trembled with his rage. "By God and Holy Church, you are not the one to speak of outrage, nor will I be disobeyed. *I* will punish Dover."

"No, my lord. You will not." Godwine's answer was firm. Final. "If you do, then I'll be hanged for the whole sheep. I will resist you."

He offered open treason. In the silence that followed, Siward rode forward, Leofric at his side, to place himself between Godwine and the king. "This is for cool heads in a cooler time. The king and Wessex are alike too hasty. Think what you say, Godwine. And you, sire. Wessex speaks good sense here, but sense or not, this is far too grave a matter to be decided in anger. Take it before the whole Witan. Wessex, will you submit to hearing before the general council?"

"Gladly. And if my peers find me unholden, I will submit to justice, but never to Boulogne." Godwine's glance skewered Robert Champart. "Or Normans. So be it."

I looked to Edward, hoping he would seal Godwine's offer with royal agreement. The king's anger seemed to have evaporated as quickly as it rose. He sat his horse, eyes roving over our massed men on the hilltops and the horsemen poised against his flank, then back to me. The shadow of something subtle passed over his visage.

"And you, Harold? You who so resoundingly declared yourself for the England which I embody? Where will you stand if the Witan finds against your father?"

I stared back into the peculiarly ravaged innocence of that face and knew everything I was or had stood in the balance against my answer. *Damn you, Edward. It is because we have been beaten, conquered, and humiliated; because we were once brutish as Eustace that we look now to law and reason first, but you'll never see that. You'd have made a lovely little king two hundred years ago with God on one shoulder and the Church on the other, and they could stain your image in glass over altars*

*and give you a pious name for posterity when you're safely
dead. But the world's not fixed; none of us believe that
anymore. If God guides a king like you, He must be blind
to shoot so wide of the mark between ideal and the actual.
You'll set us back years if we let you.*

My mouth was dry. I wet my lips, praying Edith's forgiveness because she and the children must go down with
me, but my love never married me for a title. "My lord,
Godwine speaks for me. As his fortune in this, so mine.
If Your Majesty stands on kinship, so must I, but you
have been so far misled in this matter that now you stand
in the wrong."

A pregnant silence. Leofric and Siward stared at me. In
a few words I'd placed myself with Godwine beyond the
pale of law.

Edward said with deceptive quiet, "Wrong, am I?"

No more than that. He swept his eyes again over our
men on the hilltops, then with a gesture summoned the
other earls to confer privately. This went on while our
men above stirred restlessly, no doubt wondering with me
if the next minute meant peace or civil war.

"Earl Godwine," Edward declared. "You shall have
your day before the Witan. I charge you to meet us on
the twenty-fourth by London Bridge."

I relaxed a little. We'd won, at least for the time, but
then Regenbald rode out between us, bawling at the top
of his formidable lungs: "Pray silence for the will of our
sovereign Edward. At the Crown's need, the national fyrd
is called from north and south, from east and west to join
with the king at London in the matter of Wessex, Anglia,
and Dover."

When Edward and his train rode away, Godwine and I
said nothing. The men streamed down the hills, relieved
and happy, the full import of Edward's move not yet understood by most. We hadn't won at all. We'd begun to
lose.

26 • Harold

When Edward conceded a penny, he meant to reap five in return. The calling of a national levy passed over loyalty to one's earl, requiring every thane and fyrd man to rally to Edward at London. Refusal was treason.

I sent Botulf home to Nazeing with our boats, racing eastward by horse with Godwine, both of us trying to think one move ahead of the king in a game turned suddenly against us. Doubtless Edward would have called the levy straight off had he time, but he'd not been prepared. His first news of Dover came from frothing Eustace dashing hotfoot from the coast. Edward came into the conflict like a man entering a room where two men, one a kinsman, the other an enemy, are fighting. He knows nothing of the cause, but his sympathies are predictable. Nothing for it then but improvise and call up the northern earls.

We'd outplayed him at Tetbury, but in one stroke Edward shifted the advantage to his side. The fyrds of Wessex, Anglia, and Kent melted away from us as we rode. They parted reluctantly, but unwilling to be called traitors. If my family was committed in one balance, these men hovered painfully in the middle. I could see that in their eyes as they bade farewell. Think of Teinfrith, loyal to Godwine as Swegn was false, well past forty and more used now to his peaceful fireside than rattling about in heavy arms.

"It's dread command," he mumbled, taking my father's hand. "I would not go else." Then to me: "Let Edith know that."

Think of tired, fat old Wulfwig from Slaughden, culling his few fyrd men out of our shrinking numbers, standing awkwardly before us. He said he felt no shame in leaving, as it was his duty. "But no pride either, and that's gospel." Wulfwig jammed his callused paw into mine. "And I'm passin' sick of this."

He had every right to be. When he saw his own dead lying on the sand at Slaughden, I think something tore in him. None of us can take heartbreak forever, save perhaps kings who must, or gods.

By the time we crossed Stane Street, Godwine's post riders had alerted Bosham and returned, saying Gyrth and Leofwine would meet us at Southwark. Father fretted over this; he'd not summoned them. Gyrth was old enough but Leofwine only sixteen, both of them clearly caught up in the heady air of great events roiling and thundering all about them.

We pushed on east, changing horses whenever possible at Godwine's manors along the way, resting as long as we dared at Southwark manor before our pitifully depleted force re-formed at London Bridge. We straggled, exhausted, to the point where firm ground gave way to marshy banks. While our tents were erected and grooms laid out cold food brought from the manor, we stared across the bridge to the teeming north bank.

Twenty-fourth September. Michaelmas Eve. Tomorrow was the traditional day for paying the year's debts.

"And old scores," Godwine noted. "Our king has a dark sense of humor."

"He has the lot today," Tostig worried. "Look at all of them."

We had no more than a hundred carls between us. Less than a quarter mile across Thames, for several hundred yards west of Pudding Lane, the king's ranks stretched out and out. Farther off I could see more coming down Bishopsgate.

Tostig asked no one in particular: "How many do you think?"

They might as well be a million. Whatever happened today, we had no margin for blunder.

Behind us the camp bustled with a fear-fueled urgency. Horses were strung along temporary picket lines, grooms hauled heavy buckets of grain and water for them. We didn't dare send the horses down to the river, since we might need them in a hurry. The sky matched our mood, a solid blanket of cloud drizzling intermittent rain. Back and forth across London Bridge, the tradesmen's wagons creaked between City and our position, peace bracketed by conflict and stolidly unconcerned with either side. Kings and lords might do as they pleased, but for Londoners this was a working day with rents due on the morrow. First things first.

Tostig called out: "Two horsemen coming onto the bridge."

Too far to make them out. One rode a small native pony, the other a large Flemish. Emissaries from Edward. The thing had begun.

Godwine's cry of welcome turned me back toward camp and the two young men dismounting by our picket line. Gyrth and Leofwine, both in ostentatiously bright and very new mail coats. They ran to embrace us, crying greetings.

"Good boys, good!" Godwine beamed, the first time I'd seen him happy since Tetbury. Chunky Gyrth was nineteen now, thoroughly Saxon in looks and coloring. Leofwine took after Swegn, dark and spare, promising looks as comely as Tostig's. I prayed often he'd turn out saner than the one, less devious than the other. On that day in 'fifty-one, Leofwine at sixteen was a soul of dreams yet undashed by life. With the difference of years and absence between them, he had never really known Swegn. For that reason alone, Swegn's exploits glowed with distance and glamour. Harold? Oh, Harold was familiar as Bosham, but Swegn had galloped here and there, warring in the fabled west, confounding Normans, leading armies against the wild Welsh. Swegn was a star, far and bright against darkness, Edward's treatment of him despicable.

Unflattering truth suffused in Leofwine's worship. True, Swegn killed his cousin and—well, yes, he took an abbess from her place, but Leofwine *knew* Agatha, saw her daily at Bosham. She was like any other wife with her husband gone and a baby to raise. Meanwhile, Swegn was cleansing his soul by pilgrimage to Jerusalem, staff in hand, cross sewn on his shoulder, repentance in his heart, redemption assured.

"He'll return with honor, you'll see. He'll be restored."

For Leofwine's sake I could only smother my feelings and hope with him. There'd been only one letter from Swegn, written from Bohemia. He persevered, he pressed on toward the Holy Land. So often I've wanted that picture to be true. God in heaven, not years that bend and gnarl us toward our graves but futures that might have been, cruelties that might have been avoided. Brothers who should have stood together all their lives, not cursed each other over a murdered kinsman. It is the lost things that bear us down and stoop us to age with their weight.

Leofwine and Gyrth followed hungrily the detail of grooms carrying food to Godwine's tent. Tostig hurried back from his watch over the bridge. He'd identified one of the approaching riders.

"It's Stigand. In full canonicals."

There was luck at least. My staunchest ally in Anglia was now bishop of Winchester but long out of royal favor for his anti-Norman views. I went to meet him, kneeling to kiss the offered ring as he dismounted. "Welcome to Your Grace."

"Harold. Dear oh dear, will I ever see the day when your house is not in trouble? You used to be such a affable brood."

"Fallen on hard times, old friend." I embraced him. Stigand had the kind of mien a man comes to trust early and love long. The lines of experience from forty-odd years in a world far declined from Eden, and a pessimism toward the nature of Man tempered by kindness and edged with wit. He had enough human vanity, thank God, to deny him sainthood. Stigand's hair did not grey with age but retreated from his forehead early on, leaving a grudged semicircle about the desert of his pate, which Stigand bared seldom as possible, concealed now beneath the miter of his holy office.

My father came to greet him, arms wide in welcome.

Godwine did not kneel to the episcopal ring; within my memory, he never bowed to clergy. "Come out of the rain, Stigand. They've laid a cold dinner, but may it well become you."

I lingered behind, recognizing the bishop's escort, a lank young man, the beginnings of his beard aspiring to lusher dignity, a new gilt ax in his belt.

"Aelred, well met."

"My lord earl."

"I'm glad they sent English. And good ones too."

"Champart was for sending Norman knights, but the bishop convinced 'em I'd be better. And safer." Aelred saw my eyes drop to the symbol of rank tucked in his broad belt. "My father's forthfared. Died this spring. I'm thane in north Sherwood now. May we go inside? This is my best new robe, cut by Maud herself, and it's flamin' soaked through. Been wet all day waiting on the king."

I jerked my head at the endless ranks facing us across Thames. "How bad is it?"

"The bishop bears the word, sir, but it ent good."

Within the tent Aelred discreetly joined my brothers in the background, the four of them munching cold fowl while Stigand sat to table with Godwine. Never at a loss for words, now he seemed oddly diffident, a man embarrassed by an errand he knew to be futile. The rain drummed monotonously on the tent roof.

"The king grants you trial, but the charges are now compounded. You must answer for conspiring against his life."

Father dismissed that out of hand. "The Witan knows that's absurd. He's muddying the waters."

I wondered if the Witan knew anything of the sort. Godwine had respect among them but few friends.

"Edward orders you to cross the river with no more than twelve men."

"Under safe conduct," I insisted. "And after hostages have been given us."

"Yes. Today we must have that," Godwine considered. When Stigand said nothing, he smiled wryly at the bishop. "Do you think we might have Champart and Eustace?"

Stigand shook his head. "My lord, be serious."

"Just a thought."

"Recognize the gravity of your position."

"While we're outnumbered ten to one, rest assured that is clearly seen."

Stigand's jeweled fingers worried over the lambswool pallium on his breast. "The king will give none."

"Perhaps he'd like us to come in chains," I snapped. "Just what in hell does he want?"

"In his words: 'Godwine is a traitor. I have no obligation of honor to such. He will come as commanded.' "

Tostig couldn't believe that. "Not even safe conduct? What sort of simpletons does he think us?"

"Rebels we may be, but hardly suicidal," I said. "No guarantees, but who knows how many assassins? We'd never reach the council."

"Father, would—" Leofwine's shocked disbelief overcame his manners. "Would the king *do* such a thing?"

Godwine said gently, "If not him, some around him would love to."

"They would that," Tostig confirmed in dry bitterness. "And sup and sleep well after."

Leofwine had not lived long enough to know the grime beneath the glitter of royal politics. His outrage exploded. "But he's our *brother*-in-law."

Gyrth vouchsafed him a look of pained patience. "Oh, that changes everything. Shut up and learn."

"Useless," Stigand sighed, rising. "I knew before starting out. What answer, my lord?"

My father took his time before replying. "Say to Edward that he wrongs my house to call us traitors where we are none to his people. I will stand trial before the council, on oath if possible, on ordeal if I must."

No, intolerable. I couldn't stand the idea of him, old and sick as he was, forced to undergo pain to prove his innocence. "Father, no. Please."

"No fear, son. My oath with compurgators should suffice." Godwine shook his head to clear it, gone ragged about the edges for lack of sleep. He hadn't closed his eyes for more than two uninterrupted hours since Tetbury.

Now he forced his heavy, settling frame up from the table. "Stigand, I will come with twelve men, no more. Or but six or three if the king doubts my intent. But tell him I will not harry Dover, I do not conspire to kill him, and I *will* have safe conduct and hostages before crossing London Bridge."

In Stigand's silence, I put a period to my father's will. "Your Grace will please deliver us so."

As Stigand and Aelred rode away toward the bridge, I wondered despairingly, was this the end of us? Please, God of all justice, let Edward this once put the realm before retaliation. If he didn't, how far would he go? How far would we? When the men you must fight have names and faces like Aelred or Teinfrith, the words *civil war* are bitter on the tongue and worse in the mind.

Thus I importuned God, trudging back through the rain. *Are You with him and against us? Are we cursed?*

27 • Harold

We waited.

The rain relented. Beyond our tent, spread over several acres, our men huddled in disspirited groups while a northeast wind washed over them the rank smell of the brackish river and the city. I could guess what gnawed at them. Godwine and his family were rebels, sure, but what of them? Would this unforgiving king and his Normans wreak vengeance on plain soldiers and their families?

We waited. Across Thames the bells from Saint Paul's rang the hour of nones, faintly echoed from Saint Peter's west on Thorney Isle. Unused to days spent in mail, Gyrth and Leofwine suffered in silence, loosening what buckles they could to ease the galling weight.

And we waited. At the table, the remains of supper congealed in its sauces with our hopes. When Tostig thrust into the tent, I started from tension. "What?"

"They're coming back. Three this time."

"Who's with them?"

"Some Norman."

At least one who bore my house no malice, the half-English Hugh Malet. I took his hand when he dismounted. Hugh wore mail but no weapons and bared his cropped head to me. "My lord."

"My friend. Come have some wine."

Stigand and Aelred moved wordlessly to the tent. As I followed, Hugh fell into step beside me. "Harold, a word."

I stopped and faced him. Hugh looked plainly worried. "So? What is it?"

"You're fools, you know."

"To it, man. I haven't time."

"Are your men ready to ride?"

Something chilled in my stomach. "Yes."

"Good. Because I overheard something. Archbishop Robert. His men are already mounted—see there, west of the bridge? He doesn't intend to let you escape."

"Jesus." I hurried away to the tent.

Sometimes you can read everything in men's faces and bodies. It was there in all of them: Godwine calm but stoney, Gyrth and Leofwine stricken and fearful. Tostig's mouth a bitter rictus that understood what his brothers could not. Aelred of Denby silent next to him, winding and unwinding a length of horsetail bowstring about his brown fingers. Stigand standing before my father with tears in his eyes. He's always been a worldly man, Stigand. To see such a man weep openly is to spy on a man's nakedness.

"Say it again," Godwine urged him quietly. "Harold must hear."

Stigand turned to me. "The king denies you safe conduct and hostages."

"Tell him the rest," Godwine prompted. "The doom falls on Harold as all of us."

"He said—these are Edward's words—'Godwine may have peace and pardon when he restores my brother Alfred and every innocent man murdered with him.' "

Done. Finished, and how like the man. Edward would be royal and just tomorrow, but today he would have his reckoning.

"I see." Godwine pushed the table aside and rose. He seemed to know and accept what was coming.

Stigand spoke the rest as if he would put himself at arm's length from the words. "Three times you were summoned and three times failed to appear. By the custom and law of England, the king and his council declare Wessex, Anglia, and all their kin to be outlawed."

I plied him: "All of the council?"

"No, of course not. Siward and Leofric refused. Myself, some of the clergy. Ripped down the middle, the lot of us against the king and the archbishop and the Normans. Your titles and lands are forfeit. Edward gives you five days to quit England."

"Quit? England?" To Leofwine, raised under the roof of power and plenty, the concept was unthinkable. "Can he *do* that?"

Godwine lifted his mail from the rack it rested on. "He's done it."

"Don't you see?" Stigand glared around at us as if we should have foreseen all. "He never meant to give you a trial, just to draw it out and out until your defeat was clear to all."

I could have spat my anger at anyone then, even Hugh Malet, who'd come to warn us. Instead I took my composure from Father's example and went to help him on with the mail. "Well, sir. What now?"

"Now? We go to find what friends we can."

"You have one here," Stigand warranted.

"I know." Godwine took the baldric from me and slung it over his shoulder. "We will remember that when we return. Tostig, assemble the men. Sons, get ready to ride."

"And swiftly," I remembered. "Hugh has heard something."

"Not the king," Hugh said, "but Champart and Boulogne. Their men are ready by the bridge and likely to pursue you."

"Strange kindness from a Norman," Tostig observed. "Do we trust this fellow?"

Hugh wheeled on him not in anger but urgency. "Not at all if you mislike. You needn't tell me where you ride, but *get* there with dispatch, *Anglais.*"

My father suggested we all carry away what remained of the cold fowl. Precious little time to eat or rest for the next few days. Godwine took a wing for himself, offering me a joint.

"Not to be morbid," he remarked, "but I'm irresistibly reminded of the Last Supper."

Hugh Malet strode with me toward the picket line. Our whole camp was breaking up and mounting. Tables, camp stools, many personal belongings were to be left for lack of time. If we reached Bosham or any port alive, we would have no more than a few hours of grace. Edward had given us five days but Champart far less, nor would our gracious sovereign take much heed of the disparity.

I mounted and took Hugh's outstretched hand. "Thanks for all."

He did not relinquish my grip just yet. "I don't know. Poor vavasors do not count for much, but I feel miserable in this. I am half you and half them and not knowing what is right in any of it, but I don't like what this is coming to."

"*To?* It's come, laddy. It's here or haven't you noticed? When we served him, Edward never had better. Now he's made outlaws, and he'll never know more expensive."

So much for bravado when I really wanted to weep like Stigand. I raked my fingers through Hugh's ridiculously short hair. "I know you think it immodest, but let your hair grow. Come winter, don't you catch cold?"

"Every damned year."

"Harold, haste!" Tostig swung his horse after Godwine and the rest.

"Coming! Hugh, one boon. Nazeing's but a day from London, less with a horse like yours. Can you get to Edith and tell her . . . just tell her I'll return."

"When? From where? Where do you go?"

God alone knew that. "What matter?" I called back, spurring to catch up with our swift-departing column. "You know Edith. Were she yours, what could keep you from her?"

Edith

That was how ruin came home to me. Hugh Malet, halting and reluctant, stumbling over regret as if ashamed of his duty to men who did this to us. But he'd promised Harold.

"He could not say where he was bound. Their decision had to be made in haste. There was no time."

Hugh and I were like the blind that day, speaking to each other through a darkness. I couldn't know his feelings; he could only guess at the loss as my life and family washed out from under me. *What will become of my boys?*

As the days fell one by one like a hammer on the forge and Harold's Anglian carls trickled home in twos and threes, the picture came clearer. The earls and their escort rode hard for Stane Street, detaching men and horses along the way to allow them escape and make pursuers lose time in pondering which group to follow.

"And they were following right enough, lady. The archbishop's knights and some from that Boo-loin count. The archers melted away into Kentish forest, the smaller thanes got free. 'Tweren't easy, but Earl Harold fooled 'em proper.''

At Stane, they told me, Harold made the crucial decision. Godwine, Tostig, and Gyrth would make for home on the hard Roman road, while Harold and Leofwine pushed west with enough carls to make the Normans think they followed the main party.

"And? Did it work? Where did Harold ride?"

Bristol, as they heard. None of the tired, ridden-out carls knew for certainty. They only prayed to reach home safely and go to ground out of the royal eye. Earl Harold might have embarked for North Wales, but there had been some talk of Ireland.

"No mind, lady. You'll hear straight away."

I heard nothing, but my own and the children's fate came too swiftly in the person of Edward's staller escorted by ten Norman knights who pushed in the hall doors, brushed the servants aside, and swaggered into my presence with no more civility than their kind had used at Dover. I sent the children away with a serving woman, hoping my fear didn't show.

The staller was the same corpulent fellow whom Harold had muddily inconvenienced on Lea bank. Not a Norman, merely one of those faceless men who count themselves blessed to toil in the bowels of whatever government wields power and, like flies, more at home with its grime than its pomp. He was far surer of himself this day and made no pretense of courtesy.

More accusation than query: "You are Harold's woman?"

"I am his wife," I retorted with as much defiance as I could muster. "Master staller, your vavasors need not have come armed. I will not attack them."

He blared at me like a herald's trumpet. "You are to know that the Lady of England is sent to retirement at Wilton."

Hollow deception. Eada was banished. Edward was scouring his house thoroughly of our blood, including a wife he couldn't throw out of bed fast enough. Poor Eada.

"Read, woman." The staller thrust the order at me,

written in Edward's cursive hand, the chancery seal slightly blurred in the wax like an angry summons dashed off to a debtor, niceties be damned. Edith Teinfrithsdohtor, called *Svanneshals,* consort of the former earl of East Anglia, was to attend the queen in her "retirement."

"I have a husband, home, and family of my own."

The fat staller only smirked at me. "Did you?"

"As for the queen, surely she has women of her own."

"Did she?" He relished his joke enough to repeat it while the Norman knights lounged about, snickering. "The queen will maintain no state at Wilton and only one woman in waiting. You. Well."

He roved his porcine eye about my hall. He might have been assessing house and movables for auction. "Don't be shocked, woman. Godwine, Harold, that whole brood's played God too long."

I said, "Not even the king can order me from my house. He cannot bridge common law like this."

For the first time he spoke civilly to me, almost thoughtfully. "Who's to stop him, girl? The king's now what he should have been from the start but for Wessex. Absolute, chosen of God. They always say that when they settle the crown, but it don't mean much unless the king makes it so himself. Now he has. Pack, you and your children. One small press for each. The boat is waiting."

In so little a moment life paupered me. Thank God, the boys were still too young to understand or be as afraid as I was. I said hasty farewells to my servants, trying to allay their fears and mine as well, packed no more than two changes of clothing for each of us, no room for extras, and then jolted along in a cart like a condemned felon to Lea bank.

Yes, the staller remembered Harold. He made me wade through the cold muddy water up to my waist to reach the boat, holding the children high, little Magnus frightened and whimpering in my arms.

BOOK III

The Smoke from Porlock

28 • Edith

That flattering monk who gilded the royal desolation of Eadgytha's life wrote that she was sent to Wilton Abbey for safety "with royal honors and an imperial retinue but with grief at heart." I suppose grief was in her and as close as the prudent scrivener dare come to full truth. As for honors, the Lady of England was whisked off as I was, in a small cart and a great hurry.

To Wilton again, at least to welcoming friends and a place we knew. Mother Werburgha gave up her own house to the queen. We were not inconvenienced for space. Godwine and Magnus were bewildered by all of it but too young to suffer sharply. In the first few weeks, Godwine would wonder plaintively at bedtime, "When do we go home, Mum?"

I would tuck him in with a kiss and a promise. "When your father comes for us."

If my bed was lonely, at least it was comfortable, the boys only one room away to one side, Eadgytha's chamber to the other. I asked at first if she desired me to share it with her as Clothilde often had. Eada did not.

"I sleep so little, Edith," she said. "Only a few hours a night."

Better for me as it turned out. I might not have been able to hear Magnus if he took sick in the night. And indeed, Eada slept miserably. In the mornings when I went to attend her, the couch looked like the lost Battle of the Bedclothes. Lonely as myself—Eada has been lonely all her life, yet love was not, so I thought then, what she

219

missed, but *use,* employment as well as empowerment. Her energies cried out for purpose, restless hands patting this, tugging at that. She had large plans for Wilton when she was restored, never doubting that eventuality. Things would be sorted out and she would return to her rightful place. Old Mother Werburgha had always thought her too critical, but Eadgytha crowned had become a very paradigm of disapproval and correction. When I bathed my boys in our big wooden tub, Eada had to plunge in and supervise, scrubbing the lads vigorously and wondering if I'd fed them enough at home.

"Ah, they were stuffed, the little pigs."

"Really? My nephew Magnus seems a bit thin. Give me the soap."

"Lady, with respect," I appealed in final exasperation. "Why don't you use the royal *we?* It's there even when you don't say it."

Eada was unfazed. "I like things done right. Or put right when they're not. Dry the boys properly now or they'll take cold."

For one as sure of her restoration as of the Second Coming, Eada spoke little of Edward on a personal note until that terrible night in November. She was pleased I'd been happy with Harold but deplored our "tawdry" union and the spiritual disorder of my soul. She could not consider me married.

"Now I daresay you never may be," she opined crisply as I labored to keep up with her long stride along the cloister walk. "Not while Champart sits in Canterbury. Good day, Sister Tirion, and thank you so much for the lavender! Mind, Edith, the man is positively rabid! Always sidling up to Edward with some poisonous complaint or other. Unhappy man, not entirely natural, if you ask me. He had to be courteous to me, of course, but I don't think he has much use for any woman. Well! Mother Werburgha tells me you might tutor some of the girls in French."

Indeed, anything to pass my days and deliver me for a few hours from Eada's overbearing presence.

"Isle de France, of course, as you were taught here. Teach them properly."

Truly I think Eadgytha would rather have been Wessex than queen, or more than all else to wear the miter at Canterbury. Like her darling Tostig, she could never stand by and let others err without correction. Both of them were born with a moral toothache. Naturally Eadgytha infuriated men, all the more for so often being right. It was she and Tostig against the world. Swegn she considered unspeakable and barely redeemed by his holy pilgrimage.

"Though it may count for his soul." Not all that much by the tone of her, carving it like an epitaph on his gravestone.

When I felt hag-ridden, I fled to easier company. Sister Martha Veronica was in charge of the barns and kitchen garden. The sleeves of her habit were always rolled back from work-roughened arms. Martha was still a farm wife at heart, earthy and cheerful, gossiping as she swung her pitchfork or tucked eggs neatly into her basket. Her natural acceptance of the world was balm after Eadgytha.

"But she was the same when you were young," Martha remembered as we forked hay from wagon to loft. "But *look* at my little Edith now. Grown with boys of your own. You've got a face and figure now. Shame about your Harold. Shame about all of it. God take me in my next sleep if I know what's to become of this country."

And there was the little Welsh nun, Sister Tirion, who concocted our medicines and oversaw the infirmary. Tirion always smiled as she worked with mortar and pestle, as if in return for her devotion, God shared with her some gentle joke on the world.

Sister Florence, our parchmenter, was of the scriptorium, choosing and preparing raw sheepskins for parchment with the help of several novices. Not a pleasant task with the lime water bath and smell of the skins to be scraped after curing. For this reason Sister Florence's help usually included one or two girls under discipline. The students called her Sister Fragrant. The more forthright referred to Florence as "Old Stinks."

Sister Swarboda ruled the kitchen. She had been given to Christ at twelve and perhaps always yearned for what Martha abandoned with relief. She paid far more attention to the cleanliness of her kitchen than its product, more pity to appetite. In Swarboda's view, an indifferent cook was no fault, but God help a sloven. Yet when it came to children, Swarboda was pure love. There always seemed to be a warm snack waiting for my student girls. Godwine and Magnus could always cadge a chunk of hot bread fresh from the oven and slathered with sweet pork fat. She was as generous with the poor who congregated most days about the kitchen yard; save in the winter when no one ate sumptuously, Swarboda doled them out the table leavings. If a ragged girl bore a babe in her arms, Swarboda always found an extra bit of frumenty or cheese offered with the tenderness that might have gone to her own. I think this is why she sometimes turned sharp unexpectedly, or why, at the oddest times, I saw the sudden brightness of tears in her eyes.

As autumn faded toward winter, I settled into a dull but painless round. In the mornings I helped the queen dress and did her hair, then turned out the boys and heard mass if Father Lucan was available. Then I'd climb the stone steps from the nave to the scriptorium to impart the liquid beauties of good French to our student girls. They ranged in age from ten to thirteen—giggling, wriggling, impossible daughters of carls and thanes. They found me far more interesting than lessons. To them I exuded dark glamour, the questionable lover of a banished earl and mother of his children—*but she's not his countess, do you see? They say she's not even his proper wife.*

I think the girls felt a subversive kinship with me. Some of their fathers were under suspicion as supporters of Godwine and Harold. They relished the drama of the exiled young noble who'd flung ambition to the winds for the woman he loved. From snippets of talk overheard, a titter here, whisper there, I gathered they saw me deliciously abandoned, where actually the last year had been rather thin for sin.

Loneliness was unbearable at times, the wondering where he was and how he fared. Was he dead? Night after night I lay alone, trying to conjure the warmth of him next to me, week after week as winter closed about Wilton.

From Bishop Ealdred of Worcester, no great friend to Godwine but even less to the Normans overrunning his diocese, we heard that Godwine, Gytha, Gyrth, and Tostig were safe at Baldwin's court. There was no more Wessex. Edward had seized up the family estates in great double handfuls. Whatever Godwine did not bear away was now in royal or Norman possession from sea to sea. Aelfgar, son of Leofric, was earl in East Anglia, and heaven alone knew the state of my dear little hall at Nazeing. Edward ruled alone and unchallenged. The queen never heard from him.

But Harold and Leofwine had dropped off the edge of the world. There'd been talk of Ireland, but also of terrible storms and shipwrecks. I forced my mind away from that to mundane matters, as a frightened woman might snatch up sewing to keep her hands from trembling. I must find something to do. . . .

The few clothes I'd brought from Nazeing for the boys and myself were going shabby from constant wear. Eadgytha suggested we make new ones. She sent to one of her dower estates near Winchester for bolts of wool and linen, plus a few pounds for expenses and alms. Her demands dispatched, Eada turned with her usual vigor to planning new wardrobe for the four of us.

The response was a blow in her face.

On a wet, cold day in November, Eada called me from my chamber. I found her sitting motionless in the near darkness of late afternoon, no fire and only one candle flame shuddering in the draft. Her right arm hung listlessly over the chair arm, the letter dangling from two fingers. I felt she had been motionless like this for some time. As I curtseyed, the letter slipped from her hand.

Eada asked of the wall, "He did this to me?"

"Lady?"

"Is it possible?"

I took the letter to read by the candle. The missive was brief and respectful, sent from her estate steward. Edward had confiscated the queen's possessions wherever, including all rents on hand, even the moveables. But there was more. It was common clerical gossip in Winchester that

Archbishop Robert Champart was pressing the king to divorce Eadgytha.

He had taken everything and then kicked her. She was alone. In a rush of pity I could only reach out to comfort her, but Eada shrugged me off.

"No, it's not . . . I am quite all *right,* Edith."

"No, by your leave. Oh, Eada, I am so sorry. What can I—can I bring you something? You need a fire, it's cold as death in here."

I rattled on as I struck a flint to the brazier, meaningless words to fill silence and ease her pain. I'd never seen Eada in tears or not in control. Now she labored to deny one and assert the other.

"Tell Sister Swarboda I will not take any supper but would appreciate some of the birch wine if any is left. Or whatever she has in the cellar."

That was some measure of her distress. Eada drank very little and then only the best from France.

"And Edith, I will have—that is to say, I would very much prize your good company tonight." Then what I've never heard her utter before in her life; most like she never had to. "Please?"

With two young novices and a sturdy boarding girl, I carried water for Eada's bath, laid out the oils and unguents, then helped her into the great oaken tub. She did have a fine body, long-limbed, full-breasted, and wide-hipped, hale as a young mare and made for bearing children. What an irony that a stumpy little thing like me could turn out boys like bannock cakes while Eada had none.

"I am mightily tired tonight," she breathed in a long sigh. "I feel . . . scattered."

I assured her Edward would never take such a step as divorce. Weighing the character of Champart against the king's devotion to Holy Church, she must know Edward would never fly in the face of Rome.

"You did."

I lowered my head over the wine. "You know why we had to."

"Oh, but you were lucky, Edith."

"No English king would dare such a precedent."

What hollow prattle, profoundly ignorant of where the pain gnawed at her. "You think that is it?" Eadgytha challenged. "Popes? Precedence? Edward put away his own mother. She's dying at Winchester. Finally. Here, do something constructive. Fill our cups again."

I replenished them from the silver pitcher.

"Edward has been hurt all his life," Eada said with a curious protectiveness. "There are things he can't forgive or forget. I've tried to help him. If you knew how hard I tried in the beginning, how much I wanted to give him a son."

"Surely you may yet."

"Bless you, Edith, and twice when you pray for that. Turn down the bed," she slurred drowsily. "Lord God, I could fall asleep right here and drown."

As I was preparing the bed, Eada said quite clearly: "He hasn't come to me in two years."

What could even a friend say to that?

"It was all new at first. New and lovely, and I was comely. Beautiful, some men said. But that wore off. Wore out. Nothing took its place. Tell me truly, Edith." She pulled herself up in the tub to face me. "After the first excitement, between the duty and the daily habit of affection, how did you keep Harold's love?"

The question had never occurred to me. "I don't know. We just . . . were. We love each other very much."

That sounded lame and smug before Eada's naked bewilderment. "No, it's more than that. We *like* each other."

She sank back in the tub. "Yes, there's a difference."

She talked on in a monotone as I laid her nightdress and cap on the featherbed and gathered up the broad towel to wrap and dry her.

"What could I do? Father and the Witan said to marry him, and I was excited and vain enough to think it no more than my due. Oh, it wasn't always empty. We were affectionate sometimes. I looked after Edward, turned him out right, reminded him of important things when he forgot.

"And he *tried* to like me. . . ."

Eada's voice caught on something, turning me to her in the candlelight. From her eyes squeezed tight shut, down the exquisitely sculpted cheeks, the two glistening rivulets wrote plainly what I would never have guessed.

She loved him. That arid man.

Damn you, Edward. Damn all of you.

29 • Edward Rex

No! It is not good, it is not *finished.*"

Champart lunged about the small warming house, driven by his convictions while I, cold and worn from a long hunt, stretched bare toes to the comfort of a peat brazier. Robert was here at Gloucester, like many nobles, for my Christmas court but had not ridden this day. Instead he flogged the subject of divorce yet again, a demon hunter who went on killing his quarry long after the creature expired. I'd put Eadgytha away and humbled her, but divorce was reckless sailing through dangerous shoals.

"Robert, enough."

"By your leave, it is not enough. The serpent is driven out but its egg is still in your bosom."

"Oh, desist." I rubbed at my toes, thinking how December chilled me more now than five years ago. Champart could weary one, a sour one-note trumpet on the necessity of my divorce. Acquiring the lands and livings at Merton and Wimbledon hadn't assuaged his wrath against Godwine's entire family.

"If my lord will bear with me?" The archbishop sat abruptly on a stool. Under his rich mantle and bright yellow robe, Champart had waxed corpulent in the last year.

When increase and fortune knocked at his door, austerity flew out the window. The hard, hale frame had softened and swollen, the face gone to jowl. "I have prepared a letter to His Holiness."

I barked at him: "Without our permission? Don't presume, Champart. We did not solicit such a step. Trust our competence. We have heeded your counsel and favored your interests thus far."

So far as they mirrored mine. Canterbury did not rule England, but I'd rather he woke to the fact on his own. "And now we really must prepare."

And that with some care. Duke William was in England, one more of my inexhaustible kin come to embrace his royal cousin and clarify his claim to my crown. He had paused at Winchester to see Emma, his great aunt, in her final illness. Laudable but transparent. No ruler absents himself from his suzerain in the middle of war against a formidable Anjou, or hazards a winter sea voyage just to visit a sickbed. His party was expected in Gloucester that day.

Well, I was a match for him. As that confidence firmed in mind, the door yawned wide, admitting my fat little chamberlain Hugolin and a blast of cold, wet wind. Hugolin snatched at the door and pushed it shut. "Sire?"

"Yes, what? The duke?"

"Oui, mon roi. His train has been sighted from Saint Oswald's tower."

"Tell Regenbald to meet them at Eastgate. He has full instructions. And return yourself with those garments we chose this morning."

Hopefully well selected. That was one area in which Eadgytha had been indispensable. Another boreal blast as Hugolin closed the door behind him. I must dress to receive William, while Champart had already usurped more than his share of my time. He did not follow my chamberlain; indeed he was quite ready to start in again. Tiresome man.

"My lord, we cannot be sure the queen had no part in the rebellion of Wessex."

"Or that she did. Do you think I don't know my own wife?"

"But surely Tostig will try to send letters—that one bears watching—and he is with Godwine."

"So are most of them. Vague, Robert. Very vague. You're starting at shadows."

"Well. Perhaps." Champart turned suddenly diffident, fussing with the arrangement of his mantle. "There is one clear avenue to annulment. If Your Majesty—that is, if the marriage were not consummated."

From my reaction he must have realized the absurdity of that and hurried on. "Well, a formality. His Holiness is not naive."

"Neither is the queen. She would deny it on holy relics piled high as Saint Paul's and gain more sympathy here and abroad than I can afford to lose. Not to mention a conflict with the Vatican to cost us years, and for what? A disaster."

"If Your Majesty will not be counseled—"

"But we are. Recall that we followed your counsel in removing Spearhafoc from the see of London."

That went home and stopped him short. Summarily ousted from his bishopric after Godwine's exile, the Saxon Spearhafoc had vanished, absconding with every penny of hard cash in his church's coffers, plus gold and jewels set aside for the fashioning of my new crown. Costly counsel. Far cheaper to have left the Saxon be.

"Divorce is not in our thoughts for the time. You will send no letters, lord archbishop. Pray you leave us now."

With Champart's departure, I enjoyed the rare luxury of a few moments' solitude before Hugolin returned, lovely as silence after a day of din. Champart foresaw so little. I ruled alone at last, unhampered by Godwine or any of his brood. But divorce Eadgytha and I risked losing the favor of Rome I'd laid up with such labor and cost, to say nothing of English sentiment which was always changeable. The time might come when the queen's restoration would be to my advantage or, at worst, imperative. Sometimes I missed Eadgytha. I never loved the woman, but after six years there was the *habit* of her, not always maddening or overbearing. She had been most helpful in certain areas of government, particularly the royal mints, of which she had a firm grasp.

On the other hand, my very lack of an heir was a carrot on a stick to men like William, presently knocking at my gates. This does keep the intricate game fresh. I confess complexity fascinates me.

Alone and supreme at last. Problems surely, but compensations as well. Emma lay expiring at Winchester, not expected to see another spring. Loved or loathed, there is a merciful release when your last nagging parent wafts west to glory. The catchpole lifts from your neck; you are free at last to be what you will. To *be*. Dear Emma would have a requiem mass by Stigand of Winchester. I never liked him but neither did she, so it served her right. Until that dolorous day, I would send messengers with comforts and concern, kneel finally at her bier and outweep the crocodile. I would inter my beloved mother next to Canute and Harthacanute in the old minster there. They lie near Beorn Estrithsson, who inconveniently prevented Swegn from ridding me not only of his odious self but Harold for good measure. Well—as the musty saw has it—one takes the bitter with the sweet.

But I grow old, Eadgytha. Finally rich, empowered at last, but I grow old.

A superb day for hunting, slightly overcast but dry, with just enough wind to carry scent of a red buck to our hounds. We were a brave company, William with his train, I with mine, huntsmen on foot trotting after the straining *lévrier* hounds, brawny lymerers holding back the larger bloodhounds on leashes.

Our huntsmen studied the clear track at the wood's verge, conferred on the suitability of the quarry, and presented their judgment to the duke and myself.

"A prime buck. By the width of the tracks and the scrapes, he will be fair sport."

"Send out the *lévriers*," I ordered, the thrill of the chase already skirling in my blood. "Cousin, yours will be the honor of the kill today."

We rode on. William had more than a good seat on his bay hunter; he might have been born there, no mean accomplishment, considering the stallion's spirit, but my cousin managed him easily as a fractious child. William loved the hunt as much as I, the first bond between us in understanding and affection. In his court, the office of honorary master huntsman usually went to one of knightly rank. Today it was Sire Hugh Malet, a reliable vavasor, if too friendly with Harold for my taste.

"Malet, keep close with my lance." William's huge torso swiveled from the waist as he swung a thick arm in an arc to our waiting company. *"Allons!"*

Now the leashed *lévrier* hounds were guided by their handlers in a circuitous route through the wood while we followed the stag's trail. He would be in high or late rut now, irritable and wearied from fighting for does. All morning we could hear the bugling of rival stags and the furious dry rattling of racks battered against trees or locked with other stags in competition. His tracks were ever fresher, his fume dropped only a quarter-hour past. We would be on him soon.

Exhilarating, this pursuit through forest, but always dangerous. One of William's men had already been injured ducking too tardily under a tree limb. But that is the thrill, don't you see? The quarry, noble as ourselves, has as much chance as we and often escapes us. He may drag us and the hounds through tearing brambles for half a day only to vanish, and if he puts his life before his love, we will lose him entirely with nothing to show but fatigue, torn clothing, and lathered horseflesh. But we may wear him down and the *lévriers* bring him to ground. Then in we come with the lymer hounds to lay him low with lance or arrow at the end. It is perfection, an art sublime as music, passion, and striving like the need for God. In faith, had I loved Eadgytha but a fraction as well, there'd be ten princes in line before Duke William.

Yet my young cousin is a man to reckon with, unusually tall and with awesome breadth and vigor of body. The play of his form as he rides or strides is the very stamp of virility. In manner and semblance he harks back to his

Norse ancestors who sailed up Seine, extorted a duchy from France, became passionately Christian and more French than any Frank.

Though I hadn't seen William since his early childhood, it now behooved me to know him as an opponent. To a monarch, any outside power, blood or not, is a potential enemy. William has his sore points, which one does well to avoid. On a noble but ill-timed impulse, his father, Duke Robert, departed on pilgrimage to the Holy Land, dying en route and leaving William his successor at the helpless age of seven. To Norman barons this was like leaving a treasure house without guard or lock. They swore fealty to the boy and spent the next ten years trying to kill him. But for his mother, Herleve, and her brother Walter, who hid him in one peasant croft after another, William would have been an early casualty in the baronial wars that followed.

He was fortunate, yes, but still sensitive on the matter of his illegitimate birth, the result of Robert's passion for Herleve, daughter of a Falaise tanner. One required the utmost tact in speaking of his mother, who must be respectfully named by the title assumed in her late marriage, Vicomtesse de Contiville. Once nobly wed, such women molt their past as a bird last year's feathers—except for the tanner's sharp eye to business and profit. Herleve elevated her family with her, placing them in prominent positions at Rouen and elsewhere. I do *not* approve. It is not at all wise to allow commoners into the nobility by any stair, let alone the bedchamber. Look at Godwine and, inevitably, Harold. Always for "progress," never tradition or the fitness of things.

William inherited Herleve's shrewdness, hardened by his bitter fight for survival. The English are a mystery to him. He speaks few words of our tongue, but my land he declared enchanting—reminding me of a merchant evaluating goods to be acquired. That very morning, setting out on the hunt, I congratulated him on his marriage to Matilda; in turn William inquired after my queen.

"About *la reine?* Reports are confused. One hears she

will be restored. Others say she is out of favor and you will divorce.''

I responded with my vaguest smile and manner. "What a day for riding, is it not? *Comment?* Oh, Eadgytha? I pray she can be recalled when things have settled sufficiently. Truly, Cousin, my land has been through a trying time. Her family . . ."

William's glance shot to me in sharp comprehension. "You mean the rebellion of Wessex and Anglia?"

"Yes. Unfortunate but unforgivable."

William politely brought the conversation back to the queen, but I gathered his reports were not so confused as he said. "The queen is in good health?"

I was being probed now and countered with more truth than he would guess. "No more robust or tireless lady ever consorted a king. When she returns, of course, there is what is expected of us."

William's close-cropped head swiveled too fast to mask his concern. "She is *enceinte?* A child to come?"

"Eh? Oh, no, dear me, no. Not yet. Hardly under the present circumstances."

"A pity." He sounded anything but regretful. "Perhaps when she returns."

"Through our prayers and God's help," I amended piously. "There! Listen! From the sound of the dogs—"

"They have got him!" William touched spurs to the hunter's flanks and bounded away. *There,* I thought, satisfied. *You learn exactly what I allow you.* My queen might well be recalled, hoping for an heir, but all as God disposed. Dangle, Cousin, dangle. Wait and learn and appreciate the royal art of indirection.

But one must admire him as a man. When we closed on the hound-circled stag, the quarry was already wounded near to death by the snarling dogs. Without breaking the stride of his horse, William caught the lance Malet flung him and leaped from the saddle. He took two strides, lifted the spear which barely poised at his shoulder before flying home to pin the stag between foreleg and ribs.

"Brave cast!" I cried.

"The bread!" William roared.

Three huntsmen darted in, kicking the dogs aside, stale bread in each hand. One of them slit the stag's belly and then all three plunged the bread sops into the offal and tossed them aside to draw the dogs off the kill. This done, one of them stooped to lift the stag for carrying, but the prize was far too large for him. The young duke brushed him aside, grasped the carcass by fore and rear legs and, with an effortless heave, shouldered it. As he turned to me, I swear I saw more victory in his fierce grin than a simple kill. He was showing Englishmen what kind of warrior strode his land and ours alike.

"Royal Edward! Shall they dress it here?"

Stunning young man. One feels ten times alive in his presence. A magnificent stallion himself, but I can manage him as I do my own horse.

30 • Edward Rex

A bizarre mixture of superstition and the practical, William wears his faith like a charm in which he places the trust and fear of a child, yet one could not choose a stronger man for a crown. On the first day of Christmas we heard four masses at Saint Oswald's. My cousin did not consider the number excessive, where many of my own thanes and officers nodded or dozed through the services or avoided them altogether.

There are difficulties. William cannot understand why our kings, though God-anointed with the right of blood, must be ratified by the earls. In Normandy such matters would be settled by force of arms.

"There is one towering obstacle to ruling the English," I admitted. "That is the English."

William is not strong on subtlety. Later at supper in the great hall, he turned to me for clarification. "You say they are all rebellious?"

"On my word, the least of them have the most inordinate notions of their rights and worth, not conferred by their betters but *born* in them. Like Original Sin," I compared sourly.

At the high table, flanked by William and Robert Champart, the duke's question had caught me spearing a bit of pheasant from the dish that I shared with him. The noise in the hall was deafening. Conversation was difficult at best. At the far end of the hall, dim and smoky from the firepits, singers competed with a show of puppets: the usual thing, our Saint Dunstan smiting the Devil with a club to gales of laughter from my thanes. Most of them would sleep through an inspired sermon on the same theme, but the crude puppets touched their rough humor.

As for William's rowdy young vavasors, they hardly mingled with my men. Just as well since their deportment was appalling. What they did not eat they liked to throw at each other. Apart and aloof, my thanes registered silent disapproval.

"Not rebellious in your sense," I enlarged to William. "See the wall there? That's my peasant: solid wood bending only so far before you must break it by force. See the holly draped over all? There you have my nobles: slightly more decorous but always pricking your fingers."

Reminding me that Siward and Leofric, hardly decorous in any sense, were absent from this Christmas court. Come Easter I would know their reasons. They had some sympathy for Godwine, but were they now in league with him? *Bien,* that was Easter's problem. "Now, Cousin, permit me. Esgar! The gifts."

At the steward's signal, three young women arrayed themselves before us, each bearing a garment as my gift to William. Daughters or wives of thanes loyal through the late troubles, each had been selected by Esgar for this honor. One by one they laid the gifts before William. A long winter surcoat in blue, a new saffron mantle of thick virgin wool, and a light skullcap in black samite embroidered with pearls. William thanked each of the ladies in execrable English, especially the last, who presented the cap which he donned then and there. A thoughtful present, neatly concealing the early balding patch on his pate. Some vanity in my cousin made him preen a bit for the young woman's approval.

She was not a beauty but striking, with deep-set, flashing dark eyes. She did not curtsey to William at all, accepting his thanks with a mere nod as an unsmiling equal before she withdrew.

"Très belle," William appreciated her retreating figure, "but how you say? . . ."

"Haughty," Champart grunted, watching her slip down the hall. "Amazing the disdain these people can cloak in courtesy. Who is she?"

I had to think a moment. "Oh, Denby's wife. He is my own thane in northern Sherwood."

"Haughty," Champart said again, cleaning his fingers in a bowl of water.

No, only the Saxon wall. Her husband, Aelred, was much the same. In more settled times, I resolved to make a progress through the royal forest there. My reeves in Nottingham suspected Aelred of interpreting my forest laws too liberally, allowing more game to his folk than was legal.

The thought was violently cut off by a crash and a splintering of Frankish oaths. Two young vavasors rose, the table between them. In their physical attitudes, like bristling hounds, I could see something had gone far beyond jest. The English thanes turned to watch. Several of them, unsure what this might lead to, rose tentatively.

Someone shouted *Gardez!* as the two men snatched daggers from their belts. Beside me, William merely sighed. *"Pardi.* Those two again. Pardon, Edward."

Unhurriedly he stepped down from the dais, chewing at a bit of bread. While I debated having my men intervene, one of the combatants leaped onto the table to spring at his enemy. In the same breath William caught him, slapped him hard, upended the surprised fellow, and sent him sprawling among the dogs. He turned on the other vavasor, who clearly had second thoughts about violence. He sheathed his dagger and sat down. William strolled back to his place by me and tore another bit of bread from the loaf.

"Regrets, Edward. They are not all what one would call courtiers, fine fellows though they are. My treasures, sons and nephews of our oldest houses. De Tosny, Clères, Beaumont, Montgomery. Others who joined me for lack of war at home. Each a pride in himself, but I yoked them and plowed well at Val-es-Dunes."

Champart excused himself early, due to celebrate the high mass at Saint Oswald's after compline. Impressed by William's handling of his men, I inquired after his campaign against Geoffrey of Anjou and the current siege of Domfront.

"*Ah, zut.*" William threw himself back in the chair, which creaked with the great, vital bulk of him. Only Harold's age, but one could see the strength of that mouth and line of jaw indelibly stamped with the cost of survival. "Geoffrey reaches beyond himself, but it will be an ill day when I cannot check one little Plantagenet. His ambitions do not fret me."

But should I fear yours? Who will check you, William? Holding Anjou and France at bay and reaching now for England as well? One needs an amplified term for ambition.

"Who commands at Domfront in your absence?"

"A fine soldier, Guillaume d'Arques. One of my best."

"Innocent of ambition?" There was disingenuity. William's vassals were devoid of ambition as adders of fangs.

"D'Arques is trustworthy. The ideal vassal is capable and loyal. If I must choose between those virtues, I will have loyal. In any event, men betray me only once. But what of your own family? Most of the royal house is gone, no?"

Here it comes. William proceeded obviously as the sun toward his ends. Godwine was at least a subtle adversary. "Few of us remain," I admitted dolefully. "The House of England is an ever-dwindling company."

"You mentioned a nephew?"

"Edward, the son of Edmund Ironside. He's spent most of his life in Hungary. Married there, children. They say he can't speak English anymore."

"Then there are none close."

"Only you, Cousin." Sidewise I gauged William's reaction, a telling hesitation of the wine cup midway to his lips. "Only you," I repeated as servants from the kitchen house bore in the last course of frumenty and sweetmeats.

"None but me." William set down his cup. "Then I must know where I stand."

Direct as a mounted charge. I floundered in feigned confusion, dabbing the napkin to my lips. "Ah. You go to the heart of matters."

William turned that concentrated gaze on me, to be deflected no longer. "Where, Edward?"

"By my choice alone? First after my own heirs, God willing."

"May he will so, of course."

"But again, there is my nephew—half nephew, actually." A vague gesture. "And of course the Witan . . ."

"Will you give me assurances?"

"At the moment that would be difficult."

"Edward, all Normandy is watching me now, perhaps all Europe. Asking the same question: Will I succeed you? France, Acquitaine, Anjou, Flanders, certainly Rome. Such a move would sheath England in Norman iron and keep the rest in line for years, perhaps forever. For I will have sons."

No doubt there, but William's own peril cried in the argument. He had much talked of and surely secured much credit on the possibility. Our crown assured, he would have more powerful men with than against him. Without it, he must go on sleeping with one eye open. Time for a show of candor from me while promising nothing.

"For my part, should I die without sons, there is none I should prefer before you, Cousin. Your strength, your piety—"

He was not fooled. "Your oath."

I felt backed into an untenable corner. "William, you and I were raised and think as Normans, but this is England. It is a much more intricate—ah! What have we here?''

A welcome surprise just then to see the slender boy in short, close-fitting tunic who set before us fresh bread and a dish of sturgeon's eggs. Wulfnoth Godwinesson spared me the need for quicker wit than I could command just then. I dipped a chunk of bread into the roe and savored it. ''A delicacy. Do try it, Cousin.''

Wulfnoth did not withdraw but remained, hovering before me, gangling between boy and youth in his fifteenth year. ''Sire, in this holy season, when we remember Christ's birth and his mercy, may I beg the same? I ask humbly for the pardon and recall of my family.''

Barely understanding a word of English, William inspected the slim youth. ''Who is this?''

''The queen's brother, Godwine's youngest. Wulfnoth, I bear you no ill nor any to the queen, but for your father and brothers, God will pardon Lucifer first.''

''Then may I have leave to join the queen at Wilton?''

I could hear the loneliness in his plea but would not be softened. He lived no worse than I had for so many years; far better if truth be told. *You had more years of love than I. It is a hard world, boy.* ''No, Wulfnoth. Your father is a fallen star who may yet start a fire. Go along.''

Still the boy did not move. Sadness was discernible there, but behind the frank hazel eyes, something stirred like smoke. ''Aye, sire, fallen. But before he fell, was not Lucifer heaven's brightest and best?''

''Wulfnoth, it is serious error to obscure faith with sentiment. Be off with you.''

I watched him retreat down the hall, head bent but his back straight. Well-turned thought but pernicious as any out of his father. All of Godwine's children suffered from a glut of education resulting in acute intellectual gout. No doubt the commoner in them; they all want to rise above their station. This sweet rose of a boy would grow his thorns like the rest of them.

He was still in my sight and thought when the Norman knight brushed past him, urgent with purpose, to halt and kneel before William. A young man, dirty and unshaven, obviously spent from a long journey unbroken for rest. He saluted me, then addressed the duke. *"Mon seigneur,* I am Gerald of Le Thiel in my lord's service."

William nodded. "I have seen you often at Domfront. It has fallen? Surrendered?"

"No, lord." The vavasor shifted nervously under William's scrutiny. "Sir, your loyal captains sent me. Guillaume d'Arques has raised the siege."

"Raised?" William put down his knife. His eye flashed over his men down the hall, then rested dangerously on the messenger. I would not like to have been young Gerald under the leashed lightning of that anger. "Raised? I gave no such order. What of d'Arques?"

"My lord, the count has renounced his fealty to you. He is in revolt."

William's hand fisted, but nothing else about him moved. "And my men?"

"Confusion." Gerald hung his head, miserable with what he must report. "All the months, the men, the sickness, the waste of it all and the *shame.* We could do nothing. If my lord duke had been there, d'Arques would not have dared. Your loyal men say you must return."

For one heartbeat William's body tensed as if he would fly like an arrow at the vavasor. He had just expressed his trust in Count d'Arques; now that judgment proved worthless. In my presence that could only discredit his authority. Then, when I thought he would burst with rage and frustration, William relaxed, subduing wrath easily as he had the two quarreling knights earlier.

"Merci, Le Thiel. Take your supper and rest. We depart in the morning."

A few moments later William excused himself, called for his steward Fitz-Osbern, and left the hall. I felt honest sympathy for his naked embarrassment. He was rash to leave the siege. Doubtless his captains protested and now they were disastrously proven right. His whole southern flank lay open to Anjou and France. With one traitor's defection, William had plummeted from strength to desperate vulnerability. And yet I must admire the control he exerted. There are kings and kings. I had dined with one worthy of god's holy chrism.

A long day. I was more than ready to sleep. Hugolin had warmed my bed with hot stones and looked to his own pallet in the corner with anticipation. Chaplain Peter had shriven me of no more half truths or bald lies than a king utters daily in the name of his realm. As I knelt at the prie-dieu, footsteps clumped heavily along the corridor to halt at my door. Muttered words between my guards, and a peremptory knocking. Hugolin thrust his head out the door, then back in.

"The duke, sire. Most urgent, he says."

Spare me. I needed no more of William tonight. His sheer animal force could wear one out. But . . . nothing for it. "He may enter."

The door swung wide. Behind William stood Fitz-Osbern. "Royal Edward, I must speak privately. Be so good as to send your chamberlain away."

More command than request, yet a note of uncertainty blunted the strength in William's mien. I dismissed Hugolin and sat on the edge of the bed, bare feet chilling fast in the cold room, the only warmth in the peat brazier two yards away across the cold floor. And I could not find my woolen bed socks.

William had controlled himself admirably at the news of d'Arques's betrayal and he did so now. Only the slight swaying of his body gave away any agitation. For the moment I was in the stronger position and waited for him to speak.

"My men know already. I am weakened in their eyes. I must salvage what I can, but for now—"

As if I didn't know sure as my poor feet needed warming.

"I must know my position with you."

"But I have said—"

"It must be clear, Edward." His arm swept about to the closed door. "Clear to them out there. You understand."

"Certainly."

"For lack of time, I must be direct. With respect, I

know why your queen was put away and that she will never be restored while her family is exiled. You are not young, Edward, and your queen is past thirty. Your chance for an heir recedes with each month.''

I found the bed socks where Hugolin had tucked them beneath the featherbed. ''And therefore?''

''Barring issue, I ask your oath on the succession. Cousin, you know my right; if not the nearest claimant, I am the only practical one.''

Looking up into that strong face already too hard for its years, I saw a desperate, determined man who dared not lose.

''Ethelrede gave such an oath to Emma on your behalf,'' he said.

''I was his son.''

''Canute gave her the same.''

''I was his stepson. Your great-aunt could be very persuasive, William.'' I slipped my suffering feet into the socks and padded across the icy floor to the brazier. ''And still I was passed over. So much for oaths.''

''Then I will take—''

Oh, the man was *de trop*, too much! ''You will take what I am pleased to give you, my lord duke. *I* am England. You do not demand of me.'' I met him eye for eye, unblinking that the reproof sink in. If I knew little of the English soul, William knew nothing. There is a strain in them like discord under the purity of plainsong. They will resist any foreign influence, even the Norman blood in me.

''That boy at supper, Godwine's son? We spoke of his brother Harold.''

Impatiently, William broke in. ''What has that got to do with—''

''Everything. *Every*thing. If you'd know the temper of this country, Harold's the stag to follow. No older than you but dangerous. The *cant* of that man! There is a word in our tongue: *Angel-Cynn.* Doubly meant like so many of our words, it signifies not only the English nation but the idea of the nation.''

''Idea?''

As I thought it would, the concept was lost on William. "The spirit of a nation. Harold would raise that spirit above Crown and Church alike."

"Above the Church?" William labored at the enormity but could only reject it. "He damns himself."

"Quite."

"It is impossible."

"You must come again and spend some time." Unicorns are impossible, princesses rescued from towers by athletic lovers clambering up the girl's long hair or woken from enchanted sleep by a kiss. No fact gives life to such musical lies but people's need to believe them, or to invest some passionate young man with the glamour of a hero. Harold only echoed their refrain, a nightingale lending his voice to crows.

I padded back to bed, pulling the covers up about me, but William ignored the hint, settling himself resolutely in a chair. I had seen his resolve; now he grudgingly bowed to mine. "I spoke out of urgency, not disrespect. All men know why I am here. Without some assurance, some pledge—"

"Cousin, I'm truly fatigued. Do not think me rude, but please allow me to go to bed. Do you doubt me? Your father protected me as a boy, your uncle before him. Did you think I would send you home empty-handed? An oath is impossible now, however . . ."

I trailed off and left him dangling. William leaned forward. "Yes?"

The inspiration was not sudden; its kernel had lodged in mind when Wulfnoth appeared before us at supper and borne fruit now when I spoke of Harold. "Hostages."

He hesitated only a moment. "Of high rank."

"The highest. Wulfnoth Godwinesson."

"And?"

"Godwine's grandson Hakon."

William reminded me of a hovering hawk. "And?"

He was forcing me, damn him. "Those two to return with you."

"And later?"

I hated being rushed any time, but pressure can force

inspiration from the dullest mind and this was brilliant. "Shall we say Harold's two sons?"

William lunged out of the chair, glaring at me. "Do you think me a fool?"

"Cousin, what a thought."

"Or uninformed? Wulfnoth has little worth, no hope of power, and the other three are plain bastards."

"I am tired and such matters cannot be rushed. This is England."

"I know, I know," he growled with a twist of impatience. "As you ever remind me. I could not foresee this matter of Domfront. I must be sure."

"Nor should we stain truth with hypocrisy," I parried delicately. "Your own vassals include many men more noble by nature than birth."

Not to mention his own left-handed nativity. "That any one of these children might rise in wealth and power is possible but beside the point. Godwine rose so and is still a danger, Harold fast growing beyond him, nor am I at all sure I've seen the last of Swegn. They can still raise armies against me. But if their next generation were tucked away in Normandy, that would give them pause. Certainly in how they deal with both of us."

From his hesitation, I knew I'd done it. I had him. Lymed like the stag he lanced. "Shall we say Harold's sons in September?"

I offered my hand most royally. "God be with you in all things, my lord duke. You will find Hugolin just outside. Please say I wish my chancellor to attend me."

William held on to my hand. "About my hostages?"

"To be arranged before I sleep. Give you good night, Cousin. Pray for me."

I went to my rest pleased with myself, William satisfied, and my position stronger against him and my wife's infernal family. As for Wulfnoth, he would depart England like a fleeting thought. I had nothing against him or Swegn's brat. They were payment from purse other than my own, and Harold's boys were next year's concern.

Sleep was long and sweet that night.

31 • Edith

Through grey winter into green May, life stirred and woke again. There was a softness to spring that year poignant with memories of Nazeing and the home I yearned for. Little Magnus grew stubborn about what he would or would not do. Godwine was going on five, sturdy as a pilgrim's mule. The round of my life was unchanged, shepherding the boys into the refectory morning, noon, and night, holding Godwine's hand firmly during prayers at table so he wouldn't snatch at the bread before Mother Werburgha finished reading the chapter and word of those to be prayed for in illness or misfortune. I went to mass whenever a priest came, less often to confession, having little to shrive, more pity there.

Day by tedious day I drilled my girls through French as their high, sweet voices mangled tenses and did violence to irregular verbs. And I tended Eadgytha, who had grown silent of late. No further word of any kind from Edward. Eada was alone. To occupy herself she tutored our best students in poetry, at which she was a master.

When the spring turned pleasant, my body seemed to wake, crying for use of any kind. I went forth to the fields to grub in the dirt and plant early peas, or took a weed hook to the kitchen garden, little Godwine stumbling behind, stuffing the rooted weeds into a sack for mulch. On rainy days I joined Martha Veronica on the barn threshing floor, winnowing chaff from our grain for new bedding. We received little news, but that disturbing. There were Normans in Bosham now. By way of itinerant peddlers, Teinfrith heard that some woman there, they didn't know who, had been forced to give up her infant son to William, the child literally torn out of the mother's arms despite her pleading. My father thought it might be Agatha's Hakon. I prayed God not. If Hakon, how safe were my own boys?

"Bless me, Father, for I have sinned. Yesterday and today I took our Lord's name twice in damning the king for the pain he gives his wife. For the blight of Normans he's battened on us, for the fear and loneliness I live with daily. Grant me indulgence if you can, for I'm going to damn him thrice tomorrow."

Alarmed at my vehemence, Father Lucan labored manfully to absolve me insofar as he could. Sent forth to sin no more, my black rage and fear made no promises. It *must* have been Hakon. What reason to take any other child from Bosham? So I stood on the cloister walk, dark as the day was bright—

"Edith? Edith, here!"

Down the columned walk skipped tiny Sister Tirion beside a strapping young peasant lad. Most of his face was hidden beneath a hood. All I saw was a grin surrounded by a straggle of brownish beard. I gave him little note, though it did seem his boots were fine and expensive for one in such ragged linen. Then he threw back the hood and opened his arms to me, and the sun came out of cloud to shine on my heart. "Gyrth!"

I ran to embrace, devour the sight and marvelous feel of him.

"He's just out of the kitchen which he ate bare," Tirion chirped. "Arrived on a hay wagon, no less."

"Oh, Gyrth, it is so good to—Tirion, be so kind? Fetch Godwine, he's playing in the stable. And little Magnus from his room if you would, there's a dear. They must meet their uncle."

Tirion pattered away and I looked up into the face of a smiling, swaggering young angel. "Oh, it's passing *grand* to see you. How is Harold? Where is he?"

"Safe," Gyrth warranted. "He and Leof both."

"Ireland?"

"So they are. We'll talk but I have to see Eadgytha. How has it gone with her?"

"As with me, like someone's poor relations. It's a crime."

"Don't stand so close. Siward said I'd be safer in churl's clothes." Gyrth gently set me at arm's length, indicating his sorry garments. He slipped a hand beneath the neck of the grimy tunic and scratched. "But they were still inhabited. Think I killed all the fleas but you never know. God amercy, I'd adore a bath."

"You shall have one, sir. You shall soak till you melt."

Sister Tirion returned with the children. Introduced to Godwine, Gyrth took the small hand with great courtesy—"I'm your uncle, then"—and allowed Magnus was the noblest bit of child flesh he'd ever set eye to, and now he must see Eadgytha who, Tirion informed him, had left her poetry students mid-Caedmon and commanded him upon the instant.

Their meeting in Eada's chamber was stark contrast to the warmth of ours. Gyrth bowed deeply at a respectful distance. Eadgytha inclined her head slightly in response. "Brother."

"My lady sister."

There were at least eleven years between their ages. They'd met infrequently and barely knew each other. With the queen's permission I stood discreetly to one side as she inspected Gyrth's lamentable dress. "Why so disheveled? Father cannot be so impoverished. Why didn't Tostig come?"

"He's too well known. And he's married to Baldwin's daughter."

Eadgytha brightened a little. "Then they've done it. When?"

"Last October. That much went right at least."

"What do you mean?" she caught him up anxiously. "Is something amiss with Tostig? Is he ill?"

"No, fine—I guess. You know Tostig."

"Far better than you."

"I mean he's not one for telling a body things."

"And our parents?"

Well enough for ageing folk exiled and parted from loved ones. Baldwin was an old friend and the soul of tact, deftly keeping them from too much contact with visiting Norman emissaries. For all the openness of his nature, I sensed Gyrth was carefully measuring how much he told to his sister.

"Father's sent to Edward twice asking for a trial on the Dover business. But you'd know that."

Eadgytha did not. "Edward has not come to Wilton."

"Nor written?"

"No." Eada firmly changed the subject. "And yourself? You look well, if in dire want of ablutions. What do you purpose here? It is dangerous for you."

Gyrth laughed at the notion. "No one knows me or gives a—cares a fig for Harold's ha'pny little brother. But . . ."

Eada prompted him. "Yes?"

"You haven't seen me, Sister. Father must trust your silence in this." Possibly, though I'd swear Gyrth didn't. "I went to York first."

Crossed on a trading knorr bound up Humber and Ouse to York. His mission: to gauge for Godwine the English mood, especially that of the northern earls. He'd met with Siward at Old Minster. The earl was outspoken as always.

"He and Leofric hated that business at London. So did I," Gyrth added. "Cursed near caught by the archbishop's men. Never rode so long or hard in my life. At Easter court, Siward and Leofric urged a trial and recall if the Witan found Father innocent, and you know they would. The king wouldn't hear of it. Now they're thinking, them and many like 'em: Better Godwine in Wessex than this Earl Odda and the damned Normans."

Eadgytha shook her head; to me she seemed confused, ambivalent, not like herself at all. "You have my silence, but Edward is my husband. Those Normans I have met, with few exceptions, are admirable lords."

Gyrth exploded. "*Jesus!*"

"*And* their duke a strong son of the Church," the queen bristled. "A virtue lacking in many of my own family. And you will mind your language in my presence."

Gyrth regarded his elder sister like an alien creature never encountered before. "Lady, pray you remember your own blood. William's kind have no more law than rats in a cage.''

He raked furiously at his scalp. ''There's worse. May I please sit?''

''You may.''

Gyrth waited until the queen settled herself, then dropped into a chair. ''William's making no secret among his vassals that Edward's given him some promise regarding the throne.''

Even I could not keep silent at that. ''Love of God, he wouldn't!''

Gyrth avoided Eada's eye, which had gone dangerous. ''Barring a son of his own. So they say. What Father thought—well, the queen has already reproved my language.''

''No!'' Eadgytha's fist came down hard on the chair arm. ''Edward may not *do* such a thing. Not without the Witan.''

Gyrth studied the floor at his feet. ''He has. Those just come to Bruges from Rouen say there's two hostages returned with the duke. One is Hakon.''

Then it was true. A cold hand clamped about my heart. Hakon must have been terrified of the huge strangers, Agatha mad with grief.

''The other's Wulfnoth.''

Eada was rigid in her chair. ''They were sure of the names?''

''Quite sure.''

''Wulfnoth came to court at my invitation.''

''That was a mistake for a start!''

''It was not. I meant him for the Church. Edward *knew* that. Tostig will tell you.'' The anger brought the queen out of the chair; we rose with her. ''No. I cannot believe this yet.''

''Believe it, Sister. Believe all of it. This country needs Godwine as bleeding needs a bandage.''

''Whatever Edward's reasons, I will know them, I promise you. I will write today and demand he recall them. His honor is at stake.''

Oh, Eada. Demand of Edward? William? And what of

my sons? Surely they would be more valuable to William than Hakon. Why had they been spared?

Or had they? No, never. He'd not touch my children if I had to carry them on my own back clear to the sea for safety.

Gyrth must hurry away. The trading boat would wait only so long at Southampton, but first he would make his way to Shaftesbury where the sorry mule Sister Martha spared him could be exchanged by Teinfrith for a decent horse. Sister Swarboda provided a sack of food and a little ale.

"Give my love to Teinfrith and Hildre."

"I'll that and more," he promised, leading the mule out of the stall.

"Tell me everything. What of Harold?"

Gyrth grinned at the mule waiting stoically. "Sturdy old beast's like us, Edith. Full of woes but hard to break and damned impossible to kill. There's much I didn't tell Eadgytha. Couldn't tell. You understand."

"I gathered as much."

"It's a hard thing to say, but I don't trust my sister as I do you."

I hugged him, pressing my face to the rough wool over his chest. "God go with you and protect you."

"Listen now. I must be away and there's more to tell."

More indeed. Godwine would wait no longer on Edward's justice. He'd sent Gyrth because Tostig would surely divulge too much to Eadgytha.

"And don't tell me he wouldn't. They're too close. Did you hear the woman? 'Tostig, how does he?' Nothing but Tostig. This is too important."

Backed by Baldwin and sure of support through much of the south, Godwine and Harold would return in force no later than the end of summer.

"I've carried letters to London, to Stigand and thanes in Wessex and Kent," Gyrth confided. "The wind's turned fair for our house, girl. Siward and Leofric won't oppose him, and the south's ready to welcome him home. Mostly."

"But what of Harold? What of my own boys before he comes? I'm terrified Edward intends them for William, too."

"No, he'd have taken them by now."

"Damn it, you're not a mother. I know what I feel! I've got to get them out of here."

"I wouldn't put it past Edward," he admitted with a sigh. "And Willy Bastard's known for hard bargains."

"Devil that! Where's Harold now?"

"At the court of Donough mac Brian. In Cashel, his letter said." Gyrth added with some puzzlement: "Who is married to a . . . half sister of ours?"

Now there was a thumping revelation. "What sister?"

"Never met the woman," Gyrth shrugged. "Never knew she existed. Seems Godwine had an earlier—uh—marriage of sorts over there. I tell you, Edith, this year's been an education. A whole university."

All of that. But then Harold always said their father was remarkably silent on his life before Gytha. "And Harold is well? He's truly coming this summer?"

"No later than September. He's got to gather up crews and new ships, mercenaries who won't be dainty about whom they're paid to fight."

"Fight?"

"He and Father will come peacefully if they can, fight if they have to. But they'll come."

Gyrth embraced me again before straddling the mule. "No fear about your boys."

"Easily said. Wait until you've your own. Tell Teinfrith as he loves his daughter to find me a hiding place quickly, for *I'll* be coming."

"I will. Remember," he cautioned, "not a word to the queen. Cursed if I know where her heart is. I . . . I just can't trust anything anymore."

"It's gone hard with her, Gyrth. Edward stripped her of everything. There's scarce two shillings between us. He hurt her so badly."

His smile was hard, nothing of kindness in it. "Well, there's a pity. Did she say one word for Swegn when she might have? For any of us? She may be queen but blood is blood."

I could have told him much about his sister, difficult as Edward and far less flexible. But Gyrth, for all this year had taught him, had not yet lived or hurt or wept enough for that understanding. "She still loves her husband."

Gyrth said flatly, "That's her sorrow, not ours."

Late in June came a jumble of confused reports. Godwine had landed here, landed there. Some men welcomed him, others resisted, backed by the forces of Earl Odda. Rumors trod on each other's heels. Godwine was trapped by Edward's fleet—no, he evaded them, escaped again to Flanders. But now Edward was on alert.

Coming in September. No later, Gyrth promised. Where are you, Harold?

More vague hearsay. Edward rages at Odda for allowing Godwine to slip through his fingers, but now all ports are watched. Every fishing boat in the Narrow Sea is feared to be Godwine, every curragh off Wales or Devon sure to be Harold.

A letter comes to Eadgytha from Edward, inquiring after her health and mine and, particularly, that of my sons.

Devious man. I could wait no longer. We must run now.

32 • Edith

Each sunrise I expected Edward's men at the gate and each set gave thanks for one more day's respite. My nerves frayed all the more, daring not a word to Eadgytha or the children. I filched a trimming from

Sister Florence's new parchments and scribbled a note to Teinfrith:

Come for me now or the king will have my boys.

And waited for an opportune messenger.

In high summer there are always travelers passing between Amesbury and Shaftesbury. Peddlers, carters, canny beggars who know when and where best alms are to be had. It was shearing season; the wool wagons creaked by our walls, and one blessed day a load bound for Shaftesbury rumbled through Wilton gate to tighten a loose wheel and cadge a bit of fresh bread and soup.

The driver was a burly young son of a sokeman, hoping to sell his father's excess wool to the looms of Shaftesbury. He paused in repairing the wheel to take stock of me when I joined him, no doubt gauging my sense of charity. Darker than most Saxons, most like his blood was Welsh-mixed this far west. He studied me cannily, speaking of good weather but miserly lords "and them Normans, too" and a poor year all round with Earl Ralf's crippling taxes.

"Cruel poor," he mourned, his glance sliding over the purse at my girdle, lean as his own. "Scarce able to feed three children at home."

"And a long two days to Shaftesbury."

"It is that, lady."

"What if I made it worth your while? Do you know the thane there? Teinfrith?"

The spark of his interest ignited. "For sure I know him."

"You'll carry a letter for me. There'll be a good meal and lodging. And tuppence from me now, and no haggling, mind. That's a day's wage for a good servant in a great house."

To my desperate cry for help, I silently added: *Father, give this good man a meal and whatever else you can spare, but I must get out of here soon.*

He departed with the message. I went back to my children, waiting on silent Eadgytha, and counting the hours and days. Another week passed, my prayers growing more urgent. I loved my sons fiercely with an oppressive sense of their danger. *Why* hadn't I simply tucked us away in the farmer's wagon? That would have made more sense than waiting for doom like a hog in November. Could I trust the man in the first place? I waited in raw fear.

July now, haying time, men and women gathering daily in the fields. How much time had I left? Eight days after I sent the letter, a wagon rolled into our courtyard driven by a peasant who was a study in grime slouched over the reins. But my heart swelled as I recognized three of Teinfrith's own carls riding before, heads bared in the heat but red-faced and sweating in mail. And greater joy when I saw who sat beside the wagon driver. As I hurried out from the cloister, he spoke to one of the young novices who scampered up the stairs to the chapter house.

He was the silversmith who, with his wife, handfasted me to Harold. I knew his name and hers but I am beholden and will not name them or any of their circle while I live. He jumped down from the wagon and bowed over my hand.

"Lady Edith. My wife sends her greeting."

A well-made older man in a fine linen summer tunic and loose trousers. I thought the silver cross hanging on his breast out of keeping with his own faith but put it down to diplomacy as the young novice came tripping back followed by Mother Werburgha, who held out her arms as to a dear friend. She greeted him as he knelt in reverence. "You are always too generous."

"Oh, Mother—look!" The novice hiked up the skirts of her habit to hop up onto a wheel. The driver ogled greedily at the flash of bare leg. "There's ever so much wool. And skins for old—for Sister Florence."

Far too much of either for Wilton's need. The raw skins alone were enough to keep Sister Florence and her girls ripe and sweating for weeks.

"I'll take the rest back," the smith said. Then privately to me, "Wait me in the church."

He signaled the wagon to follow him. The churl driver blew his nose copiously with his fingers, wiped the residue on a sleeve already stained from the habit, and gave me a black-toothed grin. I looked away.

It was cooler in the stone nave. When my friend came in he carefully blessed himself at the font with the smoothness of long habit, making sure we were alone.

As we walked toward the altar I said, "One would take you for devout."

"One had better. I quote Scripture better than most Christians, priests included. Come, kneel with me."

The stone floor was hard on my knees. "I almost fled with the last wagon out of here."

"Good you didn't," he whispered. "The man said he was stopped and searched. Normans."

"Edward's?"

"If not, Teinfrith expects them. Three days ago a monk from Canterbury stopped at his hall."

One of Champart's lay brothers. Nothing important, just liturgical circulars for the convent there, but asking casually if Teinfrith's daughter still waited on the queen. The cold worm in my stomach told me I'd run out of luck and time.

"Listen," the smith continued, bowed over his folded hands. "We can't wait. We leave as soon as the wagon's unloaded. You and your boys meet us in the stable. Carry nothing, just the clothes on your back."

"Werburgha will think it strange."

"I'll find a reasonable excuse. John's wife is pregnant."

"John?"

"The wagon driver, John White."

I convulsed with the thought in spite of myself. "White?"

"There's already a John Green in the village he came from. What's amusing?"

"His name. He's hardly immaculate."

"I inherited him when I bought half a hide from your father. Doesn't believe in bathing, says it invites ague and disease."

"He would seem impregnable."

"I don't expect to be stopped, not with carls and a safe conduct from Teinfrith, but if we are—"

To the end, the smith had deliberately loaded far more wool and skins than the abbey could use. Enough to bury me and the boys deep beneath the most fragrant. Between that and John White's potent effluvium, official curiosity would tend to be brief. If otherwise, the carls had their orders.

With rescue so close, I felt the danger unbearably. "For God's sake, get us away. They might come today. This hour."

The smith crossed himself and rose, giving me his arm. "Get the boys to the stable within this hour. We'll be there with the wagon. I've a donative to make to Mother Werburgha. A new silver cross for the altar." His bearded lips parted in an old joke no longer humorous. "When we pay Peter's Pence our generosity must be visible."

I took his hand to nestle it against my cheek in gratitude. An artisan's hand, square and strong but able to carve living beauty from dead metal. "Harold and I won't forget this."

"Best you do, lady. But let the earl remember his promise."

So we must. Life was dangerous and expensive for this man and his circle. When they went to mass they must be constantly aware of the deception. How that weighed on conscience, I could never imagine. Perhaps their gods are more tolerant than ours. If they were discovered, those Christians who owed them money could erase the debt by denouncing them, like hapless Jews, as eaters of Gentile children, blighters of crops, bringers of plague. When the ignorant are fearful, they need someone to die for them.

No surprise at all when Eadgytha said she would take the midday meal in her chamber. There was a baffled air to her that summer. Not the loss of place or lands killed Eada's heart but Edward's neglect and contempt. Strangely touching to see a strong woman unable to cope. Like the hanged, the solid world had dropped out from beneath her feet.

My hour waned. I fetched Godwine to our chambers and lost some precious time in deciding what clothes would serve us best, finally choosing light wool as most durable. Godwine wriggled and scratched: "It's all prickly."

"You mind!" I leveled a warning finger at him. "Today you and your brother must be men like your father. When I say be silent, good men will obey. You understand?"

"Yes, mum."

"Stay here with Magnus. In this chamber, I say. I'll be back soon."

With rescue only minutes away, I was all the more terrified. I scurried up the bell tower steps to scan the roads and country round. Only a few carters and peasants afoot, but no riders. I'd thank God for that when time allowed. Down the stone stairs and along the cloister into the busy kitchen where Sister Swarboda, amid her sweating cooks, was sampling the lentil soup and giving crisp orders.

"Wants salt, just a touch. And a kiss of basil. Edith, will the queen deign to join us at dinner or are we to be ignored as usual?"

"I'll just take her some of the soup and bread."

When I pushed in her door, Eadgytha was sitting motionless by an open window, a scrap of sewing forgotten in her lap. She didn't look up. "Dinner, lady."

Eada spared the tray a disinterested glance. "Thank you. Set it by."

"The bread's just out of the oven and Swarboda says it's the best batch of the week and that the queen should eat more."

"Did that wagon bring letters?"

"No, lady."

"No messengers? Well, I have written to Edward. He will write or visit soon."

Uttered without the old overbearing conviction. Oh, he would come, he or someone, when I went missing. I could imagine Edward in this room: thin and stoop-shouldered, glowering at his wife, now angry, now wheedling. But Eada would be his match in such a conflict. I had seen her bleed only once, then close the wound in silence. Perhaps now Edward never would.

My hour was surely gone and the smith waiting. "Do you wish anything else, lady? I must see to the boys."

The slightest movement of her head: no. The sun caught fire in a few blond wisps of hair. She didn't let me take much time over it anymore.

"Eada? I've been wanting to say . . ."

"Yes, girl?"

"I hope someday the king will know what a good friend our queen has been to me and mine."

Eada picked up the sewing like something curious dropped in her lap by a stranger. "I daresay he will. I have much to tell him myself when I return. Please see to my nephews."

The angle of her head in the light: How like her father she looked just then. *When I return . . .*

If she returned.

If I could get away safely and hide until Harold returned and we somehow reclaimed our own again.

I looked through the window into shimmering high summer. No movement or sound. In the hush, all England seemed to be holding its breath.

Then I moved and broke the hush. Time to go.

33 • Edith

The afternoon heat grew stifling. I was perspiring already, little Magnus cranky in my arms, Godwine grumbling "too hot" as he trailed from my other hand. We skirted back of the abbess's house and the church to the stable. The smith and his peasant driver had backed the wagon inside. My benefactor was worried and impatient.

"Where were you? We should have been out the gates this last quarter hour. Get the boys hidden." He lifted Magnus up onto the rolled fleeces. "And yourself until we're well away. John, help them."

Our carls waited at the open gates. The silversmith went out to give them final instructions. I was helping Godwine clamber over the side when Sister Martha Veronica loomed in the stable entrance.

"Edith? What are you doing?"

The smith chose the dinner hour to depart with as little notice as possible. I hadn't counted on Martha. I helped Godwine over the sideboard and jumped down to her. John White stared at us from the wagon, prying between his teeth with a birch splinter.

"We're leaving, Martha."

Her red moon face contorted with confusion. "Leaving the queen? Why?"

"Martha, I've not much time. The queen doesn't know and must not. Nobody, you understand? Not a word, I beg you."

"Girl, are you in trouble?"

That wrung a mirthless laugh from me. "One might say so. Someday you'll know, but for now I need a friend's silence."

"I know things aren't well between your husband and the king."

John White stared at us with his perpetual dull intensity. I wondered how much the smith had told him.

Martha would not be satisfied. "What *is* this, Edith? Mother Werburgha will be worried to death if she doesn't know."

"Remember you said it was a shame what was happening to our country? Well, it will happen to me and my sons if we don't go now." I hugged her close. "Goodbye and God bless you. Pray for us."

John held out a dirty hand to help me into the wagon. "Nobody said who you were," he allowed on a note of expectancy. "Your husband high up?"

"Just cover us over. It's going to be hot enough."

He held onto my hand longer than necessary. "You ent common folk."

"Come, boys." I lay down reluctantly on the stinking raw skins. "Cover us well, man."

He didn't move, only stared, wedging and prying that damned birch twig between the remains of his teeth. I felt a vague menace and heard the insolence in the words, but then his tone changed. "We don't want nowt to happen to the like of you then, do we?"

John White had a grin like a dirty scar. The hem of my gown was hiked up over my calf. He stared at it openly before I pushed it down, a goat contemplating available ewes. He made my skin crawl. The disgust goaded me to cruelty, imitating his speech. "In words you'll understand: I ent nobody nor you ent seen nowt. Now cover us up."

He tossed away the toothpick and spat, grabbing up a roll of fleeces and dropping them over us. I made a mistake mocking him. Such creatures feel life has done that in plenty, and women like myself are living insults to their manhood.

I lay smothering under the fleeces, hushing Magnus into silence when he began to cry. *Hist! Be still. We'll be out soon.*

After an eternity the wagon began to move.

Eadgytha Regina

But you *must* know," Edward insisted as he had for the last half hour. "Surely the perverse woman said something."

"Not to me," I repeated for the third time. "I don't know when or where. They simply vanished."

In the face of my husband's exasperation, I rendered all

the truth I knew; what I guessed was my affair. Edward would question the nuns, who would eventually remember a wagon from Shaftesbury, Edith missing the same day, and deduce as he might.

"Eadgytha, you will drive me to profanity."

"Curse away! I'll match you for Wulfnoth and Hakon. How could you?"

"That was a matter of policy and a sound one."

"Edith is not a dullard. Harold's sons would be as valuable to William, as I'm sure you pointed out to him." And no doubt thrown in to sweeten the pot for William. My husband was adept at such offers, an artist in ambiguity. "But it is good to ride with you again, my dear. We have so much to talk about."

He had finally come. Not for me, of course, never for me, though the pain of that was no longer sharp. Passing through the shire on Crown affairs, pausing incidentally to scoop up my nephews, whom God grant were now in wild Scotland. But Edward wanted me to ride the late August afternoon with him, Regenbald and Esgar pacing their horses at a respectable distance behind, followed by ten men at arms. For a king enjoying bountiful new revenues, Edward looked seedy. Without me to prompt him, my husband had fallen back into his old careless habits of grooming. His cheeks were not well shaven, and the rich green tunic I'd made myself badly wanted mending. His need of me cried in these small things, though I no longer deluded myself that he wanted me.

Riding at his knee, I glanced sidewise now and then at my brooding lord. Sad to find I no longer gladdened at the sight of him or tried to fit into the hollows of him and our marriage as before. I'd loved Edward, but as I saw the sunken cheeks and whitening beard of the man I married, I knew a corner had been turned. Foolish, futile to retrace my steps to find that place I'd thought mine by right. Exiled or even restored, henceforth I would be no more than the good Lady of England. Rather like a ghost lingering at her own funeral. But if no more, the Lady would have respect and her due.

It was pleasant to ride. We talked in banalities, skirting

carefully those things we both knew must be said. There was the comforting sight of men and women moving with scythes through remaining stands of wheat and barley. Past them to open meadows and bordering woods where green and gold were swathed with purple teasel. Edward glanced up at a flight of birds overhead.

"Lapwings. Summer goes, autumn comes."

For England and me. "Remember the old story? Were he ten times a king, Canute could not command the waves to be still on the shore. Nor can we hold back time."

"No." Edward signaled a halt to those behind us. "Madame, we must talk."

I let him hand me down from the saddle. Esgar hovered at a distance, relaxing only when Edward waved him away. We walked toward the wood's edge. Edward did not take my arm; he would not do even that much for me. He seemed to struggle with something inward. Always more direct, I took the advantage. "Indeed we must talk. Why was I stripped of my lands, even those from my father?"

"I have not enjoyed all that had to be done this year. You needed a lesson in humility the same as Godwine."

I said quietly, "Then I have had it, husband. Will you now humble me further with divorce?"

"Oh, that." Edward only shrugged. "Champart's notion."

"Vile little man."

"He has his uses. I carted him off to Canterbury."

I wondered why it still meant so much to me. "Then it is not true?"

"No, Eadgytha. Have no fear on that account."

Pale pleasure to know he wouldn't thrust me so far away. Hardly wife but still a queen, desolate victory but something. Tostig would always have a voice at court. "And Wulfnoth?"

"I'll not discuss that."

"You will, sir! I am your equal and Wulfnoth is of my blood. As are my nephews, *all* of them." I stalked back and forth before him, not concealing my outrage. "Edith has strengths I never guessed, but that wretched Agatha—

didn't you consider she's already damned in the sight of God? How could you take the one thing—"

"For once will you listen before drowning me in opinions?" Edward dropped onto a fallen log, tore the skullcap from his head, and shook out his hair. He'd not been well or recently barbered either. In many ways he was so helpless. "I am impawned to William."

"With my family as coin. You are shameless."

"Be reasonable. It has happened before."

"How impawned?"

Edward hunched forward over his bony knees, looking away at Esgar and Regenbald. "William is strongest and best to follow me."

"Failing an heir of your own," I finished for him. That didn't hurt anymore, but he would know it had. "Did you think I was made of stone? You wounded me, man. You took no lisping little fool to wife but a woman fit for a king, fit and ready to be anything you wanted. But because you hate my father—"

"Don't start on that," he flared. "Don't I have reason?"

"—I tried to be neutral, even bending to your side against my own family. Last winter I learned how little you cared. No, not so late as that. You taught me that day by day, night by night. In coldness and indifference. How can you know how a woman feels when she sees in the smallest things how her husband turns from her? How she disgusts him? How that kills her a little every day? Don't bother to deny it. You need not mourn the royal womb much longer; it isn't likely you'll have sons now, considering my age and your disinclination. You're a walking wonder, Edward. The Church may extoll your piety, but I wonder where the man went."

"In time . . ." I heard the difficulty in what he tried to frame in words. "In time I will restore your lands; some at any rate."

"All, husband. I will have something for all these years."

"*Oh good Christ, woman! Will you stop trying to be king?*"

Edward shot to his feet on strong horseman's legs and paced back and forth. "I do what I must. *I* know exile better than you, more bitterly and far longer. I know the cold sanctuary coldly offered, the hospitality that becomes unspoken debt. I hardly hoped to be king. What did I know of England? What did I find? A serpent's tangle of laws, laws, *laws* that say I am anointed and rule in all things—oh, except for this right and that ancient custom. A writ to delay me here, another to check me there in a country where men's laws come before God's. Do you know what it is like to have to rule through a Witan of earls and bishops loyal neither to me nor each other? To deal with men like Godwine who importune a king and hem him round like lawyers and unpaid creditors?"

Edward turned on me, white and seething. "And then there was my loving wife at me, at me, *hovering* over me, full of correction before I was even wrong. Love of God, I know I've made mistakes, but I don't hate you, never think that. For us . . . some men are not made for marriage. It was your father. It was . . . all of it. I'm in a game against players better than myself, but God tells me I will prevail, at least hold them at bay and wait and see. I have done nothing that cannot be undone."

"Haven't you?"

"Your father was in rebellion, the country at large clearly against him. You know he tried to return in June?"

Who hadn't heard of that colossal embarrassment? I couldn't resist the jibe. "Slipped in and out safe as houses, didn't he? Three huzzahs for the royal navy; couldn't find a crab in a bucket. Has it occurred to you that if they couldn't find Godwine, perhaps they didn't want to? That perhaps they believed he was right to land? A right to be heard?"

"Does he?"

"Sooner or later he will be heard and England will listen."

Edward reseated himself on the log, absolutely still. "Whatever the Witan thinks or peasant sentiments urge, God put England into my hands alone. Not yours. Not Godwine's."

All through our lives together there were so many times when the shadowed soul of my husband was too small for the crown, and rarer moments like this: sitting on a log and a king to his fingertips.

"Now," he said briskly, "I will return your estate near Winchester as a token of trust. That will give you some revenue."

"I need money now. It is humiliating to have to borrow fivepence from Mother Werburgha."

"Of course." Edward spread his arms. "But I need Edith's children."

"Is that a condition?"

"Eadgytha, they are promised."

"Then break your promise."

"That is an option. Eventually. But I will find Harold's children."

"You really can be a viper. When are you to deliver them?"

"Saint Michael's Day. Nothing in writing. William was pressed for time, currently not in a position of strength—and delays are commonplace. Who can foresee tomorrow?"

Yes, he enjoyed playing his intricate game, holding off the world with deft and masterly strokes. "Meanwhile it is disgraceful for your queen to be in want. Look at these clothes. I'm constantly mending. Leave me some silver."

"Is that demand or asking?"

"I should not have to ask. Don't ask me to beg."

Edward waved Esgar to join us. "What a world it is, wife. The king and queen of England haggling in a wood over what? The fate of the nation? Pocket money. Amusing."

"If you say so, but please, I'd rather not be almed by a servant like a beggar at your gate. From your own hand, if you will. Do me that much honor."

Esgar surrendered a purse to Edward, who dismissed him again, joggling the bag in his palm. "I don't think there's much here."

"When will you learn to carry enough money?"

"I never did without you to remind me."

Edward bent to kiss me. I turned my cheek, denying my lips, but the affection surprised me. "I need the children, Eadgytha. They must be visible for the time, not only for William's surety but my own. Your father will come again, sure as these lapwings will fly south. And Harold's shadow has grown long enough for Willy to notice."

Edward took my arm and led me to horse, laughing as something touched his meager sense of humor. "Willy Bastard: Isn't that what they call him here? *Nom de Dieu*, what a profane people you are."

34 • Edith

By the last days of August I was muttering desperately the old Anglian charm against high winds: "September blow soft till fruit's in the loft." When Harold comes—and let that be soon—give him good winds and safe harbor, and may I and the children endure until then.

I couldn't blame my dear silversmith. He'd chosen John White's steading for its obscurity, the haven we needed but in an open latrine hole. White's was the filthiest farm in Blackmore Vale. There was a thatched croft, which John and his wife Gerda shared across a low wattle wall with a continual squabble and flutter of chickens and their stale, dry smell. White was a boarder to the smith, rendering a regular portion of his egg yield and fattened swine to his landlord. The patch he planted for himself was indifferently tended by his sullen, pregnant wife and always weed-grown. There was a well, a hog wallow going dry, and the constant grunt and squeal of pigs more fortunate than I. They at least didn't know their candle burned at both ends as their time ran out.

There was a decaying barn, put up by a better farmer or perhaps White himself, taken once and never again with a seizure of ambition. Here in the loft, Godwine, Magnus, and I camped to wait whatever came, since the barn smelled cleaner than White's croft. From the loft I could see to the northeast the Convent of the Virgin Mary on the promontory above Shaftesbury and tell time by the bells as I did in childhood.

"And there, just a few miles north of that tower," I pointed it out to Godwine, "is where I was born and grew and married your father. Oh, there was such feasting and dancing and gifts from the earl and countess. . . ."

So near. So far. So long, but I couldn't put Teinfrith and Hildre at risk by letting them know where I was.

We were safe but miserable. The first few days we took our meals in the croft but quickly chose to eat in the barn. One needn't search out reasons for the appalling condition of White's farm. He was one of those weak, shiftless men who saw his own failings as inflicted on him by the world at large. His wife, Gerda, matched him. They cursed and whined at each other continually without strength or conviction. Now and then Gerda showed bruises on her face. I sometimes imagined her pregnancy accomplished by hurried angels disposing of some flawed miracle. That was easier to believe than the two of them making love, if love was the word. Most like they copulated with the joyless compulsion of beetles.

I felt from the first that Gerda resented my presence more than her loutish husband. Surely they'd been paid something by the smith, but they made clear to me often that it was not enough, that the boys and I ate far more than had been recompensed. That is, if one could call gluttony two bowls each daily of greasy pease porridge and two eggs among the three of us of a Sunday. I gave the eggs to my boys; when one day I asked an extra helping of porridge for Magnus, Gerda refused: They had barely enough as things were.

"Your kind always expect more."

There you had it. My "kind." Not the food but her manner added to the grinding burden of fear and disgust in me. Gerda put me at the arm's length of her hostility. I should have known why from the beginning, last on my mind though it was. John White had the mind and soul of a goat, evident in the way he stared at me that first day at Wilton. No doubt he wouldn't hesitate to satisfy himself on a convenient sheep if the need took him, but I was closer.

Fearing every day to be discovered, I had John White as far from my thoughts as distaste could put him. But in the first days of September, his actions took on an unpleasant pattern. I carried my own wash water from the well; at such times he always seemed to be close about the barn, even finding excuses to climb and peer into the loft.

"Yes? What is it?"

No answer ever, only that dull, stupid-horse look before his head disappeared below. I began to go longer between baths, collecting water during the day and washing myself and my one worn, seam-split shift after sundown. I was safe then. Like most poor folk, John and Gerda hoarded their candle ends and went to their pallet with the failing daylight to wake with its return.

Fifth September, a day I never speak of nor ever forget, miserably hot and humid. The clouds building up over Blackmore Vale promised rain but my shift was sticking to my skin before the sun was high. After the midday porridge I washed and returned the bowls, receiving no more than the usual grunt from Gerda, then sweated to haul water to the barn to scrub down my boys.

Godwine had wandered off, the little scamp. Not to worry; he never strayed far. After a slapdash effort at Magnus, who'd not yet come to view bathing as pleasant, the water was still clean enough to swab myself down quickly. I plumped Magnus in the straw naked as the day he came from me, relieving him of a long splinter of wood sharp enough to hurt him. I stripped off my kirtle and did what toilet I could in the virtuous but inefficient manner taught students at Wilton: never undressing completely but washing ourselves under the shift. Modesty before *sanitas*, and God forbid we should touch ourselves more than absolutely necessary. Marriage cured me of that, but in this place I thought it wiser.

I was splashing away, sopped but cooling, when I heard the barn door groan open. "Magnus, is that you? Stay down there, love."

No, Magnus would have answered. Sweet God, it was John. I heard the ladder rungs creak, snatched at my kirtle, pulled it hastily over my head. As it slid below my eyes, there he was, stupid-staring, loose-mouthed, the birch twig between his teeth.

I said coldly, "You could have said it was you. What do you want?"

White climbed onto the loft floor. "Don't need to want. This is my place. I can come here whenever I want. You washing?"

"That was the notion."

He grinned, honoring me with the graveyard of his teeth. "Why not nekkid like the boy?"

I turned my back on him. "We bother you as little as possible. You might give us the same courtesy. You were paid."

He took a few steps toward me. "Not enough."

"The smith will make it good; if not, my husband will. Now please leave us."

"Who're you, then?" he challenged. "You ent nobody to put on fine airs." A gleam of dull cunning. "Or maybe you are, like what I thought. Seems a great matter you get hid proper. Hid from what, woman?"

John White came even closer, almost within reach. Not revulsion alone in my stomach now but cold, grey fear that I dare not show. His kind of human weasel would relish my fear as much as any other pleasure in his gutter mind, and weasels are vicious. He was not above hurting my baby.

"You don't want to know my husband's name. You'll be in danger yourself if anything happens to me or mine."

I waited uneasily while the thought filtered through his slow mind. "From what?" he said finally.

"As I said, you don't want to know."

"You lot in trouble, ent you?"

I smoothed the kirtle down my front. His pale eyes followed the movement. I turned away from him, bending to retrieve Magnus's tunic. "Who isn't these days? If it's escaped your notice—oh!"

Breath jarred out of me as he struck, pulling me around and throwing me down on my back. Before I could recover, John White was on top of me, writhing his pelvis against mine.

"Somebody once," he rasped, gloating over me. "Now y'ent nuffin. *Nuffin*, bitch."

That open sewer drain of a mouth came down over mine as his tongue forced itself between my teeth. I would have retched if I hadn't been so terrified. I struggled, flailing at him, scratching his face, pulling his long hair. Dimly, far away, I heard Godwine's piping voice and one other and little Magnus wailing.

I cried out once before John's dirty hand slammed down hard on my mouth. He tried to hike the kirtle and shift up over my thighs. Snarling now, moaning as he tore at the drawstring of his ragged trousers.

"Bitch . . . tuppin' bitch, all you're good for. See how afraid I am? See?"

I got one hand loose and pushed his face away. He hissed and his fist hit my mouth like a rock. Diamond-hard bright lights danced an instant. I tasted blood and heard Godwine's voice below.

"Mum? Mum?"

He mustn't see this. He can't see this.

I heard Gerda's voice outside but John didn't. Beetle-concentrated, driven now by the only clear motive in his low life, he was between my thighs and I felt his penis probing frantically, then throbbing. He flailed convulsively against me, groaned, gasped as my own sex went warm-wet with the result, and I went silently mad. My outflung hand scrabbled, grasped something slim and sharp. The splinter taken from Magnus. Everything flowed together then: my son calling from below, the barn door opening, Gerda's voice, little Magnus screaming, and I plunged the splinter deep into John White's eye.

He jerked, squealing in agony, rolled off me, pawing at the splinter protruding from his left eye. The squeal rose to a wail; the wound must have been deep. His eye was gone. He twisted about on the straw, making that obscene sound. I was beyond caution now, wanting to leap on him and drive the splinter deeper, penetrate him brutally as he would have my body. Someone was cursing. I tried to snatch up whimpering Magnus and pull my clothes down at the same time—

"You whore!"

Gerda there at the top of the ladder, horrified at the sight of her husband, unable to think beyond what she saw, if she ever could.

"You dirty bitch." She came at me.

"Gerda, stop! This is not my doing."

"Kill you! What you done to him? *What you done?*"

The child in her belly was big enough to make her ungainly. As she raised her fist, my arm shot out with no conscious thought behind it, clamped on her thin neck and squeezed. A devil had loosed murder in me, driving me to grip harder, expunge the sticky, filth of that animal from between my legs, squeeze Edward, Champart, all of them from my wounded life. The blood seeped about my fingers as the nails cut into Gerda's flesh. "Enough. God damn you all, enough! You can't *do* this to me."

I don't remember releasing her. Gerda just crumpled, gasping, onto the straw beside her moaning husband. I gave them one cold glance as I struggled down the ladder with my baby. "God help you both. Godwine, take your brother."

"Wuh . . ." Gerda tried to curse me. "We'll tell . . ."

Coldly insane now, I said, "You won't, woman. Not if you don't want a eunuch for a husband. You know what he tried to do. Do yourself a mercy and let him die."

At the bottom of the ladder, Godwine stared up at me, his face stiff with fright and confusion. I took the baby from him. "Come on, boy. We're going home."

"But it's raining and Magnus is naked."

"So am I and I'm sick of it." I yanked his arm so hard

he cried out. "I don't care, you hear me? I don't give a dying damn. March!"

Babe in one arm, boy hanging from the other I lurched out into the downpour. It might have been raining rocks for all I felt, just trudged doggedly down into the vale. Magnus cried but I barely heard him or Godwine panting to keep up or the breath sawing in my own lungs as we labored up the steep northern slope. No telling how long we staggered across the open heath. Past the walls of Mary Virgin with miles yet to go. Little Godwine got his second wind and soldiered grimly on at my side.

I want to go home. I want to be clean.

I don't know how long we walked. Time had stopped. I remember a dull animal relief stumbling through the stockade gates, the mindless gratitude of a dog when someone stops beating it. Someone lifted Magnus from a numbed arm that would not straighten out again. People running—and my mother's shocked-tender gasp of pity as I fell into her open arms.

35 • Harold

Another beacon, Harold. There on the north hill." The spare figure of my brother Leofwine draped over the keel's beam as he peered through the last of night toward the hilltop fires above Porlock beach. My boatmaster, Niall mac Ciaran, had anchored us in a line just beyond bowshot. I could read Leofwine's worry in the wash of moonlight.

"If they'll just let us land, buy what we need, and go," he hoped.

"We'll see." Not likely, though I wouldn't say as

much. Whoever responded to those signal fires would be Odda's, a new earl given Godwine's western lands when Edward outlawed us. Odda was a Midlander and ambitious, commanding the naval disaster at Sandwich when Godwine slipped in and out without losing a keel or man. He wouldn't be disposed to yield anything to our family. There'd be Cornishmen on that beach, but the thanes and much of the fyrd would be Saxon.

Two nights out of Dublin and no trouble so far. We'd put in at the island of Cerrig Rhoson off Saint David's Head, rested the night offshore, and went in for water at dawn. Niall restricted his Irish and Norse mercenaries to filling our casks, though several sheep and pigs were liberated in the process.

Another easy leg to lie off Porlock overnight. Plenty of time, I thought. Barring trouble Godwine would meet us this week at Portland Bill, but trouble or not, there was no turning back now. Flanders and France had backed us with money and appeals to Edward. If we failed they'd not be eager to throw good money after lost.

Around us the twenty-four rowers on the benches dozed while their relief lay in the well fore and aft of the mast. By the lashed steerboard, the dim figure of Niall mac Ciaran rolled out of his furs, grunted, and stood up to relieve himself over the side. He and his men would relish a fight almost as much as spoils, but my orders for today were firm. Water and supplies. Fight only if we couldn't avoid it, clear?

"As a saint's conscience," Niall assured me cheerfully. "But if you say fight, you'd better mean it. My men are easier to start than stop."

Strange what this time of night did to a man's mind. Just before dawn is ebb tide in the soul. I saw it working through Leofwine now and tried to divert him. He'd matured much in the last year, wrenched from nurturing Bosham into the hard world beyond. Our stay at Cashel had not been unpleasant, mostly waiting our time. Leofwine found a willing girl for what the Irish with lyrical delicacy clept a "soldier's marriage."

"What was her name?" I asked him as we stared toward the lightening land. "The woman you were with."

"Can't remember." Leofwine's mailed chest heaved once with rueful amusement. "Couldn't pronounce it if I did."

Nor could I remember the names of the two I'd been with. Satisfaction of a sort, guilt that passed in the knowledge of how little it mattered. They were not Edith. We paid the Norse in Dublin well to convey news to us at Cashel. Edith was at Wilton with the queen. Then we heard of Wulfnoth and Hakon taken, and I suffered with Edith across the sundering miles for the lives of our own children.

We were sheltered hospitably at Cashel, stronghold of Prince Donough mac Brian, where I met his wife Driella, still unaccustomed to the existence of my half sister to whom Leofwine and I owed our welcome. She and Donough were in their middle years, generous to a fault, though conversation was difficult between folk who need an interpreter for every word. But for the distinctive mouth and chin, I wouldn't have known Driella for my sister.

"Not to ask how or when or why," Leofwine commented after meeting her, "but Father certainly got about, didn't he?"

Prince Donough, son of Brian Boru, was serenely unconcerned with English troubles but helpful where possible. "You'll be wanting the Norse crews at Baile Atha Cliath. No better ships or men, heathen as they are and uncivilized. Now, if it is the best captain for such, there's Niall mac Ciaran."

Donough sat back in his gilt chair and launched into saga. I listened in polite frustration since most of this had to filter through the interpretation of a bald little priest-scribe. I learned patience and diplomacy through dealing with such men. Donough could not know or care how desperate I was. The frightening questions hammered in my skull from waking to sleep. Had Edward taken my children? Did Gyrth fare well in Kent, and how valid was his intelligence on London and the number and condition of the fleet there? London at large was said to favor Godwine's return. How loyal would they be in fact? How many Kentish ships could we count on or impress before turning into Thames mouth?

Now, as the night died, Leofwine nudged me again. "Another beacon just lit. There to the south."

Yes. Men would be rolling out of bed, many already gathering by the beacons. And one more dark question: Must we fight today? Tomorrow? How many dirty, mean skirmishes between here and London? England's head was against us; was her heart so as well?

For no reason at all, I remarked, "At Cashel they're still sleeping warm."

"Here comes Niall."

The boatmaster took his place on my other side, a short but solid man, perhaps thirty, gripping an unlit torch. The fur cloak over his leather armor made him bulkier as he peered east toward the narrow ribbon of light widening over the Cornish hills. "You say these were once your brother's lands?"

"I'm not sure. The southern limit if they were." There might be men waiting for us who remembered and honored Swegn, but none of them in command this day.

"How many battles have you come home from, Lord Harold?"

"Only one." At Slaughden against such raiders who were with me today. Sometimes the world is a cruel and clumsy joke.

If Niall thought my experience meager, he refrained from saying so. "I've had my share. I'm good at this. If the matter comes to a fight, remember what I said."

His accent, a bizarre mixture of flat Ulster and Norse, had been difficult to follow when we first bargained and before I shook his scarred hand in agreement, though after a year with Donough, Niall's laconism was restful.

"I know this place," he said. "I've traded here before."

"Oh? That would have been helpful to know at the start."

"There's light enough. See there? The beach, the valley going back. Fishing huts just beyond the beach, village on the side of a hill farther on. Tide—"

Niall paused, peering ahead. He sniffed at the air like a hound on scent. "Tide's starting out. We should go in now. Fast."

"You say you traded here?" Leofwine asked. "Were they friendly?"

The boatmaster snorted. "To Irish? Never. Began fairly enough, but then things turned nasty. We were not ready, barely got out. Most of us. Today we are ready and not a man will show his back to Porlock."

Light enough now to see the beach clearly and some way up the broad valley between the hills. I gave the order: "Light the signal."

Booting men awake as he went, Niall strode forward to the fire on an iron plate amidships, plunged the torch into the embers, and swung the light in a wide circle. As one man the rowers bent to the oars. The longships eased forward in a line toward the beach. Our keel barely scraped bottom when the rowers backed us off gently, not to drive the prow too deeply aground.

"Come on, Leof."

We bolted over the side, Niall and fifty-odd men behind us, then those from the other boats, splashing up onto the beach over five hundred strong. Torch flaring in his grip, Niall swung it in an arc. Instantly his men fanned out in a line at the water's edge, a hundred men long, five ranks deep, front rank ready to lock shields if necessary.

In the growing daylight I saw what we'd come to. Leofwine, Niall, and I stood well forward of our ranks, watching as the dozens became hundreds swarming down toward us.

"If we outnumber them," Leofwine judged with a quaver, "it won't be by much."

Niall barked at his men. "Stand fast!"

There were carls among them, but so far as I could see, not a good sword or mail shirt in fifteen of the peasant fyrd men.

Niall did his own reckoning. "Kerns, no better. But I hope you've a silver tongue this day, Lord Harold."

Leofwine glanced back toward the lines of our men

yards behind us. Unmoving, still as death they were. "I feel naked, don't you?"

Watching the big bearded man striding toward us, scabbard rattling against his thigh, the two escorts with battle axes, I surely did, little brother.

36 • Harold

The three men halted a full five paces from us, far enough for readiness. They clearly expected trouble. The big man named himself. "Cenwold, thane to Earl Odda. This is his land."

His fyrd men straggled out in a shallow crescent perhaps fifty yards behind him. They shuffled about and jabbered among themselves. The Cornish were easy to distinguish from the Saxons: darker men in brighter clothing but poorly armed. Some brandished no more than clubs. Hardly disciplined, they brayed insults at us until Cenwold silenced them with a vehement gesture.

"I am Harold Godwinesson. My brother Leofwine."

"We know of you." Cenwold's eyes went over me like a hand feeling for a hidden blade. Cold eyes, the color of sleet in February. "And your father."

And nothing good by the sound of him. A gull swooped overhead with a scree of hard laughter as Cenwold pointed to our keels. "The tide is going out. Go with it. You have no welcome here."

Leofwine stiffened but held his tongue. "We are going," I assured Cenwold, "but we have a long voyage. We need fresh water and food, whatever you're willing to sell us."

"For hard silver," Niall added reasonably.

Cenwold threw the question at me like a stone. "Do you know what your father did, not four days gone?"

"No idea, Thane. I'm only here—"

"Landed at Wight, maybe asked the same as you. They said no, same as me. Godwine burned two villages. No one knows how many killed. His own land once, his own people. Wasted and burned for miles and then flamin' well took what he wanted."

Niall said with polite interest, "Do you tell me so?"

Leofwine could not keep silent, his voice tight with young anger. "I would not call you liar, but I know my father's heart."

"They must have attacked him," I jumped in. "Provoked him somehow under orders from Norman knights. You have the sound of a Midlander, Cenwold; you wouldn't know. Godwine is loved in the south."

He spat on the ground. "Not on Wight. Not today."

And today was no Slaughden where right was clear. This wasn't going the way I wanted. Niall waited, placid but watchful as a trained hound, still as the ranks behind us. Beyond Cenwold some of his men were pointing at us. Suddenly I could see Father and Tostig on the beach at Wight, faced with the same resistance, the same choices and chances to be taken against a shrinking margin of time. "Tell me, Cenwold. Is it Odda's order or your own disposition to deny us?"

His mailed fist rested on his sword pommel. "Both."

"And where is your earl?"

"At Wight," one of the ax men volunteered. "Succoring his people after your father's damage."

"*His* people?" All my life they'd been ours. Anger smoldered under my common sense. I tried to stamp it out as my choices narrowed cruelly. Only two, one dangerous, the other ugly. I could back away but at what cost to my authority with Niall and his men? Edward was surely calling troops to London by now. If battle were necessary, would these follow me? I couldn't risk their defection, and that left the ugly choice. Loose Niall's men and pray I never had to do it again.

Voices had risen among Cenwold's men. "Him. It's him."

The thane sent one of his carls back to their ranks. They were pointing at us again, swinging their bill hooks and clubs in front of them. The carl returned and muttered something to Cenwold. At the same time a mere nod from Niall brought his front rank forward to halve the distance between us. Leofwine whispered, "I don't like the look of this."

Cenwold jabbed an arm out at Niall. "My men know this one. One says he killed his brother two years ago. Give us this one and I'll let you go."

I gaped at him. Had the man gone stupid? Hands raised away from any weapon, I closed the distance between us and spoke privately to him. "These are his crews, not mine. I can't do that. I and my brother would be dead along with all of you and Porlock."

You can read fear and uncertainty in a man's eyes. Cenwold had neither. "There's too much at stake," he said.

For him there must have been. Most like no more than a carl when Odda was invested, Cenwold relished his piece of power and place in the world, late come and not about to be given up. In the sight of Odda and Edward, the man who stopped Harold on this beach might rise higher and faster.

I tried one last time. "Cenwold, your men are mostly farmers. Ours fight for a living, better armed, better trained. On my belt you see a sword and a full purse. Which do I use, Thane? I'll do what I must. Be wise."

Tuk!

I heard the mean whine and the impact, whirled about to see the first arrow lodged in Niall's shield, heard the breath burst painfully out of Leofwine as he reeled and fell. I couldn't see where he was hit—*he's dead my brother is dead*—but Cenwold was already drawing his sword. I leaped back, shield up, snaking my own blade from the scabbard. "Cenwold, you fool. Niall, GO!"

Our men needed no signal, already forward past me. Four spears flew at Cenwold and his carls, and then they were surrounded and down. In a breath the whole skirmish had swept past me, Niall's men charging to close with the fyrd while I turned Leofwine over. Not fatal. The arrow was high in his left arm and all the way through.

Shock-pale, Leofwine just stared at the red-smeared head and shaft protruding from his torn mail. "Jesus. Jesus . . ."

"It's nothing, Leof, nothing. Up with you! Back to the boat and stay there."

Reeling on his feet, Leofwine stumbled away toward the shallows. Nothing mattered now, the thing couldn't be stopped, nor did I wish to. They'd hurt my brother, my own blood, and for that Niall and his sea wolves could have their head.

That they did, closing with the fyrd, a steel phalanx crashing through thin wattle fence. I ran past the bodies of Cenwold and his carls, pounding toward the battle where some of the defenders were already breaking, trying to flee. A spear flew at me. I blocked it aside with my shield and ran on. The battle had already rolled far past us when I found Niall calmly detaching a silver chain from a neck no longer in need of it. He grinned up at me and the sky.

"Ah, *aimsir mhaith!* A fine day for profit."

I stared at him with sick wonder. In the middle of slaughter, the man was calm as a pond on a windless day. "They remembered you. What in hell did you do to them?"

Niall slipped his arm into his shield grips. "Did I not say things turned nasty?"

Not half as nasty as they'd turn today, by God. Where Niall was cool, I was trembling in the middle of a war of emotions, fear for Leofwine, rage and something fiery in my gut. "Up the hill and into the village. Get the water and whatever else you want. And burn that filthy place."

Niall raised his sword in salute. "With pleasure."

"You hear me? Burn it to the ground and damn them all."

His face lit up. "A grand notion. Will you be going back to your brother?"

I should with Leof wounded and miserable, but something brutal had loosed in me like a bolt from a crossbow. "No. *I'm* going to burn that place."

It was half brief battle, half rout. A dozen defenders formed themselves into a ring on an outcrop of rock. They hurled stones down on us until we cut our way through and past them, Niall and I in the lead, crying the men on up the hill toward Porlock.

Godwine made no excuse for Wight, I'll none for that horrible day. We took what we needed in food and water. What few folk hadn't fled we flushed out of their hovels and herded clear of the burning to come. Odd fragments of that morning stay with me the way some childhood fear will haunt a man all his life. I remember the shrill screams of women being dragged out of their houses, in contrast to the workmanlike silence of Niall's men, who had orders to burn, not kill. A child, a boy about Godwine's age, scurried out of a burning hut, saw me, and froze. There's no terror so naked as that in a child's face. Children must have looked so at Dover.

"Go," I rasped at him. "Go, damn you. Run!"

The boy dodged around the flaming house and vanished as I snatched a piece of burning thatch from the low roof and ran to toss it into the next house.

In half an hour, as the sun rose higher and hotter, the thing was over. Sweating in my mail, I stumbled through Niall's men streaming back down the hill, carrying neck-wrung chickens and whatever else had caught their fancy. Rarely is the absurd absent from the awful; one man had slung the shield over his broad back and carried a rickety three-legged stool upended on his head.

By now our keels were almost completely out of the water. Niall and I heaved shoulder to shoulder with our crew to float ours again. As the men clambered aboard after me, I stumbled aft along the half deck to where Leofwine huddled on a rowing bench, the broken arrow at his feet.

"I pushed it out." He reached clumsily for the clotted arrow pile and grinned feebly at me. "A keepsake. For losing my martial virginity."

"Eh, I think you'll live. Want some water?"

"God, yes. A bucket."

"We've fresh from the village. Niall! Make southwest for Land's End."

When I brought Leofwine's water, he was staring back at the smoke still rising from Porlock. The rowers needed the bench. I helped my brother to a place aft near the steerboard.

"Why did you have to burn it, Harold?"

No easy answer there. "How's the arm?"

"Why?"

The longship swung about; the oars dipped. I looked back at the smoke over what had been Porlock and knew that Leofwine's was not the only innocence we'd left on that beach. I had done to that miserable place what we refused to do at Dover, and—the thought bent in a perfect, vicious circle—for that refusal, Godwine and I must do it anyway.

No, Lord Jesus, my hands are not clean and never will be again. Worst of all, I recognized that bitterness under the soot in my nostrils and the stale taste of smoke on my tongue. Edward had pushed us all over the edge of a future like an abyss, but I would do it ten times over now if I had to. God might mourn our fall, but lying next to my brother, somehow I could not find or spare the tears.

37 • Harold

A stiff beam wind didn't help us much, but when we turned eastward around Land's End headway was swifter. I tended Leofwine's arm and worried at the inexorable march of the sun across the sky. At midmorning of the second day out of Porlock, the long, low shape of Portland Bill crept over the horizon. Niall barked an order. "Ape! Up the forestay."

The agile little Manxman they called Ape scurried forward and, without breaking stride, made a leap at the forestay line and overhanded himself up to the leather basket atop the mast. Whenever Niall was likely to encounter unknown vessels, he wanted to see them first. He signaled the other keels to fall in line on his beam, and we nosed cautiously toward the distant land. At the masthead, Ape sang out: "There's keels anchored!"

"How many?"

"Twelve I can see. No, more. I make fif—Jesus and Mary, eighteen!"

"Peel your eye for standards," Niall bellowed back, trotting forward to join Leofwine and me in the prow. In a few minutes the anchored keels were visible to us, too.

"Edward has that many ships and more," Leofwine fretted. "What if it's not Father? What if it's them?"

Niall answered him. "Then we're well and truly had, Englishman. We'd have to tack crosswind, pull like bloody hell, and pray to outrun them."

It was Godwine, had to be, if only to still Leofwine's fear. "I wish we knew," he whispered.

Niall roared up again to his lookout. "Ape! You wouldn't be dozing up there now? Can you see the buggerin' flags?"

"Almost."

"Well, don't be shy when you do." Niall grinned at my brother. "No worry, boyo. Ape can spy out a drink at five miles in fog. He'll have no trouble—"

From the masthead: "There's colors!"

I couldn't wait. I ran back to the mast and bawled up: "What colors?"

"Red and yellow. No, gold. Red and gold."

Wessex. Father. I loped back to the prow in great scissoring strides to whirl Leofwine about in my arms. "It's Godwine! We've made it."

Made it to glide in through the anchored keels amid cheers from the men on shore, splashing and floundering through the surf to embrace Godwine and Tostig over and over. Father looked far better than when last we parted.

"And how was Ireland, boy?"

"Ah, full of Irish, wouldn't you know. And a convenient sister."

"Driella, yes?" Godwine's smile was mellow with memory. "What a woman her mother was."

Leofwine showed off his wound to Tostig with studied negligence. "Got it at Porlock. Not much. Pulled it out myself. Where's Gyrth?"

"Somewhere along the coast or should be," Tostig guessed. "Our last letter from Eadgytha—"

It seemed he broke off too quickly as if he'd said more than intended. "What about Eadgytha?"

Tostig evaded, looking off toward the low limestone escarpment above the beach. "Nothing really."

"Damn you, I've heard nothing for a year. What of my wife?"

"Edward has Eadgytha watched now, but she managed to get a letter to Stigand. Edith's disappeared, she and your boys."

Through one horrible moment I knew hell. "Taken?"

"Eada said no. Edward wanted them for hostages to William—"

"No. God damn all of them, *no.*"

"—but Edith bolted too fast. As I said, disappeared."

"Well, there's a mercy. Where?"

"Somewhere in Dorset." Tostig must have read my naked anguish. "It's the succession, Harold. It's all they talk of in Flanders and Normandy. Edward's made some kind of promise to William."

With our blood he made it. "Then I feel better about what I've had to do." And what I would do now with no hesitation. After Porlock I would never again lift my hands in prayer without misgiving, but such was the price. Godwine must have felt so after Wight, but clean or not, we had hands to take and grip and hold.

With my father and brothers I waited only for the brief meal the men cooked on the ships and over fires on the beach. "Let them eat fast. I want to be at it. What's our first port of call?"

"Hastings," said Godwine.

Thirty ships strong we beat eastward along the underbelly of England. The long pebble beach at Hastings crunched under our keels and, as at Porlock, we saw the men streaming toward us, but this time women and children thronged with them. I thanked God when I saw the Lions of Wessex raised high. Men ripe for our cause, supporters and ships, and none but my brother carrying Godwine's flag—Gyrth, scraggly-bearded, tattered but exuberant, reporting that Sussex and Kent stood with their earl.

"Except for the levies of Odda and Ralf. We'll have to look sharp around Dover and Sandwich."

Gyrth wasn't sure about Pevensey or Bulverhythe. Both had good natural harbors where Godwine's thanes had maintained at least sixteen seaworthy keels. "They've goodwill toward us, but they're divided about confronting the king."

Strengthened by willing ships and crews we sailed on, our sense of imminent victory growing with each sea mile. The southwest wind prevailed with hardly a cloud in the sky, but that could spoil in less than an hour when we turned north into the Narrow Sea. Three of Niall's craft dropped back as rear guard, but no ships pursued us. We sailed into Pevensey Harbor, plugging it so tightly across the narrow mouth that neither fish nor crab could have swum or scuttled through, then swarmed up the beach to plant our banner and await friends or foes.

They were not long in coming. News of our progress had flown in advance of us. The men appeared, thanes on their stunted horses, carls and fyrd following. By then we were some fifteen hundred strong, a small army. Our fleet blocked the harbor and the armed ranks five and six deep made an impressive argument. Godwine stood before the first rank, Gyrth beside him with the Wessex banner, flanked by Tostig and me, Leofwine and Niall mac Ciaran.

But Pevensey would not join us. Their spokesman, a

Thane Oswald, was respectful but stubborn. A man of my father's age, Oswald put Pevensey's sentiments plainly.

"We hold you've been wronged, Earl, but not with how you'd right it. Not with what you did at Wight."

Niall suggested softly, "Perhaps we can persuade them, Earl."

That was not Godwine's wish. He would not make Pevensey another Wight. "Oswald, we need supplies and fresh water. If you won't follow us, don't hinder." When the old thane hesitated, Godwine said only, "I offer you the choice Wight foolishly refused."

Oswald allowed we might provision without let. Godwine called for volunteers from among the fyrd. A few joined us, mostly young fellows eager for any enterprise more adventuresome than fishing. We commandeered their five best keels, crewed them ourselves, and left Pevensey in peace.

Bulverhythe . . . Dover . . . Sandwich. By now the strain was telling on us. Godwine rested whenever he could under the hide tilts rigged for sleeping at night. Food was hastily prepared, fresh water too scarce for bathing. We went unshaven and stank. The Ape spent most of his time dangling at the masthead on watch for Edward's fleet. Gyrth thought they were still in Thames, but what if they weren't? Where were Odda's forces? Where Ralf's?

Our first ominous sign of them was atop the chalk cliffs of Dover: Norman cavalry, about a dozen. They stayed in sight long enough to count our keels before disappearing. On the beach some English greeted and rallied to us, some held back. We took on water and volunteers and were gone within the hour.

At Sandwich the cheering folk ran down the beach and far out onto the ebb tide sands to greet us. We asked nothing from them but information about Edward's troops. They'd seen Earl Ralf's horsemen patrolling the coast in some numbers but didn't know where or how many now.

Our keels turned westward into Thames mouth. In the early morning darkness of Sunday, thirteenth September, we lay well off the Isle of Sheppey, where the tide was against us. Godwine wanted to scout the shore south of the Swale. We needed to locate that reported cavalry if they were close. Although Niall could tell to the half foot the depth needed to float his shallow-draft keels off a bottom or be stranded on it, he didn't know the Swale, that narrow, marshy stretch of water separating Sheppey from the Kentish shore.

"And the tide going out," he reminded us.

All around us and on the other boats men were stirring. Niall, Godwine, and I leaned over the sidewale toward the lightening east.

My father asked Niall, "What do you think?"

"In the way of advice, sir?"

"That's what you're paid for."

"Then I'll ask you and your fine sons to wait here. I'll go in with a stripped crew and have a look. No fear. If there's a channel six yards wide, four foot deep, we'll get out."

He gave orders to lighten ship. In a few moments the ballast and cooking stones from amidships went over the side, while one of Niall's other keels slid alongside. Together with half his crew, Godwine, my brothers, and I clambered aboard. Himself at the tiller and one Sandwich fisherman who knew the Swale, Niall backed and slipped away into the grey of morning.

The tide fell lower and lower until the leadsman reported no more than a fathom depth. Our keel drew half of that. Every craft in our fleet backed to deeper water. While our father lay in the prow conserving his strength, my brothers and I crouched amidships contemplating Niall's chances. The day was already hot. None of us looked forward to donning mail.

"That Irish barbarian is certain worth his price," Gyrth reckoned.

"The man has courage," Leofwine said. "And a marvelous detachment from it all. His loyalty would be worth a place with us, were it not for sale."

"A tool is a tool," Tostig opined flatly. "You use it and put it down." But his tone betrayed the fact that he was as worried over Niall's chances as I was. "How much depth will he have now?"

Anywhere between four feet and none, but no profit in pointing that out. He got back or he didn't. "Enough," I hoped.

Leofwine wiped the sweat from his forehead. "What's on Sheppey that we'd want?"

"Father's order," I told him. "A lesson to Edward."

Full day and the sun climbing higher and hotter. We had to pull farther out yet before the longship appeared around the eastern headland of Sheppey. No wind at all; the sail hung slack, but pulling hard, Niall's crew eased in beside us within half an hour. From the steerboard he cheerfully waved us aboard. His men were sweat-soaked, insect-bitten, and badly out of sorts.

"Saw some horse, perhaps half a hundred. One company of foot. They saw us, too," Niall added, "but they were going west and wouldn't tarry."

"Didn't fancy a fight?" Tostig snickered.

"Nor did I." Niall's retort was gentle as it was serious. "Not with scant two dozen men and a bare foot of water between me and a mortal wait for tide among those devil bugs biting us to death. We fancied getting paid and drunk once more before going to a hero's death. Orders?"

I said, "We're landing at Sheppey."

His brows shot up in surprise. "Why? Is not our business at London soon as there's a decent tide?"

"Later."

He'd gotten some look at the island while scouting. Nothing much to see or take.

"There's a manor and a minster church. We're going to burn it."

"No, we are not." Niall drew a line there. "There's enough on my soul. I'll burn no church." I'd struck his moral bedrock. "Some sins are worth the price, but—"

"Not the church," I said. "Just the manor."

"Well, that's a different road entire."

"A royal manor, Niall. The personal property of our beloved Edward."

His reluctance vanished. An English king was always fair game. "Is it now? Worth a visit?"

To us it was.

38 • Harold

Sheppey was a token reckoning and a message to Edward: *If you had not brought us down, Sheppey would still be up. We are coming.*

Gyrth reasoned afterward, "Sheppey was owed us."

"Something was owed us," Leofwine agreed. Neither mentioned the rest of it. What we never planned.

No blame to Niall mac Ciaran, who relayed Godwine's orders clearly to his men. There should be no need of fighting. Sheppey was a small manor. The few carls who might be there would be foolhardy to resist us. The small church was not to be touched nor any manor folk harmed in any way, simply herded beyond the gates to safety, and the hall, stables, barn, and outbuildings burned to the ground.

It was marshy, bug-whining, Thames-side hot, but we marched in good order to Sheppey gates and sounded the ancient horn hung there. They must have seen us coming some distance away. Even before the gates were drawn back by two frightened porters, we heard commotion within, shouting men and women, the high shrieking of terrified children, doors slammed and latched.

Then silence.

With only half of us crowded into the muddy courtyard, the rest had to wait without. Godwine strode to the hall doors and pounded vigorously with the hilt of his sword. From the barn and stables, white faces peered out at us.

"Not a soldier on the place," Niall judged.

Most like all had been levied by Ralf and Odda. We'd see them at City. To the west the church bell began to clang furiously, as if there were anything to be done. One of the hall doors cracked open. A bald, fat-jowled man with a steward's silver chain about his neck peered out at us.

"Come out," Godwine invited him. "Tell all your people to come out. They'll not be harmed."

Under his light-yellow gown, the corpulent steward must have been sweating off some of his lard before we were sighted. Perspiration rolled down his jowls to meet on a thick fold under his chin. A thin, whining insect lighted on my own cheek just forward of the mail hood. I slapped at it irritably, wishing we were done with this.

"You know me, Steward?"

"Godwine. You were Wessex."

"Am Wessex," my father corrected.

"What do you mean here? This is royal property."

"I said you won't be harmed. Niall! Torches."

"But this is the king's manor," the steward protested, stepping back from Godwine. "It has been a royal dwelling since before his grandfather's time. My own father was steward here. This cannot be allowed, my lord."

Someone in our ranks laughed. Ludicrous in the face of us that this porcine lump could see only the outrage of *lèse-majesté*. Godwine laid a gentle hand on the man's shoulder, which shook with as much indignation as fear. "Please don't be difficult. We've had a frightful week already. Bring out your folk."

They crept forth from hiding, slowly at first, unsure, then faster when prodded along by Niall's men. House after house, as it emptied, was efficiently torched at points high and low. The smoke and heat became oppressive. We formed a lane to move the people along through the gates. Well dressed, most of them, royal servants like the steward, generations grown up and some grown old in the service of Sheppey manor. They dragged a few children at their sides. Some carried whatever clothes or valuables they could snatch up, eyes stung and streaming from smoke, all of us wheezing now, and over it all the futile clanging of that bloody idiotic bell.

Niall glanced up to the second floor of the hall. "There's some still up there."

I caught a glimpse of two faces, a man and woman, before they ducked aside from the casement. Niall was quicker than my own thoughts. "Where's my finest volunteer? Ape!"

"Aye, here."

"Go in. Bring them down."

The little Manxman cast one look of horrified disbelief at the smoke belching from the hall. "Volunteer my *arse!* I'll be fried in there."

"As if the Devil would have you." Niall swung him about and impelled him toward the burning hall with an inspirational boot. "Now!"

Ape plunged into that hell faster than I would have. We heard him calling, cursing hoarsely, his ragged cough as the smoke rolled into his lungs. Then for long moments nothing but the deepening roar of flame as the fire bit deeper into dry timber. A woman screamed, then two male voices sharp in contention.

The last of the manor folk were out the gate now, plodding or hurrying toward the church. Sweat-sodden and gritty in our heavy mail, we wanted to be away, but for the first time I saw a shadow of worry darken Niall's imperturbable calm as he stared at the upper hall window.

"Ape, get out," he bawled suddenly, more pleading than command. "Jesus, what are you doing? Sitting down to tea? Get *out.*"

Next to me Leofwine cried, "Watch out, the roof's going!"

And then the Ape lurched out of the burning entrance, dragging the screaming woman by the wrist. The man stumbled after, his fringed blacksmith's apron smoking.

There are horrors you can only think of long afterward in sane reflection. Then you perceive, by their elements, they could not have happened in any other manner. I suppose the couple were man and wife. They must have feared us more than the fire and by the time that changed, Ape came bounding up the stairs. No time to argue; he pulled the choking, fear-frozen woman away, guessing the man had sense enough to follow. Down the already half-consumed stairs while the woman never stopped screaming. Ape was burned, some of his hair singed off. He cleared the door and slung the woman sprawling on the ground, slapping at his flame-licked clothes.

The husband, twice Ape's size, burned badly on the face and arms, beyond thinking, saw only his woman writhing on the ground before enemies. His fear became panic and rage. He attacked the first thing he saw, little Ape himself. Wild-eyed, his mouth flecked with spittle, he charged. Niall caught him smooth as a dancer and laid him out flat with a fist to the back of the neck. The hulking blacksmith went down on all fours, shaking his head like a stunned bull. Too fast then, too quick for mind to make sense of it, let alone stop it. Only Gyrth's cry of warning and horror—

"Tostig, no. For Chri—"

—as Tostig, sword drawn, set himself beside the blacksmith like an executioner and took the man's head off with one stroke.

No one said anything. No one could. No sound but the flames and the shuddering whimper of the woman. Godwine's silence was eloquent. He took in the image of my brother standing over the corpse that still wove on all fours, then turned his back. Leofwine ducked his head away, eyes squeezed shut. The roar of flames and collapse of the gutted upper hall wrapped about the pall of our silence. Niall mac Ciaran took in the violence with the silent disgust of one who knew it unnecessary. I found I could move, must move. I shoved Tostig away from the body that finally toppled on its side.

"Why?" I choked, throat raw with smoke and worse with what he'd done. "There was to be no killing. He was down, finished. Why?"

Then I saw the horror I will never forget. I saw Swegn stir and turn to me out of Tostig's face—blank and unconscious of guilt as an adder after striking. "He looked like he might get up."

The men began to drift away toward the gates. At my

father's feet, the woman stared sightlessly. A ragged, incoherent sound came out of her that would not stop.

Godwine hooked my arm and pulled me away. "We can stand here and regret or get on."

I must have nodded, some vague movement of my head. I rubbed at my stinging eyes and sought for Gyrth and Leofwine. They both looked green. The words were an effort for Leofwine. "Tostig: look at him."

Strolling in Godwine's wake, Tostig had bared his long, luxuriant hair. He shook it out and began to draw the silver comb through it with the absorbed pleasure of a woman at bedtime.

I took Gyrth and Leofwine by the arms and propelled them toward the gates. Toward the boats, London, and Edward waiting.

39 • Harold

Tostig's senseless savagery sickened all of us, but no time to dwell on that. Late in the day when our leadsman called one and a half fathoms, our ships glided forward into Thames, silent as a school of deadly swans. Beside me in the prow of the lead ship Niall concentrated on the sinking sun and river depth.

"It's time and tide will win or lose for us now."

When Thames narrowed, on Niall's signal the other keels flattened into a slender line three abreast after us. Ape hallooed from his basket on high: "There's that village where we took on water once. What's the name of it?"

"Tilbury," I called back. "Cry out when you see London walls."

"And anything afloat larger than a log," Niall barked up at him. If Gyrth's intelligence was accurate, some half-hundred keels lay at the wharves below London Bridge, but not fully crewed and some undergoing repairs. Niall and I would believe that when we saw it.

Godwine rested aft, outwardly serene but surely aware as I of the stakes we played for and the risk. My three brothers lounged amidships beneath the barely curling sail as our rowers plied the long ashwood oars slowly and smoothly, wasting no jot of energy.

"By the mark: two fathoms."

Stripped half naked, my brothers cooled themselves with rags soaked in river water. "Bosham was never this hot," Leofwine fretted. Miserable it was, the marshes on either bank shimmering in waves of heat.

"Getting hotter still." Tostig pointed. "There. On the south bank."

Near Thamesmead, far but unmistakable, the line of Norman cavalry appeared with its long tail of foot soldiers. They kept unhurried pace with us. From aloft the Ape brayed out:

"City walls, Niall. There's the Tower."

"Niall, stand by for new orders." I loped astern through the sweating oarsmen to kneel by my father. With his weight and ailments, the heat prostrated him. He breathed with difficulty in the thick, humid air. "Father, where are the men from Kent and Sussex?"

"Those for us, if they haven't been levied by Odda, should be close to Southwark now."

"Hopefully."

"Yes."

"More cavalry on the north bank," Gyrth called out. "And foot soldiers."

I knew the banners. Earl Ralf's force. We were bracketed, but we had the depth now. If we made better speed, we could leave their infantry far behind. I took the rag from Godwine, dipped it over the side, and knelt to bathe his round, flushed face. "It's time to take up the dice, pray God's in a giving vein, and throw. Run for City."

"Just as I was thinking." Godwine took the rag and

wrung it dripping over his cheeks and bald crown. "You're not half bad at this."

"When you're home again, Gytha must make you rest. You look wretched. Have you minded your physicians?"

"I will, I will," he promised wearily. "Don't plague me now. Give the order."

"Niall, what by the mark?"

"Three fathoms."

"Double the stroke, all boats," I ordered. "We're running for London."

Niall repeated the order to the rowers, beating the faster time against the sidewale with a hammer until the rhythm caught among them like a strengthening pulse. Ape relaying the order from the masthead to the other ships, our swans knifed the river faster as we drew nigh City. I gave my brothers the order to arm. Gyrth and Leofwine obeyed reluctantly, but Tostig just lay back wiping his brow.

"It's too early and too hot for mail. I'm soaked through."

"Listen." I hauled him roughly to his feet. "I don't care if you boil like pork in cider. You may be many things I never guessed, little brother, but you will not be unready today." I scooped up his mail and threw it at him. "Arm yourself."

Our high prows sliced forward at full speed. Caesar's Tower brooded over the southeast wall of City with London Bridge ahead. Clumped together tight as sheep in a narrow pen, Edward's fleet lay at anchor. Beside me, Niall drew a deep, relieved breath and crossed himself. "Hail Mary. One of us has a saint in the family."

Certainly not me, but I thanked God anyway. "Keep toward the south bank. Hold formation."

At least fifty keels; from what I could see of the nearest, only two or three men on each. Then Niall chortled, "I think we woke them up."

Jesus, did we not? The lower city swarmed with men running toward the wharves, a few horsemen here and there to push them on. Big men, leaping from the wharves onto the near decks, bounding across from keel to close-packed keel toward the outer craft. They were vulnerable, we were deployed and moving, but their outer ring of keels was comprised of the largest and most formidable longships in Edward's fleet, shields already set along the sidewales.

"We have them!" Tostig exulted.

"Have we? Don't eat your eggs until they're laid." Niall kept his measuring gaze on the crews swarming from deck to deck. "If they have time to get underway, we've a fight on our hands." The Irishman gave me a crooked grin. "In the way of suggestions, Lord Harold, now's the time to be brilliant."

Already the first elements of Odda's Norman horse were moving between us and the Southwark end of London Bridge, while Earl Ralf's cavalry filtered through the lower city toward Pudding Lane and the wharves. Brilliance deserted me, but then Godwine was beside us, already armed. "Mac Ciaran, will you trust my judgment now?"

"Your money, my lord. Your orders."

"We can't allow them room to maneuver." Godwine's arm described a broad open loop. "Our rear keels there by the east wharves. Middle elements locked to them and bringing the line west, forward third to close the loop at the west wharves there. A solid ring about them. Minimum distance but no hostile moves."

"Minimum distance?" Leofwine worried. "They've archers aboard and we've none."

"We have shields." Godwine hoisted his. "I didn't say it would be easy. How quickly can we array?"

"Fast if it's to work at all." Niall narrowed his eyes along the far-extended line of our ships. "But quicker than they can. Hard steerboard!"

He bounded off, shouting up to his lookout. "Ape, you godless little man! Signal all boats. Tighten our line. Second boat to heave in on me."

Aloft, Ape unfolded a broad strip of green linen and brandished it. Immediately our keels flattened into a single file. When the nearest drew alongside Niall repeated the order to a man, who ran to relay it to the next. Boat to boat the command flew. Within minutes our fleet broke into three swift-wheeling elements, east, west, and center, breasting the tide to put the royal fleet in a barrel with the bung tight.

Our own craft was first in the western element. We would secure the chain on our end. Near and nearer we glided to the scurrying men on the royal decks. They saw what was happening, helpless as they were to prevent it, losing precious time as the noose of our ships tightened about them while only half of their benches were manned. Someone with his wits intact must have given an order. The first arrows whined over our heads.

"Double the stroke!" Niall roared. "Double! Get us *in* there."

From the masthead Ape brayed out at Niall, "Whyn't you *say* there was archers?"

"Ah, with one thing and another, I plain forgot. Get down and smartly."

Cursing virulently, the nimble Manxman dove out of the bucket in one leap and overhanded down the forestay line. "He's a brave man, Ape," Niall grinned. "Just he'd rather not be more than's needed. Swears I forget just to annoy him. Sometimes I do."

To my dying day I will take oath we got our money's worth from Niall and his men. Our rowers were fast closing our end of the chain, the lithe men bent forward behind the shields set along our beams. Crouched under the forward shields between Godwine and Gyrth, I admired the easy competence of Niall mac Ciaran. He snatched up a broad, round shield from the offside and set himself high in our prow, gauging distance to the nearing wharf.

"Steady . . . steady and . . . up oars!"

At no more than a dozen yards from the wharf, Niall gave "Down oars!" We felt the retarding rush as the oars braked us. An arrow thudded into the shield covering me as Niall ducked back to us. "My lords, we've got them and a good three fathoms, but that's the best of it."

No need to elaborate. The sun was low, the last of day going. If the royal keels were locked in, so were we. Hostile forces before and behind on the banks. We could hold here through most of the night, if necessary, but at morning ebb we'd all be sitting on Thames mud. On the other hand, as soon as we withdrew, the king's ships got out to fight. Not a warm consideration as the arrows thudded into our shields.

Gyrth looked pale beneath his helmet. "What can we do?"

Godwine smiled aimiably at his son. "What do you suggest? Draw swords and charge?"

Peering over the shield rim I recognized Earl Ralf wheeling his horse back and forth before his knights. The other Normans appeared agitated; they reminded me of nervous cats. Twilight deepened under a balmy breeze from the south that brought us, faint and ragged, the first ghost of a new sound.

40 • Harold

Leofwine prodded me. "Something's happening in City. Can't see too well, but there're people running."

A lull now. No more arrows flew at us from the royal keels, only the cooling south wind as I stared through fading light at the lines of Earl Odda's men across the river. Bells rang from Saint Paul's. And that other sound growing stronger on the wind.

"Dreadfully tired," Leofwine mumbled. "Was it just this morning we did for Sheppey? Seems like a year."

"Look there, Leof. East of Odda's men."

Over the horizon of high ground, so far their numbers were a mere smudge on the darkening skyline, the ranks appeared, broadening into long lines of infantry. They spilled forward toward Odda's lines, and the sound I'd heard now took on shape and rhythm from a thousand throats.

Wes-sex! Wes-sex!

"It's our levies," Gyrth exulted. "It's Kent and Sussex."

In the long twilight we strained to interpret the distant scene. Small parties went out from our men and Odda's, whose ranks now eddied about, their straight lines blurred in indecisive movement.

We waited tensely in the middle of an arena where, for the time, we were secondary to a potential broil on the southern shore. Would one attack the other? A sizable detachment of Odda's men broke off and ran for the bridge, following one man.

Gyrth leaned far over the off side. "The Kentishmen have raised the Lions."

"You're uncovered there!" Niall snapped at him. "Down, man."

Gyrth ducked back to us in the cover of the shields. "But what in hell's happening?"

Too distant to tell, a squabbling flurry of blackbirds on a far horizon. But the commotion on City shore was near and clear. Men and women, hundreds of them, poured down the narrow lanes from West Cheap toward the river. Their sheer numbers threatened to choke up Ralf's men as we had the royal ships. Despite Earl Ralf's attempts to warn or force them back, still they came on, engulfing his men, shoving, jostling around and through the foot soldiers, some of whom just broke ranks and walked away. And over it all, over the rising sound of the men marching across the bridge, the hoarse cry from the people of London—

. . . wine! God-wine!

—spilling across Pudding Lane to the water's edge, where some scrambled into small boats and pulled lustily for us. Under the roar I heard a deeper diapason as a magnificent figure astride a dappled grey approached behind the London crowd. The grey paced unhurriedly behind a staller bearing Edward's standard and a stout priest who held high a tall silver cross. Flanking the mitered prelate in white was an escort of ten priests chanting *Te deum laudamus.*

Godwine stood up in full view of the shore and the king's boats. No danger of arrows; they were watching, too, all eyes on that island of peace in a sea of pandemonium.

Tostig wondered, "Good God, is that Champart?"

Not unless Edward had gone daft. Only one prelate in southern England Godwine and I called friend, and there he was, Ralf's soldiers parting for him as the banners and cross advanced to the wharf.

I said, "God bless him. It's Stigand. Edward wants to talk."

Our family stepped from the keel to the landing with no sword drawn, escorted, at Godwine's order, only by Niall and a half dozen of his men. Whatever Earl Ralf's intentions and those of his Norman knights, the English foot soldiers showed no inclination to resist us. Choked up among screaming men and women all crying for Godwine, they could barely move, nor could we. Our own party had to push and wrestle our way through to where dismounted Stigand waited us. Never one to miss an effective moment, my father, for the first and last time in his life, knelt to the bishop and kissed the episcopal ring. We had to shout over the crowd pressing round us.

I bellowed at Ralf, hoping he heard me. "Give us some room, but don't hurt the people. Stigand, dear friend." I knelt with a clumsy swipe of a kiss at his ring, then embraced him. "Christ, man, we thought you might be—"

"Can't hear you. Speak up!"

"Thought you might be Champart!"

"Not likely. He's—"

Stigand had to roar it at me twice before I caught the gist. When Champart saw the English wouldn't oppose Godwine, he and his household Normans ran pell-mell from the palace, last seen galloping east for Aldgate and distant parts.

"The king wants terms, Godwine."

"Last year the terms were his and very harsh. Now they're ours."

"Lord love a monkey," Niall wondered, still with a

dubious eye on the Norman cavalry hovering too close. "Does this mean we've won?"

"So we have." Tostig pounded his back jubilantly. "And there are the judges. And there crossing the bridge. And there and there and *there*. Father, look at them all. Listen to them! They call for Godwine. For *you*, sir. Take the crown!"

"Why, boy? To make you a prince?"

"Why not? Better m—" He caught himself then. Recklessness was never part of Tostig. "Better one of us than William."

Niall and I struggled to keep the people from crushing us with sheer enthusiasm, the big mercenaries hard put to keep a protective ring while I fought through the press to Ralf before English sentiment did him injury. By shoulders and sheer will I reached the head of his shying, terrified horse. Ralf glared down at me, furious but uncertain as well. "Harold, stop them. Make them disperse. I have forborne, but I will loose my men."

No, he wouldn't. He wasn't that stupid. "You'll die if you do. Don't hurt them. People of London! English! Let the earl through. Way for Earl Ralf!"

Holding his bridle, I ploughed through the press of folk screaming and pawing at me, women who flung their arms around my neck, to where my father stood with Stigand and my brothers. Godwine had bared the mail from his head. His face was darkly flushed, and I knew then with a shock how much this year had cost what remained of his health; that if he had won our place again, it would likely be his last victory. He passed his sword and baldric to Stigand.

"Earl Ralf," he called. "Stigand tells me you and your knights may be the only Normans left in London. Go to Edward. Tell him I never wanted a war. Say we come now as his subjects still, but in determination as well."

He opened his arms to the folk pressing around him. "And England comes with us!"

Our torchlit procession met no resistance as we marched in good order up Aldermansbury Street toward Edward's palace. Triumph might have been disaster but for one fact that I will never allow myself to forget. Pressed into service by Odda, Teinfrith and men like him led the defection and the march across London Bridge, flatly refusing to fight Godwine.

"Stuck in my throat," Teinfrith said afterward.

And Aelred of Denby averred, "Just weren't right."

Dark now but dozens of torches held high by the Londoners striding along the ordered flanks of our march illuminated the great cross and Stigand riding ahead. After him came his priests, then Godwine and I and my brothers. Directly behind us Niall marched at the head of his small shore party. The mere sight of the hundreds striding with us made it plain to Odda, Ralf, and anyone else that whoever harmed us would be torn apart in the streets.

Through the palace gates and up the stone stairs without a Norman in sight, only a few Anglian carls and a wary staller or two who quickly scurried out of our path. Stigand strode behind the cross into the great hall, our boots echoing on the smooth flagstones, the last steps in a year-long journey that burned my father close to the end of his dwindling candle, that grew Gyrth and Leofwine taller and tougher through adversity and taught me the hard, dirty lessons of power.

There were a few stallers and servants in the hall, a handful of rough-dressed fyrd men of the northern shires on our left, Thane Aelred among them. More worrisome, to our right I recognized Earl Aelfgar, who had taken my place in East Anglia, standing pugnaciously forward of two-dozen carls. As we closed the distance to the three figures on the dais, I wished passionately that Edith and Gytha could share this moment, and Eadgytha—yes, even the shamed memory of Swegn, God guide him wherever he wandered.

With Edward were his chaplain Peter and Regenbald the chancellor, both of whom appeared decidedly apprehensive. Edward, tall and regal, betrayed no wavering in this moment. He wore the heavy formal crown, the jeweled robe of state Eadgytha designed for him, and carried the scepter. Once his eye fastened on Godwine, it never shifted.

Stigand halted at a respectful distance, raising Godwine's sword as a pledge of the truce. "Sire, the earls of Wessex and Anglia."

"Former earls," Edward corrected him. "And how come you now, Godwine? As Earl Ralf reported, as subjects? Or pernicious rebels?"

Godwine's hand fell heavily on my right shoulder. I thought he might be taken ill again, but he only meant me to kneel with him. As we did, my brothers went down in respect, Niall's men after them. Edward received the reverence with his small, acid smile and seated himself on the throne. "What, Godwine? Homage from you?"

"Sire, I kneel to you as is your royal due. Now before God, the Witan, and those English at your gates, pray you give us ours."

"Pray the king will not!" Aelfgar shouted. "They are traitors who pillaged his shores and ravaged his own property."

"If that's so, lord earl, why did Siward and your own father refuse to interfere today?" Aelred it was, contradicting Aelfgar from across the hall and advancing a few steps to Edward. "Sire, Sherwood don't hold with what they've done. Nor in good conscience with the wrong done them after Dover."

Edward turned his withering disapproval on the young forest thane. "You are a bold boy, Denby. Has Godwine bought you, too?"

The question stung Aelred visibly. He stiffened but answered with more careful respect. "I've laid my head on the king's knee and there's my loyalty. But were it not, any man could find worse to serve than Godwine."

"Could he? I hear you have an infant son, Denby. Have some heed to his future and your own." Edward took the moment, leaning on one elbow, covering his mouth with a hand while, outside, the insistent cry went up and on and on from the folk crowding against the gates.

Wes-sex! Wes-sex!

Still on one knee, Godwine inclined his head toward

the sound. "I respect Aelfgar and Aelred alike for their honesty, my king. But ask of London, Kent, and Sussex: Am I but former earl? Am I an outlaw?"

We were not. Edward—all of them—knew it. With a glance at Regenbald, Edward said, "Much pleasure as I take seeing you on your knees, old man, it appears we must come to terms."

The king rose and stood straight before us, scepter in hand, not afraid but coldly aware of defeat for the time.

"You may rise, Wessex."

BOOK IV

Promises to Keep

41 • Edith

Our wagon rolled eastward toward Bosham through
the golden last of September with the wild, joyous
bells from every small town between Shaftesbury
and Bosham in our ears, haunting us faintly even as we
passed through the cool glades of Ytena Forest. At first I
thought: *Lord, what a commotion! They can't be marrying
everywhere today.* When a Sussex sheriff joined us north
of Portsmouth, he warmed me with the truth.

"For the earl, lady. For Godwine. Calling him home."

Calling us all, me and my boys jolting in the covered
wagon as Teinfrith and his carls escorted us home. I drank
in the peal of the bells like water after long thirst. Ring
out, shires! Ring out all you south of England! Not only
reunited but restored. Harold was again lord of East Anglia. Outraged by that, Aelfgar must have spit nails and
brimstone when Botulf absented himself and two prize
Flemish horses from Nazeing's stables and rode all the
way to Shaftesbury to bring me the news. His gleeful grin
was wide enough to wrinkle up his broken nose.

"By God, things are put *right* again."

"You dear man, all this way to—how stands my hall?
How does Nazeing?"

The grin narrowed perceptibly. "Well, you know
Aelfgar."

"I do not."

"The place ent quite like when you left."

"And Harold?"

"Nor he neither." Botulf had the respectful aspect of a

man who'd blurted something too quickly. "But fine. He and his brothers, very fit."

"And you? You actually look happy."

"Never better." He sent a yearning look toward the open hall door. "Bit thirsty."

"And such magnificent horses."

"Loaned by Aelfgar, lady. More or less."

"More or—?"

"I didn't ask first."

The hills leveled out under us as we neared the turning to Bosham, and then I could hear the great bells of Chichester pealing wild and, nearer, the insistent clang from Trinity Church, like a smaller child among older sisters who will be heard come what may.

"Breathe deep," I told my sons. "Deep now. That's the sea you smell. That's Bosham."

Something squeezed tight in my chest, rose to sting at my eyes. Lovely, timeless Bosham. Gytha's hall and little Trinity Church founded by Saint Wilfrid when England was still Britain and most of our folk were still pagan. And below them, the village. From Bosham the scent of the air changed between high tide and low. It was lighter now, the tide would be in, lapping so close to the shore cottages that the nearest of them were built up on timber struts, and one might fetch up crabs from a window.

When we turned on to the last car trail toward the hall, my father reined in behind our wagon, ducking his head in to me.

"Eh, girl. Two men coming. I think it's Harold."

Instantly I was at several things in the same breath, looking to Godwine and Magnus, who were tired from the long journey and impossible all morning, patting furiously at my hair. I'd gone so slack about it without him, but I would not let his first sight of me be drooping in this wagon like a silly dove in a kitchen cote. I slapped our carter on the shoulder. "Stop, I'm getting down."

Behind us, Teinfrith's escort reined up as I lifted the boys down and, with one hanging from each hand, walked ahead toward the nearing riders. Yes, it was he, long legs sticking out from the horse's flanks, scarlet tunic brilliant

in the high noon sun, and Gyrth with him. I pulled the boys along fiercely.

"Keep up, now. Keep *up*." Magnus toddled manfully but half the time, in my eager stride, his feet were lifted clear off the ground. "It's your father come home. I told you he'd come, didn't I?"

Seeing me, Harold broke into a gallop, Gyrth cantering after. When he flung himself out of the saddle, my husband just stood for an awkward moment as if caught between wanting to engulf the three of us or just feast his eyes.

"The boys. They've grown so."

"Welcome, love."

He reached for me; we fumbled toward each other. *Why are we so shy now in this moment so prayed for?* I found the answer in Harold's eyes that mirrored so terribly what lay scarred in mine, and I knew that in some sad way that could not be voiced for years if ever, we'd grown so much more than a year older. The moment broke, dissolved, and we were in each other's arms, clinging tight to find what had been, always there but changed as the rest of us. There was a vanished time when we were that young, when we recked our joy above all else. Only a year ago? We had each other again and our boys, but the price spoke itself in our embrace.

"You're thin," I said.

He bent and lifted Magnus, tender and wondering. "I'm your father, boy."

Magnus was still too young to understand, but Godwine it was who brought us all home, brought us together. Without prompting, he plucked at Harold's sleeve. *"Hoch, Faeder."*

Harold took the small hand in his, choking with pride and delight. "Yes," he whispered. "Yes, Godwine. *Hoch,* my son."

Botulf clattered up to roar a welcome at his lord, and Gyrth saluted me from the saddle. "Welcome, Sister. All of you—let's go home. Mother's waiting."

Godwine's hall was a harbinger of what I could expect at my own. The Norman tenants had departed hastily but not before removing most of Gytha's furnishings, leaving the floors and tables chipped and stained. Her embroidered cushions were gone, her ells of linen, wool, furs, and expensive samite along with featherbeds, silver plate, and her prize tapestries from the solar. Few of the dear and familiar things were left that made Bosham home.

"Except Godwine's scriptorium," Gytha grated acidly. "Catch one of *those* reading a book."

Old Manni the steward had been livid and frustrated the year out. The Norman lord who battened on Bosham brought his own steward, a Frankish monk "who couldn't manage thruppence in account if he kept them in his own purse." All the English servants had been passed over by new foreign ones whom no one could understand. Villagers and tenants with generations of give-and-receive tradition between them and the earl now found it was all give for them and take for the new lords. Many of them simply ran away.

But we were home again. The sun shone on Bosham, and those musicians we could gather played no sad songs at dinner; in fact, Gytha had them play continuously through all meals, as if in too much silence she could hear too many of her own thoughts. Perhaps of all of us she had suffered most, given now to long walks alone or with Agatha. Gytha had aged, noticeably greyer, her progress heavier when she walked.

Agatha never gave up hope of word from Swegn. He'd reached Jerusalem; by now he should be well on his way home through Flanders, where Agatha would join him. Baldwin's daughter Matilda was now married to Duke William. As father-in-law, Baldwin might well persuade the duke to return Hakon and Wulfnoth, or Matilda might. These were lifelines of hope for Agatha. When a rider galloped in through the gates or a keel beached in the harbor, she was first at the window, then out the door. Is there news? Is there? . . .

She had been a servant under the Normans, faceless, nonexistent except for work. She never spoke of the day they took Hakon, but the silence spoke for her. Agatha had always been a serious woman, not beautiful, not even pretty, one of those souls who move through life at a fixed pace, be she abbess or wife. I often wondered what alchemy combined between her and Swegn to ignite such passion in polar opposites. Perhaps she was the firm anchor to him, he the warmth and color to her. Strength she had. The rock would not shatter, only weather and fade.

Of our lost ones, no word from court or continent. Hakon and Wulfnoth were swallowed up. No sad songs in Bosham, but our gaiety shadowed and forced. Ours was a tattered and bloodied triumph, as soldiers who limp home from battle with only the fact of victory to salve unhealable wounds. When Harold praised the loyalty of the Londoners, Gyrth responded with tongue firmly in cheek. "Yes, heartwarming. The best money could buy."

"Not true."

"True enough!" Gyrth came back sharply. "And let's not forget it."

"No, you're right," Harold conceded. "I won't. Power's not for saints, never that clean, and once you grab it, neither are you."

"I went to confession when we first got here," Leofwine told us over a mug of beer he tasted once then let go flat before him. He crossed himself with sardonic emphasis. "*Ego te absolvo.* Somehow it didn't help much."

"The way of the world," Tostig shrugged lightly. "One accepts it like the weight of armor on your back."

His brothers' reaction was something I never fully understood. Gyrth flicked cold eyes at Tostig, Leofwine just pushed his ale away and left the table, but Harold retorted with acerbic distaste, "I imagine you could get used to anything, Tostig. You have a marvelous strong stomach."

I heard his disgust and could almost taste it, acrid as smoke. From that year on, all Tostig's brothers distanced themselves from him. Not that he cared. He was jubilant, in fact, to hear of justice of a poetic cast. Eadgytha had returned to court in far more state than ever she left. Robert Champart's property was divided between our queen, Godwine, and Harold; Edward making political amends because he must. The pallium of Canterbury, abandoned by Champart in his abrupt departure from London, was draped upon our good Stigand.

Hateful and hating to the end, Champart journeyed to Rome for redress and intervention by the pope, no doubt complaining to the Alps as he crossed them. All in vain; he died the next year at Jumièges—for which, no doubt in sheer relief, daisies and dandelions, valerian and buttercups bloomed exuberantly in England.

I was graced with a small measure of vindication myself. My dear silversmith wrote expressing his happiness that all had resolved so well for me, adding a belated regret:

Your danger requiring such hasty departure from Wilton, John White was the only available carter and host to be found on brief notice. Not the most competent or fortunate of husbandmen, poor John has lost an eye through some misadventure.

I privately hoped the other eye was weak.

That was my sole and cold comfort. When Harold or Leofwine spoke of never being clean again, it was with men's meaning. At Shaftesbury, after what happened to me, I felt physically defiled in a way I could not express even to Hildre. I couldn't wash enough to feel clean. Cruelest of all, against the deep rage of violation, I felt that *I* was somehow guilty. That animal's touch was still fetid on me, chilling and blocking my feelings for Harold. Close as we were, sensitive to each other's moods, the first time he tried to make love to me, I hung back, feeling nothing but sickness and shame.

"What is it?" Puzzled, peering down at me on the bed. The first time in our life together I'd not shared this joy with an ardor equal to his. "Are you ill then?"

"No . . . no. I—it's just that it's been so long." Feeble lie. "Please just hold me. Don't say anything, just hold me until I can sleep?"

Never did I tell him what happened. The guilt faded in time, and I became pregnant again. Not rifts in our love after that year but spaces like pauses in music. Of certain places and events none of the brothers would speak much. Sheppey and Porlock became ellipses to me. When anyone asked me to describe my year of exile, I replied "Expensive" and let them translate as they might. In Harold, the old ready laughter and jesting that ever saw human absurdity in human grandeur was not gone but muted now.

Tostig left for court in October. The rest of us stayed on at Bosham, drawn tight in our need for each other. With a friendly letter to that effect, Harold gave Aelfgar more than ample time to quit Nazeing and no reason to take offense, which that touchy man took anyway all his headlong life.

Then in November, the Flemish keel beaching in our inlet, the messenger hurrying up the walk bowed forward against the wind. He bore two letters to Godwine from Baldwin, one conveying the count's deepest regrets for the other which he had received from Constantinople:

. . . died near the city in a village where contagion has already taken many others. Swegn was confessed and shriven and expired with the cross pressed to his lips.

Mercifully the letter was delivered into Godwine's hand when Gytha was absent. Only Harold and I were with the earl. Godwine simply turned away from us and poked at the scriptorium fire, which needed no help. But Harold broke down and for the second time in my life, I saw my husband sob openly, helpless with grief while I held him. Many say Harold was not a great man. If not, he still had a great humanity.

"Someone has to tell Mother and Agatha," he said. Any one of us would rather hang on the cross ourselves.

42 • Edith

The wind roared outside the windows of Godwine's study. Harold and I, Leofwine and Gyrth stood about the firepit, taking what comfort we could from the blaze. Godwine sat in the room's one backed chair, silent, crumpled, visibly ill. He rode seldom now, more often compelled to a covered chair. He knew he was dying and accepted the fact with laconic philosophy, content that he'd lived to see himself vindicated before the English and his house restored, but to outlive his firstborn son broke the man Edward could not. That dark, cold day was the first and last time I saw the old earl helpless, appealing to us, the young, where his own strength fled.

"I can't tell Gytha. She's borne so much. Edith, if you could have seen her when he left here that last time."

Leofwine uttered the obvious. "She's got to know."

"There's brilliant. Of course she must," Gyrth growled. "Harold? You're the oldest. It's your place."

"Me?" He shook his head vaguely. My heart went out to him. No one else had been so close to Swegn, loved him so much, damned him so deeply at the end, or felt such phantom pain as soldiers claim from a limb long amputated. And yet men can be so helpless at times. I found myself lifting the letters from Godwine's unprotesting hand. "I will tell them. Perhaps it will be best."

And kindest. As among men, there are things women can share without words. I chose my time when they were alone, embroidering new bed linens in the solar of the smaller hall. I read the letters to them. Gytha set her needle in the frame and read the messages herself, passing them to Agatha. As I stood there faintly shamed, knowing I'd lost nothing unrecovered, I saw Agatha shrink and die a little. She covered her face. A muffled sound escaped from behind her hands.

The wood fire hissed and crackled. Gytha handed me the letters, rose, and moved to the firepit. As I watched, her shoulders began to heave with what she would not show us. She lifted the thin gold circlet that secured her veil, and bared her head. When Harold and I were first together at Bosham, she indulged the dear vanity of hiding her grey with expensive mixtures from Egypt. After my Godwine's birth, she let me help her at the process, laughing at the folly of old women who deny besieging age until it storms their failing defenses for good. The grey showed clear now and would henceforth. Gytha stared at the veil in her hands. "I must send to Chichester, Agatha. We have no black cloth."

The stairboards groaned under a leaden tred rising from the hall. Godwine swayed at the top, breath laboring. "Ladies. You have heard then."

"I will ask a requiem mass at Trinity after vespers," Gytha declared in a tightly controlled voice. "I suppose you'll decline, but our sons will be kind enough to join me."

They exchanged wordless understanding. Pride there had always been between them, but so mellowed with wit that I'd always found their company the most delightful in England. But something hurt too much today. The veil twisted and wadded in Gytha's fingers as the words burst from her in a rush of forced lightness. "My lord has ever doubted Church authority, Agatha, both here and in heaven. He finds it difficult to believe that men like Champart bear Keys to the Kingdom when he would not trust them with a parish poor box."

Though pale, Agatha gallantly supported her. "No— was my lord so blasphemous?"

"Convicted out of my own mouth." Godwine moved heavily to join his wife. "Let us all go to church today."

Gytha kissed him on the cheek lingeringly. "You make me glad. The priest will be astonished."

"If not he, certainly God. But today I want to."

The word went out to the steadings round by messenger and the tolling of Trinity bell. Our little church, its flagstones worn from four hundred years of feet and faith, was crowded from chancel to doors. Behind the family stood Manni and the hall servants, Botulf, Godwine's carls, and as many of the cottagers, craftsmen, free and half-free folk as could travel by foot or cart in time. I stood between Harold and Gyrth, just behind the old earl and his countess. Their hands brushed together through the opening ritual and responses.

Domine Jesu Christe, Rex Gloriae—

Lord Jesus, King of Glory, deliver the souls of the dead . . .

Let not Tartarus swallow them, nor let them fall into darkness.

No, spare Swegn that. If not worthy of heaven he knew, like Lucifer, what it was to fall so far.

As the priest intoned the requiem in his nasal Sussex accent that grated on my west-country ear, Godwine's fingers found and laced with Gytha's and remained so until the service was done. I felt a rush of pity for them, anger and dark pride. Whatever else, we are survivors.

Have you learned that since Hastings, William? Did you, Edward, before you died delirious, babbling of a holy vision? Or you, Eadgytha, welcoming the Conqueror to London, and men like Aelred already bundling arrows to resist him in the north? As Gyrth said of his old Wilton mule, you can hurt us but we are very hard to kill.

Excommunicate, barred from the requiem mass at Trinity, Agatha prayed alone in Gytha's private chapel. No word ever came from her family at Leominster; they had disowned her completely. Beside the rest of us with our children and futures to get on with, Agatha was a desolate rock in a rushing stream. Concentrating on the widow's hurts to forget her own, Gytha insisted that some permanent provision should be made for Agatha, regardless of her status. Living on charity (though we took pains to minimize the fact) was additional gall to her loss. She had already brushed aside the possibility of another marriage, and began to stitch the widow's weeds she would wear to the end of her life.

Godwine and Harold readily agreed to land and a living for Agatha out of Champart's property divided among them and the queen. It was my lamentable suggestion that Eadgytha might contribute as well. Surely her year of deprivation would make her sensitive to the same in another woman. Harold and I sent her a jointly signed letter. Eada's reply was cool charity further chilled with the royal *we*:

We now bend our efforts and purse to the enlargement of Wilton for the glory of God. As our late brother was an affront to honor, so the former abbess to God and Christ. But we have well considered her plight as being near to ours in recent days, and grieve for her losses. For competence, therefore, we grant her five pounds silver per annum for life and a place as lay penitent at Wilton that she might in time be received again into Holy Church.

Harold handed me the letter. "What a gift of warmth my sister has."

"Pence and penitence." After all she suffered herself, Eada's humanity was still selective. "Five pounds and spittle in her face. No need for Agatha to see such a letter."

"She should know the queen's offer and decide for herself. You'll know what to say," Harold decided, laying the matter squarely to my trusted tact.

"Will I? I say we forget Eada altogether in this."

"Can we speak for Agatha? Do we know what she wants? Tell her."

Gytha had given Agatha a serviceable bower of her own apart from the hall, standing empty since its occupants deserted during the Normans' stay. I found her poking up the firepit vigorously, a broom in her other hand. Servants were Agatha's one difficulty at Bosham. They never got anything washed or swept to her satisfaction.

"Agatha, the earls have offered you an ample living, and the queen . . . has made an offer to help." Already I wished I'd trusted instinct and never mentioned Eadgytha. In my faltering silence, Agatha took up the mourning weeds she'd cut when black cloth came from Chichester. She sat down, spreading the garment over her lap, ready for the needle.

"Eadgytha? I heard she declared Swegn dead when we married. What does she say?"

"A living at Wilton and five pounds a year."

Agatha's needle plied steadily through the material, working a cross on the bosom in black samite thread. "How did she express herself? I would read her letter."

Lord, no. "Harold says you needn't accept; in fact I don't think you should. There's ample elsewhere, and surely you've had enough of nuns and cloisters."

She was not to be put off, a steely note in her tone. "If the queen sent word touching me, I would read it."

"No need, dear. Just her offer."

"*E*-dith." She held out her hand as if she were still an abbess and I an errant novice with her pet frog discovered. "You lie no better than Swegn. The letter please, if you have it."

I surrendered the letter from my chemise case, trying to soften its insult beforehand. "You know Eadgytha, always judgmental, and with what she's been through . . ."

Agatha read the letter through perhaps twice, standing in the middle of the room. She returned it silently but her eyes smoldered. Suddenly she seized the single lighted candle and thrust it high into a shadowed corner. "Those slovenly chamberwomen. They never see cobwebs or else they ignore them."

While I held the light, Agatha's broom brought Apocalypse to the house spiders, attacking the corner with violent strokes and shaking the remains from the broom head into the firepit. She hurled the broom away and snatched up her sewing. The needle jabbed swiftly into the material, through and out and through again.

"Five pounds for a lay penitent, is it?"

"You would read it. Refuse her."

"Oh, I will. I will. Her contempt is nothing beside mine. I'm a farm woman. We don't have much use for stock that can't breed. Go into the pot, they do. And that's our pious Lady of England, the barren bitch.'' Agatha bit off the thread end. "Hand me the other spool there. My father was poor. I wasn't much of a prize with no dowry, so it was the abbey, our holy dustbin for unwanted women. Don't deny that's what it is. I had no calling but a good head for figures. Five pounds a year is just over thruppence a day. A servant's pittance and a life on my knees, that's what she'd give me? Three pennies for the years and the pain and—oh!''

She sucked at her fingertip. "Pricked myself. No matter, put another log on the fire, there's a dear.''

I fed the fire and lighted an extra candle end. "We've at least had a life, you and I. Eada's has not been easy. I would call it pathetic. I've seen the woman with her pride down. She doesn't have much else.''

"Blessings and curses," said Agatha. "My life has been like the tale of the bride abducted by a handsome rogue on her way to wed a powerful lord and overjoyed in the outrage. I knew what I wanted, Edith. I put my mark on Swegn and he answered me. That pays for a deal of masses.''

Yes, in its own coin.

"When he was wild, he was a horse that wouldn't take bridle or bit, but never with me. With me, Swegn was gentle. He was a man who could let me know he needed me. So needy. We used to lie together for hours. Until the bad times came and the running, when we were just hunted and looking for a hole or a hope to hide in. God's mercy, Edith—''

Her head snapped back. "What am I to do? What is *left* of me?''

For a moment frozen in that despair, eyes squeezed shut. Then the farm woman who chose a man over Christ for husband rose and, with farm thrift, snuffed one of the candles. "I always hate dipping new ones, and I'll not waste. You will be answering the queen?''

"Today, yes.''

"Then say from—'' Agatha broke off to leap up again, flailing her vengeful broom against any remaining cobwebs in the high corner. "Say that the former abbess of Leominster must decline her queen's generosity with thanks. Say she blesses the queen and wishes her the bounty of happiness."

Agatha swung around to me for emphasis, a plain woman but one whose face and body bore the sure stamp of one who at least had known love. "Even as I have been blessed. Write that, Edith: As I have been blessed and with equal riches."

Oh, trust me, I did—respectful, stinging word for word. We settled Agatha on the holding of a thane at Fishbourne where she rediscovered the pleasure of working with good earth on her hands. Through Stigand she was eventually received back into the Church, and how she stood with Christ was a private matter.

But someday, God knew when or how, we had to get Hakon and Wulfnoth home.

43 • Tostig

Royal Palace, London, September 1052

My father would not live long, not a happy truth but one must be practical. Harold would have Wessex—and I, with Count Baldwin's daughter to wife, was next in line. Anglia should go to me—for a start, that is, a vantage hill from which to survey larger and greener fields. All assuming Godwine was cleared of his alleged crimes this day, but little fear he would not. A fresh wind blew over England, and what four years past was an undercurrent of sharpening resentment against Edward's Norman coterie now blew the sentiments of our countrymen toward the House of Wessex. Edward's handing of Wulfnoth and Hakon to William had effect far beyond our family. A number of highborn boys residing at court were hastily summoned home before they too became political currency.

The Witan bent with this wind. Within two weeks of our triumphal return amid the (expensive) enthusiasm of London, they gathered in extraordinary session at City in full and solemn panoply, sweeping with their trains up Aldermansbury Street to the palace, the clergy alone a pageant. Stigand, Cynesige, archbishop of York, Ealdred of Worcester. Then the earls Leofric and Siward, Odda—who would surely hate relinquishing rich Wessex—and Aelfgar, who would be as reluctant to part with Anglia. Ralf of Mantes arrived, refreshingly muted. With all of these came their functionaries, the most significant gathering in years. The very air was thick with portent and *gravitas*. The principals alone packed the palace hall, which was crowded by midmorning, a storm of voices echoing from the ancient stone walls. Esgar, the king's steward, bustled here and there, greeting the archbishops, suggesting places for the earls in order of precedence, darting to the tables where clerks were already scribbling or cutting quills and setting out inkpots. Our family was directed to stand apart to the left of the royal dais on which both chairs had been set today. Eadgytha would preside in state with Edward. Her unconditional restoration had been our first demand; our own we would try today. Interesting and perhaps a harbinger of better climate that many of those who took pains to distance themselves from our house a year earlier now gave us friendly nods here and there.

As I gazed round at the finery displayed by even common thanes and carls, I was embarrassed by our own disreputable clothing. After paying our mercenaries we were out at purse for the time. I would have begged a few shillings for a new gown, but Godwine wouldn't hear of it.

"Absolutely not. We must look shabby and worn today."

Humble but heroic. Humble always came hard to me, but I could see Father's drift. Our travel-worn garments would be sincere contrast to the opulence around us. We must look to this gathering like returned prodigals for whom, we hoped, England would kill the fatted indictment. Barring naysayers like Odda, Aelfgar, and possibly Ralf of Mantes, our former place seemed ours for the asking—in which supplication, none wilier than my father, who played on his peers that day like an inspired harper.

"His Majesty Edward, King of the English. And Her Serene Majesty Eadgytha, Lady of England."

Bearing the royal scepter, Regenbald swept through our bowing ranks. He was followed by Edward's standard, the cross of gold on a white field with two doves above the left and right arms. Then came a page bearing cushions for the state chairs. Eadgytha glided forward on Edward's arm in her favorite pale blue and white. My sister had grown thinner in exile; the sculpted cheeks were now tight and drawn. As Edward handed her to her rightful place, there was hearty applause and a drumming of dagger blades on carls' shields.

"Lay and ecclesiastical lords of England," Regenbald intoned. "Give ear now in the matter of Godwine Wulf-nothsson, accused of conspiring against the life of our royal lord, and of high treason against his rightful sovereign. Wherein Harold Godwinesson likewise stands accused."

Not to mention the rest of us. Godwine stood forth when called, supported by Harold. He staggered and might have fallen but my brother caught him. Strange; failing though he was, this had been one of Father's better mornings, his mind clear and sharp. But as the trial wore on I saw that Father was maximizing his infirmity, playing to English sympathy, an old man in clothes that might have poorly graced a cheapman, with no strength but that of his heart to sustain him. Indeed, the sight of him would have wrung my own heart had I not known where illness interwove with artifice. Shameless but effective, he made the masterful most of it for his audience.

He spoke slowly at first, as if each word were effort. "My liege and lords of the Witan, I would face my accuser."

A swell of sour laughter echoed through the hall as

Stigand stepped forward to speak. "The charge of conspiracy was brought by the former prelate of Canterbury who has quit England, and in such haste that he left the blessed pallium behind."

More laughter and louder now. I searched Eadgytha for reaction. She was impassive. King Edward merely brooded over the hall with an air of detachment, even disinterest in the whole proceeding. He and my sister seemed oblivious to each other, exchanging no word or glance. They might have been carved there.

"My accuser not present," Godwine challenged, "what lord here sustains the charge?"

Of conspiracy, that base falsehood festered out of Champart's personal malice and the king's credulity? Not one man spoke up, not even Earl Ralf, one of the few Normans still in power. Allegation abandoned, the charge was set aside, canceled with a neat stroke of the clerks' quills.

The charge of treason, however, involving the whole issue of Dover, was far graver. Regenbald read the specifications, supported by the earls Odda and Aelfgar, though I noted how Leofric frowned at his son's assertion. To his credit Earl Ralf abstained from adding his voice. As for Edward, the tide ran against him. He knew that much the night we strode into this hall with English and mercenaries at our back and all London shouting for Godwine at the gates, some paid but many of them—we flattered ourselves—in sincerity. So goes the whoring world. When I came to power and, with my sister, became *the* voice in this august council, there would be no ambivalent loyalties, simply those for Tostig or those gone.

Decending to the clerks' benches, Regenbald read in detail the grounds for the charge—yet to my mind the whole affair had the overtones of bored rote procedure, merely going through the motions. The only item with any teeth was that of Porlock and Wight. Sheppey was simply a matter of assessed damages which Regenbald, at royal pleasure, set aside. The matter of the blacksmith was not mentioned. I suspect Eadgytha had a hand in that.

When the time came for Godwine to speak in defense,

he faltered visibly, letting his voice sink at times to a reedy whisper. Offered a chair, he refused it as he summed his case.

"What Englishman here will say my action was more than their own wish regarding Dover? Was it England I resisted? Never that, but the illness battened on her from without. When I called the men of Wessex to me, I did so by law and my right—aye, and let them go without let when my king commanded their service, though few went willingly. The ill is gone, nor would I take the scourge to those Normans who have not plundered our country but served her faithfully, if with some difficulty in translation, like my lord Ralf."

That wrung a chuckle from many, even Ralf himself. Very good, Father. You have most of them on your side now. Our sister marks you, but Edward, forefinger tapping on the chair arm, reminds me of one impatient for his supper or urgently needing the latrine. What ails you, Edward? You used to be so energetically adverse.

"Since Canute invested me," Godwine said on, "I have been called many things, few of them flattering. A pawn of Denmark, seeker after more power, plotter against my king's life, even a murderer. My son Harold has been labeled *patriot* in such manner as one might cry *leper!* at the unclean.

"Well, what can I tell you? For a man born low but lucky, I *was* an opportunist, greedy as any young man who hungers for power as for a fair girl, out of lust, only to find as time passed, that there is far more in her to love than to covet."

From far back in the hall, Odda challenged: "What of Wight, Godwine? What of Porlock?"

"For Wight, for Porlock, they left us no resort but to commit the lesser crime in order to clear us today of the greater. When you are right, you cannot ration commitment or do the half thing. You must take the full risk."

"Yes!"

It was Earl Leofric of Mercia who spoke. A few men turned toward him. He said no more, but I remembered the story of Coventry, which surely taught a younger Leofric a lesson in full commitment. His countess, Godifigu, had pleaded with him to lift a heavy tax he had levied on the folk of Coventry. He replied scornfully that he would lift the tax when Godifigu rode naked one end of the town to the other. His wife did, as is known throughout England. There was commitment of a sterling cast. Never do anything by halves when all is in the balance.

"Odda need not hurl those names hard to make them stick," Godwine admitted. "Harold and I will remember them."

At his side, Harold said only, "By God, amen."

"The foreign ill is gone from us. Dover stands below her cliffs yet loyal to our king. And if to be a patriot is to be leprous, then I will take up the bell with Harold and proudly cry *unclean!* Seven days out of the week!"

Could any doubt the verdict? The tide against Normans ran so high through that assembly one could feel it like rushing water against a hand. The Witan voted overwhelmingly: full acquittal and restoration for Godwine and Harold, pardon for the rest of us. Edward gave each the kiss of peace like a man drinking vinegar. Odda and Aelfgar must seek elsewhere for livings that year. When Eadgytha rose to embrace us one by one amid a storm of cheering, I knew we'd come home at last. As her cool cheek brushed mine, she whispered, "After dinner. My chamber."

Along with the rights restored to Eadgytha were her waiting women who, like Clothilde, were all wellborn but superfluous Norman daughters otherwise doomed to a convent or inferior marriages. Clothilde was more fortunate in time. A favorite of Eadgytha, she would be profitably matched within the year by the queen herself. She greeted me like an old friend and ushered me into the privy chamber. She put a fresh peat turf on the brazier and withdrew. Though the day was bright, hinting of the first cool of autumn, the windows were closed. Eadgytha preferred dim light and fragrant peat to the rank smell of London and Thames.

"Lady." I bent my knee, then sprang up as her arms opened to receive me. "Sister, we've won."

But this close I understood the dim and kinder light. Her delicate blond beauty showed more than a few marks of harrowing time.

"Come sit at my feet as you used to," she invited. "Fetch me those cushions, I'm stiff from that cruel council chair."

When I settled at her knee she buried her fingers in my hair. "A hard road and a long one, Tostig, but we are home."

"Not all of us."

"Wulfnoth, yes. Intolerable. I have demanded, I've pleaded with Edward and, though he forbade me, wrote directly to William. For all the good that did. Had I been here I could have argued Edward out of it," Eadgytha asserted with some of her old confidence. "Or bullied him out. As it is . . . nothing."

"It's broken Mother's heart."

"Gytha is a loving woman. Even worries over that pathetic Agatha and her get."

"William's the bastard to worry us now." Cunning, infuriating Edward who alienated men even as he won others with ambiguous promises. "All worthless if you bear a son. We all pray for that."

"Can I pray that man into my bed?"

Her sharp candor surprised me. I'd long suspected as much but Eadgytha never spoke of it until now. "I see."

"There will be no heir, Tostig." If she felt regret, it was dry as dead leaves. "You are my hope now. My life."

I wished to speak of that. "Judith will be crossing soon. I must have a suitable household and prospects. Can I hope for Anglia after Harold?"

"Not Anglia, I'm sorry. Not just now."

I sat up and demanded flatly: "Why not?"

"Be patient. Edward will not antagonize Leofric by passing over his son. He must keep a balance between north and south. Anglia goes back to Aelfgar when Harold is invested."

"Little Aelfy: bouncing back and forth like a ball. You know he's a fool."

"Possibly a dangerous one," Eadgytha agreed. "Edward was forced to pardon Godwine, but he won't retreat on this. Anyway, Anglia is too obscure for your gifts.''

Save for livings and revenues I desperately needed. ''Am I to have nothing then? *I* was the one who pulled the chestnuts out of the fire at Dover and got paid out with a year of exile.''

''Oh, stop. Don't play the martyr.'' Eadgytha pushed me away and rose. ''Your exile was Babylonian beside mine. And Judith of Flanders is hardly an affliction.''

''A noble wife and an empty purse.'' The words came bitter as the gall behind them. ''What are we to have? How are we to live?''

In that much Eadgytha assured me she had provided. We were to live at court in her household for the time. Not good enough by half, I thought. Not enough for all the sweating miles, the year torn out of my life. ''I am tired of being a pensioner!''

''I said be patient, Brother. The word about court in my absence was that Aelfgar made a shambles of his charge in Anglia. A dunce, but an ambitious one. He'll be looking elsewhere and higher soon enough. Unless,'' she stressed, ''he is proven unworthy.''

Her head canted just so then, my sister's resemblance to Godwine was indeed striking. ''Fools are easy to trap,'' she said.

That held a spark of interest. ''How easy?''

''If Aelfgar were afforded enough rope, he would surely fashion his own noose and put his head in it.''

''And?''

''If you proved yourself worthy through exemplary service to Edward.''

''Interesting. Something in mind?''

''For Aelfgar? When the time comes, but see here.'' Eadgytha beckoned me to her writing table. Only just returned and already the table was piled with new business directed to her capable hands. The parchments she spread before me bore as many figures as writing, and the seals of Edward's provincial mints.

''Edward has always left certain offices to me, particularly the mints. He and the council decide policy, but I oversee practice. No one has freer access to fine silver than a minter. Consider the temptations for such a man.''

The amounts of silver represented on the schedules bore that out. "Like a fishmonger's cat. You're not suggesting theft as an avocation?''

"Oh, you.'' She cuffed me affectionately. "If the queen's loyal brother detected felony in such a place, he would quickly come to Edward's approving attention and as quickly rise. From today you have this post in my service.''

Eadgytha awarded me the accolade of a kiss on the cheek. "Study these schedules, learn these values and how and when they shift. The worth of the penny year to year is a complicated business.''

Complicated and quite vulnerable to greed. Over time, a bit here and another there, a man could accumulate quite a hoard of fine silver. "Do you suspect any of the minters?''

"Who knows? I am just returned and have no idea what might have gone slack in my absence. And the absence of proof is not in itself an absence of guilt.'' She tucked the schedules under my arm. "Who can say how honest the minters remained in that time? Or what an honest man with a sharp eye might find. You have always been diligent.''

"And avarice is one of the Seven Deadlies.'' I well understood her. God bless Eadgytha, ever the fixed pole among my guiding stars.

We expect death for a parent but are never ready for the blow when it falls. At Winchester, on Easter Monday, Godwine suffered a seizure and fell down like the very dead in front of Edward, who hardly appeared distressed. I was the first to reach Father. His lips were still moving. I and my brothers carried him to bed where he lingered three days unable to utter a sound, though his eyes were alive as ever. He never spoke again.

Never had he said he loved me, when there was no man's love and respect I craved more. Never shaped his lips to the one word that, given long ago, might have turned me one way instead of another.

Then I shall have to go without. Speak of exile, Eadgytha?

44 • Godwine

Winchester Palace, 15 April 1053

See my family about me, but I am where? Can't talk. Can't damn it all even think. Much. Edward's bedchamber. Surprisingly decent of him. If Eadgytha more . . . had spent more time here, Gytha and I might have royal grandchildren now.

What was I thinking? Hard to think, like groping through fog just to find words. There's a joke. Quickest mind in England now the slowest. God relieving me of excess vanities? Can't talk but *must* think. See each face over me, find a name to go with it. Harold. Gytha. Love you, Gytha . . .

What was I thinking? Faces.

Who is that in the corner? Shabby little man. Think Edward would turn out his servants better. Looks the sort who empties chamber pots.

How long have I been here? I would like to ask how long, but is something something is very wrong. Can't move or make a sound. Something missing between question and tongue. *Think.*

Better. Clearer.

Monday it was, at Easter court. Meant to be a show of peace and reunion. All our ladies present, even Agatha. Edith with child again and radiant. I asked her, if a son, would they honor Edward as the boy's namesake?

"No, we will not."

No mystery why. Edith's duty as subject need not include any gratitude.

The banquet went well. First time in years I had a sense of England as one whole and we part of her again. Then Edward suddenly lashed out at me with the old accusation about Alfred. Embarrassing all around, boring and in bad taste. The general feeling was, must he rake over all that now? Eadgytha tried to remonstrate, but Edward cut her off sharply. The malice is still there, part of the man, but toothless now, like the worn-down complaints of a whining wife. So much Edward could never rise above.

"Does my lord of Wessex deny it still?"

I hadn't felt well all day. Difficult to walk, worse to breathe. I wanted heartily to ignore Edward, but all were listening. I rose from the table—tried, but I seemed suddenly to weigh twice as much with no sense of balance. Then Gytha was up beside me, tremulous with concern. "Husband?"

I opened my mouth; my tongue moved in it like an ox mired in mud. "My lord . . . my lord, if I—"

Then nothing until I became aware of the passage arch passing slowly by my head. Being carried. My sons bore me to this room. That was two . . . three days gone? Been ill before, in narrow corners many times, but I will will I escape this one?

Very odd, that dismal little man in the corner. No one pays him any heed. Someone who fetches for the king's physicians? Were I given to petty irritations, I could resent the way he stares at me, grimy cap in hand, as if about to beg alms.

Harold bends over me. "Father, can you hear me? The king will come presently."

To gloat, no doubt.

Harold? Where did you go? All gone . . . no. Edith, Agatha, and Tostig's Judith are by me, sedate and sad, so like the old Welsh *tableau*, the solemn weird women grouped about dying Arthur, that I'm prompted to laugh. It emerges a dry gurgle. They must think I'm going west. Not yet, children.

As Baldwin's daughter, Judith has precedence over the other two. To her credit, the fact does not seem to impress her. "My father will mourn his friend," she promises. "And perpetual prayers will be offered for my lord in Bruges's chantries."

Decent of Baldwin, but . . .

Must have dozed. My hand is in Agatha's. "My lord, I will ever pray for you."

Why are you all so ready to pack me off? I won't be hurried out like an overstayed guest.

"And I will always remember your kindness," she vows.

Thanks, woman. Had you reached for your psalter rather than Swegn—well, that's spilt virtue now.

Dear Edith. You're a woman now, carrying another child. I can see in your eyes strength and vulnerability, all you've lived, as I can in Harold's. He was such an ordinary boy, following after Swegn, drinking and whoring. The business of that Welsh girl changed him. Guilt must have been as much a novelty as his first breath, then you came into his life like light into a dark room. He wasn't important when you fell in love. Now, like a child strayed in the path of galloping horses, history may run straight over him. Facts are rarely kind. You may lose him, Edith. What? Speak up. Bend close.

Edith whispers close to my ear. "You've been as much father to me as Teinfrith." Her lips touch my cheek. "Pardon my presumption, but God bless you, Da."

Bless you, too, but I fully intend to recov—

I've drifted off again. Something very *wrong* here. Gyrth and Leofwine hovering by me now. I wish Wulfnoth were with you. Small blessings, but we had years together at Bosham. I had the time to watch you grow into men. Take my hand, Gyrth. Try to understand you must be Peter to Harold, his rock. Leofwine, you look more like Swegn each year. He was all passion. Balance that with a mind, boy, and be there when Harold needs you.

Boys? Where did you go? Have I slept again?

Tostig, is that you? Beautifully barbered and turned out

as usual. I'm impressed. Considering the occasion, you needn't have bothered.

He sits on the side of the bed and his hand on mine is, alas, warmer than his manner, as always. Something missing in you, boy, or perhaps one dark humor too many. Swegn was a tragedy easily read, you a quandary. You should have less believed your fond sister and her foolish astrologer, while I should have taken a stick to you more often.

"I forgive you, Father."

Passing handsome of you. For what?

"Now at last I can tell you without fear you'll just turn me away with a stinging joke. I could never believe you loved me."

Not true. We loved all of you, but how could I grasp what I never understood? My wisdom's not cosmic; I'm plain human, boy. With a simpler nature I might have loved you as a matter of blind faith like utter belief in Genesis or the Resurrection. You were a puzzle as a boy. I could never find the way in, the key, though your sister must have. I admired you for Dover, but at Sheppey you frightened me. A fine spirit but too brittle to hold a lasting edge. What do you want that denies the best in you?

. . . I thinking? Where did that rather tidy thought go? Yes. Good's gone to your head, Tostig. The man too convinced of his own righteousness is a hunter who becomes his own quarry. Doubt yourself now and then; the hesitation will become you, and wiser heads like Harold will always ask for your warrant from God.

Tostig? Where did you go?

Eadgytha, I was with Tostig? Where did he go? Yes, Gytha, I'm glad you're here. Hold me wife. Wish God my—now that's *enough*. Think clearly or not at all. God, I wish I could will my tongue to sound and sense. Eadgytha, forgive me. I married you high but not happily. Seemed a brilliant stroke at the time. Yes, I know. Dynasties are clumsy and inconvenient, but as long as men maintain the absurdity that kings are God-inspired, they're all we have to work with. Our dynasty might have been clean, fresh air to blow the dust from scepter and crown. What will you do now, daughter? What will you become?

. . . slipped away again. Gytha, what a joy you've been. My lover and my friend. Rare alchemy that transformed the peasant lead of me into gold.

With enormous will and effort I can move my hand and let Gytha feel the pressure on her fingers. Oh, I loved you—and what a game it's been! Not worth the candle without you. Remember the day Canute presented me to you? You said afterward I'd overdressed and worked too hard at being agreeable. Guilty, but then I was what Edward's thought me always, jumped up and dangerously ambitious, but I met my match in you. You were easily wed, not easily won, and you kept me human. Kiss me, darling. Give me a kiss and a smile and once more the silver bell of your laugh to share between us. I'm beginning to think this a corner I can't talk myself out of. So tired. Ought to close my eyes for a wink or two . . .

Where did you go? Don't leave me, love. Thought I could will this away, but now I know there's not that much time.

Harold leaning over me now—and that *eternal* little peasant staring at me from his corner. They ought to charge him rent, he's been here that long.

Harold, listen to me. Christ, of all the times to be speechless. I've seen you grow from insignificance to a hope. You will be power now, whether you will or no. Pure banality to say power corrupts; of course it does. Only an imbecile or an Edward would say it ennobles. If you didn't sleep well after Porlock, neither did I, but now you know the truth of power, be it grimed or noble. Power as a means is a living thing that grows to purpose. As an end it stops growing and decays. You know the truth of kings now, not chosen by God but bumbling accidents of birth. Some are fine, some squalid, most ordinary like Edward. Save for scepters and samite, ermine and miniver, I've found the same men behind ploughs and market stalls.

Times change, Harold. Men and imperatives change. Remember what I taught you. God, why isn't there more time? There must ever be some enduring check on kings. Whenever Edward wants something, wrest value in return.

"I've always loved you, Father," Harold tells me. "I wouldn't have sworn it during the troubles last year, but now the people love you as deeply."

Listen, boy! I'm trying to tell—to *will* something into you if I must. In bad years when Edward needs money, and he will, that's the time to see what's needed and bargain for it. Every concession granted, every popular precedent for your folk broadens the base of the Witan's check on him. Never let him be absolute in fact, he or any who come after him. Remember the night in my study when you first took interest in the great map? Remember what I told you? Not the earls, they're only the top of the tree. Listen as well to the farmer thanes, the sokemen and carls, those plain men sitting in the shire and hundred courts, smelling of mud and manure while they respectfully but doggedly request justice of their lords. Know this common man, but *don't* sentimentalize him. Noble he can be but maddeningly stupid and treacherous at times, deserting you just when you need his support. Lately I've acquired a reputation for loving him. Actually more of a qualified affection, benevolence at arm's length. As for Edward, when you think that sainted son of Aethelrede is wrong, respectfully tell him so. He's changed since last year, not so sure of his divine mandate. Raised the scepter like God ordering the Flood and nothing happened. England said no. Think of that. Could that happen in Normandy?

"Edith will bear her child in October," Harold is saying. "Another autumn baby. I think I know what's to be done, what you'd want me to do, but I hope you will be there to show me. To help. Part of me wants what I have to be, part just wants to go home. I see some things clearly now. Swegn wasn't the one, never him. And Tostig? Once I told him I wished he'd been born in my place, but better me than him. It's a lot to carry, and I must say you lazing about in that bed for three days doesn't help at all."

That's the way, son, and thank you. You'd better know already what the expiring lump of me hasn't a prayer of teaching you now. For our lost boys, well, hostages are the way of things, hurt as they will, but Edward's promise to William has left the door open to foreign rule again. Damn the man, he's living two hundred years ago. Trying to be Charlemagne when union with the Church was the only way to unify Europe against the Moors. He does not and never will see any boundary under God between us and Normandy. You must not allow William to claim our crown. Steal the damned thing, hide it on some mountain until the Witan finds one of our own to suit, wear it yourself if you must. William on our throne will be a rent in the fabric of *Angel-Cynn* none of you will live long enough to repair.

Someone's come in. Can't move my head. Who?

Ah, Edward. Just speaking of you and other disasters.

Harold bows to the king, takes my hand once more and each of us tries, across incoherence, to read the other's heart. I search his face for understanding: Will he let Edward hand our country to a foreign duke merely by accident of kinship? I think not. I hope not. Frustrating not to know, never to know. Do we all go this way, so unfinished?

Harold kisses my forehead. "I'll just be outside."

Edward gazes down at me, and of course that hangdog lackey in the corner stares and stares. Who *is* he? I thank my lord for the loan of the royal bed, but is that churl set to watch lest I steal your money box beneath?

"Well, my lord earl. Stigand cautioned me not to tax you long. I hope you are comfortable."

He means it. How unlike Edward. He's changed since last year. So distant now, the bite and malice muted.

"They say the best revenge on enemies is to outlive them. Oddly enough that's small consolation, as if some succubus sat upon my chest in sleep and sucked the spleen from me. I hated you for Alfred. I forgive you that, Godwine."

I'll try to forgive you Wulfnoth, but not soon.

Edward leans closer over me. "What are you thinking in there, old man?"

Perhaps that in the end we could have done more together than against. Now, will he, nil he, it's up to Harold.

"Perhaps it is the long habit of suspicion, but I can't dismiss the notion that you're still scheming. No need, Godwine. I've done. I've quit."

Now what are you up to?

"Done, finished. Let things go as they will. I want only to build my edifice to God."

Edward sits on the side of the bed, shoulders hunched forward, not looking at me but through the walls toward his beloved eternity. "In a way you have won. You are restored, and Eadgytha, we are reconciled. Well . . . resigned at least. Friends of a sort. Oh, Godwine, Godwine! Kingship would have been so much simpler without you. Getting old myself, that close to fifty, and this impious, impossible land will not stand still long enough for me to get a grip on it. I have no answers. Perhaps I'm not that strong after all. But it's restful at last, like a great letting go. At least there's Westminster. I can build my abbey."

Yes, do that. But you won't build a nation on holiness any more than you'll sink bridge pilings into cloud.

"If I can accomplish that alone, I'll be content," Edward sighs. "Shall I confess something to you? You surprised me with your stand on Dover. I thought: Here is the wonder of my time. With everything to lose, Godwine does something with no possible profit to himself."

None, Edward? You heard the Londoners that day. I didn't have to buy them all.

"What's this now? Godwine weeping?"

Yes. You wouldn't understand.

"But of course. You think on eternal things now. Stigand is waiting." Edward rises, once more the king. At times he even acted like one. "Take my forgiveness, give me yours. I want to build my abbey."

No pain, nothing. I'm slipping out of time like a loose leaf from a book. Didn't see Edward leave. Stigand is here, wearing the scapular for my last unction. Wine and wafer for the lips I can't open to receive them. Doesn't look to be any middle way out this time.

Yes, old friend. I'm very glad you came.

"My lord," Stigand directs. "Blink your eyes twice if you can hear me. Good. I'm going to give you absolution.'' He winks with his old wry wit. ''In your difficult case, insofar as Canterbury can.''

He presses the crucifix to my lips. Raging hypocrisy for me to receive unction, I suppose, but at the moment I need all the reinforcements I can muster.

''I have loved you ever,'' Stigand murmurs over me. ''Thank God you came back. May the Lord be with you hereafter. I know England will be. That's a fair character for a servant to show a new master.''

I loved England, too, the unmanageable bitch.

''All the same,'' Stigand considers. ''Touching the hereafter and glib as you are, it might be wise for you to say as little as possible.''

He busies himself with crumbling the wafer, readying the wine. But now the little man emerges from the shadows to stand at the foot of my last bed, twisting the shapeless cap in his hands, for all the world like the sort a landlord sends to evict delinquent tenants. Hurry, Stigand.

Then again, no haste at all. All clear now, though He *might* have sent someone a bit more celestial.

The wafer crumbs are dry on my lips, then sweetly moistened with wine. God be with you, too, Stigand.

What, lackey? Yes, quite ready. Only their tears to come, and I'd rather avoid that. Shall we go?

45 • Edith

We were barely settled at dear Nazeing when Godwine died and Harold's importance trebled. Our return was memorable only for two meetings, one with the royal staller who evicted me so rudely.

He'd stayed on to steward the estate for Aelfgar, and I would take indecent satisfaction in reclaiming it.

With the boys and in a sturdy wagon proudly driven by Botulf, Harold rode up to the gates at the head of a dozen Wessex carls. Later March that was, and the weather changeable, but Providence granted us a day of windy sunshine, clouds scudding overhead, light and shadow chasing on each other's heels.

No one met us at the gates. Harold twisted about in the saddle to grin at his standard bearer. "Botulf, let's be old-fashioned and sound the horn."

"To it!" Botulf whooped. He bounded down from the wagon and marched to the tarnished horn hanging by the gate post. In our time the gates of Nazeing stood open all day, closed only at sunset. Even then the horn was rarely used, more tradition than function. Botulf set the horn to his lips. His first flatulent blast spewed leaf fragments from the horn's bell. The second try produced a blast that surely woke the Anglian dead. Harold roared encouragement: "Again, man! Wake them to good manners."

Rouse them Botulf did. If unmusical, he was untiring in his charge. The hall doors opened finally and a fat man bustled forth with a young girl hanging behind, peering curiously at us. She lingered in the entrance as the corpulent staller waddled to the gates and swung them open. In a year and a half he'd grown even fatter.

"Earl Harold," he puffed, short of breath. "We have expected you."

We swept past him into the grassy courtyard, hardly an impressive train. He'd evicted me with little more than the terrified children in my arms and the clothes on our backs. Knowing my husband was in flight and no courtesy needed, he gave me none. Now, with Godwine's carls at our back and his banner fluttering over the wagon, the staller was far less sure of himself. The vindictive pleasure I took in his discomfort was positively unChristian.

Harold snapped his fingers at the heavy ring hanging from the man's girdle. "The keys. Not to me, to my lady."

I thrust out a peremptory hand, received the keys, and

favored the staller with a poisonous smile. "You are dismissed. Return to your master."

"There are some few arrangements yet," he told us. "Earl Aelfgar's daughter must go with me." He indicated the girl who still eyed us warily from the hall entrance. We knew Aelfgar had sons, Edwin and Morcar, but a daughter's existence was news.

"Her name?" I asked.

"Aldyth, lady."

So I had my first glimpse of fateful Aldyth. Not more than thirteen, yet Aldyth already evinced the beginnings of what most men call desirable. As Botulf handed me down from the wagon, she came timidly to greet us, swaying with the first feminine grace that would trouble the sleep of Gruffydd ap Llywelyn before very long. The granddaughter of Leofric and Godifigu, Aldyth had the look and sound of the north, and . . . yes, I would imagine a deal of Dane in her.

"My lord." She curtseyed to us. "Lady."

"Aldyth," I returned, pleasant but pointed. "Do have a safe journey."

"Mother and my brothers are not here, but Father sent word we must go." Aldyth was not yet mature enough to hide her distress; clearly she didn't understand why they were being dispossessed, and searched Harold with huge hazel eyes for some answer. "He's ever so angry, I don't know why."

I murmured something polite, that the change was the king's will, nothing to reflect on her father. Aldyth barely noted me. I recognized her breed. Some women from childhood on will sparkle for men alone; other women will receive short shrift at their hands.

Harold bent to kiss the girl's hand. "We regret the inconvenience. Been a right tangle this year."

Aldyth stared up at him, wide-eyed. "Father says you're a rebel. Are you?"

Botulf sputtered and the staller looked even more uncomfortable, but Harold reached suddenly for the girl and lifted her to his eye level. "Only from a distance. I gather you like Nazeing."

"I love it," Aldyth confessed on a dying fall.

Harold set her down. Gravely, as to an equal, he said, "I should think you'll be back sooner than you think."

"Oh, I *do* hope so." And Aldyth skipped off, apparently satisfied with the prediction. We dismissed Botulf and the staller. Harold took my arm.

"Pretty child."

"Enchanting," I grudged.

He knew me that well and shot me a teasing glance. "She'll ornament some lord's hall."

Sorry, but I wasn't in the vein today, stiff from the wagon and out of sorts. "Yours, perhaps?"

"What? Oh come *on*, love. I'd as lief eat green pears."

No, I did not feel good at all. "Never bothered you before we were married. Nor in Ireland, I'm bound."

Harold stopped short and swung about to face me, signaling Botulf to remain with our boys. "Edith? What humor's on you today?"

I despised myself. I'd promised never to say it and could have cut my own tongue out. "Oh, I'm tired and cranky and three months' pregnant, that's what. Come, let's see what they've done to my hall."

Not a sight to lift a tidy heart. Aelfgar and his countess could not have spent much time at Nazeing. The hall had the look of casual use and infrequent cleaning. I felt desecrated. This was *my* place, the center of my life where I'd grown from girl to woman, loved a man, and borne our children. None of it easy, all uphill like staggering through the rain up the slope of Blackmore Vale, one babe in my arms and the other hanging from a numbed hand. For all that hardship, all the bitter months; for the relief of being home at last and together again; for a future uncertain as the past, I passionately felt a good soul-scouring cry welling up in me. "God's *teeth*, but this sty wants a good scrub."

In the same royal hall at Winchester where I first glimpsed Harold, I watched from the women's gallery as Harold pressed his forehead to Edward's knee in fealty, received the heavy gold chain of rank about his shoulders, and became earl of Wessex. As the coronet was set upon his head, his thanes donned their own circlets and tradition carried on. My father rarely wore his. The dulled gold had to be polished for the ceremony. Aelfgar was reinvested with Anglia.

No other earls were present, but the full court turned out. Gytha and Judith were seated some way down the gallery, but I had roved forward, as I did so long ago, to look down on Edward and the queen when Harold knelt to them. Leofwine and Gyrth stood by Harold, Tostig opposite and close to Eadgytha. He peacocked outrageously in striking black with gold trim, now Justiciar Extraordinary to the queen—rather grand title, but Tostig would have it so. Mere "staller" demeaned his high birth, and of course Eada indulged him as always. Our royal mints had already flinched under his zeal.

Vivat!—applause, and the investiture ended. I made my way back through the women, wanting to be with Harold, but recognized Aelfgar's wife, Countess Inge, and thought to congratulate her, though we'd never spoken. Aldyth's mother might have bloomed once; now, two or three years my senior, Inge was already what kindness would describe as "matronly."

Perhaps my easy intimacy with England's foremost family made me forget. I bobbed a curtsey to the countess. "A good day for all of us, isn't it? I've already met your Aldyth. She loves Nazeing so."

I was hardly prepared for Inge's rebuff. Her heavy-lidded, disdainful gaze poured over me like icy water. "You are the little handfast, are you not? The one they call 'Swan's Neck'?"

Warm spring in Winchester, but still winter in her tone. I said, "Gytha calls me that sometimes in affection."

"You mean the dowager *Countess* Gytha," she corrected, putting me in my abysmal place. "She was always too kind."

She might as well have struck me across the face, but the lesson went home. To Inge and her peers I would never be Harold's wife, let alone his countess, but only the little leman from Shaftesbury. Inge herself was illiterate and insensitive but showed me clearly how unacceptable I would always be. Shocked, livid, I could only curse the woman silently.

"As for Nazeing," she directed, "you will see my steward." Preferably at the kitchen door, her manner stated. "Pray you leave my hall as you found it."

My turn, you fat sow. "Alas, Countess, I cannot. We had to clean it thoroughly. Give you good day."

I hurried to be with Harold, but couldn't see him anywhere below. The ladies were descending to the hall now. I found Gytha and Judith making their way through the milling crowd toward Leofwine and Gyrth. The huge chamber was an echoing storm of bellowed conversations. Gytha had to shout over the clamor. "Harold has gone to—"

I lost the end of it in the noise. "Where?"

Close at my ear: "With his thanes and sheriffs."

So he would, making plans for his first progress as earl to give and receive oaths of fealty, stepping into that vast gulf left by Godwine. More time for me and the boys to miss him. Would he be with me when the new child was born?

When I told Gytha of the encounter with Inge, she only wrinkled her nose dismissively. "Ach, don't give it a thought. Inge has bad digestion and a worse marriage, but she was always a bit of a bitch."

Nevertheless, there you had my life. The insignificant mistress of obscure young Anglia was tolerable if tucked away out of sight and mind, but the woman at the side of Wessex, the king's first Witan minister, was a different matter. Saving Gytha, naturally kind and born so high she needn't care, or Eadgytha in moments when even that rigid spirit must relax to humanity, the noble ladies of England never accepted me. In time, rather than suffer their prim rejection, I remained at home more and more, sometimes resenting Harold himself. But if he was away much of the year, he always returned to my arms.

Well, Teinfrith and Hildre warned me all those years ago. I wrote home to them that spring in bitterness but new hope as well:

Some of these new foreign women at court are no better than titled cows at best, whores at worst, and with no more than surface breeding. But if I am never to be noble, I may yet be a wife before God. Stigand has kindly written to the pope for a dispensation. If Rome granted the same to William and Matilda, why not Harold? The letter's gone direct this time, Stigand most eloquent and not troubling to consult with the king. . . .

46 • Harold

But Edward heard anyway through one clerkly ferret or other, and called me to account. I was traveling that autumn with the court on the perpetual royal round of London to Winchester to Gloucester where Edward would conduct Christmas court and hunt in the Forest of Dean. Meanwhile the royal machinery would grind on as usual. In the peace and goodwill of those years there were more foreign visitors than ever traveling with the court.

A royal appanage is a cumbersome thing, tedious anytime but doubly arduous when one must ride sodden through days of cold rain. Our train stretched out for half a mile—officers of the court, royal carls and thanes, stewards and butlers, cooks and bakers—and Earl Harold envying the humblest peasant warm and dry at home. As the queen's new justiciar, Tostig rode with Eadgytha, affecting a merlin hawk on his wrist, though he was never fond either of birds or the sport. Appearances were much to him. When we finally quartered at the royal residence in Gloucester, I was wet through, exhausted and foulmooded, glad to fall into bed with Botulf on a pallet by the door. I could happily have slept next morning through, but Edward sent for me soon after eight.

His chamber was warm enough from the peat fire and smelled faintly of the harhune tea Edward was sipping for a sore throat. From his chair he wheezed, "Please sit, my lord of Wessex. We missed you at mass."

I dragged a stool close to the brazier. "I slept late."

"Um." Edward frowned and swallowed some tea. "Devotions are not to be neglected, Harold. Nor Holy Church mocked."

I knew what was coming: my inherited crown of thorns. With Godwine it had been Alfred, with me my marriage, all the more unsuitable since taking my father's place.

"Need I remind you that you are the only major noble in the Witan without a proper wife?"

"We have a legal civil marriage. For anything else, it's not for want of trying."

"Yes, we heard of Stigand's letter to Rome. After—what, seven years?—doesn't it dawn on you that your present arrangement is an affront to the Church? Or that it is insupportable in one of your rank? There is constant talk, Harold."

"Sire, after seven years and three children, it should dawn on all that Edith is as much my wife as the Church and yourself will allow."

Edward choked somewhat on his tea. "Are you going to plague me like your father? All right, so much for delicacy. Forget Rome. I've written myself saying any dispensation is directly opposed to my wishes. Oh, think, man. I know how the world goes, full of mistresses with more bastards than legitimate get. But you are no longer inconsequential."

Edward stood up, necessitating the same in me when I would dearly rather sit or sleep. "Shall I arrange an advantageous match?"

"Please. No."

"Don't be too quick. There are some excellent *demoiselles* from Normandy in the queen's train. The daughter of Count Guillaume d'Arques, for example, and it is our pleasure''—I heard the subtle stress on his point—''that we strengthen our bonds with Normandy. Fine family despite her father's unstable ambitions, and the girl is, of course, *virgo intacta*.''

My attitude of alert interest was a triumph of diplomacy. Cécilie d'Arques was intact as a sieve and, from the moment we met, had assaulted my bedroom like a cavalry objective.

I broke off half a turf to replenish the fire and give myself time before answering. For no reason in a sane world would I leave Edith. In any event urgent business would delay any such plans indefinitely.

But Edward was just beginning. ''What *is* it about your family? Swegn throws away his heritage and his soul on an unholy misalliance, and you with that thane's daughter. Who's next? Gyrth? I fully expect to hear he's lost his head over some goose girl.''

To my fatigued relief, Edward seated himself again, allowing me to do so.

''Tostig now,'' he continued with much more warmth. ''Tostig has surprised me. He has learned the business of our mints in an astonishingly short time and brought to light more than one discrepancy, I warrant you. Uncovered an appalling list of felonies.''

True. One minter in York had already had his right hand cut off when unable to account to Tostig for certain amounts of silver. In the royal eye, my brother was the man of the hour.

''Edward?''

He glanced up in some surprise. For the first time I had addressed him familiarly.

''What is the real bar between Edith and myself? Consanguinity is outmoded—''

''It is God's law!''

''—and hypocritical. All it does is cause difficulty and delay and raise the papal price on dispensations that are going to be bought anyway for political reasons. William had to kiss the pope's holy arse before he could marry Matilda, but we all knew he would. Why must you oppose mine?''

"Precedent. I know such matters can be bargained, but not in my England." Edward slipped off his shoes and stretched his thin legs and stockinged feet to the brazier. "Old serpent," he muttered. "Sins of the fathers . . ."

"Sire?"

"I mean Godwine. You have his facile tongue. You were trouble at Nazeing, trouble at Tetbury, enormous trouble roaring up Thames against me with a foreign army." He wriggled his toes vigorously. "Doesn't this country ever get warm? Freezing in here."

"No, it's quite warm, sir."

"My feet are forever frozen."

"They only want a good rubbing. Let me." I was up and down again before him, briskly massaging his toes. Edward settled back with a sigh. "That feels good. Don't forget my suggestion about the d'Arques girl. You must have met her on the appanage. Her father is looking for a good match. Shouldn't wonder, he's finished himself in Normandy. Rub harder. That's better."

And that was the posture of our relationship as Edward and I both grew older. He never approved of me or my marriage but came to depend on me more and more. When something in England wanted patching, putting down, or raising up, it was always: Send Wessex.

She writhed and moaned under me and her heels pummeled my back. She was not beautiful nor really passionate but made you forget one while imitating the other to perfection. She was not noisy in love-making, a discreet blessing within the palace walls, but extremely active— under me, over me, biting and scratching like a cat in heat. With a stunning sexual proficiency, she was not a woman an undiscriminating male was likely to forget. And, alas, she was not Edith.

Edward was not only unworldly but uninformed. Cécilie d'Arques had not been *virgo intacta* for some time, certainly not when she first fluttered her long black lashes at me on the journey to Gloucester. How she protected her reputation I never knew, but black-eyed Cécilie wafted through Edward's court stainless as the mother of Christ—

for a while at least, until Eadgytha got wind of her through watchful Clothilde.

"Tell me," Cécilie whispered against my mouth, "am I not the best you ever had?"

Not beside the ever-fresh wonder of Edith, and there is something off-putting about blatant sexual vanity. One had the impression Cécilie was performing for a dazzled audience and expected applause. Certain gallantries must be rendered. I gazed down at her, still panting from exertion. *"Tu es formidable."*

"And you, my love." Cécilie pulled my mouth down to hers, exploring it inside and out. *"Je t'adore."*

My sense of the absurd has always betrayed (or saved) me at the oddest moments. Like icy water chilling a warm bath, I remembered she was not bedding me but the vast lands of Wessex. The manic image of Cécilie whacking away feverishly at the whole south of England was too much and I rolled off her, giggling. She bounced up on one elbow, perplexed and deflated. "What is it? What is wrong?"

"Rien . . . nothing, sweet. Just feeling good."

Her father, Guillaume, was that busy man who defected from William's siege of Domfront and was now besieged himself by the unforgiving duke. I had a wager with Stigand that Arques would fall before Christmas (and won this time). Capture imminent, the count sent Cécilie to England and the best marriage she could find. In pursuit of this end, she was a single-minded huntress. Her expertise impressed, and yet bedding Cécilie was like eating an egg without salt. I was momentarily filled but unsatisfied and desperately missed the reality of Edith, to whom I wrote as often as possible.

After Christmas court, the king and conditions permitting, I will come home. Good God but I miss you, my love, and only wish I could have been with you when Edmund was born. There are so many foreigners at court now that more French than English is spoken, and all of them peacocks for style and dress. Tostig is in his glory, of course, curls his beard with hot tongs and carries his merlin on a jeweled gauntlet. Ridicu-

lous, since he never got on with the creature, nor it with him, a matter of loathe at first sight, but he is the last word in fashion.

Reach across the months and miles, my darling, and wrap your heart around me, please, please? My own shivers without it. Kiss the children for me. . . .

Down the years I've wondered how, loving Edith so much, I woke up in so many casual beds. Prolonged absence from her, I suppose, simple appetite, and so many ambitious women like Cécilie so willing to invest for profit. They considered me unmarried while I never thought myself anything else. Even Stigand's chiding now and then grew to wry exasperation.

"Adultery again? Well, only fornication, strictly speaking, but when will you put your shoulder to the wheel and confess something interesting like regicide or heresy? Something a priest can sink his ecclesiastical teeth into?"

Cécilie the Insatiable was sent from England with suspicious haste to join her father at the court of Boulogne, where he'd taken refuge from William. She married some shirttail relative of Count Eustace and settled down to produce titled offspring. They say a mother is a multitude. Hilarious to think of the names and pedigrees issuing from the voracious loins of a girl of whom my most enduring memory was her squatting over a chamber pot, washing her privates with vinegar. Somehow, against that indelible image, the splendor of *noblesse* goes dim.

At any rate, Eadgytha had now heard of my involvement, and I was summoned to the Presence. I hadn't seen much of Eada or Tostig at Gloucester, though I'd repeatedly asked for an audience regarding the minters at Shaftesbury. The Crown had monopoly on mints, but the people themselves were my responsibility. Thane Teinfrith had written strongly protesting Tostig's methods. The master minter there, he maintained, had held his post for twenty years under four kings, his honesty never questioned until now. Tostig frankly worried me. Wherever he searched he rooted out some apparent malfeasance. They couldn't *all* be felons.

And Edith had borne a son I'd not yet laid eyes on. God, I wanted to go home.

47 • Harold

When Clothilde ushered me in, Eadgytha and Tostig were just rising from prayer at the priedieu. My brother's hooded merlin brooded and muttered to herself on a perch in one corner. In addition to the usual scatter of schedules on the table were a litter of coins and a set of scales and weights.

My sister took her place in the audience chair, Tostig at her left, hands behind his back. I sensed I stood before a royal inquisition. "Hail to my lady."

"Brother. It has been too long."

"Far too long. With your permission, lady, I would speak with Tostig."

"In time," Eadgytha ruled, firmly taking charge as usual. I couldn't help noticing how my sister, at thirty-two, looked increasingly older than her years. When life and joy go out of a beautiful woman, or if they have never been there at all, she reminds one of a neglected tomb. Tostig on the other hand glowed with energy and prosperity, a large new silver clasp to his rich mantle.

"The d'Arques girl has been requested to leave our court," Eada announced meaningfully. "Quietly, of course, and with some saving excuse about duty to her father, but you know why."

I said nothing.

"You, if anyone," Eada sniffed. "The girl is a scandal! To think Edward actually put her forward as a match for you when she's no more than—well, you know what she

is. The king knows nothing of this, being wondrous innocent in some matters, but I will *not* have her in our court.
There is also the consideration of Edith. Regardless of
your moral sloth, I will not see her hurt.''

"Then why won't *you* sue to Rome for us yourself?
Stigand is with us. You and Edward together or either one
of you could make one gesture and clear our way."

"Wessex." With one reproving word, my sister became
royal and distant again. "Not as your sister but your
queen—"

"Eada—don't, please."

"Will you or no, you must be a model for our younger
and lesser nobles. As Tostig is, titled or not."

True, but I knew Tostig's appetites were other than
carnal.

"We desire amendment in you," Eadgytha continued.
"We pray you have been no stranger to the confessional."

"On my word, an habitué. May I speak to my sister
rather than the Crown?"

"If without your usual coarseness."

"Guilty as charged, *mea culpa,* but these incidents are
meaningless, Eada. I want to go home. The king keeps
me here while my own lands and family need me. Particularly in Dorset," I added to Tostig, moving to the table.
"Shaftesbury is my town. I understand you have some
question about the mint there?"

"Not really," he deflected smoothly. He joined me at
the table and chose a new penny from a scatter of them.
"Minted at Shaftesbury this year. There should be in this
coin twenty-one and a half grains of silver, fine to nine
parts in ten."

As he spoke it was clear Tostig had learned his office
well. The pennies were stamped from thin flans of silver
with circular dies. There was always some leftover which
had to be salvaged and accounted for future use, though
it was very difficult to answer for every grain of silver
when values fluctuated almost yearly.

Tostig placed the penny on the scale against two tiny
pellets of silver. "You see? A minute difference, just a

trifle light. Where did the silver go? No charges brought, just inquiring. But if the disparity persists . . ."

"As it did in York?"

He glanced up quickly, understanding me. "Or anywhere, Harold. Even Shaftesbury. By the by, do you know the master silversmith there? He made this brooch for me. Interesting man."

I recognized on the intricately worked brooch that closed Tostig's mantle the small quarter-moon benchmark of the high priest who handfasted me to Edith. "I don't know. I may have met him at Teinfrith's hall."

"Ah, Teinfrith," my brother smiled with a freighted pleasantness. "Another man of parts."

I would have asked his meaning, but Eadgytha broke in. "We only seek to regulate more closely what has been too long neglected."

"But of this minter at Shaftesbury, Teinfrith writes—"

I was interrupted by a sound between a squeal and a squawk from the merlin on its perch. Tostig took up a dish of raw meat and touched it to the hawk's sharp beak, but the merlin spurned it and pecked sharply at his hand instead.

"Ow—damn! Enough, you ungrateful slut. An end to you!" He seized the bird by the legs, tore off the jesses and hood. One quick step to push the casement open and Tostig consigned the merlin to its fate over Gloucester, live or die. "More trouble than you're—go, fly, and may you molt eternally!"

He turned to me, sucking at his finger. "Clearly you don't see the extent of our problem. Stealing silver is a Crown offense. It will cease, no matter the cost in right hands."

I was not convinced. With the blessings of peace come its ills. With no outward threats, our instinctive killers turn on their own.

By now Edith was settled again at Bosham. After Christmas court I returned by way of Winchester with a gnawing question that I must verify or lay to rest.

To speak of men of parts, Lofven of Gold Street in

Winchester was a mosaic. He owned to Danish birth and spoke English with the soft sound of Sjaelland that marked Gytha's English. Lofven claimed to have learned gold-working from Irish masters. Certainly the nimble delicacy of his hands as he fine-etched a piece of jewelry contradicted their size. By his account he'd swung a pick in the Cornish tin mines, and from the breadth of his shoulders, I believed him.

Lofven came out from behind a drape in the rear as I entered his dark shop. His establishment was tidily swept and free of dust. I'd bought Edith a gold pennanular here years ago and other baubles from time to time. The goldsmith bowed slightly to me, a man of middle years with mustaches of indeterminate shade between brown and ale-stained yellow. His saffron gown was clean as his shop.

"Earl Harold, I am honored. Something for your lady? This month I have some truly unusual pieces in Baltic amber."

"Do you know silver?"

"Do *I* know silver?" The question might have been an affront. "I have worked much in it."

"How exact are your scales?"

Again I had the fleeting impression of insult, however unintended. "Infallible. If my lord doubts any past purchase—"

"Not at all. I want you to weigh this silver for me."

Lofven set a small balance on the counter between us. The pans appeared absolutely level, but not to his merciless eye. He made a tiny adjustment. "And?"

I handed him one of the new pennies from the Shaftesbury mint, filched from Tostig's alleged evidence. "What's the exact weight of the new Edward penny?"

"Fixed by statute, twenty-one and a half grains. This one—" He set the penny on one pan and selected a silver pellet from a small tray for the other. "I keep these specially. Shave-penny dealers are worse than lice and as numerous. This penny is full weight." Lofven inspected both faces of the coin with professional admiration. "Shaftesbury does good work. But why do you ask?"

From my purse I produced the two small silver pellets

scooped up and hidden in my palm when the bad-tempered merlin providentially distracted Tostig and Eadgytha. "Weigh these against the same coin."

Lofven obliged with meticulous care. "Twenty-one and a . . . wait, then. Wait."

The pans came to rest, Tostig's weights slightly below the penny. "Lord Harold." Lofven was shocked as a man who'd detected tampering with the balance of Creation itself. "The weights are a full quarter grain heavy. May I ask where these came from?"

"From a thief." I plucked the penny from his scale, rang it on the counter, and jingled three others beside it for his trouble. "A smith at Gloucester agrees with you."

My clever Tostig. When I wrote him from Bosham, I knew Eadgytha would see the letter, and I fully meant she should. The missive was carefully worded but plain. No accusations or threats, only clear intent:

. . . twice tested, twice discrepant, and still in my possession. For now I will assume error rather than design. But you will remember I now have Godwine's responsibilities and his voice in the Witan. Out of prudence, if nothing finer, you will press no indictment at Shaftesbury nor any royal mint within Wessex without consulting me with evidence. Out of virtue you might desist elsewhere, for you stand to lose much more than the maligned minter of York.

The number of Tostig's prosecutions dwindled significantly, but at a cost. If we were uneasy allies once, Tostig was an enemy now.

How long before even I go into your balance, little brother?

48 • Harold

In the first mild weeks of spring, Edith and I took to riding together, Magnus on her saddle, Godwine on mine. We never spoiled the boys, at least Edith would not, but Godwine developed a will of his own with *Won't!* as his motto. Now and again I had to remand him to a firm but gentle servant for a birching. For a dreary stretch, *Won't!* remained my son's battle cry.

"He must get it from you, Edith. I was never that stubborn."

"Oh? A father who tells his king to go to flaming hell and then chooses exile rather than submission? Hardly from him."

"All the same, let's pray for a daughter next."

If we took some pains to ease Aelfgar's family from Nazeing, he took none in reclaiming it. With our servants and carls bustling to and from the hall, making up our train for Bosham, Edith at tearful sixes and sevens in leaving a place she loved, Aelfgar thundered through the gates, a dozen mounted carls behind him.

Of less than average height, Aelfgar compensated with pugnacity. I've found this so often true of short men, forever thrusting their virility in your face. Aelfgar bounded too athletically from the saddle and swaggered up to me at the hall entrance, shoulders swinging. Instead of a civil greeting, he challenged: "I've come for what's mine, Wessex. You are foolish to leave the gates open. Anyone could ride in."

"We're not expecting attack, my lord. My steward has the keys. Nazeing is yours."

Not even a thank you. I confess there's an imp in me that finds self-importance fair game, making me step closer to Aelfgar to emphasize the disparity in our heights. "Rather like a teeter-totter, these earldoms, aren't they? Up, down, in, out. One could feel permanently . . . impermanent, don't you think?"

Aelfgar only grunted: "Odd sense of humor you have."

I don't think he liked looking up at any man and only heaven's perverse will that he continually must. He stepped back from me. "I tell you plainly, in a few years I will be Mercia and possibly more. Your family has grown about the king like ivy on a wall, but don't look to creep north."

Possibly more? Did this crowing little rooster look toward Northumbria? Welcome to it, I thought. Aelfgar was like Tostig in that respect. In the midst of wanting more, they never paused to enjoy the moment. I took my leave courteously, but my imp could not help but pray for an apple peel now and then for his self-importance to slip on.

At tranquil Bosham time comes and passes gradually as the harbor tides, but there were Edith and Gytha and my boys. Baby Edmund was darker than his brothers, no surprise, considering Edith was west country and Hildre's grandparents had some of the Welsh in them. Many of our servants, defected from the Normans, drifted back to us, and our hall lilted with music as always. Old Manni the steward did his office as always, if slower and a shade more crotchety now. That spring of 'fifty-four was a beautiful lull. England's humor, her very weather, was fair and warm. Crops were lush, rents never a hardship. With no more drain of silver to the Danes, our country prospered.

We resolved Agatha's situation without my sister's frigid charity. One of my thanes had five hides nearby at Fishbourne, between Bosham and Chichester, from which rents in kind and silver were due me. I waived a portion of the thane's rents in return for a sturdy cottage and several arable acres, a woman servant to do for Agatha, plus several sextaries of good wine and ale per year. She also received from my various stewards eight—

"No, ten," Edith decreed with finality. "I want Eada to know we went her twice as good."

—*ten* pounds a year for life. Only an hour from Bosham, Agatha faded from the notice of Crown and clergy. By the time her disapproving father passed to paradise, Earl Ralf was dead and Leominster within my western holdings. I contested the father's disinheritance of Agatha and wrested her fair share of land from the unforgiving old bastard and his other heirs.

A mile or so south of Fishbourne was a place forever tied to my heartstrings, the ruin of a great Roman villa. Legend said it once belonged to a British client king. To enthusiastic boys like Swegn and me, it was massively grand, a treasure house for pretending. I hadn't been there in years.

One summer day, riding back from Agatha's cottage, Edith, Botulf, and I raced each other on a whim, not caring where, and found ourselves within sight of the villa. We pushed on, cantering along the broken north wall to the east entrance.

"You enter through there," I pointed for Edith. "Down across the atrium straight to the audience hall opposite. Swegn and I used to play at kings and battles here."

"Sad old pile," Botulf sniffed.

Not to the heart, friend. What is the spell cast by childhood places? What draws us back to them but to find some part of us lost there in a forgotten year?

Edith said softly, "It must have been magnificent once."

"It was a world, love. I wish . . ."

"What, darling?"

"Stay here, both of you. I'll just be a little."

I dismounted and started for the portico. Edith must have been startled to see me break into a run, but for that little time my heart led and I must follow.

Nine years old, high voice shivering back from cracked marble and faded tiles, legs churning me down the lane of bare, broken columns along the atrium path. I scooped up mud to smear my face, imagination already heating pretend to grim reality. In one bound I cleared the steps to the audience hall and staggered my last exhausted steps to kneel, gasping, before good King Swegn. "War, my lord! They've landed. Norse, Swedes, Danes, Normans, and each has a company of ogres and two of giants."

"Giants?" Swegn relished my invention. "That's good. Aye, call out our levies." He extended his ashwood sword. "Kneel again, loyal Harold, and put thy forehead to my knee. For that thou hast been steadfast, henceforth shalt thou be earl and leader of my armies."

"Let's be about it, my lord. I hear the bastards outside."

"Wait. This is the best part, inspiring my nobles."

"But they're breaking through our shield wall!" And I dashed away, Swegn and England whooping in my wake. Out we clattered, screaming terrible oaths, hacking our way through towering forests of giants, each of us a dozen times wounded but ever victorious. Nothing so glorious as imagined and painless death on the field. A treacherous thrust through my guard—

"Agh! Help me, Swegn." I staggered picturesquely and fell for the glory of England. Grief-stricken, caught up in our heroism, Swegn cradled me in his arms with unfeigned tears.

"You must not die, Brother."

"Sire," I choked, expiring, "did we win?"

"Thrice brave and loyal brother, the day is ours."

Ours. God's mercy, what life makes of us. I scoured you from my heart, all but the enduring stain of love, and you died among strangers without me.

Edith was calling me from beyond the portico. I walked slowly down the atrium and into the entrance hall, boots ringing on the age-grimed tiles.

Now, listening for lost sounds, I could look back into the atrium and clearly see two boy-fierce phantoms charge ghost armies and heroic odds with one heart before our own natures tore us apart.

Botulf called, "Lord Harold? Your lady wishes to be home."

So do I, but we never find all of it again.

* * *

In a family like ours, Gyrth and Leofwine could hardly escape ambition. They had every right to hope for some prominent place when their time came, meanwhile they learned and earned. When not hacking away with sword and shield among my experienced soldiers, they rode as nuncios between me and Edward's court or the length and breadth of Wessex on my own business. They absorbed the minutiae of duty from thanes and reeves down through half-free men and slaves, who owed what service to whom and when due. They rubbed the character of my people into their very skin along with sweat and saddle galls. As my lieutenants, they wore the golden lions of Wessex on their breast.

On a day in March of 'fifty-five, Gyrth, with an escort of three Crown carls, galloped through Bosham gates and asked to see me privately in Father's study, which I'd made mine. He surged into the chamber, threw his mantle over a chair, still windburned and reeking of horse, tearing the helmet from his tousled blond head. "There's news at court."

"Good or bad?"

Gyrth arched his back to ease the saddle stiffness. "Could be good for some like Tostig. Edward wants you in London now, before Easter court."

"What about Tostig?"

"Siward is dead."

By sheer habit I looked to the large map on the wall, already reckoning consequences. Both Siward's son and nephew had died the year before in the Scottish campaign with Malcolm against Macbeth. His second son, Waltheof, was far too young to succeed. That left Northumbria up for the asking. "Who's been put before the Witan?"

"Aelfgar and Tostig."

That took no great pondering. The earls supported our return because they feared us less than Normans, but neither they nor Edward would put the whole north into the hands of a family that already controlled the south. "It will be Aelfgar."

My brother rubbed at two days' growth of beard. "Will it, then? That's the news. Aelfgar's accused of treason."

Unlikely. "Aelfgar may be the arse end of a mule, but a traitor? I doubt it. Who's brought the charge?"

"Tostig." Gyrth shook his head in despair. "I don't know, the whole thing's a bloody bollocks. The Witan's to try it as soon as you assemble. Between gracious Edward and sweet Tostig, they've right dropped you in it, haven't they?"

Tostig's silver weights rang in memory, and I wondered how far Eadgytha's justiciar would reach for justice.

49 • Harold

The mood in the London palace hall that chilly March morning was double-edged, irritation at being summoned weeks early for Easter court, grave over the cause. Tension pervaded the hall as we waited for Edward and Eadgytha. The archbishops Stigand and Cynesige of York swept in and took their places, their retinues behind them on one side. I stood opposite with the earls and chief thanes. In the center with his compurgators, thanes prepared to swear by their property to his innocence, Earl Aelfgar was a besieged island between lay and clerical shores. Tostig entered with two monk-scribes to a table placed before the dais. Always a picture of fashion, my brother this morning was resplendent in white, the gown collared in gold wire and set with jewels under a new mantle of pale blue, the queen's colors. At my side Teinfrith muttered, "He looks like risen Jesus."

"Doesn't he always?"

The king and queen were announced. We bowed as they

entered through us and took their places on the dais. Edward shifted restlessly in the great chair, obviously anxious to be done with this. A little monk from Saint Peter's at Thorney hurried to him with a schedule. Edward read it closely, nodded, and handed it back. Probably a report on the new abbey, to which our king now devoted most of his time.

"Earl Aelfgar Leofricsson, stand forth."

Chancellor Regenbald read the indictment. On evidence to be presented before Crown and Witan, Aelfgar was accused of conspiring to attain the earldom of Northumbria by force of arms if necessary.

"How say you, my lord? Are you guilty or innocent?"

Aelfgar bit off each word. "Not guilty." This was echoed loudly by Leofric and the Mercian thanes until Regenbald rapped his staff for silence.

"Who accuses me?"

"Tostig Godwinesson, queen's justiciar."

Aelfgar laughed aloud. "I might have known! He seeks that place himself."

Tostig rose from his table, holding up a sheaf of documents for all of us to see. "With the king's permission, I appear as Crown *causidicus.* These are letters written from the accused to certain high men of the north this last year, sounding out their support for him in the event of Siward's death. *In the event,*" Tostig stressed. "The accused was already bending every effort to secure succession before the honorable earl forthfared."

Aelfgar tried to speak but was silenced by Regenbald and a fierce, squelching glance from Leofric. I listened and watched closely. The frustrated rage in Aelfgar turned livid as Tostig read each letter in turn. They were blunt and monotonous with short, bald sentences. What literacy they contained was surely from the Waltham scribe to whom they were dictated. They certainly sounded like Aelfgar:

There is no successor of age. You will agree that I am most worthy. I am heir to Mercia. I have as much Danish blood as any in Northumbria. I also speak that

**language. I am familiar with the ways of the north, the
Danes and the Scots. I—**

I, I, I.

One could feel sorry for Aelfgar as Tostig read one
letter after another soliciting the voice of this or that man
toward his preference. Tostig read in clipped, precise tones
that allowed no single syllable to be lost on any of us.
But something nagged at me. Though trumpeting Aelfgar's
purpose and ambitions, none of these writings mentioned
any armed intent, either directly or by implication.

Leofric elbowed closer to me and dug me in the ribs.
"If this is your little brother's whole case, he might as
well go home."

Tostig laid aside all the parchments but one. "Aelfgar
Leofricsson, you have admitted to these letters?"

"Of course I have!"

"And confess your guilt?"

"There *is* no guilt. Common knowledge that Siward
was old and near death. His son and nephew were dead.
I asked the support of laity and churchmen. I would not
be surprised if you'd done the same, Tostig. My claim is
stronger, my competence greater, but I never by any word
or deed plotted or planned to take the earldom by force.
You can find no jot of such in those letters. Not *one*,"
Aelfgar challenged, sweeping his gaze around the hall.
"As for treason, others"—glaring at Tostig and myself—
"others in this chamber today have been far closer to it—
aye, and that in arms and by force—than ever I dreamed.
Not guilty."

"Never?" Tostig tapped the last rolled document
against his cheek. "Never, my lord? Please the Crown and
Witan, I will read one more letter from Aelfgar to his
grace Cynesige of York."

"What?" Aelfgar's face screwed up in perplexity too
genuine to be feigned. "I sent no letters to the
archbishop."

Tostig ignored him, stepping up onto the dais by Regenbald to be seen and heard by all. "My lord archbishop,
you received this missive?"

The old man's voice rang clearly through the hall. "I did."

"Under Aelfgar's seal?"

"It was."

"When did you receive it?"

"At York, three days after our good earl died."

"From one of Earl Aelfgar's retainers?"

"So it was said. I didn't see who brought it."

"There," Leofric hissed. His eyes gleamed with vindication. *Said* is plain hearsay with no legal weight.

I stepped out from my peers. "Please the Crown, the Witan would examine those letters before any verdict is considered."

"We would that," Leofric agreed over mutterings from Ralf, Odda, and many of the thanes. Old Leofric could barely read himself. Ralf was not fluent in English to the degree of its nuances, nor were Odda or most of the others keenly literate, but the request was granted by Edward with a negligent wave of his hand. He seemed extraordinarily uninterested in the proceedings.

Then a deep voice rose out of the Northumbrian contingent: "As long as there be doubts, I'll put in mine."

The man lumbered forward from his companions. I have seen Norse traders as huge, but not many. He wore plain, undyed wool. Long, dull-yellow hair hung unbraided down his back and lankly about his face, framing fierce blue eyes. The emblem of a black raven was sewn on his breast.

Cynesige frowned at the man, whom I guessed was one of Siward's rustic thanes. "It is not your place, Ulfsson. You have no voice here."

"No fear, I'll not be long," the young giant assured him. "It's for us who have no voice in the great Witan. I'm Thane Brand Ulfsson of Brandeshal on Tees Riding," he declared to us all in a thick northern burr. "My blood's been on Tees since the old kingdom of Deira. I'll say only this: Guilty or not's no great matter to us. We want no outlander—"

Here he broke off, glaring at Aelfgar and Tostig in turn. "*No* outlander from anywhere as earl over us. There I've said and there I've done."

Shaggy Brand nodded to Cynesige and went back to his place. They're not given to many words, our Northumbrians. He'd had his say, there an end, and devil any man who disagreed. His companion thanes crowded about him, slapping his mountainous shoulders in approval. Aelfgar and Tostig alike should have learned from Ulfsson. To put any stranger over them is pouring oil on a fire.

"Lords of the Witan"—Tostig's voice cut through the babble like a new razor—"*May* I proceed?"

When the hall quieted, my brother read slowly and clearly from the one remaining letter:

Aelfgar, Earl of East Anglia to his grace Cynesige, Archbishop of York, greetings and reverence.

Surely Your Grace will know that by blood, lineage, and family ties to the lands now lordless through the forthfaring of Siward, that I am, not only by competence but in the opinion of many of Northumbria, most deserving of investiture.

Not a man among the Witan moved, listening now with acute attention. We'd heard nothing culpable in the foregoing evidence, nothing so far in this.

Aelfgar cried out: "No! That's false, a false lie. I never sent any letters to the see of York."

"My lord earl," Regenbald reproved. "You must be silent."

"Lies!"

"Silence, sir!"

"My son, restrain yourself," Leofric cautioned. "Your time will come."

Tostig held up the document. "Let me ask Your Grace once more. Did you recently receive this letter from Aelfgar?"

"I did."

"Under his known seal?" Tostig exhibited the wax seal to all of us.

"Yes."

"Then I continue and to rest the Crown's case:"

—some assurance from your grace that, my claim being favored by so many though opposed by others,

however the matter falls, I have your support even to the levying of arms.

There it was. By the letter Aelfgar plainly intended to rule Northumbria however preference fell, even to civil war. Tostig repeated the last passage with stress on *however the matter falls* and *even to the levying of arms*. A deeper silence fell on the assembly as he collected the documents together. In the pregnant hush, Saint Paul's bell rang the hour. Edward roused himself at the sound and murmured to Regenbald, who rapped with his staff as the king rose. "My lords, His Majesty is called to the new works at Westminster. This matter will be concluded tomorrow morning at the same hour, and a verdict asked of you."

With Eadgytha on his arm, Edward left the hall. I made for Tostig as Aelfgar cried out once more: "Lies! I never sent any such letter."

"Tostig?"

"Ah, Harold."

I held out my hand. "The Witan wishes to see those letters."

"Tomorrow, Harold."

"Now."

He gave me a sanguine smile. "Of course, if you insist, though you heard. The outcome is foregone."

"Possibly."

I scanned the letters in order of their dates, passing each to the other members of our body. Tomorrow Aelfgar's compurgators would swear in his defense, arguing Tostig's obvious prejudice and what other mitigation they could find, but the last alleged letter would weigh heavily against him. I studied the parchment, turned it over, even sniffed at it. Reasonable doubt did not whisper in my ear. It screamed.

50 • Harold

The session dissolved amid hubbub and argument. Leofric maintained his son's innocence. Of the others one couldn't say, but their sympathy, if not against Aelfgar, was hardly for Tostig as earl. His conflict of interest was not what disturbed me as I gathered up the letters.

Aelfgar snarled at me: "I know how you'll vote. Between you and your brother, leave my family a little in my banishment."

Before I could answer, one of Tostig's monks plucked at my sleeve. "The justiciar's evidence, my lord?"

"I'll return it myself. I'm seeing him straightaway."

The lady-in-waiting Clothilde told me that the queen and Tostig dined alone that day. Not surprising; surely they had much to discuss. Tostig rose cheerfully when I entered. "Ah, you've brought the letters. Good."

I dropped them on the table with a curt nod to my sister. Eadgytha inquired, "What is the Witan's mind in this? Not that it matters overmuch. Tostig's evidence is unshakable."

"Really, Sister? I have a few questions that might rattle it a bit."

Tostig was a study in confidence. "Oh?"

"Edward favors you, that's a given. Everyone but Leofric considers Aelfgar unfit to govern a stable."

"Very *un*stable," Tostig agreed. "Your question?"

"Just how far you'll go to win."

His expression didn't change, but Eadgytha laid down

her fruit knife, saying with dangerous calm, "I would know your meaning, Brother."

"I'm not dead set against Tostig in Northumbria, but I have grave doubts about his methods and his evidence."

His eyebrows elevated quizzically. "Specify."

I held up those missives to which Aelfgar had admitted. "I know Waltham's parchment. Far inferior to the quality of this last letter, the difference between lowland and upland sheep, Tostig."

"Highly conjectural."

"Just an interesting point if one wanted to make it. Now listen to the undoubted sound of Aelfgar himself." One by one I read the brief, bald messages of a graceless mind copied by a giftless scribe. " 'You will agree that I am most worthy.' Period. 'I am heir to Mercia.' Period. Ta-da-da-dum. Ta-da-da-*dum*. Flat and tedious as the man himself, enough to put you to sleep."

Now I took up the last, incriminating letter. Tostig's eyes flicked to Eadgytha, but I could read nothing in their silent exchange. "Suddenly Aelfgar grows literate and given to complex sentences: '. . . my claim favored by many though opposed by others, however the matter falls . . .' Strikingly inconsistent, wouldn't you say, Tostig?"

"Possibly, though it might have been written by a better-educated scribe. We know Aelfgar's ungoverned nature. He's pursued Northumbria like a dog after a rabbit. You'll agree a latitude of guilt exists."

"Or an equal one of innocence. As with your silver scales."

"Damn you!" he spat. "Are you against me, too? Not enough you have Father's title, are you jealous even of me? Those scales were never used unless suspicion of malfeasance was present, I swear it. We proved on one charge, when necessary, where we could not on another. Justice, Harold. Not haggling, ambiguous law, but justice!"

"As defined by you?"

"By me and in my hands. Right by any means remains right," Eadgytha stated as if reciting a maxim. "Tostig must be Northumbria's next earl. Edward inclines to him and you surely see the danger in Aelfgar. He will be Mercia soon enough by right. If the Midlands and north are ruled by one house . . ."

She left the rest to my understanding. "Under an idiot like Aelfgar—yes, that's clear. But what he admits is not treason. What he denies is doubtful at best. If these letters are your whole case, you're sailing in a sieve. They cry out for argument."

Tostig asked very quietly, "By you perhaps?"

"I've heard grimier suggestions today."

"You would do yourself no good." Imagination, or did I hear a note of warning from my sister? "You would lose, Harold."

"Would I? Beyond Wessex, most of the lords love our house no more than Aelfgar's. You heard that great ox from Tees. And remember, dear Sister." I leaned across the table deliberately to her. "I don't have to win, only to raise a substantial doubt."

Tostig settled his hands behind his back and gazed at me like the Archangel Michael driving the guilty pair from Eden, serenely merciless. "And will you?"

"I think not." Eadgytha poured a cup of wine, took a sip, and passed it to Tostig. "We act for the higher good. Facts, Harold. If one family must dominate England, far better us than Mercia."

Regarding Tostig I wasn't that sure, nor of Eada anymore. What I guessed of their motives and methods was anything but savory. "My God, Eada, Brother, we deal with banishment here. Have you forgotten your own exile? Not four years gone, banished without a trial, Eada stripped of everything, and the long road back that cost us all so much and killed Father? And now you'd turn around and do the same—"

"This is tedious," my brother broke in. "You raise niggling doubts over parchment and tones of letters despite the undeniable fact—" He snatched up the letters and shook them in my face—"that each bears Aelfgar's personal seal. Look for yourself. You talk of motives; you know his. You know his ambitions."

"I know yours."

"The *seal*. Look."

"No need. I could raise doubts there, too."

"How, O Solomon?"

"With his letters in your possession, and your ready access to the best diemakers in London—"

"Do you hear, Sister? Now I'm guilty of forging a seal. The Witan will swallow that whole, won't they?"

"They don't need to suspect guilt in you, only to doubt Aelfgar's." I sat down at the table and poured a small helping of wine. We were still family. I might yet appeal to the best in them. "I beg you, dismiss the case. It's been done before. Edward will likely give you the coronet in any event. He doesn't seem to have strong feelings either way."

"You're impossible." Tostig vented an exasperated sigh. "Eada, we should be angry with him."

"No, I'm pleading. I'm giving you a chance not to bury yourself too deep."

Once again Swegn looked at me out of Tostig's eyes—colder, brighter, more concentrated to purpose. "I think you're giving me an ultimatum."

"Put that way, yes. I still have your silver weights, Justiciar."

"Silver, yes." Tostig lifted his rich blue mantle from the prie-dieu. "I didn't want to do this, Sister, but he leaves me no choice."

"None," she said. "Regrettable, but there it is."

"We must dissuade him." Tostig held the cloak before me with the exquisite silver brooch forward. "You admired this. Look at the maker's mark: a quarter moon. One of many pagan symbols, but this one very powerful. A sigil, I believe it's called."

A warning whispered in my mind like clammy wind. "Many men paint suns and moons on their shields."

My brother traced a finger over the brooch. "Fine work. Amazing what can be bought with silver, even a conscience. Depressing, the venality of this world. A word here, a few shillings there. . . This smith and his good wife, would you believe, respected benefactors of Wilton

Abbey, are the leaders of a circle of witches in Shaftesbury.''

He watched me for reaction before going on. ''How wide a circle one can't say, but it appears their shadow has fallen over some undoubted Christians. Prominently placed citizens.''

Again that searching study, probing for any telltale guilt or fear in me. ''You know how it is, Brother. One small drop of soured milk and the whole bucket goes bad.''

I masked the fear by taking some wine while Eadgytha took up the argument in the same silken, solicitous tone but absolutely sure of herself. ''These pernicious servants of the devil, so it is said, performed an unholy wedding in Thane Teinfrith's hall.''

''And we know what witch-fever does to a whole shire,'' Tostig resumed. ''As with tainted milk: the whole bucket, the whole town, innocents fallen with the guilty.''

Not seen but often heard of in my youth. Such fever went through a fearful population like plague. Any ill was laid to the accused: soured milk, hens not laying, blight in cattle. Usually the victims were defenseless old widows living in hovels on the outskirts of a village, eccentric from years alone, talking to an aged cat for company. Perhaps the woman had rid a wife or maiden of an unwanted child or just skillfully used the right herbs to break a fever where a physician could not. The ''devil's mark'' is always found on her body, the cat absurdly convicted as her familiar and hanged or drowned with its owner.

But in this case the charge would be true. The wine turned to vinegar in my mouth. I felt sick and afraid. The charge would spread its shadow over Teinfrith and Hildre, over Edith and me, nor could Stigand raise one holy finger to help me. And there was my signed pledge to a man, pagan or not, who had risked his living and his life to protect Edith when the king's ferrets would have taken our sons.

''Of course,'' Tostig nudged gently, ''none of this is known beyond this room, nor need be.''

Eadgytha stretched her hand to cover mine. ''Edith is

like a sister to me, but I never dreamed you would imperil her soul and your own by such a measure."

I was a mouse between two cats who knew they could make a meal of me in the next moment if desired. I stared into the wine cup. "It was not what you think. It was a dignified ceremony, even poetic. They spoke not of duty but of love."

A long silence, then Tostig spoke. "Well, Harold? I didn't want to use this. I have some feelings, regardless of what you think of me. Am I to be earl with you or without?"

Aware of the bargain they offered, I thought: What price Northumbria, Aelfgar or Tostig? The clumsy bear or the snake. Would my brother be any more disastrous an earl than Aelfgar who could be, in his intent if not the act, just as guilty as innocent? I was only sure of underestimating my brother, who was already a master at navigating through moral twilight. I was defeated and they knew it. "Silence for silence, is that it?"

"And a verdict of guilty." Eadgytha stipulated. "In return, absolute silence and my voice added to Stigand's for papal dispensation. You and Edith may wed at last with generous gifts from your queen."

"Harold, think." Tostig leaned close over me. "It is for the immediate and future good of the country. If Aelfgar takes his medicine and behaves himself, he can be home in a year, two at most, earl in Mercia and no worse off."

His perfumed nearness repelled me. I had to stand up, away from him. "Don't. You haven't the art to sing *pro patria*. You . . . you're a pristine wonder, Tostig. Nothing bothers you, nothing sticks to you at all. One day something will. You've become everything they said our father was."

The cold judgment rolled off his back like everything else not to his own purpose. "God and the right are with me. Northumbria is wild; I'll give it law."

"Marvelous. Lady, may I withdraw? I will hold you to your promise for Edith's sake."

Eadgytha inclined her head to me. "You have leave, Brother, but—firm in our cause, I trust."

Was there a choice? "Yes."

And that, for the morally sensitive, is how Wessex upheld the good of the country. Inspiring, is it not?

Aelfgar was exiled, Tostig became Northumbria's earl. When I added my voice to the guilty verdict, old Leofric turned his back on me, as I did on Tostig, refusing to attend his investiture. My triumphant brother rode off to York in a bejeweled blaze of continental tailoring.

Home at Bosham, Edith sensed my mood. I told her of the bargain, what I'd had to do to save the folk at Shaftesbury, her own parents, and ourselves. She only put my head in her lap and said, "It will wash, love. It will wash."

She almost made me believe so.

Eadgytha kept her word and wrote to Pope Victor, pleading dispensation for us. Our hopes reared high only to be dashed again. Rome was in the thick of a deadly dispute with the Greek Church, which they anathemized as schismatic and a "synagogue of Satan." The effect on Rome and Europe was a rigid rededication to orthodoxy. When hell's fires were licking through the very floor of faith itself, what chance had Edith and I?

You angels and chroniclers, picking like ravens amid the bones of our actions, find there some trace of our intent. If what I was never came all the way clean, I never forgot what I wanted to be. Remember what we dreamed, Swegn and I, playing at kings in the old Roman villa. We wrote large across the heart's history, wise and enduring as Alfred, pure as Percival. We rescued maidens, rewarded honor, put down evil, and made England shine. The beginning was so clean before reality rolled over us and I could sit in the Witan and concur without a qualm that this or that man must die for the good of England, and even bring Edward the severed head to show it done. While men bowed to the word of great Wessex, plain Harold felt faintly fraudulent. But you can't dwell on that, only get on with what must be done now.

BOOK V

England Regrets

51 • Edward Rex

With his devilish secularity, Godwine felt anointed dynasties an impediment to efficient rule—surely excluding the dynasty *he* scattered over England before he died. After twelve years I was drowning in that wily commoner's ambitious get, while my blood kin dwindled and thinned. Of the House of England, most were women or died young. Only my half-nephew Edward stood in direct line to block William, whom Harold and the Witan would see damned before crowning him king.

Edward, called the Exile, was the son of Edmund Ironside and grandson of Ethelrede. Nearly forty himself, he'd spent almost all his life in Hungary, married to a German princess and father of three children, two daughters and little Edgar, five years old.

"Recall him and his son," Harold counseled. "Name him your heir. That will put two before William, who's already churning out sons to trouble our rest, and the daughters may be useful for alliance."

The Witan backed Harold. Actually the scheme appealed to me, though I made no promise beyond recall. William might cry *perfidy!* but not even the pope could object to a legitimate heir. If the duke raged, I would apply the calming oil of reason. "Dear William, the Witan demands thus and so, this is England, and my hands are somewhat tied." Etcetera.

Such matters require time and diplomacy. Bishop Ealdred of Worcester was dispatched, not directly to my nephew but to the German emperor Henry, whose very long arm extended to Rome. Negotiations were commenced for Edward's return. The poor fellow must have been as bewildered by the summons as I was in my time: good fortune but whence and why? He'd get the reckoning soon enough.

To speak of troublesome dynasties, with Eadgytha's family one can never close both eyes. I was forced to trust Tostig in the north and Harold in the south, enrounded by both. With Aelfgar's banishment part of Anglia went to young Gyrth Godwinesson, while I stewarded the remainder to subsidize the work on my abbey. Eadgytha plunged into rebuilding Wilton Abbey, which I gratefully encouraged. She could not harry the masons, the nuns, and me at the same time.

Dearly I would have loved to ride home from the works at Thorney without some fresh problem waiting, but there was always something. Bare weeks after his banishment, there was ominous news of Aelfgar: "He is sighted by traders in Dublin, recruiting mercenaries." "He is landed on the Welsh coast, the guest of Gruffydd ap Llywelyn." In London we sniffed the wind from the west. Welsh and exiles allied meant trouble, but where? Gloucester? Hereford? Chester? There was only one force of any size to meet them, Earl Ralf's untried new cavalry.

Then that cloudy, wind-gusted day at Winchester, the exhausted rider wilted in an anteroom chair and Regenbald handing me the dispatch hastily penned by Athelstan, bishop of Hereford.

24 October. This morning Aelfgar and Gruffydd, with perhaps two thousand mercenary and Welsh infantry, met and shamefully routed Earl Ralf's cavalry. The city and minster are under attack.

I glanced up from the hastily penned message to gravely expectant Regenbald. "The minster itself? They dare attack the bishop's own church?"

"They have, sire."

"I want the fastest messengers to Coventry, Bosham, and Nazeing. Leofric, Harold, and Gyrth are to mobilize on the instant and make for Gloucester. Wessex to command, of course.''

Regenbald hesitated. "My lord . . ."

"What, what?"

"Leofric is ill and Aelfgar is his son."

"What force has that now? If he can't go, he'll send his levies, but I want it done now." Not to begin but to prevent a war, a strong staying arm to split Gruffydd from Aelfgar and push him back into Wales. "Is that knight Malet still at court?"

"Barely. He and his knights leave for Rouen tomorrow."

"Not yet they don't," I decided firmly. "For once Normandy will be help rather than hindrance to me. He goes to Gloucester with Harold, he and his knights."

Harold would need experienced horsemen, while Earl Ralf had only a small cadre of trained vavasors. The messenger from Hereford wept with shame to tell of Earl Ralf's debacle. They had been routed without a chance to offer battle, fled back into the city, which the enemy then breached and burned. The minster church itself was besieged, hundreds dead. When he could hold out no longer, Ralf and his remaining force retreated to Gloucester.

"Easy, man." I put a consoling arm around the small man's shoulders as his tale came out in a Welsh accent ragged with disgrace. "How were they routed?"

"We do not know," he said. "Earl Ralf, he was sick with it. The horses . . . the men could not manage them in the noise. . . .''

Harold

Down the steep hills into Severn Valley, Malet and I stayed alert with patrols on both flanks. No sign of Aelfgar and Gruffydd, though we would be roughly equal in strength with our levies and Ralf's household cavalry. We breathed easier entering Gloucester along Southgate. The citizens were equally relieved to welcome us. They were a tempting target if the raiders were near. As we moved north toward the royal residence, we passed groups of dispirited soldiers hanging about in the slack, dejected attitude of men without orders or purpose. They were mostly English with a few Norman knights among them.

"*Ma foi,*" Hugh swore as we rode, "I've never seen men look so thoroughly beaten."

Botulf trotted his horse up to report. "Just been to the bridge. No guards at all. If Aelfgar's out there, he could just walk into Gloucester."

True enough. The sullen men who watched us ride through them weren't ready for any kind of fight. Shamed, resentful of our good marching order as we swung sturdily along, the broken cavalrymen turned away from us. Hugh Malet spied one of Ralf's household vavasors and called him to ride with us. Discouraged as the rest, he told us Earl Ralf was at the royal residence.

"Orders?" I plied him. "What orders has he given?"

The knight only wheeled away from us, throwing the answer over his shoulder. "None."

I had no feeling of immediate danger, but Gyrth was still a day east with the Anglian fyrd, and loyal Leofric had sent his Mercians toward Gloucester at Edward's call. We would group and probe in strength for the raiders. What worried me most was the demoralized state of Ralf's men, no longer a force but a broken mob.

At the royal residence Ralf of Mantes had secreted himself in the king's own chamber behind a bolted door. Several of his Normans hung about, frustrated as the men in the streets. No orders issued, not even for care of the horses, which Hugh considered disgrace beyond words.

"In fine," I seethed, "no one here knows what in bloody hell is happening." I pounded furiously at the locked door. "Ralf, it's Harold. Open up, we've got to talk."

The iron bolt shot back, the door cracked open. Ralf limped back to his chair by the firepit, greeting us sardonically. "Welcome to Valhalla."

The shutters were closed tight, the airless room smelled of stale wine, but Ralf appeared sober. There are times when a man cannot drink enough to escape the time. His surcoat and mail lay in a heap on the floor where they'd been discarded. On a table a bowl of soup congealed about gobbets of fat. Ralf sat listlessly, left arm in a sling, a dark stain on one leg of his tight-fitted trousers seeping from a bandage beneath a long tear in the material.

"Glad you've come," he growled. "Malet, have you brought any decent horsemen?"

"A few, my lord."

"You've got to get your men sorted out," I urged Ralf. "Some kind of discipline. A fresh start."

He might not have heard me. "A disaster."

"We heard," Hugh said. "You attempted too much, my lord, trying to make vavasors out of foot soldiers."

"You are only a knight. I am charged with the defense of the border. I did what I thought best. It would have worked if there were more time, just a little more."

Ralf would die a few years later believing that in the face of facts. History is neither kind nor farsighted. He had been trained from boyhood as a mounted knight; such youths took years learning to fight from the saddle, to fuse with the animal into a single weapon, but even there Ralf had been defeated from the start.

"I wanted a rapid striking force, but the Saxons couldn't or wouldn't take to it. And the mounts—Malet, you saw what I was forced to work with."

"Not nearly big or heavy enough."

"Border horses. Endurance and speed, but . . ."

All this time Ralf spoke mostly to Hugh, avoiding my eye. He'd stood with the king against my family. We were never friends, nor did he trust me. This humiliation must rub him raw, to be wrong in front of *me*. In his account of the battle there was an undertone of pleading.

"We met them in good order. They outnumbered us but they were almost all foot soldiers. The Irish mercenaries were in mail, the rest just Welsh tribesmen, half naked and painted. They attacked in no line, just a rabble. We could have broken them, but then they started to roar. To *scream* at us. The sound frightened the horses. They began to bolt by the dozens. My commanders couldn't keep any order."

Ralf felt gingerly at his wounded shoulder. "Do you know what hurt the most, Malet? When we got back into the city, we fought on foot. We fought *well*, Wessex, but no one will remember that or the hundreds we lost, only that Ralf of Mantes ran from a mob of wild Welsh. That he is dishonored. I can never go home."

"Ralf, get up. Look at me." I took the man by his good arm and gently raised him to his feet. "I've seen good men laugh in defeat and weep in the middle of victory for the few they lost. To hell with last week, I need you and your good men now. Shall we have a go?"

52 • Harold

Out of Severn Valley, climbing westward into the foothills. On Hugh's advice—gospel where horses were concerned—we dismounted regularly and led the animals. The laboring of our breath, clop of hooves, and muted clatter of mail as we lurched along became the rhythm of each long hour.

We were a day west of Gloucester, sniffing for any hint of the raiders. Aelred was ahead with some of his Sherwooders, reporting regularly through Leofwine. For the last half year, Leofwine had been Gyrth's liaison to me, toughening with saddle sores and experience. Now he urged the little border pony up the hill, reining to a stop before Hugh and me.

"Nothing ahead for five miles in any direction. Denby thinks we're looking in the wrong place."

So did I by now. Aelred could probably track a trout through muddy water, while two thousand men could scarcely pass anywhere without leaving a trail. "Bring them in, Leofwine. We turn north for Hereford."

Ralf and his men, few of them fit for such an expedition, had been left to defend Gloucester. Hugh Malet attached only his pick of the earl's Norman cavalry, but the last thing I wanted was a pitched battle on any scale. Aelfgar was the lesser consideration here. The man I needed to confront and contain was Gruffydd ap Llywelyn. To check the man, I had to know him.

We entered Hereford by the ancient army ford over Wye from which the town took its name. Men and women peered cautiously from their thatched huts as we rode, then came running by twos and threes to meet us in near tearful gratitude. Some of the men bore wounds, the women almost hysterical in their desire to press close, to touch us and kiss our hands, and a word rose up that in the commotion of them sounded to me like *jingle,* until one old woman caught at my right hand and pressed to it a wet, toothless kiss.

"The king . . . my lord, the king."

"They think you're Edward," Hugh laughed, waving to the crowd and leaning from the saddle to caress the face of a dirty-faced young girl.

"And why not? Likely never saw Edward," Aelred explained. "Ent like to while he's got Earl Harold to send."

We billeted most of the foot troops outside the turf-and-timber ramparts, the rest close about me in the cathedral area. The rape of the little town hurt one's eyes. Hereford lay in its own blood and ashes, barely alive. The raiders had looted and burned the royal mint, killed some of the cathedral priests and a Welsh bishop, burned the timber roof of the nave, and mortally wounded Bishop Athelstan. The old man's bedside was my first courtesy visit. Athelstan tried to rise, but I stayed him, kneeling by his side to kiss the episcopal ring. He had the bloodless pallor of a man who wouldn't last the winter, but the worst wound struck deeper than his flesh into the rage of his soul.

"My church," he railed feebly. "My priests. Did you see what they did to them? Did you see the blood in the nave?"

Stained flagstones were virtually all the raiders had left beside the gaping burned hole in the roof.

"He was so proud of this place, Gyrth," I said as we prepared to bed down amid my other officers within the nave. "His life's work it was."

"D'you suppose it's mac Ciaran's men?"

I did not. "Never. Remember Sheppey? Niall wouldn't harm a church for any man or money."

"A very principled brigand." Gyrth had shed his mail coat and was wiping with an oiled rag at the wet rust that formed continuously on the rings no matter how often one cleaned it. "He does better than us for profit."

The thin beard my brother so proudly coaxed to some kind of character was now a shapeless scraggle over his cheeks and chin. There were shadows of strain under his eyes, his mouth drawn with fatigue. "Do you know, Harold? Before I left Bosham, one of the Trinity priests gave me the usual lecture on chastity. As if I'd had time this year to drop my trousers anywhere but a latrine. My horse has more of a life than I do now."

"And mine." Leofwine snuffed his candle end and stretched out on his furs, yanking them over him. "How many stable boys would envy us if they knew the pay was so damned poor?"

The furs did little to cushion the cold stone floor. "Welcome to the realities of rank, brother mine."

I lay in the dark, watching stars through the ruined roof, listening to men sigh in sleep or shift restlessly under blankets and furs. Sleep evaded me, kept away by a grinding anger at Aelfgar and his whole heedless kind. "There has to be a better way."

"To what?" Gyrth yawned.

"To what Father worked for. Remember, he said no man should have absolute power over so much as a stone of cheese."

My brother turned over on one elbow. "Perhaps someone had too much over him once and he didn't like the way that felt."

"Ah, *merde*," Hugh growled. "I was halfway to sleep and you two want to be profound."

"It's an excellent thought, Hugh."

My friend sighed. "Life is beautifully simple, Harold. Why must you always complicate it? You were born to a certain place as I was. My honor is clean, my sword sharp, my horses the best, and all serve my duke. That is the world. *C'est ça.*"

"If that's all, Hugh, I could be home with my family but for an ass of an earl who thinks just that way, and a Welshman who might, if we're lucky, be murdered in his bed by his own lyrically savage subjects."

"Speaking of good thoughts," Gyrth yawned again, "Good rest, all."

I tried to settle myself for sleep, to think of Edith and the boys, but tomorrow would not be routed from mind and what must be done.

And with this mission we charge our trusted Wessex.

Am I trusted, Edward? And how much of my life have I given to or against you already? As Leofwine said, the pay is not enough.

God, am I too tired to sleep?

In the dark, drizzling morning I found two aldermen with some authority over what was left of Hereford, levied every available man and boy over fourteen to begin deepening the bank and ditch about the walls, and raided what was left of cathedral stores to feed my troops. Aelfgar and Gruffydd had not left much. None of us would eat well until the end of this. By noon, striding from task to task, Gyrth and Hugh Malet in my wake, I'd restored some semblance of order and hope to battered Hereford.

"They'll not come again," I promised the uplifted, frightened faces about the mounting block I stood on. "Don't tell me you're hungry, so am I. To the ditches now, there's work to do."

I set my foot troops to work with the townspeople. That would keep them too busy and fatigued to cause the usual trouble of troops foisted on a small town. We read out the penalties for rape and looting in two languages. Aelred of Denby found an undamaged grain mill, which I commandeered for a headquarters, conscious always of the marked hours sinking down the candle.

Leofwine's well-favored looks and gentle manner charmed a yard of tow linen from an alderman's wife. With this and a stub of charcoal, I drew our situation for my brothers, thanes, and Hugh Malet while cold autumn rain fell outside.

"Since we don't know where the enemy is, we make a reasonable guess and commit. God willing, we will find them and hit hard and fast. Meanwhile, look at this."

On the linen stretched by nails over a table I drew an angled oblong from the Roman road south to Hereford, a longer line southeast to Gloucester, northeast to the tiny town of Winchcombe, and closed it to the original road point. This would be our area of search.

"Winchcombe?" Teinfrith canted his head at the drawn figure. "You think they've gone for the shire mint?"

"Why not?" I reasoned. "They sacked the one here. Aelred says they're neither west nor north, and Ralf would have sent word if they passed south toward Severn. One last rich strike before they have to run west into Wales. With half their number mercenaries who must be paid, Winchcombe will be tempting to Aelfgar."

If this was their intent, then this late in the year, burdened with spoils and slaves, Aelfgar and Gruffydd would want to escape west without further confrontation. We'd probe eastward in a wide pattern until they were sighted.

"Thane Aelred, that's your charge. Ten of your best mounted men. Keep hidden, note their number and condition."

Aelred murmured something to the small, olive-skinned young bowman who stood silently at his elbow. The man wore a leathern slave collar.

"No contact, mind," I stressed to Aelred. "I need you alive and clever, not brave and dead. Get word to us. We'll be ready to march."

"If you've guessed correctly," Hugh noted dubiously. "They could be anywhere."

"Could be," Aelred drawled. "But they ent. Will says so." He tapped his companion on the shoulder. "Will Scatloch's my chief forester at Denby, but he was born here and knows every hill and valley, rock and rill in these parts."

"Somehow I am not reassured," said Hugh Malet with a tinge of scorn. Like all Normans, he considered archers a contemptible adjunct to battle and the bow a coward's weapon no man of honor would employ other than for hunting. Neither the slave nor tall young Aelred leaning on his bowstave would he trust. "Just how will you divine, *Anglais*? By prayer? Holy vision? Severn Valley is wide and thick with forest. Twice two thousand men could hide there."

Aelred regarded Hugh as if the knight had been somehow flawed in his creation. "Y'can hide from men but not animals. If there's men about, any game that walks or flies will give't out. Lord Harold, when shall I be ready to ride? At light?"

"Earlier. When the bells ring prime."

And pray I'm right.

Aelred was back after a day and a night, and I thanked heaven for his speed. We were hard-pressed to maintain discipline. Hugh's Norman's were souring for a fight with anyone, and I'd already had one or two fyrd men flogged for vandalism. There would be no more outrage against Hereford.

Nothing saps men's confidence more than indecision in their leaders. I'd already given my commanders their mustering points and order of march. We *would* attack, I promised them; when and how depended on Aelred's report. For the rest I took a lesson from Swegn: March farther and faster than they think you can, attack when and where they think you can't. Divide and conquer as Edward did to Godwine at Tetbury, as he should have done a year later when we were in much the same position as Aelfgar now—not a point I wished to dwell on, but instructive.

When we assembled at the mill, Aelred called for the linen map. The young thane was seedy and drawn, his dark-green clothes sodden with rain, but the longbow and quiver were swaddled in thick wool wrappings.

"Here," he pointed. "Halfway 'twixt Winchcombe and the road west they camped last night."

He had followed orders. His Sherwooders were still dogging Aelfgar's flanks.

"Number and condition?"

Close to the original reckoning of two thousand, now including a number of slaves, many of whom were women and children. "They struck at Winchcombe right enough. They're heavy laden. Foot and hoofprints sink deep."

"Scouts?"

"Just a few in front."

Hardened mercenaries might march twenty miles in a

day, but not encumbered with slaves and booty. They'd
be doing well to strike the Roman road by vespers, but
they wouldn't in this weather. "My lords, assemble your
men."

"Are we to know the plan of attack," Hugh inquired,
"or is it to be a mystery like the Eucharist?"

I favored him with a smile of supreme confidence.
While knowing the objective, my plan was yet only an
abstract shape, but Hugh needn't know that now. "When
it's time. Look to your men and mounts."

The rain was falling again as we left the mill. Good,
for what slowed us would hamper the raiders as well. As
I pulled up the hood of my mantle Hugh fell in step with
me, his manner halfway between concern and irritation.
"My men expected to go home, not ride clear across England to fight. I need to know what is coming, Harold."

"I wanted to celebrate my son's birthday at Bosham—
but fair enough. We're going to block the road west and
ambush them tomorrow after dark."

Hugh's jaw dropped. "After dark? Cavalry to fight in
the dark?"

"There won't be much fighting."

"No." He shook his head obstinately. "No one fights
in the dark."

"Now, is that progressive, Hugh Malet? Is that inven-
tive? They'll be tired to death, most of them asleep, and
ourselves in and out before they're on their feet."

"It is utterly mad."

"No, utterly logical. Can you think of a better time?
We're not going for a battle, but—oh, call it a lark in
lèse-majesté. We're going to kidnap a king."

53 • Harold

With Aelred ahead, we force-marched northeast up the River Frome valley to the Roman road, only twelve miles, but accomplished in just over three hours at the pace I set. The weather had cleared; that was secondary now. Like a chess bishop slashed clear across the board, we now blocked Gruffydd's road home. We rested men and horses an hour, then struck eastward until Aelred rode back to report contact with his scouts and the enemy. At midafternoon, the autumn light already paling, the thane guided our march off the road into the thick woods that verged to the south. I chose a position behind a fallen log and asked Gyrth, Aelred, and Hugh to join me. The trees still dripped rain; we were wet through but used to that now.

"Now we wait," Aelred said.

I swept my eyes across the empty road beyond. "How long?"

"Will's coomin'."

The young Welsh slave slipped down beside Aelred, a silent shadow in the same dark-green Lincoln cloth as his master. "They will camp here," he singsonged with the Gwentish lilt of his birthplace. "It is but a mile and some to the river, but this is good high ground. They would be fording in the dark with tired men who have been moving in the wet and cold since early morning, the slave women and children barely stumbling along. No, they will camp here tonight."

The enemy's advance point was less than a mile east,

Will said. He squinted up through the treetops at the fading light. "And the day is already going."

Gyrth settled his back against the log, wrapping the cloak about his shivering frame. "If we bungle here, where can we catch them?"

I was sure. "We won't bungle."

"But if we do? Best not stake everything on one throw. We need something to fall back on."

"Ask Scatloch. Gruffydd was his king."

"Never my king." The Welshman's tone was respectful but edged with ice. "In taking Gwent, he slew my prince and my own lord, who was of the prince's blood."

"And took you for slave?" Gyrth asked.

"No, Saxon. It was your brother did that." Will Scatloch's eyes, a kind of steely blue, seemed to look through Gyrth to his own thoughts. "Gruffydd is high king now, but they say no hour passed before that he did not dream on the crown. On a day that came, he had the head of our prince brought to him, and did he not dress in his finery to dip his fingers in my lord's blood?"

Scatloch studied the road beyond the forest's verge. "In blue and gold he dressed that day. It is color he loves. His tent is brightest red, scarlet as his sins. Earl Gyrth, I am lost forever out of my home because of him, but I will serve ten lords like Thane Aelred before I kneel to Gruffydd ap Llywelyn. If you lose him today, he will go west into the mountains, and such as you will be fighting him for years."

I said and meant it firmly, "No, we will not. I've my own good notion how to—"

Aelred stilled me with a finger to his lips, nodding forward. Where the road rose out of the east, the bobbing heads of the first marchers appeared. "Scouts, the point of their march," he said.

"They walk like tired men," Scatloch observed. "Did I not say?"

I gave my orders to Gyrth and Hugh Malet. "Use what remains of the light. Memorize every foot of ground before you and have your men do the same."

* * *

We had a bad moment when their leading element passed us, thinking they might go on to cross the river, but they turned off the road and just sat down heavily where they were. Half a dozen kilted tribesmen scurried off the road to the other side to erect the unmistakable red tent. In the wake of another came Gruffydd himself in scarlet cloak and blue surcoat over his mail, riding absolutely erect in the saddle beside Aelfgar, tired though he must be.

The lines plodded up and scattered over the meadow. Finally came the rear guard laden with sacks, others prodding the miserable line of tethered slaves. There were at least a hundred of them, Welsh and Saxon alike, perhaps a dozen children who must have slowed their march. Evidently Aelfgar thought the potential profit worth the delay.

By dark all my commanders were instructed and ready to move. Even dubious Hugh admired the simplicity of the plan, while to Gyrth it smacked of the headlong dash of young lovers abducting maidens.

"Going to enjoy this," he chuckled. "Going to be fun."

Not much movement in the enemy camp where most of them, plainly spent, were bedded down and bent for sleep. Here and there men sat about fires, the silhouettes of lone sentries flitting ghostly across the light. In the middle of the camp, Aelfgar's tent and a few yards west Gruffydd's lighted bright as Yule and wafting musical voices into the night.

Leofwine listened with pleasure. "They do sing well, those Welsh. Now, Harold?"

"Not yet."

We waited as movement gradually ceased in the camp and no more songs came from the convivial captains in Gruffydd's tent. Four or five men emerged and vanished into the darkness.

Behind us a detail of Hugh's vavasors stood at their horses' heads, calming the animals to absolute quiet, every hoof wrapped in sacking. At my silent signal Hugh led them out single file to take up position to the west of the enemy camp, ground already scouted by Will Scatloch. Another detachment of horse waited to the east, forward of

Gyrth's foot soldiers. My own mounted element included Leofwine, Aelred, and twenty carls. Will Scatloch grumbled at being separated from his master, but Aelred had his reasons. "Too much of a hazard. He'd kill Gruffydd that quick."

Gruffydd's death was no part of the plan. I sent the Welsh bowman with Hugh for another purpose. We walked back through the dark wood to Aelred and the waiting carls. "Form a line behind me just within the wood's verge. Easy movements. Keep those horses quiet. You know what to do and when. Follow me."

At the edge of the wood, no more than a hundred and fifty paces from our objective, Leofwine clapped me on the shoulder before mounting. "Ought to be a proper lark if we live to laugh about it. If not, I've already said my prayers."

"No fear. Hugh should be in position by now. What's delaying—?"

The knife-edged sound rose out of the night. I'd heard it in Ireland and since among the Welsh, that mournful, soul-chilling keening for the dead, and not a Celt among Gruffydd's tribesmen who wouldn't shiver before he thought. Will Scatloch's signal.

I put the horn to my lips and blew. Instantly the answering roar came from our attacking cavalry east and west of the camp, underscored by drumming hooves, then the cries of Gyrth's soldiers following. Limned in watchfire light, the sentries began to run, shouting alarm, but too late. The two files of cavalry rushed toward and through each other as the riders lay about them with sword and mace. Men scattered or fell where they were struck. Before most of them were on their feet with any weapon in hand, Gyrth's infantry was upon them.

"Now, Leofwine—go!"

I spurred my horse into a run, breaking out of the verge, Leofwine, Aelred, and my small squadron behind me. Speed, speed was the key. They mustn't have time to recover or form any sort of defense. We were to be in and out and gone before that.

Pounding across the road toward Gruffydd's tent I had

a bad moment when Leofwine cried, "Look out!" and I had to wheel aside as two of Hugh's vavasors narrowly missed colliding with me. *Damn!* He'd wheeled east again for another sweep when the orders were to join the rest of the cavalry toward the river and cover our retreat—which would be, I prayed fervently, as swift as our attack.

Gyrth's foot soldiers had formed a ring about the tent, moving aside to let us through as we dismounted. "In," I panted to Aelred and Leofwine. "In quick. To me here, Gyrth!"

My brothers, Aelred, and the carls behind me, I charged into the tent—and went sprawling as I tripped over a grass hummock just inside the entrance. Helpless for the instant, I had a flash of two men, one of them Gruffydd himself, the other a wild-eyed, red-bearded tribesman already bringing a spear to his shoulder as Gruffydd pointed to me like Judgment. I heard Leofwine cry out, then an audible rush as something flew at the spearman with lethal force. The man dropped the spear and tottered back with Aelred's throwing ax in his shoulder. Gruffydd grabbed for the sword by his bed, but Leofwine launched himself in a low dive, catching the Welsh king at the knees and tumbling him. Gyrth knelt by the struggling prince and raised his truncheon.

"Sorry, my lord." With a smart crack on the head, he sent the high king of Wales to sleep. "Horse! Who's got the horse?"

My brothers lifted the slumbering royal weight and hurried from the tent. Gruffydd would be tied over a horse, jolted and jounced through the night all the way to Hereford in his nightshirt and bed socks. So goes the glory of this world.

54 • Harold

G ruffydd was treated with a calculated mixture of respect and subtle humiliation, housed and guarded in the cathedral sacristy and allowed to ferment before I met with him. The raid and abduction had been the easier part, the escape harrowing, and all of it at a forced pace, half walk, half run, and a river to ford in the dark. When our horses limped through Saint Owen's Gate near midnight, men and animals virtually dropped in their tracks. But amazing: Hugh Malet had lost but one knight, Gyrth only three of his fyrd men. Next morning, in the roofless nave, my brothers and I offered thanks to God for our good fortune, though the task was only half done. Aelfgar must be dealt with before his mercenaries had time to recover their spirit. I sent Gyrth and a small escort under a truce flag with a message: Come to parley at Hereford, accept Edward's generous pardon or be pursued and destroyed.

"Aelfgar will come," Gyrth was sure when he returned. "Lord, but they're a sad sight! I mean, we hit them so fast they're still bloody reeling. Some of the slaves got away, there's more wounded than I could count. You know mercenaries, not all as good as mac Ciaran's lot. They want to get paid and go home. They all but forced Aelfgar to accept the parley."

Earl Aelfgar would meet us on the morrow south of Hereford. He would respect the truce, but no weapons or spoils would be surrendered.

"That's his pride, Gyrth. All he's got left beside fool's luck."

The silver looted from Hereford and Winchcombe was a small price for the peace Edward needed. He was willing to pardon and restore Aelfgar to some of his former lands in Anglia in the interests of peace, but was more concerned with Gruffydd's intentions.

Gyrth unbuckled his mail coat with the clumsy movements of a man tired to the bone. "There's little fight left in them, should never have tried for Winchcombe. Now, if my august brother has no further need of me for matters heroic, I'd love to sleep for a week."

Aelfgar's grand, foolish foray was done, my task now to deal with Gruffydd. He had recently bowed all of south Wales to his personal sway. Now he raided English lands with all the vigor of Caesar ramping through Gaul. Edward and our Witan urgently needed to curb the man and, above all, take the measure of his ambitions. Closely guarded in the sacristy, Gruffydd was shown the courtesy due a king—more or less. He had to endure a lack of privacy and the hostile stares of the cathedral priests each time they used the chamber to robe for mass. Gruffydd still wore the soiled nightshirt we took him in, though someone had donated a heavy cloak to cover him. He could wash but was denied the barber. This was calculated. The Welsh are even more meticulous about their appearance than men like Tostig. I wanted Gruffydd to stew in disarray until I was ready to see him.

There were two bored guards at the sacristy door. I set the jug of Welsh whiskey at their feet. "Have a good nip each, but leave the rest, mind."

When I entered the small chamber Gruffydd was hunched over a peat brazier, but the evening was sharp and the warmth did not spread far. Two short tallow candles burned on a table. The sacristy had the stale, drab feeling of all tiring rooms. Gruffydd did not rise but straightened on the stool as if receiving an inferior. It struck me he might expect an obeisance.

"My lord, I am Harold of Wessex."

He said nothing. Commanding black eyes swept over me with distant disdain. Between forty-odd and fifty, Gruffydd ap Llywelyn was—the Greek word must aid me here—the most *dramatic* figure I'd ever seen. Whether or not he strove for the quality, it seemed inherent. Seated in a nightshirt, old cloak, and wool stockings mud-grimed and out at the toe, he radiated dignity and vitality. In any gathering all men's eyes would be drawn to this vibrant power, and God help the women.

"Yes," he acknowledged finally in grotesquely accented English. "My executioner, is it?"

"Not at all," I assured him quickly, dragging another stool close to the fire. "Your captor for the time and your host who regrets—"

"You have not leave to sit!" The sharp command surprised and checked me a moment before he added, "But you may."

As I sat, Gruffydd stood. Clever: Like most Welshmen, he was short of stature. I would have topped him at sixteen and towered over him a year later. Now he exploited the advantage of looking down at me as I warmed my hands at the fire.

"I trust my lord enjoyed sufficient supper," I said, knowing he'd not.

He pointed to the dishes on a table. "Do you call that a meal for a king? A bowl of barley and parsnips and a few peels of onion? Or this miserable closet fit lodging?"

"None of us had much more to eat. Hereford's rather pinched this week. As for lodging, I sleep myself in the nave beyond, which—as my lord must be aware—currently suffers from no roof and a dying bishop." I looked up quickly and held his eye without blinking. "But I imagine you and Aelfgar supped and quartered well when you passed through."

He dismissed that as beneath comment. "Whatever is my fate, I am prepared."

I believed him, yet had the impression that this small, vital man was speaking not to me but to the ages and unseen bards who would set his words and deeds to music. My father had a way of undercutting such men, from Edward himself to the officious steward at Sheppey. "My lord, do sit and let's be civilized. I'm glad you speak my tongue, for I'm ignorant of yours."

"Eng-lish." He mouthed the word as if it tasted bad and should be spat out. "It is not that I wish to."

"My king has much care to the peace of his realm. When you invade us, that care becomes his chief concern—and mine."

"I have not invaded," Gruffydd answered as to a backward child. "You are the invaders." He remained standing over me.

"What? I don't follow."

"Hengest. Horsa, Cerdic, Offa, and all the rest. The whole thieving, deceiving pack of you."

"But surely you—that was five hundred years ago."

"And the spawn of pirates do not like to think on their black-handed ancestors," he countered. "How like you to think in years, as if sin faded with time. What have years to do with forever, with the eternal? You pushed us back and back, always more of you coming on. Mourning, we lost the green downs of the great Belgae, wept as we fled the rich lands of the Coritani, even those of the Atrebates and Cornovii until we could go no farther but into the sea, and those names faded from the land and all memory save mine. A long journey, Saxon, begun in such glory that Greeks once paid tribute to us, and Rome itself trembled to hear our war horns at the gates. In the end Rome was too old and weak to aid us against your kind, so *we* fought you, ourselves alone. For a time bright as it was brief, there was Artos Guletic. He gave us glory again."

For Gruffydd, as he spoke, the close walls of the sacristy seemed to dissolve into infinite vista. There were actual tears in his eyes as his voice rose and dipped like the hills and deep valleys of the only land left him. "I am but one man, but a king with a dream and the heart to follow that dream. How would you know what it is to be born with a destiny? Do you think I have warred against my own countrymen for power alone? Against you for slaves and a few bags of silver? I would build the dream again as Artos did."

As he held the mantle about his breast, face uplifted to an applauding heaven—oh, God, I understood him: infected from birth with the fever-dream, ecstatic and lightheaded with it until the glamour inevitably must consume him as such visions will. Flawed as Swegn and Tostig or noble as this small Welshman, it kills them all.

"Was it not foretold that Aelfgar would come? Betrayed as Artos was, and by your own brother?"

Discourteous or not, I could *not* keep silent for that monumental lack of judgment in any man. "Gruffydd—if I may lay lyrics aside—Aelfgar is a witless fool and an embarrassment to our king. Surely a ruler wise as yourself has seen his flaws. There are no simple answers, nor are we merely the greedy descendants of pirates. My father saw, as I've dreamed myself, a . . . nation. Ruled by a king, but where what one man proposes, another may dispute and between them find direction, order, and wisdom. Wise rider on a wiser horse that sometimes knows the way home better than his master, when to find an easier road and even compromise when needed."

"What compromise can there be with greatness?" he denied. "You are not like your brother."

"Nor as mad, sir. Unimaginative perhaps. Oh, I did have a flush of it once, very young, when Edward invested me, but no talent for the grand destiny. Not like Swegn at all but very much like my father, who taught me to see the bone of the actual under the beauty of the ideal. King Edward in friendship urges you not to trust Aelfgar. Whatever feast he promised, he's hardly a master cook, merely one of the butchers."

"I will trust him as I may." Gruffydd sat down, stretching his feet to the fire. The strength and nobility of his features altered subtly to something more like cunning. "He is a brother to me, and valuable. And his daughter, they say, is beyond loveliness."

"Aldyth? Oh, she's all of that," I confirmed heartily. "I met her as a young girl. She must be breathtaking now." And another potential problem. Poetics aside, a Welsh alliance with Mercia could be no end of trouble for England. "You and Aelfgar have some agreement in this?"

Again I received that veiled glance: me to know, you

to guess at. "Even greatness would not walk alone by choice."

I was beginning to know the cut of the man: canny and strong, but emotional, perhaps even sentimental. He and Swegn would have struck a common chord from the first. I called one of the guards and told him to bring the jug I'd left outside. The level of its contents had dropped but not by much. I offered the whiskey to Gruffydd. "From your country."

He sniffed at the liquor with surprise, then pleasure, but thrust the jug at me. "You drink, Saxon."

"Really!" I had to laugh. "Oh, for—my lord, I could take offense. If I'd orders to eliminate you, you would have died in your tent. My brother bashed you only to keep you quiet. And he did apologize." I took a substantial drink of the warm, smooth whiskey and offered the jug again. "May it well become you."

Gruffydd ventured a suspicious sip, then two good swallows, ending in a luxurious gasp of pleasure. "That is good. Just that we remember Vortigern and the Night of the Long Knives. Yours is a treacherous race."

"Practical, actually. Pass the cheer while you're reminiscing."

"It is said our drink is too strong for English stomachs."

"In my time I was too fond of it."

Gruffydd drank with thirsty relish, I more sparingly. The whiskey warmed through me and made my body remember how tired it was. We fell silent for a space in the draft-shuddering light of the candles. Gruffydd seemed far away, not gone slack with drink but like a man listening to music or some inner voice. No doubt he thrilled to the picture of his own life as a new tale for the bards: Aelfgar as his loyal Bedwyr, Aldyth as gleaming Gwynhwyfar . . . but who for Modred? I let my mind drift with the question. For such a man, honest in his motives but playing them large on an eternal stage, greatness as passion, what is noble passion without the closure of betrayal?

I rubbed at my eyes, not believing then or later that Gruffydd gave much thought to the reality of his aims, or that he had as many enemies in Wales as in England. For every loyal friend, a thousand Will Scatlochs with a mortal feud against his blood. He would see only his vision, brilliantly imagined as Arthur and as long dead, while I groped in a fog like Godwine before me toward something dim, but at least of this world and the common, comprehensible clay of men.

Gruffydd's head came up suddenly. "There."

"Um, what?"

"You did not hear?"

"No, nothing."

"I meant no sound of your world. On our mountains, in our valleys, we hear the music of forever, and eternity is never so far, but often it walks with us. Your tongue is not shaped to such sounds, nor your ear to that music. Have you never dreamed of glory, Englishman?"

I thought of Swegn and our grandiose boy games, and something stirred in my heart. "Played at it once."

"And not since?" Gruffydd passed me the whiskey again. "Is it that you never felt each day, each step was on a path destined for you? One, mayhap, that you walked before in different shoes and name?"

Lord, how did one deal with such dreamers? "Yes, I would disappoint you after Swegn. I'm an ordinary man, and to be Edward's earl is a long working year. As for destinies, I keep tripping over others like yours." I set the jug on the floor and rose. "Until tomorrow, my lord."

To my surprise, Gruffydd got up and extended his hand. "When you entered, I thought not to see another day."

"But I've said. By the king's will and on my word, that's not to be."

He regarded me curiously. "Swegn I understood with my heart, but you are yet beyond knowing, yet I could find some affection for you."

"And I for you." I gripped his hand warmly. "Savor the whiskey to keep out the cold. You leave for Rhuddlan tomorrow."

"Home." Gruffydd gave the word all the colors of its meaning. "I did not hope to see it again."

"Oh, enough of that. But heed me, Gruffydd, and take

this to heart. Edward greets you, and thus in his own words: 'We are sparing in our justice and do not raise the sword until we must. Send King Gruffydd home in peace, but if he ever troubles our land again, send us his head.' ''

The black eyes glowed. "Stones."

"Eh?"

"English words are like stone. Hard and bare. Nothing shines in them."

"Except clear meaning, I hope. Your health, my lord." I took a last drink from the jug. "Do have a care to it. I'll find suitable clothing for your journey."

He drew himself up perceptibly. "You need not trouble."

"No trouble. Nightshirts do very little for majesty."

When Gruffydd tossed the wide cloak over one shoulder, the motion was the sweep of a great bird's wing. "Learn from a king. The majesty is not in the garment."

"As you make clear to me. Good rest to my lord."

He heard only his own music until the end, seeing his name carved in stone as *Restitutor Orbis,* restorer of the world. Chiefs and clans flocking to his hall, reborn Britain adoring at his feet, Aldyth worshipful by his side and a bard immortalizing in song the deeds of the new Arthur and his queen's unmatchable beauty. Lost and gone, Gruffydd. Time's not cut to your measure anymore, and if even my Saxon ear lifts sometimes to catch that ghostly strain, it will never resound to me as to you. The world is sceptered by unmusical men like Edward who, while dreaming on heaven, hedges and bargains, complains of the weather, chilled feet, and his chronic head cold—and men like me, who must cobble and patch with whatever comes to hand.

Often after that November I thought of Gruffydd, saw him ride his fortune until it tripped on one hurdle too high and fell, crushing him. The man was strong, the man was beautiful and preposterous and doomed. What hell it must be to live in the shadow of a destiny. Rather like a constant headache—but God damn their whole kind because none of them can follow that hollow phantom without making *you* bleed for it, and that sticks in my throat.

In truth, Godwine, that may be your peasant blood in me, tuneless notes beside Gruffydd's, but set to an insistent drum.

55 • Harold

The next year, sourly recalling my prophetic advice to Earl Ralf, Edward met Gruffydd across Severn and, of course, the Welsh king insisted Edward cross the river to him.

"My ancestors once ruled where Edward sits now," he sent. To which Edward returned, "Edward now sits where his ancestors conquered," but crossed the river as an equal and confirmed Gruffydd's title in return for homage as overlord. Shortly thereafter Leofric died, succeeded by Aelfgar, who sent Aldyth to marry his sworn Welsh brother. Each was smitten with the other on sight, so bards sang, and it does make a good story. Aldyth bore Gruffydd two sons, Llywelyn and Rhodri, and then I lost track of them with time and shifting events nearer home.

Edward the Exile returned from Hungary with his German wife and three children. That was—let me think— 'fifty-seven. Though the prince was no older than I, the sea change and fetid London promptly sent him to a crypt in Saint Paul's and thence to God, leaving us to salvage what we could of the royal offspring: Margaret, the eldest at thirteen, a second sister, and five-year-old Edgar, a docile boy too young to rejoice in his good fortune as heir. Margaret we foisted on—say rather offered to—Malcolm of Scotland as a calculation of diplomacy. The young king owed Edward gratitude for Siward's help in defeating Macbeth.

With our northern door locked for the time and Gruffydd quiet in the west, a greater problem bore down on us like an iceberg, visible far away. Edward was fifty-three and declining in vigor. English hopes for the succession turned on baby Edgar—secretly, because Edward never officially repudiated his pledge to William. Though secrecy was wise for a time, Edward would not deny William even when the need became imminent; that directness was not in him, the will to solution evident only in his beloved Westminster. Stone by stone it rose as, year by year, the question spoke, shouted, and then screamed at us in the Witan: *What are we to do after Edward? There is only Edgar.*

Edgar alone. Eadgytha's astrologer cast the expected royal future for him. Stigand, though he'd provided the boy with the best tutors, predicted less in private to me.

"I would say the boy . . ." Stigand left the thought unfinished.

"Well? The boy what?"

"Well, you'll be there to help him, not that he'll be much trouble. Edgar is the most precociously mediocre child I've ever examined."

"You needn't let that get about," I cautioned.

"No need. Anyone who's met the boy for five minutes gleans the same impression. He's learned a little English and some Latin. For the rest," Stigand sighed, "he does like his horse."

"The queen's seer was more optimistic."

"The queen's seer is an overpaid mountebank," opined Stigand of Canterbury. "Or else badly misread the stars."

The word *stars* jostled something in memory. "Roland wrote an odd note on his chart. Do you believe in dreams?"

By inclination and office Stigand did not. "I've never been blessed with the kind of dreams attributed to saints. On the other hand, when I've indulged in spiced eel before retiring, they've been apocalyptic."

"Roland supported his predictions with a dream he'd had of a star with a fiery tail."

"*Cometa*, yes." Stigand recognized the reference. "Oh, there was one such seen over England the year old King Edgar died. Roland wouldn't know the star preceded a disastrous famine; I'll believe to that extent, but the present Edgar will hardly blaze in any sense."

If a dull prince, a blessedly quiet time to live through, peaceful enough for me to turn home to family and to savor like fine *brand-de-vin* the warmth of those I loved. Edith bloomed at Bosham, summer a festival through which my boys ran and gamboled and grew, carefree and independent as hound pups. Gyrth spent as much time with us as he could spare from his own lands. My widowed mother, like the rest of us in our hearts, packed her sorrows away in the bottom of a press and never spoke of them, sometimes avoiding them pointedly, as when someone mentioned Wulfnoth.

"He will be twenty-two this year," Edith reckoned over her sewing. "Isn't that right, Mother?"

"Yes. Harold, you *must* see to Leofwine's future. He needs a household and livings of his own. And fitting rank," Gytha added over her needle. "He's worn your livery long enough and time he married, by the by. And heaven's sake teach him to groom himself better than Gyrth."

"Oh, Gyrth's my own great big bear," Edith declared fondly.

"Speaking of high time, *he* ought to be married," Gytha said, not to be swerved from purpose. "There must be someone suitable in Anglia this side of the fens. Not that Gyrth would impress on first sight. Honestly: a belted earl, member of the Witan, and he dresses like someone's gardener."

I winked at Edith, who loved Gyrth as the dearest brother she never had. What can I say about him? Of *loyal* he was the very meaning of the word; to be else was not in Gyrth. As the years passed and my life stretched into its fourth decade, while I became more and more of an acting regent under fading Edward and dreamed of a nation, Gyrth *was* that nation incarnate, a thoroughly provincial lord in the casual chaos of a bachelor hall, and so unheeding of his appearance that his steward usually had to remind him that his hair and beard cried out for a barber.

Never subtle, he had nevertheless absorbed our father's style in rule, law tempered with compassion, good sense, and a natural common touch. Alas, to Gytha's despair, his habits with women recalled my own youth. Gyrth fell violently in lust on Monday, out on Tuesday, honestly in love of a Wednesday, recovered on Thursday, and by Friday was quite himself again, no more repentant than a stallion. He was sensible enough not to involve the well-born girls hopefully put before him but romped cheerfully among lesser women, who bore a growing number of children, unrecognized but whom Gyrth felt obligated to support. No furies battened on him, none of Swegn's soul-hollowing agonies. To Gyrth a love gone was a love forgotten.

"But never, *never* drink too much white wine," he cautioned me greenly after a long night of it. "The French sell it to kill us. You want to die and can't. Tell Mother I will marry. Well, I will definitely think about it. As matters are going, it's cheaper. Harold, come hunt with me in Epping this autumn."

Hugh Malet a respected exception, Gyrth abhorred most Normans on principle and was the first of the Witan to urge public proclamation of Edgar's succession. When Edward proposed a new tax toward the work at Westminster, Gyrth strongly opposed it despite sharp criticism from the clergy of Saint Peter's and Edward himself.

"My shires aren't rich," he protested. "My folk are the three plain Fs: foresters, fishermen, and farmers, and none of 'em need a new church at Thorney any more than I do. What was wrong with the *old* one?"

My boys grew apace with Edward's abbey in those tranquil years. One day captures in memory for me the best of that time. April, and all of us save Tostig were at Bosham for my birthday, the meadows bright with early flowers and the day so pleasant that Edith and Gytha decreed we dine in the fields, and duly dispatched the servants with hampers of food, cloths, and wine. Godwine took officious charge of his younger brothers and kept them more or less subdued, but the best and most beautiful moment came when Gyrth, wine-warmed and playful, stood up and cleared his throat in the pompous manner of Chancellor Regenbald calling an audience to order.

"Harrumph! Give ear, give ear! His Grace the honorable Gyrth Godwinesson, Earl of East Anglia—"

"And an impressive list of etceteras following," Leofwine proclaimed, presenting a document to Gyrth on bended knee. Gyrth unrolled it and trumpeted his will.

"—does hereby, in consideration of the birthday of gr-r-eat Wessex, give, bequeath, and donate—this."

With a flourish Gyrth delivered the parchment to Edith, who read quickly and squealed with delight. She sprang up and flung her arms around Gyrth before descending on me. "It's Nazeing! Look, he's given us back *Naze*ing!" Not just a second home, but the one place Edith loved even more than I. "It's home, love."

My lady went a little mad with happiness that day in the meadow. Gytha wove her a chaplet of flowers which she wore askew, calling for her horse. She and Gyrth and Leofwine gamboled and charged at each other in mock jousts, and Gyrth set little Magnus before him on the saddle, wheeling about the green in great circles while the boy whooped with delight. The love between us was a delicious presence as the sun swept over and down, and I watched Edith wear herself out with joy, my one arm around Gytha, the other holding little Edmund warm against me.

Sins of the father, Edward? One was the ability to love, another to wrest joy from whatever moment held any.

Winchester, 1061. I stood with my family and followers and raised a cheer as Leofwine swore his fealty to Edward and received the coronet of an earl, his lands created from portions of mine and Gyrth's.

Edward's comment was typical: "Now I am *completely* surrounded."

Teeter-totter, up and down the earldoms go as England muddles and mangles and manages somehow. Aelfgar is dead of natural causes—"Pure truculence," said Edith—replaced by his son Edwin, still a boy. William, too shrewd to repeat a mistake, will not leave Normandy to press his claim in person, but ever sends the same demand to Edward: Confirm me!

Edward dodges, placates, and improvises. Now the Witan in one body, seeing secret policy more danger than advantage, pleads with him to deny Normandy and publish Edgar's succession. Edward vacillates—"Let us wait a little longer, let us see"—but in one quarter his retribution is swift. Gruffydd ap Llywelyn has crossed Severn again, raiding into Mercia. In his Welsh heart his pact with Aelfgar was personal. The earl dead, he feels released from any promise, and fatally misreads both Edward's resolve and English character.

Christmas court, Gloucester, 1062. Edward stands before the Witan with the command every one of us knows is our only solution. Gruffydd has always been a thorn; now he grew to a spear. One by one, as the resolution goes round the table, we add our signatures—Wessex, Anglia, Mercia, Northumbria, Leofwine of Surrey, Stigand, Cynesige, Ealdred of Worcester, the combined Crown, nobles, and clergy of England—to the sentence of death.

"The earls Harold and Tostig will call their levies, pursue Gruffydd into Wales wheresoever, and run him to ground."

Our king sinks slowly into his chair, fifty-six now, his gaunt features deep-set in the cast of melancholy, advised against hunting or any undue exertion by his physicians. "I warned him. He didn't believe me. The fool . . . the fool. Bring me his head."

56 • Harold

We couldn't wait for spring. Gruffydd had wounded our west too deeply in arrant defiance. The thing cried out to be done now, but we were stymied from the start. While Tostig assembled his levies, Scots raided across his border for cattle. Malcolm regretted, of course, protesting his personal innocence, but the situation had to be met immediately. I had to march without Tostig. Gyrth and Leofwine were with me, seasoned soldiers now, but no lark flavor to this campaign. While we struck deep into Gwynedd, hunting the elusive Gruffydd, our real enemy was the terrible mountain winter.

Men's hands and feet froze in the unrelenting wind, horses went lame. Snowstorms blinded us so that Gruffydd might have walked within yards of our column or camp and never been seen. We shivered in our tents at night. Sentries were found frozen to death in the morning or so frostbitten they had to be left behind. By the time we reached Rhuddlan, Gruffydd was gone. We never saw him. Will Scatloch had spoken plain, hard truth. The man could elude us for years.

That failed campaign taught me a sobering lesson. I was thirty-seven, not twenty-one, and the years had taken their toll. Where once I could vault into the saddle in one leap, when I tried it now, I landed with a jarring thud and needed the stirrup.

"Well," Gyrth allowed, flexing the frostbitten fingers of a left hand always henceforth to be weaker than the right. "At least we threw a fright into the bastard."

"Did we?" I thought not. Gruffydd would see his escape as an episode in the dashing epic of his destiny. "How's Leof?"

"Can't leave his bed," Gyrth worried. "Can't go on like this, any of us. His cough is worse, deeper. And I've more men down with sickness."

Nor could I push men to what was now beyond them and myself. Of three thousand men, scarce half were fit to march, let alone fight. We turned and limped back to Gloucester, a sorry, sick remnant of crippled horses and spent men in rusty mail.

Edward sent to me, "We cannot accept failure in this. Rest, refit, and wait for Earl Tostig. Gruffydd must be broken."

Must be because neither that iron little king nor his people were going to trouble us again. The man reminded me of one of the great stones on Salisbury Plain: admirable, but I had one crucial advantage. Where he wouldn't learn, I could. The best school toward success is what you learn from failure. If we couldn't take Gruffydd from Wales, we would take Wales out from under him. For that, there was Tostig.

We met in Chester, from whence Tostig would launch his attack. Now in his thirty-fourth year, Tostig was in his prime, heavier, still opulent in dress, and wearing power with the consciousness of being born to it. Chester had declined much since Roman times, but its walls still rounded much of the old square fort on River Dee. Tostig and I strolled through the bedraggled town, agreeing it was the best staging area for our two-pronged attack. He would march overland into Gwynedd, raiding at opportunity but bearing toward Rhuddlan in a war of attrition while I took the fleet and scoured the coast. The object was to do so much damage that the clans and chieftains would find Gruffydd too expensive to support, and submit.

Our walk brought us to the small Roman amphitheater by Saint Mary's church. We stood poised on the overgrown bank above it when Tostig asked, "Are you ready for this, Harold?"

The condescension was so like him. Others might be

found wanting but never he. "I've been there before, Tostig."

"And failed. You're not going to have a moral headache over what must be done, are you?"

Not this time. If I wouldn't take his relish in the deed, I was as determined. We would gut Wales if we must. "We'll take hostages only when the chiefs submit. Until then, no mercy. No prisoners."

"Yes!" Glowing with excitement that burst forth in exuberant laughter, my brother bounded away down the worn stone benches into the center of the arena to whirl about, head back, teeth gleaming white and predatory beneath glossy black mustaches, arms raised in triumphant invocation. "Gruffydd ap Llywelyn! You who are about to die—salute me!"

May . . . June . . . July. From Bristol I sailed around and up the Welsh coast, burning and ravaging to break their fighting spirit. The Welsh are brave but not dogged, some inspired by Gruffydd's heady vision but none able to comprehend men who will grip and hang on simply because it must be done. While I stabbed at the coast and left it burning, Tostig's column seared and slashed a wide swath through the heart of northern Wales, burning villages and crops before they could be harvested. One by one the brightly clad chieftains came down from their strongholds, their woad-painted tribesmen behind them, and submitted, renouncing their allegiance to Gruffydd. Some of them had never seen the man who had called himself high king for eight years.

"But there is one who knows him," I was advised. "He will come if he has safe conduct."

They're subtle, the Welsh, expecting you to understand that which is not said. "And who is that?"

"Prince Cynan ap Iago," the chieftain told me. "Of the House of Gwynedd."

My soul sang *gratia Dei*. This was what I waited and prayed for, Gruffydd's own kin to sell him. "He will have safe conduct but must first render hostages."

"I am thinking he will offer more than that." The

Powys chieftain stepped in to me, close enough for me to see the scar running from chin to ear under the garish war paint. "He follows the high king, but it is that your brother gives them no rest. The king flees from one stronghold to the next, hill to hill. The clans know they cannot win. And Gruffydd it was who killed Cynan's father."

Fortunately for England there were men in Wales more practical, if less high-minded, than their king. "Let Prince Cynan come to me and quickly, for I'm to meet my brother at Rhyll."

Sixth August, 1063. Late afternoon on the sands of Rhyll at the mouth of River Clwyd, the sea murmuring in ebb from the shore, the gulls laughing still as they'd done since God created the world and let them in on the jest. The day was hot but cooler by the shore as I left Aelred and greeted Botulf at the entrance to the tent I shared with Tostig. Botulf peered up the long valley to the south. "Can't see any movement. Did the Welshman say today?"

"If he could, yes. Keep a sharp eye. Let me know when you see them."

The tent's side panels were partially rolled up to catch the cool sea air. Within, stripped to the waist and fresh from his bath, Tostig sat on a stool as his barber shaved him. His fresh linen was laid out, waiting. I felt seedy by contrast.

"What's keeping him?" my brother asked as the barber scraped delicately at his chin. "*Ai—watch* it, man! Strop that blade, will you? Where is he, Harold?"

I stripped off my linen tunic and splashed at my face and body in a ready basin. "He said he'd be here if it's done."

"If."

"I think he will. I made it worth his while. His lands will not be touched."

Tostig dismissed the barber with a curt gesture. "Out— and tomorrow be sure that razor is sharp. The idea is to shave, not excavate."

He rose and stretched lazily. Whatever Tostig did in Northumbria, life agreed with him. There were noticeable beginnings of fat about his upper hips, a slight heaviness to the cheeks and jaw. He and Judith lived well in York, but there had been rumblings of discontent from the northern thanes. Eadgytha was close-mouthed about their private correspondence, but I gathered Tostig's rigid rule did not sit well with the northerners.

He began to dress, meticulous as always, donning and smoothing each article in turn, not adding the next until each draped to his satisfaction, like a painter adding precise colors to a work of art. "Amusing, isn't it? We spend years in men, money, and bother on this bard-sung backwater when all we needed was one Welshman with a blood feud." Tostig held out the heavy chain of his rank. "Here, do this about me. I suppose you're sorry."

"I got over 'sorry' last winter when Leofwine almost died. But I can feel some regret for Gruffydd."

"You admire him, don't you?"

"Oddly enough, yes. He's one of those fabulous creatures in a wild tale, a gryphon or Beowulf's dragon. You know they're impossible in a real world, and still you half wish they lived. Listening to Gruffydd is like hearing a beautiful, dead language that no one speaks anymore. Yes, I admire him."

"Sentiment will kill you one day." Tostig slung his baldric. "If nothing else does."

Meaning himself? Ever since I submitted to him and Eadgytha in the matter of Aelfgar, my brother's manner toward me was faintly tinged with contempt. If I cried him dishonest, he could scream heresy at me and Edith.

Botulf ducked his head into the tent. "My lords, they're coming down the valley. The Welsh prince and ten others."

"Good. Tell Aelred to give the order."

I hurriedly finished dressing in the scarlet and gold, draped the chain of office about my shoulders, and slung the baldric. Two long horn notes told me Aelred was carrying out his office. Tostig and I emerged from the tent into the slant afternoon shadows to see our carls forming a lane, every man at attention as Prince Cynan neared. Botulf took up the Wessex colors and dressed on my left as Tostig's standard bearer hurried to his side. So we waited formally at the end of the lane, our flags furling in sea wind. As Cynan entered the lane, the horn sounded again and our carls knelt. It was an effective moment worthy of Godwine.

"Grand but absurd," Tostig muttered out of the side of his mouth while nodding and smiling welcome to our visitors. "I mean for one shirttail Welshman."

"The smaller the man, the more fragile his dignity. Didn't Father teach you that?"

"Father deigned to impart very little to me. We weren't close."

Cynan dismounted heavily, the scale armor rattling on his back. The brilliant blue-and-yellow-checked mantle was fastened by two large, circular brooches, and he wore a kilt over cross-gartered trousers. His family resemblance to Gruffydd was evident, though the black hair was long and straight over bushy beard and wild mustaches. The mailed chieftain dismounted and then two of his tattered escort, carrying a covered wicker basket between them.

I bowed deeply. "Welcome, Prince. The House of Gwynedd honors my tent. My brother, Earl Tostig of Northumbria."

I would have led them to the tent, but the burly chieftain who guarded his lord stepped deliberately to the fore and entered the tent first, glanced about and returned with a reassuring nod to Cynan. Inside, the two bearers set down the basket and withdrew. Cynan uncovered the contents.

"You see, Wessex, that I at least have kept my word."

Pleasure and pride fairly oozed from him. He lifted the head by the short curls. The eyes were half open in the bloodless face.

"Unlovely sight," Tostig remarked. "But we couldn't expect him to look his best."

"He was my blood and the enemy of my blood," Cynan said. "My father died by his hand, and I have answered that."

"Truly. Tostig, the writ."

I'd had the document written in Latin which, I'd been told, Cynan read far better than English. For the first time

I'd personally signed for Edward as *subregulus,* with binding powers to act in his place. "In the name of Edward, King of the English and overlord of Wales, Prince Cynan is confirmed in all lands and titles held by him under Gruffydd, and his hostages are released to return with him."

Cynan read the document at least three times over, not trusting what he could not see for himself. The writ misrepresented nothing, so far as it went. The wilier part of our Welsh policy, partly conceived by myself, was to keep such little men happy while neutralizing the more powerful. There would be no more high king. Gwynedd would be divided between Gruffydd's two half brothers, Rhiwallon and Bleddyn. Concerning those southern lands conquered by Gwynedd, our policy was purposefully vague. In short, the Welsh would be fighting each other for years and unlikely to unite against England. His lands safe and his pride salved, Prince Cynan wouldn't realize for those years, if ever, that we'd broken his country's back.

This is why you're dead, Gruffydd, fine as you were. You wouldn't learn and couldn't change. Legends may love you, but history doesn't give a damn. So sing with the Welsh heroes and forgive my lack of charity, but I've seen how much men like you cost.

The tent flap barely rustled, and then Aelred appeared at my side, gazing with placid blue eyes at the sorry object in the basket.

"Yes, Thane?"

"Pardon, Earl Harold. I promised Will Scatloch I'd see this and tell'm it's done."

"As you see. Please tell my guards to release Prince Cynan's people immediately."

"So I will." Aelred slipped out of the tent. Their matter concluded, Cynan and his chieftain merely grunted at us and left the tent, making ready to depart. With the same pomp observed on his arrival, the prince left our camp amid kneeling carls, blaring horns, and bowed earls, his freed hostages trudging in his royal wake.

"Tostig?" I asked, waving courteous farewells. "Did you glean the impression he doesn't trust us?"

"Distinctly, but would you trust someone who'd just bribed you to kill your own kin?"

We'd bought Edward's security with assassination, a grimy truth that gave Tostig no qualms whatsoever. "Such was good enough for Brutus."

"Brutus bore the knife himself."

"Only you would haggle the point. I am the only sane man in a mad world." Tostig turned to a more immediate problem. "We'll have to pack Gruffydd in salt, if we can find enough, else he'll never keep till Winchester."

57 • Harold

Only one task left before I could escape to Nazeing and Edith. Something about my wife troubled me like a disturbing dream one can't quite recall beyond the malaise that lingers after waking. I would look at Edith as she moved about the hall or busied herself with the boys, and reassure myself that we *were* happy, only to know in the next breath that young joy in each other had faded to contentment. No, be honest, less than that. You cannot live so many years with a woman and not sense distance growing between you, but so damned indefinable that neither can name the ill, let alone speak a remedy, and silence deepens.

I know I'm away more and more of the year, but the king . . .

Always the king, ever that heaven-obsessed old man. Always the nation to be served through him. I was his dog fetching back the stick from wherever it was flung. Here, Edward: I've brought you Gruffydd's head. Stuff and mount it on your mantel for all I care, for I'm going home.

Fortunately Eadgytha was visiting her own estate outside Winchester. Just as well; she needn't see this. I waited in the great hall with two servants carrying the covered basket between them, while the time came and passed for my audience. A full hour later a priest entered from the far end of the great hall. I had to look twice to recognize Archbishop Stigand in the plainest of brown monk's robes. He hurried to me, his forehead creased with concern. I knelt and kissed his ring.

"Harold, he'll see you now, but . . ."

"What is it?"

My old friend swerved his eyes at the two servants and drew me aside. "Don't overtax Edward, he's ill. He didn't even dress this morning, saw no one but his chaplain."

"Should I return later?"

"No, he insisted you attend him now. Another letter from Duke William."

When Hugolin admitted me, I dismissed the two lackeys who guessed what they carried and were happy to abandon the gruesome charge. I knelt to Edward, appalled at his appearance. His color was ashen, forehead wrapped in a bandage. He sat on the edge of the large, curtained bed where my father had died, pinched and withered in his nightshirt, sipping from a steaming cup.

"Just willowbark," he informed me. "I've had a beastly headache all night. Hardly slept."

More than that. A mere headache wouldn't leave him looking like death.

"It just gets worse," Edward fretted in a feeble voice as he rose with an effort and approached the basket. "Open it."

We'd managed to find a certain amount of salt but barely enough. Edward squinted nearsightedly at the head, then stumbled back to his bed. His hands shook taking up the tea again, and he seemed unable to keep his eyes all the way open, as if light were painful to them. "Have it set on a pike on London Bridge. Always something. We bolt one door and someone forces another."

As he fumbled for the lead-sealed document beside him on the rumpled bed, I would have sworn he couldn't see it, reaching clear past the document at first. "From the duke."

With bare civility William questioned the status of Edgar in our court, tediously reasserting his own right and at a loss to understand why Edward had not answered him on the matter before this. Patience exhausted and suspicions rising, William cited Wulfnoth and Hakon, reminding Edward of the penalty both might incur if his word proved false, even hinting at stronger measures forthcoming.

"Harold?" The reedy voice was aged as Edward looked. "All is secure in Gwynedd?"

"Yes, sire."

"Lady Aldyth?"

"She and her sons were sent home to Coventry. We— Edward!" I leaped to help him as he wilted and crumpled in a ball on the bed, hands pressed to his head.

"Lord God," he gasped. "Never this bad."

"I'll call your physicians."

"No . . . no, we will finish here first. Harold, I can barely see." Edward levered himself up again and took the mug of tea I placed in his hand. "I need you now. You must deal with William."

"Yes. We can wait no longer to proclaim the Aetheling." So much was clear, though I might be condemning my brother and nephew to death or life in a dungeon. "This week. Now."

"Yes, I will. I will think on it." An indecisive wavering of his head. "But not now."

It has to be now. You did this to us, you and your supposed cleverness. "If William's intent is firm as his letters, then 'stronger measures' might mean he's prepared to go to war."

"I don't know, Harold. I don't seem to be able to draw any of it together today. Can't think."

Ill as he was, I couldn't spare him now. His was the royal place for which men bowed to him, and he must honor and fill it. "Then let me, Edward. We have two alternatives, neither pleasant. Proclaim Edgar and risk a war, or confirm William and make war inevitable.''

Edward tottered to his feet, weaving back and forth. "You think he would dare? He would be so bold?''

"You know him best, but I know our people. Men like Gyrth and Aelred and Teinfrith will never submit. *I* will never—good God, how could you have put us in such a position?''

"I thought to gain time. The queen and I might still be reconciled, still might have a son.''

Nor did Edward believe then in that year of his absolute power that Godwine and I would return with all the nation behind us. Our cunning royal dove had outclevered himself at last.

"I thought of every possibility,'' Edward reasoned. "Who knew the Exile would step off the boat and die within weeks? It seemed the best policy at the time. Perhaps I was wrong.''

"More than wrong, Edward, you were irresponsible.''

"Wessex—remember your place.''

"I can't. I dare not. By the thread of that promise, you hung a sword over all of us.''

"It was our royal decision.''

There it was: one man's crippled thinking against a people's crying need. "I know you hated Godwine—''

"I did not, not at the end. I forgave him.''

"—but did you learn nothing from him? You had no *right*. No English king has the right to bequeath our crown as a personal fief.''

" 'Our' crown?'' Scarce more than a whisper, Edward's answer held a ghost of his old spleen. "*Ours,* Wessex?''

What could I say to this querulous old man, frail and foolish in his nightshirt. "That was the word. Have you learned so little of us that you must ask?''

"I knew you'd say that. I *knew* it. Godwine's miserable brat to the end! To the bitter . . .'' Edward trailed off weakly, groping blindly for his bed. I jumped to catch him as he collapsed in my arms.

"Chamberlain! Hugolin, come quickly!''

As Hugolin threw open the door, I lifted the thin body

of our king and laid him down on the bed. His eyes fluttered open. "Harold . . ."

"Hurry, Hugolin. Summon the king's physicians. Hop it, damn you!"

"You must send for Eadgytha," Edward whispered. "Do what you think best, Harold. I cannot decide anything now. What you think best."

The court hovered in fear for a day and a night before Edward rallied to general relief and *Te Deum Laudamus*. But then, so like the maddening man, he insisted the Witan make no proclamation of Edgar without his consent, which he was pleased to withhold for the nonce. Delegating so much of government to me, he couldn't resist reasserting his power just to let me know Edward still ruled. The unresolved question held dangers all too imminent, as Stigand put to me walking slowly together toward my boat waiting at the quay.

"We have a dying king. Make no mistake, this was a seizure much like to your father's. The next one will kill him, or the next. If Edgar were a paragon, he'd still come to the throne a callow boy with no support among the nobles. And William?" Stigand dismissed that insanity, throwing his hands to heaven. "Why, Harold? Why are we always at the bottom of a pit with no ladder?"

I said, "If we have to, we can overrule Edward in the Witan. Proclaim Edgar and hope for the best."

A weak best and well we knew it. While Edward vacillated and faded, William would eventually know he'd been cozened and prepare accordingly. He'd made too many promises to his vassals and Rome on the strength of Edward's word, his power and prestige staked to the hilt on the succession. In the Witan we watched his every move in Rouen and saw to all the grubby backstairs matters that secured kingdoms: intercepted letters, bought informers, and cultivated those Normans here or abroad deep enough in trouble, debt, or grudge to listen to the jingle of silver. We knew it significant when Hugh Malet was permanently recalled by Rouen. Stigand drew a very clear picture walking with me down to River Itchen and my waiting keel.

"There is a third alternative, a middle way if you will. You have been king in fact for several years. How far a step to king in name? No, no, don't tell me it hasn't occurred to you, Harold. You're more human than that, the more since it's staring you in the face. Nor can it have escaped your notice that you are not only the most experienced noble in England, but now the eldest."

That was dryly amusing. "I never thought of that. At thirty-seven, a patriarch."

"I'm serious." Stigand hooked my arm and brought me to a halt. "Gyrth and Leofwine will support you. So will I and the English Church; most at any rate, but who else *is* there? Waltheof of Huntingdon is a mere boy, Edwin of Mercia little more, and his brother Morcar still a child."

"There's Tostig," I said.

In the urgent rush of Stigand's argument, I'd fetched him up hard against that stumbling block. "Yes. There is Tostig. I suppose."

"You think he and my dear sister will placidly agree to my coronation?"

"No," said Stigand after a moment. "We couldn't be sure of that."

One could be sure of nothing in my brother but ambition. There was no one but me.

Edith

Not a warming truth that in the past several years I'd seen more of Gyrth than my husband. Edmund asked constantly when his father was coming home. Godwine practiced daily at sword and shield with our carls. Sometimes when he strode into the hall at evening, the likeness to Harold in gait and carriage was a pang of memory. But always Gyrth would ride over from Epping to roar and wrestle with the boys and pass the hours with me. He cheerfully agreed that, yes, he *ought* to marry, but gave the matter no more weight than what horse to ride of a morning. Concerned with developments at court, he hardly sensed my loneliness. There was trouble coming in Northumbria and Tostig at the root.

"Not good," he grumbled over his ale. "They say Tostig's too arrogant by half, that he's imprisoned men for personal reasons. The Witan is blocked because Eada won't hear a word against her angel. She and Harold are barely speaking, and Edward? Ha! If you need him for anything, y'must send clear to Thorney."

Frustrating in that it meant one more delay to keep Harold from home. "What's the broil in Northumbria?"

None of the Witan could say, but ugly reports were coming out of York from Cynesige to Stigand. "It's a muddle, that's all I know. Tostig writes mostly to Eada, to Edward only when he must, but men are being hanged, more of 'em paupered and their land seized, and some say Tostig's growing rich."

"And this keeps Harold at court?"

"Well, that and . . ."

I read his pause for reluctance while my heart whispered the answer. I despised myself for asking and yet must. "And what? Some lady?"

I wanted to believe the surprise that washed over his open face. "Is that what you—?"

"Someone young?"

"No, by God." Instantly Gyrth was out of his chair and kneeling by mine. "No, Edith. I give you my word, not a bit of it, but he can't leave court now. Harold must be there because Edward's all but abdicated. On my word, so it seems. There was an Eye-talian envoy last week addressed Harold as 'Royal Edwardi' because he didn't know any better, and small wonder. Harold has to deal with everything, be so many places at once that people are beginning to think of him as the real king. Then there's the Normandy business. Duke William writes every other week, hammering on the succession. While our royal saint of a king putters and prays in his abbey, he's given us the most dangerous 'stability' you ever saw, and done it with our own kin to boot, the bastard.''

When Harold came home at last, he was with us and not with us really, ever preoccupied. He'd grown thinner, the face I loved cut deeper with lines of concern, the body I cleaved to galled at both shoulders from iron worn too long. The deeper side of his nature he'd always masked with laughter. Now care could no longer be hidden, and it had aged him. For all this, we went through the motions of a happy reunion. Harold was overjoyed to see the boys, cut notches in the doorpost to mark their growth, swearing that no fifteen-year-old ever grew as fast as up-shooting Magnus or took to Latin with more facility than Edmund. He talked and walked for hours with Godwine, listening to the boy with grave courtesy, and they went at sword and shield with furious glee, Harold whooping with delight when Godwine bested him at least once. Harold and I rode together and made love, but not with the old, wild sweetness. I missed *us,* grieved and raged silently, sure with no proof at all that there was another woman, reasoned it aside as foolish and forgave him, all without a word.

Without a word: There lay our trouble. What happens to two people so right together, so long as one? Two arms entwined but slipping apart, down the limb, the elbow, until fingertips brush alone, then nothing but the phantom ache of love.

I thought for us that love was forever, but forever is not that far anymore. I can trace the lines about my eyes and mouth, the nipples gone brown and dark on breasts beginning to sag. I can see the pinched creases of worry and care on you, but that's only time, my love. What is there that cannot share as it used to? Know it or not, you are leaving me, letting me fade out of you. You can't lie to a wife about that.

We came to the truth one summer night in the darkened hall when for some reason I remembered a Saint Mark's Eve years before, and on a tender whim brought some wine and barley cakes to the table where Harold sat alone, brooding by a single candle. The night was murmurous with summer sounds as I set the wine and cakes before him. Harold glanced up, surprised.

"Remember?" I leaned to caress and then kiss his mouth. "Saint Mark's and my divining cake?"

Harold drew me down beside him but still with an absent air. "Yes, the night before Edward came."

"I was carrying Godwine and wondered would the cake tell me in a dream if I was to have a boy or girl. But I dreamed of the king instead, a strange, unhappy dream. You said it was only because I'd put in too much salt."

"Did I?"

"Seeing you here made me remember. What are you doing?"

"Thinking."

"May I share the thought or doesn't our *subregulus* stoop so far?"

Harold flared at me. "You can be cruel as Tostig." Then he checked himself, poured me some wine, and I read a kind of resolution in the attitude of his body as he turned to me. "Don't. Don't, love. Listen. There's that I must say. I can't put it off any longer."

How much you can sense in a single moment, with or without a word. *Here it is. Whatever, I'm to know now.*

"I love you. I love you and our boys so much."

As bad as that? He's leaving me. He's going to leave us.

"Edith, I may have to . . ."

With my eyes cast down on the wine goblet, I would say it before he did; it might hurt less that way. "Put us aside?"

"No, I'll never leave you. Would I choose to leave life? Listen, please. Only Stigand and a few bishops know what I'm telling you, and they're sworn on holy relics to secrecy."

"What, Harold? Are we going to be at war?"

"We could be when Edward dies, because the country won't crown William or a dull little boy. There's only one man they'll follow."

Did he hear my heart stop in that moment, hearing so

much more than he said, and the truth grinding and tearing under it. "And you want it, don't you?"

A bare whisper: "Yes." My husband couldn't look at me. "God help me, but I do. I'm Godwine's son. He taught me so much, and I can *do* so much, Edith. I can finish what he began, king and Witan working together instead of a council hampered by a sick old man in love with heaven and nothing else. The only bar—"

"Is me. I see."

"Then you see more than I do," he choked. "Edith, I want it because it has to be, but I can't give you up."

"Thank you for that much, my love. They will make you put me aside. You'll have no choice."

"I won't!" Harold thrust himself up off the bench into the darkness beyond the candle, as if saying what he must were too painful in the light. His voice came to me like the grieving of angels over lost Eden. "But that's the rock I break on. Now I know what Swegn felt when he had to give up Agatha and could not. Oh, I could say *must* so easily then. I've thought and thought but just go about in circles, coming back to the same answer. I must wear the crown. There's no one else."

Suddenly he loomed over me again, urgently catching me up in his arms, and I crushed myself to him, buried my face in his chest so he wouldn't see my pain. "I know you've been lonely," he whispered. "That you've felt me drifting away. I've felt it, too, but like a coward I didn't say a word. I still can't, because I don't *know* what I can do. Help me, Edith."

I'll try, yes, because that's what love does, but there is nothing to be done. You want this and you will pay the price as your father would, and I will say what will ease your heart at the cost of mine. "We can only hope and pray and wait. Come to bed, love."

We made love that night, and the need that made us cling for hours was stronger and darker for its desperation, and our hungry exploration of each other's bodies with lips and tongue was the licking of wounds by hurt animals. Love was a mourning that night, nor did we sleep before Waltham bells rang matins. When I wept, turned away from my sleeping lover in the bed, was it for what we had or what he must take from me?

Breath by breath, hour by hour, managing through the day, see the lady of Nazeing turn out her sons for their father's departure. Listen as she mouths the proper sentiments before he leaves, and, oh, hear his pain and the limping reasons.

"I can't deal with this now, Edith. My thanes need me, and I've had to neglect my lands, so much heaping up in the shire and forest courts. I'm needed at Bosham."

Yes, the earldom's troubles and the Crown's are so much easier to allay than our own. I rage at you in my soul and know in the next breath it is not you or me alone but what must be, that prayer will be no more answered than those from hell, nor hope make one moment more bearable.

Yet see the lady of Nazeing riding to her husband's proud new church in Waltham, overseeing in village and kitchen, visiting the poor, praying with her sons, consulting her stewards, counting and folding the ells of linen, giving bread and alms at the kitchen-house door, trimming candle tallow, turning the tiresome glass where the sand whispers down, bearing her on its current toward the end.

Seeing so much, quiet as she was, did anyone see that unobtrusive death?

Had she been there, Agatha might have, or even Eadgytha.

58 • Harold

We fly from what we fear has no remedy as a dying man will deny the blood brought up by the wracking cough that will kill him sometime, but surely not today. I had no answers for Edith beyond love and what must be, so I sailed to Bosham with Botulf and a small company of carls to bury the impossible in the soluble affairs of Wessex.

Had I remained at Nazeing, Gyrth's invitation to hunt in Epping Forest would have entailed an hour by horse rather than two days by keel up the Narrow Sea. That September of 'sixty-four my brother's request came as an open door out of the dilemma wherein I plodded endlessly between the problems of the Crown and Edith. That late summer just before the season turned, when the first faint smokiness in the air always reminded me of childhood, I shrugged off the troubles in one convulsive heave, said to hell with it all, and went hunting, even sent a brief notice of rebellion to Stigand:

Your Grace and my dear friend, trusting that Canterbury and the Witan can avoid national disaster for the next few weeks, I propose for a refreshing change to hawk and hunt at Epping with Gyrth. At least there I will know exactly what I'm doing. H.

We fitted two keels, one for horses, luggage, mewskeeper, and several favorite hawks, the other for Botulf and me and the ten or so carls who accompanied us. We would sail with the morning tide at half ebb. I bade farewell to Gytha and of course old Manni, who insisted on hobbling down to the inlet to wish me well. With Botulf behind, I tucked up the skirts of my tunic and waded out to clamber aboard, and the boatmaster Edric shouted the order to back us out to deeper water.

"Lively now, pull! We're fair scraping bottom."

Twenty-five years in the sea service of Wessex, Edric had been with Tostig when they were storm-driven onto Dover beach and discovered the outrage committed there by Eustace of Boulogne. There was no foot of the southern coast or Narrow Sea he hadn't navigated, nor any sight, smell, or danger of its treacherous waters he didn't know.

"Not much wind." Edric squinted at the barely rippling sail. "We'll take her out a mite farther."

He kept glancing to the southwest. "You look worried," I said.

"I don't know. I don't know," Edric muttered, stumping aft, shaking his head.

The sea motionless under a warm sun, the men rowing at an easy stroke, toward noon we lay perhaps fifteen miles off Wight on a windless, mirror-smooth sea.

"Easier on the horses," Botulf remarked, waving to our second boat far astern. "Look there, my lord."

Fairly close to our beam, a fat plaice broke the tranquil surface and plopped back again, followed quickly by another. The urge was irresistible. "Botulf, there is nothing in this world so delicious as fried plaice. Let's break out fishing lines."

My friend needed no persuasion, smacking his lips. "Douse 'em in ale and we'll have a grand feast."

Some of the off-watch rowers joined in, and shortly half a dozen lines were baited and dropped. Within the hour eight or ten fish were wriggling their last on the deck planks. Edric suggested we make east, but the sun was warm overhead, the fish fair in love with our crab bait, I wallowing in the luxury of nowhere to go in a hurry for once, yet Edric seemed curiously baffled.

"Shouldn't rain, but she's going to." He followed the flashing arc of a fish breaking water, then two more, leaping and diving. "When they feed this close to the surface, she's going to rain."

"Nowhere I can see." Not a cloud in the flat blue sky, but I trusted Edric's sea wisdom. "Right, then. Let's go."

The order was relayed to the second craft. The watch laid on oars and slipped us forward at an easy three knots, bearing for Pevensey. In the prow Botulf and I felt rising swells pitch the keel more deeply as a freshening breeze filled the square sail.

"Tide's running swifter." Botulf yawned and stretched in the drowsy afternoon warmth. "Edric's wrong about rain. Not a cloud any—"

He was cut off by a cry from our lookout in the leather basket atop the mast. "Boatmaster! Storm signal from the keel astern."

"Ah, he's daft," I laughed, but Edric bounded aft through the idle men off watch as our keel began to spank forward before a stiffening wind. We must have seen it at the same time, that long, dirty smudge of cloud looming toward us over the southwest horizon, growing even as we watched.

Edric bawled his order: "Oars! Lay on your oars and pull! Steersman, two points to port. Earl Harold"—as he fetched up beside me—"I've seen this before. Knew I was worried by something. This time of year they come out of the ocean sea like the hand of God and that quick. We've got to pull for Pevensey and wait it out. God help the other boat. Those horses will go mad."

"What can we do?"

"Run before it and pray."

"Edric," said Botulf with an audible quaver, "I'll never doubt your eye again."

"If that catches us," Edric jerked his chin at the approaching storm, nearer even as we spoke, "you may never have the chance. Rowers, lay on! I'll give you the beat. Lookout, down! Get down now!"

Edric scooped up a hammer and pounded out the stroke on the beam plank. Faster and faster he hammered until the men labored and panted, all the while his eye on our tautening sail. "Relief rowers stand ready."

"I'll take an oar," Botulf volunteered.

"And I." I peered anxiously astern where our second

craft, already drenched in the leading edge of the storm, was pitching wildly. "Never mind rank, Edric. I can drown easily as anyone."

"Don't say that," Botulf beseeched in a peculiarly tight voice. "I can't swim. I can't swim a stroke."

The two of us relieved panting rowers on one port bench and pulled with all our strength, no breath left for anything but the oar, until Botulf gasped: "The mast! *Look!*"

Bellied out tight as a drum head, the square sail strained our mast to where I could see the stout pine shaft actually bending. Edric saw it, too. He and another man, fighting for balance, flattened against the beams by the shrieking wind, tried to loose the side stays, then just cut them. The sail collapsed, but at least the mast wouldn't snap.

Impossible to tell how long I strained over the oar. No one could see the second boat at all now, just a dark wall lashing out at us with rain and salt spray. When someone chucked me on the shoulder and I surrendered the oar, I simply fell down out of the way, exhausted. Botulf staggered aft to the small tilt erected for sleeping, and brought our cloaks.

Edric himself doubling on the tiller with the helmsman, we could no longer hope to make Pevensey even if we'd been able to find it. Oars were useless now. In the mountainous seas about us, the men could only cling to the benches. I looked past Botulf's white face to Edric and the helmsman laboring to keep the steerboard level. Drenched and wind-battered, they seemed crucified to the tiller as the squall drove us east and east.

The men fought their way regularly in pairs along the careening deck to relieve at the steerboard. When Edric stumbled forward to collapse by me, I shouted over the wind, "Can you tell where we are?"

"No way sure. Wind feels sou'west by west. Tide runs about five knots usually, but maybe seven or more with this blow. We're closer to Normandy than home."

Hours since we'd had any sight of the second keel, if it was still afloat, storm-battered for hours with no sign of the squall blowing itself out. Making my way toward Botulf where he'd wedged himself between two rowing benches, suddenly I felt the deck roll sickeningly under me, and I fell against him. The last thing I heard was Edric's warning. "Tiller! Tiller!"

Their footing lost, both helmsmen sprawled on the wet deck while the steerboard swung wildly in the churning sea. Our keel yawed sickeningly as they fought to regain their footing and the tiller, but too late. The killing wave loomed high, rushing down on our beam. Edric wrapped his arm about a bench, screaming at me, "Hold on!"

I saw Botulf, eyes closed, lips moving rapidly, and I snatched at a rag-end of prayer myself, but the port beam tilted high, ours dipped. We were hurled toward death with incredible force, then the cold sea closed over me.

—lungs starved for air as I tore at the bronze clasp that closed my mantle, finally wrenched it free over my head, fighting up through black cold toward blessed air, gasping as my head broke surface. Dimly, yards away, I saw the capsized keel and heads bobbing in the water.

"Botulf, where are you? Call *out*."

I heard the strangled sound of water-filled lungs, and floundered toward it. A head rose out of the dark water, then disappeared again. For a horrible, sick instant I thought my friend was gone.

"Ha-Harold, help! Can't swim!"

"Here, I'm here! Don't fight. Go limp. Float."

I windmilled through the swirling water toward him, but my shoes were like lead on my feet. I gulped a deep chestful of air and sank, tearing the shoes off and fighting for the surface again. In the common mistake of approaching the drowning man from the front, I almost let Botulf kill us both. He seized on me with a panicked death grip that dragged us both under. Sheer, cold will to survive took me. I slammed a fist into his stomach and heard the faint *oh!* as air burst from his lungs. I kicked furiously, ducking under his arms, and came up behind him. One arm wrapped about his chest, I thrashed us both toward the surface.

"Can't swim, I can't swim—"

"Shut *up*, Goddamn you, you stupid ox. Go limp. Edric! Where are you, Edric?"

Swallowed in the roar of the storm, I might not have heard an answering voice. No more heads dotted the water anywhere, only the capsized keel drawing farther away on the swift current.

"Help me, Botulf. Kick with your legs."

Nearer to Normandy than home, Edric reckoned, but how much nearer? Nothing but to swim and swear by Jesus bloody Christ I wasn't going to drown without a fight. When the huge swells bore us high, I tried to see ahead. Once in the near dark I thought there was a shape, a line that didn't melt into the next wave, then down again, trying to keep from swallowing water as it crashed over us. Fighting upward again just to breathe. To tire, to surrender meant death for us both.

Drowning's easy, they say. The siren sea whispers her song in your ear and holds out her arms and you sink into them. Holy Mary, Saint Wilfrid, have mercy on us. I did build the church as I promised, and the chantry priests pray for Eirianell. I never thought it would end so, Edith, and Christ my witness, I'm sorry for everything, for every day I wasn't there for you and the boys. God, dear God, give me one more chance pleasepleaseplease . . .

Borne up on a high wave, I saw the dim shape of land and this time a tiny light. Suddenly fear boiled into rage such as I'd never known before, an elemental fury to survive. With my arms going numb, I brushed against something solid. A rock. The next time the wave rushed us forward, my feet touched firm bottom. Then Botulf and I were floundering, holding each other up, choking and spluttering through waist-high surf that pushed us forward like clumsy dolls toward the beach until we stumbled through shallows to pebbles and sand and collapsed facedown.

A long time we lay on the dark beach, high water lapping about us and the wind howling, before I had the strength to raise my head and seek out that blessed light. Still there, but a long way off. Too far to go now.

Botulf labored to his knees, wracked by strangled coughing from the acrid salt burning his lungs.

"Where . . . wherever I'm to die," he rasped, "God be praised it ent today. H-help me pray."

I wanted to pray and surely tried. Nothing emerged but a grateful wheeze.

We weren't saved. We had beached near Saint Valéry-sur-Somme. The light I'd seen was a coastal guard port for Guy, Count of Ponthieu. The next day we were taken north to Castle Beaurain near the town of Montreuil. Guy's practical policy was to hold any unlucky traveler for ransom, the more important the better. When he recognized me, the price went up.

59 • Harold

Aelred of Denby said once he could never abide stone walls for long, and I could agree. We English don't build our homes so, wood being more natural to our hand and heart, but the Normans won't consider anything else. If I had built a walled castle at Bosham and surrounded the whole with a ditch, my thanes would have wondered, "Look 'ere, what are you expecting? Armageddon?"

In Normandy and Ponthieu, however, every lord, large or small, has his stone keep, no matter how dark, damp, and oppressive. Botulf and I were delivered straightaway to the tower and the dungeon beneath, little more than a pit under the ground floor reached by a rude ladder. When the trap was dropped shut, we were left in total darkness and had to feel out our bearings. There was a bucket partially filled with stinking water, a stone shelf to sleep on, but no blankets. The bucket was the only convenience in our darkness, but after the first day hardly necessary since we were given no food or water. For two days—it felt like that long—we remained so. Frightening how quickly darkness and deprivation steal one's sense of time and sap the will. When I woke for the second time to the fetid air over me, I nudged Botulf with my bare foot.

"Are you awake?"

"Yes. Hungry enough to wish I wasn't."

"I imagine the count wants us this way. No food, no light. The notion is, I'll be weak enough to agree to anything."

"Bastard." Botulf snuffled and coughed. "Does he know what he's doing? Does he know who you are?"

"He does." I felt with one hand at the other where my seal and wedding rings had been stripped from me. "Customary here, sort of legalized piracy. Ransom's a filthy business."

Botulf stirred restlessly and swung his feet off the stone bench. "Just wish we could get away from the stink. We should have gone overland."

I thanked him for keen hindsight. "At least there're no rats. No self-respecting rodent would frequent this place."

"Lord Harold, did any of the others make shore, you think?"

"I don't know. I can't even say how we made it except God didn't want us dead yet."

More unmeasured time dragged by. The only sounds we heard were occasional muffled footsteps on the floor timbers overhead, now and then the faintest suggestion of a voice. Then the trap flew open, spearing a shaft of dingy light into the pit. Not bright but I still had to shut my eyes against it. The ladder thudded on the earthen floor.

"Out, you two. Come out!"

We stumbled toward and up the ladder, hardly able to stand the cruel sunlight from the open outer door to the keep. We were marched under guard across the bailey toward the stone hall. The long chamber was filled with people, clergy and knights, some in mail, the galleries that ran above on both sides crowded with a chattering gaggle of women in brightly colored gowns. The guards pushed us forward to a dais where, in a short red tunic and tight trousers draped with a short black mantle, Guy, Count of Ponthieu lounged, inspecting us with negligent disdain.

Filthy, shoeless, our clothes stained and stiff with salt, we presented a forlorn sight, no doubt part of our deliberate humiliation, as I had left Gruffydd though with much more humane treatment. The women above pointed and tittered at us. Botulf, always stiffish with strangers, straightened his back and snarled out of the side of his mouth—

"Who are those doxes anyway? Ought to be home keeping house."

"Dames des choisies," I told him. "The noble ladies of Ponthieu. Don't suppose they find much diversion."

"God, I'm so hungry I'm weak."

"So am I. Bear up, friend. One way or another you may be paying for my sins."

A dwarf, garishly dressed in motley, waddled toward us, cackling and brandishing a wooden sword, paying us sharp whacks about the legs while the count of Ponthieu and all the others roared with laughter. I focused what will I could muster on Count Guy, one leg slung languidly over the arm of his state chair. He couldn't quite bring off Gruffydd's regal scorn. I recalled what our continental informers had learned of Guy: pugnacious, troublesome to his nominal lord, William, considered himself independent and a nonpareil among warrior lords. I guessed the assessments of his character to be correct. There was not much intelligence to be read in Guy's face, nor indeed in his treatment of Edward's first minister. He might have reaped some diplomatic profit from returning us to England; instead he prisoned me like a felon and would most like go for the immediate gain of ransom.

"This you may keep." Guy tossed at my feet the ring Edith had put on my finger at our marriage, holding up the seal ring of Wessex. "This I retain. England will pay well for your release, and of course I will be reasonable. *Within* reason, at least." He looked about to see who else relished his joke. "England is a mercantile nation and trade is trade."

"Are you so sure?" I challenged, trying to sound stronger than I felt. "When my king hears of this, to say nothing of my brother earls, I may prove more expensive than profitable, Count.''

A dicey argument, though Guy needn't know. Gyrth, Leofwine, and all Wessex I could count on, far less on Edward, Eada or Tostig, who might pay Guy to have me disappear.

The count jabbed a finger at Botulf. ''Who is this, some serf?''

''My standard-bearer, a freeman known to our court. And my friend.''

''What did you purpose here? How dare you bask upon my sovereign shore like a trespassing seal?''

''By accident. The storm blew us off course and we capsized. I was bound for East Anglia.''

''Oh, I think not.'' Guy sat back, obviously enjoying his moment of cat-and-mouse. ''Not this time of year and its tides. I think you were bound for Flanders. Since Baldwin is my enemy and England hardly a friend, I should know what passes between them, *n'est-ce pas?*''

''My purpose was to hunt in Epping Forest, my trespass the result of a poor choice, no more.''

''Choice or no, *Anglais*, law is law, right is right. You are subject to penalty in Ponthieu. William has his laws, I have mine.''

Drooping with weakness in spite of himself, Botulf understood none of the rapid exchange in French. ''Lord, what's he saying?''

''We're in trouble. Count Guy, we have eaten nothing for over two days, and my man is ill. Would it bend your laws to allow us a little soup and bread?''

''*Rien!* Allow them nothing.'' A grizzled, heavy-set older knight stepped out before Guy, thrusting an accusing finger at me. ''This Harold is our enemy. He and his father have always fought the presence of Normans in England. I was at Tetbury with Count Eustace when Godwine's entire family rebelled. Archbishop Robert had to flee for his life when these rebels besieged London and their own king with foreign troops.''

And if you were at Dover with Eustace, laddy, you bloody well know why.

"Food?" the knight jeered. "Let him chew leather and drink his own piss."

"What's *he* on about?" Botulf muttered.

"I'm not popular. Breakfast may be late."

"Good my lord." From one side of the hall, a little butterball of a priest moved forward to entreat Guy. After a moment of hesitation a young man in the simple grey tunic and short mantle of a servant followed him. "Regardless of policy or sentiment, will you deny them the charity any would afford a poor traveling monk?"

"May I add my voice to that of the good father," the servant urged. "Please you, I will see to them myself."

I blessed them both for their humanity. For Guy, he hardly seemed to care, dismissing them both with a permissive gesture. "You have leave, Remi—but not *too* generous. I never overfeed prize stock."

This was greeted with raucous laughter, the dwarf prancing about us and neighing like a horse. Botulf flinched as a well-aimed apple core, launched from the women's gallery, struck him in the face. He glared up at them with one of the visceral epithets for which our folk have a gritty talent.

"Cunting bitch."

"Easy on, Botulf. I think we'll eat."

"And then?"

Who could say? We were herded from the hall by our guards and trundled again down into the rank darkness of our cell to wait for we knew not what, hoping only that the count's word was good and someone would bring food. Our ordeal began to take its toll. I found it hard to think clearly. Botulf's persistent cough worried me. Weak and demoralized, he gave in to remorse about his wife and the life he'd led her.

"Not there half the time, always someplace we had to go. I don't blame you, lord, but I should—" He broke off with the deep coughing that brayed from his lungs. When he could speak again, his normally robust voice was reed-frail in the darkness. "I should have been with her more. I'll make it up to her when we get home. Boring as the woman is, that's a promise before God."

Before God. I touched Edith's ring, wanting to promise the same despite that heavier ornament I must wear someday. Bright, cruel crown that can afford content only to the worst of its wearers, like Harefoot or Harthacanute, and only misery to the best. Did Edward know one happy day under it? Did Eadgytha? Would I, kneeling before Stigand and answering *volo* while he bound me before God to a queen other than Edith?

Overhead the trap swung back and the ladder dropped. One man descended with a fat lamp, followed by another with a small bucket hooked over one arm. I recognized the young serving man from the hall. As soon as the first man set the lighted lamp on the stone ledge, the other dismissed him. "Go on up; I'll set this out."

When he opened the bucket, the odor of hot, fresh vegetables and meat was maddening, and all I could do to keep from snatching and gulping it all down. The servant produced two small fresh loaves from one inner pocket of his mantle, two bowls from another. When the other man had vanished up the ladder, he divided the soup into the bowls, whispering quickly, "*Pas de peur,* my lord. You won't be here long if I know the duke."

I mumbled through a mouthful of bread, "Who are you?"

"*N'importe pas,* but William will know. The news you're here is already on its way to Rouen. I can bring you food, but I must go now."

I gripped his hand. "We thank you."

"It is nothing. I am well paid."

Between gulps of soup: "Dare one ask by whom?"

"One should not," he countered coolly with a gleam of ironic humor from intelligent eyes. "Count Guy is not stupid, merely of average gifts, which is at best depressing as this world goes. Does my lord think the duke would allow such a vassal to go unwatched? *Bon appetit.*"

He moved quickly to the ladder and climbed up, calling for a hand at the top.

Days went by, made more tolerable with food and a little light and once, some water to wash with. Our benefactor, whoever he was, fed us once a day and even furnished a blanket apiece, but for further news, we might not have spoken at all. Then, at least a week or more after our capture, as he set out our food he whispered two words: *"Demain. Turold."*

I hoped *tomorrow* meant deliverance. The name Turold was not unknown in England. The knight ranked high in William's service. He seemed to the duke roughly what I was to Edward, first to be sent in the ducal name and authority.

The next day Botulf and I were rousted up from the dungeon and marched, stumbling, Botulf leaning on me and clutching his blanket about him, both of us half blind in the light, to where a tall vavasor, magnificently mounted at the head of an escort of ten mailed men, waited to take us in charge. From the sullen look of those watching the Normans, I don't think they were too welcome, but no one dared interfere.

"It is the pleasure of my lord William, Duke of Normandy, Maine, and overlord of Ponthieu, that you shall accompany me to his presence and remain as his guest. Count Harold, I am to render you any service I can."

"Thank you."

Botulf broke into a fit of painful coughing, bent double with it. He didn't look well enough to ride far. *"Merci, bon vavasor, mais je vous en prie,* my friend is ill. He needs a surgeon as soon as possible, and the count did not see fit to provide one."

"There is a monastery at Fécamp. He must bear up until then."

I helped Botulf mount and then took the horse provided for me.

I never saw the servant again, which was regrettable, nor Guy of Ponthieu, which was not, but however Turold put the duke's demand, it must have been potent. And still I pondered the difference between being prisoner to one and "guest" to the other. I'd never met William and could have forgone acquaintance indefinitely. It was my ill fortune to meet him at a huge disadvantage, that of owing him my freedom, and William always collected on debts.

60 • Duke William

B y the face of God, what unbelievable luck! The first lord of England dropped like a foundling babe at my door. I could not longer doubt God was with me in my claim. Guy of Ponthieu gave me no trouble when Turold bore him my intent: Release Harold to this vavasor or what I do in Brittany, I will do in Ponthieu.

I had no direct quarrel with Count Conan of Brittany, but a threat and an opportunity. Few men credited Edward's promise, and as my own trust faded with unanswered letters, I set about gathering support in the event my English claim must be asserted by force. God and all men knew I didn't want that. The expense, the incalculable risk of the sea venture alone before a man was landed or a blow struck, made the undertaking insanity in the eyes of prudent men.

The stupid and greedy, of course, leaped at the idea of English titles and fiefs. Wiser heads gave it long thought and no immediate approval, but Conan of Brittany openly opposed me. First, he argued, I could never concentrate the huge fleet necessary in one place to land an effective force before the swift Saxon navy destroyed us in detail. Second, if by some miracle we secured a foothold, we would fight for months or even years in hostile country where every wagon load of forage and other supply would be a constant problem, if not totally destroyed by the defenders beforehand. Third, Conan boasted, his proud forebears came from Britain, driven out by advancing Saxons, to find safety in the Roman settlements of Armorica. The ancestral island was holy to him; he would not see his blood subjugated again by anyone. Finally he told me to my face that if I left Normandy, he would surely take it from me. There you have the man: niggling, sentimental, stubborn, and dangerous. But Conan had a certain gift of tongue that made men listen to him. When Rhiwallon of Dol rebelled against him, Conan besieged the small castle. Rhiwallon pleaded for my help, which I found very convenient to extend. I would raise the siege and bring Conan to heel.

I was on the point of setting out from Rouen when the news of Harold reached me. My orders to Turold: Secure his freedom and bring him to me at Falaise on our line of march.

Turold's detail did not appear where ordered, nor could I wait for him. Soon the autumn rains would set in, stalemating me and Conan alike in front of Dol.

"What is *keeping* them?"

Certainly not the weather or the roads, both clear and dry. Day by day we inched southwest toward the Brittany border, five hundred horse, a thousand foot soldiers, and war engines, luggage, a mile-long train. We were camped a few miles south of Avranches when Turold's messenger overtook us with the news that they would arrive the next day. And high time! In less than three days we could be in contact with Conan, at River Couesnon in less than two. Yet I gave more thought and plain curiosity to this Harold than the crossing of the Couesnon estuary where tides and quicksands were a formidable threat.

I didn't bother to conceal my irritation from the messenger, a mere squire, very young and earnest, exhausted from a hard ride. "Well, what hindered him? Why did they not join us at Falaise?"

"My lord, they were delayed at Fécamp, the monastery. Illness . . ."

I wanted to leap down the callow boy's throat and drag the facts from him. "Did Ponthieu harm the earl in any way? Speak!"

"Not at all, sir, but his companion was very ill, barely able to ride."

I'd had no word of any other survivor of the shipwreck. "What lord is that?"

The squire fidgeted under my scrutiny his muddy shoes. "No lord but a peasant, sir. Very rough fellow, very surly. He fell ill in the dungeon and could barely ride to Fécamp. The earl would not leave until he knew the man was tended to and out of danger."

Still, I was hardly used to men ignoring my orders, no matter what their rank. "*Would* not?"

"Flatly refused, sir."

I returned to my tent. When Fitz-Osbern entered to ask if I required anything, I shared the news of the incoming guest. My steward gave me a knowing smile.

"Edward's *subregulus* himself. This should be profitable."

"It will be. It must."

I needed solitude to think and sent him away with orders to inspect my personal guard every hour, and that every commander of horse would be personally responsible for any desertions within his squadron. Unquestioning trust had died young in me. Trust of any sort perished at Domfront. Nothing in my life came easily—until this month and the windfall gift of Harold in my hand. God sent him to me and I would use him, but first I must know him.

Over the years Hugh Malet had told me much and really nothing about the man. "Doesn't ride well, but none of them do, not as we would judge. Good swordsman, an absolute genius with the shield."

But the man himself? In later life Malet was as vague as ever about his good friend. "Before he married Edith, he drank to excess, but even drunk you had the impression the man distanced himself behind good manners. Affable, informal with equals and commons alike. Close and distant at once, as hard to grasp as a phantom in a fog."

And still later—

"Good soldier, excellent strategist, but very unconventional. Takes incredible risks to do the unexpected, as in his capture of King Gruffydd. When I called him mad, he answered with a jest. Disconcerting: One never knows when Harold is altogether serious or not."

But the core of the man, his beliefs, passions? Where is his heart?

There Malet was more definite. "With Edith and his sons, for the little he sees of them."

And the tales of his lechery, his whoring?

"Oh, that." The vavasor turned his hands over and back in a so-so gesture. "As these things go among the English, far less than gossip would savor in report—and, if I know Harold that much, of no more significance than myself snatching a quick meal away from my own table."

Edward said that to know England, Harold was the stag to follow. He leads the Witan, he is next to the throne. Is he ambitious?

Again Malet would not answer at once. "Ambitious? I do not think that the *mot juste,* my lord. There is a room at Bosham with a large map of his country, the borders painted in red, which has hung there since Godwine's time. All his life Harold has known that shape, seen it change as Danes came and went, earldoms grew or shrank, but the red borders remained inviolate, as Gruffydd learned at the cost of his head. Harold went against Edward, endured banishment, risked ruin, not for power but because he thought the king wrong. His heart, my lord? That map, that shape on the wall."

In its own way a life extraordinary as my own. A spoiled second son become a statesman, first hated by Edward and then chief and trusted pillar of the realm, a man who supported but questioned the God-given rights of his king, and yet—I found myself smiling at the thought—one who would not leave an ailing servant even for me. I felt so about my Uncle Walter, who risked his life for years to keep me safe. Part of us must love and trust completely somewhere. But frugally, Harold. Sparingly. I will read your heart. No longer a crude, impetuous boy to bray out my first impulse like a donkey, I will not judge you quickly. I will be your good and generous host for as long as it takes to accomplish my end, but with you or without you, I will have England.

* * *

Weather held fair, but the treacherous sands of Couesnon estuary shifted and ran through my dreams at night. No other place to cross the river with heavy war engines, and where, *where* was Turold? His party rode in toward evening of the next day, and I marked the tall man riding at his knee, dressed in ill-assorted clothing of our fashion but too small for him. To put Harold at ease, I had Malet with me to greet and reassure him. When the earl recognized Hugh, he flung himself out of the saddle and ran to embrace his friend. In their exuberant reunion I was quite forgotten for the moment.

"Hugh, well met!"

"You great ox! *Mon Dieu,* but you are lucky. Rescued from the sea and Ponthieu all in one week. And Botulf?"

"Mending, mending well. We'd never been in a dungeon before. Awfully hard on the health. Eh, what's so funny?"

"Those clothes. Couldn't the abbey find something larger?"

"None to be had. The hosteler swore I was damnably hard to fit. But forgive me, my lord duke." Harold stepped to me, his eyes on a level with mine, friendly and open as he extended his hand, with no hint of apprehension about his situation, quite at home I would say. Not as thick as I through the chest and shoulders, but his grip was firm. "I am in your debt."

So you are. "But I must chide you, my lord earl, for tarrying so long at Fécamp. I expected you days ago."

"Sorry," Harold dismissed the notion casually. "That wasn't possible. I pray my lord will pardon the breach. I thank you again for my freedom. My king will be grateful as I."

Possibly, until his king got my bill. "Come, dine with me. Malet, you also. Turold, bring your chief vavasors. Fitz-Osbern! Tell my chaplain we will hear early mass and march by the hour of terce tomorrow."

I learned more of this Harold as the evening lengthened and the supper candles burned down. Never had I seen a man so at ease among strangers with no great love for his kind, men who well knew his opposition to Normans at home. He showed concern only when asking about any possible survivors from his ships. None had been reported. A shadow of regret passed over his countenance, then faded. One got the impression that Harold immensely enjoyed the simple state of being alive. He had a zest, a *brio,* as Italians say. When he drank wine, he savored it. Though hungry as a horse when he sat to supper, he wolfed nothing but tasted every morsel. His fingers, moving from the common dish shared with me to the herb-scented finger bowl, were a delicate dance of propriety.

He spoke effortless Frank with a liquid sound more of Paris than Rouen, yet stretched and strained to an English cadence, like a lithe cat forced to trot like a dog. Only half noble like myself, yet he wore the quality of *noblesse* with more ease than Edward and so offhandedly one would think he donned it only for the working day and doffed it on returning to his hearth.

I am not a lighthearted man. Mora has the wit in our house. She would take well to this Englishman. Before supper was done, two things about the man were clear to me. He had neither arrogance—as far from that as Rouen from Jerusalem—nor any vanity among men. Toward the middle of the supper when jests flew thick about the table, Harold held his own. He recounted common occurrences and made them sparkle with humor, talking of the things every man or soldier knows and endures: needing to relieve yourself suddenly while in full armor and having to hold it; the night his lady shattered his composure by secreting a frog in their bed; how he dove full tilt into the tent of King Gruffydd and sprawled unheroically on his face. Finally, how Hugh Malet once so bested him at sword, he had to resort to trickery to win.

"I protest. Not so," Hugh cried down the table. "You bashed me properly. Did I not say as much, *Seigneur Guillaume?* A wizard with a shield."

Harold objected modestly. As a raconteur he charmed the table of rough, hard horsemen who doubtless measured him by their own iron rule. But in each recollection, Harold made himself the butt of the joke, baring his own foibles and, through them, those of the blundering world.

His story of bargaining with his lady's father for her hand made me laugh long and heartily, recalling my endless negotiations with Baldwin for Mora.

"My lord earl?" Turold set aside his cup. "I am intrigued. Are you truly, as Malet declares, a sorcerer with the shield?"

"He was being generous," Harold responded politely. "Ours are round, designed for fighting on foot. Hugh is used to your longer shield."

"On foot then," Turold persisted. "Even on foot, you think your shield could fend me off?"

The laughter about the table eddied out as my men sensed a sporting challenge and perhaps a few bruises. Harold sat back, cleaning his fingers fastidiously. "Oh . . ."

The men waited and so did I, frankly interested.

"I should think so, yes," Harold drawled.

Turold pounced. "What wager?"

Harold spread his hands. "Dear sir, I washed up on the beach without a farthing."

"Take his wager," I urged. "Turold, I will back the earl to a full pound English silver."

"Oh, hardly," Harold demurred. "That's unfair to the worthy vavasor."

"Unfair?" Turold bridled slightly. "To me or to you? Could it be my lord has doubts? The wager suits me, for I have none."

I caught a sudden *froideur* in Harold's glance, the barest chill in his reply. "Perhaps you would rephrase that, Sire Turold? I thought to spare your purse. Surely the duke does not pay you more than one shilling ten per diem on campaign."

"I care not, *Anglais!* Ten shillings then. My sword against yours on foot."

"Sword?" Harold's brows shot up in sudden comprehension. "I'm to have a sword as well? In that case, I'll go the full pound."

Malet sputtered with laughter, but then he alone among us understood the English sense of humor, which has been variously described as mocking, cruel, or plain bizarre.

The wager was played off later in Rouen, but before that an incident occurred at the Couesnon estuary that made the man much clearer and even admirable to me.

Interesting, though. His estimate of Turold's daily pay was a little generous but not by much. I could not help reflecting that an Englishman who knew what I paid my vavasors doubtless knew far more about my rule and intent.

Trust Harold? No, that came later, but liking? Man to man, it was impossible *not* to like him.

61 • Duke William

Our train reached the Couesnon estuary at ebb tide, cavalry before, foot soldiers urged along at a smart pace, ox-drawn catapults lumbering in our wake. I spurred to Harold, who sat his horse gazing out across the vast tidal flats to where the sudden, majestic wonder of Mont-Saint-Michel thrust itself high like a prayer to heaven. Harold did not cross himself as I did, but I heard the awe in his voice. "Travelers have told me of this, but . . ."

"But nothing like the sight, I know. The abbey is new, but the mount has always been a holy place. Saint Michael himself commanded its building. The sea has stolen much of this land, but when those flats were still forest, the religious hermits on the mount used to light a fire to signal their need for supplies, which were brought on a donkey. One day a wolf attacked and killed the donkey and would have eaten the beast, but God directed it to carry needed provisions to the mount to the end of its life."

"Poor wolf," Harold remarked. "Must have felt himself ill used."

This was not my first encounter with casual English profanation. "I assure you the story is true. But then Edward said your family was hardly devout."

Earl Harold dropped his eyes then raised them to meet mine steadily. "Devotion is difficult when both king and Church are convinced of your villainy. My father's objections were toward the clergy, not God. He considered Robert Champart a venomous liar and our own Eadsige a turgid old bore."

I silently agreed with him concerning Champart, may his fevered soul find peace. "Now I will show you something less magnificent. From here the tide goes out more than five miles, but the sand and mud are left waterlogged in many places."

"Quicksand?"

"Very quick. Men and horses have been sucked under and—*fini*. I will mark a safe crossing with stakes." I looked to Harold, whose eyes were now narrowed past me on the Breton shore half a mile beyond, challenging him delicately. "Will you join me? You will gain much respect among my men."

He answered absently. "What? Oh, to be sure. Delighted. If that's Conan's land yonder, those must be his men."

Harold had keen eyes. But for the pale sunlight glinting on their mail, I might have missed the half-dozen motionless riders observing us. "Yes. No doubt a reconnaissance."

"So much for surprise."

Surprise was no part of my plan. I wanted Conan to wait and worry. When I finished sweeping Conan away from Dol, every Frank and Breton, Gaul and Norman in the northwest would know I was supreme. Harold would report the fact to Edward—when I let him go.

Harold reined the horse's head upstream. "Something's afoot back there."

They were several hundred yards away, but I recognized Turold and Hugh Malet by their surcoats, in furious argument with some dozen knights in full armor despite my command to strip it off for lighter crossing. One of them swept an arm out at the Breton knights on the far bank and drew his sword. Then he spurred his horse into the water followed by nine or ten others, whooping and brandishing swords in challenge.

"Come." We cantered forward to meet Turold and Malet as they dashed for us and reined short in a spray of mud. "What is it? Don't those fools know—are they mad?"

Turold swore, livid. "*Zut alors!* De Tosny and some of the younger pups. They knew the orders, but they're out for glory."

"Oh, yes," Malet seethed. "We told them to stand fast. They just laughed at us."

Did they so? By God's face, that would be their last laugh for many a day. "Follow me!"

The four of us dashed back along the bank. Galloping at my knee, Harold shouted, "How deep is it there?"

"Only a foot or two. That's not the danger. Quicksand. Keep back, keep away!" I bellowed at the other knights on the shore. "We will get them."

As we dashed from the bank into the shallows, the young idiots were already halfway across, but their heavy horses were breaking gait ominously as the sands sucked at their hooves.

"Keep downstream," I warned those with me. "Feels firmer."

God help them. Even as we watched, the whole insane sortie lost speed, foundering. One mount, then another sank to its haunches. One went down at the head, pitching its rider forward. His head came up once, then no more than a frantic arm clutching at nothing before it disappeared. He never came up again.

To those young knights still on firm footing but their bravado vanished, I roared, "Back! Back to the bank. Keep downstream."

One man gone already, a wholly avoidable disaster, ludicrous to the watching Bretons. Leaping from the saddle, Harold swashed through the shallow water toward de

Tosny, half pinned under his sinking horse, wild-eyed and screaming for help. Harold called for Malet to help him. "Take the bridle, Hugh, while I—*up* with you, sir!"

With one great heave, Harold hauled the lucky dolt to safety. A high-pitched scream whirled me about, a sound I knew surely as Mora's own voice. My own Flemish had floundered into a sinkhole, already under to the haunches. Harold was between us. I cried out to him, "Harold, save—"

He'd seen already and dove not for the bridle but the destrier's nearer hindquarters already submerged. As I struggled toward him, Harold lurched and sank himself. "Stay clear!" he shouted. He hurled himself flat across the horse's croup and sank completely out of sight. All too quick, the animal's eyes rolling white with terror, then Harold's head reemerging, spitting muddy water and curses.

"You bloody, stupid mule—*allez!*"

With an anguished shriek surely heard on the Breton shore, my horse shot like a geyser out of the hole, Harold clinging to his tail. They were free, the horse shying nervously about. I caught his bridle and calmed him. "*La,* boy, *la.* Easy. I must reward you, Harold. This is far more than a horse to me. He is a dear friend."

Harold sputtered and pushed the sopped long hair back from his face. "Who was that boy who went down?"

"I'm not sure, but I thought you were truly gone as well."

"So did I. Pray the rest of your vavasors are more intelligent than these, else you'd be wiser to knight the horse. This old fellow," he patted the horse's mane, "he knew when to move when I suggested."

"Move? Good God, he *erupted*. What did you do?"

"I inspired him with my dagger up his arse. I fear he'll need a bit of ointment."

I winced at the method, but a wounded *derrière* is preferable to a dead one. I forgave Harold on the spot, clapping him on the shoulder. "Let us go get dry. There is a clutch of arrant fools who require a word or two."

And that they got, arrayed before me on the bank, miserable, soaked, and penitent. I loomed over each in turn like the sword of Michael, saving de Tosny for last.

"Undisciplined! Disobedient! You dishonor me, all of you. Were it not for us, you'd be under ten feet of mud now, and no one would care, *compris?* No one! What report will this earl make to England of Normandy's vavasors? Or those Bretons yonder who will tell Conan that no army but a fool's parade of clowns comes against him. *Pardi,* you all deserve to drown. Turold, send these idiots to the rear and let us hope they can escort the luggage without mishap. God forfend, I will not put such in my first line."

Not knowing when he was well off, young de Tosny protested hotly. "I beg you, my lord duke. My father is your strongest ally. You know his quality and I would prove mine. How can I tell him I was denied a place in the first line?"

"Your mistake, boy. You find a way. Turold, who was it we lost?"

"I think Jean de Lignières. He is the only one not here."

"Which Sire de Tosny can also explain to Jean's father. Disobey once again and I will break you from my service like an untrainable hound. Go!"

Defiance and rage seethed in the boy and might well have boiled over, but Harold's calm tone carried a caution.

"Sire de Tosny? If I may."

Drying his hair on a horse blanket, the earl strolled to the fuming youth. "I was happy to save you for another day when your quality no doubt will outshine many others. Glory is sweet to find along the way, but so are flowers, wives, and children, and much more enduring. Before you hark to the raven, listen a while for the lark. Your lord has ordered you to the rear. Cut along then, there's a good fellow."

In his few wise words to the boy I heard a mature man speaking his heart. And mine. I have come to find glory no more than a thin patina on the struggle for power or merely to stay alive. That day on the bank of Couesnon,

I felt more than gratitude toward Harold. I might almost wish this man for a brother. He did take risks, seemed careless and frivolous at times, as if to be too serious were embarrassment or bad taste. Beside men like mine he was beyond unconventional, he was plain radical. Yet in odd moments, when tired, when he thought no one watching, the lightness would slough from his face, and I saw the man himself: aging, serious, watchful of the world about him, and burdened with sadness he would rather turn to jest but for its weight.

I must have much from this man, but offer much in return.

62 • Harold

My rescue by William was only subtler imprisonment, my face stiff from smiling and playing the affable guest oblivious to his host's intent. I admired William personally; he controlled men well because he had learned to control himself. I received from him every courtesy, but only a matter of time before he broached the matter of succession. Until then I walked on eggs while sharper worries gnawed at me.

Did they know in England? Did Edith know? That she might believe me dead was torture made tenfold worse by the manner of our parting. With a kiss I evaded the painful question and fled the brutal answer. *And I left you so. Our eyes knew the truth and, knowing, couldn't meet with the old honesty. How can I speak of courage hereafter or you ever feel safe again? How did we come to this?*

Speak of egg-walking. As he vowed, William himself marked the way across the dangerous estuary, and I with him, an honor I dared not refuse in front of his knights, though after losing one of their companions in that deadly mire, no one clamored for my place. We led two mules loaded with bundles of birch rods, every dozen yards or so marking a firm path across the sands, through which the low-ebbing river now ran in thin tidal rivulets. Every movement was tentative. Each time my foot sank or the mule floundered on the brink of danger, I aged a year.

For William's part, he was *sang-froid* itself. "The quicksands shift, you know. Now here, now there, one tide to the next. One can never be sure."

Overhead the sun was a milky disc behind cloud, like a cataractous eye, but even now the autumn light began to fade. The two of us snailed forward, ten or so yards between us, while his men and the Breton knights observed our course, no doubt speculating when one or both of us would take a fatal step.

As much to defy them as anything else, William shouted jauntily: "How goes it with you, Harold?"

"Never better. Just feeling a bit naked out here."

"*Prenez garde!* Quicksand here. Move left. Left!" William jammed another rod into the sand well away from the sinkhole. On my side I inched cautiously to my left and did the same.

"Is it true in England they call me Willy Bastard?"

"Not to worry, my lord. They call me worse in Wales."

At length the scornful Bretons tired of our crawling progress and trotted away up the bank just as my mule lurched suddenly and sank to the hocks in sucking mire, and I had to haul him out by the bridle. He resisted at first, braying abominably, and I was at the wrong end for the dagger cure. "You ridiculous, goddamned—come *on.*"

I pulled with all my strength and gave a prayer of thanks as the struggling beast found firm purchase again. But William had halted again, frozen.

"No farther, Harold." Carefully he probed to his front and right side in an exploratory arc. "All around me."

Christ, I could see it: directly athwart our path, a swath of death yards wide and God knew how long, that actually swayed and trembled with the waters beneath. "A belt of the stuff, see? We have to go round."

"If we can." William looked across at me with a glint of cold humor. "*N'avez-vous pas peur,* Harold?"

The question caught me too short for manners. "There's a fool question for a start. Not scared in the middle of a riverbed full of quicksand? The word *panic* comes to mind."

"Me, too," William admitted with a sour grin. "But you should never curse at animals."

"Pure envy. *He* doesn't know the trouble we're in. I do."

Suddenly, out of nowhere and nothing we both began to laugh for no good reason but that we shared peril and for that moment were bonded by it. I backed carefully until William had ample room to swing left with me. "Firm here."

An endless time later we reached the Breton bank and gazed back across the lethal flats at the staggered lane we'd pocked into it. William brandished one of his rods as a signal for Turold to start crossing. "If we had waited for tomorrow, the quicksands would have shifted under the new tide."

We were very vulnerable alone on the bank and Turold only now leading the first elements through the lane, dismounted, men holding on to horse bridles. The war engines and trailing infantry would be crossing in near dark. "If Conan had enough archers nearby, he could inflict considerable damage."

"The patrol hasn't reached him yet," William said confidently. "He would have to force a march twelve miles from Dol and deal with the dark the same as we. He will not come."

"I would. I'd be waiting for you here. You'd never gain the bank."

William nodded thoughtful agreement. "Some would think it unknightly, but I will remember that."

"War is simple, William. It's peace that's difficult. In war you only have to destroy. In peace you must maneuver to preserve."

"*Bien*, Malet said you were unorthodox. Turold! Speed them! By God, if we can do it, you can. Haste!"

Any profound thought on peace and war would be lost on Norman and Breton knights. The next day we arrayed before the high, besieged castle on Mount Dol, our lines a longer, stronger crescent curved about Conan's siege-worn force, and for several days the only danger was boredom and bad food. Nothing moved, utterly static. We observed Conan, he observed us. From the castle battlements, complacently sure of relief now, Rhiwallon yawned down on all of us. Compared to the frozen hell of the Welsh mountains or the no-quarter savagery of Porlock, Dol was a dull holiday.

We arrived on a Saturday in the middle of a local institution called the Truce of God, which by Church statute and sacred oath prohibited private warfare from Wednesday evening until Monday morning. William was exempt from this, but Conan was not. He might have ignored the holy injunction but for several bishops present to keep him honest. Fresher and far superior in strength, William did not attack, merely hovered there, letting Conan worry. Of course, punctually on Monday morning our catapults began to pelt his ranks, and mounted sorties clashed in brief engagements. Prisoners were taken on both sides, Breton knights glumly trudging through the churned-up mud into our camp, bound by honor to remain captive until their families ransomed them. For all their fire-eating sentiments, vavasors are as mercenary as whores. To me it seemed an absurd parody of war, half courtesy, half carnage.

With Dol still untaken, prevented by William from foraging for supply, Conan reluctantly came to terms. He lifted the siege, gave hostages for his promise to keep the peace. The lesson was salted in, and William went home. The real winners at Dol that year would be the serfs who would reap a windfall in the horse manure that ripened the trampled field, or at least those not butchered in the next "war."

*   *   *

Across Seine, William's palace and the priory of Saint Gervais dominated Rouen from atop a long, sloping hill. William and I were on the first ferry barge to cross to the north bank. My heart leaped at sight of the welcome figure wrapped in a dun cloak, long hair whipping in the wind and, amid waiting Norman functionaries, his broken nose aloofly in the air.

"Botulf!" I jumped from the barge to the quay to swallow him in my arms. "How is it with you?"

"Ach, my lord, I was sick to death but better now."

He was still wan from the illness but at least still with me. "And Edric? Any of the others?"

"No, sir. God was not that generous."

"We must pray for them."

Botulf glanced about and lowered his voice. "And us while we're at it. I don't feel safe. Wherever I go, there's always someone watching."

A welcoming procession of palace dignitaries and monks escorted us through the narrow streets of the city up to the palace gates, within which the Duchess Matilda waited, flanked by her women and William's children, the daughters Cécilie and Adelaide and the presumptive dukeling Robert, his younger brother Richard, and four-year-old William toddling on the arm of his nurse. Plainly William was a man of enormous energy. Beside putting his stamp deep on western France, he was heeding Genesis, being fruitful and replenishing the earth. I noted the familiar bulge under Matilda's loose-flowing garments.

The sight of her next to her husband was comical. William had the height and bulk of his Norse ancestors. Matilda was, to employ Botulf's pungent description, the "smallest damned woman I ever saw, nigh to a bleedin' midget."

But a fertile one. Matilda had churned out children like grain from a mill since marriage, a dynasty in herself. I was presented to her warmly by William after he'd swept her up like a child in his arms and kissed each of his progeny. Matilda inclined her head to me, then surveyed my ill-fitting clothes which by then were ready to be buried or burned.

"*Ma foi*, Earl Harold, but you look like all England stuffed into a very small sack."

"So I feel, madame."

Matilda's form alone lacked stature. With a peremptory snap of tiny fingers, a waiting woman was at her elbow. "Send for the duke's tailors. I want them here with their best materials this evening."

In a few days I was provided with excellent clothing of the Norman cut, and even Botulf, at my request, was rendered presentable, though Matilda thought my concern for a peasant odd and unseemly. Beyond that she feted me as an honored guest. She had enormous personal charm, if now and then the sharp edges poked through. She had known my parents in Bruges as a girl. We passed many hours before her fire, and only when I tried adroitly to mention departure was Matilda vague or indirect.

One evening will serve to illustrate. It was late, Matilda and I chatting before the hearth in one of her private chambers. William had retired early, always his custom since he was up and busy long before light. We drank mulled cider while I pondered a fresh approach to the subject of my departure.

"Madame, is it not possible at least for my man to attempt a crossing with news of me. The king and my family surely think I'm dead by now."

"Really, my lord." Matilda seemed mildly offended. "Are you so anxious to leave us? Believe me, we have made inquiries. I sympathize deeply, but no craft are sailing."

"Not one? Surely—"

"But I forget me." Matilda eased her pregnant weight out of the chair, smoothing the surcoat over her gown. "I must be up early as William tomorrow. We receive emissaries from Denmark and the Holy See. *La*, but you men are lucky not to have to bear children. William has especially asked you attend him at mass in the morning. *A demain*, Lord Harold."

"Madame." I bowed after her. Once more denial had been glazed with honey. To get home, I might well have to swim.

William always heard mass at six of the morning, a Spartan devotion in the unheated palace chapel. His chaplain, an unctuous fellow from Poitiers, offered to hear my confession. I obliged, hoping it wasn't to be my last, and was then directed to a small consistory off the chapel where William waited alone, warming his hands over a brazier.

"Ah, Harold. Let us breakfast together. You slept well?"

"Very well, thank you."

"Good, good. Sit. I have something to tell you." William positively beamed at me, but he had a hard face which a smile did little to warm. "When I asked you to risk the river with me, I meant to find for myself the kind of man you are. By the time we crossed, I knew. I must reward you."

"Really, that's not—unless you can get us home."

"With arms," William bore on. "The best sword and mail in my armory—you will find our mail better than English—and your pick of my stables for mount. The duchess herself will buckle on your spurs."

"Spurs?" A warning whispered in my brain. "You mean a knighthood?"

"I mean no less, Harold."

"It is a great honor, but . . ."

The smile vanished. "But what? What?"

"I must decline, William. A matter of fealty. How can I become your knight when I'm sworn to Edward?"

"And to his successor, no? What difficulty?"

William's frown deepened; he seemed to be hovering. I took my time framing an answer. "Why do I feel I'm still surrounded by quicksand?"

A subtler man might have laughed quickly to put me at ease, but not single-minded William. "How? Where? I know you are educated, but do not insult my intelligence. Take the honors or leave them lie, but you know of what we speak."

If I must lie prodigiously that day, I dared not do so stupidly. "I do."

"Then why? Tell my *why* is Edward silent when I have

sent letter after letter? When your own brother is pawned on his promise. Why, Harold?''

William paced about the small chamber like an agitated cat. He was well informed, he knew Edgar's age to the month and how little promise he showed. Surely our Witan would not entrust the kingdom to *him*. Now that the Exile was dead, there was only himself in the royal line. And always, always William hammered on Edward's promise. Listening, a deep, sick rage surged through me at that pious, inconstant old man playing with his new abbey like a child building sandcastles, bastioning his hope of heaven and to hell with England.

Abruptly William loomed up over me, demanding: ''Well? You are premier lord of his Witan. What are you going to do about it?''

In swordplay and politics, one learns to sidestep. ''At the moment? I was saved from the sea by God and from the lion's den by your generosity. Is this the price?''

''Do not play the *naif*, Harold.''

''You'd be surprised. May I naively ask to see my brother? It's been years.''

''Perhaps,'' William considered. ''When I have your assurance of England. But my friend—and I call you that with a ready heart—many things would be easier for both of us then. Otherwise . . .''

Elided but clear enough. Otherwise I would be a hostage myself at best. At worst I might not leave Normandy alive. William knew the uses of power and how to rule, but of England no more than a goose. Amazing: As much as he had gleaned of *what*, the man was blind to the *why* of us and how we think. When our country is at stake, we do not scruple to sink the knife in the danger's front or back, whichever is toward us. I bought Gruffydd's murder, much as I admired him. I would sell William on the same block. I rose and looked into the man's strong face with blank innocence. ''What does Your Grace imply?''

''I know you have blocked Edward's will before,'' William declared. ''He said you—aye, and your father before you—had ideas that were radical, even dangerous. But hear me, Harold. Your council of earls, three of whom are your own brothers, will have no force against my right. The pope himself will back me. You know he will."

I chose my words very carefully, sure William was testing me with instincts keen as his mind. "You are mistaken, my lord. We are difficult for foreigners to understand, I know. The Witan may oppose the Crown on many matters but never on the succession. We must choose from the royal house. So we brought back Edward and his nephew. After Edgar there is you and no one else."

William sighed and turned away from me. "You're not dealing honestly with me, Harold. There is you. You are the best they have."

"Me?" I hoped my surprised laughter convinced him. "Good God, my own brothers would laugh at the notion. The very chrism would steam dropping on my head. My grandfather was little more than a peasant."

"Mine was a tanner. Don't palter with me, Harold. Will you support me or not?"

"Against a doltish boy? I have already put your claim before the Witan and will do so again." True, and their volcanic response would have given William a seizure. True, I would mention the matter again, receive the same reaction, and prepare for war. "Of course they will oppose you, but I will not. We've fair run out of kings."

William peered dubiously at me. "I do not question your honor, but I must be satisfied your promise is worth more than Edward's. I must have your word on that."

No room, no choice. The knife must go into his back. I uttered the damning words with the practiced ease of Satan. "My oath on it."

The lie dangled like bait between us. William stared at me for a space, then extended his hand to clasp mine. "So be it. You have said. Your oath before witnesses."

William is not a complex man. For England's sake, thank God he believed me. Were I to utter such treason and mean it, gentle Leofwine himself would coil the noose to hang me. But William took my words as laid on God's altar and made his offer in return. I was to be his regent in England, uncrowned king with fealty to him alone.

"I have heard many opinions of you, but I know what I have seen myself. Twice you went into quicksand for a noble horse and a brainless boy, then followed me out again where there was no honor or repute waiting, only miserable death. I could not find a better man, Harold. You will uphold my power in England. You will *be* my power in England, and none save God shall prevail against us."

When such a man opens his heart, you cannot fail to be moved, yet he reached for my country for no other reason than his personal rights. William is ten times a king, God's own mold for one, but not in England were he Christ incarnate. As for Botulf, fretting to be home, chafing at all things foreign, I could take him only so far into confidence now.

"Friend, listen. I've negotiated with William. We're to go home as soon as crossing is safe."

"Oh, good," he sighed. I heard long misery dissolve in relief. "What of Wulfnoth and Hakon?"

"I said listen! Until we sail, whatever you see me do or hear me say—however it appears, you know nothing. You say nothing."

"Going home . . ."

"Do you hear? What I'm telling you is the difference between going home and not ever."

Botulf saw only the green meadows of Nazeing. "Only you could've done it. I am proud to be your man."

Will you be so hereafter? "Botulf, at this moment in a cold November in this clammy tomb of a palace, I would rather be your man, call you earl, and carry your standard instead."

He was shocked at the notion, taken aback. "Well, I never! Going home, my lord says, looking happy as a plague death and talking of—damn me, sir, if you ent flat beyond me sometimes."

Damn you, Botulf? If you knew the half of what I must do toward damnation, you'd scrub out my forswearing mouth and soul with lye. "Just remember. Silence. By the bye, Turold's sent to remind me of our wager when time and weather agree. Pray you won't bet against me.''

63 • Harold

E*h, la!''*
Once more Turold's sword came out of nowhere. Once more I blocked with the old round shield, both of us sweating under mail and padded coats. A drop of perspiration tickled its way down my face under the helmet's noseguard. Turold was younger and faster, handling the oval shield expertly, but if I cut low at his off side, he had to cant the shield sideways to block, else it dragged on the ground. For all that, his strength and speed would eventually tell on me.

"La!''

Again the stroke almost too fast to see. I blocked it barely in time.

"No point!'' William ruled from the midst of the knights and squires ringed widely about us on the practice field below the palace. Turold had chosen this, the first dry and unseasonably warm day in March to play out our wager. Pride demanded he win. The matter weighed less with me, but as the bout went on and on, I began to tire. Unable to get past my shield, Turold grew more and more frustrated. He wove before me, shifting his weight from one foot to the other like a dancer, his mouth a grimace of insolence.

"You are old, *Anglais.* You are already short of breath.''

Only thirty-nine, but I felt every year of it and had spent far less time at sword than Turold. I could only hope to find some weakness and exploit it quickly. A quick sweep of Turold's shield knocked mine aside. He charged in with an overhand chop. I was just quick enough to block, but his shield slammed into my chest, jarring me cruelly. I had to give ground before his complex attack. Against his youth I had only the cunning of foot-to-foot combat. While Turold was constantly encouraged by the other knights, only two voices cheered me on, William and loyal Botulf.

"Stay with him, my lord!" Botulf bellowed. "You'll wear him down."

A roar from the Normans as Turold attacked again, his blows battering my shield with the thudding rhythm of a giant hammer. Blocking a sudden direct thrust, I parried him aslant and whirled in a complete circle, forcing him to turn.

Twice he's come out of slash into straight thrust. That takes an iron wrist. Next time I'll use that to surprise him. I'd better or it's all up. Wait for the thrust . . .

"Sire Turold, finish him," de Tosny laughed. "I'm getting thirsty out here."

"Ah, but it is meager sport at best," Turold retorted, putting the best face on his inability to hit the "old" *Anglais.* "I must prolong it to get any exercise at all."

Not much sport left in me. We wielded practice swords, edgeless and dull pointed, but of full iron weight. My arms became harder to lift; it had to be now. With all the flagging speed I could muster, I went on the attack, knowing that any one of Turold's parries could begin his counterattack if I presented the smallest opening.

So be it. I went for a head chop which Turold easily deflected, countering in a diagonal slash. God, he was quick! As the slash came level with my chest Turold lunged in a straight thrust that would have scored, but I expected it. Rather than strike his blade aside, I slid mine under and along it, wrenching my wrist far outward in a painfully unnatural turn. His sword aslant, the move threw Turold's whole balance to his off side as my shield crashed into his helmeted head and shoulder. Before he could recover, my point, already leveled just below his breastbone, went home hard, forcing an *oof!* of expelled wind from his lungs as Turold went down hard on his rump.

"Point and match!" William exclaimed jubilantly. "Turold, I'll have the silver or one of your best horses for this."

The circle broke inward, knights and squires running to Turold where he sat on the ground, holding his middle and trying to catch his breath. In a moment Botulf was at my side, pounding me on the back, William bearing down to pump my gauntleted hand in congratulation. *"Magnifique! Merveilleux!"*

Botulf busied himself removing my gauntlets and helmet, unbuckling the mail coat. "Never had a doubt, sir, never. Think to best you, would he? Aye, and we'll have snow in June. How is it with you? What's the matter with your hand?"

"Damn wrist's nigh sprung out of the socket. I'll be wanting a basin of the hottest water you can fetch to my chamber."

Free of the mail I went to Turold, who stood disconsolately among his comrades, still holding his belly. From the sour mutterings around him, I gathered more than his wager with William had been lost. Still, there was the sporting way to do these things. I offered him my hand. "Well run, Sire Turold. Well played. You wore me to a shadow."

After a cold hesitation he reluctantly gripped my hand. "Next time I will, Earl Harold. Next time it will be real."

Christmas had passed, then Candlemas and Lady Day while I waited for the ax to fall when William would demand my oath. Late in March I took to walking the palace roof in the morning to read the weather. Yes, it was turning, not quite so damp or cold, the wind less often from the north. Boats would soon be venturing back and forth in the Narrow Sea and, at whatever cost, Botulf and I could go home.

One morning early in April as I walked the battlements, the sentries pretending not to watch, the bells from Saint Gervais went on in a steady clamor long after ringing the hour of terce. A stream of horsemen, nobles, clergy on palfreys and mules, and covered carts wending up the hill toward the priory. Certainly a gathering of note, but what occasion?

I asked of the sentries, "Is there to be a wedding?"

They didn't know, and the damned bells were becoming tedious. I went down from the roof to my own chamber, where a cheery brazier on a tripod dispelled the morning chill but made the room damnably smoky since no one had remembered to draw back the tapestry before the stone casement. Pushing it aside I learned far out, inhaling a sweet telltale warmth beyond the stink of Rouen. No doubt of it, winter was broken.

"Lord Harold?"

Botulf stood just inside the open door with a slender youth in a long dun surcoat bearing the blazon of Mortain, one of William's kinsmen. "This lad just arrived, sir. Guards said—I *think* their drift was I should bring him to you. Something about release?"

"Release? Who—?" Before my thoughts connected, the dark-haired boy bowed with tentative courtesy.

"Mon oncle?"

Something in blood knew before my mind. "Good God, of course." I grasped him by his narrow shoulders. "Hakon?"

"Oui."

"Botulf, this . . . really, this is wonderful. This is my nephew, Swegn's son, Hakon. By the mass I'm glad to see you. So long it's been. You were just a babe."

Hakon endured my torrent in blank confusion. *"Comment?"*

Stupid of me. In my eagerness I'd rattled on in English and suddenly chilled to remember Hakon was taken from us before he really knew his native tongue. *"Bien,* my boy. Released you say?"

"The duke says I may return with you."

"Alors, we will tolerate his tongue for now, but we'll have you sounding the proper Saxon in good time."

"I am most pleased to greet you, Uncle," the boy said

gravely. "So many questions, so much I have forgotten or never knew."

"Certainly, certainly. Botulf, please excuse us for the time. We must speak in French."

"Aye, sir, and all gibberish to me. I'll be just outside."

I invited Hakon to sit by the brazier, pouring him some spiced cider. He never took his eyes from my face at first, as if trying to find all his own life there. "It is peculiar to see my kin for the first time. It has been so long. All my life."

"You were very young. What do you remember?"

"There was . . . a boat. When I try very hard to remember, there is always a boat and strangers I couldn't understand. I was terrified. I could not stop crying."

"Do you remember Wulfnoth?" I pressed. "They brought him here with you. He was fifteen then."

No, Hakon had no memory of any such boy nor ever heard the name. They'd housed him in one castle after another over the years: Bayeux, Avranches, finally at Mortain, where he was treated well enough but alone most of the time with no friends, no one to talk with except the guards. Listening to him, I sank into a silent, icy rage at Edward and William alike for robbing this boy of his childhood and his heritage which I must try to restore. "Do you remember your mother, Agatha?"

Hakon brightened with a new eagerness. "There was someone, yes, and I knew she was my mother. She was always there, talking to me even though I could not understand. What was her name? They never told me."

Mercy of God, all those years. "Agatha of Leominster. She gave up much—someday you will appreciate how much—to follow your father and bear you. She loved you dearly."

"I wish to think that," he murmured, "that someone did. Sometimes when I close my eyes and try very hard, sometimes just before sleep, I almost see her bending over me, but her face is dim. Aga-ssa."

Hakon smiled with bright pleasure for the first time since entering. Of all he'd lost, I'd given him back one small piece. "She is yet alive?"

"Alive and well, tough as weed like all English country folk. You'll live with her at Fishbourne close to your grandmother's estate and we'll see each other often."

"*Où est cet village,* Fish-burr?"

"In the south, the loveliest part of our island, where Agatha has her own cottage."

"They told me she was a *putain.*"

I could only stare at him. "A whore? Your mother?"

"They said—"

"Devil what they said. They lied, the bastards. *I* say she was none. Before God, not one day of her life. I might as well tell you, she was a religious before she married Swegn, an abbess at Leominster."

"But they said terrible things about her and my father. There was an old priest at Mortain who always stunk of bad wine. He said my father was Satan's own, that he had a demon in him."

"If a demon, then an angel as well who defeated that demon in the end." I must tell Hakon larger truth, drawn not from shabby fact but from the heart. "True, your father, Swegn, never got on well with Normans, but there was so much more. Did they tell you he went barefoot on pilgrimage to the Holy Land? Did they recount how, on the Via Dolorosa, at each station of the Cross, he prayed on his knees? Swegn Godwinesson. No man was a greater soldier, none was more human."

"Was? Is he not yet alive?"

"No, he is dead, Hakon. He died returning from Jerusalem, but not . . ." Words failed, I had to stop. Hakon leaned forward, prompting eagerly. "But what, Uncle?"

"Not before paying for more sins than ever he committed. Lord, boy, which of us doesn't house heaven and clay, angel and demon together? We are the unfortunate heirs of Genesis; that's why we prize love and forgiveness. Your parents gave up all for each other and for the sake of you. They placed much value on love."

A light, quick tap at the door and Botulf ducked his head in. "Lord, the watch've all jumped back in their proper places, smart and alert the way they do when the duke's comin'. Right enough it's him and the midget."

Faint from the corridor I heard William's penetrating voice, then the high, crisp sound of Matilda. A bit thick coming here himself instead of sending for me to attend him. More trusting friendship?

I drew Hakon to one side as William swept into the chamber, tiny Matilda on his arm. "Ah, the boy himself, and you've been getting acquainted. Good, good. As you see, I kept my word, Harold. He may return to England with you."

"After far too long I fear," Matilda said as Hakon bowed over her hand. "We regret so many things that must be, but now it is over."

"All but the last." William struck one hand against the other. "Your promise, Harold. Come with me to Saint Gervais. I must now have your oath."

The silent question gleamed in Botulf's eyes: *oath?* I tried to thrust my will into his memory: *Whatever you hear.* Hakon was free, Wulfnoth not mentioned, nor this the time to insist. William's friendship did not extend to parting with his last surety. For what I bought, this was the price. "Botulf, my mantle."

Swear to you, Willy? With all the poisoned pain in my soul. Yesterday I would have lied for my country alone, but this boy makes it personal for what your ambition stole from him and fouled what little memory remained of his parents. Angel and demon equal in all, you've waked the devil in me. Swear to you, take false oath before God and your hand in manly accord? Just watch me, Willy. You're a strong man, a fine man, but may you be damned hereafter surely as I am. For the rest, England regrets.

Botulf fixed the mantle's clasp at my shoulder and stepped back. "Your Grace," I assured the duke, "with all my heart."

64 • Harold

Some men hone their wits with education, some on
the grindstone of the world. Of the latter school,
William knew precisely where faith and reality met
and joined, arranging my oath for the most solemnity and
effect. I was led in formal procession from the palace to
the priory church, walking between two bishops, Hugh of
Lisieux and Odo of Bayeux, William's half brother, with
a gaggle of chanting monks going before us. I was followed by William and Matilda, their son Robert and, I
gathered, as many notable witnesses from court as William
could press into service. Then Turold and twenty knights
all clad in white. Lesser folk of the court brought up the
rear, Botulf and Hakon among them.

The assembly waiting in the church nave was no less
impressive. The prior and subprior were ranged to the left
of the high altar, chamberlain, almoner, and other officers
to the right, and I approached the chancel through a black-
robed lane of obedientiary monks. A writing desk with
quills and ink had been placed to one side, while two
small tables, their samite covers reaching to the flagstones,
stood side by side before the choir steps, each bearing a
closed reliquary.

William joined me and, together, we genuflected to the
crucifix and crossed ourselves. I recognized the wizened,
dry-as-dust monk waiting by the two tables: the priory
sacrist who'd requested frequent audiences with William
during the winter and spring. As William addressed me,
voice ringing through every corner and eave of the
crowded nave, the priory precentor took his place at the

writing desk, that no syllable of my oath be lost to record. Further, that there be no possible confusion or evasion, one tongue to another, the precentor would translate aloud into English each stipulation of the oath, which would be written in both languages.

"Harold, Earl of Wessex, first lord of England," William began, "I charge you remember that you speak in the presence of God. You are prepared to render oath?"

"I am."

"Sacrist?"

The cadaverous sacrist, whose entry into any chamber had always reminded me of a blast of stale air, opened the reliquaries before me. Each contained small bones and skull fragments. "These are the sacred remains of two missionaries from your own land. Fleeing persecution from the heathen Danes, they sought refuge in pagan Neustria but were martyred for their faith instead. Against these holy relics is your oath impawned, my lord. Therefore, if your heart hold any reservation, conceal any let, remember that Judgment hears your oath."

"There is no let."

The sacrist closed the reliquaries. "Then stand between the tables with a hand to each holy cask."

I placed myself so, facing the crucifix. *Eirianell, poor sufferer, it seems surer than ever that we'll meet again.*

"Firstly," said William. "Do you swear while Edward lives, to be my *vicarius* in England and to advance my rightful claim before all pretenders?"

"My lord, I so swear."

"Secondly." The hard voice of a hard man hammering the last nails in the edifice of his destiny. "After Edward's death, do you swear to uphold the conditions of his pledge and to support my coronation howsoever opposed?"

"I do so swear."

That thoughtful man, Stigand, observed long afterward, "The act strains irony to its root. One self-serving man would steal England in good faith, while another saved it with a lie."

Thirdly I was to continue as *subregulus* in England and

to do William homage for Wessex when he became king. But then he went too far.

"Lastly swear that, on your return to England, and at your own expense, you will fortify the town and surrounding heights of Dover as a recognized Norman garrison enclave."

What he demanded was preposterous. Edward himself backed by God and a Witan of archangels couldn't shove that down England's throat. I opened my mouth to protest, but the denial that ripped through the air of the nave came not from me.

"NO!"

I turned with everyone else to where Botulf hovered, at once outraged and shocked by his own boldness. "Lord Harold. My lord, you . . ."

"Botulf, be silent."

"You cannot, sir. You *dare* not."

William's arm shot out in command. "Turold, restrain that man!"

"No, leave him be." I strode forward as Turold and two others moved on my friend. "You hear me. *Leave him alone.* He's mine to deal with." I pushed through the crowd to confront and grip Botulf by both arms. The man need not have said one word more. All the horror of my treason was naked in his eyes. "As you are my man, as you are loyal and love me, be silent."

His mouth shaped the word soundlessly, stunned: *Loyal?*

"Trust me," I whispered, leading him back to his place by Hakon.

"Trust what?" Botulf shook off my arm, refusing to look at me. I returned to William amid a sibilant rush of whispering from the assembly, and spoke for the duke's ear alone.

"You must pardon my servant, an ignorant provincial whom I have labored in vain to gentle."

"Give him a stick across his back."

"For too much honest care to my soul? All else I can swear with good conscience, but you know Dover is impossible. To attempt this while Edward lives would kill your cause at the start.''

William must have known that. He only shrugged. "Dover now or later, no matter, but worth a try. Precentor?''

The precentor-scribe took up what he had copied and read in a high, clear voice those articles sworn to by me. Then the thin old sacrist glided forward again, solemn as death. "Once more, Earl Harold, on our soul's salvation, have you freely sworn to fulfill these conditions?''

"Upon that salvation have I sworn.''

"Indeed." William turned up the covering cloth of each table. On the bottom shelf of each rested a single, small fragment of wood. "You have.''

Crossing himself, William took up the first piece. "This is from the tree trunk that carried to Fécamp the phials containing the blood and sweat of Jesus' agony on Golgotha. You have heard of that miracle." Again he crossed himself and held up the second relic. "And here is a fragment of the True Cross. The sacrist has been months collecting them from other houses. On no less than these have you sworn.''

I've since heard that witnesses saw me falter and turn pale before such potent holiness, but the Norman soul is more primitive than ours, their piety feral as their love of war. I was trapped in a deadly game and could save England only by saving myself, and what price damnation now? Long damned for Eirianell, one more eternity in hell was redundant.

As William waited, positively oozing triumph and satisfaction, I held out both hands. "Let me hold them.''

In each hand rested one of the holiest objects in Christendom. I looked long and closely at each before pressing it to my lips. From that day to this, God has not thundered nor Christ bled anew for shame.

William kept his word; we were allowed to leave that week. Hakon was excited, chattering at me thirteen to the dozen, but Botulf kept his sullen distance. He suppressed his outrage until our boat stood well out from Seine mouth for England, frightened, confused, and sick with my betrayal.

"I daren't think on what you've done to England and yourself. I've borne your standard for nigh twenty years. You were the last man in God's world I'd call a traitor. Edward might touch lepers to heal them, but you—you and your father, bless his memory—I've seen people weep for pride if you just smiled at them when riding by. Why? Damn it, sir, I've earned the right to ask. Why?"

"I can do nothing for England dead, nor can you."

Botulf turned away from me. Bitterly: "Beside what you've done, is death so bad?"

"Nobly said but more tardily paid. Damn your smugness anyway! Had I been so righteous as you, I would somehow disappear like Wulfnoth, and you would shortly meet with accident. Didn't I say to trust me? Didn't I pound that into your thick Anglian skull months ago: 'Whatever I say, whatever you hear.'"

I drew him to me by the sidewale. "I know it's all been worse on you than me, but hear me out. William will never rule England. *That* you can trust. But he believed me. *That* is our victory. Yes, it means war, but we knew that a year ago, and if I ever doubted, Turold told me himself after the sword match. 'Next time,' he said. 'Next time it will be real.' As if he knew what was coming and couldn't wait."

Still Botulf feared for my soul. "Right, then. So be it, but falsely sworn on holy relics. I couldn't keep silent, no mind what you told me. You've damned yourself ten times over."

"Long since, Botulf, but not this week." I leaned out over the sidewale, loving the southwest wind through my hair that brought me, stronger with each hour, the familiar smell of home waters.

"Holy relics? Let me share with you a shabby truth absorbed with what the duke would call my decadent education. The sale of saints' and martyrs' bones to credulous clerics is shameful but ever lucrative. Those bones were not whitened enough to be old as that sacrist said. And the holy tree of Fécamp was a fig, not a chestnut, nor the

True Cross of oak such as I held in my hands. Oh, William believes, and the sacrist and the lot of them at Saint Gervais, else they'd not have used them to make my oath more terrible and binding. For the rest, my friend, there is no end to the mendacity of this world.''

Just then our lookout hailed from the masthead: ''La-and ho! Pevensey dead ahead.''

''Hakon! Now where the devil is that boy? Hakon, you'll want to see this. Quickly, I say.''

The boy was already running down the deck toward us, leaping through the rowers, shouting joyously. ''I see it, Uncle. I can *see* it.''

''By God, Botulf, are you weeping?''

''I am not, sir.''

''Then pray you'll pardon me if I do, just a little.''

With my arm about Hakon's shoulder and Botulf perhaps beginning to understand on my other side, I watched England rise, long and low, out of the north.

I am a servant like you, Botulf, if I can't afford your principles. If Wulfnoth is lost to us, Hakon is home again. I lost some, I preserved much, and only in heaven and hell do all scales balance.

BOOK VI

Lord of Sunset

65 • Harold

Aventuresome trading keel a week in advance of us left the news of our return at Pevensey, from whence it spread to Bosham, Fishbourne, and north to London and Nazeing like fire in joyful tinder.

Every rare now and then a particular time of your life, like a well-told tale, comes to such satisfying closure that your heart sings with the angels: This was well done. When Agatha hurried from her cottage to see Hakon, the joy that trembled in her cry went on paying me long after for so many things. She clung to the boy, who understood not a word of her loving torrent but tried to return it. For all the years and loss, they had a life again, someone to share with, and I turned away with a few cleansing tears of my own.

Agatha tried to do a dozen things at once, calling us into her house, ordering her old woman servant to pour the ale, unwrap the cheese, fire the oven for fresh bannocks. This was the sweeter part, but there was my mother yet to see and far less happiness to lay before her.

Yet that one dear interlude at Fishbourne: Agatha couldn't take her eyes or hands from Hakon. While I translated, yet not so swiftly as their meanings and hearts ran, Agatha looked to devour her son whole with her heart, drink in every line of him to find again the child come from her body, while Hakon glowed brighter with each passing hour.

Before I left them Agatha took me aside, past forty now and so long alone that she'd become careless of her appearance: no veil, hair caught up in a simple grey-shot twist, spending her days in the garden or bickering aimiably with the stolid old companion servant. But that one day some of the light that must have once shone for Swegn rekindled in her eyes.

"Archbishop Stigand has received me back into the Church, but were I still excommunicate, I would pray for you, Harold. From this night until my last. Kiss me good-bye."

"You are kind, Agatha." Against her cheek I entreated, "Considering the request, please pray very hard."

"My uncle needs no extra prayers," Hakon warranted heartily at my stirrup. "I was there in the church and saw what William made you do. *Vraiment,* may it cost Bastard a hundred years' purgatory. Let me be more than nephew. Let me be Duke Harold's man."

I gripped his offered hand gratefully. "The word is *earl,* Hakon. As your first duty to me, learn your mother's tongue. She's so much to tell you."

"I'll come when you need me," he promised, then cried after as Botulf and I rode away, "I can ride any vavasor into the ground. Without a saddle!"

At Bosham Gytha greeted me bowed over a cane. For Hakon's return she showed grave pleasure, graver resignation at the loss of Wulfnoth which, barring miracle, we must now see permanent as the pain in her fingers, the stiffness in her knees. My mother endured all without show or undue complaint. "Vinegar and water each night before retiring. Wretched stuff, but it helps. I can sleep so little now. Who would think so natural a thing would become such a blessing? All may be the will of heaven, but sometimes I wonder why God doesn't just let an old woman go to sleep for good."

"Nonsense. You'll outlive me."

"The prospect does not shimmer," my mother declared with some of her own old vinegar. I lifted her legs onto a footstool.

"There now. You must come often to Nazeing. Promise me."

"No, you must all come to me now," Gytha said. "Unlike good wine, I no longer travel well. Now kiss me and be off. Edith will be beside herself if you stay longer from home.''

Knowing Botulf yearned for wife and home more than he confessed, I'd sent him on ahead and would have furnished a good swift keel, but Botulf declined. He'd had his bellyful of the sea, thanks the same, and left boats to me. All the way around Kent into Thames mouth my eagerness could fill the sail or row the keel by itself. I was in a fever when we turned into River Lea. Only a few hours more. So much to do, say, touch, and share. Godwine? He was going on eighteen this year. Magnus sixteen, and Edmund with whom I'd spent so little time in the last years, already twelve. How much time had I spent with any of them? Where was I, and where did the years go like deserters from a vowed cause?

"Lay on!" I roared at the sweating lithsmen, straining their goodwill along with their backs. "Lay on!"

The landing quay to Sigward's hall glided past while his goose girl waved and the geese honked. I honked back raucously, and when I could hear nones bells from Waltham Church, I knew I was home.

"Lord Harold," the boatmaster sang out. "Up ahead. Three riders coming along the bank."

Botulf it was, carrying my standard, the Lions curling over his head, badge of his office as much as mine. Magnus, too, proud in the saddle, and Edmund jolting up and down and trying for all the world to look the seasoned horseman.

"Boys! Here! Rowers, into the bank."

"No need. The quay's just ahead," the boatmaster called back.

"To hell with that. In now. Boys, here!"

As the keel swerved into the bank, I leaped the side, alas, with more joy than judgment, landed short of firm ground and got soaked to the hips. Uncaring, I floundered up the bank, arms wide to grab Magnus, both of us grinning idiotically, whirling around as Edmund tore into me with an avalanche of affection.

"My God, let me look. Lord, you've both grown so.''

"Mum's waiting," Edmund piped, front teeth squirrel-prominent in his grin. "And Uncle Gyrth and Leofwine."

"No! Really?"

"And all the servants and cottagers have turned out to welcome you," Magnus took it up. "And Uncle Gyrth's brought a monster boar from Epping, turning on the spit now, and there's to be such a feast."

"And your mother, Magnus? She's well?"

"Never better and at the gate since we rode out."

"And Godwine?"

Something spilled the wind out of Magnus's enthusiasm. In his pause, Edmund blurted, "He didn't come."

"But he's there with Mum," Magnus recovered.

Botulf stepped down, furling the standard and offering me his horse. "You and the boys go on, sir."

"Ta for that. How is it with your wife, man?"

"Oh," Botulf squinted at me, "perhaps it's just being used to the damned woman or almost drowning or just getting old, but I don't seem to mind so much when she natters at me."

"After almost drowning, perhaps you listen more." I cuffed his shoulder in farewell. "Anon."

As we drew near Nazeing's gate, I could see that the entire household and folk from the near cottages were there, ranged behind Edith, Gyrth, Leofwine, and the unsmiling youth at my wife's side. Though I had eyes for Edith alone, my brothers descended on me and dragged me from the saddle, smothering me in rough love, incoherent with welcome, Gyrth vowing, "I'm not much for church, but devil if I don't go tomorrow."

"Ach, the sight of you both. Edith!"

As I brushed past him, Leofwine's words blurred in my ear: "—got to talk. There's trouble."

"I'll not hear a serious word today. Edith, love!"

Her hands flew to her mouth to hold back too much feeling or tender dismay at the Lea-soaked sight of me dripping before her, then her arms went about my neck and crushed me to her like life itself. "It was so terrible. They said—"

"It's all right, love. I'm home."

"—that you were dead, but I wouldn't believe them."

"There was no way to get word, I swear."

"When I heard, it was like coming alive again. Why are you all over wet?"

"Because I can't jump as far as I feel anymore."

Edith threw back her head, flung her arm out to our people as she had to me on our wedding night. "My folk! *Hoch* to your lord who is home again. All come feast!"

As their cheer went up, men tearing the caps from their heads and throwing them high, Edith beckoned Godwine, who had hung back so far. "And here is your firstborn son grown nigh tall as his father."

"Godwine, boy."

He seemed more to suffer my embrace than return it. "It is good to have you home, Father."

My son didn't sound that glad, but then Magnus and Edmund surrounded me, prattling of Gyrth's hunt and the boar and how we were going to crowd the hall to the rafters tonight and feast to bursting, and only when I led Edith to the hall on my arm did I have a chance to ask, "What ails Godwine? You'd think I was a stranger."

"He's a little—well, it's a long story and can wait."

All weighty matter must wait at the door that night, for I'd have nothing but joy. The hall doors were thrown wide, tables filled, the great tun of ale rolled in. All invited from Waltham Church, one of their priests gave the most heartfelt grace I ever amened, then I roared out the ancient cheer to all and watched them fall to. Giving most of my starved attention to Edith and my boys, Leofwine became downright annoying. Twice my brother rose from his place, bending over me to whisper something urgent about Tostig, but I'd none of it.

"Leave off, will you? Just this one night, get a little drunk and forget worry. We can talk tomorrow."

I could barely sit still myself, jumping up to lean over my sons in their places at the high table, running down the hall to greet old friends. When the musicians struck up a dancing measure, I led Edith down amid cheers. Didn't we *dance* that night, whirled till we sweated, Edith springing gaily on my arm through late afternoon into twilight. The servants lighted extra beeswax candles to add their scent to that of the fire, the boar, ale, wine, and happy people.

Edith whispered breathlessly as I seated her again, "Do you remember our wedding, how we slipped away?" Her warm breath and lips tickled my ear. "Let's do it again. So long since I dared to feel this happy. I want to be a bride again. And I've a surprise for you outside."

As we left the table, Gyrth and Leofwine raised their cups in approval. Godwine's eyes met mine sullenly, then dropped again. Seeing us leave, the hall sent up a rousing good night. Flushed and happy, I swept her up in my arms and carried her grandly through the tables and out into soft April evening.

"You great fool," she giggled. "Put me down."

"You wanted to be a bride again. Which way?"

"Past the kitchen house."

"My love, you've gained a bit of weight."

"Since we're being ungallant, so have you."

"Norman cooking."

"Not that being close to forty has aught to do with it. Come, put me down, you're puffing already."

Beyond the kitchen house stood a new bower that hadn't been there the year before. The single chamber was warm from a small fire in a new brazier. Edith lighted a single candle from it, moving about the chamber with that feminine purposefulness so unconsciously sensual in a woman. She lighted a single candle from it and then the rush lights in their stands on either side of the bed, holding the candle high so I could see the whole room in a warm glow, and her single word held all the pride and love that had gone into this little room. "See?"

A plain bedchamber, but every line of it spoke of loving care. Wattle and daub walls had been meticulously plastered over. Our own bed was there and other furniture from our old chamber with a new bolster and featherbed laid on. In one corner stood Edith's small prie-dieu from Shaftesbury. Great fool indeed: I thought of all the years she slept uncomplaining in the room and bed where I'd loved Eirianell, asking only that I scour from it all intrusive memories. Oh, years . . .

Edith set down the candle and began to undress, turning down the bed. When we were both bare, I sat on the edge of the bed, drawing her to me, pressing my grateful mouth to her stomach and breasts, breathing in the beautifully familiar musk of her skin. Edith trembled slightly, speaking to me out of a deep place.

"I was so miserable when you left. Then they were so sure you were lost in that storm. Weeks and then months with no word, until *wouldn't* believe became *had* to believe, and I knew I'd go mad without something to do. I built this bower."

Drew the plans, gathered the workmen, put her own heart and sweat into the labor, cutting and carrying wattle herself, mixing daub, troweling plaster with her own hands and, at the end, leading the procession of servants with the furniture.

"I found a kind of sanity again. Are you pleased?"

There were no words. In her womanly way Edith's heart and roots had sunk in Nazeing and in me.

"Don't say anything," she breathed. "I died a little when you left."

"So did I. When I was with you I couldn't say or do anything right, couldn't find what I meant or felt. I'm so sorry."

"This place was yours, then ours. Now it is mine as you are mine. I earned it, Harold. I kept resurrecting day after meaingless day without Lazarus' gratitude, moving through the hours somehow, always talking to you, loving and hating in the same breath. No, don't speak. So easy, so frustrating to find the right words after you part, all the things you should have said. Then you can cry the emptiness out of you when it's all too late, and you know that never again, never . . . then when you're still enough at last to listen, the truth comes."

Her cool, strong fingers covered my mouth tenderly. "You said you must be king. Accept that and we must accept what follows. Pray God I can when the time comes.

I don't know, Harold. Can I love you so and be that strong in the same day? There's no promise, my darling."

"It won't be tomorrow, there's blessing at least."

"Yes, time can be that kind." Edith slipped into bed, pulling me over her. In the dim light her eyes were huge and fathomless. "For this night I don't care a damn for England. You're home and we have now. Be with me now. Come into me."

Loving over twenty years is not always ecstasy. One or the other can be tired or distracted. Small irritations or unspoken anger with each other can pall the pleasure, or worry over a sick child, anything. Then there are those enchanted nights when you can't get enough and take each other again and again, and then the smallest part of the need is mere desire. Such times bring from you all you mean and all you are. You wake scrubbed clean, and for the rest God must take a promise.

"It's morning, love."

Edith twisted sleepily against me. "Mm . . ."

"I didn't think to feel this good ever again."

"Or I." Edith raised her arms overhead in a long, luxurious stretch and yawn. "I feel like a great, soft, beautiful horse ran over me."

When I slid out of bed to use the chamber pot, I noticed the dispatch case lying on a chair. "What's this?"

Edith sat up, pushing the tangle of hair back from her face. "From Canterbury yesterday. Didn't want to bother you, and we certainly had better things to do. Come back here."

She was sleep-warm in my arms and desirable as a young girl, murmuring against my mouth, "Doesn't this bower have advantages? Lovely thick walls, noisy as we were."

"To wake the dead." We kissed for a long time. "Thank you."

"Entirely my pleasure, my lord. Good morning."

"Wonder what Stigand wants."

"Let it wait."

"I'll just have a look." I broke the Canterbury seal and scanned the archbishop's brief message:

I have thanked God hourly since learning you were safe. Imperative we confer at your earliest convenience on the worsening situation in Northumbria.

God, not now, not so soon. Just a few days of my own life if England would be so kind. "Nothing that can't wait." I pulled the covers and Edith to me again. "You are a marvelously wanton wench when the humor's on you."

"It's been so long."

"I'll send for breakfast. Been ages since we ate in bed."

"Later." Edith smoothed her hand down my stomach to caress between my thighs. "Much later, love."

After much and lovely later, when we'd had our fill of each other and breakfast, Edith showed me the second letter with some reluctance. "From Thane Sigward. I wanted you in a good mood before dealing with it."

"What could be so bad on a day like this?" I broke the seal, read, and found out. In any mood, for this I was not ready, but no parent can be.

66 • Harold

When we'd washed and dressed I took up Sigward's letter again. Written on an old palimpsest by a priest of Waltham, the thane's message regretted presenting such a problem on my homecoming but left it to me to take proper action in the matter of Godwine and Elfring's daughter Anna, who would be inconveniently fruitful later in the year. I appealed to Edith. "Godwine and a slave girl?"

Edith's brows arched with delicate irony. "Beyond a vivid *déjà-vu*, what will you do about it?"

The letter described the lot of Sigward's thrall. Apparently shiftless as well as unlucky, Elfring had sold himself from the status of churl farmer into slavery for the payment of his debts. He had six children and knew he had no real claim, yet he'd been further unfortunate in trying to marry Anna off and begged any relief the good earl might render in the name of Christ Jesus and compassion for a poor man.

"He was so frightened," Edith remembered. "He came on a day when Gyrth was here. Your brother's a good heart, bless him, but no example for your son, having occupied more beds than a corn-husk mattress. He would have thrown the wretch out the door, but I forbade him and sent for Godwine. Poor Elfring, trembling there before us, twisting his dirty cap in his hands. And Godwine admitted it."

Edith vented a hiss of disgust. "It was the *way* he said it: casually, as if I'd asked him if he'd had enough supper. And Gyrth just laughed. But you will not, dear husband."

I set the letter aside with a sigh. "Thanks for not saying 'like father.' "

"No, but you must heed me now." When Edith opened the bower door, whatever feelings she harbored were battened tight under determination that brooked no argument. "You married beneath your class and could have done far worse in your own, if I do say it myself. Your parents had the power to make such problems vanish. I can't blame them for putting their sons first, but we do things differently in Shaftesbury, and I say neither Godwine nor Magnus nor Edmund will come to manhood as you and Swegn did, thinking you could ramp where you pleased without a price. They will *not*, husband. I taught them French and how to write and what is proper. Together we will teach them this."

Edith swung the door wider, letting in the morning sun. "Let Godwine know this will cost him. Now. Today. I'll send him to you straight."

Still off balance, I had no clear idea what I might say to Godwine beyond the obvious, nor would I embarrass both of us with a soppy recitation of Eirianell and my own guilt. However, when I heard the tentative knock at the open door, I surely knew what Godwine Haroldsson was going to do forthwith. "Come in, son."

Godwine was a mirror before me: my coloring and cast of features, even the faint hint of amusement about lips too ready to curl with laughter. The same long legs and expressive hands. "I was just off to hunt with Uncle Gyrth."

"He'll have to do without you. Sit down. You know why you're here."

My son dropped into a chair, eyes lowered. "Yes."

"You've made a proper mess, haven't you?"

"You should know, Father."

The insolence stung. "What was that?"

"Mum told me you did the same more than once. And Uncle Swegn."

"Damn your impudence, you little whelp. Who in Christly hell do you think you are? A spoiled brat with too little responsibility, that's what, and not too big to take a birch to. I may not have been a good example—"

"None at all," Godwine flared back, the anger flushing his cheeks. "Not good, not bad, just not. Never here at all. I hardly know you. And Mum—"

He caught himself, bit off the words, but I couldn't spare him or myself. "Your mother what? Out with it, boy. What did she say?"

"What she doesn't say, never says." This seemed to pain Godwine more than any matter of a slave girl. "I've had little time with you but all my life with her. And I remember. I know loneliness when I see it."

Yes, that was one root of his resentment, old enough to know the smell of the world, but too young to deal with it. "This . . . business of Anna. Only a part of it."

"I see. Then I won't bore you with pious slop about keeping your trousers up. It hasn't been easy to raise a family, neither for your mother nor for me. I went where I must, did what I had to for my own father or the king. You think you're the only man to feel alone, lonely? Sorry about that, but you haven't earned any *mea culpas* from me about women or anything else. I never had the chance to put things right when it mattered. You will.''

The child, if it lived, would legally belong to Sigward, but Godwine would contribute to its support. ''You'll begin by selling your horse.''

''Sell Brutus?'' Sheer outrage. ''Do you know how much that gelding cost? More than Anna's whole family.''

''Shut up. That's just for a start. Absent or not, I know where your living comes from, most from your mother's hides, some from mine. If you've suffered for lack of a father, you haven't lacked much else, by God. We'll arrange with our stewards to subtract some each quarter for the child. You won't see the money at all. The child won't have your name, but you might now and again let the little soul know it has some kind of father.''

''I'd like to know how that feels myself,'' Godwine said. ''When I was little it was mostly trying to remember how you looked, what you said, how it felt to have you here. Then that year in Wilton when you were exiled, listening to Magnus cry himself to sleep because he didn't know where he was, just frightened in a strange place. And hiding in that filthy barn in Blackmore Vale—''

''You know why that was. Our family had one choice: exile or destruction. You think I didn't miss you all painfully every day? That I don't love you now?''

''Well, there's the meat of it.'' Godwine said it so quietly, I knew he spoke from his heart. ''How can I love what I've never had a chance to know?''

No mercy then. What careless faith children have in a parent's strength. No matter how hard they strike, they think we can't be hurt. ''Your brothers manage that well enough. Perhaps one day you'll grow to forgive me, later perhaps even understand. Meanwhile, you've a horse to sell. Try Sigward, he's always fancied Brutus.''

Godwine rose with me and, as our eyes met, I saw with pleasure that he had almost attained my own height and well might exceed it. ''Father, I'm sorry for—well, for anything I've said. I know I'll never have your title or be any kind of lord after you. I just wanted you home.''

"So did I, Son. Every day." I gave him a reconciling hug. "Go do what you have to."

Godwine sighed. "So I will. But damn! Such a devilish *good* horse."

"Men have paid more. Ask Gyrth. And I'll look about for a good marriage. Obviously it's time."

"Marriage?" My son flashed an all too familiar grin. "Who'd have me, poor as I'm going to be?"

The stablers told me Leofwine was off giving his horse a run, and my border mare nickered for exercise herself. Cantering along the muddy road toward Epping Forest, I felt I hadn't dealt all that harshly with Godwine. Accepting responsibility for Anna would make him pause next time his eye lighted on some rustic nymphet. His grandfather dealt with Swegn out of hard necessity, the very tack to drive my blundering brother to his last follies. If passion burned him out, thank God my son could step back and laugh at himself. If never to be lord, at least a man.

"Harold! Hi, Bess—go!"

I reined in as Leofwine galloped toward me across the neighboring meadow, scattering sheep before him. He jumped a low stone wall and pulled up short, spattering mud. "Did you see Gyrth?"

"No, he's off hunting."

"You know there's a problem."

Christ, another one? "That's a refreshing change. The one thing I've lacked this whole year past is a good problem. What in hell is it this time?"

"Very funny," my brother snapped. "I mean Tostig and the north. Stigand must have written."

"Not in detail."

"Very strange reports from York all year. That's a pot bound to boil over, Harold. I don't know. Some say Tostig's rule is hard but honest, others swear it's just a matter of time before his thanes revolt. And that's not all."

My brother slid his slender form from the saddle to inspect his cinch, busying himself with the task longer than necessary, as if he didn't like what he must say. "Stigand heard from our informers in Tostig's household.

Two thanes, Ulf and Gammell—you know them—were slain in Tostig's own chamber while under safe conduct.''

An assurance of safe conduct could only mean there was hostility to begin with. "Murder plain and simple," Leofwine said. "Word has it they'd gone to protest some new tax." He gave the cinch a last tug and remounted. "Remember Sheppey? Tostig wouldn't hesitate or lose an hour's sleep after.''

"And Edward?"

"Nothing." My brother shook his head. "Apparently he doesn't know the half, and what difference? Tostig's his darling these days. When he's not ill, he's at Westminster. But someone at court is burying most of the news from York."

Not hard to guess at *someone*. "Our beloved sister."

"I don't want to imagine how deep she's in it. Thane Gospatric was at Christmas court last year, waiting on a private audience with Edward. Three days after Christmas—" Leofwine grimaced with the black coincidence,— "Holy Innocents Day, mind, murdered in his bed."

Fact by damning fact Leofwine laid the crime and its sequel before me. He had spoken himself with Gospatric only hours before the man was killed. "Guarded in what he said, but plain to see he and many others had had a gutful of Tostig. I think he came to lay it all before the king but never got the chance."

Guilt did not point directly to Tostig, who'd stayed that night at Canterbury with Edward. When the king heard, he demanded an investigation—which, because of pressing business at Westminster, he delegated to Eadgytha. Our sister made a visible show of seeking out the malefactors but "found" Gospatric's death the work of persons unknown. She sent sincere condolences to the widow.

"Decent of her, yes?" Leofwine stripped off a glove and turned up his palm. "I was always proud of the blood in my veins. Lately I've wondered how much is on our hands."

"That hardly bears thinking on."

"We have to, Harold. Too damned much is just too damned queer. Remember that rat-faced little lackey of

Eada's? Henry his name was, the sort who creeps in and out of back doors, catches rats, empties chamber pots. Always skulking about, listening to conversations as if his natural home were behind a tapestry. Well, Henry's gone from court all of a sudden.''

More, according to our informants in Bruges, Henry surfaced there in no one's service, but having his clothes cut by fashionable Flemish tailors.

Fact by fact, all of them fitting too well. "You think Eadgytha gave the order?''

Leofwine's reply was quick and cold. "You doubt her capable? I don't. There's nothing she wouldn't do for Tostig.''

"Even murder?'' I queried with a pitiful lack of conviction. "You could be wrong.''

"I hope so.'' Leofwine wheeled his horse about, waving me to ride home with him. "But you've been months gone. Edward does nothing but play with his new abbey and count the days till Paradise calls. He sees only what Eada lets him see. You're the real king, got to be. Hell take all, Harold, *do* something. And watch your back.''

67 • Harold

In the north Tostig was only the visible swelling over a deeper infection. Separatism always roiled in its sentiments.

Stigand worried privately to me, "If independence is their aim or separate alliance with Denmark, then Tostig is a blessing to their cause. Think of Scotland ten years ago. What better excuse than a Macbeth to rally around a Malcolm?''

Summer and early autumn of 'sixty-five had the eerie, unreal quality of sunlight between storm clouds. There was blood on Tostig's hands and, though none dare whisper it, I feared the same stain on Eada's. More blackly absurd, in my absence from England, some little monk-scribbler had begun a life of Edward clearly meant to deify the royal pair and our whole family. Partially in verse and wholly washed in the gilt of panegyric, Edward emerged a saint, my father a Solomon, Tostig and I harmonious pillars of state, Eadgytha all of these—

"And so cloying *sweet,*" Gyrth winced over the pages. "What utter rot."

When Edward tore himself away from God's work at Westminster, he called the Witan to London and sat apart with Eadgytha while the council, as expected, gave Duke William's claim short shrift. Tostig was prudently absent, but young Earl Edwin attended with Gyrth, Leofwine, and Stigand. I moved up and down the long table with William's written demands, quite a sheaf of them by now and all saying the same thing. I recall that Edwin said very little that day. Considering what followed shortly, one can see why.

"My lords, I promised the duke I would lay his claim before you for consideration and decision."

Eloquent silence wryly broken by Gyrth. "Yes. There it lies."

"For our consideration," Leofwine mused over the apple he peeled. "I'm considering."

More silence. I asked Edward directly, "Has my lord aught to suggest in this?"

"We would think not," he replied pleasantly. "We rely wholly on the wisdom of our council."

Another hiatus. At length Stigand spoke. "Well, having considered—"

The table exploded in guffaws.

"—what else must we address?"

So much for William. In a fever to complete Westminster as his last enduring act, Edward had professed himself overjoyed to see me safe. No doubt he, Eadgytha, and Tostig alike would have been as delirious had I vanished down some Norman *oubliette*. Edward asked surprisingly little about my stay with William. "You did take oath to him?"

"To support his succession, yes. As you saw, I supported him as far as the Witan where he collapsed."

Edward's dry cackle trailed off into coughing. "Swore under duress of course."

"And on very questionable relics."

"Not binding then, is it? Remarkable man, my cousin."

"I liked him well, but he has no sense of reality."

"I wish I knew. I wish I knew," Edward fretted vaguely. "At least we have gained time. Come, you must see the tomb they are building for me."

Emaciated and failing, the man would need it soon.

Oh, yes: Godwine's restitution, firmly helmed by Edith from the start. On the appointed day our procession rode out of Nazeing's gates and down Lea to the holding of Thane Sigward. By Edith's wish Magnus joined us to profit from his brother's lesson. Botulf rode behind my wife and me, the Lions uncased but limp in the windless morning, while Godwine brought up the rear with his brother.

Sigward waited us with Elfring, Anna, and his reeve beneath an ancient oak favored for his summer hallmoots. Suffering from painful rheumatism, the old thane required a chair. He tried to rise in respect, but I wouldn't hear of it.

"Don't stir. I know it bothers you."

He fell back gratefully. "Thanks, my lord. It is a constant misery."

"Yes, I've a touch myself."

Such formality over a pregnant slave was hardly usual, but I'd never seen Edith more adamant since banishing the Welsh thralls from Nazeing. Terms had been written, signed by Godwine and sealed by me. Elfring would be showered with a comparative embarrassment of legal riches. He stood to one side in threadbare best linen, bobbing his head eagerly as the reeve read out each article to him. Then it was time for my son's part.

"Godwine, Anna," I beckoned them, "stand before me."

Buxom and buck-toothed, Anna came forward, the bulge of things to come already evident beneath her frayed and faded kirtle. No more than fifteen, plain as an oatcake and already foursquare as a cow, I wondered if she were Godwine's first, and inwardly sympathized with him. For so brief a now, what a tedious tomorrow. Anna didn't even blush or seem discomfited, and why would she? She'd marry someone like herself, bear child after child, her life grinding on toward death like slow water through an endless marsh. But Godwine's discomfort was obvious, humbling himself before slaves.

"Anna, before our fathers and these witnesses, I take responsibility for your child. By my faith and name, I will honor these articles."

The girl mumbled something, bob of Elfring's head. From his expression he might already be calculating his profit. "You," I warned him, "if you've more daughters at home, don't be tempted to make a going trade out of this."

"I will say amen to that." Edith stalked forward stonily to stand almost nose to nose with Anna. "Reeve, read again the last article. Slowly."

If the child died at birth or in the first year, no further payment could be claimed. He or she could not take Godwine's name nor would Anna, on pain of flogging, come henceforth nearer than a mile to our son. Edith lifted the girl's fleshy chin, repeating each condition after the reeve. "Never, you understand?"

Anna dropped a clumsy curtsey and "Yes'm," and that was all. I helped Siward from the chair to his waiting wagon. Elfring stumped away, with Anna trudging stolidly behind. Godwine's shoulders sagged in visible relief. Hardly a parting of fated lovers. As we prepared to ride home Botulf passed an unfortunate remark within Edith's hearing: "Lot of bother over not much done."

Edith blazed at him. "He did enough and fool enough. Do you mark me, Godwine? Aye, and you, Magnus. As for you, Master Botulf, look to your own hearth and I'll to mine. Magnus! Leg me up and let's be home."

That evening I needed a tax roll I'd left in our bower

and, to save time, went to fetch it myself. Edith was there, seated over a basin while one of her women, hands brown-stained to the wrists, worked henna into her hair.

"You catch me cheating," Edith confessed crisply. "Your mother resisted grey while she could, so do I. Honestly, I could just spit."

"Over a few grey hairs? Really now."

"I mean that fat cow. Not even comely."

"No, but Godwine's put it right."

"But how could he—what could he possibly see in her?"

"You're not a man, Edith."

"You're not a mother," she denied from the depths of the basin. "Common little *lump*. Of course, were it *your daughter*, you'd be at the boy with castrating irons."

Perhaps. I suppose mothers and fathers have different blind spots. Edith saw nothing to tolerate or understand in the matter. Privately I could feel for Godwine and the girl alike. As my son led Brutus out of the stable and handed him over to Sigward's reeve in sale, my tender smile was more for passing time and the way of things than anything else.

Edward and his court went west early that autumn to the royal estate of Britford, Edward desiring to hawk on Salisbury Plain before Christmas court at Gloucester. Tostig joined them in late September, a ruinous mistake on his part as it turned out, but sufficient to keep me at home. What I suspected of my brother and sister would sunder an already strained family tie.

That day in October was cloudy and cool and, throughout my near estates, all were slaughtering and salting their mast-fattened hogs. I sent Godwine with Botulf to see that my hall and Waltham Church receive our due by week's end. On his way to the armory for sword practice, Magnus paused to hail his brother an earthy farewell.

"Eh, Goddy! One of those sows wiggles her bum at you, be strong, brother. England is watching!"

Then to some promised time with Edmund. The miracle of children is seeing them grow into people. If *won't* was once Godwine's motto, Edmund's was *why?* A thoughtful boy with Edith's Welsh strain in his dark coloring, Edmund wanted to know the *why* of everything, where it came from and why it worked just so. His incessant curiosity fascinated, seeing his mind revolve on my answers, turning them this way and that, chewing them thoroughly before swallowing. Edith thought the boy's keen mind would be well used in the Church, but Edmund would stick at accepting so much dogma without question.

Amid the falcons and hawks in the darkened mews: "Why does the keeper sew their eyes shut?"

Because sight is her sharpest sense, I explained. Her eyes are closed at first only to hone the others, touch, taste, and hearing. "Close your eyes. *Hear* me move one way or the other. Smell the air, feel it change as I move this way and that about you."

"Her. Why are females better for sport? Wouldn't it be better 'tother way round?"

"The female is larger and more aggressive."

Edmund frowned over something that didn't balance in his experience. "Mum's not bigger than you, and I can't recall I ever saw her terrible angry."

I wrestled him close, one arm about him. Riches like Edmund could keep me home forever. "If you ever do, boy, get out of her way. Come, let's go in to dinner."

"Wizard! I'm hungry."

I remember the perfection of that day with its tang of woodsmoke from the kitchen house and the warm company of my son. While I dared to be complacent, naturally God laughed as usual. Trotting toward the hall, Edmund riding on my shoulders, a carl at the gate shouted to me: "Earl Harold? Messengers from the north. Crown thane, he says, name of Aelred."

Before I banished him to dinner Edmund peered curiously at the two unshaven men walking their horses toward us, full quivers slung on their backs, bowstaves packed on the mule stoically plodding behind. They dismounted stiffly.

"Aelred, greetings. And this fellow I recall from Hereford."

"Will Scatloch, sir," the Welshman refreshed me in his singsong English. "Forester to the thane himself."

"Bless me if you don't look done in. What news?"

Aelred rested his spare frame against the horse, which seemed exhausted enough to resent it. "*Done*'s the word, sir. Riding from Dunstable, and Towcester before that, all the way from Nottingham. That was . . . days ago," he calculated wearily. "You're closer than the king, and all we could do to get this far."

"Why, man? What?"

"They've risen up in York, hundreds of 'em, and it's spreading like blight in cattle. Broke into Tostig's armory and treasure house, looted 'em clean. And that ent the worst."

Abruptly Aelred's legs folded under him and he dropped on his rump like a sack of sand, followed by Scatloch. Aelred rubbed at his saddle-chafed thighs, speaking to the ground between them. "Pardon, lord, but we're that run out. They stormed Tostig's own house, killed all they could find."

"Jesus, his wife? Judith? Did they—?"

"No." Aelred shook his head heavily. "They spared her, least that's what they said marching through Nottingham. Not blood they want but justice of the king. And a new lord. Just luck Will and I were there."

"Marching through? Where bound?"

"Coomin' south, bound for the king. They've called Earl Edwin's little brother Morcar to be their earl."

"Morcar? He's not old enough to raise a mustache."

"He's fifteen, like to my own Robin." Aelred raised desolate eyes to mine. "But he jumped quick enough when Edwin joined them. Hundreds, maybe thousands now with the Mercians. Of all the times for the king to be in flamin' Salisbury when the whole north's falling about his ears."

He got up, joint by exhausted joint, pulling Scatloch to his feet. "Earl Harold, you're first lord after the king. What should we do?"

What indeed? I had to get to those determined marchers and then before them to Edward, or our whole country could break asunder in the middle.

68 • Aelred of Denby

Five and seventy, five and seventy miles, the horse under me eating them up twixt Britford manor and Oxford. Lord, but I'm tired. Slaughtering the hogs at home—well, Robin can manage well enough with Will gone home to help. He says the boy's a natural forester and may make a good thane in time if he can learn to deal with men like Little John without getting their backs up.

I want to be home, but my place is here. Never since old Godwine faced Edward across London Bridge has our country been so close to civil war. Right and wrong on both sides then, the same now, and not for me to judge, but I lay most of this to Earl Tostig. If he broke thieves, he's broken good men as well with cruel taxes and swung them from gallows who'd done nowt to deserve death save they were in his way. Now it's come home to him like locusts over Egypt in the Bible, as the rebels burn and loot their way south.

I can't believe half I hear: men dragged out of their homes and hanged or ambushed and beaten to death because they were carls or servants or just friends of Earl Tostig. The earl himself outlawed, a green boy set in his place, Mercia in league with them, coming on to demand of Edward that he banish a sinful lord. I know Edward of old, seldom strong when he should be, stubborn when he shouldn't, and with his own cruel streak. In Sherwood once he made me cut the hand off a poacher before his eyes and enjoyed it.

Eh, he won't enjoy this. Tostig's like a sheepdog my da bought once down Linby Dale, a big, black-tempered brute with the wolf strain in him. That's common in our parts, but you don't want more than quarter wolf blood in a dog or you can't trust them not to turn. That was one keen dog, flat wizard at handling sheep. Run off foxes, scared away hawks, even wolves in winter. That were the problem. One day that grey-brown devil killed three or four of our sheep. No reason, not even hungry, just his nature coming out, and there you have Earl Tostig: one part of him turning all the rest, raging to the king in Britford—*do something!*—but Edward's deaf and blind until I bring word from Earl Harold up with the rebels. Great doings, history being writ all about, and me in the middle. I'd be excited were I not so flamin' tired. I know you're near done, horse, but go, *run!*

Weary's one thing, cold-sweat scared another. Harold, Gyrth, and Leofwine have good carls with them, but not near the thousands behind Edwin and Morcar. Harold's a cool head who doesn't bridle or raise his voice to these boy earls skittish as unbroken horses, but patiently asks they listen to the royal word I've brought: "From the king: Do no more harm to any man or town, but lay down your arms and I will deal justly with you."

Which likes neither Edwin of Mercia nor his little pup of a brother with the new gold chain gleaming on his half-grown chest. From the saddle Edwin spits on the ground before me and gives his answer: "Dismiss Tostig, who can no longer be tolerated in England. Confirm Morcar or we will look on you as enemy and make war on you."

Brave words, but clear to me Edwin ent any Godwine for brain. Harold knows he's dealing with dangerous fools who'd split the country down the middle, and his answer is that of a man who knows whereof he speaks: "Think long, Edwin, before you hack off England's one arm with her other. I know your cause and how much right is on your side, but do not raise your hand against Edward's majesty. The head of an earl comes off as easily as that of a king."

Then, says he, he'll haste back to the king and present their side if Edwin and Morcar will hold at Oxford and harm no more of the king's folk or lands. Guarantees of truce are exchanged, the rebels will wait for a time, but they're like bristling hounds with the smell of blood in their noses, checked only by the limit of a leash like to snap anytime. They'll be patient for the nonce, but time is running out, and as we saddle to ride I'm that glad to be away from wild-eyed thanes like Brand Ulfsson and his sons, leaning on great battle axes and itching for war. Ulfsson himself told the king they wanted no foreigner from the south as lord over them.

"I'm the king's man right enough," I tell Harold as I haul my sore bones onto a fresh horse. "But it's a heavy honor for a farmer who only wants to be home more than he's gone."

"I know what you mean," Harold says, waving his brothers and the dozen carls to ride. "I do, Aelred."

Does he then? A great earl whom men already wish for king, what would he know of small men and dreams like mine, small enough to lose in Sherwood? He and his brothers, gold-chained and high-placed, how could such ever be homesick?

But these brothers are hardy enough, sparing themselves or the horses no mercy as we dash through dry-leaf autumn, through wind and rain. Change horses twice, a bare hour to rest, bolt barley soup and bread, then on and on toward Britford, hoping Edward will be wise, praying the rebels will keep their word and wait. Those monks who write our history year by year, how will they color 'sixty-five and we who tumbled through it? No matter there, I couldn't read it anyway, and for sure they'll not write my name.

Britford at last, where the king's men sprawl out in tents beyond the manor walls or crowd and cram under every roof, sleeping three to a bed or anywhere in the hall there's room. Huntsmen, carls, stallers, none of them expecting what's come on them, the courtyard alive with men as worried as stirred-up bees around a threatened hive. We almost fall from the horses, lurch and stagger through welcoming hands clutching at us, eager for news. "What word? What from Oxford? Na, don't hinder us now. Where's the king?"

Limping, saddle-stiff, we push our way into a hall jammed with men in arms, where Edward and the queen wait at the far end, and then Regenbald bawls out:

"Lord King, the earls of Wessex, of Surrey and Anglia!"

The crowd parts for us, and we drop to one knee before thin old Edward. Tostig moves to stand by his sister. It's said they've neither of them any love for Harold, nor can I see any now as Harold raises up, and the waiting hall falls silent, as tense as a drawn bow.

"My lord, I've heard the rebels out. They have outlawed Tostig and will proclaim Your Grace enemy as well unless he is banished. They demand your just answer."

You can't get plainer than that, but the queen is rising even as Earl Harold speaks. Whatever mood's on her, the woman crackles with it. "No! Never!"

"Proclaim?" Edward grips the chair arms till his bony knuckles go white. "They demand of their anointed king?"

"Sire, it's gone beyond that," Earl Gyrth breaks in. "It's Edwin and all of Mercia with them."

Tostig glares at Harold. "No doubt. How convenient when I attend the king with only a few men. This was planned. You are in it with them."

"Tostig, I am not. For God's sake—"

"Liar!"

The air in the hall is like dry heath live with summer lightning that stands the hair on end, ready to strike fire anywhere you look. Already the men about us are edging this way and that, drawing apart into their own loyalties. I swear Tostig might spring at Harold any moment. Gyrth and Leofwine move closer about him, I behind and ready.

Harold sounds sadder than angry. "I will take oath I'm no part of this, but I agree with them. Lord Edward, they've burned and wasted for over a hundred miles to let you know they will have Tostig outlawed. They've not harmed your wife, Brother. They want you gone, not dead. Sire, by your answer they will call you king or enemy. My brother must leave England now, else I cannot answer for peace."

There all and there enough. Light the Yule log without me, wife, for I won't be home for Christmas.

69 • Harold

Edward rose with obvious difficulty. "You, Harold? You who voted for Tostig's investiture now ask me to banish your own brother?"

"Why not?" Tostig challenged. "He's turned his back on a brother before."

"Swegn was hard," I countered. "You are easier. Tostig, for once think beyond yourself and go. The rebels will not harm your wife. They wait on the king's justice, but not for long. There is too much evidence against you. Thane Gospatric who was slain in London—"

"We ourselves led that inquiry." Eadgytha leveled her dagger glance at me. "Gospatric was killed by persons unknown."

"He was of my own following," Tostig protested to the court at large. "It must have been a private quarrel. The man had enemies and far too sharp a tongue."

"Or too sharp an eye," I said. "Someone didn't want the king to hear what he had to say."

"On my oath before the king and these witnesses, I had no hand in that."

"Or Ulf and Gammell? What were they, another obscure quarrel?"

My brother left Eadgytha and came down close to me, whispering his warning. "Take heed, Harold. Bring down my house and yours falls with it."

My eye slid to Eadgytha taut in her chair, ready to fight as Tostig and more dangerous. "You offered me that choice once before. At least Swegn killed in blind rage. I think you did it smiling."

"As I smile now, because you're dead. You, Edith, your sons—all. Just watch me." Tostig whirled away from me, raising his voice for all to hear. "You accuse me of murder then?"

"I do."

"And I," Gyrth echoed.

"Brother, step down," Leofwine implored. "Were you innocent as Virgin Mary, it's too late for anything else."

"I will not." Instead Tostig knelt before Edward. "Sire, you know my worth. I ask for trial by compurgation, even ordeal if I must."

"No," I denied. "While you argue and delay we'll lose half of England."

"Wessex!" Edward screeched with piercing vehemence. His venomous glare riveted on me. "You do not dictate in our presence. These rebels know our mind. We will not bend to such . . ." Edward's hands lifted toward his head. "To such . . ."

He faltered. His lips worked but no sound emerged. Eadgytha sprang up. "Esgar, the king is ill."

A general murmur of concern whispered through the hall as Tostig and Esgar helped Edward to his chair again, where he feebly waved them away. "No . . . no, I am recovered."

"I am glad, my lord." Eadgytha spoke for every ear in the hall. "There has been much said here to distress you, but in my conscience I must burden you with another ugly truth."

She appealed to the assembly before her. "What force to these charges when uttered by a heretic so closely in league with the enemies of Christ that he was married by witches in unholy rites?"

If God had descended on us in a thunderclap He could not have produced more profound shock in Edward. His chaplain, Peter, went pale and crossed himself. The rebels at Oxford might be a May dance for all they mattered to our king at this moment. "Lady, you know what you say?"

"I do. Though Edith was my friend, let Harold deny he was joined to her by the cursed of God. If he dares."

Like morality players on a stage, Eadgytha and Tostig stood arm in arm, symbolic pillars of virtue. "I am at fault for not disclosing this before, but I am only a woman and too loving toward my family."

There must be such a thing as moral nausea; I felt faintly ill. "Eada, I asked once of God if all our blood was cursed. This must be His answer."

"When?" Edward pressed, shaken. "When did you discover this?"

"Long since," Tostig said, a masterful study in regret. "We loved our brother even as we are loyal to our king, and torn in our duty."

Eadgytha matched his pious reluctance. "Pray God and our lord forgive us."

"You are silent, Wessex." Edward made to rise again but lacked the strength. "Though we do not wonder. If, as men say, you take oaths too blithely, it is not curious in one who spits on the heavenly source of their power."

"Can't you see?" I tried desperately. "Can't you see what Tostig is doing, what he's done since you invested him? He's used the law to make a mockery of law."

"And little Morcar can do better?" Tostig laughed.

"At least our king will have a whole country left," Leofwine shot back. "Whatever Harold's done, there's no more respected lord in England."

"Nor finer wife than Edith," Gyrth added vigorously. "Tostig, you're unspeakable. Never call me brother again."

But Edward's merciless attention battened on me alone. "Is it true?"

Despair, urgency, and years of useless hope for Edith and myself tore the truth out of me. "Yes! Yes, it is true, my lord. Because of you and holy thieves like Champart. Because you blocked and would still block us from holy sacrament, no other reason, though we begged you for years."

"For holy law, Harold! For love of my Church."

"And hatred of my father."

"From which tree the blighted branch has not fallen far."

"My lords, crave pardon." Aelred spoke for the first time, his common sense cold water in the flushed face of turmoil. "If those rebels are not dealt with now, saved or damned won't signify much. They'll come on. We must act now."

Sibilant agreement murmured through the hall: practical men less concerned with demons and damnation then rebels and now.

"So we will." Edward managed to push his gaunt frame out of the chair. "You think us too ill, too feeble to yet rule where we reign? Hear me all! Were these rebels ten thousand, we will put them down. Saved or damned, Wessex will prove his loyalty. We declare Edwin and Morcar and all who follow them guilty of high treason, and we call a general levy of all the forces of Wessex, of Anglia and Sussex and Huntingdon and all Crown thanes and their fyrd in support of Earl Tostig. How say you to our royal command?"

A silence fell over the men behind me. In this way, at Tetbury, Edward had crippled and exiled our family. Now I and the two brothers at my side were the real power of the south, while Edward played without a strong Norman faction or any sympathy for Tostig. Just as Godwine must have felt at London Bridge when Stigand brought nothing from Edward but harsh refusal and contempt. Backed against a principle with nowhere to turn, my father could make no other reply then. I couldn't now.

"Sire, when loyalty means civil war and ruin, the price would be too high if we outnumbered Edwin five to one. Damned I may be, but all here know I am for England first. No brother's blood nor king's rule is above that care. I will not levy for Tostig."

Gyrth said clearly, "Nor Anglia."

"Nor Surrey," Leofwine refused. "Tostig, if you have any love for your country's peace, leave her whole while there's yet honor left you. Don't wound her like this."

"Three blind mice," Tostig laughed. "Following a dark star."

"And you, Denby," Edward turned on Aelred querulously. "My own thane. You were there, you saw the threat. Will you follow your sworn lord or will you too not stick at treason?''

Poor Aelred, dropped into the sizzling pan, holding his small lands directly from Edward and with a wife, family, and homely folk to protect. I couldn't blame him for yielding.

"I'm the king's man, sir."

"We are thankful that some loyalty remains."

Aelred was not finished. "But as your thane, I say the earls here have the right of it. I won't go gladly in a wrongful cause."

Edward stared at him, livid. "Will you not? Is this the humor of all of you? Is it? Are we king or not?" His voice splintered with rage. *"Chancellor!"*

He tore the white staff from Regenbald's hand. "Hear us! Wessex, Anglia, and Surrey having refused our call, we charge them alike with treason, and we will—"

Edward stormed at me, the staff raised to strike. It hissed through the air but fell on my shoulder with no force behind it. "Godwine," he slurred. "Godwine, you evil . . ."

Still staring wide-eyed, cursing me with soundless lips, Edward went limp and fell sideways. I sprang to catch him, lowering him gently to the floor as other lords gathered about us. Edward's eyes were open but sightless in the first of the final seizures that took him from the world. He would be mostly bedridden from that day, and dead at the turning of the year.

70 • Aelred

No Gloucester Christmas court this year. Edward wishes to be carried back to Thorney to be near his abbey. He won't hunt this winter, nor any other, that's clear.

The king's own rage brought him to his bed and this end. I've seen what the man becomes when rage takes him: frothing, spittle flying. Mile by mile east toward Silchester, Edward slumps in his litter like a man broken across. Harold gave him every respect save what he wanted, and bless the earl for that. I'd be fighting with half a heart against what's right. The king mutters in his sickness, calls it treason, and still he won't understand. It ent just the earls against Tostig but the whole country, voices and minds of our own that will say to a king's face, *Damn it, enough!* Praise Harold, he said it for all of us. He is already our king.

Back goes Harold to the rebels at Oxford. With no army willing to fight, Edward has no choice but to give in and banish Tostig, but showers him with money and gifts even as the writ is sealed. Satisfied, Edwin and Morcar give Tostig and his lady safe conduct to ship. The queen's beside herself, cursing Harold with every black name within her dignity and some beyond. Tostig, cold as a viper, wastes no long breath on his brother.

"This is but begun," he promised Harold. "We will meet."

If I know them, so they will. Sad to think of it so, savior and Judas out of the same manger.

At Thorney Isle, two miles up Thames from City, Edward takes his fitful rest at the old palace he's rebuilt in part to be near the work of his heart. Would his folk had been as close. The seedy deadhouse of past kings and bishops creaks and leaks in the rain, and the draft whistling through every chamber smells musty. No mind, for on the tower spire above the abbey transept, the new weather vane is fixed to sign an end to the labor.

"Done," Edward whispered with tears in his eyes, as all of us knelt about his litter. "Boundless be thy mercy, Lord, who let me live to see it."

The great work is to be consecrated the third day after Christmas, Holy Innocents Day, but Edward is surely finished as his abbey. Men gather from all parts of the realm for the consecration, the death watch, and the necessary crowning of a new king. Not much talk of the choosing, but much of the danger in delay, and there's only one serious choice, he who's been the real king for years.

On Christmas Eve our king was taken with another seizure. We thought it was the end but he recovered the next day to lead us to his beloved new church to hear high mass. Holy or not, the cold stone of the place is not for me. The new masonry smells clammy and damp. Already the workmen waited with picks to open the deep pit before the altar for the royal tomb. But Edward was like a man brushed by an angel's wing and with that angel's voice in his ear, face uplifted in the grey light from one arched casement. He seemed in good spirits at the banquet but fell ill again that evening, took to his bed, and never left it again. The queen, nobles, clergy, and we thanes witnessed the abbey's consecration without him.

Boundless be thy mercy, Lord, who let me see this.

I couldn't love the man, but even I can wonder: Was God so merciful, any more than to Moses at the end? Moses could see the Promised Land at his death, but God forbade him to enter with his folk after all those wandering years. For all the praying Edward did, you'd think God might have spared the old man a few more days. Seems mean, at least equal to Edward's own spite, but rest his soul, for he can't last the week.

Harold

Stigand said, "The king is waking."

We gathered closer about the bed: Stigand, Eadgytha, and I, the stewards Rodbert and Esgar, Chaplain Peter and Regenbald. Edward's eyes fluttered open but being so near the next world, I doubted he marked much more in this one.

"Dear husband, let me bathe your face." Eadgytha took a damp cloth and gently patted it over his sunken cheeks. "How is it with you?"

"Cold." Though two braziers warmed the chamber, Edward shuddered. Eadgytha knelt at the foot of the bed, massaging his feet under the covers.

"But I have seen." Eyes unnaturally bright, he muttered feverishly. "I tell you, think not of my end but rather on your own. Harold? Stigand, all of you, I have *seen.*"

Stigand and I exchanged silent understanding. Edward was plainly delirious, but then in a calm and reasonable voice he asked, "How went the consecration?"

"All you would have wished," Eadgytha assured him. "Are your feet warmer? Mother Werburgha and the nuns of Wilton were there in duty and sorrow for your illness. But the gifts of gold and silver were beyond counting."

"And the lands bequeathed to your abbey from Harold and his brothers," Chaplain Peter put in. "Aye, from every noble in England."

"Rich or poor, it mattered not," Regenbald exulted. "Cups and chalices, jewels without number. The great man's acres or the widow's mite, all freely given to God."

"I have seen," Edward croaked at us in his febrile

voice. "Even now in a dream two monks of Normandy came to me. Men I know . . . knew, for they are dead. Sadly they regarded me and said that England's days were few."

"Not so, my lord," Regenbald denied. "England stands tall and strong as her ancient oaks."

"And so I answered them." Edward's colorless lips trembled. "They only shook their heads. They know, heaven knows, this land and its priests and nobles are in the service of the Devil. But I said no—no, I will not let this happen. Harold, you mark me? I will bring the people back to God. But again they denied me, saying this land would not repent nor God pardon until the tree . . ."

Edward trailed off, muttering and plucking fitfully at his beard. He reached with a bloodless hand to draw me closer. "The tree. They prophesied that God would not pardon England any more than Gomorrah until the tree had been felled halfway up the trunk, the parts separated and joined together again without the labor of men. Mark me: A year and a day from my death, demons will sweep this land and flatten it like wheat in a gale. So said the holy monks who spake with the voice of God."

I put my ear close to his lips to hear, but Edward had lost consciousness again. Stigand motioned Esgar to bring the wine and wafers for extreme unction.

"It must be soon," he reckoned. "He is close to the end."

"Yet I believe his vision," my sister said in an iron voice, glaring at me. "Heaven has threatened doom and it will fall as my husband saw. *You* have done this to us. You have opened England's door to Satan."

"No," Stigand contradicted respectfully. "The king speaks out of fever and dreams. We can give no weight to such."

"Do I? Help me, Esgar."

We all turned at the quiet entreaty. Edward's eyes were open again and focused on us. "Pillows, Rodbert. Help me to sit up."

The stewards jumped to his bidding, supporting the king with pillows at his back. "My mind is clear, Stigand.

Harold, take my hand. And you, dear wife, come close. Quickly, I say. I am still your king.''

With our two hands in his, Edward appealed to me. ''Into your hands, Harold, I commend the keeping of this good woman my queen, and all the kingdom to your protection.''

He uttered each word distinctly; everyone heard them. I said, ''My lord, do you name me your successor?''

''Uh . . . what?'' Edward's attention wandered. He looked away as if no longer interested in worldly matters, but ambiguous to the last. ''I have said. A doom is on this land and all are culled out with the goats. I have seen what will be, and yield to what must be. You will take the crown anyway.''

Something of his old acid returned as he cackled suddenly: ''And the burden and the guilt. That will be a fly in your wine, Godwinesson. And William's. Willy Bastard, he'll take this hard. He doesn't manage frustration well.''

That was all. Edward drifted off again like an exhausted child. Stigand bade us all leave for the time. When the king woke again, unction must no longer be delayed. After Eadgytha and the others had withdrawn to wait without, Stigand stayed me.

''A moment, Harold. We must move swiftly to your coronation. William will know in a matter of days. We dare not wait.'' Stigand gently tucked the rumpled covers under Edward's chin. ''Not even a decent interval of mourning. We have days, no more.''

He went to close the chamber door pointedly in the face of servants and stallers hovering there. ''Already your troubles begin. Edwin and Morcar will support you, but . . .''

''They want something in return. Those cubs learn fast. What's their price?''

''An alliance with Mercia. Sealed by marriage to Aldyth.'' Stigand said no more, knowing full well how that fell on my ear.

''Their dear, negotiable sister. No other way?''

''Not unless you want them to cry for Edgar.''

"Oh, that's—"

"Ridiculous and no more than delay, true, but we need the north, and there's no time."

I gazed down at our king in his shriveled innocence, quite at peace and ready for the heaven he craved. *Pray it's all you hoped for. Damn you, if you'd been less of a saint and more of a king. You know the mess you've left to me. By God, I could almost think you planned it so.*

"Tell Edwin and Morcar they'll have their price."

However unseemly our haste, time was vital. Edward died in the small hours of fifth January and was buried the same morning. While the abbey bells tolled through his requiem mass, echoed by Saint Paul's, preparations hurried on for my coronation. Weeks would pass before the west and north knew one king was dead and another crowned, but William would know much sooner.

A raw, grey day, wind sharp off Thames as the long procession formed outside the abbey before the unfinished cloister walks. As the monks sang "Let Thy Hand Be Strengthened," Stigand and Cynesige each took one of my hands, and we followed the chanting monks into the nave. After us came the assembled bishops of the land, more priests, abbots, and the nuns of Eada's Wilton clad in sackcloth mourning, then the earls and, finally, the thanes like Aelred, ballast and backbone to our state.

As I stepped past the flagstones closed over Edward mere hours ago, I wondered if he writhed and snarled in his grave at the thought of his crown on my head. The same thought might have occurred to Stigand; he murmured out of the side of his mouth, "It is well done, my king. Now England works to become whole."

The three of us turned to face the assembled strength of England: earls in their finery, from the sleek sable of my brothers to the mangy marten pelts and homespun of men like Aelred, passed down by his father. Each held his coronet in front of him, to be donned only when the crown settled on mine.

Stigand waited until the echoing nave stilled, then spoke loudly and clearly the ritual question: "Earls and thanes of the kingdom of Angles and Saxons, do you accept Harold as your king?"

Thundering through the nave: "We do!"

Cold in the vast space. I could swear old Cynesige shivered as he waited with the holy oil and Stigand gave the traditional instructions on my duties to Holy Church. His words only half sounded in my mind. I caught sight, far back in the crowd, of the head and shoulders of my tall son Godwine in the dark-brown mantle Edith herself made for him last year.

"—so let the Church be ever your first counsel at the nation's need."

"So will I and name their graces of Canterbury and York to that place." *Edith, are you here, too?*

"I will ever pursue justice for my people and take in hand, even as great Alfred did, the best laws and customs of the land." *Don't be here, my love. This is not us or anything we can share.*

Cynesige hovered, whispering. "My lord, the chrism."

I held out my hands. The archbishop anointed my head, shoulders, and palms, joining me in the ancient covenant between God and kings. Now Stigand slipped onto the index finger of my right hand the ring of unity. Cynesige proffered the sword of royal protection, Stigand in turn the scepter rod of equity, both of which I must hold erect throughout the ceremony. I stared ahead with distant majesty but really searching for that tall figure I had seen. Godwine was gone.

At last Stigand lifted the crown from its cushion, raised it high over my head, and settled it on my brow—heavily down and down, golden prison setting me forever above and apart from other men, from Edith and all the happiness I'd ever known. The assembled nobles raised and donned their coronets. The thing was done, the kingdom continued, and however strong or valid William's rights of blood, he could whistle for them now.

"God save King Harold of England!"

"Vivat!"

"May the king live forever!"

But my son had stolen away, and I was alone in a

reverent multitude with *Te Deum Laudamus* holy and harsh in my ears.

In the unheated sacristy after the interminable swearing of fealties, Gyrth and Leofwine, in triumphant spirits, did the honors in divesting me of the regalia. "Did you mark Aelred when he swore to you?" Gyrth chortled. "Never saw him look so proud."

I better remembered Eadgytha kneeling in her sackcloth and looking anything but. "Did you know Godwine was here? Did either of you?—" I bit off the question, but Leofwine divined my thought as he fastened the warm mantle at my shoulder. "Edith? No, I didn't see her."

Just as well. Botulf entered, bowing awkwardly. My old friend who shared so much with me over the years never learned how to bow with grace, reminding me of a man ducking under a low lintel to avoid banging his head. "Sir . . . sire, Queen Eadgytha begs private audience with the king."

Leofwine sighed, Gyrth's brows lifted eloquently. I wanted Eada's presence less than having my teeth drawn, but as my brothers withdrew, I stayed Botulf. "Old friend, once a man dons a crown, those men are few he can trust. Stay close and bear my standard with that trust. We leave for York when weather permits."

Botulf digested the thought, nodding approval. "That's well thought. The old king never bothered to go there."

"That's why I must. Bring me my gloves."

"I must be getting old," Botulf admitted, slipping the gloves onto my hands. "I will miss my wife and the warm smell of the kitchen. There ent an inch of this new church but it's freezing."

All of that, and I'd spent more time than Botulf missing a wife. "Admit Lady Eadgytha."

I could feel fleeting, detached pity for my sister when she knelt to me in the coarse sackcloth of her mourning, drab and drawn from the long, sleepless vigil over Edward. Exhaustion deepened the lines beneath her eyes and about the mouth long since set in the bitter line of her life. She made her obeisance with sardonic precision. "My brother and lord has his desire at last."

"Something less than that. There was no one else."

"There was," Eada flared. "Edward spoke true. The felled tree was my banished brother."

Ever her Tostig. Between the funeral and the endless coronation I'd had little more sleep than she and felt weary as Eada looked. "Sister, the Tostig you dreamed never existed beyond your frustrated ambitions and the maundering of a foolish astrologer. You coddled and kissed him into believing himself thrice what he was. Martyr him, crown him with thorns if you will, but he's finished."

Whatever her emotions, Eada kept her icy control. "And I?"

"You heard Edward's will. I'll deprive you of nothing. Save to leave the country, dwell where you please, Wilton or one of your estates. But away from me."

She was that much of a realist. "I thought as much. How you must enjoy this."

"No, but to save your precious Tostig you'd have destroyed Edith and me. You always were a bitch, Eada, but now it's over. I've no time to hate you. You don't matter anymore."

"Tostig should have been king."

"You must have arrangements to make. Leave me, Eada."

"He will return, never fear, and I will give him tenfold that fealty I choked on today."

That much I believed of Tostig. Already we'd heard he scurried feverishly about Flanders, trying to recruit what support he could. "He'll have to stand in line, Eada. Denmark may try, William certainly, but Tostig's stars have passed him over."

"Ungrateful!" she burst out. "There was a time when we could have crushed you like a fly."

But spared me at a price that dingy day when they forced me to throttle conscience for the sake of Tostig's diseased ambition. I wouldn't punish Eada with that now, however sweet the urge. "Oh, you'll have your moral victory, lady. I have to bind the north to me by marriage to a woman I can't love and who may well despise me. It should please you and God to have me back in the sacramental fold.''

Her expression was inscrutable. ''So one hears. Poor Edith.''

''Christ, try not to weep. You know what you've done. Were I not who and where I am, Edith and I might be hanging at a crossroads for crows to peck at. Leave us, lady. And do not come to court again.''

''No, my lord.'' Once more my sister dipped low in perfect curtsey and glided to the door. ''But you will get used to the cold, Harold. I did long ago.''

I sat alone in the unheated sacristy thinking of what must be done today, tomorrow, what men seen and bound to me, but agreeing with my sister. *It begins, Edith, as we knew it must. I'm cold. The only warmth is England like a beating heart in my hand, but ambition is chill and bleak as this shabby little room.*

71 • Duke William

January 1066

HAROLD: I cannot believe the news from London. Edward's pledge to me was clear as my right, my trust in you and your oath so firm I will not credit these tidings until I hear from you. Our bond demands your earliest answer.

And I received in reply Harold's reasons, English reasons. If he had sinned, he wrote, the sin was in taking the oath, not in breaking what the Witan would never ratify. He had been chosen by the country at large, the *Angel-Cynn* (that slippery phrase again) and anointed by the Church. He even cast doubts upon the authenticity of those relics on which he was forced to swear.

Forcefully persuaded, I admit, but I can't stop now; the wheel I turned now moves by itself. Already too many have heard and the whispering begun: William is cozened, bilked of his inheritance by a crafty, lying Saxon who set the stone over Edward and himself on the throne between one sunset and the next.

I stumbled about the palace, Harold's treachery a sickness in my bowels, avoiding even Matilda, seething for something or someone to break for this. But I've drawn better wisdom from a hard life. Not the blaze but the steady fire and slow-turning spit best cooks the meat. Rouen was abuzz with the news yesterday. Tomorrow Paris, Maine, Anjou, Ponthieu, and Flanders will know. They will mark how I answer this. If I do nothing, they will hold me light and laugh at me. Such laughter is dangerous as the speculation that will follow. *William is in his fortieth year and perhaps begins to decline. What good his promises to us of English fiefs when he cannot keep his own? Touching Normandy, perhaps we should make alliances of our own elsewhere.*

I know such men. In their sight I must never break stride but proceed as if I'd expected this, summon my clients and chief men, respeak and even enlarge their promised portions, commission the timber, set the shipwrights to their labor, build the fleet, and sail for England.

Still there is the rage, the wounded thing. I know men and never met a better. How could I be so blind?

Use the pain, man. Pump the bellows, blow the fire white not to revenge but purpose. Anointed by the Church, Harold said. Yet our own prelates say the English Church is a pit of sloth, a contradiction in terms. Remember Godwine: the old serpent, Edward called him, who once bit the king's brother fatally. I'll touch on that in my reasons and let Odo, Montgomery, Mortain, and the rest believe the hatchling sons shared in the kill. Remind them of Champart and other Norman clerics driven from England by that family's hate. Many of them were present in the church when Harold placed his hands lightly on the reliquaries and as lightly damned himself forever. Add that his "marriage" was incestuous and adultery not beyond the scope of his sins. Morality and right are my strongest weapons. If I can convince Rome that this is a holy crusade to cleanse the Church in England and sweep a blasphemer from her throne, is that less than truth? Rome with me and Harold excommunicate, how eagerly will men follow him when done at peril of their souls?

Policy clear, plans made, the war council gathered, still something sticks in me, something remains unsalved. You struck at *me*, Harold. You hurt me. I would have raised you high, preferred you before so many others, but you put my very life in the balance. Before I tear the crown from your head, you will account to my face, man. You will tell me *why*.

Edith

Merry bells peeled from Chichester on Easter Sunday, longer than usual to mark the Resurrection, as my son rode in through our gate and dismounted by me. I'd sent Godwine to Fishbourne with fresh loaves and comfits for Agatha and hadn't looked for him home before dark, nor the sullen manner of him as he lifted the horse's off forehoof to pry loose a stone. "I thought you would take dinner with your aunt."

"No," he grunted while Chichester bells went on clanging in the distance. "Hakon was just back from town."

"Is he learning English well?"

"Well enough for what he had to say. That's what the bells are for." My son dug angrily at the hoof. "Our liege lord's married Aldyth of Mercia." One last twist of the knife and the stone came free. "Bastard."

I couldn't feel anything just then. ". . . What?"

"At York, Hakon said. In one churchly stroke, I'm bastard and you—"

"Godwine—don't."

I saw the flush of anger hectic on his brown cheeks. "I may have been born one, but Harold? He works at it."

"Don't be a child. You love your father."

Still numb as my son crushed me in trembling young arms. "I don't know what I feel."

Nor did I. "Let me . . . I would be alone."

"Mum, no."

"Please. Just for the time."

My son led the horse away, bitterness like mist about him. "Hakon's off to seek a place with the king. There's patriotism, and welcome to it."

What then? I placed one foot before the other, no real sense of where I went. From somewhere behind me Edmund called a greeting. Then the legs went out from under me, and my son, startled into running, saw his mother on her knees, choking and retching out her last meal to spatter on the ground.

Through two days of physical purgatory nothing would stay in my stomach, not even milk. My chamberwomen worried; they all knew by then.

"Will you not eat something, lady? At least a little wine or ale?"

"Get out."

I felt numb, remembering Eada in her pain when Edward dashed her across the face with rejection and poverty. Stunned she was, and now my body learned the same lesson. Mind can be that nimble, step apart, and say, *He only did what he must. He loves you as ever. But she is young and must be beautiful now, and the little bitch has bedded a king before. Oh, she is young . . .* But dumb flesh can only ache with no remedy for the pain, the sleep that will not come, the drink turned flat, the food the mouth cannot swallow.

Still there is responsibility, the rounds of each day. If I

couldn't look at the food brought to my bower only to go cold, there were the poor who always huddled for alms at the kitchen-house door. Even as I dispensed the soggy bread trenchers and broken meats, mumbling a blessing by rote, my smile fixed and empty, I hated them in Harold's place. The goddamned everlasting poor, they outlast us all with nothing to pray for but survival. In the darkening April dusk I couldn't see their blunt, needy faces, only the outstretched hands—as the frantic bells began to ring from Waltham Church, not merrily as from Chichester, but shrill as the scream of a terrified child. Hurry! they shrieked. Hurry to the shelter of God! And from the kitchen yard, the waiting folk, gaping and gasping out one huge *oh!*, forgot hunger and fled toward the alarum of the bells.

The old cook put down her soup crock and peered out the door. "Jesu, lady, what is it? Where are they running?"

I stepped out into the kitchen yard after them. More folk were streaming from the outbuildings, servants and carls alike, to stop, transfixed, staring in horror at the sky.

Vivid against the soft blue of evening, its tail a long, milky smudge among the stars, the comet blazed over England.

When Godwine and Magnus found me, I was still rooted there. "Edmund is saddling your mare. You must come," Magnus urged. "The folk are afraid and want you to lead them to the church."

I answered without thinking. "Yes. Certainly. Go quickly and get mounted."

That pale stain on the stars, how redundant it was, hastening to warn the sky will fall on me when I stood already in the ruin of my house. Staring up at that superfluous doom, something in my pain unlocked and let flow the life-saving tears at last. I led my folk out to pray, eyes swimming and blind with the blessed relief.

The comet burned for a week in our sky. When fear ebbed with its fading light and men could reason again, learned savants like Stigand chided the gibbering doomsayers, recalling how the comet had appeared before, but while it ignited heaven, they babbled of dire portents. Years later Norman scribblers deemed it God's punishment for unrepentant England and a just verdict on the usurper Harold. So it seems with wonders, revealing to each his own belief, guilt or folly.

So it surely appeared to mad Tostig. An old woman can still remember the Shaftesbury girl for whom a beautiful boy was an hour's dazzling. Eada's chronicler said he had no vices. What then brought him down but virtues blighted before they bloomed? How pathetic he seemed that last year, a preposterous embarrassment hammering at the doors of uninterested kings, swearing to the end he was conspired against. He must have taken the fiery star as his own harbinger and plucked it from heaven to blazon his shield in that last gamble.

In May while we prayed for peace and Harold prepared for war with William, Tostig's fleet appeared out of the morning mist off the Isle of Wight.

72 • Harold

Tostig's raid confused the folk of Wight who didn't know how to respond to his demands for supplies but submitted as the easiest way out of an awkward position. By the time word reached my council in London, he'd already raided at Pevensey and Hastings.

Leofwine frowned over the map of our southeastern coastline. "He's following the old route we took with Father coming home. Romney and Dover might be next."

"We'll never get there in time," Gyrth knew.

No, but we might stop Tostig at Sandwich. "Gyrth,

Leof, give the order to march. I want us across Thames and on Watling Street by midafternoon.''

I felt Gyrth's hand on my shoulder. ''You're limping worse.''

''Damned nuisance, yes. To your men.''

We would levy the fyrd for coast defense later. To deal with Tostig, the household carls of my brothers and myself, over twelve hundred strong, would be enough. We rattled across London Bridge through warm May afternoon and made good time on the Dover road, eyes smarting with the dust of foragers gone before to commandeer provender. I worried over the effect Tostig's raids would have on our defense against William. Wind and tide would favor the duke until the middle of September; later than that his chances dwindled rapidly, but the shores would bristle with our men all summer—carls, thanes, farmer-levies, and as much of a fleet as I could gather. Then, no matter where he landed, we could take William in the rear, burn his boats, trap him between us and our land forces and, as Gyrth colorfully predicted, ''kick his Norman arse up betwixt his ears.''

But just where would he try us, and when? This week? Next?

By midmorning of the next day we were north of Canterbury, close to the fork where the Dover road turns for Sandwich. The weather was unusually hot, sending waves of heat off the dusty road. More for the horses than ourselves, I called a halt. A little rest, then we'd lead them on foot for a half hour or so, little as I looked forward to walking. We were a disheveled lot, armor folded and tied behind saddles, damp hair straggling limp, mustaches sweat-sodden. We were about to move on when Gyrth shaded his eyes and peered ahead.

''Rider coming fast. Damned fool, he'll kill the horse and himself.''

One look sufficed. I grinned, wiping the sweat from my neck. ''Not Hakon. He'll ride a whirlwind into the ground.''

You must be young and immortal to ride so. He begged a place with me and no idle court sinecure. None of my

young post riders had as good a seat or unerring eye for
a fast horse. To lighten weight, he rode without a saddle
or weapons, clad in the lightest clothing and soft shoes,
virtually flat over the horse's neck. Gyrth sometimes
thought the youth's panting zeal a bit much but understood
whence it came.

"Poor little sod. Got you to live up to and Swegn to
live down."

When my nephew clattered up to us, his lithe body
flexed and flipped him clear of the horse onto the ground
before the animal was full halted. He knelt before me.
"Sire, I've come from Sandwich."

"Good lad. Botulf, fetch him some water."

The sweat-streaked linen shirt flapped loose about Hakon's narrow waist and his breeches were out at the knee,
but he was in high spirits. "No need at Sandwich. Your
brother is gone."

Hakon scooped only a handful from the water bucket
himself before tendering it to his white-lathered horse.
"Easy, *mon ami*," he soothed. "Not too much, not too
fast. They held them, Uncle. The local thane and his men,
they drove Tostig off. *Ma foi*, but it was marvelous."

How many men did Tostig have? How many ships?

"All done when I got there, but our men counted eighteen, perhaps twenty craft, no more. Not longships but
how you say . . . boats of fishing, *comme ça*. They fled
away from our men and put out again."

"North," Leofwine guessed. "Wind's against anywhere else."

Gyrth said, "Then he could strike my shores next."

We held a hurried council there in the road. Tostig
might well raid Anglian shores or farther north. Neither
Edwin nor Morcar were experienced battle commanders
and Humber mouth very tempting to men in need of water
and supplies. Yet we dare not be drawn away from the
south right now.

"We'll divide here. I've got to make a show of strength
starting at Sandwich, let the folk know we're ready. Gyrth,
Leof, take your carls and ride for Bosham. I want every
thane and fyrd man from Sussex and Kent assembled as

quickly as possible and an unbroken line of sea watch from Sandwich to Wight. I want every royal ship and any vessel capable of carrying twenty men gathered in The Solent."

"No," Gyrth worried. "What if Tostig raids *my* coast? Those were your people once."

"I was there to act, Brother. You can't be."

"But—"

"Gyrth." The decision wasn't any easier than the order I gave him. I knew the frustration Gyrth must feel and the price in plunder and deaths. "Those villages must be expendable. We can't waste time chasing Tostig now. I'm sorry, Gyrth, but that's a command. You'll make for Bosham. I'll join you there."

I rode south and west through English summer while the folk ran from the steadings to line the roads and cheer us on. Now and then as I rested to ease my leg, the old and sick, the black-toothed country faces would collect shyly before me, hoping I could affect cure for their ailments as they heard Edward had often done for suppliants. God alone knows where such fables began. The only saintly thing about that perverse man was his hunger for the quality. Still, most of these folk passed all their lives without ever setting eyes on a king. There in the dusty roads of Sussex, I hope they saw something in me to give them faith.

Word went before us. Often as we rode we met the southern thanes riding over the downs to muster, sun-browned fyrd men trudging after with ancient seax knives, farm axes, or mere cudgels on their broad shoulders. They spread in a thin line along our cliffs, through the marshes, over the beaches, settling down to watch for William. Though crowned, I remained earl of Wessex and now made heavy demands on my home folk. When local farmers grumbled at the amounts of food we needed, I reminded them that William's demands would be higher and less graciously acknowledged.

Beside the strain of waiting we had the usual trouble with bored men fighting among themselves or having a go at the local maids. On the green downs above the beaches they played violent ballgames, collecting bruises and a few broken bones. Like all hardworking men they were glad to be free for a rowdy, unfettered time, but as summer stretched on, they fretted over their home fields and harvests.

May . . . June . . . July. Still William did not come.

At Bosham we were glad to be reunited with our mother, who moved with difficulty these days, pretending indignation when one of us lifted her and whisked her up or downstairs. I think she relished the attention, being lonely for so long. Attention she now had in abundance with three sons and an army spilling out of the old barracks into a city of tents beyond her gates, and Hakon ever galloping in with relayed reports. His English expanded every day, not always untainted.

"I cannot yet think in it," he admitted to me. "But the men, they are so profane. Goddamn this and rutting that. Do all English curse so?"

"From the cradle, alas. Means nothing."

One day Gytha began: "Edith usually visits this time of—" And cut off the rest.

Eager for more, I had to urge, "You've heard from her?"

"She writes often. The boys are well."

But of me or for me in those letters, nothing but silence.

"Son, fetch my cane." When I helped Gytha to her feet, she kissed me. "Dear Harold, no man should ever envy a king. Especially one who needs a cane himself."

"Not wise, Mum. The men mustn't see me ailing."

Loving but strained summer with gaping holes in our family fabric. If Edith never mentioned me, our mother never spoke of Tostig. When jubilant Hakon brought news of him relayed from London, we shushed him because Gytha was in the solar just above.

"What, man. A rout you say?"

"*C'est vrai.* Complete."

"Keep your voice down," Gyrth hissed. "Where? Anglia?"

"No, Uncle. He tried Humber, but Edwin and Morcar

came out against him in such strength Tostig had to flee back to his ships. What remained of them.''

"Fine," Leofwine exulted. "We undervalued those boys."

They should be fine. I paid high for them. "Go on, Hakon."

By Edwin's count no more than ten or twelve small craft remained to the raiders. Futile Tostig was now a toothless menace. I breathed easier, Leofwine did not. Thirty-one now and just taking on the bulk of his prime, he'd always been the most reflective among us. "I've heard adders lose their fangs only to grow new ones. From the first Tostig felt the world was against him and must be overcome. Always something *missing* in that man. It's inconceivable to him that he could be wrong or lose."

August Lammastide came. The men grew restive, wanting to get home to their own steadings. Supplies had to be brought from farther inland, for the coast was now a bare larder. "Yet a little longer," I exhorted them, testing the wind each day. "These weeks are William's last hope of sure winds. Soon the odds turn in our favor."

The loyal men stayed as August became September. An ancient farmer's homily holds that fine weather on ninth September presages forty more fair days. The ninth dawned, maddeningly perfect and extending William's chances, but the fyrd and ships' crews had already served long beyond required duty and could be held no longer. I gave the order to disperse.

On thirteenth September the winds turned with a vengeance, as if the boreal north sucked in one deep, icy breath and blasted it forth across the Narrow Sea. Some of my homeward-bound ships were never seen again. Before leaving for London, I went alone to Trinity to pray for the lost men. It's said God never sends more affliction than we can bear and often large blessings mixed in. The gale that drowned my crews brought more north winds to keep William pinned on his coast. So much for weather wisdom.

The stone floor of the empty nave pained my knee cruelly as I knelt to pray. *Blessed Mary, mother of God, intercede for the souls of my good men lost to the sea. Heed the chantry prayers on their behalf, for they were brave and steadfast, putting my need before their own. Lord God, I thank you for delivering us so far. Let your hand stretch forth a little longer over this isle and its folk. Be with them, if not with me. Lord, if you heed my prayers, you know my doubts. I don't know how you weigh a man's soul, or if, in your eyes, I have any right to this crown. I'm only a man who, when the grain went under the grinding stone, had to choose one sin over a greater.*

The pain in my leg had robbed me of sleep for some days, and I must ride two days to London without proper rest. Aldyth wouldn't bother me overmuch, there was blessing. That day in York on the green hard by Micklegate, when Edwin handed his sister to me, we mouthed the high, hollow phrases that sanctify such royal grime. Oh, Aldyth had changed. In the prime of her beauty now, yet the fetching lightness was gone, the sweet mouth harder, the violet-blue eyes no longer wide or trusting. We regarded each other like alien creatures between whom joining is unthinkable but necessary. . . .

"Sire?"

I glanced around to see Botulf blessing himself with water at the font, my sword and baldric under one arm. "Is it time?"

"Your train's made up and your lady mother wishes to say farewell."

Trying to rise, the pain lanced through my knee. "*Damn* this. Botulf, friend, help me up."

73 • Harold

Drinking watered vinegar is not a joy, but after two days in the saddle only that and strong willow-bark tea dulled the ague enough to let me sleep. In the London palace my mornings were much like Edward's but far swifter paced. On my insistence Chaplain Peter bit a scandalized tongue and abbreviated his daily matins.

"In all reverence, Father, God has eternity to work. We do not. Just a brief chapter and prayer."

Which I heard that particular morning while spooning fresh blackberries in cream. The priest had just said amen when Regenbald entered to advise me of audiences waiting. For convenience I'd kept the major crown servants. After years with God-obsessed Edward, chaplain and chancellor must surely clepe me a slothful Christian and far too informal for kingly *gravitas*.

"The queen and the archbishop, sire. His Grace begged you hear him first." Regenbald's glance slid to Peter as he silently mouthed: *alone*.

Stigand wouldn't ask precedence of the queen without cause. "Father Peter, we thank you. Regenbald, tell my lady I know her errand and will see her shortly. Ask His Grace to come in."

Stigand slumped in, seedy and stubble-cheeked, his plain monk's habit sodden with rain and splashed with mud. By his sour mien he brought no happy news.

"My God, Stigand. Did you sleep in the rain?"

"What sleep? The nuncios reached Canterbury after midnight. I've been riding since."

"Here, sit down by the fire. What is it?"

"A papal decree." He produced it from the pocket of his mantle. "Alexander has excommunicated you."

I might have expected the usual damning phrases that canceled my salvation and cast me into outer darkness:

On complaint of the most Christian Duke William . . . your incestuous union . . . usurpation of his rightful throne . . . cut off from the body of the Church.

I dropped into a chair not knowing what to say, only what must be forestalled. "This news will spread from every pulpit, but no need to hurry it."

I was terrified as any Christian would be, the bottom gone out of my soul for a nightmare moment before my father's common sense whispered through life and memory. God's turnkey had slammed the heavenly door, but that portal had closed on kings before. Rome usually reprieved them at the price of new churches, rich donations, and much public groveling. "However black William painted me, he must have used the whole bucket. What can we do?"

Stigand shrugged helplessly. "Whatever can be done. I must publish this, but you are a popular king. Their sympathies will be with you. Later, appeal, give reasons, but the pope has already taken sides. He's sent the papal banner to William. Our spies saw them parade it through the streets of Rouen."

Yes, William would do that, raise high the sign by which he could now rape my country with God's blessing. "Do they know where he is now?"

"Last reported at Dives, but since the storm no one knows."

Too much to hope he'd been lost at sea with my own keels, but wherever, William wrestled with the problems I'd faced all summer, feeding an impatient army and daily scraping up tons of provender for horses, safe sailing weather past. I heaved out of the chair. "He'd be mad to try now. As for this"—I slapped the decree into Stigand's hand—"we'll deal with Rome. These things are seldom final, just expensive. Pardon me, friend, the queen is waiting. I've asked her to fashion something with her women.''

"The new flag, yes. I glimpsed it outside. Handsome.''

"She and her ladies are accomplished with needle, and it . . .''

When I trailed off, my old friend studied me cannily. "Yes?''

"Gives her something to do,'' I finished lamely.

"Do you know you never refer to Aldyth by name or speak much of her at all? I know what this cost you, Harold. Truly, how is it between you?''

Like grey November with only feeble sunlight and no warmth. "I broke her father's ambition and bought her husband's death. How should it be? I try to be kind. She tries to be dutiful. She will present me with a child in spring.'' I could hear my own lack of enthusiasm. "Stay and greet her.''

Aldyth entered, followed by one of her Mercian ladies bearing a dark-blue bundle. My queen knelt to the archbishop's ring, unable to miss his disheveled state. "Your Grace seems quite . . . distressed.''

"A lack of sleep, madam.''

"Indeed? My lord, your standard is ready.''

The women spread the banner before me. Considering I'd spent every day since Edward's death preparing for invasion, my device was fitting: On the deep-blue field, each border winking with four inset jewels, an armored warrior strode with battle ax upraised to strike.

Aldyth asked, "My lord is pleased?''

"More than pleased, lady.''

"Only the PAX is missing,'' Stigand suggested. "For the peace we pray for.''

Aldyth ventured a puzzled criticism. "A fighting man rampant over peace? Most surely wrong.''

"Madam, peace is the general idea,'' I snapped. Why I erupted at her I can't say. The news from Rome, the persistent pain in my leg, and now a growing noise of shouting men beyond the unshuttered casement, roiling nearer from the direction of Cripplegate—all of the frustration boiled over.

"What does this pope think we'll do, Stigand? Hide under the bed and quake? 'Beg pardon, sorry, all a terrible mistake,' and hand our crown to William? By God, but he knows little of us. He can forbid mass, bind or loose, but he will not *stop* us."

"Pope?" Aldyth looked from me to Stigand, bewildered. "What is this of forbidding mass?"

I snatched the decree from Stigand and waved it before her. "Just that, lady. Read for yourself. I'm a spiritual leper whom you may now avoid with a clear conscience."

With the briefest knock the door flung open, and Botulf all but fell into the chamber. Though startling us, his obvious haste was apology enough. "Sir, there's a messenger just through Cripplegate. It's bad, sir."

My first thought was William. Against all odds, reason, and weather, my enemy had landed. "Where, Dover? Pevensey?"

"Scarborough in the north, sir, but it ent the duke. It's the king of Norway. The messenger's just outside."

The young man who dropped to one knee before me had clearly ridden far and hard. He held out a folded square of parchment. In his haste Morcar's clerk had been reduced to minor sacrilege, tearing a page from a psalter and scribbling the back with no time for amenities.

LORD KING—this morning, fifteenth September, King Harald of Norway in league with the former earl Tostig, and with more than a hundred ships, landed near Scarborough and sacked and burned the town. Earl Edwin's levies and my own will meet them, but as Tostig will surely attack York, we beg the king's soonest aid. MORCAR, EARL

Harald Hardrada, that crafty old berserker. For fifteen years he'd tried to bring Denmark under his sway. Now, somehow Tostig had talked him into having a go at me. *The adder's grown his new fangs, Leofwine.*

I sent the messenger to eat and rest, then read Morcar's appeal to Stigand. What can I say of that moment? Hardly fresh news that I'd worked at damnation for years, but to be pronounced so and invaded all in one morning—at such a time a man can laugh, curse, or break altogether. I went to the open casement and stared out at a lowering sky.

"Tostig, Norway—and now it's going to rain again."

My desperate laughter, joined by Stigand and Botulf, took the curse off disaster for a moment, though Aldyth remained stonily unamused. "I admire your composure, madam. You seem unfazed by this."

"God disposes all, my lord. Even kings."

I felt the sting of vindication in her words and should have expected no better. Mourning one marriage across the desert of a second joyless as a crypt, this paid me out for Gruffydd and her children bereft of a father. For this empty alliance she never wanted, for bearing my weight in duty alone, this was her recompense. That she was pregnant with my child gave new meaning to an embarrassment of riches. Because I could match her in broken lives, she loosed something acid in me now.

"Thank you, madam. Never have I heard anyone so profoundly state the obvious. God will dispose, yes, but not before *I* dispose and put things right. Botulf!"

His name whip-cracked loud enough to make him jump. "Sir."

I tore the Fighting Man standard from the waiting-woman's hands and thrust it at him. "Find a staff and carry this for me." A quick glare knifed at Aldyth. "Dispose, madam? Not by God nor Edward nor priest nor pope, but as my father alone schooled me in the meaning of the word, we are *sovereign*. We will render to God, but we apologize to none for being our own nation. You'll pardon me now. I must go pull your little brothers out of the fire. We've lived with an ax over our heads for nine months. Aren't you damned sick of it, Botulf?"

He gathered our proud new flag to his breast. "I am that."

"Me, too. Ready the carls to ride and let's clean house."

74 • Botulf

That was three—no, four days ago. When the sun came up over Thames again, we were out of Bishopsgate, moving fast up the north road, levies joining us as we went. Tadcaster now, only nine miles from York, men and horses just dropped down in our tracks, hundreds of us scattered along Wharfe bank like wash drying in the sun. We won't have much time to rest, but I'll have a tale for the woman when I get home. None of us thought it could be done, marching day and night, an hour's rest here, bare doze there. From London nigh to York in four days, riders on our flanks crying through every town and village, *"Rally to the king!"*

And a king he is. Don't care what that pope wrote to my lord. The pope ent here, but God must be because Harold's leg stopped paining him, and the raider fleet at Riccall where Ouse meets Humber, they don't know we're even close. Trouble is, we don't know what's happened in York. The sailors from our keels who got chased upriver by the raiders, they think there was a battle somewhere near the city, but we can't be sure until Hakon gets back.

I lie here on the riverbank with the flag propped against a tree and me resting against my horse's back. Poor brute just lies still, too flaming tired to switch at flies with his tail. All along the bank hardly a man on his feet. Sunday morning bells ringing from Tadcaster church. Wish they'd stop and let me sleep if I can. Don't know how we're going to fight if that comes today. Can't get the horse up,

531

can't get me up, and even young Hakon setting out for York, he sighs all forlorn—

"Now I know what it is to feel old."

—and I have to leg him up like someone's grandfather. Too tired to sleep. The men about me look dead, but there's one still on his feet: Lord Harold stripped down to his belly, walking down to the river to wash. Poor sod, I don't know where he finds the strength, but since they set the crown on his head, he don't dare show less. I know that man standing there in the shallows. How slowly he moves, scooping up water to wash himself, clumsy as a man half asleep. Closed his eyes less than any of us since London, I'm bound. Thinner these days, all the ease worn out of him. Doesn't laugh quick or easy much as he used to, and no great wonder. No man came to a throne with more troubles, and the queen—well, she ent grim as my lord's sister but not a patch along of Lady Edith. Odd, a lump like me feeling sorry for a king, but Harold and I have traveled many a mile together.

Don't know or care what some duke says about his right to the crown, as if we'd let some foreigner decide for us. Harold saved my life, kept my spirits up in Count Somebody's stinking dungeon, kept the duke twiddling his thumbs while he sat by my sickbed, and that's just what he did for one friend, mind. He's gone against his own blood, against King Edward for England, mayhap forsworn himself to hell for England, worn himself out for her. He's a right to her clear as a man's right to his own wife, and none deserves her more.

What noise now? Halloos from up the village road. From where the road curves down into Tadcaster from the south there's men running toward us, new levies coming in, those in front wearing mail coats, and a hundred or more bobbing behind them. Someone ought to meet them with proper show, but Lord Harold's up to his knees in the river and pissing calm as you please, which ent any way to greet levies. I tug at my horse's bridle. The poor beast wobbles up no happier about it than me, and the men about are muttering and hauling themselves up to see who's coming in.

I meet them at the river bridge, mounted with the Fighting Man in its socket. When they see me the young fellow in front lopes forward, sword swinging from his baldric, mail chinking as he comes. "Standard-bearer, is the king by?"

"Might be. Whose men are you?"

He pulls off his helmet and the red hair flops over his brow. "Thane Aelle. This is my village and these men are from the near holdings. Where's the king?"

"Here, man!"

Lord Harold swings up the bank toward us, and Aelle's mouth drops open. Country lad, most like never saw a king before and for sure not one half naked. The men go down on their knees in a wave like wind through tall grass, but Harold won't have that. "Rise up, rise. Aelle is it? Good to have you with us. We move as soon as my scout returns."

"Sire." Aelle takes the hand the king extends but right ginger about it, as if't might burn him. "We heard of a battle while we were gathering. If there's to be another, we want to be there."

"Then let's see what sort of men you've brought me."

Lord Harold moves among the fyrd men crowding round, staying them when they want to kneel again, glad they've brought provisions, glad for the offered swig of ale from one man, a bit of cheese from another. He seems to gain new strength. His chest swells out with a deep, free breath, and he laughs loud through a mouthful when Aelle makes a joke about Norse needing to thaw their stones in winter before going at a woman. But then he always had that touch with men, same as his father, able to lay his power by without you forgetting it's there, like he's one of you. Whatever Aelle and his lot expected to see in a king, they know it's a man they've come to serve.

As Lord Harold passes me the ale skin, I see Hakon barely creeping along the riverbank, and the way his horse favors a foreleg, it's run its last mile for many a day. "Scout's back. Hakon, here!"

Harold hooks a foot into my stirrup and steps up to see

the boy hobbling along. "He looks hurt. Eh, Nephew! My old gran was slow, but she was seventy. Come *on*, then."

Hakon drops the reins and tries to run, like a man dead drunk or dead tired, and when he staggers through the parting press of men the lad's purely done in, with a big, dirt-smeared bruise on the right side of his face. Pushed the horse too hard getting back, says he. Went clean out from under him, and he took a fall.

The king's no time for that. "What about York? Edwin and Morcar? Is Hardrada in the city?"

A hopeless wagging of the lad's head: no. "Come and gone. There was a battle. It is chaos, my lord. The earls are beaten. The city of York is a whipped dog turned on its own masters. They want to hang Edwin and Morcar."

Harold

If Edwin and Morcar weren't veterans before, they are now. They faced Hardrada and Tostig a mile south of York on the bank of River Ouse. Morcar—how old is he, sixteen?—charged first with his wing, broke the Norse flank and almost won a victory, but Tostig's feeble summer raid and seasoned Vikings are very different matters. Hardrada rallied his men and went on the attack. The defenders had never faced shrieking, ax-swinging madmen plunging into their ranks with utter disregard for their own lives. The English broke and fled back to the city, what remained of them, with no choice but to open the gates to their conquerors.

How Tostig must have savored that moment in his poisoned heart, striding up Micklegate, vindictive and seething, spying this way and that for former enemies, to halt contemptuously before the shaken young earls despised by their own for what many considered cowardly submission. Depressing how many unhurt bystanders are always brave enough to throw blame and call for a rope, but by their surrender the earls saved York.

We entered the city that afternoon, our infantry swinging along lustily behind us, marching in good order to give hope to the demoralized citizens. Hakon confirmed that Tostig and Hardrada, after four days, had withdrawn to Riccall, nine miles to the south without leaving any men in York.

"Four days? I've heard Hardrada is craftier than he's bright," I told the men before we marched. "This is the first sure proof."

The second? Incredibly, Tostig and the Norse king still had no inkling we were anywhere near York, much less ready to fall on them—couldn't have, else they'd never dare quit the city.

Riding over Ouse Bridge, Botulf saw the peril clearly as I did in the sullen faces that lined our way, giving ground reluctantly before our advance cavalry, who had to shoulder their horses through the press. "Not a happy thought, sir, but we may have to fight York before we even see Norway."

"Where are the aldermen? Got to restore some kind of order and that quickly. You there!" I called to the grizzled carl reining up before me. "Have you found the earls?"

"Aye, sire. In Stonegate. They've their housecarls for guard, but there's a passin' ugly crowd about the house. Some of them have ropes."

He looked familiar, a middle-aged man with a battered, beer-flushed face and a fresh bruise on his neck where someone had flung a stone or clod. "What's your name, soldier?"

"Einhelm, sir. I served under your father."

"Now I remember. Einhelm, take your company through the city, flush out every goddamned alderman who may be hiding under his bed, and bring them all to me in Stonegate." I glared about at the citizens within earshot and raised my voice. "Drag them if necessary. Deal with any trouble as you see fit. Any fool with a rope in his hand, he drops it or hangs from it, clear?"

"Damn right, my lord."

"Move."

Einhelm drew his sword with visible relish and rode forward, shouting orders to his men.

The surging crowds grew larger and louder as we drew nigh Stonegate. Before the house where Edwin and Morcar had taken refuge their carls stood in tense lines four deep with spears and drawn swords, blocking flung stones with their shields. Botulf forced his way through, wheeling about to challenge the mob, the Fighting Man furling over him. "Give place! Give way for King Harold. Be still, you men. Peace, I say!"

I stood erect in my stirrups to address them. "Put down those stones. *Down*, damn you. I'll hang the next man who throws one. Soldiers forward! Force them back."

Gradually, with shields, spear butts, and sword hilts, the guards pushed the mob back. They were quieter now but still exuded the anger of their fear like rank sweat. I was burning the last of my strength, fatigue a heavy mantle closing about me, and still the earls and aldermen to stiffen with resolve before I could sleep.

"What are you men afraid of? Your city's not sacked, not burning, you're still alive. You've lost one battle, but you'll win the war. Who here hasn't been knocked down in a fight and got up again to win? A bloody nose just got you madder, right? Then *get* mad, but where it'll do the most good. Who talks of hanging your earls? For sure no man who fought with them. I tell you for truth I'd rather them for brothers than that traitor at Riccall. Tomorrow they and I, Wessex, Mercia, and York together will teach Hardrada a lesson in English manners he'll never forget. I promise you. Disperse now, go to your homes, and let's get on with winning."

When I entered the house I recognized the chief stewards and captains who always accompanied the earls. Seasoned men, what they felt about the defeat and surrender they kept to themselves, conducting me to the main room where Edwin and Morcar came forward with touching gratitude to kneel before me. They looked stricken, shame vivid in their faces as the red welt left by a blow. A wave of paternal pity washed over me. At their age I was tupping slave girls, trying to outdrink Swegn, and could have done no better than they at Fulford.

I took each by the elbow and raised them gently. "Thank God you're safe. Botulf, all of you, leave us. Sit down, my lords. This isn't half so bad as you must feel."

Like Aldyth, Edwin had his fair looks from his mother, while Morcar took after Aelfgar, stocky as Gyrth as a boy. Scarce a year gone they dictated their terms to me with puppy-fierce arrogance. The difference now was stark as a bloodstain. They'd been harrowed through battle and seen too many friends die. Like new metal scorched by fire, they'd never shine as brightly again.

"Earl Morcar? Condition?"

The boy shot an unsure glance at his brother. "Edwin did most of it."

"This is your city. I'm asking you."

"Well, I—I thought of Stamford Bridge."

I read the remnant of pride in Edwin's wan smile. "For four days we drew it out, hoping you could get here."

"We didn't really believe you could, but then Tostig wasn't in any haste to depart. That murdering bastard, he—" Morcar caught himself. "Pardon me, my lord."

"Not at all. I call him worse. Go on."

"He expected his friends to come forward, so sure they would. As if he had one left."

"And the Norweyan king," Edwin took it up. "He just sat tossing down his beer and nodding *ja* now and then. Biggest man I ever saw and the coldest. They made us swear to join our men with theirs and attack London. No choice with bloody huge pirates all over us, breathing down our necks. We didn't know one moment if we wouldn't die the next. We did what we could."

"We delayed." Morcar sucked in air like one with a new respect for breathing. "They demanded five hundred hostages to secure the surrender, and then Tostig argued with Hardrada about which to take. He wanted every personal enemy who'd ever crossed him. He had a list."

Morcar agreed to send the hostages to Stamford Bridge in two days. Tostig knew the place, a small village seven miles east of the city out of Monkgate. "They'll have a good walk getting there. For what it's worth," the boy concluded, "just a little more time."

They fell silent, hunched side by side on the bench. Edwin's tremulous whisper came to me like that of a troubled ghost. "When I looked back . . ."

"What, son?"

"At Fulford. They were throwing the bodies of our men into the marsh. Dancing on them. We did try. We fought. We didn't know it could be so . . ."

"No one does, Edwin. Ready to try again with better odds?"

What a question. Look twice on horror, wade through it once more? Edwin knuckled at red-rimmed eyes. "We have to, don't we? The people cursed us in the streets. I wanted to die."

"But my lord came in time," Morcar breathed. "I'm glad I've been regular to mass. God *is* with us."

If God wasn't by now we'd just have to muddle through alone, but I could wish our excommunicating pope had raced with us from London at the pace I set. Besides sweating some of the lard off his holy Roman rump, he mightn't be so free with condemnation. I laughed suddenly at another truth, one I could freely share with my earls.

"You know, lads? One thing Tostig always hated was surprises. And tomorrow my unspeakable little brother is fated for the surprise of his life."

75 • Tostig

Stamford Bridge, 25 September 1066

From the top of the rise, River Derwent behind me, the road from York is still empty in the noonday sun. We reached here an hour past; the hostages should appear soon. Hardrada's men are scattered on both sides of the rivers, swimming or lying about in the sun. You'd think we were on holiday, yet my mind misgives.

I've learned to trust first thoughts on waking. When I opened my eyes this morning at Riccall and beheld Hardrada placidly munching his breakfast, I knew we'd gone from beginning to victory too swiftly only because we'd overlooked something. What was it?

Hardrada hasn't a qualm, of course, not a twitch. The man loves fighting more than taking breath. To a warrior who's ramped from Russia to Byzantium and Africa, this is just one more grand adventure with victory foregone. We'll simply gather our hostages, take the boy earls and their levies in tow, and march south to more conquest and glory, one-two-three. So confident he left a third of our force at Riccall, and his men marched here with weapons and helms alone, leaving their mail coats on the ships because the day is so warm. I stowed mine behind my saddle all the same. My stars hold true, the curve of the Easter comet's tail was heaven's smile bent upon me, yet I won't press fortune too far. Before Hardrada, luck was all bad.

Baldwin welcomed me in Bruges but, with silken regret, refused to support my return. Malcolm of Scotland the same, honoring our friendship but reluctant to cross Harold. Not much left of my "force" by the time Edwin and his little brother chased me into the sea. Finally to Norway, to Oslofjord, knowing too well Harald Hardrada my last chance, but winning on the last throw of the dice.

Not easy to convince the Norse king for all of that. I've never dealt with a legend before, nor one with the rough bark still on him. Hardrada looks his reputation, well over six feet in height, broad and solid as Micklegate Bar. That blue tunic he donned this morning must have required twice the linen needed for a middling man. Nor is he stupid. I needed all my wit to convince him of this voyage, a losing argument until I asked myself: What does *he* want? Where is he vulnerable? From then on I steered a sure course.

Hardrada is a man born centuries after his time. More Viking than king, he would rather sack a city than rule it, and given to composing verse on his exploits. But the man is fifty now. After futile years trying to subdue Denmark, he must know glory is behind him but stubbornly pushes that truth and his age aside. For a fact he dyes his hair and beard; the auburn tint is too even and goes carroty every few weeks. All the more reason to be tempted by one more prize, one last ringing refrain to the colorful mayhem of his life.

"After such vain effort in Denmark," I posed, "why hesitate when England could be yours for the taking?"

He has sleety eyes, this aging hero, and he seems to look quite through me. "Then why did you fail when you tried last summer?"

"I was only testing the waters. Besides, I had not enough men or ships. I am no more royal than Harold—that place will be yours—nor do I wish any more than he deprived me of."

The prospect of new adventure lighted Hardrada's imagination more than halfway to my cause, but he's still dubious. "What of the Norman duke? His ambitions are well known. Will we not have to fight him as well?"

Not the time to mention my failure to secure William's aid or even his ear when his own preparations were shaking all of France. I spread my arms before Hardrada, showing my reasons transparent as spring water. "My lord, I am half Dane myself, as is much of England, and know whereof I speak. They'll cleave to you before Normans they hate."

So we sailed, slaughtered, and won York—yet all seems too quick and easy. Perhaps I tarried too long in the city, waiting for "friends" I counted on then but no more. Those flatterers who fattened at my board in better days, not one could be found. Where are they? More disturbing, where is Harold?

We should have sent mounted scouts in every direction the moment we anchored at Riccall. Harold will, wherever he is. His Wessex men are the best foot soldiers in Europe, their horses mostly of the Welsh border breed, hardy as the men. I've campaigned with them and know how swiftly they can move. But Hardrada feels royally secure. I warned against complacency this morning, but he just brushed the concern aside as womanish, gave the order to move, and the men marched off singing to this misbegotten bridge.

"At best we take England," my lord of Norway allowed. "At worst we carve a new kingdom from her north."

Wait. Something glinting far back on the road. Movement?

Yes, they're coming, the hostages. I whistle and wave at Hardrada, pointing down the York road. He strolls to his horse, Fredrik his standard-bearer following after. They start for me at a leisurely pace; when they arrive, I've had time to make an uncomfortable discovery. No mere five hundred hostages, not that mile-long human snake writhing toward us, sunlight flashing from countless spear points and burnished mail.

Hardrada gazes his fill at them. "That is an army."

Oh, brilliant.

"Where did they come from, *Jarl?* That cannot be your brother."

Alas, I must cloud his sky. "That *is* King Harold, that *is* the army he could not possibly field so soon, and I would think this the time for swift decisions."

"Such as?"

"We can't fight them here. We haven't the men and those we have are without armor. We must retreat to the ships and fight them there."

"Retreat, *Jarl* Tostig?" I might have spoken a word foreign to him. Hardrada assesses the nearing force, and now among the banners fluttering over them, I recognize those of Northumbria and Mercia. Hardrada smiles with genuine pleasure. "They come for battle. We will give them one. This king, I will crack his skull and sup on his brains."

A simple victory would suffice me, but there you have a Norse warrior with a reputation to uphold. One may read *Beowulf* with delight, but living with his incarnation is a strain.

He barks at his standard-bearer. "Fredrik!"

The man wheels his horse about, anticipating orders and action. *"Ja."*

"Put three men on our fastest horses. We need the armor and every man from the boats but a bare guard. Now!"

Fredrik slaps the horse's flank and gallops down the hill, screaming a war cry to rouse the men below. Hardrada turns to me. It is a good day for him, his kind of day. His expression is positively beatific. "You fought well outside York, but perhaps you do not wish to fight your own blood. Will you retire to Riccall?"

Does he insult me, thinking me so afraid of Harold that I would skulk in guilty fear? "Thank you, no. I must stay and greet my dear brother. Today he is mine."

And I will have him or he me. This day will Harold's stars or mine ascend or fall. We canter down the slope toward the river, where our men are moving with purpose now, looking to their weapons as our messengers dash away to the southwest.

Harold

From the last rise above Derwent we saw Hardrada's lines drawn and waiting us in the meadow below, some this side of the stream, the rest across the narrow timber bridge that spanned the river. *Wrong.* Why didn't they occupy this ridge and make us fight uphill? More baffling still, I estimated no more than a thousand men and none in armor. Why? Where in hell were the rest of them? The obvious blunder must be Hardrada's doing. Tostig knew the value of high ground and would never choose such a vulnerable position.

Botulf gasped in disbelief at the sight. "Are they gone stupid?"

"The men from Tees are just behind us. Ask Thane Brand to fetch me his best archer."

Morcar trotted his horse up to me and pointed. "There is Hardrada. The big man in blue by the raven standard. Land Waster he calls it."

The boy's face was thin and pale beneath his helmet. He must have grown years in the last hellish week. "Frightened, Morcar?"

"Yes," he declared honestly. "But more ashamed. There are things to put right. We wait your orders, sire." Morcar jerked the reins and rode away.

Across the meadow the towering Norse king was difficult to miss, though I couldn't make out Tostig anywhere. Botulf returned with Brand Ulfsson and a spare little fyrd man whose bow was longer than himself.

"Peter Fletchersson, my lord." Brand shook the fellow's shoulder in sour affection. "I'd hang him ten times over for poaching but he's too good a hunter."

"Fine. Archer, can you put a shaft just there, about seventy-five paces to our front?"

Peter gauged the distance with an extended thumb and fitted a shaft. With no pause between press and loose, the arrow whistled through windless air and lodged within a pace of my mark.

Our troops had become mixed during the march. They had to re-form under their own flags on that line, Edwin to the left, Morcar right, Wessex in the center. "And hold there. I'm going to try parley first."

"Hardrada will never listen," Edwin said.

"No, but Tostig may have more sense. He can see what they're facing."

Moving forward with my lines, I tried to read as much as possible from the flat meadow, the only elevation a grassy knoll on the far bank. Those on this side, if we flanked them, would have only the bridge for retreat. If parley failed, our attack must squeeze them toward that one point, leaving no room for those on the far bank to get into action.

I half hoped my brother wasn't here at all today, but the wish was faint. *No, he's here. He won't shrink from this. Neither can I.*

"Give me the standard, Botulf."

Surprised and offended, "That's my place, sir."

"Just this once, friend. I'm going to play nuncio."

My brother wouldn't know the new flag. With the nose-guard of my helmet down, none of the Norse would recognize me at all. I twitched the reins and rode forward with the Fighting Man gripped firmly, already soaked with sweat under my mail coat. Below, Hardrada stepped forward and waved me on in insolent invitation. I halted midway between the lines.

"I speak for Harold of England. Is Tostig Godwinesson among you?"

The answer came back in the lightly mocking tones I'd known since boyhood. "Did Harold think I would be elsewhere today?"

Their ranks parted for the only armored man in their throng. He brought his horse forward at a walk, removing his helm and shaking out the oil-gleaming black hair. Most like he'd scented it, too. We greeted each other as he drew up before me.

"*Hoch*, Tostig."

"I recognized your voice. Hot day for a fight."

"You're well turned-out as always."

"Devilish hard in this heat. Our men smell vilely. One tries to stay upwind." Tostig surveyed the flag with an appreciative nod. "Lovely banner. Have to carry your own these days?"

"Why not? You've been waving yours in my face all your life. I didn't want one of your bowmen to recognize me."

"No fear, Harold," Tostig allowed with a sweetly acid smirk. "No one will ever take you for a king. How does our sister? Deprived as myself, I suppose."

"Only of the power she abused."

"Said the usurper."

"Listen and mark me. You see our numbers, almost two to one, and yours are without mail—God knows why, but there it is."

Tostig vented a grunt of resignation. "Hardrada ordered the dispositions. He's bad at chess, too."

"I never slighted your mind, Tostig. You know we can avoid this. Lay down your arms and treat for terms before we destroy you."

"Terms?" he shot back. "Just what can you offer me that we won't take ourselves today? You ruined me with Edward, shipped me out in disgrace, and gave my lands to a snotnose boy. I'll give you terms. Restore me, set the coronet once again on my head, and then I'll call you king."

Absurd; for an instant I felt an impossible urge to conciliate, to compromise and avoid the death hovering about us, and to save what vestige of family remained in us. But there was nothing left. We'd been years traveling to this hostile riverbank. "You're blind mad to hope for that. The north spit you out without my help. They'd do it again and me with you. I offer you life, man. Take it, leave England, and never return."

"Oh, Harold." A slow, regretful shaking of his head. "You were much better at bargains in Wales. What to Norway for all his pains?"

This wasn't going well at all. My anger boiled up hot as the sun overhead. "You speak of pains, you and that murdering pirate?" I checked the rage with an effort. Behind me waited the long curve of my army, a like wall in front, both deadly quiet, as if every man knew this sweltering moment only a respite before the inevitable. And Tostig before me, mocking, sure as always of his superiority, unable to believe this the end of him.

"The same as to you," I answered. "Leave England while he can or never leave at all."

Tostig glanced round at the massive figure of Hardrada resting ham hands on the butt of his long-handled ax. "No, I don't think so. The king looks forward to this. He's lyrical as Gruffydd, did you know? Already composing a poem on your death."

"Best be a short one. He hasn't a chance."

"You think not?" Tostig backed his horse. "The rest of our men are hurrying here from Riccall, and my stars tell me I'm lucky today."

Too much for me. I burst out with it. "What happened to you? What makes you rather die than see truth? What did I have that you didn't? You turn me sick, Tostig. You could have been so much more."

"When? How?" The sardonic smile vanished as he resettled his helmet, showing only hard eyes and a mouth set. "Never in your shadow. You forget how hard I tried. God's truth, what perverted irony put the crown on your head? You were always too soft—except with me, forbore with all save me, forgave all save me, loved Swegn but never me. Godwine's brightest, Gytha's golden boy. All my life, there was only Eada. All of you . . . blind. So come down if you dare, Harold."

I looked down at my reins, unable to speak. Finished now, all of it. "Then this is good-bye."

"Not quite. When you come, look for me." Tostig turned and rode back to his lines.

When I dismounted again among my own men, I took my shield from Brand Ulfsson. "What's their mind," he plied, eagerness naked. "Will the beggars fight?"

"I thought my brother would listen. I was wrong. Thane, it's going to be a long day. Return to Earl Morcar. Tell him he's to attack when the horn sounds. Hakon, to me!"

My nephew came forward leading his border pony, dressed in the plain shirt and breeches that had become his badge and livery as my scout. He'd begged for mail and weapons this morning but I refused. Whatever befell us today, his mother would not suffer another loss. "Down the line to Earl Edwin. He'll attack on Botulf's horn. Tell him Morcar and I will push them, but he's got to turn their flank toward the bridge. Maintain contact and *turn* them, understand? Then I want you out a mile or so to the southwest. Find a good vantage point. Tostig has reinforcements coming from Riccall. I need your earliest warning."

Hakon scratched at the light scruff of first beard darkening his dirty cheek. "You will have it, Uncle."

"And stay clear of battle. I need your eyes and speed." I hugged him close. "God keep you, boy."

He leaped the horse's back agile as a cat and galloped down the line, calling for Edwin. All about me men were sliding swords from scabbards, others leading horses to the rear, silent but for the rustling clatter of preparation and the warm September air thick with tension. I tried to wet dry lips with a dryer tongue.

Botulf dismounted to carry the Fighting Man at my side. "Lord?" He held out a wicked little throwing ax. "Picked it up in York. These have saved many a life thought lost. Please carry it, sir."

Why not? "Thanks. Ready your horn."

He tried to grin at me, but fell somewhere short. "Christ, but it's hot. Why is it, when there's a battle, it's always too hot or too cold?"

I whispered a brief prayer and drew my sword. "Now."

The horn blared its challenge and we poured down the slope like water through a broken dam.

76 • Harold

We broke their line with our first charge and gave them no chance to recover, pressing them relentlessly back toward the bridge while the Northumbrians, Brand Ulfsson in the van, encircled their ragged flank and forced them back on their own ranks behind. The men rushed from the opposite bank onto the bridge to get at us but only bogged down in the congestion of retreating comrades.

Time stopped for all of us—minutes, hours, I could no longer tell. At my side, the Fighting Man dropped somewhere, Botulf emitted a steady stream of low curses. There was only the hot sun above screaming, slaughtering men.

First you fight to stay alive, then you cease to feel fear or any sane emotion, only the droning voice in your mind: You must win, you *must*. You tire at first in the punishing heat, then there is no fatigue as you block and cut your way through the shrinking knot of enemy giving ground toward the bridge. At some point you've gone coldly mad. Hardrada is there just ahead, and he's yours. Now there are few left this side of the bridge, then none at all as they fall back step by step behind a giant of a berserker, his green tunic slashed and bloody but the ax in his thick arms a murdering mill wheel none can stand against.

Botulf stumbled and went down. Our men surged past me as I dragged him out of their way, but he shook me off, wild-eyed. "Leave off. I ent hurt, just tripped."

In that moment of sunlit hell, I caught a glimpse of

Tostig across the river, and some of Hardrada's men leaping into the stream to escape. One by one the floundering men jerked and went limp.

"Look at him," Botulf croaked. "Jesus, look."

At the water's edge, unhurried as a boy tossing pebbles into a pond, Peter Fletchersson drew and loosed, methodically dispatching the swimmers.

On the bridge the Viking in green still held, the deadly flailing of his ax mowing down all who tried against him. Only a few of his men behind him, but in front a barrier of dead English high enough that to reach him our men now had to leap atop corpses, only to fall themselves.

"Brave man." Botulf spat on the ground. "But he's in the way."

He scooped up a fallen spear and leaped down the bank, running for a small boat bobbing in the shallows. He hauled himself aboard and, with the single oar, paddled furiously for the bridge. Not far from me lay the Wessex standard where the bearer had fallen. Four young men knelt beside him.

"You men leave him. There's no time. Follow me."

I snatched up the Lions and we ran for the bridge, battering through those falling back from the lone berserker's ax. Foam flecked his lips as he screamed high, wordless rage, but his moment of glory was done. As I charged with the flagstaff to knock him off balance, a spear shaft thrust up through the bridge planks into his belly. He convulsed; the spear skewered him again. He tried once more to lift the ax, but I ran at him with the flag, hitting him square in the chest. He went over backward like a felled oak, and the tide bounded forward behind me.

"A Wessex! A Wessex!"

The Norse were re-forming on the far side, rallying around Hardrada and the raven standard. Through a sweat-stung blur I saw Tostig trying to restrain the king. Hardrada shoved him away and strode forward to take his stand alone, pointing at me.

"You! Godwinesson!"

The men behind him didn't move. This was to be personal combat, then. None but their king could have me.

Only the flagstaff in my hands, a hacked and blunted sword at my side, but I didn't care. Like pain, fear can mount only so high before spirit numbs. I held the Lions across my chest, walking toward Hardrada while cold wisdom whispered: *He loves rage. He feeds on it. Fight him with your head.*

I met the white heat of him with casual insolence. "You glorified old donkey. Did your mother ever have any legitimate children?"

Hardrada snarled and started for me at a clumsy run, ax raised over his head. The force of his blow would have gone through my helm to the collar bone, but I blocked it midway up the haft with the flagstaff and felt the stout wood crack. I kicked at Hardrada and backhanded him across the mouth. Suddenly he jerked sideways, stumbled, and fell heavily. Only then did I see the arrow protruding fore and aft from his throat.

A hand gripped my shoulder: Botulf, still dripping water from his foray under the bridge, thrust a shield into my hand and took the flag. "Will you take *care,* for God's sake? Here."

I remember grasping the shield but not why my legs went out from under me. Something burned dully low on my left calf. Botulf helped me up as our men ran past me to take forward positions. From the din of battle I blinked suddenly in eerie silence at Tostig and the men around him on the knoll half a hundred paces away. So numbed, I had to gather simplest thought one piece at a time. Our two forces faced each other, unmoving. Sheer exhaustion alone had called a halt, as lovers spent by passion will break apart from each other only because they can't go on. I wheeled a weary arm at my men still in the meadow to join us, then lurched like a drunkard to Hardrada's body, picking up his ax. *Greedy old man. Is this enough glory at last?*

"Lay him out, Botulf."

He needed another man to help stretch the huge carcass prone. I lifted the ax and brought it down. The head jumped like a lopped end of wood, rolled, and lay still. I carried it by the long red hair through the unmoving lines of my men.

"Tostig? Do you see?"

High on the knoll by Land Waster, Tostig waved his sword in response. "Come again, big brother."

"You're losing. You've lost all day. For the love of God and sanity, will you yield?"

"Not while my own head still works very well, thank you. But King Hardrada's men ask a truce to claim his body. A few minutes, no more. Then come and die."

Behind me my men stood with shields and swords hanging at arm's length, so still they might have grown there, but Tostig would not trick me. He must be staking all on the men reaching him from his ships. I slung the head toward their lines. "No truce! Botulf, tell the earls I want every man this side of the bridge now. And hop it, man. We're going to finish this."

The Norse had their breathing space anyway. Tired men can move only so fast. Some tried to run but fell down, utterly spent. Brand Ulfsson lumbered across at the head of Tees fyrd, a red-sodden tangle of hair hanging from his belt, sporting the most contented smile I'd seen all week.

"What in hell have you to laugh at, then?"

"Eh, it was Peter did for their king, my lord."

"There's luck. Thank him for me."

"No luck to it, sire," Brand asserted. "I did see him miss once, but that's five years gone."

"What is that horrid thing you're carrying?"

He patted the grisly prize at his belt. "This? You might say in the way of sentiment, sir. These bastards' ancestors once raided up Tees on Brandeshal land. My family took scalps then to shame them before Woden. They never dared us again. Sorry if it offends my lord."

Brand swung his arm toward the enemy. "That scum there, this was their doing, not ours."

Shadows slanted longer as our lines formed and the killing beast took shape again. Botulf set himself beside me as he had from the beginning of the battle. The Norse arrayed before the knoll, their ranks far thinner now. Earl

Edwin jogged up to me, sword clutched in a bloody hand. "Mercians formed."

A bare moment later Brand Ulfsson returned to report Morcar's Northumbrians ready. "And the earl begs that no prisoners be taken."

"None," Edwin agreed bitterly. "No mercy. Not to them." He swung away down the line. Our cubs had lost their milk teeth very quickly.

"Brand, look after Morcar," I urged. "Sixteen's young for tasting blood. Don't let him be careless."

The big thane nodded, squinting at the low sun. "I've lost all track, can't tell how long we've been fighting or what hour now—hey, there! Your scout coming back."

Hakon plunged his horse down the slope, slowing to avoid the bodies strewn over the meadow, clattered across the bridge and leaped to the ground before me in his usual breakneck manner. "They come, Uncle. A mile away. Less by now."

About five hundred by his reckoning, all in arms and burdened with extra mail coats, running like men who must fight for every breath. Spent or fresh, within minutes half a thousand men would come down behind us on the York side of Derwent and force us to divide our remaining strength, possibly go on the defensive. Tostig must be counting on just that.

"Nephew, do me one more service. To all earls and commanders: I want every last archer and arrow from all wings back there on the ridge now. Array as they see best to prevent that force from hitting our rear."

"Not many shafts among them," Hakon worried. "When those are gone?"

"What would you do?"

Hakon wiped at the sweat on his sunburned brow, only streaking the road grime in a different pattern across his narrow face. "Me? I would run like a rabbit."

"So will they. Meanwhile, they'll gain us time. Go, boy."

He turned with no enthusiasm to a horse drooping as himself. "*Allons, bébé.* One more time."

The archers were dispatched, no more than forty or fifty all told, scurrying back across the bridge toward the rise, scavenging fallen arrows as they ran to cut off Tostig's last hope. I hefted my shield, wheeled my sword in a high arc toward the knoll where my brother waited. As we ran, Edwin's clear young voice rang high over the roar of our charge. *No prisoners! No mercy!*

What do I say about the worst day of my life, the most violent England has known? The sun dipped lower as we fought, left us in shadow as we circled and tightened a death grip about the last men on that little rise.

What do I say about killing my own brother? The thing was there to be done. I felt nothing. There by Land Waster in his last moments, armor torn, wielding a red sword two-handed and bloody-minded as the king he bought, Tostig saw me and screamed his challenge.

"Harold, I am here! Give me back what is mine!"

My foot skidded over the blood-slippery ground, throwing me down awkwardly to one knee. Tostig loomed over me; I had only an instant. I threw my shield in his face and clawed the little throwing ax from my belt. An old trick and a desperate one that worked in play years ago with Hugh Malet. In that instant Tostig was blind. As he cast the shield aside, the ax already flew, striking him just below the right eye. Tostig staggered, pawing at the missile protruding grotesquely from his face, and a spear from one of my men finished him.

A few of those from Riccall got through our archers but not enough or soon enough to count, most too run out to fight. I'm told farmers found bodies strewn along their path for the last several miles, men who died from exertion before they could strike a blow. When the long September twilight deepened, the thing was all over, simply petered out for lack of men or strength to fight. The dull thud and clatter of the last individual fights thinned and went silent. A few of the Norse, seeing it hopeless, escaped downriver in darkness. I sat on the disputed knoll by Tostig's body, conscious of a burning low in my left leg, a deep laceration just above the boot. When did that happen? I couldn't remember.

Tostig lay with the ax still protruding from his cheek,

eyes wide open in angry shock at his big brother for having the cosmic impudence to come between himself and his destiny. Under my mail the sweat had dried stiff on my linen, and I felt cold.

Hobbling like an old man, Botulf labored up the knoll with the Fighting Man, Hakon moving stiffly in his wake. They sat down heavily beside me.

"I suppose we ought to pray," Hakon mumbled.

Just then I couldn't recall the first word of a single prayer. I covered Tostig with a mantle, shivering under his indifferent stars.

We buried our own dead, as many as possible, but there were simply too many Norse. Perhaps the farmers of Stamford Bridge dragged them away for compost.

Morcar believed God was with us. I wonder. When we limped back to York, the young earls argued with me and each other over division of the Norse ships and the prisoners taken from them. I'd enough of blood and simply took their oaths never to set foot in England again. Norway was broken, their king dead, their entire fleet in our hands. They would never come again.

A week after Stamford, tending my leg amid bickering earls and soldiers, the news came that William had landed at Pevensey. He too had done the impossible. God with whom, Morcar?

77 • Harold

Our army had already wrung miracles from its heart, a forced march into battle, another swift progress home, staggering into London to lick our wounds for all too brief a time before it must all be done again.

Leofwine and Gyrth joined me on sixth October in the small chapel consistory of the palace, aghast at the mauled, limping sight of me.

"Please sit." Gyrth dragged a chair close for me. "You, too, Botulf. You look half dead. What of Tostig?"

"He chose to play his chances," I said. "I left him with his friends. Where are your levies mustered?"

"At Southwark," Leofwine said. He cleared his throat in some awkwardness. "Bad news. There's been more than the usual number of desertions. Stigand could no longer delay publishing the pope's decree."

Gyrth avoided my eyes. "I was with Edith when the priest read it out in Waltham Church. She wouldn't believe it. Later she had to."

My Edith. After all of this brutal year, the thought of her was like remembering a former life. "How is she, Gyrth?"

"Well. Tolerable."

"No, really. Tell me."

"They're getting on. Where's that map?"

I wanted desperately to hear more, but as Gyrth spread the map of Kent before us, there simply was no time. The desertions plainly meant men were unwilling to fight against God and the Church. The rest would be divided and frightened. We must move quickly. I tried to haul myself out of the chair, but Gyrth stayed me. "Please don't. You hobble like a ruined horse. Rest."

I sank back gratefully. "Well, Job had his afflictions."

"Not to mention our sovereign lord is no longer a spring lamb," Leofwine observed.

"Nor my little brother very tactful, thanks."

"You're worn out. Rely on Gyrth in this. He has a good plan."

Gyrth used his dagger to demonstrate on the map. "We can't wait for men to wrestle with conscience, and we can't hazard losing you in one pitched fight." He and Leofwine would engage William as far south as possible. While they defeated or at least stalemated him, I would destroy all supplies between Hastings and London. Either way William would face winter and starvation in hostile country.

"So would our folk, Gyrth. Report estimates he's over seven thousand men, almost half of it cavalry. If you lost, I could never hold him with Wessex alone."

"But sir, there's Mercia and the Northumbrians coming," Botulf reminded me hopefully.

"Promised but where are they? Too many ifs, too many churches tolling my spiritual death, too many men who may lose the heart they have while we delay. No, we march together and stop William dead. That's all, my lords. I'll join you tomorrow at Southwark."

When my brothers departed, I asked Botulf to fetch the cane discreetly hidden under the consistory lectern. "Help me up, man."

"Bad today then?"

"Bad enough. Pass my orders to the Wessex carls."

"Aye, sir." But Botulf didn't move.

"Something?"

He bit his lip, casting his eyes about the chamber. "The Church is one thing, but men deserting is a crime all round. If any man thinks it's right and holy to leave us now, no need of foreigners, for they're killing themselves."

"Thanks, friend. Pray God agrees with you."

He said *us*. Not deserting me but *us*. Then and later that stayed in my mind.

Thirteenth October—six miles north of Hastings. And so we wait on this ridge straddling the London road. We know of William's progress toward us: Bexhill to Filsham, Wilting to Crowhurst, his locust army eats its way north, destroying as they come on.

We reached our position by evening, deploying in a wall across the road with more men joining us hourly to find a place in line and build their fires for the night. As I passed among them they looked to me with the silent question: Are we enough to meet them tomorrow?

"We're as many as them," I encouraged, "and more coming."

But in every face there was the other question none dare voice and to which only God can reply. Alone in my tent I collapsed on my pallet, arm flung over closed eyes, needing to rest. Trying to pray.

God, Blessed Jesus, Holy Mary, hear me. Stop this pain in my leg that gnaws at me until I can't think. My courage burns low and gutters out, and with darkness come the doubts where none were before.

What if I'm wrong? Does a bishop in Rome truly have the power to deny me heaven? Was it mere caprice of weather or your hand that turned the north wind southerly for William?

God, forgo priests now and listen, I beg you. I've never doubted nor feared hell so much as tonight, and that's a double burden when I dare not show it before soldiers come to this place with their own misgiving. They know I'm cut off from you but followed anyway, I think, for something not beyond but apart from salvation, something no other men have in this age, a sense of freedom and the right to say, *This is mine and no man can take it from me.* Remember how Botulf said *us.* If he can't write the first letter of the idea, such men have no need when the belief is bred in their guts. They are what my father sacrificed for, what Edward never knew and William never will. Who is he to ramp over England as sanctified restorer of a perfect world? There are no such saviors, only clumsy carpenters like myself, laboring with blunted tools from incomplete plans toward an obscure end.

The misery in my leg's quieted some. Thank you, Lord. Perhaps you do hear me now.

Yet, why do I ask when what's to do has no question about it? I know life comes down to love in the end, what gives a man meaning and what he'll pay for it. We're told to love you, love your Church, love each other. Then why are we so much better at killing? Is love so perilous? There was a girl long ago, and I pray she's with you now. Not a day since that I haven't remembered Eirianell with guilt and awe. Who would choose hell for love of the ignorant fool I was then? Orpheus went into Hades to rescue Eurydice, but who would willfully embark and burn the boat behind them? There must be that in us that neither writ nor angels can reckon, for Eirianell paid the price.

The night she put her neck in the noose and kicked the stool away, she knew what she did, and so do I. That is why, despite mortal fear and demons whispering that William is right and myself on the brink of hell, that I must fight him tomorrow and let you decide between us. Love is worth the price and, as our merchants would say, the price is right. Amen.

"Harold?"

I'd been drifting toward sleep. She had to call me twice. "Husband."

I opened my eyes, peering past the lamplight into the shadows as she came forward. "Poor love," Edith said, "you look so miserable."

I grabbed for my stick and rose to squeeze her tight to me. "Edith. Oh my—I don't know how you came, but thank God."

"I had to. Just going on day to day, trying not to think or hear about you. Then they read that filthy writ at Waltham after Gyrth said you'd gone north against Tostig. Now William. It was too much for you to bear alone."

"Bless you forever." I dropped another turf on the peat brazier. "Here, sit by me. I want to look at you."

"Don't. We've ridden two days. I'm a sight."

"Not you, not ever. Who is with you? The boys?"

"Two monks of Waltham."

"Let me look at you." My love had aged. I knew every line and plane of that dear face and could read where each had deepened or turned down, saw the first wrinkles left by time in the lovely throat Gytha once likened to a swan's, and how the light betrayed the grey in her hair. Edith's hand strayed to it.

"I gave up vanity when you left."

"I never left you for a day, you or the boys. How are they?"

"They manage, but it's difficult. After the writ Godwine felt guilty for not allowing you closer to him."

"He's always close to me. And Magnus?"

"Like you, always a jest, but he was sick over the pope's decree, and Edmund flatly refused to go on with his Latin. Said it was personal between him and Rome."

Edith bent to touch the bandage on my leg. "From the battle?"

"Yes, but devil if I know just when."

"That's no mere scratch. How can you not remember?"

"Love, you've no idea how busy we were."

She picked up my cane. "Gyrth said your ague's come back."

"Lying down helps. Here, come rest with me."

We stretched out close together on the pallet, and I felt tears coming for weariness, for the miracle of Edith in my arms. She kissed the rivulets that stained my dirty cheek. "You need much rest, my darling."

"It's enough you're here. I couldn't have faced tomorrow without you. Not much of a hero king. Purely run to ground. Do you know how it feels to be flat out of strength and courage when those are the very things that men need of you?"

Her head moved slightly against mine. "Yes. When you married Aldyth. How I hated you then, and how it hurt hearing she was with child. I felt the bitch had stolen what was mine. Even the good times were painful to remember then."

Remember all of us, the good and the bad. No love worth the loving that didn't hate at some time and none more bitterly. "Girl, I was alone from the day I left you."

"Not now," she breathed. "Not this night. Cover me?"

I pulled the fleece blanket over us. "We had a peat fire on our wedding night, remember?"

"Aye, lovely. We did everything but sleep." Edith's tiny chuckle trailed off in drowsy contentment. "We'll sleep well tonight."

And I'll wake next to you once more. Lord, you hear me after all, blessed my arms with her this night and gave me a simple answer. In the last moment of this world, as in the first, a man will reach to you for meaning and his hand will close about all he can ever grasp, a woman and a hope.

78 • Harold

14 October 1066

Botulf shook me gently, "Sir?"

I unwound myself from the warmth of Edith. "Um . . . time?"

"Light's coming up. The monks from Waltham are praying with the men, and I've cider and bannocks on the fire."

"Botulf?" Edith sat up, fuzzy and yawning. "Thanks, that's heavenly of you."

He turned to the entrance. "A few more levies came in late last night and Thane Aelred with his Sherwooders."

I groped for my boots. "Edwin and Morcar?"

"Not a sign. You and Lady Edith should come eat while there's time." Botulf vanished out-of-doors.

Edith pulled me back down to her. "Must you go just yet?"

"William will be moving by now."

"Keep me warm. When can you come home to Nazeing?"

"Soon." We lay together while the appetizing smell of bannock cakes and spiced apple drifted in to us. Yes, soon. I'd encourage Aldyth to visit her family, not that she'd require urging. My absence never burdened her.

Edith buried her face in my shoulder. "Do you know what I want most? Please don't laugh. Before I'm too old, I want to have another child."

And give her back a little of the happiness we shared long ago. "Lovely thought, but we're a bit rushed today."

"Idiot. There." She packed me off with a kiss. "I ban-

560

ish you from my bed and demand a few moments' privacy.''

Outside the air was clear and cold as day came up, stung with woodsmoke from cooking fires. Botulf brought my mail coat and while he strapped me behind, I studied our ground. All along the ridge for several hundred yards in both directions, men stood or sat about their fires, some just waking now to wheeze, grumble, and turn out, but each with his weapons to hand. Farther back along the London road other men forked out hay or fed buckets of grain to our horses.

This ridge was well chosen. Below us the valley floor had patches of marsh to slow a cavalry charge, then they'd have to push those heavy warhorses a hundred yards uphill to get at us.

Wrapped in a thick Welsh cloak, Hakon munched his breakfast by the fire. ''You sent for me, Uncle?''

My nephew had never asked for much, not even new clothes which he sorely needed, but I suspect Hakon was impervious to fashion. ''When this is over, you shall go home to Fishbourne with a full purse, but now I need you to ride.''

Hakon sighed through a mouthful. ''Our horses dread the sight of me coming with a bridle. They know it will be another day in hell. Where, my lord?''

''I want to know the moment the duke is sighted, what forces comprise his van, and anything else you can read at a distance. At a distance, mind. You're not immortal.''

All along our lines the stir of men increased as morning lightened. Edith hugged and kissed Gyrth and Leofwine when they rode up to join us, Leofwine in good spirits, Gyrth still dubious of committing all to this one fight. About the cheery little fire, Botulf turning out bannocks as fast as we could gobble them down, we were family again, crying good luck to Hakon as he galloped down the slope and up the other side to vanish over the brow of Telham Hill.

''Swegn should be here,'' Leofwine said. ''He'd be proud of his boy.''

''Proud's fine for soldiers,'' Edith said. ''For me it's

enough to be here with the men I've loved all my life."
She took the mug of hot cider Botulf offered, smiling at
him over the brim. "And you too, growly old Botulf."

"A little respect," I informed her. "I intend to make
Botulf a Crown thane."

He beamed at Edith in confirmation. "A man of rank,
no less. Won't my old woman puff up fair to burst with
that?"

Small, loving family talk to warm us all, yet my brothers and I kept glancing southward. Perhaps Edith sensed
the tension in us. "Do you know what day this is?"

Gyrth shrugged. "Uh . . . fourteenth?"

"Ach, you heathen. This is the feast of Saint Calixtus,
who absolved sins all others damned as unforgivable. It is
to him I'll pray this day."

She held out her cup to the long ranks of our men, then
to us. "Calixtus, bless every man on this hill and absolve
their sins whatsoever, for they know why they've come.
Bless my Gyrth and Leofwine for being brothers and
warmth to me, and Botulf for the loyalty lords pray for
but seldom find. Saint Calixtus, bless Harold for being my
husband and so much more. Your life teaches us that without a heart, faith is only a word and nothing done through
love is unforgivable."

She passed the cup for each of us to share the benediction. We mumbled *amen* and crossed ourselves. Let the
saint bless us with all his vigor today, needful as we were.

Up and down the line the army drew together like
bunching muscle, fyrd men jostling with carls for a
place—Kentish fishermen smelling of their trade, farmers
with Wessex dirt under their nails, west-country men with
more than a hint of Briton in their looks. Blades ringing
on whetstones, the *snap!* of our banners in crisp October
air. Gazing south with so many others, I saw the two
riders break over the brow of Telham Hill. "It's Hakon."

The other man rode in mail with a long, tapered shield.

"Bloody Norman cheek!" I hadn't heard Aelred come
up beside me, leaning on his bowstave. "Prancin' up to
let us know they've coom. Like we didn't know."

As they drew closer I recognized the hammer device on the vavasor's shield. "That's an old friend, Thane."

By the sun it must have gone nine or close on. As Hakon and Hugh Malet started up the slope the first elements of William's cavalry appeared over Telham Hill, widening in a line east and west, foot soldiers and archers trudging after.

"Sound the horns, Gyrth. Stand them to."

The lines on our ridge straightened and stiffened into a long, formidable spine.

Hugh Malet took my hand, removing his helmet. "I was on my way to you when I recognized the boy before one of our archers put a shaft in him."

He surveyed our army, the silent men waiting for that force deploying across the valley, archers to the fore. "I've long known this day would come, but by the good God I regret."

This must be awkward for Hugh. I tried to ease the moment. "You've grown stouter, Sire Malet."

"And you too thin, my lord. How goes your mother?"

"So much the better, so much the worse. I'll tell her you asked. What from the duke?"

"These are William's words. 'Tell Harold I wear the ring of Saint Peter and carry the holy relics by which he perjured his soul—' "

"Lies!" Botulf exploded. "I was there."

"Botulf, be silent," I commanded.

"They would have killed him."

"I said be still, man. Go on, Sire Malet."

Hugh pointed to a rider cantering through the thickening ranks of foot soldiers toward the archers in the valley. He was flanked by two standard-bearers. "His words again. 'The flag of Rome comes with me. Tell Harold I would avoid this battle. Secure in my right, I will let English law decide my cause, or if he dares, before God in single combat between us.' "

I looked down at my boots, unable to conceal a sad smile. "All this way, all this misery for one man's sense of his right. What William knows of English law you could put on your tongue and never taste. Tell him—''

''*Zut*, have I not tried?'' Hugh hissed in frustration. ''It has gone too far. It is no longer William alone. He is bound hand and foot by promises. And his pride.''

And now William sat his horse in that valley, waiting my answer. ''Botulf, fetch our mounts and the standard. I'll tell him myself, Hugh. Thank you for looking after Hakon.''

Botulf returned shortly, leading the horses, Thane Aelred cradling the Fighting Man in his arms. As he handed up the flag, Aelred glowered at the distant lines poised to move on us. ''Be damned to him. English law is it?''

He swung about and came to my stirrup. ''My lord, I've sworn to two kings in my life but gladly only to one. When you meet that manny down there, will you tell him summ'at for Aelred of Denby?''

The thought struck me right. ''A word from you might be instructive today.''

''Tell him King Edward on his deathbed passed the kingdom to you, the best deed he ever did. No man may gainsay a dying wish, *that's* the law.'' He glared at Hugh Malet. ''And does he think we'll care tuppence for any single combat? Jesus, has the man no learning at all? He's wrong, Norman, wrong by miles. Tell him if my lord were not here to lead us, we would have come by ourselves, for he ent earned this place.''

''He has not,'' Gyrth sealed it. ''But let him come try.''

I reached to clasp Aelred's callused hand in both of mine. ''In your name and words. No man could put it better. Please see my lady and those monks safely off the ridge.''

I blew a kiss to Edith, who stood nearby with the monks of Waltham, her veil fluttering in the wind. She crossed her arms over her heart, gathering me to her once more, and her lips silently shaped *I love you* toward all our promised tomorrows. Then, between Botulf and Hugh Malet, I rode down the slope to deny that intractable man who had not earned this place.

This earth is theirs, William, not mine. Before you draw

your last breath, pray you grasp that. I may not surrender anything to you. Men like Aelred won't let me. They just won't have it.

79 • Edith

The years fade and fall like dry leaves in this changed land where court and lords speak Frankish now, while our own tongue is despised and left to peasants. My boys are long grown and gone. For a time, raiding the west country already risen up against William, they earned the name of outlaw. Godwine, Magnus, and Edmund shared that lonely honor with Aelred, who fell at York, and his son whom northern folk now story and sing as Robin Hood.

The wind blows over that last ridge where they say on certain nights it carries the sound of grieving women who search the field for their dead. Harold and his brothers, Hakon and Botulf, may walk there still and my heart with them. We are all ghosts.

For King William, I know he never exorcized his own guilt over Harold and perhaps other things. He left me my hall and livings but gave my husband's body into the charge of Hugh Malet who wrote:

—with orders to inter it at Hastings. "Let him rest by the shore he defended so well," the king said. I will never know if he spoke thus in bitterness or respect, but one will be as true as the other.

I took Harold to a cliff where the new castle motte stands within the older defenses. Hard by the castle the downs grow green to the very cliff's edge, and one can see miles of pebble beach and sea. Peasants from Hastings stood with bared heads, kept at a distance by the soldiers save two who begged permission to prepare the grave. Though William ordered that no rites be allowed, one of the laborers whispered the requiem mass. He was a Saxon priest who had put aside his vestments in order to honor his king. Whatever God's will, I say that was well done. I will show you the grave when time permits.

Surely you must know my feelings in this. Harold was a friend to me much of my life. Our own prelates revile his memory with the name of usurper, but I have seen him among men, how they followed him, and heard myself what Denby said to him before the battle. If Harold was not royal, let none ever say he was not a king. May God bless him and yourself—HUGH MALET.

My love lies at Hastings. As time passes and William's heart softens or searches for some redeeming kindness to shorten purgatory, I'll go to him and ask the body to be buried at Waltham. That hard old man should remember Calixtus and relent. Until then there are bitter days but as many warmer nights when all my dear ghosts stride into the hall and Harold gives the cheer.

Until the last day, Aldyth, it was me he loved. . . .

What a foolish old woman I am. Aldyth ages in Coventry like Eadgytha at Wilton. She never wanted him anyway, and the twin boys she bore him as a widow are only afterthoughts. We were all dropped in the path of headlong history that simply ran us down. So be it.

Now my remnant life stands guard over pointless time, but these late years when I think of Harold, there is Aelred as he was on that last day. *We would have come by ourselves.* There is a kingdom not God's alone, a place in the heart that looks not only up but onward, where no odor of sanctity can smother the rich smell of our own earth or any king tear our deep roots from this ground.

For the rest, Lord God, receive my dear shadows gently and say to those churchly liars who curse my lover's memory in a foreign tongue: "I hear you. Nevertheless."